A Ballplayer

Samuel H. Grant

About the Author

Christ follower, husband, father, and veteran: Samuel H. Grant is a retired U.S. military veteran residing in Western Pennsylvania with his wife and four children. He blogs at https://www.samuelhgrant.com

Acknowledgments and Dedication

For Mom and Dad, who taught us everything essential before we were ten. And for the lifetime since, trying with God's help to understand and live it.

For my wife, my steadfast supporter, confidant, and sounding board. You are my true love and my best friend.

For my friends Nicole, Dennis, Graham, and for my children. For all of you, I pray God's grace and wisdom in the choice you must make, as all men must.

~

In honor of Jackie Robinson, the most important sportsman in American history. He is a true hero, whose sacrifices both inspire and dare us to look at each other as brothers and sisters, equal in the eyes of God.

"Now the Lord God had formed out of the ground all the wild animals and all the birds in the sky. He brought them to the man to see what he would name them; and whatever the man called each living creature, that was its name."
— Genesis 2:19 NIV

"Your name is the most important thing you own. Don't ever do anything to disgrace or cheapen it."
— Ben Hogan.

"Good name in man and woman is the immediate jewel of their souls."
— William Shakespeare, "Othello."

"A good name is rather to be chosen than riches."
— King Solomon.

One

It was a glorious spring day in Western Pennsylvania. In the past week, all turned from gray to green as new growth punched through the barely thawed countryside. The warm rays of sunlight danced through windows, coaxing the locals out of their houses, famished bears exiting their caves after winter's hibernation. Unlike Punxsutawney Phil six weeks before, they dare not see their shadow and turn back, not now, not when spring was so close. Every cold-blooded Pittsburgher shed heavy clothing for too-light summer wear. Their shivering bodies willed the world to fast-forward, seeking the warmth of promised summer yet to come.

Saul "Pops" Samuelson sat quietly at the batting cages of the Pittsburgh Pirates' unofficial hangout, a sports complex on the south side, where a few of his best players just departed. Years ago, he found "Bruno's Sports and Games Emporium" as an assistant coach and struck up a friendship with the owner, Bruno Shulz. Over the years, he and Bruno came to a unique relationship of mutual benefit as Pops leveraged Bruno's desire to promote his business, while Pops got a chance to test his players clear from other teams' scouts or prying reporters' questions. Pops supplied Bruno with a one-of-a-kind pitching machine, a high-speed pitching monster, right in the center of the complex. Pops ordered it specially built to his specifications. It came with a remote rigged to control the pitching from Pops' seat in the bleachers overlooking the cage. The monster fired its missiles inside a batting cage with a vast three-dimensional painted field on a curved backdrop. The field stretched onto a layered wall with almost invisible netting to absorb batted balls. From the hitter's perspective, it appeared as if he was batting in a full-size baseball stadium. Over the entrance were the words, "Pro Level." With its whirring, buzzing, bending metal and painted plastic pieces remaining partly hidden in the shadows of the painted backstop, the machine took on a mysterious life all its own.

The players named Pops' menacing machine "Goliath." Goliath's pitches were perfectly wicked. It produced big-league curveballs that dropped like scraps of meat falling from a Viking banquet table to waiting underfed dogs. Just when the players thought they had "Uncle Charlie" figured out, Pops would hit them with a laser-beam fastball that seemed to rise as it approached. Goliath's manufacturer even got the monster to throw a wicked "special" resembling a Mariano Rivera cut slider, nearly fastball velocity with a nasty sharp break at the very end. Finally, Pops could drop the occasional changeup, looking every bit a fastball, but slowed and dying down towards the dirt at the last moment. Sitting in the stands, Pops could select the pitches and their position, or he could set Goliath to random and let the remorseless machine choose the pitches and placement.

Pops designed the cage with targets in the outfield. When they lit up, batters tried to direct their hits for situational hitting bonus points. However, the reality of hitting Goliath was much like facing the living aces from other pro teams. The Pirates struggled to hit Goliath and barely put a third of its wicked and relentless rocket deliveries into play.

Bruno allowed Goliath to go into "Pro-Level" mode only when Pops brought his players and switched the remote on. In full Goliath mode, the monster pitching machine glowed with a single red light in the Pitcher's eye, like a one-eyed demon displaying the beast of ballplayers' nightmares possessed the mechanical monster. Goliath brought repeatable ferocity and perfection no human pitcher could replicate. It never grew tired, and it never hung a curve. When its red eye stared unblinking at the batter, a passionless fire of pitching perfection, the batter knew he was in the omni-gaze of the ace of aces. All who entered should prepare more than even Mighty Casey, or they would face a similar unceremonious dismissal.

Once finished and Pops shut off his controls, the red light would extinguish, the demon would sleep, and the machine slowed down to where mere mortals could hit its muted deliveries. This prevented Bruno's patrons from growing discouraged, deciding not to purchase more of his slightly overpriced tickets. Bruno, in turn, gave Pops and his players free access because the local crowds would come to watch, inevitably adding to Bruno's sales.

Typically, Pops would have left shortly after his players, but something held him in his seat today. His customary twin radar guns rested heavy in his lap like two cement bricks, holding him anchored in his seat. Pops was now a living legend in Pittsburgh. He grew up in the "hill district," facing tough odds, persevering, and graduating from Trinity Christian High School as a two-sport star athlete. His stature and baseball prowess caused classmates to bestow the "Pops" moniker at a young age because he resembled Pirate hero Wilber "Pops" Stargell. This Pops dreamed of becoming another Stargell or Clemente for Pittsburgh but signed with the San Francisco Giants, who offered his only professional contract after graduating high school. As his baseball prowess grew, his love of Pittsburgh and his Pirates never faded. He asked to be traded to Pittsburgh when he saw the opportunity early in his career, not long after the Pirates' last World Series victory in '79 and the original Pops' retirement.

After almost a decade as a Pirate, injuries led to his early retirement without a championship. However, his love for the game and his hometown organization continued. He secured a job as a batting coach for Pittsburgh in the Minor Leagues. During nearly 20 years in the minors, Pops honed his skills and finally got the call back to the majors. He quickly advanced, earning a shot to lead the club. This hometown son accepted the job of rescuing the Pirates from decades of mediocrity at the Major League level. His daunting task was simple. Take the perennial loser and make them a contender. Pops put his heart and soul into it and amazingly led the Pirates to a triumphant return to the playoffs in only his second complete year as a big-league manager. Despite an early playoff exit, expectations of a return trip to the World Series ran high. After making the playoffs two years straight, Pops and the Pirates' last two seasons headed in the wrong direction. They failed to make the playoffs, and the hope and promise of two seasons ago seemed like a distant dream from another life.

Now another spring training passed into the books with a sub .500 campaign. When asked by reporters, Pops explained the lackluster spring performance on his focus developing new talent while letting the players get to know each other. It was a similar story he told the media the previous few years. Pops remembered the newspapers rejoicing after the Pirates' playoff berth. Now, the three-year-old Tribune-Review® article predicting the Pirates soon to be "Champions on a budget" became an albatross around his neck. It dragged him down with bouts of sadness and doubt as rumors inside the organization flew. Poorly veiled whispers hinted at owners' impatience. The Pirates' finances depended on putting fans in the seats, and fans didn't come to Pirates games if they weren't winning—or capable of winning.

Pittsburgh was blue-collar through and through, and while Pops loved Pittsburgh's hearty, stubborn character, he knew all too well, here in Pittsburgh, football was king. In baseball, where their winning ways left decades ago with the departure of the original Pops, this Pops was running out of time. Pops knew he must return the Pirates to contenders if he hoped to keep his job.

Deep down inside, Pop's concern was more personal, a validation of sorts. Thirty-five years in pro ball, working his way up through the ranks, honing his skill and knowledge, failed to produce that most coveted moniker of all, "Champion."

Since he was a boy, Saul dreamed of making it to the big-leagues, of making the game-saving catch, or even better—the game-winning hit in game seven of the World Series. After his injury, Saul now dreamed of coaching his team to that same elusive goal. No matter what the individual awards, Saul, like any true ballplayer, wanted most of all to taste victory's sweet nectar and hold the World Series trophy high above his head. But after this spring, despite what he told the media and even his players, his keen baseball mind knew what his baseball heart could never accept. The Pirates overachieved three years ago, and his roster wasn't good enough to win it all. Today, Goliath only confirmed Saul's doubts. His best players were good support players, but there was no hitting "Ace" to lead the Pirates, no pure hitter who could throw opponents' pitching staffs into disarray. He saw clearly in his mind, despite his encouraging words, his team would again struggle this season.

The evidence was clear—perhaps it was always clear, ever since he took over as chief architect of the comeback of his beloved team. Maybe, he told himself, they could make up for their lack of a hitting star through guts and determination, but the last few years showed Saul it was not enough to carry them to a championship. The Pirates were good, but against the best, they lacked a hitter who could keep the other teams off-balance, unable to pitch around the heart of his batting order. Saul shared kind words of encouragement to his departing players as they left, but this realization struck him like a lightning bolt after five years of denial. It turned his grit and sand to crystal, instantly freezing him statue-like, where he sat, thunderstruck by this revelation of unrelenting truth. There was nothing he could do. Saul did not have enough bullets in his gun. Most importantly, he lacked that rarest of batters, the elusive silver bullet to slay the great beast. Opening day was little more than a week away, the clock was approaching high noon, and his six-shooter was all but empty.

Two

J oshua Green enjoyed a rare, delightful, lighthearted day with his daughter Ruth. Over the last few years, his family struggles nearly forced him into a constant state melancholy. First, he struggled to finish his USAF special operations tactical air controller career after multiple deployments to the war-torn Middle East. This USAF elite warrior spent a lifetime embedded with the special force units of black ops legend—harnessing the fast-moving close air support aircraft to place their deadly ordnance on target. Time and time again, his skill in controlling those ghostly apparitions saved him and his team from death. When the fight turned deadly, he would call on his aircraft, seen only by an occasional contrail, appearing suddenly at his call, screeching down with a high pitch howl, then tearing away, vanishing as quickly as they came. He placed their life-saving ordnance, threading the needle and expertly targeting the enemy while protecting his comrades and nearby civilians.

Josh's swift and accurate control of the aircraft often brought his team back from the precipice of death, catching the enemy just before their poisoned arrows and clutching tendrils reached out to drag his team to their doom. He thought of his flyboys as modern-day cavalry, knights on winged steeds, electronic eagle eyes spying out the enemy as they snuck up on his team. His knights strained against their surly bonds, leaning forward, waiting for his radio calls, their bugle's charge, to bolt and strike just in time. Yes, his knights of the sky delivered timely justice, sent the enemy back into the shadows, and turned possible defeat into victory.

Josh's teammates trusted him to call down his air warriors when things turned ugly and save the day. Together, Josh and his Special Operations Force (SOF) brothers moved through countless engagements with an evil enemy who hid like parasites embedded amongst the populace in strange foreign cities and villages spread throughout rogue nations and failed states. After years embedded with SOF teams in combat, Josh saw the term "Terrorists" as simply a new name given to an ancient foe. This twenty-first-century scourge was but the latest incarnation of biblical evil he first read about as a child. He saw them unmasked and exposed as evil men, hell-bent on doing as much damage, gaining as much power, and enslaving their fellow man in totalitarian misery and carnage. The only way to defeat such evil was to summon courage, determination, and fortitude, and stand and fight.

Josh recognized these thugs and brutes as evil men, trying to wrap their cruel ways in a false religion. With twisted hearts bent on destroying all who opposed them, they hated the Creator they falsely claimed to worship. While the evil they did in the name of God appalled Josh, the destruction they caused the surrounding societies saddened him more. They dragged their fellow citizens headlong into an evil abyss, barely this side of hell. Children lost their innocence in the twisted religion and often their lives. Fathers forced sons to choose far too early between joining them as a new generation of jihadists and hate mongers or resist and face their fathers' wrath. Justice was nonexistent in their macabre world, where life was cheap. Josh's great-uncles fought the Nazis, their version of such evil. Almost overnight, once proud Germany, birthplace of the Renaissance and the Reformation, descended into a decayed and degraded society that brutalized and murdered without remorse. The Nazis would never stop until confronted by good and just men. Even though the Nazis were their nation's minority, they pulled down and destroyed it in less than a decade, to the ruin and loss of millions of lives. Now Joshua dealt with societies ruled by generations of twisted beliefs leading to a descent into evil. Josh knew these "Islamic extremists" for who they were, that same old wolf, recreating itself as it did since the first time man rebelled against God in Genesis, wrapped in yet another cloak of hate and brutality, revisiting the same hideous sins.

If fighting nearly continuously in combat wasn't enough to push Josh into a depressed state, losing his beloved wife, Naomi, could have been a fatal blow. After years of being his rock and anchor from the storm, always waiting for his return, she contracted cancer. At first, Naomi hid it from him while he completed his fifth combat tour since 2001. When he returned two years ago, she was already undergoing treatment. Josh met Naomi seven years previously while stationed in Japan. She was the widow of a former member of Josh's new unit, killed in a tragic training accident before Josh arrived. This life of a combat airman was rewarding but dangerous, and Josh knew well the associated risks.

Josh flashed back to his closest call during his third tour. His team conducted a direct assault in an urban area on the outskirts of Ar Ramadi, Iraq. Initially, all seemed to go well as the assault captured a lightly defended improvised explosive device manufacturing center. The simple, nondescript house was a homegrown shop of horrors, used for building makeshift bombs to wound and kill travelers on the town's highways and paths. However, the calm didn't last long. The enemy used a tunnel system nearby to sneak up and surprise Josh's team as they cleared the booby-trapped area. Suddenly, a young teen, exiting a hidden entrance, popped up over a short wall and launched a rocket-propelled grenade at almost point-blank range. Josh pushed a comrade away with a split-second reaction, diving to the side as the explosion lifted and threw him against a wall. Shrapnel sliced through his helmet, cutting dangerously down his cheek but somehow missing the rest of Josh's head and shoulders, opening his left hip and thigh like a fillet knife. Dazed and unable to walk, Josh followed his training, kept calm, and called upon his cavalry.

Holding a bandage to staunch the blood flow from his face while a medic worked on his leg, Josh directed his air knights and ended the fight with a well-placed bomb. Though not life-threatening, the injury to his leg required rehabilitation, and Josh returned home to his newly assigned unit in Okinawa. While rehabbing, Josh learned the sad story of another American hero who survived his own combat tour, only to die tragically in a training accident. The fellow airman's wife, Naomi, and their three-year-old daughter, Ruth, were at the base hospital when Josh came for physical therapy on his injured leg. Little Ruth sparkled with life as she bravely fought through her therapy sessions to help combat a genetic muscle condition that robbed her legs of strength, and she wore metal braces to this day.

The little girl's courage would make her father proud. Her mother's infinite kindness, love, and patience with the little girl drew in Josh. Even more amazing to Josh, despite a culture and family pushing Naomi to abandon her brief American life, she opened her heart a second time to another kind American warrior. Josh grew to admire and love this gentle yet resolute Japanese beauty, whose courage and steadfast faith in Christ became an inspiration and a foundation for the much-deployed airman. Josh accepted Christ as his personal Lord and Savior as a young child. Upon graduating high school, he joined the military, believing it to be his calling. As he witnessed the strength Christ gave Naomi, he found new respect and renewal in his faith. Much to his surprise, Naomi said yes to his request to marry him after a short courtship. Their eight-year marriage and watching little Ruth grow with courage and strength, despite her physical struggles, became the bedrock of his life. When deployed, he maintained that perfect picture in his mind; Naomi and Ruth, safe and happy at home, waiting only for his return from war to make them a complete family again. It was that peaceful picture that saw him through battle after battle. But the evil in this world found Naomi in a form even Josh could not overcome. He could not protect her from cancer, and after eighteen months of valiant fighting, Ruth and Josh lost both mother and wife.

Josh could have descended into a deep depression, but his faith in Christ and his daughter's love saved him. However, he was far from healed, still suffering the unseen wounds of Naomi's passing and enduring memories of so many close calls, so many battles, and too many lost friends.

Perhaps because of her physical struggles or merely inheriting her mother's great faith and courage, Ruth seemed more resilient and better able to carry the grief. She became Josh's steadfast encourager, piercing the shroud of his malaise as she reminded her father, as a 12-year-old, she could take care of herself, and he should "go out and have some fun." But Josh was reluctant to leave the house when off duty, afraid equally of losing his daughter and how he would act back in the real world. As he learned to cope with life without Naomi, Josh realized he could not continue to put himself at risk now that he was Ruth's lone surviving parent. He reached the magic 20-year mark of his military career and retired as a 38-year-old combat vet.

That was nearly six months ago. Strengthened by his faith and his daughter's persistent encouragement and led by the Holy Spirit's quiet voice, Josh saw through the fugue of sadness caused by his wife's death and realized he needed a fresh start. He moved away from the familiar Special Ops roots of his long-time duty location of Fort Bragg, North Carolina, and returned to Western Pennsylvania, far from the military. Josh returned home for the first time in twenty years, near where he grew up. However, the job market in Pittsburgh was discouraging, and his veteran status seemed more of a burden than a help. Although he was one of the nation's most valued and uniquely skilled warfighters, public praise of "Thank you for your service," became a snub in private. Behind industries' closed doors, comments like "not enough experience" and "try something you are more qualified for" flowed from potential employers. Josh sensed these "would be" bosses silently wondered how this nearly middle-aged, scarred-face rookie with a slightly distant look of a man who saw too much could handle the pressure of a new career.

Sitting in the interview hot seat, Josh sometimes flashed back to intense moments of combat. Instead of the interviewer, he saw his comrades' desperate faces as they placed their lives in his hands. They depended on Josh's ability to target a large warhead dropped from a high-speed warbird on an enemy all too close to their position. The devious thugs used their favorite tactic, hitting the Americans late in the game, from civilian homes and dwellings where the closeness of their fellow citizens and even family members caused not them, but the Americans, concern. Wolves in sheep's clothing, just out of sight, waiting until the Americans were close. Only then would they attack, hoping to negate the U.S. air attack advantage. Memories of this close-in enemy infiltrated Josh's mind as waking nightmares. One moment he was at a job interview in the States, the next, transported half a world away, his team's weapons firing desperate shots as the commander shouted for him to bring down hell before they all died. His sure, steady voice on the radio, conveyed not fear but urgency, passing precise coordinates of the evil menacing his position, mere meters away. Josh implored his high-flying aviators to speed the delivery of their life-saving ordnance.

Josh barely recognized his current location as silent seconds ticked by, simultaneously in the present and the past, as sweat beaded on his forehead. The interviewer wondered what delayed his reply to some question pertinent only to the mundane job. Josh continued to stare through this civilian ghost, seeing more clearly the memories of bearded men and young men unable yet to grow beards but trying just as desperately to kill him and his friends.

Silently the interviewer pondered whether he should call for security or could afford to wait a while longer to see if Josh could give the "secret reply" expected, providing the elusive phrase he needed to hear before offering Josh employment. Yet Josh looked far beyond the interviewer's unseeing eyes, mere orbs of translucence, reflecting his past and his teammates' desperate glances, pleading without words for him to release the airpower and save them all. Though his team usually escaped unscathed, sometimes the cost for those precious seconds, before the bombs silenced the enemy, was paid in a teammate's blood. As Josh emerged from his waking dream, he saw the interviewer sitting across from him with a slightly concerned look. Josh wondered if he would accept the words, "Danger Close Approved, Cleared Hot!" shouted back as an answer to the hypothetical question. Josh did not think so. Instead, he thanked him for his time and quietly slipped away, jobless for sure, but at least out of the dreary building and offices, back into the light of a blue sky equally devoid of warplanes and enemy rocket-propelled grenades.

Three

Ruth reveled in the warmth and sunshine of the glorious spring day. "C'mon, Daddy," she told Josh, "Let's go visit Pittsburgh!" Her infectious smile and bright eyes always softened Josh's heart, and he gave in. They left their old foursquare home in Greensburg and drove downtown to the burgh via one of the many arteries that sliced through the mountains, depositing them into a maze of roads and bridges, confounding all logic. Armed with a good GPS and hoping to prove to his daughter he was a true Pittsburgher, Josh carefully navigated the maze, only twice retracing his steps. First, they rode the incline and gazed down on three rivers from Mount Washington. Then, while stopped at a favorite sandwich shop to enjoy a Primanti's® sandwich, Ruth spied an advertisement for buy one get one free putt-putt golf at Bruno's Sports and Games Emporium. Ruth was a bit of an American sports buff and liked to compete with her dad whenever she got the chance. She begged him to take her. How could Josh say no to her bright-eyed imploring?

"All right, all right. We'll go, but the winner buys ice cream," said Josh.

"Deal," she squealed, but in a serious reply, "But you have to try your best, Dad. No letting me win!"

"Let you win?" Josh replied with a shocked look on his face. "I don't know what you are talking about—you're too good!"

His wife Naomi remarked that the often repeated argument from his beloved daughter, who wanted no quarter for her disability, must have come from him and his stubborn resolve to overcome any obstacle. Josh saw it as more than a bit of Naomi, although he was smart enough not to argue the point. Despite her braces, Ruth sparkled with uncanny optimism, and she moved around the putt-putt course with a single-mindedness bent on showing her dad she would beat him, just as she was beating her braced legs. If she caught Josh easing off on a few shots or showed he might not be trying hard enough, she would chastise him and tell him he needed to mind the motto that he often told her, "Do your best and let God take care of the rest."

After they finished the course and Josh inevitably bought the ice cream for Ruth, she noticed the interesting batting cages next to the golf course. Baseball was one of her favorite sports, and she liked learning all the statistics behind its history. She was an amazing precocious kid, and Josh sometimes wondered where her love of baseball came from, although he did enjoy watching it with her on TV. "Daddy, Mom used to say you were a baseball player when you were a kid; is that true?"

"I suppose it is," replied Josh, reminiscing wistfully. "I was pretty good once, but I haven't played since I was 16." In his usual understated way, Josh hid the passion and dreams he once held but let go of so many years ago. Decades passed since Josh even thought about his playing days, too busy with the nation's important work, he surmised. Today was different. Today, he remembered the passion of his youth. As a young teenager, Josh was an excellent ballplayer with much promise. Baseball was *his* sport, a love shared with his father, David. He thought back to one of his earliest memories, sharing his dad's passion as a young boy, having a catch with his dad on the road outside his house in their quiet neighborhood. He remembered endless days in Pennsylvania passing ball, shagging flies, and heading to the local ballpark for batting practice. His dad would pitch to him until sunset, or he finally wore out his dad's arm. As he got older, he would sock ball after ball over the ever-shortening fences. "Son, life is like baseball; it's hard and takes lots of work. Sometimes you'll fail, but when you get it right, it makes all the work worth it." Josh thought about his dad more often these days. Dad taught him virtually everything Josh found important in life at an early age. Love of God, country, and baseball. Baseball was their "thing." Together, they enjoyed each year of Josh's childhood playing baseball. Josh once dreamed of turning pro as a standout player in his hometown, but his dreams ended one fateful day with Josh pulled off the ball field at school to dreadful news. His beloved father, the picture of strength and health, suffered a heart attack at work. Never one to complain, Josh's father was a laborer at one of the few factories that remained in Western PA after the fall of U.S. Steel. None were stronger and more skilled in Josh's mind, but the unseen silent killer caught Josh's father unaware, and he passed without ever regaining consciousness. That was Josh's last day playing baseball. He was the oldest of five kids, and his mom needed help to raise the rest of the family and pay the bills, so Josh took a job after school to help her make ends meet. Losing his dad was one of the main reasons Josh joined the Air Force after graduating. He continued to send money to his mom as she raised his brothers and sisters and even helped put some of them through college. Josh never felt slighted. That wasn't his way. Josh did what he must, but he never played baseball again.

"Dad, I think you ought to go hit some baseballs and show me how good you are," said Ruth.

"Oh, hon, I don't know. I haven't touched a bat for over 20 years. I don't know if I can anymore," replied Josh.

"C'mon, Dad, you know you always tell me we must try our best, and it's good to try new things. I want to see you go out there and whack some balls like Babe Ruth, like Hammering Hank!"

Josh thought now how Ruth sounded a lot like his dad. "I suppose you won't let me rest until I do." Josh walked up to the window between the putt-putt and batting cages as his daughter sat on a bench eating her ice cream nearby. Bruno was working on cleaning up behind the counter. A door led to the back room on one side of the rear wall. Bruno propped it open with a tall basket of wooden bats as he moved some supplies in and out after the Pirate players left. Peeking through the propped open door was a small office in the back room. Josh noted a black-and-white picture above the desk, of people from long ago, overseas. It was a portrait of an old storefront with foreign writing on the sign above and two grown men with two younger boys looking at the camera. The old cars in the photo gave it a 1930s look, just before the war. The frame was ornate, and Josh could see the Star of David carved into its dark border. Bruno stood up from shoving some supplies into the counter beneath the back of the booth and turned to see Josh looking at him patiently.

Bruno was probably fifty-five-ish, with a large, bushy, old-time mustache and a slight Yiddish accent. "Sorry. Didn't hear you approach. Normally, my daughter would be helping me, but I gave her the day off. What'll it be?"

Josh replied, "I'd like to try my luck hitting balls in your batting cages."

Bruno nodded and sized him up for a helmet selected from the shelf. As Bruno handed it to Josh, he asked, "What kind of bat do you want? We have all kinds of aluminum bats, even one they call a 'Cherry Bomb' for hitting the big home runs."

Josh looked around the booth until his eyes fell on the bin of wooden bats by the back door to the office. "How about the wooden ones?" Josh asked.

"Well," said Bruno, "Our patrons don't normally use those. They're for...ah, you know...special occasions." Bruno hedged, as these were the Pittsburgh Pirates bats. He hadn't put them away in the back office yet. Suddenly Ruth called out as she ambled up behind her dad.

"My dad's a great hitter. You ought to let him use a wooden bat like Babe Ruth. He'll put on a show for you!"

This little spitfire of a girl, a picture of contrast to the man, with her slight Asian frame and braced legs, yet with a look on her face, half smiling, half sheer determination, took Bruno aback. He glanced somewhat pleadingly at Pops, the lone audience, sitting several rows behind home plate in the bleachers. Pops, however, was unusually quiet and unmoving, as if deep in thought. Bruno looked back at the man the girl called "Dad." Bruno tried but failed to place this man's background or heritage. He was tall, with long wavy dark hair. He displayed a prominent hawkish nose on a dark face, and his lean body looked hard as a rock. Bruno noted a jagged scar, tracing a pale line down the side of his face. He wore a tan baseball cap with a barely visible subdued American flag above the brim. Then the man tilted his head up for the first time, and Bruno got his first look into his eyes. For the rest of his life, Bruno would not forget that look. Although the man looked late 30s, Bruno saw in his eyes, someone much older, much wiser, looking back. The man's eyes pierced straight into Bruno and, for a moment, saw his true heart. It wasn't unnerving. Instead, it seemed to be a deep understanding, a connection with Bruno's soul. Bruno remembered feeling something similar when his father first brought him to visit his grandfather. Without a word, he knew his grandfather could tell what was true and what was not about him with just a glance.

The memory surprised Bruno. Disarmed by this train of thought, Bruno acquiesced, walked back to the basket, and looked through the bats. One particularly beautiful Louisville Slugger stood out. He should have picked one of the less valuable bats, and normally he would, but he looked back at the big man. His hat brim now hid his eyes, but Bruno could not forget; those eyes that knew so much, just out of sight. The man stood looking down at his daughter, arm resting gently across her shoulders. He appeared a swarthy Greek god, resolute as a chiseled statue, were it not for those kind, hidden eyes. He completely contrasted his slightly built daughter with her leg braces. She smiled lovingly up at him, waiting expectantly. Bruno could not disappoint either. He reached in against his usually frugal nature, grabbed the beautiful bat, walked back to the man, and handed it to him.

"Here you go, take care of it; it belongs to a star player that comes here occasionally," said Bruno, eyes down, trying not to match the man's gaze again. "Which cage do you want? We have five different levels."

Before Josh could reply, Ruth squealed, "What's the hardest?"

"Well, the Pro-Level is, but I don't think you want to start there. You'd be better trying one of the amateur cages," replied Bruno.

"We'll take the Pro," said Ruth. "Dad likes them as fast as possible!" Again, Bruno looked pleadingly towards Pops, but Saul never moved his gaze, staring into the bleachers of the Pro-Level false backstop.

"OK," shrugged Bruno, "but don't say I didn't warn you."

Josh took hold of the 36-ounce Louisville Slugger, admiring the smooth ash wood barrel and pine tar on its handle. It felt good in his hands, an organic feel, carved from life versus the cold-rolled metal bats with their rubberized grips. He realized, genuinely surprised, this may be the first time he picked up a bat in over 20 years. Somehow, this piece of ash, sanded to perfection, rekindled happy memories of days gone by. He walked toward the batting cage centered in the facility and raised the bat admiringly, smiling at it. He could hear the words of his father. "Say a prayer before you step up to the plate, then do what God created you to do, just like we practiced. Take a good swing and let Him take care of the result." Josh turned towards the cage. It looked like a miniature baseball park, with the standard distance to the mound of 60 feet 6 inches. The "field" was a background of netting and fake painted bleachers behind an outfield with several targets. The manufacturer cleverly designed the field from the batter's perspective giving the illusion of a full-size ballpark filled with cheering fans, urging the hitter to "Hit one to me!" On the mound, half-built into the false backdrop, stood a mechanical pitcher unlike anything Josh had ever seen. Partly obscured by shadows, it looked like an old-timey pitcher, all bulging muscles and brawn, frozen in wild, mid-delivery. Josh heard quietly whirring components, half visible behind the hidden pitching arm and a single bright red light in the shadowy face where the pitcher's eye should be.

Pops only partially noticed the man and little girl leave Bruno's ticket booth. He gazed almost without seeing as the girl sat down on the first row of bleachers in front of him, directly across from Goliath's cage. He was still brooding over this morning's revelation, unaware of Bruno's pleading eyes as he tried to dissuade the man from the wooden bats and Pro-Level cage. Pops watched unconsciously, a passive bystander.

Pops thought what an odd combination the two customers made. The girl was slight of frame, with straight black hair, Asian features, and metal braces on her legs. She hobbled slightly but capably made her way by the man's side. He thought, "man," at first, not dad, because they couldn't have looked more different. He was a big man, probably in his late 30s, thought Pops, but one thing piqued Pop's attention enough to bring him part ways out of his reverie. Unlike the ordinary Joe American of his age, there was no fat on him. As slight as the girl was, he looked solid as an oak tree. He was tall, about 6'4", not huge, but muscularly cut, about 210 lbs., lanky and hardened as if chiseled from granite. His hair was a curly wave, dark but not quite jet black, like the little girl's. In his mind, Pops thought he might be a man of some African American descent, like many of the kids in Pop's old neighborhood. He walked strangely light for such a big man, almost stalking. He wore cutoff pants with a desert camo pattern and an old light-beige T-shirt, stretched and faded as if exposed to extreme sunlight. He looked like a hawk, wary of his surroundings, not quite relaxed, ready for action at any moment.

Pops still sat with his radar guns and remote. Unmoved since his players left, Pops didn't bother to turn off the remote. Goliath rested, its soft, whirling noises hidden just out of sight, patiently awaiting its next victim. Josh put on the helmet, gripped his bat, and paused, looking at the bat. Momentarily in profile, Pops got a good look at his face. It looked older than he expected, and although he couldn't quite make out the dark eyes under the hat's brim, he could see a prominent white scar extending just above the man's ear, across his cheek, close to his left eye, ragged and cutting the otherwise ordinary dark face. It all struck Pops as curious, the strange pair, this young petite disabled Asian girl, and the dark, swarthy god entering the cage.

Suddenly, the girl drew Pop's attention. "C'mon, Dad," she cried as the man closed the gate, "Hit a home run for me!" It surprised Pops to hear her call the man, "Dad." The man smiled as he settled into the batter's box, then the smile faded as he took his stance. After decades scouting players, the coach in Pops automatically conducted the same analysis of this batter he used a thousand times. This right-hander exhibited a neutral, upright batting position, no hitch, little bat movement, quiet hands, and no apparent flaws. Pops was a hitting expert, and like an opposing pitcher, he would evaluate a batter for any potential weakness to exploit. Unusually, especially for an amateur, this batter showed none. Pops watched absently as the machine used its laser-guided aiming sensors to determine the man's position and size, set the computed strike zone, and prepared the first pitch. Pops gazed on, a passive observer of the scene, unable to break out of his melancholy trance. Though the red light glowed with the machine still set to Goliath mode, Pop's mind did not register the man now faced the scourge of baseball batters' nightmares, come to life.

As Josh stood in the batter's box, it surprised him that his days as a combat controller, not his time as a baseball player, returned to him. He remembered coaching a younger controller during live training drops. He observed the incoming plane and his trainee trying to determine if it lined up on the right target. Josh's abilities continually improved over the years after hundreds of controls of fast-moving aircraft in peace and combat. He attained a level of prowess even his peers found hard to comprehend. Josh found he knew before the planes dropped their munitions, and before any of the other controllers, if the aircraft were properly on or off the correct trajectory. During the heat of battle, this ability saved him and his teammates' lives on several occasions when he waved off a bad drop, narrowly averting disaster. It was a difficult skill to teach to his young controllers. As he gained experience, Josh realized it was a talent one could only refine, not build from scratch where it did not exist.

Josh remembered the seeds of the same raw gift as a boy watching a pitch from his father travel towards the plate. Until now, he never realized they were flip sides of the same coin. After years of honing his skill in combat, Josh knew he could tell the ball's trajectory like the cavalry charge of his flying knights with their lethal projectiles. When the whirling pitching machine started its launch, he saw the jet rolling off the perch to attack, and he could see whether or not the jet was on target. But this wasn't a 500-mile-an-hour warbird. This was only a baseball. At first, the pitching machine stood idle, sizing him up, then it started to move.

Pops' reverie broke as the machine began its pitching motion, realizing too late, the red light still shined brightly on Goliath. The bullet was firing from the gun, and it was impossible to stop.

For Josh, like those moments when the aircraft descended to deliver its munition, time slowed. The machine's delivery arm seemed half-human, half-machine, as it rotated and released the ball from artificial fingers above the pitcher's head in an outstretched, off-center semicircle. Josh saw the ball, a white spinning orb of leather and stitches, almost in slow motion. He saw the path it was taking in his mind's eye and could see himself placing the bat in motion. It was as if he saw multiple choices, frozen in time, on the ball's trajectory to his bat and swing. If he selected one, it would foul the ball off high or low. Speed up his swing, and it would pull the ball down the third baseline. Slow it down, and he could slice away to the opposite field. Josh instantly saw all the options and made the best selection. To those watching, Josh's body suddenly struck like an uncoiling snake, releasing his swing in one beautiful, fluid motion. Josh chose which of the "possibilities" he saw as the best chance to hit. For this pitch, hard and fast on the inside of the plate, Josh chose. He moved his hips through his swing quickly, placing the wide barrel, not the narrow handle, of the bat on the ball. Struck sharply, the ball's perfect impact with Josh's bat delivered an unmistakable sound; A clean, crisp "CRACK!" The natural sound resounded throughout the surrounding area as the unbending hardwood of the Louisville Slugger accelerated through the spinning leather orb, redirecting its flight like a sledgehammer pounding a tack. The ball, launched like a cannon, flew laser-beam straight into the netted artificial left field bleachers.

Out of habit, Pops fired the radar guns. It wasn't until the loud crack of the bat he awoke fully from his trance-like state. Pop's previously slumped position snapped erect as he watched the ball deposit in the left field bleachers. He leaned forward, squinting in disbelief behind his dark sunglasses. What just happened? Had the machine somehow slowed out of the pro mode? He stared for a second at the bright red light shining above Goliath. Then Pop looked down at the radar gun readings. One read the speed of the incoming pitch, and the other, if hit, read the speed of the outgoing ball. Pops could scarcely believe the numbers. Goliath was indeed alive and well. The pitch came in at 98 MPH, but, more astonishingly, exited at 106 MPH. Pops sat stunned. This man hit a world-class fastball, on the inside corner, into the bleachers. Such a hit in an actual game would easily be a home run in any Major League Park. There wasn't much time, as Goliath would soon fire the next pitch.

Josh was still in the zone when he saw the first ball smack into the outfield bleachers painted on the back wall. "Hooray, Daddy!" called Ruth as she gushed admiringly at her father, "I knew you could do it!" Then she turned toward Bruno, who watched the first pitch from the ticket booth while rubbing some bat handles with an old oily rag. "See! I told you so! Just like Babe Ruth, like Hank Aaron!" Bruno looked back with puzzled, bushy eyebrows scrunched below a furrowed brow, scrutinizing the scene. Bruno watched Pops put his players through the machine many times before, with Goliath inevitably coming out on top. How could this guy hit Goliath in full pro mode? He glanced up at Pops and nearly dropped the bat he was cleaning as his expression changed to shock when he realized Pops looked as amazed as he was.

Josh smiled at his daughter's shouts of glee, but he quickly realized it was only the first pitch, and another was soon winding up inside the machine.

As Pops leaned forward in the seat, coming to his senses, he realized he needed to make a decision. Prudence would have him turn off the monster and let it slow to a more hittable speed, but he hesitated with his finger over the off switch. He would often wonder years later about the motivation for his decision, but in those next few seconds, though he recognized the red light was still on, Pops left the machine set to full Goliath mode. For some time afterwards, he told himself it was to prove the first hit was just a fluke. But as the years rolled by, he looked back on his decision as an unconscious plea, a desperate hope, into his little world wandered a true hitter, like a miracle and an answer to prayer. In the present, however, he didn't have time to decide. Instead, he selected a different Goliath pitch. How would the man react to an off-speed pitch? Pops selected a curveball on the outside corner.

Josh watched as the machine whirled and gyrated, then launched the ball. Again, with the ball's release, time slowed. Josh distinctly picked up the ball's seams, this time not spinning straight up but canted at a forty-five-degree angle away from him. Although the ball seemed aimed center-in on the plate, he realized it would break down and away from him, catching the outer corner. It was slower than the last pitch as it curved and dropped toward the bottom of the zone. He again saw the possibilities and chose to meet the ball as it crossed the plate, knee level, lying back on his swing and waiting. The pitch arced like a perfect, wicked rainbow as it ducked deviously toward the ground at the last second. After facing the fastball, most of Pops' players would swing too early and high to hit the wicked curve. Josh was not deceived. He met the curve perfectly. Once more, his tan ash bat placed its full barrel on center, striking the spinning leather ball with another loud, crisp, crack, shattering the still spring day. As Josh intended, the ball was driven solidly down the right field line, up and out of the park, into the seats on the painted right field bleachers with a resounding thud. Pops looked down at his radar guns, already in disbelief. The off-speed curve came in at 86 MPH, and went back out at 102 MPH, another home run.

Pops watched eight more pitches for the man he began to think of as some kind of machine himself. Curves and fastballs, a changeup mixed in with a couple of specials. He made the machine paint the corners of the strike zone, but the miracle man hit the ball no matter what he threw or where he threw it. Every hit resounded with the same solid "WHACK" of perfection. Four were home runs, and the others were line drives, no misses, no strikes, not even a foul ball. Impossible! Pops checked his radar guns with each hit to verify what his eyes and mind could scarcely believe. Pops began selecting his various situational targets toward the end. The batter immediately got the gist, narrowly missing the first, then hitting the last three. All too soon, the batter finished his ten balls. Pops sat stunned. He could hardly believe what he just witnessed. The batter hit every pitch type, every location, without a miss. This man achieved what even his best professional players facing Goliath never approached; Hitting Perfection.

During his time in the cage, Josh forgot the world and its current problems. After a couple of swings, life became simple again, and he was back with his dad at batting practice. Josh watched each pitch and saw the options in his mind's eye. Like a surgeon wielding his scalpel, like an artist painting with his brush, he selected the most satisfying arc and swung. When the targets lit up, he was back with his airman students, training them to hit the desired target. His swing was a bomb drop matched to a target, a simple choice of the proper intersecting solution. Too soon, the pitches stopped, bringing Josh back into the present. With a tinge of regret, he turned from the simple truth of spinning leather and stitches, flying smoothly toward him, inviting him to intercept their arc with his smooth, swift swing. He was a warrior effortlessly slicing his broadsword through the waiting, massless orb, enjoying each satisfying "CRACK." As Goliath's arm returned to the parked position, Josh reluctantly lowered his bat, sheathed his sword, and turned back to the immeasurably more complicated world of real life.

Four

Briefly frozen in his seat after the last hit pitch, Josh's movement out of the batting cage spurred Pops to life. He rose out of his seat, almost dropping the radar guns. Roughly gaining control, he placed them on the bleacher beside him and hurried down the stairs. Josh's daughter ran despite her braces and gave her dad a big bear hug.

"I knew you could do it. You're the best, Dad!" cried Ruth.

Josh smiled and picked up the girl in his arms as if she were weightless. "Just for you, Kiddo. I guess your dad still has some hits left in him after all."

Josh noticed an older black man rushing down out of the bleachers overlooking the cages. The man wore a collared black sports shirt trimmed in gold, a pair of blue jeans, and a black Pittsburgh Pirates ball cap. He was an inch or two shorter than Josh, barrel-chested, with a muscular, athletic-looking build for a man in his late 50s or early 60s, and there was something vaguely familiar about him. He removed his aviator sunglasses and placed them on top of his cap. The man approached Josh directly as he and Ruth walked back to the ticket counter to turn in his bat and helmet. Josh handed his bat back to a puzzled-looking Bruno, who ceased cleaning the bats to watch Joshua's entire turn in the cage.

Meanwhile, the man from the bleachers finally caught up to Josh and his daughter. The man looked earnestly at Josh.

"Excuse me, sir. Can I talk to you for a moment?" Pops exclaimed, slightly out of breath.

Josh thanked Bruno and turned back to the man with the Pirate hat. "Sure," replied Josh, smiling. "What can I do for you?"

Pops collected himself slightly and said, "Impressive hitting out there. How long have you been playing baseball?"

"This is our first time here," Josh answered.

"No," said Pops, "That's not what I mean." Suddenly Pops was at a loss for words, struggling with how to proceed. "What team do you play for?"

Josh chuckled a bit out loud. He wasn't sure if this guy was putting him on or not. The man stared back at him seriously.

"Well, sir," Josh replied more soberly, "I don't play on any team. As a matter of fact, this is the first I've tried to hit a baseball since I was back in school."

Pops looked back, dumbfounded and silent. At this point, Ruth turned around and looked up at Pops. Suddenly, she stopped. "Coach Samuelson?" Ruth blurted out questioningly. She waited for a moment, but Pops still stared at Josh. "You're Pops Samuelson, aren't you?" she said.

Josh did a double-take. He did not follow sports lately. With the start of his repeated combat tours overseas, Josh lost contact with most pop culture and found it less and less relevant to the world of life and death. Even after he retired, he rarely watched sports or anything on TV, as he preferred not to get caught up in current events. However, his daughter adopted all the Pittsburgh teams as her teams since she found out her dad was from Pittsburgh. Her mom and her background in Japan did not lend to sports appreciation. Yet Ruth always held an affinity with sports. While her disability hindered her opportunities, she longed to take part. When they lived in North Carolina, she followed the Pittsburgh teams, constantly watching and reporting to her dad when he got a chance to Skype back from some overseas location. Although Josh initially didn't follow the teams, his daughter's enthusiasm discussing their highlights and stats always amused and encouraged him. He often had her describe some play, like a seasoned sportscaster, as only she could. Leave it to her to recognize the Pirates coach—he realized now why he looked so familiar. She was right. It was Pops.

Finally, Pops broke his stare at Josh and looked down at his daughter. "Yes, young lady," said Pops affably, relieved to have someone help fill the space where he was at a loss for words. "I am Coach Samuelson, and who might you be?"

"I am Ruth, and this here is my dad, Josh. Joshua Green. He's a great baseball player."

"Now, hon," Josh said, slightly embarrassed, looking at his daughter and placing his arm around her shoulders, "I'm sure Coach Samuelson has many talented baseball players and just wanted to say hello."

"Actually," said Pops, "I haven't seen anyone hit like you just did, Mr. Green. Ever. Can I ask what it is you do?"

Josh carefully replied, "Nothing at the moment. I'm between jobs."

"I might have some work for you. How would you like to come to the ballpark tomorrow during our practice?" queried Pops.

"To PNC Park?" Josh responded. Now it was his turn to look surprised. Pops nodded back. "Sir, would this be for an interview?" asked Josh, mystified.

"You could say that, but it will be an on-field interview—bring your baseball gear and come at 8 AM."

"Coach, I'm sorry, but I don't have any gear—like I said, I haven't played in...years."

"OK, make it 7:00 am at the right field entrance and show them this card." Pops handed him a golden card with black lettering. It said "Saul P. Samuelson, Pittsburgh Pirates," with a phone number and email on the back.

"Dad, can I come and watch the practice?" Ruth blurted out, looking at her dad but glancing sideways at Pops.

Before Josh could answer, Pops stepped in, almost laughing. "Sure, bring her along. She can sit right behind the dugout." Pops turned back to Josh. "So, I'll see you tomorrow, right?" Pops tried to say it in a level tone, but it sounded more like a plea for help.

Josh paused for a moment and looked down at his admiring daughter. How could he say no when he saw the excitement in her eyes? "OK, Coach, we'll see you tomorrow at 7 AM."

Five

J osh got up early, mostly because he scarcely slept. He drove quietly, listening as Ruth excitedly discussed seeing the Pirate players up close during practice. Josh smiled as she rattled off their names, stats, and even some rumors of their off-field personalities. Meanwhile, Josh kept thinking, "Lord, what is it you want me to do here? Please help me do what you would have for me to do. Help me be the man and the father you want me to be." Finally, Josh prayed one of his oldest prayers, a prayer he often heard from his father during family devotions. "Whatever your will is, Lord, let me find and follow it." Again, his dad's words came back to him. "Just do your best, Josh, and let God take care of the rest." He smiled sheepishly at the thought as Ruth recounted the players, hoping to get their autographs. Josh thought, "At least Ruthie should have a good time."

They arrived at the appointed time—something not easily done as they got stuck in the typical early morning traffic coming through the Squirrel Hill tunnels. Josh and Ruth walked up to the right field gate. There was a single security guard there, reading the morning Tribune-Review.® Josh rattled the closed gate to get his attention.

"There is no admittance today—it's a closed practice."

"I have an invitation from Coach Samuelson. He told us to be here at 7 O'clock. Here's his card." The security guard walked over and took the card through the fence. He looked at it, then pulled out a walkie-talkie and asked someone called "Parrot 1" if the coach said to expect a man and a kid visitor. The reply was prompt to let them in and send them to the home locker area.

Josh and Ruth were partway down the entrance corridor, looking for signs to the lockers, when a young man with wavy brown hair, khakis, and a polo shirt with the Pirates emblem met them.

"Hello, sir. Are you Josh Green?"

"Yes," Josh replied, "And this is my daughter Ruth."

"Great. My name is Mark Johnson. I oversee player relations for the Pirates." He gestured down the hallway. "If you follow this hallway, second door on the left, they will get you set up with some gear. I can take Ruth to her seat behind the dugout. She'll be able to see everything going on, and Martha, one of our interns, will show her around all day and get her anything she needs."

Ruth spurted out, "I'd like to see the players. Can I get a few autographs before they get started?"

Mark laughed, "Well, miss, I suspect you can get just about any player's autograph today. The only people watching will be Pirates staff and a few stadium employees since today is a closed practice."

Ruth turned and reached up to Josh. He bent over, and she hugged his neck, whispering in his ear, "Knock 'em out of the park, Dad!"

Ruth joined Mark, and as they walked down the hallway, he said over his shoulder, "Go on in and ask for Pete—He may act the old curmudgeon, but there is nothing he doesn't know about getting a player ready to play!"

Josh watched with some trepidation as Ruth ambled alongside Mark, but something about the young man's demeanor put Josh at ease. Mark came across almost with innocence, even younger than his years conveyed. It didn't take long for Josh to remember Ruth adapted to new experiences better than he did. Josh could almost see the spring in her braced legs as she began asking Mark about what he did, about the many Pirates, verifying the players' details she seemed to know better than a Pirate radio announcer. The last thing Josh heard was Ruth asking Mark if they had any openings for a batboy on the team. Josh turned with a half-smile as they moved out of sight and followed the path Mark specified.

Josh found his mind drifting, much as it did since Pops invited him to come. What exactly did the coach have in mind? As he approached the door and raised his hand to knock, he noticed this door bore a picture unlike most of the blank doors and generic signs he passed. On it were portraits of Clemente, Mazeroski, Stargell, and Honus Wagner.[1] Below the picture was a small plaque that read, "Champions aren't made in gyms. Champions are made from something they have deep inside them-a desire, a dream, a vision. They have to have the skill and the will. But the will must be stronger than the skill."[2] Josh didn't consider himself a sports buff, but he was a student of men. He remembered the man who made this quote.

Josh knocked on the door and heard a gruff reply from the other side. "Come on in!" Josh opened the door. The office was a small glassed-in annex overlooking a large, combined weight room, whirlpool, and massage area, with lockers around

---

1. Four Pirate Hall of Famers: Clemente, Mazeroski, Stargell, and Honus Wagner

2. Quote of Muhammad Ali

the edges. It looked like the gym teacher's office in high school, but with much better equipment in view beyond the glass. Josh saw players, coaches, and trainers getting dressed, stretching, or doing light workouts, preparing for the day's activities.

The office itself was part desk, part lounge, and part historical Pirates' paraphernalia. Behind the desk sat a late 60s, early 70s, gnarled old-timer wearing a faded yellow and black pillbox Pirate cap circa the 1970s. It even came replete and partially adorned with Stargell Stars—the kind Pops Stargell gave out to players for doing things to help the team in critical situations. Holding a ball glove, the man worked some ointment into it with an old rag using his hands and a blackened softball that saw better days sitting close by. He was about 6-foot-tall, Josh estimated, with a thick chest and strong-looking forearms. Josh couldn't help but think he looked like a black Popeye sitting there with a chewed but unlit cigar in his mouth.

Josh introduced himself. "Hello, I am Josh Green. Are you Pete?"

Pete turned his gaze from working the leather glove and smiled around his cigar as he put down the rag and stood up to shake Josh's hand. "The one and only! Saul said to expect a new rookie. Pleased to meet you." Pete took Josh's hand and gave it a good, firm shake. He didn't let go immediately but pulled Josh slightly forward and seemed to look deep into his eyes for a moment, as if sizing him up. His gaze strayed to the scar on the side of Josh's face, but Josh held his eyes steadily on Pete's, and it was Pete who looked away first. Pete gestured to an old, mahogany-covered chair amid various pieces of baseball and other sports equipment strewn around his office. "Have a seat, Son. Let's talk."

Pete sat back down, and this time picked up the softball sitting on his desk. He began pounding it into the glove. Josh could see by the stains on the ball, it was an oft-repeated process. Pete saw Josh watching him work the glove.

"Just breaking in a new one for use. I tie up the glove with the softball in it overnight and leave it dunked in a bucket of my secret concoction—gets about 60% of the break-in done. Then I dry it, oil it, and pound it into submission—only way to break in something new is to do it right the first time. Otherwise, you work twice as hard to reshape it." Pete pounded the glove with the softball for a few moments. "Saul tells me you're a hitter," he said finally, looking up at Josh with a slightly accusatory tone.

As Pete would learn, Josh paused and contemplated his response before speaking. He replied, "I used to be one once, but it's been a while."

"Where'd you play ball?" Pete asked.

"To be honest, Pete, when I say, 'a while', I mean it; the last time I played regularly was right here in Western PA."

"Mmm-hmm," Pete nodded his response, lips clenched around his cigar. "You're about to get another chance to play with this lot of Western Pennsylvania ballplayers," Pete gestured out the windows at the men slowly filing out of the room toward the field. Josh surveyed the room outside the glass, giving Pete, who never took his eyes off Josh, a chance to give him a once-over. As he pounded the ball into the glove, Pete studied Josh's scarred face and taut figure, and those eyes, taking in everything. There was something about the eyes. Pete suddenly felt a distant echo from his past, of ghosted figures he could barely see on the edge of a moonlit rice paddy. He was only a boy when he found himself thrust into the midst of an unpopular war.

When Josh first entered Pete's office, he noticed it was all about baseball. All that is, except for a small, faded picture on a shelf over Pete's shoulder. It was a hilly jungle setting as a group of men in fatigues, carrying weapons, paused for what looked like a last-minute photo before heading out. On the corner of the picture frame was a small Marine Corps crest. The bottom of the frame stated, "K company 26/3, Khe Sahn 1968." As Pete looked at Josh's face, glancing out the windowed office, Pete caught a glimpse of those men, his old comrades, and especially his gunny, who he hung onto since showing up on a troop transport as a replacement marine in late '67. The Gunny kept him safe and taught him what he needed to know in those early days. It saved his life more than once during his tour, but alas, the Gunny perished on hill 861 in Khe Sahn. It was Josh's eyes that sparked Pete's memory. Those eyes held the look of someone who saw so much and would soon see more again. Suddenly Pete realized he was staring at the ball sitting idly in his glove, bringing him back to the present.

Pete looked back at Josh, who watched with those same penetrating eyes, now fixed on him, waiting patiently. For a moment, it was Gunny, looking at him knowingly, seeing everything good and not so, all his dreams and mistakes, yet not judging. It was a kind but penetrating look that could see right to your core. Pete cleared his throat uncomfortably and sat up, trying to break Josh's gaze by pounding the softball into the glove a few more times.

Finally, as if deciding, Pete continued. "Saul said you're worth a look, and he rarely wastes our time—especially so close to the start of the season, so he must have seen something in you at the cages." Pete resumed pounding the ball as the memories of Gunny and Vietnam receded. Pete looked back at Josh. "Before we get started, can I ask you one more question?" Josh nodded, a slight smile on his face. Pete abruptly paused the monotonous pounding of the ball into the glove, sat both on his old desk, and leaned forward as he motioned at Josh with his cigar. *"Why are you here?"*

It was an odd question, but what struck Josh was he asked himself the same question all morning. In fact, in some ways, he was asking the Lord, in something of an unspoken prayer, to help him understand. Josh turned his head and looked out through the glass at the professional athletes getting ready to play. Many were more than a decade younger and passed all the tests for professional baseball players, finally leading them here to the Major League. Josh did none of those things. But Josh passed a different test, one that brought him to this place at this time. Suddenly, he knew whatever happened today, he was right where the Lord led and meant him to be. A peace came over Josh as he chose again to place his life in God's hands. This same peace Josh felt in the chaos of battle when fear sometimes paralyzed others. Josh heard the Lord saying, "My yoke is easy, and my burden is light." He could almost feel His smile as He again said those inviting words to Josh:

Follow Me.

Josh's doubt washed away. He looked back at Pete, smiled, and said, "Pete, I'm here to play ball."

Six

Pete and a few staff took Josh around to the various bins to get him a full uniform, right down to his socks. When Pete asked Josh if he owned any gear, Josh replied, "No, Pete, nothing left from my playing days survived."

"No worries, kid. I've broken in a glove I was gonna give to my grandson—just turned 15, and he's going out for varsity this year—you can use it, and I'll give him the one I was just breaking in. How bout bats?"

"No sir, sorry," Josh said a bit sheepishly.

"OK, we just sent a couple of guys back down to the minors. What size?"

"I used a nice 36-ounce ash Louisville Slugger at the cages."

"Sounds like Judah's," Pete frowned slightly. "I have a few of his still in boxes. I'll break them out, but I'll warn you, he's a little *particular* about his gear." Pete paused for a moment, thinking. "If he says anything, tell him I got it for you," he hurried on. "Get dressed, and I'll put it in the dugout bin with your name taped on it—you'll be in the field to start."

Before Pete let Josh get ready, he took him for one last stop to the medical area just off the locker room. A short, bald, slightly plump gentleman was head down, earnestly mixing some foul-smelling concoction. "This here is Dr. Luke," Pete said as an introduction. "He's a cross between a doc, a physical therapist, and a camp counselor. Hey Doc, you got a nice pair of those squeezy shorts you gave me last year that'll fit Josh? It might help 'em as he's a little more...," Pete searched for the right words, "Well-traveled than our average rookie."

Doctor Luke looked up from his mixture and glanced at Josh, smiling. Josh could now see his face. He was an upper-50s bespectacled man with a contemplative look and a hint of sparkle in his eye. "Hello, Josh. Let's have a look," said the doctor, sizing Josh up. "I'd say about a 32-inch waist and 38-inch inseam—the reverse of old Pete here," he deadpanned, and Pete grimaced a little around his cigar. Doc Luke moved deftly through the cluttered medical room. "Here ya go," he said after rummaging in one of several boxes haphazardly spread around his office. "Wear it under your uniform. It'll keep your muscles and everything else where it's supposed to be;— Hold on!" He searched through a few other bins. He grabbed various articles of clothing and a small plastic bottle, which he then filled with the concoction he'd been mixing. "Here's some post-workout compression gear for your legs and arm. You'll find they help you recover more quickly. Rub a small layer of this natural home remedy if you get real sore—my grandma's special recipe. It smells like mothballs and old socks, but it got grandpa through forty years of working bent over in the mines. And if you need anything else, come see me. If I can keep old Pete and Coach Saul going after all their aches and complaints, I should be able to help a young rookie like you!"

By the time Josh and Pete returned to the locker/gym area, all the players were gone. Pete dropped his half of the goods in the last locker catty-cornered from his office. "Get dressed, and I'll walk you out to the field." Josh hesitated as he looked around with a few nervous butterflies. "Don't worry, playing ball is 90 percent muscle memory," counseled Pete.

Josh relaxed slightly and thought, "How hard can it be—at least no one's trying to kill me, and I haven't played any games for ages. This should at least be fun."

Pete walked back into his office and reached for the glove as he sat down in his chair. Doc Luke came in from the hallway and closed the door.

"So, what do you make of Saul's find?" said the Doc.

Pete turned slightly to see Josh as he put on his compression shorts. Both men could see a long scar running haphazardly down his left abdomen and thigh, stopping just above the knee. Even Doc Luke gulped a little in surprise, as Josh showed no other sign, the scar on his face paired with a much larger twin on his leg. Neither man said a word. Suddenly, the phone on Pete's desk rang, and both men jumped. The two-digit number indicated it was from the dugout. Finally, Pete hit the speaker button. Coach Samuelson's voice was unmistakable. "How's he coming?"

After a momentary pause, Pete replied, "Just got his gear together. He's getting dressed."

"What do you think so far?" asked Saul.

Pete chewed on his cigar and looked away from Doc toward Josh. It was an odd question from Saul, as he typically asked Pete this type of question only after seeing a player in action. Pete recognized the plea in Saul's voice. He wanted some reassurance he wasn't crazy. For a moment, Pete thought to mention the scar and the significant injury it represented, but he hesitated, remembering instead the look in Josh's eyes. His Gunny was a man like no other. Only death itself could stop him. "Pops, let's just see what he can do. We'll be up in ten," Pete finished, hanging up the phone.

Doc looked at him for a second, then he smiled, nodded, and said, "Call me when you need me." Luke walked back out of Pete's office, closing the door quietly behind him.

Seven

I t was a cool 60 degrees in Pittsburgh as the team took the field, but the sun shone brightly. With few observers beyond some staff in the stands, the stadium was unusually quiet. The breeze carried the smells and sounds of a city beginning its workweek. Josh walked out of the tunnel into the dugout. The rest of the team, already on the field, tossed balls, stretched, or ran light laps. Pops stood at the edge of the dugout talking to one of his coaches and turned to see Josh and Pete. Pops walked over to Josh, looking him up and down and nodding in approval to Pete for the gear he supplied.

"Well, you sure look like a ballplayer. Ready to get back at it?" said Pops.

"Ready, Skipper. Where do you want me?"

A quizzical look came over his face, and Pops replied in a low voice only Josh and Pete could hear. "Josh, I never asked you what positions you played. I thought I might start you out in right field. How's that suit you?"

"Sounds fine, Coach. I loved playing the outfield as a kid."

"OK, head out to center. Coach Phil is working with the outfielders warming up."

Josh left the dugout, took a quick look at the infield, then jogged towards center, where several players and a coach were lightly jogging and warming up.

As Josh arrived in center, he spied the coach and jogged up to him as Coach Phil watched his half dozen players running back and forth. Phil sported a large mustache and looked about mid-30s, only slightly older than the players he was coaching. He turned as Josh jogged up. "Coach Phil, the skipper said I should work out with the outfielders."

Phil looked back at the dugout and could see Saul looking at him. "OK, Rookie. Pops said to expect you." Phil then looked Josh up and down, halting at his middle-aged face where he expected to see someone much younger. He, too, dropped his voice down so only Josh could hear. "Good grief, Pops said to expect a rookie, but I wasn't expecting a geriatric one! Where did you come from?"

Josh smiled and shrugged, "Overseas mostly, here and there."

"OK, best take some three-quarter runs between center and right—get the blood flowing, and then we'll stretch as a group in 10 minutes."

One thing Josh could do was run. Many of these men were ten or even fifteen years his junior, but Josh ran with a deceptively easy gate. He ran a fast 400-meter in track and field in high school as a freshman at nearly state-level quality, only running track to stay in shape for other sports. The track coach pleaded with his mom to let Josh return after his father passed, but Josh already began working an after-school job. In the military, besides his gifted eyesight, his speed, despite his heavy gear, often surprised his SOF brothers. His team leader once told him to lead the way back out of a dangerous situation, back to the landing zone, yelling at him to haul ass and get on the radio to bring back the helicopter. Josh dashed back and radioed the helo so quickly, the team arrived, huffing and puffing, shaking their heads at the lanky greyhound sitting idly in the helicopter waiting. He just smiled and waved them on board. His teammates called him "Flash" after that. They reminded him of his moniker after his injury and challenged him to return to where he could "smoke" them. It took him three surgeries and twenty months of rehab, but he finally led from the front of the pack again. If he lost a step, it didn't show, and he still worked hard on his runs through the hilly Western PA landscape since moving back home. He warmed up quickly to acceptable standards with all the young guns.

After ten minutes, Pops gathered the entire club for a team stretch. It was a tradition Pops kept, starting not with baseball but during his football days in high school. "All right, fellas. Before the captains take over, I want to introduce you to Joshua Green. Josh will play with us this week during practice. You'll see him work out in right field. Josh hasn't played baseball in a few years, but he has some skills we want to look at." All the players looked at Josh with varying degrees of surprise, skepticism, and perhaps even some thinly veiled animosity. Bringing in a new player this late in spring training was highly unusual. More surprising was taking a rookie nobody straight to the Major League club without some tune-up in the minors. Whatever their thoughts, Pops didn't give them much time to challenge him as he waved to Andrew and Thomas, his captains, to start the team stretch.

The captains were the star center fielder, Andrew, and the starting catcher, Thomas. Andrew was the Pirates' perennial all-star, just past mid-career. He grew up a star player out of rural Louisiana. As a standout shortstop at LSU, Andrew led the Tigers to two NCAA national championships in three years before signing with the Pirates. Soon he became the team's lone All-Star, leading the Pirates back to the playoffs and winning the League MVP four years ago. For nearly a decade, Andrew set the standard of hard work and excellence in the Pirates organization for everyone to follow. Thomas was a former journeyman catcher, coming to the Pirates late in his career. He led with his hustle and brilliant appraisals of friendly and opposing pitching. Thomas proudly claimed the title one reporter gave him; "team overachiever." Tough and scrappy, previous teams thought him limited by lack of size and speed, but he kept playing, awaiting his chance. Pop saw something in him he liked, traded for him, and Thomas started nearly every game for the last three years.

Andrew was slightly shorter than Josh, slighter of build, and moved with lithe, effortless grace. He walked forward, stopped in front of Josh, and looked him in the eyes. Andrew would talk about this moment years later to whoever would listen.

"As I approached Josh, I remember this hawk of a man, older, weathered, and well-traveled. I thought he must have lived a tough life, a different life than most ballplayers. I'm not sure why I felt that. Maybe it was how he held himself, like a statue, cocked and ready to let loose. But just when I thought to walk past him and start the workout, I caught my first good look under his hat brim. His skin was a dark coffee and cream, with wavy brown hair spilling down, a hawkish nose broadening to his cheeks, and a jagged white scar pointing to one eye. Those eyes: They instantly drew me in, and despite the hard curves and edges saying this man was hewn out of rock, the eyes brought me up short. They said something entirely different. Here I was, so sure of myself; veteran ballplayer, team captain, All-Star, and League MVP. The team leader, but his eyes fully disarmed me. Whatever I thought I was, I wanted..., no, I needed to get to know this man. I'll never forget it. I stopped, dead in my tracks, reached out my hand, and said,"

"Welcome, Josh."

With a twinkle in his kind, old, knowing eyes, Josh took Andrew's hand firmly and said softly, "Thank you, Andrew. Glad to meet you."

As the years passed, Andrew recalled, "His handshake was like meeting an old friend again. People say he held my hand for a long time, but I tell you, it was I who delayed letting go. It was his eyes. They caught me and held me. They knew me and said kind things to me—those things that know you well, that know you true, that let you know everything was going to be alright, like he knew what I needed and was ready to help me. I should have been leading and teaching him. After all, I was the All-Star. But I knew, at that moment, with a brief glimpse into those eyes, it would be the other way around, and somehow, that made my heart fill with joy. His eyes took away my doubt of failure to lead this team, to be what they needed me to be. That fear washed right out of me. It was like he knew what I thought, and his eyes said everything would be alright, as they did every time thereafter, when I bothered to focus on him. I never quite understood why I knew it, but I knew I just met a man, no, met a friend I could trust, without fail."

Andrew caught himself thinking these things but realized, to his back, the other 25 players were watching and wondering why he stood still for so long. He recovered and said, "Well, Rook, why don't we stretch out these old muscles so we can get down to business?"

"Sounds like a good idea, Captain," Josh smiled in reply. He walked out to the space Andrew vacated, with skeptical looks from the other players eying him up and down. Andrew and Thomas started the warm-up with their teammates in a semicircle. Andrew went through the paces like a good team captain, with a nod and a grin, letting Thomas do most of the callouts, making a quip here or there toward one or another of his teammates to wake them up and get them going. But honestly, he kept thinking about the old rookie in their midst and those all-knowing, understanding, kind eyes.

Eight

O nce the team finished the group stretch, Pops stood up in front of the players to set the agenda and tone for the day.

"OK, let's take about 45 minutes for positional warm-ups with your coaches. Then we'll get going on a mock game. Utility players, you're clear to keep your scheduled position rotation today or see me if you need to switch. Everyone's cleared off to work with your position coaches as they direct."

Saul released the players, and Josh followed five others, including Andrew, working with Coach Phil in the outfield. They circled Coach Phil, and he was about to say something when one player walked in front of the others and spoke bluntly. "Phil, what's the deal with Pops saying this rookie would work right field? Does he intend to give this guy a chance to start?" The player's back partially blocked his expression, but all could sense his red-hot anger.

"Judah, you know I don't know what's on Pop's mind any more than the rest of the coaches—he's the boss, and when he is ready to tell us who he intends to start, he will."

"Look," said Judah, "I've paid my dues and done what is necessary to earn the starting spot in right field. It's been mine the last two seasons, and I did whatever Coach asked. Just because a few of my stats fell off last year doesn't mean I haven't earned the spot. This is my last year under contract, and I am ready to prove my worth. But I can't do that unless you give me a chance!"

Phil looked back at Josh, then said to Judah, "Look, Judah, you'll get a chance, but Pops decides when and how—just do your job!" Louder now, Phil shouted at the others, "OK, line up two rows in left, and I'll hit some flies—let's see some good throws and hit your cutoff here!"

The outfielders turned to jog back out to left with Andrew leading the way, and Josh turned slowly. Judah caught him in stride. Trailing the others, Judah turned his head slightly to Josh so only he could hear.

"You may be Pop's new favorite, but don't expect us to bow down to you when he's not around. Stay out of my way, or you'll find yourself in a hole so quick, you'll never know who hit you. Understand? This is my outfield, and no no-name, washed-up, old rookie will take my position away!" Judah said as his ruddy, dark skin burned even darker, plainly displaying anger and hostility.

Josh listened, looking straight ahead, then as Judah finished, he turned back to meet Judah's intensely malevolent gaze. Judah caught the big man's eyes in his own for a split-second, and his iron resolve faded to confusion. Josh's look was not what he expected. Judah looked away quickly, as he too, would never forget Josh's first look into his eyes. Where Judah expected to see responding anger and defiance, there was only a sense of peace and even sadness for him in those eyes. Judah saw neither fear nor confusion but concern, with a patient, fatherly kindness toward a hurting, wayward child. It took Judah aback. He did not understand how this rookie from nowhere could make him feel like he was the one with much to learn. Judah turned away, unsettled over his future, not just with the team.

Andrew pulled the men up short and turned around to face them. "Judah and Barney with me, J.J., you take your twin there and Josh. Show him how it's done."

Barney shouted at the three men who peeled away, "Alright, you guys, don't forget, best shooters eat free at the next road dinner." Barney was smiling at the other three guys with a twinkle in his eye, saying he was playfully egging them on.

The two men with Josh grinned at Barney and moved off to one side as one looked over his shoulder, "C'mon Josh, you're with us," said J.J.

James Jr. and Juan were "up and coming" young players in their mid-twenties with skills to play both infield and outfield. Coach Saul saw their fast bats and easy smiles as diamonds in the rough and potential stars on the team. He fought to find them starting positions and groomed them to discipline their big-league skills. They weren't really brothers but came from similar long-shot backgrounds. James was from Miami, and Juan was from the Dominican Republic. Pirate players and coaches, however, called them the "Thunder Brothers." They looked and talked alike and played the game with the same youthful joy and intense fun of little leaguers. Their style and friendly rivalry were infectious, reminding everyone why they loved the game.

"What do you say, Juan? Do you think we should show the "Rook" what the Thunder Brothers can do?" smiled J.J. as the three men gathered to await Coach Phil's first hit.

"Sounds good to me, Bro," said Juan as he turned to Josh. "Dju see dat basket mounted chest high with a net around it, next to Coach Phil?"

Josh noticed it earlier and nodded. "That's Coach Phil's cutoff-man. Barney always challenges us on who can hit it the most times every day."

"Yeah," piped James, "Whichever group throws the most balls into the basket wins the best "Shooter" for the day, and the other outfielders have to buy their next road dinner. Oh, but there is one automatic win—that thing is made from bamboo—some kind of weird basket Phil brought home from who knows where. He said no one can break it. It's magic. So, it's an automatic win if anyone does. Don't worry about the wager too much. We've got the best arms on the team, and we'll carry you–remember though, whoever gets the most points also gets to pick the restaurant, and you know who gets to pick the most?" "I do!" they both said simultaneously and laughed as they shoved each other good-naturedly.

They looked at Josh expectantly, trying to see underneath his cap visor. He turned toward them, and the scar caught their eyes for the first time, curtailing their smiles, but then he raised his head so they could see the rest of his face. Josh's eyes smiled back as he replied, "Sounds good to me." Their smiles returned, and they high-fived each other.

Barney shouted across to them, "Standard bet, Thunder Brothers?"

"Dju got it, man!" Juan smiled back. "We plan on eating da best Mofongo in Saint Lewy come next Monday!"

"We'll see about that!" laughed Barney back. "Good luck, Rook!" he said towards Josh and smiled as Josh waved back.

Coach Phil returned from the dugout after retrieving a fungo bat and bucket of balls. He set up along the right field foul line a few steps from the basket, turned to his players, and yelled, "Heads up, fellas, let's get started!"

Nine

Coach Phil yelled, "Alright, guys—three-quarter speed, let your arms finish warming up for the first couple of throws." He hit the first ball toward Andrew's threesome, and Andrew stepped out and caught it. The captain, lithe as a gazelle, possessed a graceful, natural lope, making everything look smooth and easy. He caught the fly ball, charging towards Phil, and in one continuous motion, made an arcing throw towards the basket. The ball sailed neatly into the strangely shaped cornucopia with a reedy sound of bamboo ricochet.

The next hit went to the other group. Juan shouted, "You got it, J.J.," and his "brother" charged the off-line sinking drive, catching it just before it hit the ground. He continued his forward momentum and planted his foot to redirect his body toward the basket. J.J. threw more aggressively than Andrew, more of a line drive hard throw, and the ball entered the basket hard, at an angle. You could hear the ball rebound inside the basket with several muffled "Thunks" of bamboo. "That's a tie with the captain," J.J. said, smiling and holding one finger at the other threesome of players. "One apiece!"

Barnabas, or Barney as his teammates called him, was more of a fireplug utility player. He scrambled after the line drive Coach Phil hit to his right, reached across his body to catch it on the first hop, and fired back at the basket. He was still moving right when he released, and the ball sailed slightly right of the basket, hitting the wider net instead. Head down slightly, Barney returned to his group, and it was Juan's turn.

Coach Phil hit Juan a pop fly to his left. Juan got a good jump on it and flagged it down easily. He was slightly off-balance as he caught it and redirected his body to throw. The throw was on-line but slightly below the basket opening, hitting its outside and landing in the net.

Judah was next with a look of sheer determination on his face and stance, on the balls of his feet, ready to pounce. Coach Phil struck the ball, producing a sinking line drive. He intended to make it a one-hopper, but Judah held other ideas. He got a great jump on the ball, charged in, and made a shoestring catch, coming up firing for the basket. This was no three-quarter throw but a full-out strike, and it made a satisfying "thwack" as it sunk directly into the center of the basket. "Nice play Judah! Way to pick us up one!" Barney said.

"That's how it's done, Rook!" Judah yelled, looking in Josh's direction. "That's how we play here. Don't bring it weak!" he shouted accusingly.

Josh went last as he loped out into the open field. As he took his position, he saw in his mind's eye the many times he walked to a training position on some remote military range, ready to conduct calls for fire with his beloved "fast movers" overhead. His eagle eyes rested patiently on Coach Phil. He waited to assess the arc of the ball, his quarry, to dictate the course of his attack. He would reverse what he did with his aircraft, ready to place himself in line of the strike. To see how Josh judged fly balls, Coach Phil hit the ball harder and deeper than he intended, straight back over Josh's position. For an outfielder, this was the hardest ball to judge. Without hesitation, Josh took off with a drop step and quickly came up to speed. The ball went deep, almost to the left field foul side, forcing Josh to use full speed and every inch of his 6'4" frame to make a difficult, cross-body backhand catch. He quickly slowed, stopped, and reversed direction. Coach Phil said three-quarter speed, but somehow Josh didn't think that would do. He made a strong move toward the distant basket and let fly a powerful arcing throw. The other five outfielders looked on as the ball sailed true, entering the basket neatly and bouncing deep into its interior with a series of "thwacks."

If Josh's teammates were a little surprised, they didn't show it, as even some of his competitors for the shooter competition seemed pleased. Barney shouted, "Nice play Josh!" Only Judah looked back with disdain, hands-on-hips, and disgust on his face. If he was going to say anything to Josh, he never got the chance. Andrew stepped out between them and tipped his hat to Josh. "Nice play, Rook—keep it up."

Josh jogged back to his two teammates, and the Thunder Brothers gave him some generous smacks on the back while Juan exclaimed, "Way to pick me up for my miss Josh."

"Yeah, Bro, we are even with them thanks to you," followed J.J.

As the practice continued, Josh's presence and excellent play seemed to spur everyone to play their best and represent the Pirates well. Even Judah, in his anger, made some of his best efforts of spring training, and everyone fought hard to make the play and "shoot" the basket on each try. Finally, Pops, who watched and moved around to all other parts of the Pirates warm-ups with pensive hidden glances to the outfield, arrived at Coach Phil's side.

"How are they doing?" asked Pops.

"Great, Coach," said Phil, "It's the best they've looked all spring."

"And the Rookie?" Pops begged at a level only Phil could hear.

"See for yourself, Pops," replied Phil. It was Josh's turn. Phil lined a sinking liner to Josh's left. Josh got another good jump, long legs pumping strong, speedily chasing the ball as it tried to dive and slice away. Josh was quick enough and caught the ball at the knees. Moving deftly forward, he used his momentum and made a full-bodied throw at the basket without breaking stride. Displaying the smoothness of a seasoned veteran, Josh used his long frame and released the ball with every ounce of power, like a massive bow uncoiling its arrow with tremendous force. The proverbial frozen rope, it entered the basket dead center at a high velocity. Unlike most other throws, there wasn't the typical "thwack" of the bamboo but a loud single "thunk" of the ball striking other balls already in the basket. The basket seemed to flex back more than usual before rebounding. Because of its deep and twisted back-end design, the basket rarely released its previously ingested balls. This time, however, either because it was overfull or the chance positioning of previous contributions, the force of Josh's throw was so powerful not one, but two balls shot back out of the basket. It acted as if punched in the gut, forced to cough up its treasure back onto the field. Phil and Saul looked on, surprised at the noise and the basket's reaction to Josh's throw. Phil walked over to inspect the basket with a slight look of concern.

"Would you look at that!" said Phil at a level only Saul could hear. Pops walked over to stand beside Phil as Phil gestured to the back of the basket. There, peeking out and wedged through the tightly woven bamboo, a baseball, approximately one-third visible, stuck through the basket weave.

Pop's eyebrows rose slightly as Phil continued to stare at the basket. "In the three years I've been using this thing, I've never seen a ball go through like that," Phil said. He stared for a moment, finally shook his head, and turned towards Pops, away from his players in the field. With a sheepish look on his face only Pops could see, Phil chuckled a little and said in a low voice, "Coach, I don't know how he hits, but this 'kid' sure can catch and throw a ball. As far as playing outfield is concerned—he's doing fine!"

Ten

P ops pulled the coaches together to review the mock game plan. Since it was Monday, and the opener was the following week, he planned to use his ace pitcher and give him a good, strong outing before switching him out. Pops debated with himself about how to do this, entirely because of Josh. He saw two problems as far as he was concerned: Josh's untested bat under live pitching; and his players' response to Josh's position in the lineup. He knew many would resent Josh's presence wherever he placed him. While mindful of the team's emotions and chemistry, Pops felt Josh's play would make or break his acceptance in most of their eyes. Josh's bat stunned Coach Saul yesterday. He prayed it would translate to live big-league pitching. Still, he was uneasy of his own opinion and filled with self-doubt, he placed Josh seventh in the lineup today.

Josh would start in right field. The top spot in the order was Zach, the starting shortstop. Next, Pops sandwiched the Thunder Brothers, Juan and J.J., around the captain, Andrew, holding down the third spot in the lineup. Judah would bat fifth today, followed by a young Oklahoma native, Nathan Fisher, a strong-arm third baseman and a country boy with a deft skill of snagging hard-hit balls in the hot corner. With only 12 fielders available on the Pirate 26-man roster, Josh would play the field until relieved by Judah after Judah batted.

Pirates ace, Samson "Slayer" Gibson, would start on the mound. Next to Andrew, Samson was probably the most recognizable Pirate. He was in the final year of his original Major League contract. Samson was a brawny 6'6" African American fire-baller from Georgia with long braided hair, who came to the Pirates as a coveted first-round draft pick straight out of high school. Samson spent only a brief stint in the minors primarily to work on a second pitch, a changeup, devastating because of its visual similarity to his fastball. His high velocity, lively fastball, matched with a now perfected changeup, made his rise to the big-leagues rapid in his first year of pro ball. With each season, Samson's legend grew, famously hurling unhittable fastballs, and on his off days, entertaining fans by holding five baseballs in one huge hand. His nickname off the field was Smiling Sammy because of his playful demeanor, and he quickly became a fan favorite and ladies' man. He spent two full seasons with the Pirates in the majors after his brief time in the minors and fell just three votes short of the Cy Young award last year after a 17-5 overall record on a middle-of-the-road team that didn't make the playoffs. During winter training, Samson added a third pitch, a slider, which he introduced this spring and was a lone bright spot in the Pirates' spring training with a 0.68 ERA. If Andrew was the long-term star and face of the Pirates, Samson was its star of the moment.

Samson looked good during warm-ups, and he was ready to face Zacchaeus Purqana[1] to start the game. Zach was known for lithe, graceful play at shortstop, speed on the bases and in the field, and as one of the few prominent baseball players to come out as gay. Zach was the son of a migrant Mexican worker and a black nurse who met when the worker almost died in a freak accident on a Texas ranch. His parents raised their two children in a rugged, dusty west Texas town, and though poor, taught their sons the value of hard work and perseverance. Zach became a two-sport star; a speedy, diminutive, black sprinter for a small AA high school and baseball standout, and played college baseball for the Texas A&M Aggies. Despite being a virtual unknown, he came on the Pirates' radar when he placed second in the state championship 100 meters and was consistently the fastest to 60 meters, where his size lost out to the taller sprinters. The baseball coach from Texas A&M was an old teammate and long-time friend of Saul Samuelson from his San Francisco farm team days years ago and called Saul, saying he should take a look. Saul kept an eye on the small kid from Texas and saw enough to have the Pirates sign him during his junior year at Texas A&M with deferment until he graduated. Zach did not disappoint and started in the big-leagues primarily because of his excellent defensive play, after a year and a half in the minors. Zach quickly gained a reputation as one of the best athletic shortstops in the League, and more than one analyst remarked how his play resembled St. Louis great Ozzie Smith, the Hall of Fame shortstop, as both his size and style were similar.

Now in his third year, Zach perfected his short slap swing to put the ball into play at a high rate and use his speed to gain first base increasing his consistently good on-base percentage over last year. Zach's diminutive size and small strike zone, combined with his speed, made him a problematic first out, and he was also near the top of the League leaders with infield hits. Once on, he was a threat to steal, finishing second in the National League last year in stolen bases. Since Zach and Samson both came up from the same Minor League team together, Zach roomed with Samson on the road. Their teammates often laughed at the look of two polar opposites in size and demeanor. Sammy was the big outgoing, lovable

---

1. Purqana is Aramaic for 'Deliverance, redemption'

giant, while Zach was the diminutive introvert. Sammy was overpowering in his play, while Zach was all about finesse. Somehow, despite their differences, they found in each other a kindred spirit. Both came from challenging backgrounds but made a great career out of very different physical talents.

The practice game began with a different, almost desperate feeling. It seemed as if the team was straining to find something about themselves, something that was missing. Though few wanted to admit it, each player sensed the team needed something more if they were going to contend this season. With this underlying tension, Thomas called for the first pitch, and Sammy started Zach off with a high inside fastball, clocking 98 MPH on the scoreboard radar gun, brushing Zach back off the plate. It was not exactly what Zach expected from his roommate, and Zach stepped back and shook his head.

"Sorry, Zach," said a smiling Sammy. "Just tryin' to get your attention. Can't take it easy on you just cause you're my roomie," came the half wink, half threat, as Samson returned to his ready position. Zach frowned down at Thomas, but Thomas just shrugged, suggesting the pitching location wasn't always his decision. Zach shook his head. Samson was a teddy bear off the field but a fierce competitor once he took the mound. More determined than ever, Zach showed no intimidation and stepped back into the box, slightly closer to the plate. The second pitch was knee high and a little outside. Zach reached out and barely made late contact, fouling the pitch down the third baseline. 1-1 was the count, as Sammy's next delivery was a high fastball centered over the plate. Zach could not quite catch up but fouled the ball off up and behind home plate. Still, with a 1-2 count from 3 fastballs prior, which Zach poorly handled, Zach expected the overconfident young fireballer to want to finish him off with another missile. Samson let loose with a pitch on the outside of the plate, and Zach swung quickly, trying to catch up to the expected fastball. Unfortunately, the ace threw his off-speed changeup. Realizing his mistake too late, Zach awkwardly tried to slow his bat, but it passed high and harmlessly out in front as the late drooping delivery dove down toward the plate. Zach left the batter's box meekly as Samson turned his back, rubbing the ball hard as he awaited his next victim.

Juan fared even worse than Zach, as Sammy threw Fastball, Fastball, Slider, all strikes with the slider's late cut away, off the plate and far from Juan's swing. Next up was the captain. Andrew was a wily veteran, used to patiently waiting for his pitch. Samson tried painting just outside the plate twice with his fastball and no swing from Andrew. He brought a third fastball inside to the captain, who fouled it off hard down the third baseline. Samson came back with a changeup in the dirt, but the captain didn't bite. Finally, at 3-1, Samson delivered a hard fastball outside again, just in the strike zone, with the radar gun recording 99 MPH. Considering its velocity, the captain got a pretty good swing on the ball but got slightly under it, popping it up meekly into right field. Josh tracked it down easily and caught it for the third out of the fake inning.

Inning two started much the same. First, J.J. swung late at two fastballs on the outside corners of the plate, missing one, then fouling another off. He then held up on a slider that broke out of the strike zone but could not resist the changeup next that died down into the dirt, striking out meekly. As Judah came to bat, Slayer Samson was on a roll, perhaps overconfident, efficiently handling the top of the lineup. With his crooked nose, ruddy complexion, and sour disposition, Judah played baseball like an angry brawler ready to fight. He took a defiant stance against Samson as he stood in the batter's box, snapping the bat up and slowly lowering it back to his shoulder again, as was his custom. Judah used a squatty open stance, allowing an excellent two-eyed view of the delivery. Thomas called for a slider outside against Judah, a notorious first-pitch swinger, who seemed even more ready to swing than usual. But this was ego against ego for Samson, and his early success today made him brash. He shook Thomas off and waited for the fastball sign. Thomas relented and waited for the delivery. Samson threw his hardest pitch of the day at 100 MPH, but his location was not good; belt high out over the plate, and Judah hammered the pitch into left-center. He managed an easy standup double, and the offense gained its first baserunner.

Thomas called time and walked out to the mound to chat with his pitcher. He stood with his mask on so no one could see him speak, but Thomas stepped in close for emphasis. Thomas did not mince words. "Samson, you're a great pitcher, but sometimes you let your ego get the better of you. I know every one of these hitters by heart except one. That hit was on you because you wouldn't listen to me, and you tried to blow a fastball by a guy who loves fastballs on the first pitch. Let me call the game, and we'll beat everyone we face this year."

Samson paused for a moment, shocked by his catcher's forthrightness. But he knew what Thomas said was true, and he smiled back at Thomas, whispering, "You're right, Tommy. My bad—keep me honest."

Thomas walked back to the plate, and Sammy followed his signals without question for the next batter. On the first pitch, Nate swung late, missing the fastball badly, then swung far out in front and over the subsequent changeup, much like Zach. He struck out on a wicked slider breaking outside Nate's swing by a good six inches. Nate left the batter's box, shaking his head, feeling slightly foolish. Slayer Samson was back on track, recovered from his one mistake pitch to Judah, and looked to sail through the rest of the lineup. After Nate's at-bat, Pops called time, sending a baserunner so Judah could replace Josh in the field. Josh ran into the dugout as Pops directed him to the cubbyhole with a taped-over name "Green" on it. As he deposited his borrowed glove and pulled out the bat left there, Judah turned around from swapping out his helmet for hat and glove. Judah's expressive face looked at Josh, then the bat.

"Where'd you get that!" Judah accused, face flushed.

Before Josh could answer, Pops, leaning on the railing and looking over his shoulder at the two, said, "It's one of our extras, Judah. Relax!"

Judah stared angrily back at Josh, then broke into an evil grin. "That's OK. I doubt it's in any danger against Slayer Samson. It probably will remain untouched!" Josh said nothing as Judah turned on his heel and ran out to right.

Josh was about to leave the dugout when Pops said quietly, "All right, Josh?"

"Fine, Skipper," Josh said without hesitating.

"Pick your pitch and just do what you did in the cages," Pops said, almost too matter-of-factly. Normally calm and secure on the field, Saul felt more nervous than a rookie. He couldn't help but have far too high hopes resting on Josh's ability to hit in the big-leagues. Worse, Saul suspected his team full of pros and coaches wondered what exactly Josh was doing here and if Coach Saul had lost his mind. Saul then added one more thing he would wonder, in years to come, if it was prophecy or desperate hope. "If ever a man was put on this earth to hit a baseball, Josh, it's you," said Pops, surprising himself. Josh smiled back in a way that said he would never forget.

After a few quick practice swings with a heavy bat in the on-deck circle, Josh walked to the plate. Thomas watched him steadily as Josh drew closer. Thomas knew nothing about this player, but he knew any rookie must be nervous facing a big-league pitcher like Pirate ace Samson Gibson. There were two outs, and Josh was an unknown rookie. Time to serve the best pitch and see what Josh could do with a world-class fastball.

It was quiet, with hardly a soul in the stands. Josh paused and looked out over the field, seeing the Pirates team staring back at him in all its big-league glory. He could feel their questioning eyes on him. Who was this rookie Pops brought, and what in the world could he do against Slayer Samson Gibson on the mound? Josh tried to think of the batting cages and the calm serenity he found there but could not capture his nerves. For a moment, Josh doubted he could match up against these professional ballplayers. What *was* he doing here, Josh thought? He looked at the world around him and stepped back out of the box before getting set. As a batter, he felt totally alone, sinking into the sea during a storm.

Josh's hesitation was enough time for the only occupants in the stadium bleachers to get his attention. His back was to the home dugout as the Pirates bucked tradition and placed their dugout along the third baseline, giving the home team a beautiful view of the city skyline. Above the dugout, Ruth walked in with Martha, the intern, and Mark, the PR agent. After wandering PNC Park looking at the various Pirate artifacts, they arrived just in time to see Josh walk out to bat. Little Ruth's voice broke the silence and turned Josh and the rest of the team toward her.

"C'mon, Dad. You can do it!" Ruth cheered.

The players were a little surprised as families were not usually allowed at the closed practices, and they all turned and looked at the diminutive Asian girl with her braced legs, then back at Josh. More than a few raised their eyebrows.

Josh's sinking feeling stopped. Little Ruthie's cheer placed him on solid ground again, and he waved back and smiled. Before he turned to step into the batter's box, he saw two men walk out of the dugout tunnel and join Pops standing by the rail. It was Doc Luke and old Pete. During warm-ups and the early at-bats of the game, Doc watched the field on a monitor in his office, noting when Judah and Josh began switching to let Josh bat. Luke jumped up, spurred by some burning curiosity, and walked down the hall to Pete's office. Knocking, he stuck his head in.

"Josh is about to face Gibson. You want to go watch?"

Pete hesitated for a moment. He and Doc typically stayed behind the scenes during the practice games, but he also felt he needed to see the rookie with his own eyes. "Yeah, I'm comin'."

Doc turned and hurried out. Pete instinctively grabbed for the pillbox Pirate hat he customarily wore when he went out on the field but sat it slowly back down as the old, faded picture of his U.S. Marine Corps company caught his eye. Instead, he swiveled on his chair and opened the bottom left desk drawer grabbing a dark blue baseball cap he was gifted years ago. It bore a faded red and yellow patch with a blue V and the numbers 3/26 with the "Path-Finders'[2] logo at the bottom, Pete's old unit flash. He stared at it for a moment, not quite sure why he felt like wearing it. Finally, he put it on and scrambled after Doc Luke. He wore it as he walked out, just after Ruth shouted at her dad. Josh smiled back at his daughter, then looked at Pete as Pete settled into place next to Pops.

Pete met Josh's eyes and, for a moment, saw his gunny again. At first, slightly surprised, Josh shifted back to a knowing look of quiet confidence as if understanding his position despite the whirlwind surrounding him. All was again right with the world. Josh smiled at old Pete—and Pete remembered the feeling of Gunny smiling at him when he did something to make Gunny proud.

Seeing Pete and his USMC hat made Josh realize he was back in the world again. He lived through hell, and this was a beautiful day on his hometown baseball field. Josh took a deep breath and focused on the moment. He realized feeling alone in the batter's box was a lie, straight from the pit of hell. This was just a game, but

---

2. 26 Marine Regiment / 3rd Battalion

it was *his* game, and he was good at it. Though he didn't understand the entire plan, Josh knew God wanted him here, today. He turned back towards the plate and bent down. As the players watched, Josh kneeled on his right knee, grabbed some dirt in his right hand, held his bat in his left hand by the handle, end straight down, like a sword shoved into the earth, and bowed his head in prayer. It was much as he did before a combat mission, with a rifle instead of a bat. But this was a different prayer. It was the same prayer his father taught him to say when he was a kid playing ball in Little League. "Dear Lord, help me do my best for your honor and glory today." Peace settled over him. As he rose, he gripped the bat tightly in his two hands. Looking up at it, he no longer worried about the world around him or doubted his purpose. He looked far beyond, to the One immovable and timeless, who held all things in His control. Josh realized again; he was never alone. Finding His peace, he breathed deeply, stepped into the batter's box, and turned to face the pitcher.

Pops watched as Josh took the neutral stance he saw at the batting cage the previous day. Thomas signaled to Samson for his fastball on the outside corner. That moment, time seemed to freeze, and all the players years later would reminisce about what happened next. Before the pitch, the Pirate players and coaches were each skeptics, as this hawk of a rookie carried the bat like a stick and faced their ace pitcher. Each would see this first at-bat, indeed, this first pitch, in their mind's eye forever. Samson wound up, took a deep breath, then huffed a strong exhale, his lungs great bellows of a blacksmith's forge blowing out of his powerful chest as he released his fastball. Like a spinning rock hurled from Samson's massive sling, it sliced through the crisp spring air clocking 100 mph on the overhead scoreboard. The ball torpedoed for the plate at knee level, aiming precisely to clip the outside corner of the strike zone. The empty stadium was so quiet many thought they could hear a slight ripping of the wind from the hyper-fast delivery. However, it was the next concussive noise that was truly unforgettable. On a cool bright day, the last week of March, quiet Pittsburgh heard a new sound for the first time.

"THWAACCKK!"

The stunning sound of a perfectly timed swing from a Teutonic lance against a high-speed bullet burst through the stadium, echoing off the empty stands and reverberating through the bodies of those few present, like a tuning fork resonating to a perfectly struck chord. If time stood still as Samson made the pitch, it jolted violently into motion, all a-frenzy, spurred on by the explosion of a leather wound orb striking the impenetrable, polished ash of the Louisville Slugger. The ball launched high toward the right-center field sky. As players and witnesses stared transfixed, it rocketed into the air, arching far above the 21-foot Clemente wall, past the bleachers, and beyond, out over the turbid Allegheny River. Sailing far out of sight of the mere mortals in the stadium, the ball flew farther than any before, disappearing into the distance before plunging into the cold, rapid spring waters.

Eleven

The mammoth shot into the Allegheny pulled the gaze of everyone in PNC Park toward the sky in right field. As the ball disappeared from their views, all stared at where they last saw the shooting star hurtling into the crisp morning Pittsburgh sky. While the rest stared out toward the city beyond the outfield wall, Josh stepped out of the batter's box, turned, and walked back towards the dugout; there was no need to run the bases. At first, there was only stunned silence. The witnesses now looked back at Josh as if he were an impossible apparition, soon to vanish after his supernatural appearance. It was Zach, still in the dugout, first to move and break the spell. He walked up the stairs to meet Josh as he walked back and reached out his hand to shake Josh's.

"Greatest thing I ever saw, Josh," said Zach.

At first, the brim of his helmet shielded Josh's face as he walked head down, but now he raised his eyes to meet Zach's. Like many before, Zach saw in Josh's eyes an immeasurably kind soul smiling back at him. Josh shook Zach's hand warmly, and their movements suddenly spurred everyone to life.

Pete and the rest of the dugout, frozen statues made suddenly alive, moved to greet Josh and began almost giddily back-slapping him as he walked down the steps.

"You sure can swing a bat, partner!" said old Pete, taking Josh's hand in both his own and shaking it vigorously. "Guess we'll have to order a few extra bats—if you keep abusing them like that, they'll cry uncle sooner than later!" Doc Luke and the other players in the dugout swarmed Josh. The Thunder Brothers were next.

"Holy cow, Rook, Dju knocked tha thing halfway to Santo Domingo!" Juan laughed as he gave Josh a one-armed air clasp like an arm wrestler grinning from ear to ear.

J.J. stepped up behind him and picked up Josh in a bear hug. "Bro, Wheaties called and said they want you on their box!"

Nate and Phil both laughed and patted him boisterously. The big third base-man slapped his shoulder so hard he almost knocked him over. "Hey Rook, Sammy's lookin' for the number of the bus that just hammered into his pitch—you may have to apologize for murdering his delivery!"

Andrew was last, standing with his hands on his hips at the end of the gauntlet of congratulations, looking very serious. Josh turned to the captain, and Andrew stared at him for a moment. Andrew broke the silence with a face-splitting grin. "Good grief, Rook. Where have you been hiding all our lives? That was a heck of a homer—Think you can do it a few more times?"

Josh laughed as Andrew reached out, shaking his hand with one arm, giving his shoulder a friendly squeeze with the other. "I'll give it a shot, Captain," was Josh's understated response.

Only Coach Saul held back, unmoving. He stood with his hands gripping the dugout railing tightly, still not taking his eyes off the distant spot in the heavens where the ball disappeared. Finally, he released his grip to look back at Josh, now surrounded by his teammates and coaches in jubilant commotion. Something inside Saul didn't quite believe his hopes and dreams had come true. He questioned himself and his motivations after seeing Josh's extraordinary talent at the cages. Overnight, he began to doubt and wonder if he was so desperate to find a hitter, someone who could put the Pirates over the top, he somehow dreamed what Josh did. Now, Josh faced one of the best pitchers in the big-leagues, and the result was floating down the Allegheny, to the Ohio and beyond—to the endless river and a sea of possibilities.

Twelve

J osh's homer entirely changed the complexion of the practice game and the team. Everyone seemed to relax as hope and promise of a new season replaced the trepidation and desperation before Josh stepped to the plate. The Pirate coaches and players came alive. Everyone played their best ball as the failures of spring training faded away. For the rest of the day, Josh alternated between the outfield and trips to the plate. He made three more plate appearances. Samson faced him again and tried to make Josh bite on a changeup in the dirt after a high and tight fastball, but Josh wouldn't take the bait, unfazed and ready for the next delivery, a would-be-strike of a slider on the outside corner. Josh placed it neatly down the right field line for a stand-up double. Next, Josh faced one of the Pirate's better middle relievers, an off-speed junker they often used after Samson because of his polar opposite delivery and arsenal. He, too, tried to throw Josh several breaking balls out of the strike zone, but Josh showed a good eye, refusing to bite on the pitches until the pitcher tried a large slow curve breaking just over the outside corner of the plate. As Pops witnessed when Josh faced Goliath, Josh waited on the pitch. He caught it cleanly with an effortlessly smooth but powerful swing. Its high rainbow arch carried the center field fence and dropped just over the green batter's eye wall behind, banging off the roof of Manny's Barbeque. This time, the Pirate players just laughed and high-fived each other.

Finally, in a simulated ninth inning, one-run game, Josh faced a right-handed reliever working with no one on. On Pop's orders, Thomas gave the signal and intentionally walked Josh. The reliever and catcher tried to work from the stretch, and Pops signaled the third base coach to put the hit and run on. The batter missed the pitch, and Pops expected Josh to get thrown out, but he got a good jump on the pitcher and was deceptively fast. Thomas made a hard but slightly high throw. Zach, playing short, tried to snap the tag down, but the quick old rookie slid in on a close play. Since there was no actual umpire at the base, it was Zach's call. He looked down at the rookie, surprised by his speed. With a growing smile of amused disbelief, Zach signaled back toward Thomas, shaking his head. "Sorry, T, the Rook got in under my tag." Thomas looked over at Pops as they shared a pleasant surprise. Their "Old Rookie" could run the bases as well.

The practice game became electric as everyone felt loose, playing at a high level. Josh's presence and performance pushed them all to do their best. Still, not everyone was glad. Judah approached Coach Saul with a serious, concerned tone when he caught Pops relatively alone towards the end of the game.

"Pops, I would like to know where I stand and your intentions?" said Judah, adding, "I've brought a lot to this team, and I think I deserve to know."

"Judah, I know what you have brought to this team. That's why you're here. It's a long season. We are trying to field the best team with the best lineup. You know things change during the season, and we'll continue making decisions that best contribute to winning." Judah looked pensively at Pops. "Look, nothing is decided. We will let you know when everyone else does, and I promise I'll make the best call for the team and review as the year progresses."

Judah didn't seem very satisfied but nodded and returned to the field. In the end, Pops wrapped up the day with little fanfare. He told everyone to get a good night's rest as they would have the more typical position practice tomorrow starting at 1030 AM.

Pops grabbed Josh and directed him to see Doc Luke first, then Pete, to establish his post-game routine. Pops stopped the two captains, asking them to stay behind in the dugout. The rest of the team headed to the locker room. Saul waited for everyone else to depart. "Gents," Saul began, "We have a unique situation here."

Thomas smiled, and Andrew chuckled. "You can say that again, Coach. Where the heck did you find this guy?" Andrew expressed what everyone was thinking.

Saul almost said he stumbled onto Josh like manna lying outside his tent, a gift from heaven. Instead, he brushed the thought away quickly, trying to compose himself. "Just a new prospect we luckily came across before anyone else," Pops said in what may be the greatest understatement of his long coaching career. "Look," he hurried on, "I want you two to take him under your wings—Andrew, you help teach him the ropes on what to expect as a big-league player. He has...," Saul fought for the right words, "Limited experience with professional ball." Both players looked back at Saul, slightly stunned. "Tommy, I want you to take the book you work on with Coach Caleb and start schooling Josh on what he will face." Coach Caleb's keen eye for the future saw the desire and potential to become a successful coach in Thomas. Both spent time together writing "The Book" on the opposition's pitching staff, sharing it with the team. "Start with St. Louis, since we face them next Monday in the opener. Catch him at the start of practice tomorrow and set up some time for the two of you to work."

"So, he's signed then, Coach?" Andrew asked.

"Not exactly, Andrew, but I feel we'll have him on board in a few days." Saul paused, looking down at his hands for a second. He knew his work was just getting started. To begin with, he must face the stingy owners with a whopper of a request for an unknown player. "One step at a time, partner," Saul could almost hear old Pete say, "Don't get ahead of yourself."

Saul nodded to himself, then raised his gaze finally and asked, "Any more questions?"

"Nope," Andrew spoke for both of them. "I am glad you found him, Coach. After what we saw today, I'd hate to look across at the opposing dugout and see him there."

"You and me both, Andrew," said Saul, preparing for the long evening and long week ahead, accomplishing everything to make Josh a Pittsburgh Pirate by opening day.

Saul followed his captains to the locker room and walked through with words of encouragement to his players. Samson, in particular, looked a little nonplussed as he began his post-game ice bath treatment on his arm and body. Pops stopped to see how he was doing. "I felt good, Skipper, but I got knocked around some today."

Thomas, who dropped his gear nearby before his own ice bath, said, "Other than your pitch to Judah in the second inning, you pitched a solid outing, Sammy."

"From what I saw, you pitched strong, Samson," Coach Saul agreed. "You gave up three hits total, and two of them were on tough pitches. I've got a feeling you won't be facing many like Josh that can hit those regularly. You looked good out there, and I expect you to do fine on opening day."

"Thanks, Coach. Glad I won't be facing Josh on an opposing team," Samson said honestly.

Saul smiled and nodded before continuing to Pete's office door. He knocked, and Luke, listening to Pete, stood aside, opening the door for Saul. Pete continued his directions with Doc Luke around his unlit cigar. "...and make sure you get him started with a good 'old guy' post-game regime. His body is probably not used to baseball workout...." They paused as Saul took the old mahogany chair Josh sat in earlier. Luke could see Saul had a lot on his mind.

Luke finished quickly, "Right. Better grab him and get started." He nodded to Saul and headed out towards Josh's locker, closing the glass door. The two men watched through the glass as Doc Luke spoke to Josh. The windows were thick enough one side couldn't hear the other, and the two coaches looked on silently for a moment as Doc seemed to ask Josh some questions. Luke then pointed to the ice bath areas, giving him some instructions. Finally, Saul turned to talk to Pete as Josh nodded and began peeling off his gear.

"So, what do you think of our new recruit?" Saul asked for openers.

"What do I think?" Pete harrumphed around his cigar, still hands behind his head, looking at Josh. "I think...," Pete said in a low gravelly voice as he turned and leaned forward, taking his cigar out of his mouth, gesturing toward Josh, "You better sign him pretty quick!"

"I know," Saul said, nodding and looking down at his hands with concern.

"What's the matter?" Pete said, wrinkling his brow as he sat back, placing his cigar back in his mouth, eying Saul while picking up a glove, pounding the old softball into it.

"Just want to make sure we are doing the right thing. I have to go to the owners and sell them on signing a guy no one ever heard of that we saw play his first and only practice, with no background and no history," Saul said, summing up the daunting task and decision in front of him.

"Oh, he definitely has a history, all right. We just don't know what it is," said Pete cautiously as he hesitated, looking out past Saul to the locker room. "I am not trying to make your job any harder - but you might want to ensure he passes his physical with Doc when you go to the owners." Saul looked up from his hands to Pete with a furrowed brow of some confusion. "Don't make it obvious, Pops, but take another look at your *rookie*," said Pete with a slight nod towards Josh.

Doc Luke walked over to talk to some players working with the trainers in the workout areas and the ice baths—specifically Samson and Thomas. It appeared Luke directed Josh to get an ice bath as well. Josh stripped down to the pair of compression shorts Doc gave him before practice and stood up from his bench to walk over to the cold water tanks. His body could have been the model for Michael Angelo's David, save for the long white scar hidden by his clothing. It ran jaggedly down the side of his left abdomen and hip, continued onto his thigh, and stopped just above his left knee. Stripped now, it was clearly visible, a long, large twin to the one on Josh's face. Saul whistled, inhaling between clenched teeth in surprise, catching his first glimpse.

Both men sat quietly for a few moments as Pete flashed back to the wounds of many friends he visited after returning from Vietnam. The scars weren't just physical. What they carried went far beyond the flogging of flesh and sinew. Pete shook himself quickly out of his reverie. "Look, Pops," he said as he recognized Saul's concern, "Whatever baggage this kid has, we saw him run and play the field fine today. Extraordinary even. Between you and me, we have over 75 years scouting talent all around this country—and around the world, for that matter. You saw something in the rookie at the cages to bring him to practice today, a week before opening day. And now we saw him against our best pitchers. Be honest; Have you ever seen anyone do what he did these last two days?"

Pops looked back at Pete. "No," he said without hesitation, "I've never seen anyone do what he did today and yesterday—Not even close."

Pete stopped pounding the ball into the glove and sat forward again, looking directly at Saul, who focused on him.

"Neither have I. In fact, I've never even heard of someone hitting like that," Pete said with finality. Saul nodded, and they both looked back out through the glass. After a few moments, Pete spoke again softly. "My friend, I don't often give you advice...," Saul looked back at him, quickly hiding a slight smile. He knew Pete was never one to hold back what he thought when they were alone, which is why Saul often came to have these discussions since he was a young player on the roster. Pete looked back at Saul and continued as if he hadn't noticed, "...But whatever his story, you have to take a chance on this guy, no matter the costs."

Saul nodded as clarity replaced doubt. Pete confirmed what Saul already knew but needed to hear from his old friend and mentor. He was resolute again. Standing up, Saul said, "You're right, Pete. Thanks. I guess it's time to get to work and earn my paycheck."

Thirteen

Samson and Thomas discussed the day's events, reviewing the game as they endured cool baths. Tommy often worked with his pitchers on their mental approach when time and their personalities allowed. Thomas took a particular interest in Samson since the young man rose quickly to the big-leagues. Samson, the young phenom, valued Tommy's experience and wisdom in calling the game. The rest of the locker room emptied as they sat in the ice-cold baths in their post-game regimen.

Doc told Josh to hit the tub for 10-15 minutes while he talked to their physical therapy team next door to schedule a massage and rub down. Doc walked Josh over to the ice baths, briefly explaining their operation as the two other players paused their discussion. As Josh entered the tub, Doc headed to the massage area. Samson and Thomas stared sideways at the scar lancing down Josh's left side.

Just before Doc reached the massage door, Saul exited Pete's office into the locker room. "Doc, what have you got planned for Josh?" Saul said.

"We're starting him with a good ice-down, and I'm about to ask Cy to give him the 'old man special'—figure his arm and legs will hurt in the morning, but it'll help. He's probably got an hour or so until he's ready to leave."

"OK, sounds like a plan. Thanks," said Pops. "Oh, and Doc!" Saul called back to Luke, who stuck his head out of the therapy room's open door. "We need to schedule Josh ASAP for a player physical—think you can set that up?"

Doc nodded. "I think I can call in a favor or two and get everything going tomorrow if you like."

"Thanks." Saul then turned towards Josh. "Josh, I need to talk to you after you get done. I'll check back with you before you leave, OK?"

"OK, Coach," Josh said, smiling and shivering slightly from the ice-cold water.

Samson and Thomas stayed quiet until after Doc and Pops exited. Samson sat in the tub with his elbow wrapped in a cold gel pack. As big as the tubs were, his oversized frame made them seem almost small. He was smiling as always. Never one to hold back, Samson spoke first. "Well, after the way you hit my fastball today, I thought you were Superman, but that scar on you makes me think maybe you're Robocop, eh Josh?"

Josh smiled slightly at the young man's quip. "A little accident a few years back," Josh said, trying and failing to get used to the cold water.

"In the future, have Doc get you one of these beanies," Thomas said, pointing to the one on his head. "They look goofy, but when you're in the cold bath, they keep your head warm, and it helps you survive a little better."

"Thanks, I will," said Josh.

Thomas continued, "So Josh, what's your story? Where'd you come from?"

Josh paused before answering. "I grew up in western Pennsylvania. I left home after high school and just moved back recently."

Samson laughed, "Why come back? Why not go somewhere warmer—go where the action is!" He laughed, and Thomas smirked and shook his head. Samson was always dreaming of the bright lights and big city. Everyone expected the Pirates to lose their star pitcher once his contract was up—signing with one of the big clubs from a large city that could afford the large salary and provide the type of "big" lifestyle the young Samson yearned to find.

"I've been all around the world since I left home," said Josh, "But after seeing it all, I realized what I wanted most was to come home. It's a great, safe place where I could raise my daughter and give her a chance to grow up like I did and have a wonderful life."

"Not me, man—I am ready to live La Vida Loca!" said Samson, smiling at Thomas. "Know what I mean, Bro?" Thomas shook his head with a wry smile, looking back at Josh.

"I think you will find, the world and its offerings aren't all they are cracked up to be," Josh countered, "and don't forget, where your treasure is, there your heart will be also."[1]

"Ahhh, old Mathew 6:21, eh Josh?" said Samson smiling, and Thomas looked at him, surprised. "That's right. I was a good Baptist boy. Never missed a Sunday, so you don't have to preach to me, Bro. Or are you trying to be like my dear ole grandma back in Georgia? Wantin' me to stay on the 'straight and narrow'?" asked Samson with arched eyebrows and a grin at Josh.

"Just how I see things. But if you don't take the Bible's word for it, I have also found a mother or grandma wants the very best for her kids. Perhaps it's good to listen to what she has to say as well?"

"Ah, I will listen when I am grown old, like you and Thomas here! Until then, I have to sow my wild oats!"

---

1. Matthew 6:21

"Then I guess you remember the one about reaping what you sow,[2] Samson?" Josh asked calmly. His dark brown eyes, steady on Samson, neither accusing nor condemning, holding Samson's eyes in his own. Samson saw the man across from him clearly for the first time. He couldn't quite make out what manner of man he was. Josh was dark-skinned, with wavy dark brown hair and a broad hawkish nose. Something ethnic about him—maybe Eastern European or Middle Eastern, Samson thought, but he can't be a black guy, could he? He took another look at Josh's face—it was a kind face—kind, despite the jagged scar. Josh held Samson's gaze. Samson, for the first time, looked at Josh deeply. Those eyes conveyed honesty and clarity of sight that seemed to bore right down to his soul. They reminded him of his grandma, who raised him after his mother died of a heart attack, far too young.

"Yeah, I remember that one too," Samson said more quietly and paused momentarily, then dropped his eyes from Josh's gaze, looking down at the pool of water. His smile faded a bit as he withdrew into his thoughts.

"Well," said Thomas, trying to break the silence and change the subject. "So that was your daughter in the stands, Josh?" Josh nodded. "How'd you and her mom meet?"

"We met while I was working overseas," said Josh.

"Where's her mom today—I didn't see her in the stands?" said Thomas.

"She passed away a year and a half ago. It's just Ruth and me now," answered Josh.

"Oh," said Thomas awkwardly, "I am sorry to hear that."

"It's OK," said Josh smiling sadly. "We'll see each other again one day."

---

2. Galatians 6:7-8

Fourteen

Saul left the owners' offices with the impression he had just spent the last of his personal favors. The owners made clear their investment' better pay back quickly and handsomely. A group of several partners controlled the Pirates, but the Chief Partner and Pirate President was now Cai Annason. Cai recently took over for his father-in-law, who held the office for many years and still exerted his power from retirement. Because Cai held his position primarily through his father-in-law's good graces, he was a stickler for the detailed rules his father-in-law established for the entire organization. Cai expected Saul to discuss every move with him ahead of time, especially one as significant as bringing a new player to the majors.

It was little surprise that Saul's request to sign an unknown directly to the big-league club did not go over well. Cai would have blocked Saul's unexpected request as a show of power over Saul's arrogance, asking to sign the unknown rookie without asking Cai's permission first. However, Saul advised Cai and the other shareholders, passing on Josh would be the miss of a lifetime. Though Cai remained skeptical, Saul intimated that if Josh went elsewhere, it would eventually get out Mr. Annason passed on signing Josh. Cai's fear of looking foolish in front of his father-in-law and the other owners was even greater than his desire to oppose Saul's leadership and strengthen his power and position over the respected coach. Cai begrudgingly acquiesced. Still, Saul's request to offer Josh nearly double the League minimum guaranteed, plus impossible performance-based bonuses, shocked the normally taciturn Cai. In return, Cai demanded the performance bonuses set at play plateaus beyond the abilities of even a star player.

"If he is as good as you say he is, Saul—let him perform these miracles you describe, and then we'll believe he's truly the great player and savior for *your* team," Cai pronounced with thinly veiled ire. Saul did not miss the emphasis by Cai this was Saul's guy, not his, and he left with the distinct feeling Mr. Annason and the others didn't allow him to hire Josh out of trust—instead, they gave him an extension of rope with which to hang himself should Josh fail to perform.

Still, signing Josh was far from a done deal, as Saul understood the offer would be much less than just about any other club in the league. Saul did have two things going for him. Josh was a local, and Saul hoped he wanted to play for his hometown team. Hometown loyalty was uncommon today in professional sports, where stars often go to the highest bidder. But Saul felt Josh might be a kindred spirit, as he too once worked to get back to the burgh. Second, as far as he knew, no other club knew Josh existed, or they would have scooped him up long ago.

Pops stopped back at his office before heading to the team locker area. He flipped through his old Rolodex, preferring to keep the paper kind rather than going digital, and spun to a name unused for a while. Joseph Arima. Joe represented Pops from the time he first turned pro. A local Pittsburgher, Joe came to watch Saul back when he played ball in high school. He was a little Jewish guy with a little Jewish wife, but looks were deceiving. Saul soon realized Joe possessed an amazing mind for baseball, talent, and life lessons. The faculty at Trinity Christian High School recommended Joe to Saul's father. Joe talked with Saul's dad often as Saul developed, and the pros started taking notice. Saul's dad advised his son of his confidence in Joe as a man Saul could trust.

When Saul turned 18, signing with Joe after getting to know him for the last several seasons was easy. Although Joe didn't look much like a sportsman, Saul came to admire Joe's understanding of both the game and the business of baseball. Joe always steered Saul in the right direction through the years, even when Saul's vision was less clear. Joe was semi-retired now, but he still kept up with Pops and visited the park often, where he and his wife were long-time season ticket holders behind the dugout. As one of the more successful agents, many players sought to make Joe their own over the years, but Joe kept his client list short. Instead of moving to a big market city, Joe stayed a Pittsburgher in both occupation and spirit. He represented players mainly for the Pirates or Pittsburgh talent over the years so he could stay close to home. Joe and his wife still lived in the same house in Squirrel Hill they purchased nearly fifty years ago. Pops knew Joe stopped taking new clients for the last seven or eight years, but he made the call anyway.

The phone rang a few times, and Joe answered. "Hello, Saul. Beth and I were just talking about you." Elizabeth and Joe brought young Saul over to their house regularly since they first met, and although Saul's visits were more infrequent since becoming a coach, he still loved every time he went. They always made him feel at home just as much as when he was a young high school ballplayer so many years ago. It never mattered to Joe and Elizabeth that Saul was a black kid from the tough side of town. Saul saw the Arimas as second parents to him now that both his parents passed, and he trusted no one more.

"Joe, I am glad you were because I have wanted to call you all day. How's Miss Elizabeth doing?"

"She's doing well. We're enjoying the spring weather and looking forward to being at the park to see you and your men soon. Now I know you're a busy man and have something more specific on your mind, so what can I do for you, Coach?" replied Joe.

"Joe, I know you're retired now, but I need you to come out of retirement—and before you say anything, hear me out...."

Saul spent the next twenty minutes telling Joe how he came across Josh at the cages and his performance there and on the field today. Joe listened patiently. When Saul finished his review of Josh's playing abilities, Joe asked several questions about Josh's background. Saul realized he knew very little about the man. Saul told Joe that Josh's only family was a middle-school-aged daughter, and Josh originally grew up in the area, but Saul reluctantly admitted he knew little else. Finally, Saul ended, "Joe, this guy's older. He's older than any of my players, and, well..., he seems to come from a difficult past. I don't know what it is, but I know this—Josh's talent for baseball is exceptional. However, he is still a rookie and new to the business. He needs the best to represent him and his needs—to look out for him. He needs you, Joe. There's no one else I trust to handle this player."

Joe, as always, thoughtfully considered what Saul told him. Joe meant it when he said Elizabeth and he were talking about Saul. Thoughts of Saul troubled them all day, even though they hadn't seen him since the team went to spring training in Florida. Something was nagging them both. Joe and Elizabeth became messianic Jews as young adults. Many from their lifelong Jewish roots subsequently rejected them because they accepted Christ as the Messiah. As a result, they turned to several Christian organizations to invest their time and effort and made many friends, including Trinity Christian High School, Saul's alma mater. Although they couldn't have children, Joe and Elizabeth loved working with young people at Trinity, where they both volunteered for decades. They helped the city's underprivileged children and sponsored poor students to attend the school. They found young Saul as a teenager at Trinity and grew to love Saul like their own son. Elizabeth said to Joe before Saul called, "You ought to give Saul a call—we've both been worried about him all day. I think the Lord wants us to talk to him and see if he's OK."

Saul waited for Joe to answer. His silence made Saul more than a little nervous. However, Joe was only confirming in his mind and heart, this was what the Lord wanted him to do. Hearing Saul's request as he described the situation, quieted the troubled spirit Joe felt and replaced it with a sense of peace. "OK, Saul," Joe said in agreement with the Spirit, "Bring Josh over to see me tomorrow after practice. Remember, if I take him on, I will get the deal he needs, right?"

More than a little relieved, Saul replied, "That's all I want, Joe—I will have him there by 6:00 PM."

"Sounds good. We'll have dinner waiting for you both—but yours will be to go—Capiche?"

"Understood—and thanks. We'll be there!"

Joe hung up the phone, and Elizabeth, who was knitting quietly next to him, listening to Joe's side of the conversation, paused and looked at him over her reading glasses expectedly.

"Looks like everything's alright with Saul, but we may have another young man to take care of dear—would that be all right?" said Joe to Beth's silent question.

"That'll be fine, dear," she said, smiling, as she returned to her knitting. God was in his heaven, and all was right with the world in the Arima house again.

Fifteen

P ops descended back into the team area and found himself outside Pete's door. He could hear him talking with Doc Luke in muffled tones. He reached up to knock and saw the four Pirates Hall of Famers' picture on the door. Was he on the brink of signing another member to add to that storied legacy?

Saul knocked, and Pete said, "Come in." Saul entered as Doc started to rise from the mahogany chair. Pops waved him back down as he needed to catch Josh.

"OK, Pops, how'd it go with the money—did they tighten their grip or swing for the fences?" snarled Pete around the cigar.

"Well, they are more than a little skeptical, but I assured them he was a game-changer," said Saul. Pete knew there was probably more to it than Saul's simple pronouncement, but he did not press. "How's he doing?" Saul asked Luke.

"OK, basically—the usual middle-age aches and pains, I think—he told me about his workout regimen. It's complete, well-rounded, and he's obviously disciplined in executing it, or he wouldn't be in such good shape. Primarily, I think he will be sore in his throwing arm—I would restrict that tomorrow if I were you. The rest is standard issues and no worse than any of our 30 and over guys. He's over next door, finishing a massage with Cy. Little Ruthie's there too. She's a pip!"

"Right, I should head over. I'll say goodnight and see you guys in the morning."

Saul moved through the locker room to an open door where Josh was lying on a massage bed, and Simon, the Pirate head physical therapist, and a licensed masseur, worked on Josh. Simon Cyrene, or Cy, as most called him, was the club's gentle giant. He was a tall, strong African American and rivaled Samson with overlarge hands and a solid upper body, but a polar opposite to Samson with an introverted, quiet personality. He used his strength to great effect, manipulating the Pirate's stable of athletes with ease. Cy worked on Josh, finishing his famous "old man special." Pops himself got one or two a month—no one hurt you so well as Cy. Saul often thought afterwards, Cy may be the most important member of his staff, and many of his older players and coaches probably agreed. Little Ruth sat on a chair nearby, regaling her dad and Cy of everything she saw and the staff and players she met. Ruth collected several souvenirs today, including Andrew's signed Jersey. She pulled it on over her clothes, and it extended almost to her knees. The men weren't getting many words in, but Cy smiled and nodded as she explained her day in detail. Josh occasionally grimaced as Cy found and worked out a particularly troubling knot in Josh's muscular back. Cy looked up at Saul as he arrived.

"Hello Coach, just about finished here with Josh. He'll be as good as new and ready for a good night's sleep tonight!" Cy said in a deep bass voice.

"Doing all right there, Josh?"

"Fine, Coach," Josh said between slightly clenched teeth. "Remembering a few muscles, I must have forgotten."

"And how bout you, young lady," asked Saul. "Did you have a good day with Mark and Martha?"

"I'm great, Coach. Mark took me all over the stadium and got me all this cool stuff. I especially like the radio broadcaster's booth. I can't wait to meet the broadcasters when they're here. Someday I would like to be one. Martha was great. She bought me a burger, fries, and a coke from Riverwalk Grill. It was delicious. They even brought us peanuts and some cotton candy during the practice game. Look, Andrew gave me his jersey, and he even signed it! It's a little big, but I'll grow into it! Did you see my dad hit those home runs, Coach? Just like I said he could!"

"Yep, I saw it, Ruth, just like you said."

Cy finished and patted Josh on the shoulder. "You're good to go, Chief,"

Josh sat up, saying, "Thanks, Cy...I think?" Cy looked slightly concerned, but Josh smiled sheepishly at the big man with a reassuring grin.

Cy laughed, "No pain, no gain, my friend—believe me, you'll thank me in a few hours when you go to bed. Between Doc Luke and I, we'll keep you going for 162 and then some."

"Cy, would you mind taking Ruth next door to Pete's? We'll be there in a minute."

"No problem, Coach," he said, "Come on, Ruthie. Time you met the oldest curmudgeon on the Team—nobody knows more about the Pirates than him."

Ruth grabbed her bag of goodies and reached her little hand out for Cy's enormous one. He helped her up, and she walked with him out the door towards Pete's. "See you in a minute, Dad!" she smiled back at Josh and Coach Saul.

Saul turned to Josh. "So how are you *really* doin', Son?"

"Pretty good, Coach," said Josh. Pops looked somewhat skeptical. "Seriously—my arm's feeling it a bit, not used to so much throwing, but the rest of me feels pretty good. Cy is..." He wrinkled his brow.

Pops chimed in, "I know, it hurts while he's doing it, but after he's done and you start to recover, you feel a ton better."

"Yeah? Guess I am still recovering," said Josh. After a momentary pause, Josh looked up at Saul and said, "So what's the plan now, Coach?"

"Finish getting dressed, take Ruthie home, and get a good night's rest. Come back here tomorrow for a 10:00 AM start. We'll have some position play, take some batting practice, and then I cut 'em loose for individual workouts. Except for you. You and I have a date with your agent."

"I don't have an agent, Coach."

"You do now, and he's the best. For one thing, he's the toughest for management to say no to.—I know because he was mine when I played—great for a player, tough if you're the owner."

"Or the coach?"

"Yeah, well, he keeps me honest."

"Coach, what about Ruthie—she's with me everywhere I go."

"Doesn't she have school?"

"Yes, but I don't have anyone to watch her afterwards—I let her skip today...." Josh and Pops were alone now, but Josh dropped his voice a little and continued quietly. "Coach, Ruthie's my world now. She and I only have each other, and I will take her with me regardless of where I go...."

Saul nodded thoughtfully and contemplated Josh's words as he looked around the room. Cy's masseur annex of the locker room was an oasis for the players and staff. It held several couches and chairs beside the three masseur tables where Cy and his two assistants worked on the players. Cy furnished it as a nice relaxing lounge area and a place of solitude for people to withdraw and relax. While the press was permitted into the locker room, the team would close the door to this area as it was off-limits. Pops allowed the players their privacy here, and it also became a sanctuary where the team chaplain, Pastor Timothy, would meet with the players occasionally. In the room's corner was a semi-circle of comfy chairs with a coffee table in the middle. On it was some reading material, and an old, worn black Bible with a cross embossed on its cover. Saul observed Cy reading it many times—he struck such an unusual picture when he did, putting on a pair of delicate half-rimmed glasses. A giant of a man with giant hands gently cradling the book, making it look tiny. When he saw Cy's Bible, Saul thought of Ms. Phoebe from Oakland Christian School. It closely matched her ever-present, well-worn Bible with a similar leather cover and embossed cross. Ms. Phoebe, as a long-time teacher at the school and deaconess at a large Pittsburgh church, was an old friend who helped Saul's little sister get through school and out of the mean streets of the hill district safely. Phoebe helped her get a good start at college, eventually leading to a distinguished career as a lawyer. Ms. Phoebe was still active throughout the community and in several Christian organizations. An idea began to formulate in Saul's mind.

"I understand, Josh," Saul said finally. "Look, I have an idea about that. Let me make some phone calls tonight. Tell you what. We will send Martha to get Ruthie after school tomorrow and bring her to meet us at your agent's house. Meanwhile, let me see what I can do for Ruth."

"OK, Coach. I can give you our address, so you can give it to Martha to pick up Ruth after school."

"Sounds good. Why don't you get changed, and you and Ruth head home? You're in for a big day tomorrow."

They both walked out into the locker room. Saul got the address and said his goodbyes to Josh and Ruth. Leaving them with Pete, Saul hurried back to his office. He needed to look up one more number in his old Rolodex. It was even longer since he called this phone number. He hoped Ms. Phoebe was still available. Saul got a twinge in his gut, though, as he knew Ms. Phoebe was a tough nut, and she would ask him if he was faithfully attending Church. Baseball and life sometimes got the better of him, and Saul sadly admitted his church attendance waned in recent years. Being a little afraid of the old Christian teacher's opinion of him made Saul chuckle, but he knew, deep down, her tough veneer covered a soft heart. However, Saul suspected even if she could help, there would be a price to pay. It always surprised him what she got people to do, who needed her help. He knew it was worth it and dialed the old, faded number. On the other end, a familiar voice answered, "Hello Saul, it's been a long time since you visited. Where've you been...?"

Sixteen

As Ms. Phoebe hung up the phone with Saul, she contemplated their conversation. A player found, out of the blue, with great potential. But Saul wanted someone to care for the player's daughter while traveling with the team. Saul needed a nanny with teaching/home-schooling certification. He knew Phoebe worked many programs, a few she ran in Pittsburgh, and others she held connections and supported throughout the area. The coach sounded desperate—something unusual for Saul, whom she knew for decades. Saul knew he could trust anyone Phoebe recommended. Saul promised to make good on her finder's fee, and at that thought, she smiled. She first met the Samuelsons when she shepherded Saul's sister through school and into a bright future. Once Saul could afford it, he always gave generously and supported her many Christian causes, often donating his time and financial support when Phoebe needed a patron. She was one of the few who knew of Saul's generosities over the years. Truth be told, she probably owed him. Still, this was a tall order. Strangely enough, someone already came to mind, but it was a slightly delicate situation.

Ever the organizer and volunteer, Ms. Phoebe worked for many charitable organizations. She met Mary Dalene on a chilly night a decade ago, right off the streets. Phoebe helped her find shelter at the Light of Life Rescue Mission on Pittsburgh's North Side, where she volunteered. Mary was a teen runaway trapped by sex trafficking and drugs who escaped the street life through the help of the Mission. When Phoebe first met Mary a decade ago, she was a broken young girl with no self-esteem, searching desperately for help; Help out of addiction and help out of the life of abuse and neglect. Mary needed a miracle, and she found it, beginning with their meeting and Phoebe introducing her to Jesus.

During her time at the mission, Mary started her new life in the grace Christ offered. Despite Phoebe's many responsibilities, she took a special interest in Mary, as it seemed God placed her on Phoebe's heart to help, heal, and love. Slowly, the young, frightened, broken girl recovered, and her life renewed in the Christian setting. Mary gave her life to Christ while at the mission. She completed the Light of Life program and earned her GED. After a year at a community college, Mary received a scholarship to Grove City College, PA. Mary recently graduated with her teaching certificate and a degree in education, with a minor in special education. Mary wanted desperately to teach young children and return the favor of love and education she received. She was still developing her self-confidence and trying to find what Christ could do with her new life. Phoebe talked to Mary only a week ago. Mary was a meticulous, hard worker with an even greater love for children than most, but Phoebe knew the young girl was still trying to find her way.

As Phoebe prayed this week, she could not shake the feeling, God spoke to her quietly, saying, *Wait and see.* Now, Phoebe saw the circumstances of Saul's and Mary's unknown future not as random coincidences, but more like the Creator's providence, as two pieces of a puzzle put together perfectly in His timing. Phoebe picked up the phone and dialed. A familiar voice answered quietly on the other end, "Hello, Ms. Phoebe, how are you?" said Mary.

"I am wonderful, Mary, and I think I have found you an employment opportunity you will want to consider...."

Seventeen

As practice began at ten o'clock the next day, the Pirates played with light-hearted jubilation. Opening day was a few days away, and the frustration of a mediocre spring seemed left behind as the team carried a new hope this season could be extraordinary. If they were honest, it was something few felt most of this spring. Josh's play seemed to elevate those around him and renew their spirits.

Position play went well for Josh as he continued to impress coaches and players. Coach Saul told Coach Phil to keep it at three-quarter speed or less. Coach Phil removed the basket, making the players throttle back by rotating through as a cut-off man. Still, Josh's fielding displayed solid decisions on his initial jump on the ball, surprising range, and accurate big-league throws.

Batting practice was more suspenseful than usual as Saul held Josh to bat last. Saul wanted to prevent a letdown from any players who would follow Josh. The team's energy grew with anticipation. Finally came Josh's turn. As the players looked on from their various position work, all other practices came to a standstill. Besides the regular onlookers, Cai Annason and several key partners were high in the secluded owner's box, enjoying a catered lunch while watching practice. Josh did not disappoint. For his 25 pitches, Josh swung 18 times. Josh hit all 18 sharply, scattering nine around the outfield and knocking nine out of the park. Two homers wound up in the river, and one blast to left field hammered into PNC Park's large scoreboard above the left field bleachers, knocking out several pixels, leaving a dark dead spot on the board. Even skeptical Cai raised an eyebrow at that prodigious blast.

While Josh's performance elated most of the team, some harbored personal concerns. Only 26 make each big-league roster, and with Josh's arrival, someone must go. Judah was chief among those, with a noticeable chip on his shoulder. He was the Pirate right fielder and a starter for most of the last two seasons. Judah played an up-and-down season last year, starting poorly, but after a short stint on the disabled list in July, he returned with a strong August and September to finish with decent numbers overall. Still, in this final year of his current contract, he must prove himself to the organization to get the long-term offer he felt he deserved. As he watched Josh's excellent play, a simmering resentment took hold in Judah. How could this aged rookie, out of nowhere, walk onto the team and become the team darling? Judah feared he could lose everything if Josh continued to do well.

After Josh's batting, the practice drew to a close. Saul kept the day short since the team flew out tomorrow morning back to Bradenton to complete three more preseason games Thursday, Friday, and Saturday. The Pirates would travel on Sunday for the season opener in St. Louis, Monday, at Busch Stadium. Pops dismissed the team to their individual post-practice work, reminding them it was an early start tomorrow morning.

After cutting the team loose, Saul grabbed Josh and pulled him aside. "You have an appointment with your new agent, Joe Arima, at 6:00 PM. We should leave by 5:30 sharp to get to his house in Squirrel Hill. I have already told Martha to bring Ruth after school. Joe's wife will entertain her, and a prospective nanny recommended by an experienced friend of mine in the local area."

"Coach, I am not sure about a nanny—how will I afford it?" Josh replied.

"Josh, while I can only offer so much to an untested rookie in the way of salary, I told your agent of your need to have your daughter with you. This contact is a Christian teacher and administrator at one of the area's schools I have known since I was a kid. She took care of my sister's education needs, and she says this nanny is top-notch, with all the credentials as a teacher. Your agent and I both trust Ms. Phoebe—she keeps more contacts around the city than we have put together. If she vouches for this nanny, you'll do well to meet her."

"If this nanny meets your approval, Joe said we could include her full pay, plus the costs for Ruth and her to travel with the team, in your contract. It's unusual, but it's a clever way to keep your salary at a level the owners can accept and still meet your needs." Saul didn't go into the details of the tight fist the owners placed on him and the offer he could make. Joe planned to add the nanny and Ruth's expenses to the miscellaneous labor costs counseling Saul to use this method to keep the salary limit Cai gave Saul. Saul knew it would not please Cai when he noticed the rider, but Saul decided he would rather beg forgiveness than ask for permission.

"OK, Coach. Sounds like you have it all thought out. I'll be ready by 5:20 pm," said Josh.

"I'll meet you at the exit. You can follow me over there—I'll introduce you to the Arimas, and then I'll head out—this meeting is for you and Ruth. Joe will call me later tonight, and we'll see where we stand."

Eighteen

Mary Dalene arrived at the Arima house at 3:30 pm. It was a pretty house made of red brick familiar to the early twentieth century found throughout the area. The lot was typically narrow, with a small front yard. However, this street of houses enjoyed lots substantially longer than many in the city. The beautiful backyard was one of the main reasons Joe and Elizabeth bought on this street decades ago. The house featured full-length front and rear porches and a long backyard, fenced off with similar red brick to the house, just high enough to keep a family pet in but low enough to encourage neighborly house-to-house discussions on warm summer days. Like many houses on the block, a detached garage stood opening onto the alley behind.

Joe escorted young Mary through the house, decorated with simple homely décor from the 1950s and 60s, and onto the large back porch. From the porch led a winding walkway surrounded by flower trellises for perennials Elizabeth planted, not yet in bloom. The walkway continued down the side of the lot along an open picnic area and beyond. It passed through a vegetable garden ending at a small, pergola-covered garden sink attached to the rear of the garage. The pergola featured two climbing rose plants, one growing from each side, showing early spring growth. The weather was again glorious, though moderately chilly. Elizabeth worked in their vegetable garden since Joe finished tilling the ground yesterday.

Elizabeth always wished for children and prayed to God for many years to have her own, but unfortunately, medical issues kept Elizabeth from carrying a child to term. Instead, she and Joe began helping with kids in the area. They met a young Ms. Phoebe at a shelter they volunteered at decades ago. Even then, Phoebe was already a well-known Christian activist whose spiritual gifts and organizational skills influenced many of the city's charitable organizations and outreach programs. She introduced them to two programs she worked with: The Children's Home of Pittsburgh and The Children's Institute. The Arima family fostered many children over the years from these organizations, including three they wound up adopting, one a special needs teenager with MS. The children were now adults, but when they visited on special occasions, they often teased

Elizabeth about her attempts to keep them from falling into her pride and joy gardens. The gardens boxed in both sides of the picnic area, once the children's play area. Elizabeth especially missed their noisy life in the backyard but took solace in their kids' accomplishments and the fact that her garden was now considerably safer.

Joe considered himself an expert in sizing up his athletes professionally, but he always deferred to Elizabeth and her gift of understanding their personal needs and situation. Elizabeth suggested she interview the prospective nanny/teacher for his new rookie and mediate the introduction of Josh's daughter, Ruth. Joe and Elizabeth worked with Ms. Phoebe for nearly forty years, and the three made a good team. Joe knew that if Phoebe vouched for this girl, Mary carried the credentials necessary to be an excellent teacher and nanny. He just needed to see how she did with the child. As soon as he hung up with Phoebe, Joe devised the plan with Elizabeth to have Mary and Ruth over before Josh arrived. This way, Elizabeth could let the girls get to know each other and observe how they got along. While Joe worked with Josh that evening, Elizabeth would ensure the daughter and nanny were compatible. Joe and Elizabeth worked this way all their lives, complimenting each other's strengths, covering their weaknesses, leading to the Arimas' many successful outcomes.

Mary was a pretty, reserved young lady, quietly respectful as Joe introduced her to Elizabeth. Elizabeth sat on an old flat-top wagon that looked like something out of an old mine. Low to the ground, it was a perfect width to fit between the garden rows, and the low height allowed Elizabeth to sit and plant her garden with seeds or seedlings. She would plant and pull the cart through the rows and, later in the season, use the same process to weed and finally pick her rewards.

Elizabeth stood and greeted Mary. They were quite a contrast; one a five-foot-nothing gentle Jew nearing 70, with grayed hair peeking out of a colorful babushka and baggy overalls with a heavy cotton sweatshirt; The other, a tall, thin brunette, mid-twenties with her long dark hair pulled up in a bun wearing black horned rimmed glasses, a colorful crocheted hat, slightly frayed jeans, and a navy waistcoat you might find in a military surplus store. Elizabeth couldn't help but feel that Mary looked a bit like Mary Poppins if Mary Poppins was a hippy.

Elizabeth pulled off a glove and reached for Mary's hand. "Hello, young lady. I'm Elizabeth Arima, but my friends call me Beth."

"Hello, ma'am, it's a pleasure to meet you," Mary said quietly, eyes diverting quickly from Elizabeth's. "You have a beautiful house here."

"Well, thank you. Joe and I are very blessed. You aren't seeing it at its best—This garden is where the real beauty lies, but winter's touch still hides it. I am just getting it started again. Would you like to help?"

"I would, but I don't know much about gardening. I am afraid I was a city kid without a yard." Mary trailed off.

"It's OK, dear," Elizabeth said as she cleared a space for Mary to sit on her wagon. "You just need some elbow grease and love. God does the rest. Sit, and I'll show you." Mary smiled and sat next to Elizabeth. Beth handed her a pair of gloves and a small trowel.

About a half-hour later, young Ruth arrived. Martha escorted her to the door, carrying her book bag. Joe was there to meet her. "Mr. Arima, this is Ruth Green. Ruth, this is Mr. Arima. He's going to be working with your dad this afternoon."

"Welcome to you both," said Joe. Little Ruthie took Joe's hand and shook it vigorously. "Hello, Mr. Arima!" she said with a bright smile.

"Please to meet you, Ruth, and please call me Joe. Won't you both come in?" Joe replied.

"Mr. Arima," Martha said formally, "If it's all right with you, I would like to leave Ruth with you and Mrs. Arima. I have a bunch of work to catch up on." Martha was polite with Ruth after picking her up at school, but Ruth got the distinct feeling there were other things she would rather do.

"That's fine, Martha. I'll take Ruth out back, and she can meet Beth and Mary. They are working in the garden. We'll get to know one another until Josh arrives."

"Thanks, Mr. Arima. I appreciate it. I must stop at the ballpark before heading to another workshop I volunteer for tonight. No rest for the weary!" she said as she handed Ruth her backpack.

Ruth said, "Thank you," to Martha as she turned to go.

Martha replied, "Good luck, Ruth!" over her shoulder and hurried back to her Prius.

Ruth looked back at Joe with slightly raised eyebrows. "Well, Joe, Pops says you've known a lot of ballplayers over the years."

"I suppose that's true, Ruth. Some were my clients, and many others were my friends," replied Joe.

"May I ask who were your favorites?" Ruth said as Joe escorted her through the house.

Joe laughed, "I liked most of the ones I got to know, but certainly, Coach Saul was special." Ruth continued to grill him on his many baseball memories and the players he represented. Joe chuckled at how Ruthie knew so much about baseball and the Pirates players and was delighted with her spunky way of expressing herself. It was, quite frankly, a refreshing surprise as her bubbly personality and positive spirit were in stark contrast to the picture of a diminutive young Asian girl with braced legs. She seemed to light up the room. Her questions and comments quickly showed her bright mind with an excellent understanding of baseball and a curious, outgoing personality, trying to take in all the world offered.

Joe and Ruth dropped Ruth's backpack in the house and joined Mary and Beth in the backyard. After introductions, Joe played the server role, running to fetch some light snacks and drinks and an occasional gardening tool or supplies as the ladies worked as a team in the garden. Joe sat in the picnic area working on some papers and a laptop, with one ear listening to the girls' conversation. He noted Ruth jumped right into the challenges Elizabeth gave her and Mary to accomplish. As usual, Beth used a well-planned set of tasks for the girls, allowing Mary and Ruth a chance to work together. Elizabeth could then observe how they got along. Ruth continued to be a bubbly personality but remained focused on the work at hand as Mary gently guided her with some things Beth taught her to do before Ruth arrived. Mary continued with soft words of encouragement as Ruth navigated the physical work despite her braces. Elizabeth caught Joe's eye when the two girls were working on something. Elizabeth smiled and nodded to his unspoken question. Joe smiled back and returned to his work. Ruth and Mary showed the makings of a fine pair.

Nineteen

After practice, Josh followed Saul to the Arimas' house. It was nearly 6:00 pm when they arrived. Saul climbed out of his Chevy Tahoe and watched as Josh exited his old Jeep Cherokee. It was a plain four-door, nondescript vehicle. Although it looked well maintained, it must be at least 15 years old. Josh walked up to join Saul, and they continued up the steps to the house.

Joe answered the door after a few moments. Saul was in front, and Joe shook his hand warmly. "Hello Saul, it's good to see you."

"Good to see you too, Joe," said Saul. "Thanks for meeting with us on short notice."

"No problem, son, now let's have a look at this rookie of yours," Joe said matter-of-factly as he let both men into the front entryway.

Joe was about 5 foot 6, so he was used to looking up at his athletic clients, but he was still a little surprised when he finally got a good look at Josh. Josh wore a Pirates cap and turned from letting the glass storm door close behind him as Joe sized him up. Josh stood about 6 foot 4 inches tall, with a muscular, lean body, coffee-colored skin, and long curly dark hair framing his face. As he turned, Joe noted a broad yet hooked nose with a pale scar tracing jaggedly down Josh's cheekbone. Josh struck an imposing figure, the intimidating warrior, like a dark version of Jack Lambert, one of Joe's favorite Steeler Hall of Fame linebackers from days gone by. But just then, Josh turned and looked at Joe. For a second, Joe caught those dark brown eyes in his own. Brimming with kindness, they appeared as two dark pools of knowledge and understanding far beyond his years. They held Joe's gaze, penetrating to his soul. Something stirred in Joe's memory, and he hesitated momentarily, trying to place where, but then Josh smiled and reached out his hand. "Hello, Joe," Josh said with a smile on his face and in those kind, ancient eyes.

Joe reached out his hand automatically in response, and the memory evaporated. "Nice to meet you, Josh. Welcome to our home."

Saul watched as the two men shook, and there was a quiet moment. He broke the silence and said, "Joe, if I can, I'd like to say hello to Miss Elizabeth and the others before I head home. I must do a few things tonight before we leave tomorrow."

Saul's question ended Joe's vision of Josh for the moment, and Joe answered, "That's fine, Saul. Beth, Mary, and Ruth are in the kitchen. Beth's making her mother's famous Noodle Kugel and some brisket in the pressure cooker. It should be ready in a few minutes, but I think they are snacking on some of the leftover hamantaschen Beth made for Purim."

"Well, I don't know what hamantaschen is," said Saul to Josh as they walked through the living room, "But I can tell you, Josh, Beth's Noodle Kugel is delicious." Josh smiled back at Saul and Joe.

"Hamantaschen are triangular, jelly-filled cookies, and they're delicious as well," said Josh. Joe and Saul both did a double-take, but Josh didn't seem to notice. As they approached the kitchen, they could hear the girl's voices and Beth's laughter at a story Ruth was telling with exuberance.

As they entered the kitchen, the smell of cinnamon and raisins filled the air as the oven-baked Kugel neared completion. Mary smiled at little Ruth as she recounted her dad's at-bat against Samson from the practice game. Ruth sat on a barstool at the kitchen center island as Mary leaned against the counter. Both munched on the triangular treats, Ruthie speaking through cookie bites. When the men walked in, she stopped her story and jumped out of her chair, exclaiming, "Dad! Wait till you try these cookies Beth baked. They're amazing!" Josh met her outstretched arms with an engulfing hug.

"OK, Ruthie, just don't ruin my dinner. Whatever is cooking smells incredible," said Josh as he hugged his daughter.

Joe introduced Josh and Saul to Mary. After saying hello, Saul turned to Beth and said, "Just wanted to stop in to say hello to you, Miss Beth. It's been a while...."

"Too long, Saul," Elizabeth said. "You're as bad as our kids—you need to stop by more than once in a blue moon." Beth opened the oven door, flooding the kitchen with delicious smells.

Saul smiled. "Well, I have been busy in Florida for the past couple of months...."

"That's no excuse," Elizabeth replied over her shoulder as she pulled the casserole dish out, setting it on the stovetop. The aroma shot up strongly now that the Kugel emerged, and Saul couldn't help but think of the special holidays he spent with the Arimas and their brood of foster kids over the years. Elizabeth turned toward him and took off her oven mitts. She put her hands on her hips for a moment, looking at Saul. Then she smiled and opened her arms, and the coach bent down to accept a warm hug from the diminutive but strong woman. It *had* been a while, and he felt a tinge of regret as he knew his coaching job took significant time away from many of the friends he made over the years, like the Arimas and Ms. Phoebe.

Elizabeth pulled back and held Saul's face in her small hands. "Oh, don't look so sad, Saul," she said forgivingly as she studied his face. Finally, she turned back to the stove, letting him go. "I know you must go, but you look like you've slimmed down in Florida with no one to cook for you properly. I already sliced off a piece of brisket, and I'll add a scoop," she looked back at Saul, continuing, "*Two* scoops of Kugel to your 'To Go' bag." Saul tried to protest to no avail as Elizabeth did just as she said, and she wrapped three or four hamantaschen cookies in as well. "Here you go," she said, sounding like a mother to the coach. "Now remember," she said with a stern finger to his face, "This doesn't count as a visit, so you need to stop back for a real one as soon as spring training ends and you and the boys come home."

"OK, OK," replied Saul, as he knew when he lost a negotiation. "I'll be back soon, I promise." She smiled and hugged him quickly before he turned back towards the front door.

"I'll see you out," said Joe as he followed Saul. "If you can all help Elizabeth get the table set, I'll be back in a minute," said Joe over his shoulder.

Joe walked Saul back through the house to the front door. "Any thoughts on our player's situation," said Saul.

"I think Mary is the answer you need—Ms. Phoebe knows her stuff, as usual," said Saul.

"Good. I hoped so," said Saul, with a pronounced relief.

"So truthfully, what have I got here since I haven't seen him play?" said Joe.

"Honest Joe?"

"We've been at this long enough, and this really is my last time, so yes, off the record, what have we got?"

"Off the record...," Saul looked around at the front room. Its décor was mid-twentieth century or older. It was pretty and ornate and very much the Arima house he remembered as a young man. The room displayed many pictures with quite a few Pirates of the last half-century with Joe and Beth, many who were his clients. There were pictures of Joe with members of the 71 and 79 world champions, including one with Beth, Manny Sanguillen, Kent Tekulve, and Willie Stargell at what appeared to be a cookout in the Arimas' backyard. These were the legends of Pittsburgh's championship past. He turned back to Joe. "If we sign him, you'll be putting his picture on the mantle with these others, and I believe he'll fit right in."

"And you found him, out of the blue, at the batting cages?" said Joe, eyebrows raised slightly at what Saul said.

"Yes. To be honest, Joe, he makes me want to believe in miracles again," said Saul quietly.

"Well, Saul, miracles never cease. You just got to remember to look for them," Joe reminded.

Saul nodded and shook Joe's hand as best he could, careful not to drop the hot Kugel. "I'll be up for a while, so call me and let me know. We leave tomorrow for our last games in Bradenton. I would like Josh to catch up with us there."

Joe shook Saul's hand. "We'll work it out. Let me talk with the lad, and I'll call you back."

Saul nodded and walked out the door to his truck parked down the street. This evening brought back many memories and the hope to make some future ones. For Saul, it was always about taking the next step and winning it all, but this short evening at the Arimas made him remember there was more to life than just the wins. He put so much into playing the game, but he knew, win or lose, it would end someday. Memories flooded back of the many characters on and off the field and friendships over the years. As he pulled away from the curb and headed home, Saul felt richly blessed, reminiscing about past and present baseball players and friends in this glorious game.

Twenty

The Arimas owned an old round kitchen table made from dark brown heavy hardwood, with a large center pedestal divided into four carved legs. It fit snuggly in the kitchen corner in a three-sided bay window overlooking the backyard. A large "Lazy Susan" was in the center of the table, and Beth placed the various dishes on it. The three guests and Arimas sat down, with Ruth sitting between Mary and Josh, then Beth and Joe next to Mary. Joe asked them to hold hands for the blessing, as he did many times when the foster children filled their house in years past.

"It's nice to have a full table for a change," said Beth after Joe finished blessing the meal.

"Yes, it's usually just Beth and I eating now since everyone is grown and gone," said Joe wistfully. "Although we still get together on special occasions."

"I think it's great here!" said Ruth. "Dad and I rarely have company either, and our dinner menu is..., well, a bit limited...."

"What Ruth is trying to say is my culinary skills leave somewhat to be desired," said Josh sheepishly.

"I love your cooking, Dad, and you're getting better!" replied Ruth, patting her dad on his hand lovingly.

"Oh, I love to cook!" said Mary somewhat abruptly. Then she caught herself and looked down.

"What kind of cooking do you like?" said Beth encouragingly.

"Well, I roomed with three other girls at school. I had little opportunity to cook when I was younger. To be truthful, I was often hungry," she said, slightly embarrassed at her honesty. She hurried on, "I always jumped at the chance to cook at school. My roommates called me the house mom, and I would try out different recipes for them. They usually liked it, but I had a few failures...."

"Like what?" asked Ruth.

"Well, I tried a souffle that turned into a giant cheese brick, and then there was a sinking sponge cake I tried to make for my roommates' birthday...."

"Didn't go so well?" asked Ruth.

"Well, let's just say it sunk, and we buried it at sea," Mary laughed at herself.

"I'm so sorry!" said Ruth.

Mary shrugged and replied, "It's OK. I've had many more successes since then, and I always say, you don't know until you try."

"That's a good motto," said Beth. "Perhaps sometime we could cook together."

"That would be wonderful," said Mary. "I am unfamiliar with most of the food you made tonight, and I love learning new recipes."

"How about you, Josh? What do you like to eat?" broke in Joe.

"Oh, pretty much anything I don't have to cook," Josh replied.

"Me too, Dad," quipped Ruth, and they all laughed.

"Well, I do a pretty good fried fish. My dad was a big fisherman, and it was the only time he would cook—mostly because mom didn't want to deal with it. I would help him after we went fishing. I still love fish 'til this day."

"Yes. I look forward to your fish fry night. It's one of our best meals," said Ruth honestly, and Josh reached over and hugged his daughter.

The dinner continued as the five sat together and passed the evening meal. The three newcomers to the house ate a wonderful Jewish meal as Joe led the discussion. He pulled as much out of Josh and Mary as he could, but while Josh answered the questions Joe pitched at him, he avoided most of the discussion of his adult past, focusing more on his childhood. Mary was happy to talk about her recent past at school, preparing to be a teacher, but said nothing of her early life. They were interesting opposites, thought Joe. One focused on his daughter, not wanting to talk about his adult life, and one focused on her future, unwilling to talk about her childhood. There was pain for both in their past, and Joe was sure there were wounds unhealed.

Still, it was a wonderful evening, and the five enjoyed each other's company. As they finished, Elizabeth brought out one of her most famous desserts, chocolate babka, which she made fresh yesterday and heated for a few minutes in the oven before serving. As she cut into the twisted bread, the aroma in the kitchen took on a distinct mixture of dark chocolate and cinnamon. Joe asked if anyone wanted some decaf coffee. Josh raised his hand, and Joe brewed them each a cup. As Elizabeth served the babka, Joe took the plate Beth offered him and said to Josh, "Why don't you follow me into the study with your babka and coffee, and we'll chat?"

Josh looked at his daughter Ruth, who joined Mary in tasting the delicious bread. "It's fine, Dad. Beth, Mary, and I will be a little busy taking care of this dessert!"

Josh smiled, picked up his dessert plate and coffee cup, and followed Joe. They entered an extensive study, and Joe slid the old pocket doors closed. The study was a book repository with various baseball memorabilia half-hidden around the room. A somewhat disheveled desk and several old wooden filing cabinets were to one side. The room featured floor-to-ceiling bookcases like an old library out of an English novel, complete with a rolling ladder. Two high-backed leather chairs with a large ornate table and lamp sat opposite the cluttered cherry and mahogany desk.

Joe offered Josh one of the high-back chairs as he took the other. Setting down his babka, Joe sipped his coffee. Josh instead took his first bite of the babka.

"Oh my!" said Josh.

"Good?" asked Joe over his cup.

"This is incredible!" replied Josh.

"I know," said Joe. "She doesn't bake it often, and you don't want to know how many calories are in there, but I think the first time she made it for me when we just started dating, I knew I must marry this girl," he smiled, and Josh laughed.

"Can't say that I blame you. This is something else." Josh sat the plate down and picked up his coffee cup.

After a few moments, Joe began, "OK, Josh, so perhaps we can talk some baseball, and by baseball, I mean the business side of it."

"Sure, Joe."

"This is what I know," began Joe. "I've known Saul since he was a teenager. He signed with me, and I got him his first contract right out of high school. He was with me throughout his playing career. When he retired as a player, I helped him get his contract as a coach, although I put him with a friend of mine when he moved back up to the head job as the big-league coach, partly because I was moving to retire, and partly because I was always a player's agent. We both didn't want there to be a conflict of interest. He is still one of my oldest friends and clients, even though he no longer pays me. Are you comfortable with this?"

"Sounds fine, Joe. Coach Samuelson strikes me as a straight shooter," replied Josh, "And so do you."

"Fine," continued Joe. "So, when he called me the other day, understand I haven't taken a new client in nearly eight years and didn't expect him to ask me to take you. My last Major Leaguer retired almost five years ago. I have kept up with the club as they still bring me in on consultations now and again, and I have worked with three other younger agents getting them established over the years in the business, and they are all still active. Bottom line, I am still up to speed with the business side of the game. I agreed to Saul's request to talk with you, and I will represent you if you want. But you can say no at any time, and I can at least recommend some other younger agents."

"Pops thinks highly of you, and he has been a stand-up guy for the short time I have known him—if it's all the same to you, I'd like to hear you out first, Joe," replied Josh.

"OK, so look. As I said, I never expected to take another client. But when Saul called me, he said some things to make me think I should meet and talk with you."

Josh nodded encouragement for Joe to continue but did not comment.

"Josh, Coach Samuelson told me that when he saw you hit the other day, he's never seen anything like it. He told me you were a once-in-a-lifetime player. He also said your life history was very different from most ballplayers. Here you are, late 30s, I presume, walking in off the street, causing one of the best baseball minds I know to say, 'I have never seen a guy hit like this guy hits.' Yet no one has ever heard of you or seen you play. That's intriguing, to say the least."

Josh sat the coffee down on the table next to him and sat back in his chair. He offered no further explanation of his past, instead asking, "Where do we go from here, Joe?"

"Well, Saul will do just about anything to sign you, and I can tell you he has probably staked his future to get you this offer, but it's on the table." Joe pulled out some papers. "Bottom line, it's a million dollars for one year, with some near impossible bonuses if you were to make the all-stars, win an MVP, win a batting title, lead the League in home runs, or break some hitting records. And it adds some bonuses for playoff performances. I'll be honest, if you were any other player, I would say the million is all you can count on as a rookie, and it's a lot more than the Pirate owners probably wanted to pay, but Saul honestly believes that some bonuses are within your reach."

Joe paused and took a drink of his coffee. He watched as Josh sat back and looked around the room. There was a calm, somewhat distant look on Josh's face. Joe thought it was an old face, older than his age belied. Joe couldn't help but look deeply at that face, with the scar, the broad hooked nose, the long dark curly brown hair. Again, Joe tried to fix Josh in his mind. It was as if he knew him from somewhere in his distant past. A man with Jewish or Arabic ancestry, perhaps? Like many he observed when he and Elizabeth took trips to Israel and walked Jerusalem's ancient streets. Josh would fit right in with his dark complexion and facial features. He could be a child of the holy land. If you placed a robe and sandals on him, Josh would look like he stepped out of a movie about an ancient Jewish hero. Joe caught himself, realizing he kept silent for some time. Josh's eyes were fixed on him, kind eyes looking deeply and thoughtfully at Joe, waiting patiently.

Joe began again. "Josh, look, I know nothing about you, and frankly, that is not how I like to do business with my clients. I always get to know them over time to best represent them and their priorities when negotiating a potential contract. This time is different since the season starts in a few days. I ask you plainly, do you want to play baseball for the Pirates, and what do they need to offer you to close the deal?"

"I understand," Josh nodded and replied. "Joe, this is what you need to know. I am a Christian. I've spent my life trying to seek the Lord first and do what the Lord has for me to do, to bring honor and glory to His name. This meant taking care of my family and my fellow man. Since her mother passed away, I am now the sole provider for my daughter. I think the Lord brought me to this place, bumping into Coach Samuelson, to give me this opportunity to play baseball again. You say they want to offer me one million dollars for a one-year contract?" Joe nodded. "Well, Joe, that is more money than I made the last 10 to 15 years combined, under very tough circumstances. And it's enough to set Ruthie and I up for life. The money is fine. I need to know that Ruthie is taken care of, and she gets a good education and the medical care she needs. Joe, I want to be there for her. I missed much of her young life, so I would ask that she come with me when the team is on the road."

"If you're open to it, I can write the contract to pay Mary's salary as a live-in nanny and schoolteacher and provide her and Ruth travel accommodations when the team is on the road. Mary has all the proper teaching credentials. I haven't asked her yet, but she knows this is an interview for such a position. What do you think?" Joe asked tentatively.

"I will have to run this all by Ruth, but they seem to get along well. I think Ruth and I could give it a shot for a season."

"OK, Josh, I will talk to Mary. You discuss it with Ruth tonight, and I will write up the proposed contract. If you give me the go-ahead, I can run it by Saul and the team. Is it OK with you if I call you tomorrow morning around 9:00 AM to discuss?" added Joe.

Josh smiled and nodded, "That sounds fine, Joe." He paused, then added, "I guess Ruth and I have some things to discuss tonight. Perhaps we ought to get going."

"I'll have Beth wrap some babka for you two to take with you," said Joe as they rose together. Josh reached out his hand to Joe, who took it and shook it warmly. "We're glad to have met you and Ruthie, and I look forward to seeing you both soon."

Josh and Ruth said their goodbyes and headed home. As promised, Joe sat with Mary and discussed her offer to be the teacher for Ruth and accompany Ruth as her nanny when the team was on the road. They discussed her role and salary and that this contract would carry through the baseball season as a trial employment. Mary asked several questions, but in the end, she and Joe came to an acceptable tentative offer to include in Josh's contract proposal.

Meanwhile, Josh talked to Ruth about her day as they drove home. She excitedly talked about meeting the Arimas and Mary and all the wonderful things she, Mary, and Beth discussed. When they arrived home, Josh helped Ruth get ready for bed. "Hon, I have an offer from the Pirates to play for them in the Major Leagues, but I told Joe I would do it only if you could come with me. It will be a challenge with all the travel involved, and if you don't want to come, it's OK; I won't take the offer. What do you think?"

"As long as we're together, Dad. Where you go, I will go, and where you stay, I will stay. The Lord will take care of us.[1] Besides, this means I can come and watch you and the Pirates the entire season, Dad!" exclaimed Ruth.

"Well, I want you to have someone with you while I am playing. What do you think about Mary being your teacher and living with us as your nanny?"

"Oh, Dad, I think that would be wonderful. She seems really nice."

"As long as you think you can work with Mary and keep up with all your schoolwork, hon," he looked at Ruthie, and she nodded emphatically. "OK, I guess we should give it a try," said Josh.

"Dad, it will be wonderful, and school only lasts through May. After that, it will be all about baseball and seeing all those cities and stadiums and games!" Ruth sounded more excited with each as she said it.

"We will have to find ways to continue your therapy while on the road. And remember, therapy and schoolwork come first—then baseball," reminded Josh.

"I know, Dad—I know. But you know I am a great student, and I'll show those road Doctors a thing or two about what I can do when we go for PT. You just watch me!"

Josh laughed at his daughter's exuberance. "Well, all right, I guess you like the idea, huh, Ruthie?" he asked.

"As long as you do, Dad, I am definitely up for it!" said Ruth excitedly, making Josh smile. Ruth's encouragement and loyalty always put Josh in the right mind-set.

"OK, let's pray about it and sleep on it, then we'll talk about it in the morning," replied Josh. They said their prayers, and Josh hugged his daughter and kissed her goodnight. Little Ruth fell asleep with visions of beautiful baseball stadiums in her eyes, the sound of "Take me out to the ballgame" in her ears, the taste of a fully loaded hot dog, on her tongue, and the smell of popcorn and nachos nearby as someone yelled, "Get your ice-cold Coke here!"

---

1. Ruth 1:16-17

Twenty One

The following day, Josh and Ruth ate an early breakfast.

"OK, kiddo. Do you still want your dad to play ball for the Pirates?" Josh asked Ruth as she sat at the table anxiously waiting to eat the scrambled eggs mixed with vegetables Josh cooked.

"Yes, Dad, I think you ought to go for it," said Ruth through chomps of a crisp piece of toast she stole from Josh as he worked on his version of a vegetable omelet, "It's a once-in-a-lifetime opportunity, and you're not getting any younger you know!"

Josh chuckled while buttering toast after it popped out of the toaster. "Well, when you say it that way, I guess I should. And you're still OK if Miss Mary comes as your nanny and teacher so you can attend the games?"

"As long as we can be together, I think it will be great—time for a new adventure!" said Ruth, smiling at her dad.

After Josh saw Ruth off to school, he called Joe. "Joe, if you can make it happen as you described last night, Ruth and I are ready to play ball."

"Great! The team is heading out today for their last few spring training games, but I talked to Saul last night in anticipation of your call. We added Mary's allowance as a paid employee rider to your contract with her salary and travel accommodations. Do you have space for her to live at your house when you are in town?"

"Yes, actually. We bought an old house with a decent spare bedroom and a room set up already as a study that Mary and Ruth could use for schoolwork. Plus, we're just a few blocks from the Greensburg Art Museum. Ruth loves going there, and the local Library is just a few more blocks away."

"OK, Josh, why don't we do this? I'll finish drawing up the contract with the Pirates today. We'll have it ready for you to review tonight, and you can come downtown and sign it tomorrow. I'll see if Mary can visit you and Ruth this afternoon at your house. You can show her around and discuss her duties."

"OK, Joe, Ruth gets home at 3:30 pm. Mary could come over after that and get a look at the house."

"Sounds good. I will get to work and call Mary and have her call you. Are you good with meeting at the stadium at 10:00 AM tomorrow?" asked Joe.

"Yes. That's fine," replied Josh.

That afternoon, Mary arrived at the Greens' house, and Ruth was already waiting at the door. She let her in and began showing her around with Josh in tow. During the day, Josh cleaned out the attic spare bedroom and bathroom. Josh moved his old military gear and other items unpacked from their recent move to the basement. Josh and Ruth furnished the house with Asian art and furniture, reminders of their beloved Naomi. Adding to the eclectic mix were several eras of second-hand American furniture. However, Mary noticed, here and there, pieces of well-built, good-looking wood furniture. They included two end tables and a coffee table in the living room, and an ornately carved cabinet and table in the dining room. The table featured an inlaid wood top, delicate curving legs, and sculpted decorations along the table's edge. It was a lovely piece. Mary, who was mostly silent until now, commented on its ornate beauty.

"Oh, this is my dad's table," said Ruth admiringly.

Mary looked confused. "What Ruth means is, I made the table," explained Josh. "My dad was a master machinist at the mill, but he taught himself woodworking in his spare time at home. There was nothing Dad couldn't do with his hands. Besides teaching me baseball, my dad taught me woodwork in his carpentry shop in our basement at home. Unfortunately, he passed when I was in high school, but I inherited his tools. My wife encouraged me to take up a hobby when I was home from...working on the road, and I started woodworking again a few years ago. I made the coffee table and those two end tables you saw in the living room, the cabinet here, and finally, this table. It was something my wife asked me to build just before she died. She said she wanted me to make a nice big dining room table so that Ruthie and I would have a place for friends on special occasions. I worked on it for some time and just got it how I wanted it a few weeks ago. I hope to try my hand at making chairs, but all we have now are these I found at a couple of thrift shops."

Mary looked again at the table and could only imagine the hours of work that went into making it. "Where do you do your woodwork?" she asked.

"I converted the detached garage out back into a small shop."

"And I helped!" chimed in Ruth.

"Yes, you did," smiled Josh approvingly at his daughter. "We have a fairly decent-sized backyard for being in town. After yesterday, Ruth and I discussed building a little garden out back, nothing as big as Miss Elizabeth's, but Ruth enjoyed working in her garden yesterday. Maybe that is something you might like to help her with?" said Josh.

"I think that would be a great spring project for us. We could both learn together, take what we learn from Miss Elizabeth and apply it here," said Mary.

They continued to show Mary the house. Finally reaching the top floor, the attic door opened onto a sizable bedroom with a little kitchenette, small bathroom, and shower. A second set of narrow stairs ran down to a back door with a lock and key. It looked as if the previous owner intended it as a sublet. Josh commented, "You can have this as your living space and private entrance if you think it's all right?"

"This is probably nicer than the little apartment I have been sharing. It will do just fine," Mary said kindly, smiling.

They walked back downstairs. "Ruth, why don't you go into the living room so Mary and I can talk for a bit in the kitchen?"

"OK, Dad, but don't be long. It's almost time to start dinner!"

Ruth took off for the front of the house, and they could hear a TV turn on. The kitchen, circa 1970, contained a small center island with two chairs tucked under it. Josh offered one to Mary and took the other.

"Mary, I just want to make sure you understand what you would be doing. Ruthie is a bright girl, and I understand you have excellent teaching credentials. But that would only be part of your job. Ruth has physical therapy appointments twice a week. Once a month, she also sees the doctor at the hospital for treatment. You will have to take her to all those appointments when I am unable. Joe is writing your responsibilities into the contract with proper compensation. I talked to the doctor; he wants Ruth to keep up with her treatments when we are at away games. Being her nanny means, when I cannot help, you must take Ruth to her treatments, here and on the road. It's a full-time job."

"I think I understand, Mr. Green," said Mary.

Josh nodded. "I just wanted you to realize this is more than just being a teacher. And please, call me Josh. Mr. Green was my father."

Mary smiled, "OK, Josh, Joe told me most of this yesterday, and the salary includes allowances for room and board. I am quite happy with the arrangement and pay. Ruthie seems like a wonderful young lady. There is just one thing," she said hesitantly.

"What's that?" said Josh, concerned.

"Well, Josh," she said somewhat timidly, "I hate to say it, but when I talked to Ruth yesterday, I realized how much she was into baseball, and well, I thought you should know...," and she trailed off.

"What is it, Mary?" asked Josh.

"I just don't know much about the game!" She blurted out. "I mean, I barely know the basics. I didn't have any brothers, and not really a father if I am honest, and I never paid much attention to the sport—and well…, Ruth seems to know everything about it!" said Mary pleadingly.

Josh laughed, relieved. "Yeah, well, that's Ruthie. I guess it's become her favorite sport—she may know more about it than I do, so you are not alone there. She won't mind teaching you about it. She'll probably enjoy it!"

"Well, I just didn't want you to be offended, being your occupation and all," Mary replied.

"Mary, until a week ago, I had thought little about baseball for over 20 years. What's important to me is Ruth and giving her a good upbringing and a chance for a great life. I think you will be a wonderful help. As far as baseball is concerned, it will be a learning experience for us both."

"OK, Mr.…OK, Josh, if you're game to try it, I would love to be Ruth's teacher and nanny."

"Then it's settled. I'll tell Joe tonight, and we'll arrange to get you settled in here with us tomorrow."

"Thank you, Josh," said Mary. As they shook hands, Mary thought of her life's many twists and turns to get to this point. A week ago, she was afraid of ever finding the right job as a young college graduate from a difficult background. Now she looked forward to the adventure of living with the Greens and seeing the country while teaching this young girl. God's plan was amazing, and the future suddenly seemed bright indeed.

Twenty Two

J osh met Joe at the ballpark the following day. They walked together through the entrance, and Joe led the way to an elevator to the executive offices. "With the team and coaches in Florida, we may meet the principal owner, Cai Annason. Just a note of caution, Josh. Cai is a businessman, first and foremost. He is in the position largely because of the influence of his father-in-law on the other partners. This makes him more than a little concerned about keeping his position. Also, the owners demand the Pirates operate on a tight budget. Cai must show he is in control and keeping the Pirates profitable. If you fit into helping the team toward what Cai sees as a profitable future, he will support you. If he sees you as a threat to his position or the club's profitability, he can become...difficult."

Josh looked nonplused at Joe. "What I mean to say is, try to stay on his good side, follow his lead, and you'll be fine. Oh yeah, playing well would be a good thing also!" Joe said with a half-hearted grin and a shrug of his shoulders.

Mark Johnson met them in the executive suites waiting area. "Hello Josh, good to see you again. We have the contract and other forms ready for signatures in the conference room. Once you and Joe are satisfied everything is how you expect it, we can get started.

Mark escorted them into the conference room. The Pirates' legal advisor, Nechemia Demus, waited for them. He was an older gentleman with a short gray beard and wispy gray hair. "Josh," Mark said, "This is Nick, our team lawyer. He's drawn up the contract with Joe and is here to help you through all the paperwork and answer your questions."

"Good to see you, Nick," said Joe as he shook Nick's hand.

Nick smiled kindly as he patted Joe on the shoulder. "It's been too long, my old friend. How's Miss Elizabeth?"

"Happy to have me working again. Gets me out from under her feet!" said Joe as Nick laughed, "How's your son Ezra? I haven't talked to him for a while."

"He's flourishing, following more in your footsteps, I think, than mine, and making quite a name for himself in the big apple. We talk regularly, and he told me to say hello to you when you came in, and he was delighted to hear you were still keeping your foot in the business. He told me to tell you again how much he appreciates what he learned working for you those first few years out of school."

Joe turned to Josh. "Nick's son was my brilliant assistant when he first graduated law school for a few years until I couldn't hold onto him anymore, as too many big-name clients heard about my young protégé. Ah well, now his dad and I hear about his famous client list when he makes the occasional visit back home."

"Well, let's have a look at our new star here," said Nick.

"Nice to meet you, Nick," said Josh as he approached Nick with an outreached hand. Nick took his hand and held it momentarily, looking intensely at Josh's face. He saw a thirty-something man with penetrating, deep brown eyes. To Nick, those eyes had the look of a much older man, despite the fact Josh was 30 years his junior. Nick observed the dark skin, curly hair, and white trace of a scar down Josh's face and wondered what life journey brought this man here today. Nick looked deeply at that face, and it struck him that he wanted to know this man and his story. He reluctantly released Josh's hand as Mark brought him back to the moment.

"Gentlemen, shall we get started?" said young Mark Johnson, breaking the silence.

Joe and Nick led Josh through the various contract forms. The contract granted everything Josh and Joe requested, including the rider for hiring and supporting Mary's employment, plus Mary and Ruth's travel accommodations throughout the season. Nick walked Josh through the signatures as Joe reviewed each page. Along with the contract were several personnel forms. Mark explained the forms to Josh as he filled in the information. They included standard disclosure statements for employment and an Equal Opportunity Employment form. As Josh filled in the data, he checked the form's "choose not to disclose" box. Mark piped up at that.

"Josh, you are, of course, not required to disclose, but we as an organization must fill out observed racial information if our employees check the non-disclosure box as part of our filing with the government. Just so you know...," Mark trailed off.

"Mark, I understand the team may have a policy, but I prefer just to be a part of the human race, nothing more," replied Josh, smiling back at Mark.

"OK, that's fine," Mark agreed somewhat awkwardly. He knew he would be required to put the "observed" race on his filing for the team, and frankly, as he looked at Josh, he realized he could not easily guess the answer to the question. At least, he certainly wasn't sure. Josh's features and colorations seemed to defy a single race evaluation, and Mark knew nothing about Josh's background. Josh's daughter was clearly Asian, but she looked nothing like Josh if Mark was honest. Mark uncomfortably thought his requirement to place observed race would go beyond just the Department of Labor filing required. Mark's job was to understand the public nature of professional sports, and he could foresee it would be an issue the press would eventually discuss. For Mark, that meant he, as the team's lead PR man, would also have to deal with the press when they asked questions.

When they got to the final signature page, there were places for Josh, Joe, and the team president to sign. Mark spoke up. "Although Mr. Demus can sign on his behalf, Mr. Annason asked me to bring him in for the signature, as he wanted to say hello. So please, give me a moment. I will go find him and bring him in," said Mark as he rose to exit.

"Well, I can only imagine Cai and Pops' conversation over signing a rookie straight to the big-leagues," said Joe to Nick as the three men sat waiting.

"I wasn't present during Saul's discussion with the owners, but I understand from some people in the room, it was quite a memorable meeting." Nick paused, looking at his hands, contemplating his next words. "You know Josh, as I heard, Saul ultimately told the owners to sign or risk losing the best prospect he ever saw. Off the record and just for us here in the room, Mr. Annason made it clear it was Saul's call, and his reputation and job were riding on it."

As the men reflected on Nick's statement, Mark opened the door to the conference room and held it for Cai Annason. "Josh," Mark said formally, "I would like to introduce the Pirates President, representing the team's owners, Mr. Cai Annason."

Cai wore a three-piece black suit of impeccable taste. He was a slightly built man in his late fifties with oval black glasses. His hair was jet black with a black mustache and goatee, perfectly trimmed, tight and clean to his narrow face. As Cai approached, the three men rose, and as Josh was closer, he held out his hand. "Nice to meet you, Mr. Annason," said Josh.

"Nice to meet you, Mr. Green," said Mr. Annason while keeping his hands clasped. "If you don't mind, I make it a policy not to shake hands to avoid spreading germs." Josh dropped his hand but continued to smile. "Why don't we all take a seat," continued Mr. Annason as he waited for Mark to ease his chair out.

"Well," stated Mr. Annason, "Coach Samuelson tells me you are quite the ballplayer. Guaranteed to take the League by storm, he promised?"

"I am thankful for the opportunity to play for the Pirates and Coach Samuelson's faith in my abilities," said Josh.

"Oh yes, Saul certainly made it clear to all the owners you were a player we could not afford to pass on."

"I hope to help the team this year and validate your trust in Coach's assessment," replied Josh.

"I am sure Saul will make good on our investment," said Mr. Annason, pausing for effect, "One way or the other." Cai continued, looking steadily at Josh. "Tell me, Mr. Green, what's your background? Saul was vague on why we haven't seen you in any leagues before now, given your age?" Cai trailed off, waiting expectantly for an answer.

"I worked overseas for much of my adult life and recently moved back to Pennsylvania with my daughter. You are correct. I have not played baseball professionally," Josh replied dispassionately to Cai.

Cai observed Josh, trying to read his responses since entering the room. As he watched him, he thought how odd he acted and appeared. He met many gifted athletes in the big-leagues. Today's modern big-leaguers all carried a similar swagger as highly paid and prized rare talents, though they came from diverse backgrounds. Even for a so-called small market town like Pittsburgh, professional baseball players made at least ten times the salary of the average person off the streets. Josh was about to sign a contract for a guaranteed one million dollars, a large sum for a Pittsburgh rookie, though it was relatively average for the big-leagues. However, Cai was used to seeing athletes signing with a big-league team bring big egos or at least the expectation they were different now that they "arrived." They were stars, ready to tell their story to the world.

Josh didn't seem to fit the mold as he sat across from Cai. He seemed down to earth, without the usual bravado. Cai liked to remain cold and distant in his interactions with rookies. He felt it better to keep all but the star players on his roster, slightly off-balanced and concerned with their status in his eyes. Cai believed doing so made them feel they must play hard to earn his approval and justify their position on the team and corresponding salary. He made exceptions only with underpaid stars, such as Andrew and Samson, because he knew they brought in fans and increased his bottom line. However, as he sat looking at Josh in the silence of the room, he couldn't help but think this man, who he tried to put in the hot seat, could not have looked less concerned. That bothered Cai. He meant to put the fear of God into Josh, to make him realize his place was not secure, yet Josh looked impassively back at Cai, almost making him feel as if he, rather than Josh, was the one being evaluated and found wanting.

Cai decided Josh must be a fool, not realizing what was at stake. Fine. If Josh turned out to be a bust, Cai could hang it on Saul and get rid of the old coach with the powerful personality and a city full of admirers. Cai envied and feared the weight of Saul's power and saw it as a threat to his legitimacy because Saul was a hometown son, a former star player, and a surprisingly successful coach. If Josh turned out to be a skillful player but was a fool, Cai determined to bend Josh to his will and get what he wanted out of him. Either way worked for Cai, he decided. Ultimately, the team's success didn't really enter the equation. It was all about staying in and accruing power. Cai would use Josh, whether bust or fool, to his own ends.

Cai realized the room remained sufficiently quiet longer than intended. As he looked across at Josh, Josh's eyes showed neither fear nor concern. Instead, they showed peace. Cai didn't understand why, and it was disconcerting. Mark cleared his throat somewhat uncomfortably. "Sir, we have the paperwork here if you would like to look at it?" he motioned hesitantly.

Cai was relieved to drop his gaze as he pretended to focus on the paperwork. Of course, he read it meticulously the night before, looking for loopholes to the position Saul forced upon Cai in front of the owners. However, with Joe Arima deftly writing the contract, Cai failed to find a way out of signing Josh per Saul's wishes. This frustrated and angered Cai. He silently vowed, then and there, it would never happen again. Outwardly, he displayed complete calm as he pretended to read the contract for the first time. "Ah yes, Joe, you have a reputation for driving some hard bargains in the past, although they were with my father-in-law while he held this position." Cai continued, "But I see now your reputation is well earned. Garnering your man a nice paycheck with some unusual allowances, like the rider for daughter and nanny accommodations as well?" he said, glancing at Joe over his glasses.

"As your father-in-law, I think, would attest, I always made fair deals for my clients that paid off for the team, Mr. Annason.

"Yes, well, that was my father-in-law," Cai said with an insincere-looking smile at Joe. "Since we have no history for Mr. Green, this would not be my first decision...," and Cai paused for effect, looking back at the contract. Finally, he looked up at the group, "But Coach Samuelson persuaded the owners, he is a good judge of talent, and we agree to give him *one final chance* to prove it with Josh this season," said Cai ominously as he came to the signature page. Cai pulled out an expensive-looking Montblanc-style pen from his breast pocket and signed, returning his pen to his pocket. Cai slid the contract to Mark rather than Josh. Mark searched quickly for the pen he was using with Josh on previous forms and, finding it, slid both to Joe. Joe signed and handed paper and pen to Josh, who also signed.

"If that's all, I will leave Mark to assist you with anything further you need to catch up with the team. It was nice meeting you, Josh. I expect to hear great things about your success with the team this year," said Cai as he rose to leave.

"Thank you," said Josh with a faint smile, and they all stood as it seemed it was what Cai expected. Mark got the door for him as he left and closed it quietly, returning to the table. "Well, folks, thank you for that," he said apologetically, palms up with a little shrug. Clearly, dealing with Cai was a difficult part of Mark's job.

"I thought his father-in-law was a tough nut, but he has nothing on Cai," said Joe with a wrinkled brow.

"No, indeed he does not," said Nick, shaking his head, affirming his friend's impression. "Sometimes our children have a hard time walking in the footsteps of their forebears. And getting the job because of who your father-in-law is," Nick said and shrugged, "Can be difficult."

"Yes, well, anyway, Mr. Annason has a somewhat unique way of doing business," Mark said, followed quickly with a smile. "However, on behalf of Coach Samuelson and the rest of the organization, we are delighted to make you a Pittsburgh Pirate!" Mark's youth and enthusiasm placed smiles back on everyone's faces and distilled some of the chill in the room. Mark extended his hand to Josh and Joe, shaking each hand enthusiastically and saying to Josh, "Welcome aboard, Josh!"

"Thank you, Mark," said Josh as he smiled back at the young man. "Let's play some ball!"

Twenty Three

Over the next day, Mary settled into the Green's house, moving her limited belongings with the help of a few friends and a small rental trailer. Josh and Mary visited Ruth's school and collected her remaining assignments so that Ruth could complete the school year under Mary's supervision. Despite the rapid work, the last few days of spring season ticked off, and the Greens and Mary found themselves on a late-night flight out of Pittsburgh to Tampa to allow Josh to play the last spring season game with the team in Bradenton.

They arrived at the team hotel near the ballpark at almost midnight, and Coach Saul was sitting in the lobby with a laptop. Ruthie fell asleep in the team vehicle that picked them up from the airport for the long drive south. "Glad you are on board, Josh," said Saul as he rose from poring over several documents and shook Josh's hand warmly.

"Thanks, Coach, it's been a long journey," replied Josh, somewhat sleepily. "What's the plan?"

"Well, here are your room keys. You're already checked in," replied Saul, handing him a key, then one to Mary. "We got two rooms, one for the girls and your room adjacent. They are pretty basic, but they'll do for your brief stay. Josh, the team normally rides a bus to and from the stadium, but I have a rental car for you. If you leave by 9:30 am, you can follow me. Pete has gotten his folks to get all the gear you need to play. The game starts at noon. Other than that, breakfast is included and starts at 7:00 AM. Is there anything else you need?" said Saul.

Josh and Mary shook their heads, and they all said their goodnights, heading to their rooms. The Greens and Mary got settled, and soon Josh was tucking Ruthie into bed. "Dad," said Ruth, more than a little sleepy, "Make sure you wake me for breakfast. I want to go with you."

"OK, kiddo, I'll slide by here about 9 o'clock?" Josh said questioningly to Mary. Mary nodded and smiled back. "You two get some sleep, and I will try to as well; I am right next door if you need anything."

"Can we say our prayers, Dad?" asked Ruth.

"Sure, hon, you start," said Josh.

"Dear Lord, thank you for getting us here safe. Please help Dad do his best to help the Pirates win tomorrow!" said Ruthie. Josh couldn't help but smile.

"Dear Lord, thank you for all you have done in our lives. Let our lives bring honor and glory to your name, keep us safe and help us do your will. In Jesus' name, I pray, Amen," said Josh. Josh rose to leave, and Ruth said, "What about Mary?"

Mary nodded, and Josh said, "Of course, I am sorry, Mary."

Mary bowed her head. "Dear Lord, thank you for all you have given me, bringing me to this place with this family. I pray you watch over and use us to be light to this world and salt of this earth. And help Josh tomorrow do his best in the game, in Jesus' name I pray," and they all said, "Amen."

Twenty Four

The last day of the preseason dawned bright and beautiful, a typical Florida spring sunshiny morning. Pete met Josh and Saul as they arrived at Bradenton stadium at 0945. He wore dark aviator sunglasses, his Pirate hat and game shirt, and a pair of tan Bermuda shorts and sandals. "What's this? A new alternate uniform, Pete?" Pops said, half joking, half disconcerted.

"Game's not for two hours, and I have been bustin' my hump pulling everything together—It's too dang hot in Florida," Pete said around the unlit cigar in his mouth. He looked like something out of Coppola's *Apocalypse Now.*

"Well, it's still getting down to the low forties up north, so don't complain when we get to St. Louis tonight," reminded Saul.

"Ain't complaining—just statin' facts. I'm old and sweatin' buckets. I'll switch on my game pants, so you won't have to see my knobby knees after we take care of Josh." Pete led the way into the Pirate players' area, a smaller, less lavish version of the big-league stadium. He directed Josh to a locker with Josh's playing clothes arrayed with several optional items. Doc Luke was waiting for them as they entered, but the room was otherwise empty of people as the rest of the team would arrive on the bus in about a half-hour. Doc and Pete talked with Pops as Josh went through fitting his gear. When Josh finished, Doc said, "Take it easy on warm-ups and gameplay. This is preseason for one more day, so ease into it."

Pete agreed, "No use getting hurt now. It will take a few games to figure out a good routine to warm everything up right at the beginning. In that box is a bunch of cold-weather gear for the trip to St. Louis. The high will only be about sixty for the game, so you'll need it." Josh picked up the glove, put it on, and pounded a fist into it. It was the same one Pete gave him the first day.

"How do you feel, Josh?" asked Saul.

"I'm ready to play, Coach. How's this going to work?"

"I wanted to talk to you about that. I plan to start you in right field, as I think it will be a good fit for you at home at PNC Park. You'll bat seventh for now. I am moving Judah to left." Pops hurried on, trying not to think about Judah's hurt ego. "I plan to keep the Thunder Brother bats in the game, so I am pulling them into first and second base, where they both platooned last season and have some history playing in the minors. This should give us some good options for the batting lineup as the season progresses."

"OK, Coach, that all sounds fine to me," said Josh. He sensed the other two men looked at Coach Saul, expecting something more. "Is there anything else, Coach?" Josh asked.

"Well," said Saul, "You don't need to worry about it, but Judah is not exactly happy being moved to left as he has played right for the last three seasons. But I wanted to keep you in right—it'll work better in our home field, I think, for you to play, with less ground to cover, and you played it well for us in the practice game. I'll handle Judah but try to steer clear of him.... Hey, one more thing. I don't plan to have you speak to the press after this game, but there will be...questions. I'll field those, but you and I, and probably Mark Johnson, should talk about it before opening day in St. Louis. I'll have the three of us sit together when we fly out tonight. Bottom line, this is the big-leagues, Josh, and the press is your window to the fans. They will want to know your backstory. Coming out of nowhere to play in the big-leagues will spark interest. You need to start thinking about what you are going to say. I don't want this to become a distraction, but rookies get a bit of trial by fire, especially depending on their play. We'll keep you out of it today, but it's part of this game. Right now, do your best to focus on having a good game today."

"OK, Coach. Sounds like a plan," replied Josh, and left it at that.

The rest of the team arrived as Josh was finishing getting dressed. Most greeted Josh with enthusiasm, with Judah the noticeable exception, and his silence spoke volumes as he looked more than a little antagonistic. Josh accepted the welcomes with a smile and a few handshakes. "Rook, why don't you talk to Tommy about the pitchers you can expect to see today and then meet me on the field so we can warm up together? I'll show you the ropes," said Andrew.

"Sounds good, Cap," said Josh, smiling.

Josh shook Thomas's hand as he was getting dressed. Thomas pulled out the notebook he developed with Coach Caleb and reviewed the starting and relief pitchers for the Red Sox, their opponent for this last day of spring training.

The game started with public announcements introducing each lineup. Both teams primarily used their regular season starting lineup except for the pitchers, saving their ace for opening day. As the teams posted their starting roster, the broadcast announcers expressed surprise with the Pirates lineup.

"Well, folks, here we are on the last day of spring training, and Coach Samuelson, the Pirates skipper, decided to make it interesting. What do you think about the lineup Matt?" offered Roman Josephus. Roman was the Pittsburgh beat reporter for Sports News Network, America's largest and most influential sports channel. Roman also doubled as an announcer for the network during their spring training coverage.

"It's surprising, RJ. The Pirates are notoriously traditional bringing in new talent and maintaining consistent lineups. However, unlike most teams at this point in the preseason, Pops has changed his lineup and positions. He's moved a few players around and added a new player. This new player hasn't even been on the roster all spring. His name is Joshua Green, and he's starting in right field, batting seventh," replied Roman's brother commentator Matthias Apphus.

"OK, folks, Pirates are breaking with tradition, starting an unknown on the last day of spring training. This may get interesting," said Roman.

Generally, the last game of the spring training season plays out with little drama as teams are essentially looking ahead to opening day, but with the sudden shift in positions and a new player, the Pirate fans watching and listening on the radio were more than a little curious. It was 2-0 Red Sox when Josh led off the third inning for the Bucs against the Red Sox pitcher who, so far, held the Pirates hitless. Pops spoke to Josh as he walked out to the on-deck circle before the inning started. "OK, Josh, wait for a good pitch and drive it. No pressure here, just one at-bat."

"Got It, Coach, it'll be all right," Josh said with a smile.

"Go get him, Dad!" Ruthie yelled from behind the dugout in the seats the team provided.

Josh swung his bat with a donut weight on it to warm up. It was a bright Florida day, low 80s, and muggy. Josh knocked the weight off the bat and approached the batter's box as the Red Sox and umpires got ready to start the inning. Just as he reached the dirt surrounding home plate, Josh dropped to one knee and bowed his head silently for a moment, just as he did in the practice game in Pittsburgh.

"Interesting pre-batting routine from this rookie, Joshua Green; eh RJ?" said Matt.

"Yes, well, maybe he's praying for divine help against the Red Sox pitcher—He's owned the first six Pirates number today."

"Let's go, Rook," said the umpire, somewhat impatiently.

Josh rose. His right hand clutched a small amount of dirt, and he rubbed it on the bat's handle, looking at its smooth ash, and branded Louisville seal. He stepped into the batter's box, holding up his hand, and took his natural neutral stance. Most fans watched with little concern as nothing piqued their interest, but the Pirate players were unusually attentive, sitting or standing still with eyes locked on Josh.

The first pitch came at him, breaking off the corner of the plate. Josh watched it go by as the umpire called, "Strike!"

Josh stepped out and looked at his bat. The pitch looked a little low and outside in his view. He said nothing but realized the strike zone may be a little bigger than the book for him today. He stepped back in.

The next pitch was similar but slightly more off the plate, breaking down toward the dirt. "Ball!" yelled the ump. So, the zone was a little bigger, but not too much.

Josh stepped out for a moment again. Looking at his bat, he realized he was not seeing the predictive pitch traveling like practice and in the cages. His mind was all over the place, thinking about too many things. "Come back to the moment," he told himself. "It's still a game, and you can hit just like before."

Josh took a deep breath, closed his eyes briefly, and said one more silent prayer reciting, "I can do all things through Christ who strengthens me."[1] Then he stepped back into the box. The pitcher wound up and let fly his pitch. This wasn't an off-speed pitch on the outside. It was a fastball chest high and inside on Josh. Well thrown, it could handcuff him, but Josh brought his hips through quickly and caught the ball slightly out in front of the plate. Josh struck the ball with the meat of the bat, resulting in a loud "THWACK." The ball rocketed down the third base line over the head of the infielder, struck the ground just inside the foul line, and Josh was off and running. He made it to second with an easy standup double. The Pirates, almost in unison, rose and clapped their hands. As Josh turned back, Andrew gave him a thumbs up, smiling, and Josh tipped his hat back. So began the Green era for the Pittsburgh Pirates.

---

1. Philippians 4:13

Twenty Five

As fate would have it, Josh drew a walk in his next at-bat, and before he came up again, afternoon thundershowers hit the west coast of Florida. As the last preseason game, the umpires called the game in the seventh inning, and like that, the preseason ended. The team gathered for some instructions from the coaching staff on meeting for the flight tomorrow to St. Louis for opening day the following day.

There was a brief post-game press conference that only Pops attended on behalf of the team. Though unusual, Pops wanted to control the initial onslaught of questions about Josh. For better or worse, few outside loyal Pittsburgh fans considered the Pirates contenders. Limited press remained to cover the game, as most already traveled to the big-league home parks for opening day.

Coach Saul gave a brief statement about how the team was ready for the start of the season and looked forward to the first game in two days at St. Louis. He then opened the floor to questions from the half-dozen reporters gathered. The first question was predictable and came from SPNN reporter Roman Josephus. "Coach, tell us about this new right fielder. Who is he, and do you expect to start him come opening day?"

"His name is Joshua Green, and yes, he will start for us," replied Pops.

"Where'd he come from, Coach? Who'd he play for before coming to the club?"

"He's a local Pittsburgh prospect we worked with, and we just signed him for the season."

"Coach, what kind of background does he have at the professional level?" asked another reporter.

"As I said, he's a local Pittsburgh prospect we signed directly to the big-league team. He was not playing ball professionally before his signing. I can tell you he's a great hitter and plays a solid outfield. He'll start for us in right field in St. Louis."

"Coach, you have a solid farm system and, until today, normally keep a stable lineup. Why the sudden change with this player?" cut in Roman with another question.

"I made a few changes today, Roman. We felt it was a good opportunity to add offense to our roster," said Saul.

"You moved Judah to left and brought Juan into first. Do you plan to keep those position changes, and who are you dropping to get to the 26-man roster?" continued Roman before anyone else could ask.

"Roman, you know I don't usually advertise my lineup ahead of time, but I will say we moved Justus Barabbas, one of our middle relievers, back to AAA Indianapolis to make room for Green."

"Coach, any more details about Green?" asked another reporter.

"You'll have to ask him yourself after opening day in St. Louis," said Pops, and he nodded to Mark Johnson.

"All right, folks, that's all for today. Coach Samuelson and the team have to prepare for the move to St. Louis, so we'll see you there in two days," said Mark, signaling the press conference was over.

Saul walked down the hall to the staff room. Pete packed up a rolling duffel bag and looked up as Pops entered.

"How'd it go?"

"Well, Josh better be ready to field some questions because he will get hit with them the first chance they get."

"Let's hope he has a good game, and they want to talk to him about his play," said Pete.

"Yeah, but I think sooner or later, they're gonna' want to know about him, where he came from, and his background," said Saul, concern on his face.

"And what's the answer to that, Pops?" said Pete.

Pops shrugged his shoulders. He knew no answer and realized no one else in the organization did either. "I honestly don't know, Pete. I just don't know," Pops said, concern in his voice. One thing was for sure. It made for an interesting start to the season.

Twenty Six

It was a cool 60° F in St. Louis for the noon start of opening day and bore all the promise and hope of a new season for both teams. Above, white puffy clouds drifted through a bright blue sky, witnesses to a boisterous and festive atmosphere. The capacity crowd soaked in the sounds and sights of the city, with the Gateway Arch glinting over the center field wall. Fans drank Coca-Cola, crunched Cracker Jacks, and ate hot dogs smothered with their favorite condiments, enjoying a moment filled with happy dreams of a bright future. Out on the pristinely manicured diamond of Mississippi earth, a blues band accompanied the national anthem singer just after midday as Busch Stadium became electric with anticipation.

St. Louis was excited about their Cardinal baseball team. As a big market franchise, St. Louis fielded an expensive roster of athletes with high expectations. One of baseball's powerful and storied franchises, the Cardinals consistently sold-out Busch Stadium and were perennial contenders for the National League pennant.

As a franchise, the Pirates were one of baseball's oldest, but their economic situation placed them consistently on a tight budget as a small market team. As usual, for Major League Baseball, the small market Pirates would play on the road for opening day against one of the big market divisional rivals. The Cardinals were one of Major League Baseball's most storied franchises, able to pay for star players and field a contender every year. Today, however, the Pirate players sensed something different, something new. With an extra spring in their step, Pirate players and coaches eagerly anticipated opening a new chapter in Pirate history.

Pops still held back on several last-minute decisions. His gut told him to go with his youth and start his two youngest players, J.J. at second and Juan at first, to bring their bats into the starting lineup. They finished the spring season with quality at-bats and hit well over .300 for the last few weeks. Like the last spring training game, Pops placed Josh batting seventh, starting in right field. Zach led off for the Pirates in the top of the first against the St. Louis ace pitcher, a high 90s fastballer with a hard slider and wicked changeup "out" pitch he would sneak in on unsuspecting aggressive batters. In some ways, he was the human version of Goliath, Bruno's pitching machine. The ace worked Zach to a 2-2 count with a combination of bristling fastballs and sliders. Zach was protecting with two strikes and bit off on a nasty changeup, looking like a fastball but flying softly and diving at the end, fooling Zach completely as he swung early and awkwardly. The St. Louis fans erupted with applause as Zach humbly exited the batter's box. Next, J.J. jumped on a first-pitch fastball up in the zone but couldn't quite catch up, popping out to right field, bringing more cheers from the St. Louis crowd. Hitting third came the captain, Andrew. He was more patient and let a similar high fastball go for a ball. Next, the pitcher served up a hard slider that broke late and away, but the wily veteran held off, and the pitch was called a ball just off the plate. At two balls, no strikes, a hitter's count, the pitcher tried to come inside for a strike on the hands, but Andrew fought it off with a good inside-out swing, and the ball cracked neatly back over the left side of the infield just out of reach of the shortstop as the Pirates recorded their first hit.

The few Pirate fans in the stands rejoiced with applause, many unleashing the traditional Pittsburgh Terrible Towel, adopted from the Steelers' legendary sports commentator, Myron Cope. You could almost hear a few lone fans shout "YOI!" in Cope's most unusual way as the St. Louis fans looked at them like aliens and shook their heads. But Buc fans' elation was short-lived as Pops got aggressive and put the hit and run on, trying to catch the Cardinals off guard. Unfortunately, Juan missed the fastball entirely, and St. Louis's All-Star catcher threw Andrew out, sliding into second.

The Pirates took to the field with their ace, "Slayer" Samson Gibson, on the mound. On the radio broadcast back to Pittsburgh, the Pirate-friendly announcers discussed the Pirates' recently changed roster.

"Well, folks, here's a first look at your Pittsburgh Pirates, and Pops has thrown us a curveball, eh Greg?"

"You're right, Bob. Most of the time we've seen him as head coach, Pops took a conservative approach grooming younger players before starting them. However, after missing the playoffs the last two years, he's thrown caution to the wind, going with youth and an unknown rookie."

"Yep, that's right. First, Pops pulled two veteran infielders for the Thunder Brothers, J.J. at second and Juan at first, both in just their second year in the big-leagues," announced Bob.

"Well, they swung hot bats all spring, and the Pirates were desperate for offensive infusion after the team's anemic batting average last year. After all, Pops platooned them in both infield and outfield at the end of last season—but what do you know of this so-called rookie?" questioned Greg.

"My notes are few," said Bob, and Greg hit a button on his sound console that made a paper-shuffling noise. Bob continued, unperturbed. "But what I do have is..., well, the coaching staff gave us nothing on this 'out of nowhere' pickup,

Joshua Green, the Pirates new right fielder. He didn't play until the last spring training game, and apparently, the Pirates signed him directly to the big-league team, something unheard of, especially for the Pirates," commented Bob. "Lest you think this 'Rookie' is a young phenom out of some unknown high school somewhere, think again, Pirate fans. Get a load of what little we know, Greg. The Pirates PR rep listed him today as a 6 foot 4, 210-pounder; bats right, throws right; out of Greensburg, PA. And listen to this, Greg. He's 38 years old!" Bob exclaimed.

"Wow! What's going on with the Pirates and Pops Samuelson all of a sudden? First, they take a leap of faith by starting a couple of young prospects in the infield, who only came up last year, and as outfielders no less. Now they sign an unknown rookie old guy to start in right field. Folks, he looks more like an old-timey Steelers Linebacker than a baseball player. What else do we know about him, Bob, anything?"

"Not much, Greg, just that he was a local prospect from Western PA, signed by the Pirates last week. They don't even have any stats on his play with other teams. We saw him at the last spring training game against Boston, where he went 1 for 1 with a double and a walk. Other than that, he's an unknown," Bob offered.

"Welp, at least that means he's batting a thousand then, folks!" said Greg, and both men laughed.

"Yeah, I guess that's true, Greg. Better than going 'O' for 1. But what do you make of Coach Samuelson's decisions?

"Only time will tell if Pop's bold decisions will right the Pirates ship after two seasons of decreasing wins and missing the playoffs or...," hesitated Greg with effect.

"Yes?" questioned Bob.

"Or whether Pops, in desperation, has lost his ever lovin' mind!" finished Greg.

The Pittsburgh ace, Samson, who looked good all spring, did not disappoint the Pirates faithful. Samson blew two fastballs by the Cardinals first batter, the first looking, the second swinging far too late. He finished him off with a hard slider breaking off the plate, which the batter missed by six inches. The number two hitter fared no better as he mixed him up with a series of overpowering fastballs in the upper 90s, laced with a few teasing sliders off the plate and un-touchable. Both batters looked overwhelmed with poor swings and left without touching a pitch. The St. Louis fans were eager for a hit to break the all-star pitcher's mystique, and they carried good reason for hope as the Cardinals third batter, a perennial all-star, came in second for the batting title last year. As the number three hitter, he saw quite a few good pitches, hitting just in front of another Cardinal big-name star, the clean-up hitter who often challenged for the League lead in home runs. Samson started with an outside fastball waist-high just off the plate, but this Cardinals batter stayed disciplined and took the pitch for a ball. Next, Samson tried his hard slider, and the right-hander fouled it off into the dugout on the first base side. At 1-1, Tommy, the catcher, called for a fastball low and outside. Samson delivered, but instead of keeping it low, the 99 MPH fastball was belt high, and the hitter was ready. "CRACK," went the bat as he hammered the ball hard toward the right field line. In Busch Stadium, the seats in right field hug the foul line for about 20 rows before the foul pole as the warning track turns the corner, running along the right field foul line and outfield wall.

"OH! There's a hard-hit line drive down the right field line...," reported Bob on Pirates radio. Josh shaded somewhat towards the line because of Samson's velocity and pregame preparation with Thomas on the St. Louis hitters. At the crack of the bat, he got a good jump on the ball. "It's hit well towards the corner. Green's after it.... He's diving just before the seats! Did he catch it?" questioned Bob excitedly on Pirates radio.

A cloud of dust came up as Josh dove outstretched at full gallop, reaching his full 76-inch frame toward the ball, catching it just before he slammed into the ground near the foul line. The right field fans leaned over the railing to see the old rookie slide and half crash into the bleacher wall, waiting to see if he held onto the ball. The crowd held their collective breath as the umpire ran down the line to see the results.

Josh's momentum carried him hard through the dirt as he slid into the wall, catching it awkwardly with his free right hand. He barreled into the wall, curling up after landing, trying to decrease the impact and popping up in one motion back towards the infield, left glove hand still hidden as he stood. He turned around to the umpire running towards him from the infield and raised his glove, presenting the ball at the very top of the webbing, neatly secured. The St. Louis crowd groaned in unison as the hitter, rounding first, ripped off his hat in disbelief. What seemed to be a sure extra-base hit was a very hard-hit third out, ending the inning.

"Oh my! YES SIR RE Bob, Green dove and made a SPEC-TAC-ULAR diving catch right up against the right field bleachers, sliding headfirst into the wall! HOW A-BOUT THAT!" exclaimed Greg.

As the Pirates jogged off the field, Andrew, running from center to right to back up Josh as he dove, caught up to the rookie as he started toward the dugout. Andrew grasped him around the shoulders and shook him good-naturedly, playfully dusting off the dirt on his back. Josh, surprised, looked at the captain and smiled. "Nice catch Josh!" yelled Andrew over the still buzzing crowd, "You OK?"

"Yeah, I'm good, Andrew. Just got to dust off a little," Josh replied. Samson did not leave the field, waiting for them in the infield. He held up his glove and high-fived Josh as he came in. "You saved me on that one, Josh. Outstanding catch, brother!"

"Just doing my job, Samson. After all, I couldn't be the one to let your Perfect Game get away!" said Josh, smiling.

"Oh, now you've done it, Rook—don't jinx me!" laughed Samson.

"No jinx Samson, I've seen your fastball. It's legit!" smiled Josh back.

On the radios back to Pittsburgh, the announcers continued to discuss "the catch." "Wow, what a way to start your career, eh Greg?" said Bob.

"I'll say so, Bob! That was a brilliant catch. It will make more than a few top ten lists tonight, I'll wager!" replied Greg.

"What do you think of this Old Rookie, Josh Green, now?" queried Bob.

"He's startin' to grow on me, Bob; 'course we haven't seen him hit yet," answered Greg.

"We'll be starting with the cleanup hitter in the top of the second, folks, and Josh Green would hit fourth, so he needs someone to get it started for him to make his first big-league at-bat," said Bob.

"Let's see if Pop's wager pays off, and the Pirates can get something going here. It's zero-zero, folks, but something tells me Pirates baseball will be a wild ride in ole St. Lou, so stay tuned!" finished Greg with a flourish.

Twenty Seven

The top of the second inning brought the Pirates number four batter, Juan, back up to the plate. He determined to make up for letting Andrew down by missing the fastball in the first inning, causing his caught stealing. Juan was 6'1" and looked like a bodybuilder with a long torso and muscular arms. He resembled Albert Pujols, his favorite Dominican Republic born big-leaguer, and used a similar squatty batting stance. The St. Louis pitcher started Juan off with a slider outside followed by a high outside fastball, but Juan showed a good eye and refused to chase either. With a 2-0 count, the next pitch was a changeup, and Juan was able at the last second to ease off his bat speed and make good contact with the ball. The St. Louis infield was shading Juan, a right-hander, to pull the ball toward the left side of the diamond as he often did, but the unusual, slowed bat meeting the changeup punched the ball to the right side. The second baseman could not reach it, and Juan earned the Pirates' second hit of the game.

Next came Judah to bat. Of all the Pirates, he was the least happy with Josh joining the team and taking his position in the field. Still, with the chip on his shoulder, he hit well the last week in spring training and historically hit this pitcher decently. The St. Louis ace started Judah off with two fastballs, one on the outside of the plate, which Judah fouled off, and another on the inside, called a ball. Next, he threw Judah a changeup, which dropped out of the zone, but Judah did not bite on it. At 2-1, Judah received a hard fastball delivered on the outside of the plate, and he was ready for it, promptly swatting it back to the right side over the first baseman's head for another single, placing runners at first and second with no outs.

The Oklahoman Nathan Fisher, the Pirates third baseman, known for his Mickey Mantle good looks and shy demeanor, was next. The first pitch was again a fastball away, and Fisher jumped on it, hitting it high to right field near the foul line. He got underneath it just enough to allow the right fielder to catch it at the warning track for the first out, but Juan tagged up at second and made it safely to third.

"The Pirates have runners at the corners, and one out for Josh Green, the man from nowhere," Greg, the color commentator, said over Pittsburgh Radio.

"Actually, Greg, it says he's from Greensburg, apparently," Bob chimed in.

"That's pretty much nowhere, isn't it, Bob?" replied Greg.

"My Grandma was from Greensburg, Greg. It's a friendly town—Named after General Nathanael Greene," Bob responded.

"Who's that, you say? Was he Mean Joe Green's dad?" asked Greg.

"No, no. He was the great revolutionary war General, Greg. C'mon, now. Greensburg was named after him—it's the county seat of Westmoreland County."

"There's your geography and history lesson for the day, folks. Let's see if this Greensburg rookie learned to hit out there in the Laurel Highlands."

Josh took his last practice swings in the on-deck circle and was about to walk to the batter's box when Thomas came out behind him. He reminded, "OK, Josh, the first pitch has been fastball outside to every batter. So, look for it, but watch out for his slider. He likes to throw it off the plate early to see if you'll bite."

"Roger, Captain," Josh said almost reflexively. Thomas looked at the big man, and Josh turned for a moment, realizing his response was what he would say to his team leader after receiving orders for battle. Josh recovered quickly back to the present. He smiled at Thomas—it was something Thomas would never forget. Josh's smile said, "Don't worry; all will be as it should."

Josh turned and walked towards the batter's box. The scoreboard flashed up with only his name and number. Unlike all the other players, his picture wasn't yet available, and there were no player stats. *"Now Batting, number 3, Joshua Green,"* glared the stadium's public announcement system. Though tense, the crowd was relatively quiet, and just then, from behind the dugout, Josh, and the few nearby, heard Ruth's small yet strong, high-pitched voice. "C'mon, Dad, bring them home!"

Josh turned around, spying his daughter standing just a few rows back next to Mary. They waved, and he smiled and tipped his helmet. Josh turned and strolled towards the plate. He made it to the edge of the batter's box. He did not hesitate; instead, he knelt down on one knee, like the practice game, head bowed, one hand on the bat and the other grasping the fertile, brownish-red Mississippi dirt of Busch stadium.

"Here comes Green, and it looks like he's seeking divine intervention, Greg," said Bob on Pirates radio.

"Yes, folks, Joshua Green kneeled down next to home plate for a moment. Looks like he might have said a prayer. He kinda' pulled a Tim Tebow, wouldn't you say there, Bob?" queried Greg.

"Yeah, but the question is, does he know Tebow did that after he scored, not before?" replied Bob, chuckling.

"He probably feels he needs all the help he can get, facing one of the League's best pitchers when the chips are down. We've seen this pitcher throw some of his nastiest stuff when backed against the wall. Let's see if the Pirate rookie can put them on the board."

The Cardinals pitcher was dialed in. He knew the number eight hitter, Thomas, was next, followed by the pitcher. With second base open, the conservative approach would keep any good pitches from this batter, but he was a rookie, after all, and never faced his world-class fastball.

"C'mon, Rook, let's go!" said the umpire gruffly through his mask. Josh stood and entered the batter's box. The Cardinals catcher looked up at Josh as he stared out toward the pitcher. Like the Pirates catcher, Thomas, the St. Louis catcher was a League veteran. In fact, he was a five-time all-star, considered one of the best catchers in baseball. Like the pitcher, he knew nothing about this hitter. He saw the neutral, quiet stance Josh took. His demeanor, and more specifically, his eyes, showed no fear. They showed just the opposite. He saw a man calm, quiet, confident, and relaxed, yet his eyes showed total concentration and resolute purpose. It shocked the veteran catcher, and he instinctively thought, "Best give this guy a wide berth, nothing to hit. Let's start with a slider outside."

The catcher flashed the signal to his pitcher, the team ace, who promptly shook him off. It was unusual for his ace to do so, but he understood his thinking. This guy was a rookie. However, the catcher felt uneasy about what he saw up close to this giant of a man. Still, he acquiesced and put up the sign of a fastball outside.

"And here's the pitch...," started Bob on the radio.

The St. Louis pitcher wound up and threw his hardest fastball of the game, 99 MPH. It blazed for the plate, a knee-high bullet, threatening to paint the outside corner of the strike zone.

Josh was at peace. He asked the Lord to help him do his best for *His* glory, not Josh's. He stood relaxed but ready, watching the pitcher as all else faded away. The roaring crowd noise became a distant, muted sound. Nothing penetrated Josh's tunnel focus on the ball, and nothing could break his concentration. Time slowed. As the pitcher released the ball, Josh was back on a live-fire bombing range, directing an F-16 and gauging its run-in to drop ordnance. At that moment, empty of all his surroundings, Josh saw the ball's path, the swing he would make, and the track the ball would travel back in the opposite direction. Nothing else in his mind mattered; no sight, no sound; Just the spinning orb angling toward his bat. Josh swung the 36 oz. Louisville Slugger effortlessly. His swing flowed with his powerful will and released his entire 6-foot-4-inch frame from his neutral stance in a graceful explosion of energy and strength. He felt no weight, no resistance, as his left arm stayed hooked in perfect compact motion until he rotated his hips, uncoiling his sinewy core in a perfect arc through the ball. Josh's body motions collectively released their massive energy through his bat to wipe away the ball as if it were not there. He barely felt the perfect contact as the ball obligingly compressed, absorbing the pent-up energy in Josh's bat, transferring to the ball, then rocketing back in the opposite direction.

"THHWAACCK!"

To the onlookers, it happened so fast it seemed almost a blur to the naked eye, but suddenly came that sound. It caught everyone, players and fans alike, off guard, and it froze St. Louis's heart. It was as if someone fired a strange gun. The ball shot high into the sky, deep and just left of dead center field.

"THERE'S a drive to DEEP LEFT CENTER, WAYYYY BACK; THAT BALL IS HAMMERED INTO ORBIT!" exclaimed Bob excitedly.

"HOL-LY-COW! That ball went CLEAN out of the STADIUM, folks! Over the bleachers in left-center. It's on its way to Clark Avenue, for goodness' sake! Gigantic cannonball coming! That might have made the roof at Cardinals Nation across the street! I don't believe how hard Green hit that thing! Did you see that, Bob?"

"I saw it, I heard it, but I don't believe it—Look at that, Greg. The Statcast® system here at the ballpark shows the pitch coming in at 99 MPH, but look at that exit velocity. 116 MPH! What? The Statcast® system shows a mammoth 545 feet distance—YOI!"

"YOI, Bob? That's at least a Double YOI, ain't it?" exclaimed Greg.

"Heck, I think if ole Myron Cope were here, he might even break out the rarest—Triple YOI! Greg," replied Bob.

"I think he might," said Greg, and even he said, "Bob, I got to tell you, I'm speechless!"

"Well, folks, in 26 years of working the booth with Greg here, that may be the Rarest of the Rare!—not the hit, but Greg at a loss for words! Well, there ya have it, Bucco's Fans. In his first Major League at-bat, a gargantuan home run by the unknown 38-year-old rookie puts the Pirates on the board 3-0 with a three-run blast, here in the top of the second inning. The Cardinals call a time-out as a coach walks out to the mound. He doesn't seem to want to take his ace out just yet, but this ballpark is abuzz with what we just saw. I think the coach is trying to give them a chance to compose themselves. This is not what the Cardinals were hoping for to open the season, but to all our fans listening at home, I think ol' Myron would be out swinging his Terrible Towel, shouting, LET'S GO BUCS after that one. Stay tuned while we take a quick break for our sponsors," finished Bob in the broadcast booth as they went to a thirty-second commercial.

The Cardinals pitcher regrouped, getting the next two hitters out, ending the inning. The following two innings renewed the pitcher dual, with little offense on either side. Josh led off the fifth, watching the first four pitches, waiting for his pitch. The pitcher threw another good slider breaking off the plate, but with two strikes, Josh was on it with a stretched-out swing and lifted it neatly over the second baseman's outstretched arm for a base hit. Then, as the pitcher worked Thomas, the next batter, he ignored Josh at first. To everyone's surprise, Josh got a good jump on the second pitch to Thomas and stole second on a no-throw by the catcher. Thomas hit a grounder to second base, advancing Josh to third. The pitcher struck out, but the lead-off hitter, Zach, the switch-hitting shortstop, did what he often did. He slapped a pitch the opposite way, deep into the hole between shortstop and third, and beat out the long throw to first base, scoring Josh.

J.J. was up next and drove a fastball into right-center for a standup double. The St. Louis ace's day was over, and the Cardinals skipper pulled him as the Pirates held a four-run lead on six hits and looked to score again. The rest of the game was downhill for the Cards, with the Pirates scoring four more times. Josh drove in two more in the eighth with a standup double, finishing the day three for three. Pitching for the Pirates, Samson was almost untouchable with 13 strikeouts, sprinkling two walks, and just two hits in a complete-game shutout. St. Louis never got past second base, and what started as high drama for St. Louis fans ended in a blowout watching the Pirates celebrate around Samson on their mound after an 8-0 victory. Today, with Josh's hitting and Samson's pitching, the Pirates raised the Jolly Roger, and the Cardinals surrendered.

"Folks, the Pirates are celebrating on the mound after a gem of a shutout on two hits and a complete game by "Slayer" Samson Gibson," summed up Bob.

"Yep, Bob, but he got a lot of help from the offense today, and it all started with Josh Green, our unknown rookie, and his prodigious blast in the second. The Cards never really recovered," chimed in Greg.

"He sure had himself a game! Green went three for three, driving in five runs and scoring twice, while every Pirate but the pitcher ended up with a hit," replied Bob.

"Quite an opening day for us, but not what the Cards wanted from their Ace, to be sure. We know you Pittsburgh fans are celebrating as you raise the Jolly Roger back in the Burgh! Be sure to tune in tomorrow when we get to do it all over again. Let's see if the Buccos can keep up this momentum," said Greg.

"Yes sir, folks, bring your ears right here tomorrow for another 1:10 PM start as the Bucs try to make it two in a row in ole St. Lou!" finished Bob.

Twenty Eight

The Pirates' locker room was light and jubilant, with the players smiling and laughing at their excellent play. Coach Samuelson pulled them together for a moment before letting in the press. "Men, we have 161 more games to go, but I like what I saw today. I want you to remember how it felt. We just faced one of the toughest teams and their best pitcher today, and we chased him until he was gone. And then we put our foot on the gas and gave them no chance to come back. That's the way you win. We can beat anyone if we can do this to St. Louis on the road. Remember this day. You veterans know the season is long, with plenty ups and downs. If you ever think you can't do it or someone's better than you, remember what you all did today. You play like this, and there's no limit to what we can accomplish. And let me tell you, my goal for you is the highest of goals. It's up to you to choose that goal—make the deliberate choice every day. Choose to be the best you can be, one step at a time, one game at a time. All right?"

Everyone nodded at Pops as he looked at them sternly. "Now, change of gears. Again, you veterans know this, but you youngsters need to learn it and learn it fast. I am about to let the press in, and the better you play, the more questions we are bound to get. Be ready and think about what you say before you say it. You probably can't help us with what you say, but you can hurt us. Remember, the press wants a story, and they'll take anything that draws an audience to sell their product. We are your teammates and friends; They Are Not! Be careful, and when in doubt, push their question back to me. Understood?" Pops paused and looked around at his players, and to varying degrees, they again nodded. "OK, you get twenty minutes or so to yourselves, then we'll release the hounds. Grab your showers and take care of the necessities. Mark Johnson will give a 5-minute warning before we let them in."

Josh turned from his locker, intending to take a shower. Samson's locker was across from him. Dr. Luke watched Cy wrap Samson's pitching arm in an ice pack. "Hey Josh, you were great out there today," said Samson to Josh as he walked towards the whirlpool therapy tub. Josh veered over towards Samson. "I mean, most of the guys loved your offense. Don't get me wrong, it was great, but the way you laid out for the catch early on—that's when I knew we were going to have a good day—that's the game-changer for me," said Samson in sincere gratitude.

Josh took Samson's free hand in a cross grip shake. "Just doing my part—I'll always be there for you, brother, whenever you need me," Josh said, looking Samson in the eye. Samson thought of a big brother when Josh smiled back, and the thought struck Samson right to his core. Samson secretly always wanted a big brother. He was an only child whose father left shortly after he was born. His mom did her best, working two jobs in Athens, Georgia. His granny watched and primarily raised him. Samson lacked a male role model or mentor to look out for him. Samson was a roly-poly baby and an overweight grade school kid when he was young. Until he shot up late in Junior High, kids bullied him, and he felt defenseless without a father or older brothers. Samson couldn't bring himself to think about missing the father he never knew, but an older brother, that he could imagine. For all his strength and bravado, Samson remained wounded, never quite getting over the lack of a father to protect him—someone to set the example of what kind of man he could be. Josh's kind eyes and face reflected what Samson imagined his brother would look like; a giant, kind, middle-aged, black man, able to defend him from all foes, someone to watch out for him as good big brothers did. Samson squeezed Josh's hand tight. "Thanks, Bro," Samson said, "I'll be needing you about 30 times this summer! What do you say?"

"Sounds good, Sammy, but maybe you ought to broaden your expectations," Josh smiled back at Samson as he headed to the showers. When Josh turned away, Samson pondered Josh's reply. As he sat down in the cool waters, he thought at first Josh must mean adding games for the playoffs, but something nagged at him. He settled back into the whirlpool and remembered the way Josh spoke and looked at him. Samson wondered if Josh wasn't talking about baseball at all. As the cold, turbid waters of the cool pool massaged his tired body, Josh's words penetrated even deeper, reaching out to touch his wounded soul.

Twenty Nine

Mark Johnson gave the players a five-minute warning as many settled down from their post-game activities, dressing at their lockers. Coach Samuelson gave him the nod, and Mark opened the door. In poured a dozen reporters, some from the local St. Louis news affiliates, some traveling reporters from Pittsburgh, and a few from national sporting news outlets. Many were in St. Louis to cover the St. Louis Cardinals home opener, not expecting the turn of events in the game, putting the focus on the Pirates. Like all reporters, they went to the breaking news. Today, it was the small-market Pittsburgh Pirates making the big splash.

Coach Samuelson placed himself close to the reporters' entrance to catch some of the flack coming his players' way. Mark tried to usher and corral the reporters in his direction. The questions began in earnest.

"Coach, what's your thoughts on today's game?" asked a veteran Pittsburgh reporter friendly to the Pirates.

"I thought our team played up to our expectations. We got a strong outing from Sammy, and our offense was nice and balanced throughout the game, especially considering who we were going against."

"Coach, what can you tell us about your change of the lineup and the addition of Joshua Green?" asked a sporting news reporter from their St. Louis desk.

"We've been looking to get Josh into the rhythm of our lineup, as he was a late addition to the team this spring. As you can see, he's a special talent, and we think he will be a significant contributor to our club this year," replied Saul.

Roman, the SPNN reporter, cut in, "Coach, it's unusual for a rookie to come out of nowhere and start on a big-league club. Can you tell us how the team acquired Green and his background?"

"We're always out looking for talent, as you know, and Josh's hitting abilities impressed from the start. Once we got a look at his fielding and all-around play, his skills convinced us he could help us right now. After that, we just needed to sign him and get him ready to play today."

"Coach a follow-up," injected Roman, cutting off another reporter. "Where'd you find him, and what brought him to your attention?"

"Listen, we aren't going to give out how we scout prospects in this organization, but I can tell you we have a pretty good history of finding talent, and Josh's skills immediately impressed us."

"Coach, you didn't answer about Josh's background?" said another reporter.

"No, I didn't. That's up to Josh; you can ask him," was Pop's curt response, displaying he wouldn't answer further details about Josh. "Folks, we just beat one of the best pitchers and teams in baseball. Do you have some questions about the game?" continued Pops, slightly annoyed.

Another reporter stepped up. "Coach. Gibson delivered a dominating performance but finished with 108 pitches. What made you decide to let him stay in for the ninth?"

"We checked with him about how he felt starting after the seventh. He was at 99 pitches after the eighth. I told him I would pull him for relief if his pitch count got much higher. With that type of lead, we could afford a base runner, but as you saw, no one got past first the last three innings, and he retired the side in the ninth."

"That seems like some wear and tear for your ace—think he can hold up like that for the rest of the season," the reporter countered.

"I probably would have pulled him after the eighth were it any other regular-season game. But you must understand something about baseball and our team. We're a proud club. Tonight, we played a great game against a great team. Sammy wanted to stay and finish. You don't get many opportunities in your career to have a dominating performance on a big stage opening day. I know it's a long season better than most. Sammy wanted a shot to complete the game. That was good enough for me. He earned his chance, and he finished strong. That's the kind of attitude that breeds success. I think everyone felt it tonight, and that's something we can build on for the future. Also, I'll say this. No one worked harder in the off-season preparing for the year than Sammy. You all know or will soon know he's done a bunch of work with Pitching Coach Eli Aaronson, adding a pretty good slider this off-season. Beyond that, he's followed Eli's regimen and pitch count all spring. So, we know he was good to go today," finished Saul. He gave the nod to Mark, and Mark stepped in.

"Folks, we have a busy day tomorrow, so I would ask you to talk to the players for about ten minutes. We'll cut you guys out so the players can get some rest this evening," said Mark.

The reporters scrambled to get position on the players they most wanted to interview, Josh and Samson. Josh was the surprise star of the moment, and the reporters were on him like vultures on fresh meat.

Roman Josephus, the SPNN reporter with the Pirates, raced to the head of the line. Roman wore a dark blue tailored suit and kept his dark brown curly hair slicked back, showcasing his impeccably close-trimmed beard hugging a triangular face and hooked nose. He came complete with a "TV" tan, unnatural for the often overcast Pennsylvania spring, even with the spring training in sunny Florida. Roman always prepared for a close-up or an extended TV interview. Then again, Roman carried far bigger ambitions than being a beat reporter for little Pittsburgh and was prepared to do whatever it took to make it to TV "big-leagues."

An aggressive smooth-talking newshound, Roman never feared drumming up a little controversy with his questions if it elevated an otherwise mundane news story. He planned to move up to a large market team or break a big news story with national attention and secure his shot at one of SPNN's coveted national broadcast spots. To do this any time soon, Roman needed a big story with this small-town club. He toiled hopelessly for two years, looking for some news story to hype and punch his ticket to bigger and better assignments. A week ago, such a break seemed impossible, but suddenly, Roman smelled his chance to make some news with this unknown rookie. Before anyone else could get started, he took the first stab at climbing his ladder of success.

"Josh, I'm Roman Josephus with SPNN. Can you tell the fans a little about yourself, like where you're from and how you ended up playing for the Pirates?"

Josh was sitting in a chair beside his locker, tying his shoes. He wore a pair of weathered beige ripstop utility pants over the compression shorts Doc Luke gave him and a black compression shirt with long sleeves and a small Pittsburgh Pirates logo on the left breast. He donned a Pirates cap sporting a digital camo scheme Pete found for him from a stash of last year's alternate uniforms. The hat shielded Josh's face as the reporters and their news cameras got their first good look at the hawk of a man. Josh wore his hat pulled low, but his flowing dark black curly hair peaked well below his cap. At first, they could only see part of his broad, slightly hooked nose as the brim of his ball cap hid his eyes until he finished tying his shoes. Like his entire frame, his cheeks appeared angularly chiseled without an ounce of excess fat.

As he finished tying his shoes and sat up, the reporters saw a scar traced jaggedly from behind his left eye down his left cheek. It stood out, a stark contrast to his dark complexion in the room's bright lights. Josh's entire countenance might seem formidable and unapproachable, if not for his eyes. They spoke of someone old and wise. They were kind eyes and inviting. Josh's eyes dispelled his daunting physical traits and welcomed you like an old friend, glad to see you again.

Josh's warm voice drew all to him as he calmly responded in a bright baritone voice. "I grew up in Western PA but left home shortly after high school and only recently moved back into the area with my daughter. I suppose you could say the Pirates saw me this spring as a possible addition to the club and invited me to try out for a position on the roster. Coach Samuelson signed me last week, and I joined the team just before the end of spring training."

"Josh, can you tell us who you played with before coming to the Pirates?" a local reporter asked.

"I have not played baseball professionally previously," answered Josh.

There were more than a few blank stares at this remark and even a few open mouths as Josh surprised the veteran sports reporters. To his credit, the reporter recovered and followed up with, "What did you do then?"

"I worked in the government sector," replied Josh, smiling.

Roman Josephus cut back in before the other reporter, "Josh, it seems more than a little odd that you've come out of nowhere to start for the Pirates during the season opener. Yet you managed to go three for three and hit a tape-measure home run off the Cardinal ace pitcher. Can you tell the fans more about your story, background, and what you hope to accomplish as a Pittsburgh Pirate?"

"I am sorry, Roman, but there's not much to tell. Pops saw me and thought I could help the club. My only goal is to make the team better and try to contribute at every opportunity."

"C'mon, Josh, give something for our fans and listeners," pressed a skeptical Roman.

"I have a 12-year-old daughter, Ruth. Apart from my family, I guess I would say, most importantly, I am a Christian, first and foremost, just trying to do what the Lord has for me to do, to make the world a better place and give Him all honor and glory. I am delighted to get the opportunity to play ball for my hometown Pirates, and I hope to continue contributing to the club positively."

Mark Johnson watched the informal question and answers from the reporters and realized Josh was unwilling to give much of his personal life history. He spoke up from the sides, trying to bring the reporters back to the game. "Perhaps someone would like to ask Josh about the game?"

"Josh, what was it like to play in your first big-league game?" asked the beat reporter from the Pittsburgh Tribune-Review,® breaking in after Roman's questions.

"Pretty amazing to be out there in front of such a large crowd here at Busch stadium. There were a few butterflies in the first inning, to say the least."

"Can you take us through the catch you made on the ball hit down the line?" followed the same reporter.

"Yeah, that was a hard-hit ball. To be honest, it was all reactionary. With it being early in the game, I wanted to keep it initially from getting past me to the wall. I got a good jump on it and thought all the time I might have a chance at snagging it. I didn't think much about the wall—probably should have, but as you know, I am still new to the park. I dove for it—The good thing was I could keep the wall in my field of view as I chased down the ball. I felt I could glove it, but I didn't know how far I would slide. It all worked out in the end. I got good and dirty, and that play helped chase the butterflies away. It was just a game again. It gave me the right perspective. Regardless of the crowds, it's the same game we play as little leaguers. No one will die if we don't win or I drop the ball. I told myself to play the game I love, play it hard, have fun, and good things will happen."

"Any thought you might hit the wall before you dove or if the ball got by you?"

Josh was thoughtful and replied, "One thing Andrew told me was don't be afraid to get after a hit if I thought I could make a play. He talked to me about each backing the other on any diving play. With no one on and the heart of the order coming up, it was a little risky, but I knew Andrew wouldn't be far behind if I dove and missed. Pops talks to us about taking good risks—leaving it all on the field. He said we want to be smart, but we also want to challenge on every play, every at-bat. He promised to have our backs on taking good risks and pulling the trigger. I like that—it's kind of like when you teach youngsters playing this game; go down swinging. You never forget watching a called strike three without a swing. That's kinda' what Pops and Andrew said to me. So, I was confident to go all out on the play. It's a good feeling on this team, everybody pushing to get the most out of our opportunities, and I am enthusiastic about our chances."

"Josh, while that play was great—I think the fans want to know about the home run," asked another reporter. "What'd it feel like to crush that St. Louis pitch into orbit?"

Josh shrugged. "I just went up to bat feeling locked in, seeing the pitches well. Again, the team showed a lot of confidence in me, and it helped me stay loose. I figured, being the newbie, the Cards might want to test me with a high-quality fastball. I got what I expected and caught it cleanly. As far as how it felt—great contact on a ball always feels the same to me—the better you connect with a ball at the peak of your swing, the less you feel. On that pitch, I felt almost nothing."

"What was with taking a knee before entering the batter's box? Some people said you looked a little like Tim Tebow in the end zone," tickled Roman, trying to get a rise out of Josh.

Josh's eyes smiled back at the skeptic Roman and chuckled, "We're talking to the same man, I'd say. Just thanking Him for all He does and asking Him to help us do our best for His honor and glory. It's just something that I do..., Something I have always done before I..., go to work, so to speak." Josh paused for a moment, with a thousand thoughts, but decided against saying them. "No, I like Tim Tebow. I am a big fan, so if people see that in me when I bow my head, that's fine. Like I told you, Roman, I am a Christian. It's the core of who I am. I always ask for the Father's guidance and help. That's what lights my path, and in every sense, brought me here today."

Mark Johnson looked between Josh and Pops, waiting for the signal. Pops nodded to him. "One last question for the players before we let them get out of here for some rest tonight, folks."

"Josh, any thoughts on tomorrow's game," said the Trib reporter.

"Well, it's going to be fun. I am looking forward to it. Tell the fans to tune in. I don't think they'll be disappointed," replied Josh.

"Guaranteeing another victory then, Josh?" quipped Roman, trying to get an edge to what he would report.

Mark grimaced from behind and looked pleadingly at Josh. "Don't take the bait," he thought, hoping Josh read his thoughts.

Roman's goading didn't fool Josh. "I only guarantee the same hard play you saw from all of us today. When you play with that kind of heart and attitude, I think good things can happen," Josh answered.

Mark breathed a sigh of relief and said, "All right, folks, that'll be all for today. We'll see you tomorrow back at the ballpark.

Thirty

After the reporters were gone and the team was alone again, Pops cleared everyone to complete their post-game routines. Players made arrangements to eat together at the team hotel restaurant. The Pirates set up several shuttles, allowing for players who took more time with physical therapy after the game. Josh was one of the last to finish and caught the final shuttle back to the hotel, finally getting to the room just before 6:00 PM.

Ruth, excited as always to see her dad, ran to greet him when he entered their hotel suite.

"Dad, you were awesome today. What a way to start the season! The Cardinals never knew what hit them!" said Ruth as Josh embraced his daughter in his customary bear hug.

"Yep. We got off to a great start, didn't we, sweetheart?" Josh said, picking her up effortlessly. "How's everything going here?" Josh asked Mary, who closed her tablet the girls used for schoolwork and stood smiling at them.

"All's well here, Josh," Mary replied. "Ruth and I were reading for one of her history assignments. She seems to have found something she wants to study."

"Yeah, Dad, our history course allows us to select optional studies on various topics. One of them is the history of Jews in Europe and America. I thought we could learn about how they migrated and their customs and maybe have something to discuss with Joe and Beth."

"That's a terrific idea, hon. I bet they would like that," replied Josh, always buoyed by his daughter's endless enthusiasm. Josh released little Ruth. "OK, what's our schedule look like tonight?" he asked with a hint of expectation.

Before arriving in St. Louis, Josh asked Mary to work with the Pittsburgh medical facility where Ruth went for treatments to help establish contacts in the various cities on their schedule. When Mary called the facility, they contacted a St. Louis facility administrator they recommended, who volunteered to meet with them today after the game.

"The patient advocate at the St. Louis Children's Hospital agreed to meet us at 6:30 PM," replied Mary. "She said she will be just finishing with a patient but understands our time constraints with your schedule and would be happy to spend 30 minutes with us. I got Ruth's PA to send the medical records to the hospital, and the advocate talked with one doctor there early today. She planned for Ruth to match what she would get in Pittsburgh. We can meet tonight, and I can take her to PT tomorrow at 10:00 if you are happy with what we see tonight."

Ruth wrinkled her nose. "You know, Dad, I could always skip a treatment or two when we're on the road," she said hopefully. Though the PT did her good, it also was tough on her.

"I know PT isn't much fun for you, hon, but it always makes you stronger and more able to do the things you want to do—and I know you have big plans for the future."

"Like earning a varsity letter in high school?" asked Ruth hopefully, as she still wanted to be an athlete despite her disability. Her competitive nature was a driving force in working through the PT regimen to strengthen her muscles.

"Well, I know the Lord tells us to do our best at whatever we do, so if you want to do a sport, you've got to keep working on the therapy just like the doctor says to you every time we go. And look—you know you've seen improvement in your leg strength since we moved; We've got to keep it going even when we're on the road, OK?"

"You're right, Dad. Let's go check it out," Ruth said with renewed determination.

"That's my girl!" Josh smiled at Ruth, and she gave him a high five.

"Well, good, because I have already ordered an Uber to get us to the hospital. It should be here soon, just in time to get us over there for the appointment," chimed in Mary.

"Wow, you're on top of it there, Mary!" said Josh, with a little laugh.

"Just earning my keep, Mr. Green," Mary shot back with just a little punctuation to Josh's wry remark.

"OK, let me drop my bag, and we can head out. Maybe we can get some Italian on the way home. I'm hungry," said Josh.

"If you mean pizza, Dad, I'm in!"

Josh laughed again, smiling as he walked to his room to deposit his things. Mary and Ruth proved a formidable team with everything well in hand.

Thirty One

The meeting with the patient advocate, Ms. Linda Richards, went very well. Ruth's health history and treatment intrigued her, and Ms. Richards was sympathetic to their needs. As they learned, she was something of a legend. A nurse for 45 years at St. Louis Children's Hospital before "retiring," as she called it, Ms. Richards was now the full-time Patient Advocate. Linda listened intently to Josh's concerns about moving around throughout the season while trying to ensure Ruth continued her treatments. Ms. Richards then took the Greens and Mary on a brief tour of the facilities where Ruth would come tomorrow.

"You know folks," Ms. Richards said casually as they returned to her office. "I have access to an extensive nationwide system and colleagues around the country. Mary probably found it difficult to identify and schedule treatment here in St. Louis, and this is just your first city. Could I suggest, Mr. Green, you let me work with Mary? Together, we can match your schedule with appropriate facilities and arrange treatments. Mary and I could easily set it up together using my system and contacts. After being in this business almost fifty years, I know a lot of doctors, and most owe me!" Linda said, smiling.

The offer took Josh aback. "Ms. Richards, that would be a great help to us. But it's also above and beyond what we expected today. I am not sure I can ask you to spend so much time on us."

"Well, Josh, I have a thought about that. I have a proposition on how you might repay me," Linda said with a twinkle in her eye.

"Oh really?" said Josh. "What do you have in mind?"

"Would you consider visiting some of our kids staying at the hospital and our more long-term, critical patients? I know many would love to get a visit from a Major League Baseball player?"

"Oh, Dad, just think of all the kids you could help cheer up while I get my treatment," said Ruth.

"Well, it sounds like a wonderful opportunity," Josh agreed, and turned to Mary. "What do you think, Mary? Think you could use Nurse Richards's help?"

"I absolutely could," said Mary, visibly relieved to have help with what seemed like an impossible task, trying to work a schedule for Ruth with all their travel.

"OK, Ms. Richards, what do you want us to do?" Josh replied.

"If you have a few minutes, let's all take a walk...."

Thirty Two

Nurse Richards led the Greens and Mary to the children's ward, where they treated many children with challenging childhood diseases. As they entered the ward, a doctor talked with two nurses at the nurse's station. She told one of the nurses something, pointing to a chart they were pouring over, and he nodded as the other nurse annotated the sheet. Doctor Thyatira looked up at the four newcomers approaching the nurse's station. Doctor Thyatira was a striking figure, with classic Eastern European features, dark eyes, and wavy dark black hair with an accent of silver back one side, belying her roughly 60 years of age. She wore dark purple scrubs, and although diminutive in size, her presence was formidable. To the newcomers, the two nurses showed great deference to her comments and orders for their patients. When she heard the foursome approach and looked over her shoulder at them, she turned and placed her hands on her hips, smiling up at them yet still commanding the room.

"So here is our famous base-baller, eh Linda?" the doctor said with a wry smile and a slight accent, Greek perhaps, thought Josh based on his travels.

"Yes, Doctor Thyatira. These are our newcomers, Josh and Ruth Green and Mary Dalene," replied Nurse Richards. Josh looked at Linda sideways as it seemed apparent the two ladies discussed Josh's visit before he even showed up. "Please call me Lydia," said the doctor as she reached out her hand, looking up at Josh.

Though Josh towered over Doctor Thyatira, Mary and Ruth could tell Josh was the one being scrutinized. He reached out and took the doctor's hand, and she gripped it firmly despite her size. Unlike many others, Lydia Thyatira did not hesitate to look deeply into Josh's eyes, drinking them in. Lydia cared little about the man's looks. She wanted to see him like she saw her many young patients. The eyes always told the story, for their story was where the doctor cultivated seeds for each patient's success. In Josh's eyes, she saw a story filled with kindness, strength, and profound wisdom. Her smile turned to a serious but motherly look as she clenched his hand even tighter, pulling him slightly down to her. "Welcome, Josh. I think you will make a splendid gift to our patients when they meet you," she said to Josh, who saw Lydia's story of kindness and healing echoed in her deep, dark eyes.

"I'll happily try, Lydia," Josh replied. "What would you have me do?"

Dr. Thyatira released Josh's hand and put her hands on her hips, turning first to Ruth. "First, let me say hello to your daughter. Hello Ruth. Nurse Linda shared your profile with me today, and I think the plan she made will do well for you. How are you enjoying being on the road with your dad and this base-baller team?" she said to Ruth.

"Oh, it's been a great first trip so far," said Ruth, "Especially since Dad played a great game today."

"Yes, so I heard, and even though I have lived in America for the last twenty-five years, I still don't quite understand this national pastime. I am a big football fan, but of course, that's European football, and you don't see that so much over here!" said Lydia, much to the chagrin of the male nurse who talked to the doctor as they came in and now was shaking his head sheepishly. Dr. Thyatira looked between him and Josh as she continued in her Greek accent. "I heard your dad single-handedly spoiled our Red Birds' first game—what's it called?" she said, looking over at the nurse.

Obviously, the nurse told Dr. Thyatira countless baseball facts before, which she casually pretended to forget. He wore a Cardinals lanyard with his ID badge, and his scrub cap was Cardinal Red and bore the Cardinals logo. He rolled his eyes, smiling, and shook his head.

"You mean home opener, Doc?"

Dr. Thyatira played up her supposed lack of understanding of baseball just to frustrate her nurse friend, an obvious Cardinals fan.

"Ah yes, yes, that's it," said Lydia, "The home opener spoiled by; what is it, Josh, when you hit the ball very far?"

"A home run?" said Josh, smiling as he played along.

"Ahh, yes. Young Reuben here was coming on shift when you hit this home run, and everyone was talking about how far it went. He seemed a little sad about that, as I recall. You are still recovering, eh Reuben?" said Lydia, looking up at Reuben as he shook his head, smiling.

"Sorry about ruining your day, Reuben," replied Josh sheepishly.

"No problem, Mr. Green," Reuben replied. "Can you just try not to make it a habit?"

"Well, no promises, I'm afraid," said Josh, and they both laughed.

"Dr. Thyatira, since it's a little late, I thought we could just show Josh to a couple of your patients since Josh, Ruth, and Mary's day was a long one with another tomorrow."

"That's fine, Linda, and for Pete's sake, you have to start calling me Lydia to—You are the only one around here who's been here longer than I have, and you're retired now—let these young nurses call me Doctor Thyatira, you've been mentoring me for twenty years."

"Now, Josh," said Lydia as she took Josh by the arm, patting his big hand as she led him, and the rest followed, "I see you came prepared." Josh looked questioningly. "Your hat," said Lydia, nodding up at Josh's Pirate hat. "You wore your hat."

"Well, I guess that depends on what you want me to do," said Josh.

"Mostly take their mind off what they are doing for a little while. Give them a chance to focus on something else. Just be their hero for the day."

Though Dr. Thyatira surprised the others, Josh, unfazed, smiled and nodded. "I will, Lydia. Where do we start?"

Josh, Mary, and Ruth spent the next 30 minutes in a children's cancer ward. The male nurse, Reuben, escorted them as Doctor Thyatira broke away to make rounds and promised to catch up to them when she finished. Reuben prepared the kids by rounding them up to meet Josh in the patient common area. Reuben also came prepared with a box of St. Louis Cardinals paraphernalia. He explained, "Sorry, Mr. Green, but I only found out you were coming a few hours ago. The Cards sent this stuff over at the end of last season as a gift to give to the kids when we saw fit. Since Linda and Doc Thyatira made this plan to, well..., get you to come here as a surprise, and it's been quite a while since a Cardinal player visited, I thought maybe you could hand some of it out?" Reuben said somewhat hesitantly. "I know, Mr. Green, probably a bad idea, right?–You playing for the other guys and all." Reuben trailed off saying it, as it seemed presumptuous, but Josh put him at ease.

"Not at all, Reuben," Josh said and laughed at Reuben's relief. "I'll be happy to hand it out, and now that I know what to expect, I'll bring some Pirates stuff with me next time to replace it. And please, it's just Josh."

"Thanks, Josh. Many of the kids are pretty young and don't know a lot about the game. I didn't tell them you were from the other team, just that you were a pro baseball player who played today."

Reuben stepped out to get the kids assembled as Josh and Mary sat on a bench while Ruth walked around, looking at the various gaming tables and other kid things filling the room. It was half a recreational, half a communal treatment area.

Josh said quietly to Mary, "What do you think?"

"Nurse Richards volunteering to help with the contacts at the other cities is huge. I didn't say anything to you, but when Ruth's doctor in Greensburg got a response from her directly, he told me he heard of her by reputation. She apparently is a legend in the nursing community, known in the children's hospital circles around the country. He heard her speak as a visiting lecturer to pediatric doctors at Johns Hopkins when he attended a symposium there several years ago.

He said she was top-notch and was delighted she would meet us at our first stop. Honestly, I am relieved to have her help."

"I think she's got some good planning skills, seeing how she and probably Doc Lydia planned this entire visit. I suspect it will be PT combined with more patient visits for us as we go."

"I know," replied Mary. "Do you mind?"

"Oh no, not at all. I think this will be great for all three of us. Ruthie always wants to help others, and I am sure it will help us keep a good perspective. It sounds like the kind of opportunity the Lord gives when we follow His will. I will pray He blesses all with these visits."

Suddenly, Reuben opened the door, and eleven kids from 16 down to 6 years old came piling into the room. Many were undergoing treatment, two pushed two of the smaller kids in wheelchairs, and two pulled intravenous drips along as they came. Either a parent or guardian accompanied each child. They all sat down or gathered around Josh.

Reuben walked to the front. "Thanks, everyone, for taking a moment out of your treatments to meet our guest. His name is Josh Green, and he's a star baseball player with the Pittsburgh Pirates. Some of you may have seen the opener today, where Josh and the Pirates beat our Cards. Doctor Thyatira will be here in a few minutes as she is attending to a few other children who couldn't come to the recreation room. She asked Josh to say hello to you. Plus, I have some Cardinals' stuff you can pick from and take with you—Josh, would you like to introduce yourself?"

Josh stood up, so everyone got a good look at the hawk of a man for the first time. Tall, lean, strong, and muscular, the scar on his cheek caught their attention. He might intimidate some with his large, rugged build, save for his eyes. Once he turned his kind eyes on them, the children warmed to his presence, looking on expectantly.

"Hello everyone. Thanks for gathering here. Doc Lydia told me you all are going through some tough treatments today but would like it if I could come and meet you all. Reuben's got this great box of goodies from your hometown team, and I would be happy to hand it out and even sign something. I am sorry, this was a bit of a surprise for me, so I didn't bring anything from the Pirates.—I'll do that when I return to St. Louis next time. I want to say hello and hopefully have a little fun with you here today."

As Reuben predicted, many kids didn't know who Josh was. After all, he just made his debut. But they were ecstatic to get to talk to him. Meanwhile, Mary busily searched for a highlight reel from the game. She quickly found one from the local news on her phone and cast it on the TV screen. Everyone watched as the news replayed the "Rookie from Pittsburgh" story. The newscast showed

Josh's great catch and incredible home run onto Clark Avenue. After the video, the children turned back to Josh with a sense of awe. Many excitedly shook his hand, asking him what it was like to be a baseball player.

Reuben, a favorite big brother to many patients, especially the younger kids, produced a gold sharpie, and Josh began signing whatever the kids picked out of the box. Balls, caps, a pennant, a couple of mini bats, and even a Cardinals shirt or two. It didn't seem to matter the stuff was Cardinal gear, as the kids were happy to talk to a real ballplayer. Josh did his best to answer all their questions. Though he was a brand-new rookie player, he seemed to know the right words to encourage each child and their family.

After about 20 minutes, Dr. Thyatira joined the group and watched as Josh chatted with the patients and families. She finally spoke up as Josh and Reuben finished giving gifts to all the patients in the room. "Josh, would you like to come and meet a few other patients who couldn't leave their hospital rooms? I am sure they would like a chance to chat with you.

Josh said his goodbyes to the patients and told them he would be back to visit the next time the Pirates came through town, but he hoped and prayed their treatment would be successful and they wouldn't be in the hospital for too long.

Dr. Thyatira took the Greens and Mary to several rooms where children received treatment. He greeted each one with a similar cheerful countenance, giving kind words and taking their minds off their illness, if just for a while.

In the last room was a sleeping child who looked to be about eight years old. She was well into late-stage cancer treatment, bald and swollen from the effects of the treatment. She wore a little white crocheted cap on her head, with a pink flower sewn on the front, to keep her head warm. The girl's mother and father sat with their daughter as she slept. Dr. Thyatira entered first, as Josh, Ruthie, and Mary followed. The woman looked up and smiled tiredly. "Hello, Dr. Thyatira."

"Hello, Mrs. Sidon, I was just making my rounds with some visitors, but we can come back if you prefer."

"No, it's OK, Lydia. She is just resting. She sleeps a lot now," she said, her voice trailing off. The four watched quietly as the girl's father sat by the other side of the bed, his hand gently resting on her shoulder.

With her braced legs, Ruth ambled up next to Mrs. Sidon and broke the silence. "Mrs. Sidon, my name is Ruth. Thank you for allowing us to come into your daughter's room. Is there anything we can do for you? Anything your daughter needs?" Somehow, the way Ruth asked, kindness entered the room with her words.

"Oh Ruth, I am not sure there's anything to be done. Our little Tyre fought a good fight for three years against this cancer, but it has returned. She's just three days shy of her twelfth birthday, and she always loves birthdays. She was hoping to get a bike to ride. Tyre loved riding her bike before she got sick the first time...," Mrs. Sidon paused, composing her breaking voice as she idly stroked her daughter's forehead, repositioning her beanie ever so slightly. She sat back and continued, "I am sorry. I was thinking about how Tyre was still talking about riding a bike this morning before falling asleep." Mrs. Sidon stopped and looked back at Ruth. "I guess, Ruth, she could use your prayers. We all could."

"We can do that," said Ruth, and she walked closer to the bedside and took Tyre's hand. Ruth reached out to Mary, standing behind her with her other hand, and Mary immediately stepped forward. "Come help, Dad," said Ruth. Josh walked to the foot of the bed, touched the little girl's foot, and placed an arm around Mary to grasp Ruthie's shoulder. It was Ruth who prayed as they all bowed their heads.

"Dear Lord, please help Tyre, be with her, hold her close, and heal her if it is your will. Please be with her mom and dad and care for them in the days ahead. In Jesus' name, we pray," and everyone said, "Amen."

After a few moments, the group moved back from the bedside, and Ruth leaned over and hugged Mrs. Sidon.

"Thank you," Mrs. Sidon said with tears in her eyes.

They exited the room, and Dr. Thyatira walked them back toward the ward's exit. They were quiet as she explained, "Tyre has been such a fighter. When the fight is long, it takes a toll on the patient and family."

She turned to the three with a smile and a hint of regret. "Josh, I know Linda and I kind of waylaid you today, and you have been very generous, not just with your time but with taking this all in," she turned to Mary and Ruth. "You all have. Thank you very much. These children and their families often struggle for hope, and you brought more than a little with you today, I think."

Josh smiled down at Dr. Thyatira. "I suspect you, Reuben, and the staff we met here bring hope to them and their families every day. And it is we who should thank you, Doc."

Dr. Lydia Thyatira gazed up at the big man and again took his offered hand in that same warm handshake she gave when they met. She peered deeply into those kind eyes and knew there was something old and wise beyond years as Josh smiled back knowingly. She reached up and patted him softly on his cheek. "Now I'll know if you play well and win your ball game tomorrow because Reuben will be all mopey when I see him. But that's OK. Just bring yourself back when you're in town because there is nothing he would rather see than his kids getting a kick out of seeing you."

They said their goodbyes and began walking to exit the ward. After a minute, Josh paused and handed the keys to Mary, saying, "You guys go on. I'll catch up with you."

Mary and Ruth returned to their car just as Josh arrived, rushing to catch up. As he helped his daughter, opening the door for her to get in, Mary noticed he was missing his Pirates cap. She watched Ruth turn and give Josh a big hug. Mary was unsure how the experience affected Ruth, but now watching Ruth reminded Mary of Ruth's strength and incredible positive spirit. Mary thought she must get it from her mom and dad. "Thank you for making those kids' day today, Dad. You did good," Ruth said to Josh.

He smiled admiringly back at his little girl, "So did you, hon. I think it's a reminder to us all just how blessed we are and how thankful we should be."

Mary looked on, taking it all in as she often did, not speaking but pondering all that happened in her heart.

Thirty Three

On a typical mid-west spring morning, the day dawned chillier than expected as the Cardinals and Pirates took the field at a brisk, windy 55 degrees Fahrenheit. Busch Stadium was rocking almost as much as opening day. Pops made one significant change to the lineup. Going with his gut and what he saw for the last week, Pops moved Josh up three spots to the number four position.

Lead-off man Zach started the game, slapping a single to the opposite field in the top of the first. J.J. jumped on the first pitch fastball and hit a grounder deep into the hole at short, but the shortstop gloved the ball and made an off-balance throwback to second to force out Zach. J.J., however, beat the throw to first. The captain, Andrew, came up and worked the count to full, with a couple of foul balls down the left field line. He got a decent fastball over the outside corner and drove it into right field, placing runners on first and second.

The Pirate announcers discussed Coach Samuelson's lineup decisions between batters. "Two on, one out for the Pirates, bringing the rookie Green to the plate, batting in the cleanup position. Pops moved ol' Green up to fourth after starting him seventh yesterday. What do you think about that, Greg?" asked Bob.

"Well, he played a heck of a first game, Bob. Pops already showed us a few surprises, starting J.J. and Juan in the infield. It appears he's going with youth and the old rookie, after how they did yesterday. I guess we have to wait and see if yesterday was a fluke or if Pops is on to something here," Greg responded noncommittally.

"What do you think the Cards will do with the rookie Green for this at-bat—too early to walk the bases loaded, don't you think?" wondered Bob aloud.

"The rook is a rookie, after all, and Juan's behind him after having a good game yesterday and a great spring training. I think you got to pitch to him. 'Course, that home run's got to stick in the back of your mind," answered Greg.

Josh approached the plate and again kneeled to pray just as he did for his first at-bat yesterday. Today he got more than a few boos.

"Green's pulling a Tebow again, Greg, and the crowd is letting him hear it today," stated Bob.

"Yeah, well, it's unorthodox, and it will be interesting to see if the League has something to say about it if he keeps it up," Greg opined.

Josh stepped into the batter's box to face the Cardinals pitcher. This pitcher was known for his off-speed prowess, painting the corners and dropping a nasty curve or a changeup mixed with a low 90s fastball. The catcher saw enough from Josh and the fastball yesterday. He decided to start him out on a diet of off-speed pitches.

"Here's the pitch, a curveball on the outside, just a little low, and Green didn't bite. One ball, no strikes," said Bob.

"Cautious approach. Looks like the Cards are playing coy with the rookie," commented Greg.

As planned in the pregame, the catcher signaled for a fastball high, just above the zone. The pitcher executed the pitch, but Josh took the pitch for ball two.

Bob shook his head. "Well, it looks like they *are* going to pitch around Green."

"Yeah, it looks like it. The pitcher is hitting the glove, but Green's showing a surprisingly good eye. Let's see if they will load the bases," Greg sounded disappointed.

The catcher called for the changeup down and in. Standard baseball wisdom said Josh would swing over and in front of the slower pitch after the high fastball.

Josh was at peace. He saw both previous pitches clearly in their arc to the plate, knowing they were not in the strike zone. Focused as only Josh could, Josh saw in this delivery, a slight delay as the ball spun and traveled a looser, slower trajectory than the previous fastball. Josh's body, perfectly tuned to his mind's eye, delayed movement slightly, waiting patiently to hit this deceptively plunging offering. It was inside but slightly higher than the pitcher intended, just above the bottom of the strike zone. Josh's swing and hip turn, tuned to its delayed approach, uncoiled his arms late with a long, sweet stroke. His bat intercepted the slower pitch as it traveled downward, catching it on the bat's barrel just out in front of the plate, yanking it down the third baseline.

"THWHaacckkk."

Unlike yesterday's concussive blast of the fastball, the smoothness of Josh's swing against the slower changeup belied its power, and the perfect contact sent the ball arching just inside the foul line, high toward the left field bleachers.

"There's a drive!" shouted Bob into the mike. "Down the left field line, curving, curving... if it's fair, it's gone!.... It's FAIR!" he exclaimed. "Josh Green just deposited the Cards offering into the left field stands!"

"HO-LY COW! What a start for the rookie, Bob! Two games, two three-run homers!" followed Greg in amazement.

"Cannonball coming Bucco Nation, Green puts the Pirates on the board with another three-run dinger!" Bob announced excitedly.

"Bob, do you notice how silent this crowd is now? Man, you could barely hear yourself think to start the game, and now you could hear a pin drop," commented Greg.

"Everywhere but in the Pirate dugout, Greg, they're whooping it up and high-fiving each other like they just made the playoffs!" said Bob.

"Well, if Green keeps this up, who knows?" replied Greg.

The game continued as a back-and-forth affair. Josh followed up his three-run home run with a double in the second. When the Cardinals intentionally walked him in the seventh, he scored after a hit-and-run single by Juan, and a Judah sacrifice fly. In the top of the ninth, he lined sharply to left field for a single and later scored again. The Pirates held on in the bottom of the inning for a 9-7 victory. Josh finished three-for-three, and the Pirates had the makings of a bona fide star.

Thirty Four

T he post-game scene was chaotic. If anything, the crowd of reporters was even greater than opening day. As usual, Pops took the first questions before opening the locker room to the press. More interviews were going on, as many of the Pirates produced good offensive outputs today. Still, as soon as Pops finished taking questions and Mark Johnson released the reporters, most grabbed territory as fast as they could around Josh's locker area.

The Tribune beat reporter was first to fire a volley. "Josh, two games, two big home runs. How's it feel to be the talk of the town?"

"Well, I am glad to contribute to our success, sir. The team is playing well, and we are fortunate to be sitting at 2-0 playing a good team like St. Louis."

"Can you take us through your first at-bat, Josh? What did you see, and were you looking for the changeup?" asked another reporter.

"Well, I know he throws a lot of great off-speed pitches, but to be honest, his fastball is pretty good too. I always look for a pitch in the zone I can hit. He threw me away and away before, with the second being a high fastball. It seemed like he might try something off-speed. I think he was a little high on his placement, and I told myself to slow it down and get the hips through since it was a little on the inside. I made good contact with the barrel, and my swing kept it just fair. I was happy to take advantage of a bit of a mistake there, as I know he doesn't make many."

Roman Josephus finally saw his chance. "Hey, Josh. You started with your Tebow move again. You've done it twice now, and the result has been a three-run homer each time. Are you claiming divine intervention with those at-bats and swings?"

The other reporters chuckled, and Mark Johnson and Pops, watching from the side of the room, paused in their conversation as Mark grimaced slightly.

Josh smiled, "The good Lord isn't concerned too much about how the baseball game goes, I think, Roman, but I want to give him all the honor and glory. I ask Him to allow me to do my best to that end. That's all. Believe me, whether I strike out or hit a homer, it's all because of Him, I'm even here, getting to play this game. I feel very blessed."

"Yeah, but Josh, two home runs, and you're currently six for six, batting a thousand. That, in anybody's book, is a pretty good start. Especially for a thirty-eight-year-old rookie. Some might even call it a miracle," said Roman, trying to stir the pot. He needed Josh to say something controversial to garner national attention.

"Roman, don't get me wrong, I believe in miracles, and you might say my being here, playing for the Pirates, is one, but I am just a ballplayer with a half dozen good at-bats. I've made some good swings, and I'm happy to contribute. Again, the team is playing very well, and we want to keep that momentum."

"Josh, you've made some excellent plays in the field; A diving catch and a stolen base yesterday, and you went to third on a hit-and-run today. Can you tell us more about your physical approach to the game, since you're the oldest starter on the field?" asked another reporter.

"When you put it like that, are you trying to say I'm old?" replied Josh, staring back at the reporter.

"Well, I just thought...," said the reporter hesitantly.

Josh broke into a grin, "I am just kidding with you," he said as the reporter looked relieved, "No, you are right, I am not a spring chicken, but I have worked to keep my body in the best shape I can, and we have some great trainers and medical support here with the Pirates. Between Doc Luke and our physical therapist, Cy, they've kept an eye on me in training and recovery. However, I have always been able to run well. A lot of baseball is about timing and putting yourself in the best position. Our captains, Andrew and Thomas, have worked overtime with me to know where to position, based on the batters and pitchers. I am still learning, but so far, it's paid off."

"Has that always been a part of your game, then?" asked Roman, trying to work an angle.

"Well, you must use the gifts God gave you, and I've managed to stay in shape. I'm still pretty quick. So, I would say, yes."

"Josh, we still know little about your earlier playing days. Can you tell us some more about your background? Where did you play before? Where did you come from?"

"Good ole Western PA, Roman. I was away from the game for a while before returning to it in Pittsburgh."

"Away doing what?" pressed Roman bluntly.

"Just living life and working to help my family."

"Not going to share your history with us, then?"

"I will try to answer your questions. There is just not much to say. I am happy to talk about the game, and you have witnessed my total body of work playing professionally, Roman. What else can I say?" Josh finished, shrugging his shoulders.

"Then let's get back to the kneeling and prayer at the beginning of the game—has the League said anything about it?"

"No, not that I am aware of," Josh replied, eyeing Roman with no outward sign of emotion. "Why do you ask?"

"The League often frowns on public displays of controversial or offending gestures, comments, or visible signs outside those authorized by the League. For example, Tebow received a lot of flak for similar displays in the NFL. Are you worried the same might happen to you?"

"I hope my faith isn't considered controversial. We live in America, and the first amendment guarantees our freedom of religion. I don't see how bowing a knee to the Lord for a few seconds would be considered controversial or offensive."

Coach Samuelson whispered to Mark, and Mark stepped forward from their side view, speaking loud enough for the reporters to hear. "Any more *baseball* questions for Josh, folks?" he said, firmly emphasizing baseball.

"What's it feel like to be batting a thousand, Josh?" asked the Tribune-Review® reporter, breaking Roman's streak of questions.

Josh smiled again. "Feels pretty good while it lasts. I am glad to see the ball so well these first two games. As long as that continues and I make good swings, hopefully, I will continue to contribute."

"Any predictions on the series finale tomorrow night?" asked another reporter.

"Just the same as last time," Josh chuckled as the reporter smiled. "I guarantee we will give it our best, so come out and watch the show. I think you'll enjoy another great game." The reporter nodded back, acknowledging Josh wouldn't give him anything to spur the opponent.

Mark Johnson walked to the front with that answer, "All right, folks, that will be all for tonight." Mark escorted the reporters out. Saul walked back towards the visiting manager's office area. He noticed Old Pete was chomping on his unlit cigar, standing in the hallway, arms crossed, observing the locker room interviews. As Pops walked close with no others in earshot, Pete spoke softly. "You might want to keep an eye on that," he said.

Pops paused and looked back at where Pete nodded. "What's that?" he replied.

"That reporter, he's looking for an angle," Pete replied.

"What angle?" queried Pops.

"Doesn't matter," was Pete's terse reply. "He doesn't care as long as he's got one. That one's searching for a story, and he'll do anything to get it."

"So, what else is new? He's a reporter," answered Pops, and was about to move on.

"There are reporters, and then there are *reporters*." Pete said with emphasis as he looked directly at Saul now, with a look that said, "Pay Attention!" Saul knew Pete was talking about Roman. The man made no secret this Pirates beat was just a temporary steppingstone.

"Watch him," continued Pete earnestly, "He has big plans, and being the Pittsburgh Pirates reporter ain't big enough for him! He'll make the story go national any way he can, mark my words," he warned.

Pops looked out on the locker room as it cleared. He knew Pete was right. Pops himself warned the players of guys like Roman. He should take his own advice and pay special attention to this guy. "OK, Pete, I know what you mean. I'll pull Josh aside tomorrow and talk to him." Chomping on his cigar, Pete nodded, releasing Pops from his gaze, and walked back to the equipment room.

Pops stared out over the room for a moment. He thought, "We're 2-0, and I would rather have an overeager reporter trying to find dirt out about a player than talking to us after starting the season with a couple of losses." Still, as he continued toward his office, he couldn't shake the uneasy feeling he failed to recognize until a few moments ago.

Thirty Five

Quint Pilate's day was busy as usual for the beginning of the regular season. He didn't complain, though. It came with the job. As Commissioner of Major League Baseball, he was only a few years into his reign. However, his long history in the League taught Quint he must carefully nurture the season start to stoke interest and ensure the best possible League attendance for the entire long season. Bottom line, he walked a tricky tightrope satisfying the owners who hired and fired the commissioner, and the public, who generated the MLB market revenues and, ultimately, their profits. Opening week was busy. He needed the owners and the public to see the commissioner engaged throughout the League, managing MLB's image.

He started the year off in Boston in their opener against Tampa Bay before returning to New York. For day two, he had just returned from watching the Nationals play the Mets, with a much shorter trip between MLB offices on Park Avenue and the ballpark. After the game, Quint returned to the office. Since this was Saturday, he hoped to conduct further business from home, but his number two, the VP for Operations and Media, Herald Gripp, called him as the game ended and said they needed to talk. This was code something of concern came up and couldn't wait.

Quint's position was somewhat precarious as the commissioner. If things went well, he got little credit but excellent pay and all the perks of being commissioner of the U.S.'s oldest professional sports league. However, thirty very disparate owners with different needs and concerns voted him into the job. Quint's climb from once being an MLB intern to the top spot was as improbable as it was inspiring to anyone who followed professional sports. It was a challenging, lifelong journey for Quint. In a league that often favored tradition for the commissioner position, Quint was a long shot. It took a man who truly understood the ins and outs of the business, from the 30 franchise owners to the players and the fans. Some would say Quint leveraged the owners to vote for him, but Quint knew those were the losers he defeated to get to the top. He played the game the best.

Quint learned to balance an unequal league with wealthy owners and big-market and small-market teams, giving the public what they wanted. As the child of a first-generation immigrant, Quint grew up on the rough streets of Brooklyn. Despite the difficulties such a young life faced, he inherited his father's drive to make a better life for himself and his family. A previous MLB commissioner noticed the young, talented, hard-charging student intern from City College of NY and hired Quint after graduation. Quint worked hard to get ahead in this ultra-competitive business, climbing MLB's corporate ladder, eventually earning a reputation as a tough but fair negotiator as VP for player relations by hammering out the latest players' collective bargaining agreement for the League. The owners selected him as the new commissioner based mainly on what they saw as his ability to sway the players to conform to the owners' desires. Ultimately, this was a business, and when the owners made and kept their money, Quint kept his job.

Herald Gripp, Quint's number two, followed a very different path to his MLB position. Herald was legacy old-school baseball. His father's family was part owner of the Houston Astros and Texas Rangers. They were as close to baseball royalty as you could get, owning the Houston team in particular, since it entered the League in 1962. Herald's great-grandfather made his money in the oil business. His grandfather became commissioner of the American League in the '70s after agreeing to trade majority ownership of the Astros for minority ownership in both Texas teams. Herald was a charismatic personality who grew up around his family's team and learned to nurture owner support around the League as a young heir to one of the League's old families. With his likable personality and family heritage, Herald Gripp garnered a direct appointment to the deputy commissioner's position as VP for Operations and Media, concurrent with Quint's posting as the commissioner. While the two got along, Quint fully understood the meaning behind the dual appointment as Herald was a favorite of the owners and acted both as a spy for them and a number two to Quint. Should the owners decide it was time for Quint to leave, Herald was an obvious heir apparent. Despite this competing background, the two men worked surprisingly well together. Their tenure saw the League increase market value and profits for the three years since taking their current positions.

Quint arrived at the MLB offices on Park Avenue and went straight to his office on the 31st floor. Herald was already there waiting for him, speaking with Quint's assistant, who worked the weekend shift. It occasionally struck Quint that young Cassius reminded him of himself some twenty-plus years ago.

"Herald, good to see you. Shall we go in?" said Quint.

They walked into the commissioner's office, and Quint held the door for his subordinate. It was an expansive office with a conference area and table off to one side and a large mahogany desk with two leather-backed chairs opposite. Around and behind the desk were the commissioner's various baseball artifacts and bona fides, including pictures of him with some elites of baseball past, other VIPs, and two U.S. presidents. As Quint took his desk chair, Herald took one of the two leather chairs. Intentionally or not, the office could intimidate an uninitiated visitor.

"OK, Herald, I assume this isn't the kind of news that could wait for Monday. What do we have?" started Quint.

"I know you have been busy with some of the big draw openings, Quint, but have you caught the highlights of the St. Louis, Pittsburgh series?"

Quint bristled a little at Herald calling him by his first name. He was ten years his senior and, by any measure, held much more experience in MLB management. Herald was the only one in the organization who did so and got away with it, and Quint supposed that was why Herald did it. Quint was slightly irritated but told himself he needed to get over it after three years. "I heard about the home run and a good catch from opening day by the new rookie...what's his name?" Quint answered, trying to focus on the matter at hand.

"Joshua Green, the Pirates new starting right fielder. Yes, he has made quite a splash, not just in the opener. He is six for six, with a three-run homer in each of the first two games."

"OK, that's a little unusual, especially since I don't remember hearing about this guy before, but what's the problem?"

"Well, that's part of it. Green's an unknown, literally. He's a rookie, but not a normal one."

"What do you mean, Herald?"

"Well, for starters, he's thirty-eight years old," replied Herald.

Quint paused opening his office laptop computer, stopped, and looked up at Herald. "That is odd," he said, his irritation washing away, replaced with concern. Quint did not expect to learn this kind of information from someone else, let alone his VP. Quint grew up knowing all about the players, especially those who impacted the League, better than his competitors. Rarely did someone blindside him with this kind of information. He prided himself on being the first to know and get a jump on knowledge used to his advantage.

"Who did he play for before coming up to the 'Bigs'? I know a lot about the Pirates' farm prospects, and I don't remember this guy being on the radar," Quint asked, irritated with trying to catch up.

"That's just it. Nobody's heard of him. I just asked young Cassius to look up all the Joshua Greens in the minors before the start of the season: Long story short, there isn't one."

"Overseas or Mexican League?"

"Checked; no hits."

"OK, that's definitely odd. What info do you have from the Pirates?"

"We just got a copy of the contract filing yesterday," said Herald, handing a copy of the contract he pulled from his briefcase to Quint. "Not much to it as far as background; An interesting lack of info at that, actually," stated Herald somewhat coyly.

Quint felt Herald was enjoying one-upping him in the information department, and he also felt Herald still held his biggest bombshell of all. "Yes?" Quint couldn't help but ask.

"It's all legitimate," Herald started hesitantly, "Although there are some unique clauses for some pretty heady bonus levels for MVP awards, etc. It wouldn't be unusual for a current League star, but surely not reachable for a thirty-eight-year-old rookie. And he has a rider paying for a live-in nanny for his daughter. They are traveling with the team. Apparently, he's a single father of a child with special needs."

"Who's his agent?" asked Quint as he scanned the documents.

Herald replied, "Ah, it's on one of the last pages. I think it was a Joseph Arima?" replied Herald.

Quint stopped short and looked up at Herald, surprised. Herald was young as an exec in this business, not raised on player-agent relations like Quint. Quint cycled quickly to the end of the documents and saw, sure enough, Arima's name and signature. Quint sat back as the name sank in, remembering the old man. He thought Arima retired and was glad for it. Joseph Arima was one of the toughest agents in the business, and most formidable. Arima was certainly no fool, quite the contrary, and his players always seemed to get the better part of the deal. This was troublesome news indeed, yet Quint knew there was something more Herald held back.

"Odd, but still not that eye-opening. What else?" Quint was losing his patience.

"That's just it—we have almost nothing, no background. No next of kin, no beneficiaries other than his child, and when he filled out the Equal Opportunity Employment...," hesitating, Herald looked down at his hands.

"Yes?" asked Quint impatiently, rapidly scanning the document, trying to understand.

Herald looked back up. "Well," he hesitated again, "He checked the box 'Prefer not to disclose.'"

"And did the Pirates Player Relations executive fill in the observed race per our policy?" It was rare for a player not to disclose, and the League was very sensitive to race relations. You must be.

"They wrote 'Unknown.'"

Irritated, Quint thought this conversation was the epitome of strange and unexpected. Quint never liked the unexpected. It gave him no time to plan or get ahead of everyone else.

"What's he look like, for goodness' sake?" Quint asked, letting his exasperation show.

"I figured you would ask that. Plus, videos best show why I called you. Check your business email. I asked Cassius to cut and splice the relevant clips."

Quint pulled up the email. He swung the computer around. "Is this it?"

"Yes, that's the one. Take a look."

Quint watched the footage Cassius cut from their MLB Network and got his first glimpse of Mr. Green. He saw a tall, imposing player approach the batter's box at Busch Stadium. "This is from the opener," said Herald.

The announcer called out his name, "Now batting, the right fielder, number 3, Joshua Green." Quint leaned in as Josh walked towards the batter's box, then dropped to his knee, head bowed. Today's broadcast technology was superb. The center field high-definition camera zoomed in as the announcer commented. Quint Pilate got his first good look at the ballplayer. His face was a little weatherworn, thought Quint, and on his left cheek was an apparent jagged white scar from the corner of his eye and forehead running down to his chin. His skin color was dark brown, almost black, with curly dark hair sticking out from his batter's helmet. The hair framed his chiseled face. His nose was broad and slightly hooked, hawkish looking, possibly broken at some point. Quint would not call him handsome, but perhaps rugged and a little foreboding, actually. His eyes were closed as he kneeled and prayed, like a knight, Quint thought suddenly. Why did he think that? Quint shook it off. Green rose and stepped into the batter's box. The camera pulled back to standard zoom for the first pitched, and Quint watched as the St. Louis Ace and four-time all-star threw a fastball to the low outside corner of the box. The impact of Josh's swing on the ball, even on the laptop, made Quint's eyebrows raise, and the sheer height and distance of the home run were enough to make this seasoned baseball expert think twice. He looked up at Herald.

Herald nodded as the video continued, saying, "Yeah, and just like the announcer said, it made it to the Cardinals Nation Club across Clark Street. Longest ever recorded in the stadium by Statcast®—545 feet."

After watching it again, Quint said, "OK, so he hit a giant home run."

"Yes, on his first at-bat, first pitch, as a rookie in the Majors," followed Herald.

"And he kneeled to pray beforehand," said Quint, still studying the man on the video.

"Yep," affirmed Herald, "They are calling it a 'Tebow.'"

Quint winced at that slightly. "OK. What else?"

"Well..., here's today." Herald motioned to the other attachment on the email. They both turned back to watch the spliced video of today, and they saw a similar kneeling for several seconds, then Green stepping into the batter's box. After a few balls he didn't swing at, another monstrous swing and a home run. While not as deep, still a remarkable piece of hitting.

"And you say he's six for six?" asked Quint.

"Yeah, and that's six swings for six hits total," said Herald, with emphasis, adding, "Against two pitchers that were a combined 35 and 8 last year, with 2.8 and 3.1 ERA, respectively."

"And he's kneeling before each at-bat?"

"No, he's only done it before his first at-bat in each game."

"The at-bats when he homered?"

"That's right."

Quint sat and looked back at the screen. He backed up the video to where the coverage showed a pretty good zoom on Josh standing in the batter's box. Quint saw his face clearly, but his dark brown eyes threw him off. He wasn't sure why. They seemed out of place with the rest of his stark hawkish demeanor, with almost a sad or ancient look, something Quint found disconcerting. At least he understood why the Pirates PR exec put "unknown" in the race block. There was something ethnic about him, for sure, but what? Green, what background would "Green" be? Maybe African American, or perhaps something else, American Indian? Middle eastern? Looking at the video, all seemed possible.

"You said he had a daughter?"

"Yes," said Herald.

"Can you get me a picture, discreetly," Herald nodded as Quint scanned the contract, "And this nanny, too, if they are with him at the games. Maybe they can help us figure this out. Where's the wife?"

"We're not sure. Apparently, she's not in the picture," replied Herald.

Quint nodded. The first home run passed by on the video again. "Anything else?" he asked, pausing the video and looking up at Herald, who watched him patiently.

"After today's game, our PR office got a call from an SPNN reporter that works the Pirates beat, a Roman Josephus."

Quint was sharp again at this point. Now up to speed, he guessed what was coming. "Don't tell me. He asked if the League would like to comment about the kneeling and show of faith before entering the batter's box."

Herald smiled at his boss. Quint was a lot of things, but he always admired his quick mind and understanding of the world they lived in and not just the world of baseball. He nodded affirmatively. "You guessed it."

Quint looked back at the video, now paused on a frozen close-up of Josh. "What do you think our stance should be? Do you think this meets the threshold of the "detrimental to MLB image" clause in the bargaining agreement?" Quint asked Herald. He always tried to get Herald to take a stance and get some skin in the game. Herald often shrewdly took a middle road to his credit, not wanting to commit to something controversial if he could help it.

"I asked Cassius to pull out any precedence with our senior lawyers. You know, we previously asked the lawyers about what happens if players or coaches decide to kneel during the anthem without our prior consent. It hasn't yet become an issue, with the owners giving their own stern warning about this behind closed doors after the NFL debacle a few years ago. The lawyers say we're on shaky ground if we try to use the detrimental clause for anthem kneelers."

"So, how do you think this would go?"

"We probably don't want to find out."

Quint thought about it and said finally, "Agreed. But we currently don't have any anthem kneelers, and very few in the past do we."

"It's been a few years since someone has tried," Herald replied. "But times and the nation have changed in the few years since kneeling started in the NFL. How we handle something like this may be seen under a different lens."

Quint sat back and looked out the window. Race-based kneeling was a valid concern and a potential revenue threat. You need only look at the once invulnerable NFL and see them taken down a few pegs by what happened. However, as Herald implied, the world was changing. The last thing Quint wanted to do was place Major League Baseball on the wrong side of history.

As the country became more progressive and socially aware, Quint must seriously consider what to do the next time a major story broke of an African American death by a cop, especially if it occurred during baseball's regular season. Baseball's history was patchy when it came to race. Quint needed the League on the right side of fan support. He was concerned over the polling of the fans, especially those 16 to 35, who bought much of the MLB merchandise. They were also the generation to court if Baseball was to survive and prosper. Race relations were one of the League's primary concerns. Quint didn't want to alienate fans, and he didn't want to test the waters with an overt MLB stance against a religious show of faith. He knew many of the older fans still clung to their religious beliefs. Religion in private was one thing, but Quint feared an overzealous Christian might become a lightning rod. The American public clearly moved away from some of the more controversial conservative beliefs. Frankly, current culture left old-school Christianity behind twenty years ago, at least. Quint didn't want fans exposed to those beliefs they found offensive. Either way, if Baseball responded with a firm stance, MLB would likely lose.

Quint needed to be careful, and he assumed this was likely a Christian player with strong beliefs, ready to stand or, in this case, kneel despite fan ire. Joe Arima was a well-known Messianic Jew and one of the players' best-known and successful agents. Arima's belief in Christ might be the only thing stronger than his legal prowess for his clients. His unshakable faith gave Quint headaches during negotiations on more than one player contract.

The NFL shut down Tebow reasonably well in the end, but it helped that Tebow's NFL career fizzled. He did not want this to spiral into a League versus Christians situation, especially if this guy turned out to be a star. A chill at the thought ran through Quint. He quickly calmed himself, thinking, "Let's not jump the gun." The fans may be much more accepting of denying a public display of faith than denying a race statement, but he didn't want to test those unknown waters—publicly, at least. There were options, and he was already forming an idea as he finally looked back at Herald and smiled. "Well, maybe it's time I called our good friend Cai Annason. We haven't talked since the owners meeting in February."

Herald nodded and thought about this as his boss smiled at him. He could appreciate the implication of Quint's approach. "And a response to the reporter's question?" he asked.

Quint thought for a moment, looking down at his hands as he leaned back in his seat. "This is Major League Baseball, the favorite pastime and oldest professional sport of the United States. Like all our fans, we love our country and respect all Americans' rights. As long as it doesn't disrupt the game or adversely affect the fans watching, we have no issue with a player saying a silent prayer," finished Quint.

"OK, if I quote you on that?" Herald said as he was quickly typing on an electronic tablet. Herald was pushing Quint to go on record.

Quint didn't take the bait. "Just have Cassius give it to our PR guys to distribute as a statement from MLB. No need to put my name on it," replied Quint without emotion.

Herald nodded. "Right, Boss," and stood to leave. Once again, Herald admired Quint's savvy. He was no fool, Herald thought. Quint won't make a personal statement about kneeling if he doesn't have to. Herald learned a lot from watching Quint and planned to remember every bit of it.

Quint watched as Herald took his briefcase and walked to the door. "Oh, and Herald, have Cassius get Cai's personal cell phone number for me. It should be in the secretary's phone register."

"Will do, Boss," said Herald as he left, pulling the door shut behind him.

Quint leaned back and waited for the number. There were three types of owners: The Yankees, who cornered the largest baseball market franchise and did anything they wanted; the other big market fat cats from the Red Sox, the Dodgers, the Cubs, and the like, that could pretty much do what they wanted because the League needed them to be on board; and then the rest of the League. The Pirates were near the bottom of that last group. How the League went, so went they all, Quint knew. Occasionally, a small market team would surprise you with a few good years and maybe even a World Series appearance. Everybody loves an underdog. It kept the hope up for all those smaller markets and their fans and was good for business—up to a point.

In reality, small-market teams towed a fine line between profitability and paying too much for a contender. To the commissioner's office, these "third tier" teams were the most malleable of all. Not only were the Pirates a prime example of such a team, but he knew Cai was in the position of principal for the owners only because his father-in-law said so. Quint knew he could count on Cai to get the information he needed and spread the word to the coach to ease back this Green fellow's spiritual proclivities. The League didn't need the potential distraction of turning off the fan base by kneeling to pray, especially not at the beginning of an otherwise promising start to the season. Cai was the kind of guy who understood and would get this done quietly. Quint already knew what to say. This would be a quick conversation, and he would still get home in time to catch a late dinner, sit back and enjoy the rest of the evening games.

Thirty Six

S aul was frowning as he hung up the phone, sitting on the sofa in his hotel suite. In the best of times, talking to Cai Annason was a chore. A careful walk through a minefield would be more enjoyable. It wasn't just Cai's unpalatable demand. It was the way Cai delivered it. No congratulations on the Pirates' start, or "Josh Green is doing well," just the admonition, "Green must stop his controversial actions before his first at-bats. You need to rein your player in!" When Pops reminded Cai those at-bats represented game-changing home runs, Saul could almost hear Cai scoff through the phone.

Cai made it clear. He expected a player's religious beliefs to be non-public and off the radar. He said he "allowed" Pops the luxury of the team's private area with a chaplain outside of public view for such purposes. However, in public view, players were to refrain from anything that might be offensive to the fans. When Saul asked how kneeling in prayer was offensive, Cai responded, "Keep the prayers for the rabbi or the priest, and the home plate umpire was neither." That was interesting to Pops since outwardly, Cai Annason's family were devout Jews, even somewhat of a so-called "pillar" of the Jewish Pittsburgh community. It was a partial excuse for why the Annason family didn't associate with Joe and Beth Arima due to their "radical" departure from the community as Messianic Jews.

Saul argued he saw nothing in the player's agreement granting management the right to stop silent public prayers. Cai replied, "Figure it out. That's your job." Thanks for that, thought Saul. It wasn't just that Saul hated how Cai played politics instead of worrying about wins and losses. Cai also expected Saul to take a position against the act itself, which Saul found repugnant. Saul's faith lapsed somewhat over the years. Saul admitted that life got busy, and he stopped making time for God and faith. Now this "order" from Cai raised serious concerns in Saul's conscience. First, to deny someone the right to pray seemed damnable at some level on its own. Also, it just seemed un-American. He was concerned when all MLB players contemplated whether they should take a stand with those kneeling in the NFL. By the time the baseball season started, all 30 clubs had "the talk." In his opinion, MLB prepared to fight if the players joined suit and knelt. Not kneeling for a brief prayer seemed even worse to prohibit.

Saul thought about what Pete would think about it. Even when he disagreed with someone's views, Pete was pretty black and white about first amendment rights as a Vietnam combat vet. Saul knew what some of his other mentors, like Ms. Phoebe and Joe Arima, would think; shoot–even his mum and dad if they were still here.

Saul got up, walked over to the bed, and sat down. The team looked good–great even, especially after a weak spring training performance. They were only two games in, but this group showed true potential and real chemistry. Saul should feel good about the team prospects, but something was missing. Even before the phone call, something was nagging at him. He opened the nightstand drawer to put away his watch and wallet. Inside, the Gideon Bible slid into view. Although out of practice, Saul grew up on a steady diet of Sunday school and prayer meetings and knew the contents well. Still, it was a long time since he habitually read.

Saul took out the book. It looked relatively new and unused. He opened the cover and heard the spine creaking as if rarely opened. He thought of Josh. Joshua Green was like a book whose cover was rough and difficult to penetrate. Who was Josh, really? Saul knew hardly anything about him. Joshua Green, the unknown baseball player, the old rookie and would-be savior of the Pittsburgh Pirates. The man who swung a bat like no one else. A hawk of a man. An African American man, like him, perhaps? Well, if he was, that was where the similarities ended. Josh looked like a chiseled gladiator in a baseball uniform. Yes, a Pennsylvanian warrior with a scar from his knee to his eye. That description fit. That is, until you looked into those eyes. Why did they look so out of place in that old warrior's frame? They carried so much knowledge. They sang to your soul like an old friend who knew your true heart. How was that possible, this unknown man, this enigma? "Tell me, please," thought Saul, "How can I ask you to stop praying before batting, Joshua Green...?" Joshua.

Saul stared at the Bible he held, suddenly coming back into focus. He unconsciously turned and flipped pages. Saul realized he now stared at Josh's namesake, the book of Joshua. He was near its end and slowed, stopping on the last chapter, chapter 24. Despite its unused appearance, someone had opened this Bible because there was a pencil outline under verses 14-15. Saul read, *"Now fear the Lord and serve him with all faithfulness. Throw away the gods your ancestors worshipped...and serve the Lord. But if serving the Lord seems undesirable to you, then choose for yourselves this day whom you will serve...But for me and my household, we will serve the Lord."*

Saul sat still as those verses penetrated his soul. He knew the book of Joshua. This was Joshua's "goodbye" speech after leading the Israelites to take over the Promised Land. These verses were both a warning and a promise to the children of God. As Saul thought about those verses, he remembered the one thing his Joshua, Joshua Green, said of himself to the world. "I guess I would say that I am a Christian, first and foremost, just trying to do what the Lord has for me to do, to make the world a better place and give Him all honor and glory."

Saul reminisced talking long ago with Joe Arima about his name, Saul, and its use in the Bible. The Bible contains two prominent Sauls. One in the Old Testament, Israel's first king, who could have received the kingdom forever but walked away from God in disobedience and was never the same. And the one in the New Testament, who first rejected God as Christ, then turned wholeheartedly to him and became the great evangelist of the New Testament. Saul remembered Joe asked him what the difference was between the two. Saul thought about it and answered each made a choice or even a series of choices. One chose to follow God in faith. The other, swayed by the people, went astray. Yes, in the Old Testament, Saul made a lot of excuses, he thought. What excuses did Saul Samuelson make? Why did his faith wane, and what did he choose instead of serving the Lord? Baseball? Pursuit of a championship? Which Saul was he now choosing to be?

Finally, Saul surmised, I may not know much about Josh, but I doubt I could change his mind if Josh believes his actions were what he was "meant to do." "I guess we all choose one way or the other," thought Saul aloud. He would talk to Josh, but it wouldn't be what Cai expected him to say. As Saul closed the Bible, he suspected there would be more than a few twists and turns to the season. It might even give an old saint like Joshua a run for his money to get to the Promised Land. But he also knew Joshua would have said, "It's not up to me to succeed or fail, just to choose, trust, and obey." It was time for Saul to choose, and as he lay down to sleep, Saul prayed to God to help him be the New Testament Saul that became Paul and choose the Lord's path.

Thirty Seven

The team had the morning off, as the third and final game before heading back to Pittsburgh was a Saturday night game at Busch. Most players arrived relatively early to take advantage of some extra batting practice the late start offered. The players were getting dressed in cold-weather gear for the expected falling temperatures, and Coach Saul spoke with Old Pete when Josh arrived. Pete nodded to Pops and turned to catch up to Josh as he walked to his locker. "Josh, here are a couple of extra outerwear you might need if the temperature drops tonight." As Josh took the gear, Pete leaned in so the other players couldn't hear. "Josh, Pops needs to speak to you a moment. Drop your gear and head over to his office."

"Sure, Pete, and thanks for the clothes," said Josh.

Pete headed back towards the field, so only Saul waited when Josh entered the office. "Close the door and have a seat, Josh."

Josh did as instructed. As the visiting team, Pops' office was relatively small, with two chairs on the other side of a small desk.

"How are you handling everything—how do you feel?"

"I feel great, Coach. So far, so good."

"How're the accommodations working for you and yours at the hotel?"

"Couldn't be better. Mary and Ruthie are getting along wonderfully, and the trip to the local hospital went well. Ruth's physical therapy was as good as we get at home, and the staff went above and beyond to help us. We are doing better than I anticipated, and Ruthie loves coming to the games. Thanks again for this setup, Coach."

"I am glad to hear the road arrangements are working so well. Your play has been nothing short of spectacular."

"Well, let's pray I can keep that up," said Josh, smiling.

"Look, Josh, I want you to know we, the coaching staff, are here to support you in every way," said Saul, voice trailing off as he looked down, searching for the right words.

"Thanks, Pops, but it sounds like there's a 'but' in there somewhere?" Josh asked.

"No buts," Pops hesitated, "Well, sorta. Look, here's the deal." Pops plowed on. "We support you, but the management sometimes has different perspectives than the coaches and players. So, I want you to know what's going on. The media asked the League about your kneeling in prayer before your at-bats. This, in turn, meant they called the owners' group and your friend and mine, Cai Annason."

"And he gave you a call," Josh finished for Saul.

"Yes," replied Pops. He continued, "If you read the full players' collective bargaining agreement, and it would surprise me if you did, there is a no-detri-mental clause in the current agreement. Basically, it says the League won't act against a player as long as their actions during or outside of the game do not negatively reflect on the League. Now, here's the kicker. The current agreement left it fairly vaguely defined. Believe me, it was a bone of contention and may not have passed if the NFL kneeling issues occurred before the current agreement, but fortunately, that came later. Bottom line, the League officially has no position on your kneeling to say a silent prayer—yet."

"And what about the Pirate owners?" asked Josh.

"Plain and simple, Cai wants you voluntarily to stop—do it out of public sight. I will also say he's on a precarious legal standing, especially if the League won't come out officially against it, but here's what you need to know. Cai does nothing independently without considering his position with the owners' group and the League. He will do whatever it takes to keep his position and strengthen it, if possible. The League wants to see this go away, and Cai will pressure us to stop it."

"What do you think, Coach?" asked Josh. Saul tried, as he spoke, to read what Josh was thinking, but couldn't. Josh listened but showed no emotions one way or the other, and now he poured those deep and penetrating eyes directly into Saul. Strangely, it was not a bad thing. In fact, it was a calming influence on Saul, who decided what he would do last night—Albeit, after some considerable prayer, the first for him in a long time.

"Honestly, Josh, it could make life more difficult than I would like, but, you know, I'm also a bit stubborn. Quite frankly, old Pete will never let me hear the end of it, trying to deny you the right to pray. By the way, he and I are the only ones who know all of this, and I will keep it that way as long as I can. I think, as long as you keep it short like you're doing and it doesn't impact the flow of the game, well...," Saul paused for a moment, trying to make the conscious decision to be New Testament Saul as he promised Joe all those years ago. Saul's silence lasted longer than he intended, thinking about many things, but he returned to the same question. Who do you choose to be? Saul looked back at Josh finally, with resolve. He didn't know much, but he wanted to be the new Paul, not the old Saul. He continued, "...They can go pound sand as far as I am concerned. Just don't be surprised if the press turns up the heat on you and starts asking more questions."

Josh smiled. "It's OK, Coach. I can handle the questions."

"Fine, let me handle the owners and the League, and I'll let you know if and when it gets more than what it is." Saul reached out to shake Josh's hand as they both stood. "One more thing," Saul said as he pulled him slightly closer. "Focus on your play—It'll be a whole lot more difficult for the League and Cai to say something negative if you become the people's choice because you keep spanking the opposition! Everybody loves a winner, Josh."

"And if we don't, Pops?"

"Aw shoot, Josh. That's what baseball's all about!" Saul said with a shrug and a laugh. He was back to being the veteran ballplayer and coach players loved and respected so much. "It's best not to overthink it too much; It's a long season, but the way you've been hitting the ball, it looks like they're throwing softballs up there. So, I say, forget all the other stuff and just swing away!"

Thirty Eight

J osh would again bat fourth for the Pirates to start the game. Zach started the game by grounding out on the second pitch, and J.J. hit a pop-up to shallow right field. With two outs and Josh hitting fourth, the Cardinals decided to pitch to the captain, Andrew, and get the third out of the inning. Andrew responded by hitting a 1-1 fastball out over the plate to the gap in right-center for an easy standup double. Like the last two games, Josh approached the plate and took a knee, head bowed, left hand on bat pointed straight down into the dirt, and right hand grasping the earth. The crowd responded with audible boos as the Pittsburgh Radio team discussed the scene.

"Well, folks, Green is making friends again here in St. Louis, taking a knee as he has the first two games, saying an apparent silent prayer. The crowd isn't so silent this time as they let him hear the boos," commented Bob.

In Pittsburgh, Cai Annason watched with his wife in his stately home in Squirrel Hill. "I thought you discussed that with the manager?" she said coyly. He did not respond. Unlike the announcers, he did not find the situation amusing, not at all.

Greg added, "Yep, I get the feeling Green doesn't back down much from what his stance, or in this case, kneeling, means. Now we'll see if he can quiet those boos with another nice piece of hitting. The Cardinals have yet to get the man out, as Green pounded the Cards with six hits and two home runs in the first two games."

The Cardinals must choose to pitch to Josh or put him on to get to Juan, but Juan started the season 3 for 9 with 4 RBIs, making him a tough out. They chose to pitch to Josh but give him nothing good to hit. The Cardinals pitcher, a right-handed fast-baller with a good curve, started Josh with a fastball off the plate. Josh took the pitch for ball one. The pitcher stayed away from Josh with a curve on the outside corner, breaking late off the plate. It would have been folly for a typical right-handed hitter to swing at a breaking ball away, but not Josh. His long reach allowed him to hit outside the zone and still get enough contact on the ball to lift it down the right field line for a single. Andrew, running on contact with two outs, scored easily. Josh was still batting a thousand, and the Pirates were on the board.

The game remained a tight affair. The Pirates started a young lefty pitcher who survived a couple of tough innings, sprinkling hits while giving up just a single run thanks to two inning-ending double plays. Meanwhile, the Cards' pitcher allowed no hits after Josh's RBI single in the first. In the top of the fourth, J.J. led off with a bouncer to deep short. He legged it out and beat the throw for an infield single. Andrew came up again with a great at-bat. He worked the count to full after starting 0-2, with a couple of foul balls, finally drawing a walk. With two on, no outs, and Josh coming to the plate, the Cardinal pitching coach took to the field to talk to his pitcher and infielders.

"Well, Greg, what do you think? Do they pitch to him or load the bases for Juan?" suggested Bob.

"Not a great choice. The rookie beat you twice in this same situation with a home run, and there's no sign of getting him out. Of course, Juan is hitting well and hits many fly balls, although this pitcher is known for getting hitters to hit ground balls and double plays on his curve. If you walk Green and load the bases with no outs, a fly ball from Juan or even a double-play ball still scores a run, assuming Juan doesn't take you deep. Juan hit ten home runs in his last sixty at-bats last year, and one of those was a big one off this very pitcher last September here at Busch Stadium. In his first at-bat today, he hit one to the warning track." responded Greg.

"So, you're saying.... What?" asked Bob after Greg's lengthy analysis.

"Well, I don't know!" admitted Greg, then finished quickly, "But I wouldn't want to be in the Cards' shoes right now."

"There you have it, folks, all the stats you could ask for, finished off with Greg's stunning insight," quipped Bob. "We'll soon find out as the coach is returning to the Cards' dugout."

Josh took his position. He was calm and at peace. The first pitch challenged his peace as the fastball came in at 96 MPH high, inside, and tailing right at Josh's upper torso. Josh saw the ball about to clock him and started his dive away and down from the pitch. The pitcher and catcher made no unusual movements, perhaps revealing their intent. Josh's quick reaction avoided the beanball pitch, but it was extremely close and ended with him face down in the back of the batter's box. This brought the entire Pirates' dugout to their feet, and Pops quickly climbed the stairs of the dugout, waving back the players behind him but on the top step as the umpire called time. Josh slowly got up and dusted himself off.

Today's home plate umpire, Jim Centurion, was one of the oldest and most re-spected MLB umpires. Without hesitation, he issued warnings to both dugouts, and he would eject the manager and their pitcher if he surmised they intentionally threw at the hitter. Throwing at a batter was as old as baseball, but there was a time and a location. In today's game, throwing inside was a given, but throwing at someone's head was tantamount to asking for a fight.

Pops stood, arms crossed, glaring at the opposing dugout. He might have said something, but Josh waved him down as he dusted himself off, giving him a one-hand sign indicating everything was all right.

After staring down both benches, Jim Centurion turned slightly to Josh while putting his mask back on and said, "Take as much time as you need, Rook." Josh nodded at the ump, smiling slightly, before stepping back into the batter's box. Josh's smile caught both the umpire and the catcher off guard.

"Well, that was close. They tried to put the first one in Green's ear, and I thought we were about to have a little brew-ha-ha there, Greg. Let's see what happens now, shall we?" asked Bob.

"Yep, to say things are a bit tense here folks, would be an understatement. The crowd is buzzing after that chin music to the old rookie. Everyone's returned to their corners, but all the Pirates are standing in the dugout as Green steps back into the batter's box. Here we go," stated Greg.

"Maybe we should be the ones taking a knee, Greg," quipped Bob.

"What's that?" replied Greg.

"To pray for Green's protection," responded Bob, only half kidding.

As the St. Louis catcher crouched and waited for his pitcher, he peeked sideways up at Josh as Josh came to rest in his hitting stance. Josh displayed the same calm demeanor the catcher saw each time he batted the last three games. Before Josh's at-bat, the seasoned catcher almost voiced his concerns when they conferenced on the mound with their pitching coach. Despite his misgivings, the catcher kept quiet when the coach said, "No one is going to come here and hit an outside curveball by leaning out over the plate, not in our ballpark."

They planned to throw the first high and tight pitch to intimidate Josh. The well-used tactic often worked against hitters on a hot streak, and his coach expected the untried rookie to lose concentration. However, the catcher saw Josh's demeanor up close and personal. The catcher's heart warned him of this rookie. Josh Green came from some place and background no one understood, carrying an unshakable faith. The catcher sensed nothing would deter Josh from completing his mission. Josh's soul held something intangible, protecting him against the fears other players, even superb ones, fought. Josh's smile just confirmed it.

They underestimated Josh's athletic ability to hit a curve outside the zone in the first at-bat. 99 out of 100 other hitters would miss or foul off such a pitch, but Josh hit it for a hard single down the line. After the high and tight pitch, the plan was another fastball, high, just at the top of the strike zone, hoping Josh

would be gun-shy after the chin music. The catcher worried they underestimated Josh's supernatural ability to maintain peace in the storm. His quick
peek at Josh's peaceful eyes and calm face proved it was the Cardinals who
should fear what this man would do, but the catcher felt he had no choice, the
die already cast. With much trepidation, he called for the fastball, setting up
his target to be above slightly rather than at Josh's top of the strike zone, still
inside but just over the plate. Make it unhittable, thought the catcher, and the
pitcher executed the pitch perfectly.

"Here's the pitch!" Bob told Pirates radio fans as the pitcher released the
high fastball.

Of all the pitches Josh saw this year, this may have been the hardest to hit
well. The previous delivery looked little different, yet Josh saw this pitch would
stay just over the plate, high and even with the top of Josh's shoulders. Josh
needed to quickly move his body inside to get the thick part of the bat barrel
on the ball, or he would hit the handle of his bat and likely shatter it. He
also needed to rise, or he would swing under the pitch and pop it up. He
did both necessary movements, stepping quickly through and slightly down
the third baseline instead of striding straight through the swing. Josh ever
so slightly raised his body to meet the ball square as it crossed high over the
inside of the plate. If anything, Josh swung harder, his body exploding up
and through the swing to make the necessary adjustments in time. To those
watching, this motion was hard to follow, lightning-quick, like an over-taut
longbow uncoiling with ferocious speed and force. A few days earlier, Josh's
first home run at Busch stadium left an unusual sound of smooth transference
of incredible power. This time, the sound of Josh's bat hitting the 98 MPH
offering dead on with all his strength was almost violent, like a point-blank
gunshot, straight to the heart of all Cardinal fans.

"kaPOW!"

"GREEN HAMMERS one DEEP to left field," yelled Bob into the mike
out of sheer reaction. "NOOOO DOUBT about IT. That ball is CRUSHED!"

"WOW, that thing was BELTED, and I do mean BELTED into orbit, Bob!
Another moonshot, folks, clean out of Busch Stadium," an incredulous Greg
chimed in.

"Another Gargantuan Green Cannonball coming and another three-run
homer for the rookie!" Bob continued loudly.

"Turns out Green didn't need your prayer for protection after all, Bob," said
Greg excitedly, turning to Bob.

"Nope, but the Cards sure did. Look at the Statcast® system on the scoreboard,
Greg!" commented Bob excitedly. "Green's homer tracked at a whopping 537
feet, 118 MPH, that's slightly shorter than the one opening day, but folks, this

one was so high, I think St. Louis International Airport just issued it a flight clearance!"

"WOW! As Green finishes his home run trot, there's almost no noise here, like the air was sucked out of what was a loud, boisterous crowd just a moment ago. All the St. Louis fans sat down like Green kicked them in the gut, and all that's left are the few crazy Pirate fans swinging their terrible towels and generally going bonkers while the rest of the crowd looks like their dog died!" exclaimed Greg.

"Yeah, Greg, the crowd was lively after that brush-back pitch drew the Ump's warning. Now they're either quiet or booing," replied Bob. "Who do you think they are booing, Green, as he trots around the bases or their Cards?" he asked.

"I'd say it's a bit of both, Greg. Cardinal fans aren't used to starting the season off at home, losing three in a row, especially to a team that hasn't made the playoffs the last two seasons, and after Green's home run, it's not looking good for the Cards."

The game remained a close contest. The Pirates pitcher settled down, making it to the seventh inning before St. Louis got a run back, and Pops brought in a reliever to end the inning. Josh came to bat in the top of the eighth, but the Cardinals saw enough and intentionally walked him. It was to no avail as Juan hit a double to right, scoring the unexpectedly fleet-footed Green. St. Louis got one run back in the ninth and threatened with two on before the Pirates bullpen finally finished with a game-ending strikeout, winning 5-3. The Pirates swept last year's central division champs to start the season and were 3-0, heading home.

The jubilant Pittsburgh fans were ready to welcome the team home for their opener. All that is, except for Cai Annason. Josh's kneeling was a brewing problem for Cai, compounded by Josh starting the season so dramatically. Cai would have to have another discussion with Saul before this rookie set a precedent he couldn't walk back. However, Josh's play made it difficult. Cai could not let the local fans get behind Green. Cai feared the fans and what they might do if they found out he tried to stop Josh from living his faith.

Meanwhile, the 38-year-old rookie Josh Green was the talk of the sporting world, with three, 3-run homers, 12 RBIs, and a slew of hits in his first three games in the "Bigs." SPNN's sports center led off with game three highlights. Their news report centered on the rookie sensation out of nowhere, Joshua Green. After playing the tape of Green's three-run homer to lead off the segment, the in-studio sportscaster, Guy "Tac" Cornelius, turned to the on-screen correspondent, Roman Josephus, standing on the infield of the now nearly empty Busch Stadium, back in St. Louis.

"Roman, what's the story with this unknown rookie the Pirates signed? He seems to be making mayhem in St. Louis," Tac asked.

"That's right, Tac," replied an impeccably dressed Roman. "Joshua Green is on fire here for the Pirates. He started the season, going an amazing 8 for 8, hitting three home runs, and driving in 12 in his first three games in the majors; All records for a rookie in their first three games."

"Tell us about Green, Roman, what's his background, where'd he come from, and why hasn't anyone heard of him before?" asked Tac.

"Well, that's the 64-thousand dollar question, Tac. The Pirates are not very forthcoming with much information. We know they signed him just before the season started, joining the club during the last week of spring training. Coach Samuelson said he was a local prospect the Pirates became aware of late this spring. Some say Josh may have been overseas and only recently returned. Josh tells us he is originally from Western Pennsylvania. We can't find a record of him playing professionally at any level before this season. The Pirates list him as a 6'4", 210 Lbs. Outfielder, Bat's Right, Throws Right, and here's the kicker, Tac. According to the Pirates, Green's 38 years old!"

"Wow, pretty old for a rookie, Roman!"

"You bet, Tac, and he is playing like anything but a rookie. He is hitting moon shots and hitting for perfection—8 for 8. Despite his age, Green runs well with better-than-average speed on the bases and in the outfield, making a spectacular diving catch on opening day. This rookie looks like a superstar in the making, and the Pirates look like an entirely different team, sweeping the Cards here at Busch Stadium."

"We'll be sure to tune in to watch the Pirates' home opener the day after tomorrow against the Cubs. Hopefully, you can bring us more about this old rookie phenom, Josh Green," said Tac.

"You can count on it!" finished Roman, ending the segment.

Pops decided not to give the press access to the locker room. He left the interviews to a few on-field, post-game discussions, allowing the players to pack their gear to catch the late flight home to Pittsburgh. Josh and the other players gratefully accepted the press reprieve. Despite the high energy of beating the Cards three straight, the players were exhausted. Though tired, the Pirates enjoyed their victories and looked forward to the rest of the season with newfound hope.

Thirty Nine

Pops planned a light practice on their off day at PNC Park, similar to a pregame approach, starting at 11:00 AM, so he could let the players hit their physical therapy and personal workouts that afternoon. Press coverage was so unruly it threatened to disrupt the practice. Pops once again tried to keep the press at bay, allowing them only to talk to him in his office after practice. Pops worried about greater pressure on his team, especially from the national sporting press, and he hoped to protect the players and Josh if he could.

Saul brought Mark Johnson in to discuss the press with his core "old guy" brain trust, as he called them, Pete and Doc Luke, in Pete's office before practice started. "Boss, I understand your reluctance with letting the press in—but eventually, you'll have to let them talk to the players at length," said Mark after hearing Saul argue his plan. When Saul first met Mark, the young, brash PR agent for the Pirates, Saul was unsure how Mark would work as the team's head press agent. Saul first joined the staff as an assistant coach, and young Mark, a new hire, was relatively untested. Mark played a brief stint in the Minor League system before plateauing and falling back on his college degree, starting as the Pirate junior media agent. Mark was a cousin to Pirates journeyman player Barney, with a similarly upbeat and infectious personality. Though passionate, Mark's youthful exuberance and lack of experience sometimes caused a misfire during his early days with the Pirates, and the young man became discouraged. Saul doubted he would be a good long-term fit for the team. Barney, one of Saul's favorite players, convinced Saul to give Mark a second chance.

Barney appealed to Saul, Pete, and Luke, memorably bursting into a late-night meeting in Pete's office to make an impassioned plea. The three still laughed about Barney's impressive peacemaking personality to persuade the three old guys. Barney finished by reminding them of Mark's understanding of the younger generation and promised Mark would become an asset to the organization and grow the Pirates' image and appeal.

Ironically, it was old Pete who stepped up and took Mark under his wing, like a young Saul, when Pops first came to the Pirates. Pete helped Mark overcome his inexperience and shaky start, mentoring Mark through the ins and outs of big-league ball. The "kid," in turn, showed Saul how to appeal to the younger generation, just as Barney promised. Both Saul and Pete talked with Mark during many conversations over the years. They taught young Mark how to deal with a big-league team and players' egos. Mark developed his own style and learned to run the gambit of modern sports press relations. Saul now admitted Mark's progress slowly gained his confidence, reversing his early doubts. He now relied on Mark's gift of understanding people, press personalities, and public relations in the modern sports broadcasting era. Just shy of thirty, Mark matured through the bumps and bruises, becoming a strong and successful PR man for small-market Pittsburgh. Saul's old guy brain trust listened carefully as Mark provided the voice of youthful fans to the three older men, benefiting from the experience they planted and nurtured in him.

One thing Mark did was use his easygoing personality to develop an understanding of the egos and needs of the individuals in the press corps. In some ways, Pops found them to be worse than the egos of his players, and Mark possessed an understanding of people that came naturally, much like his cousin, Barney.

In the present, the old guy brain trust listened to Mark's thoughts as Saul nodded, encouraging Mark as Pete pounded on yet another glove. "Who's the biggest problem?" asked Saul.

Mark smiled back at Coach knowingly, raising his hands and shrugging his shoulders in an unspoken answer.

"Let me guess," Pete cut in through clenched teeth. "Roman. That man is a real pain in the derriere, excuse my French," he said, chomping on his unlit cigar. They all knew the answer was correct.

Mark continued, "He's been pressing hard to get some 'face time' with Josh." Pops could tell Mark wanted to say something more.

"Go on, Mark," said the coach.

Mark wrinkled his forehead slightly. One thing Pops saw as growth in the young man, Mark now contemplated what he said before saying it. It was a trait many of his generation never seemed to learn.

"Coach, my biggest concern is always the background or information I don't know. I worry about a player getting blindsided when I don't know their history. I can't help them prepare and deflect the impact. The bottom line is Josh is pretty much an unknown to us," Mark said, receiving nods from the "old guys." He continued, "Roman will keep pressing for answers. I am not saying there are any problems, but we don't know what we don't know, and eventually, it all comes out. It would be better to learn as much as we can early."

"The lad's got a point, Saul," Pete said between his rhythmic glove pounding.

"I know," Saul replied, thinking and furrowing his brow. "But Josh is pretty private about his history. I am obliged to keep his privacy as much as possible," said Pops.

"I understand, Coach," said Mark, "We need to understand and make Josh understand the press will keep pushing for background and an angle, especially Roman. He's got a chip on his shoulder as much as any player I know. He'll keep looking for something until he gets a story, even if he must make it himself. Roman's aggressive and relatively unscrupulous. I think he sees Josh as his ticket for bigger and better exposure. As long as he gets a story, positive or negative, it doesn't matter to Roman."

"And with a guy like that, controversy is probably a better story than just a great player playing well," said Luke, voicing what they all felt.

"Yes, Doc," said Mark, "Roman's worst kept secret is he wants the limelight of a big city or national coverage. For the first time since he's been here, the Pirates, with Josh's play, are that kind of story, and he will get it, one way or the other."

Doc Luke was a good listener, always capturing details and subtle meaning others missed. Saul knew, when he spoke, it was usually with wise insight. "What about using the Arimas as a venue to get Josh to open up?" Luke offered.

Saul smiled after digesting what Luke said, and Pete nodded in agreement while Mark looked confused.

"Yes. Yes, I like that idea, Doc, and I think Joe would understand and oblige," said Saul to the other two, then turned to Mark. "OK, since our best bet is to get to know Josh as well as we can, before the press, we'll hold them off at practice today. In the meantime, Mark, why don't you plan on going over to the Arimas for dinner after practice tonight?" said Saul, looking at Mark with a twinkle in his eye.

"Boss?" said Mark questioningly.

"They are hosting the Greens and Mary for dinner. I was to be a plus one, but I think I'll send you in my place. I'll let Joe know and tell him to induce some good discussions so you can get to know Josh to help fend off these press vultures."

Mark looked a little perplexed. He met the Arimas on several occasions as they played a large part in Pirate players in the past, but he hadn't been invited to their house before.

"C'mon, Mark, it'll be good for you," said Pete, smiling around his cigar. "You haven't seen the Arimas in a while, and if you want to know sports and players in this town, they know all the best agents in the business. Besides that, Beth's probably the best cook on the east side," Pete said fondly, reminiscing. "As a matter of fact, I haven't seen them in a while. I sure could go for some babka and coffee...," he said, trailing off with a distant look in his eyes.

"She made some when we were there last week," said Pops, smiling.

Old Pete harrumphed at his loss and Saul's good luck, pounding his glove especially hard. Pete turned back to Mark. "Go on, kid, take Saul's offer up. Meet the Greens with Joe and Miss Elizabeth. If you ever get someone to lower their guard, it will be eating dinner hosted by the Arimas. Worst case, you'll have the best meal since..., well, since your grandma made you one last!"

Gruff old Pete dismissed the lot of them with the last word, pulling out the cigar and waving in the air. "Now, let's stop running on about the press. We all know they're not to be trusted farther than we can throw 'em! This team is a family, and right now, we're on a roll. It's up to us to take the pressure from outside and deflect it away, so they can play ball—besides, it's time for practice, so..., let's get movin'!"

Forty

Practice went well, and the team was loose and excited. Tomorrow was the home opener, and the Pirates came with a renewed sense of purpose, different from what the team felt just a few weeks ago. True to his intentions, Pops told the press corps he would be the only one taking questions today. The press was ambivalent and asked Pops to go on record about his decision. As expected, Roman led the charge for more access, but Pops held his ground, saying he didn't want the players distracted before their opener. Pops told Roman it was a long season, with many opportunities to talk with the players, but not today. Roman tried to argue with Pops, but Pops said, "Asked and answered, Roman. Does anyone have other questions about the team they would like me to answer? If not, we can call it a day." Perplexed, Roman said nothing, allowing the local press a foot in the door. They asked several baseball questions of the coach. Saul took each in stride, completing the press question-and-answer session. Saul knew Mark was right; they would soon have to allow the press access to the team, particularly Josh.

While the team went about their various individual workout and physical therapy routines after practice, Saul closed the office door after the press conference and dialed up Joe Arima.

"Hello Saul, how'd the first-place Pirates' first home practice of the season go?" said Joe with a smile in his voice.

"Fine, Joe. At least on the field, that is."

"Oh?" Joe replied, listening.

"I needed to fend off the dogs in the post-practice press conference," said Pops after a brief sigh, grumbling.

"You never did like the press, but as I told you way back when you began playing, this sport is a game—and the people watching are what pays everyone's salary. The press knows it, and they get paid based on the best story they can find. Right now, that story is in Pittsburgh, and that's a good thing," replied Joe.

"Yeah, I know, and I guess it's a lot better than answering why we lost, but I still find it..., well, let's just say it's not my favorite part of the job."

"Skippers always take the brunt of the press wave, Saul. Hang with it. I suspect this team will give you many good things to talk about this year. The best thing is to take the pressure off the players and be their shield."

"That's what I wanted to talk to you about," said Saul. "Mark Johnson talked with me before practice. We've been trying to keep the interviews to a minimum, especially with Josh. However, Josh's extraordinary play makes fending off the press difficult," said Saul, unsure how to continue.

"And you're concerned you can't protect him forever. Eventually, the press will start asking tough questions," finished Joe knowingly.

"You have it exactly. With an ordinary player or someone whose history we knew, we could gauge where the press might go, or at least where the answers might lead them, but with Josh...."

"You know nothing about him, and that's a potential problem." Again, Joe's wisdom shined through.

"Yes. Mark said as much to Doc, Pete, and I today in a little powwow session before practice. Mark is right. The best thing for us is to get to know Josh. Help him prepare for the onslaught that's bound to happen when the press gets a good chance to interview him."

"What can I do, Saul?" asked Joe.

"I would like to send Mark to you for dinner with the Greens. Mark has a personality that lets people open up. Maybe we can find out a little more about Josh between you, Miss Elizabeth, and Mark and understand him better," Pops said thoughtfully.

"And maybe we can gently persuade him on what he should and should not say when the press is around?" Joe partly asked, partly stated.

"Something like that. Yes," replied Saul.

"Hmmm," thought Joe out loud. "Mark's idea?"

"He suggested it. I thought Mark might be better for getting to know Josh," Pops responded.

"Well, Mark's a thoughtful young man, and as you and others have told me, he's grown into a good press handler. He has good instincts. But I want to warn you about something, Saul," said Joe.

"What's that, Joe?" asked Saul.

"I talked to Josh several times, but that doesn't mean I know him well. One thing I have noted, he's pretty comfortable about who he is and what he's about; I don't know what Josh's life's been like, but Josh strikes me as unlikely to change the way he believes, and therefore what he says." Joe paused, thinking about looking at Josh that first time and those eyes that knew far beyond his years. Joe tried to form his thoughts on Josh aloud to Saul, but everything that came to mind seemed inadequate. Finally, Joe continued, "It feels like whatever life's lessons he's learned, Josh is a man who's been through the fire. And Saul, when that happens, it does two things. First, as our Bible says, it burns away the dross, removing everything not worth saving, and second...," began Joe.

"Whatever is left is strong and well-formed—tempered and hardened by the fire," finished Saul. Saul sensed something similar about Josh every time they talked, but it took Joe's wise words to coalesce what he felt.

Joe broke the silence. "You see? I *have* taught you well. Of course, Ms. Phoebe and a few others may have contributed," said Joe, trying to dispel the somewhat serious mood. "Look, Saul," Joe resumed, "Send Mark over early. He and I can talk, develop a game plan and see how it goes. But I got to be honest with you. We will learn about Josh as we go along, and I don't think it will disappoint us. Quite the opposite. I've got a feeling he may teach us a thing or two." Joe paused, wondering, then hurried on, "Just know, I think he's got a pretty solid foundation, fire-proofed if you will. I suspect he'll bring strength and goodness to us, and baseball is only one part. A long time ago, to a much younger you, I told you what was most important about baseball. Do you remember?"

Saul remembered the answer, and as he got older and closer to the end, it meant more and more. "In the end, baseball's a wonderful game, but only that, just a game. Who you are is much more important than what you do, especially when you are a guy who plays a kids' game and makes a living off it."

Again, Saul could hear Joe smiling through the phone when he said, "Yep. And it's still the most important perspective we can have—and there's one thing more I know about Josh," said Joe.

"What's that, Joe?" asked Saul.

"He already knows it," Joe replied.

Forty One

As Saul and Joe discussed, Mark arrived at the Arimas promptly at 4:45 pm. The Greens and Mary weren't due until 5:30 PM, so Mark and Joe could discuss his task. Mark talked at length with Joe and Elizabeth. "I guess you could say," Mark summarized, "I just want to get to know Josh better. Find out what he's like, where he comes from, and what might come up when the press starts digging into who he is or what he thinks," replied Mark, as Elizabeth and Joe moved around the kitchen making dinner.

"We will do our best to help make the Greens and Mary feel comfortable to talk with you, Mark," said Beth, "But don't get your hopes up on prying Josh's background out of him. I get the feeling he's not keen on getting deep into his personal history. He's been consistently private about that when he's been with us. What do you think, Joe?"

"I talked with him at length now on several occasions. He'll tell you what he thinks on most topics, but he keeps Ruthie and his history close to the chest. His privacy means something to him. I know he was married to Ruth's mom, and she died of cancer less than two years ago. Everything he does puts Ruth's well-being central in their lives. I infer from what little he said they've traveled a tough road, but it's created a tight bond between them."

"One thing seems to ring true. If Josh is good at not talking about his past to us, then he's unlikely to volunteer that to the press," thought Mark out loud.

"Look, I don't get the feeling Josh is uncomfortable with his past—just private about it—if it's any consolation, I don't get the feeling it's something embarrassing or bad. If I had to guess, I'd say military," Joe said thoughtfully.

Elizabeth looked up from a pot she was stirring and nodded at Joe. "Yes, that fits. He reminds me of the Vietnam Vets we work with at the community center. Not as old, obviously, but the same demeanor."

"That would be a good angle if true, a plus for our PR," said Mark.

"Don't get your hopes up on Josh agreeing to that, Mark," said Beth. "I work extensively with these vets, and many went 25 or more years without talking to non-vets about their experience and history. If Josh is a recent vet, it's likely something that takes a while, perhaps years, for him to discuss."

"Yes, and even then, he may never talk with the media about it," added Joe.

"Well, my job, my goal, is to protect Josh if I can and help him navigate the media minefield as they search for stories. Unfortunately, his lack of a baseball background makes the media even more curious. Some will kill for a story or a headline if they can find something about his background to pique the public's interest—especially if he continues his brilliant play." Mark changed gears and asked, "What about Ruth and Mary?"

"Do you think the media will turn to them?" asked Elizabeth, concerned.

"I think if Josh stonewalls the media, some less scrupulous will look for another angle, and eventually, they will ask questions...."

"Because the situation looks different?" said Joe.

"Yes," Mark hesitated to go further.

"What do you see from the press's point of view," said Joe. He already suspected where this was going.

"OK, I will treat you folks like Pops said—as trusted agents. Joe, your reputation for these things precedes you, so this is between us. First, you know Josh refused to identify his race on his EEO form. The Pirates' normal policy, handed down by the League, is to follow the national guidelines and place an 'observed' race. Let's just say, for a player, this is...unusual. After his selection, my job required me to write the 'observed' race. For the first time in my career, I honestly couldn't answer. We filed, listing his race as 'Unknown.' I can tell you, Mr. Annason was not happy, but I honestly couldn't tell, and Josh wasn't of a mind to help us. However, when it comes to Ruth, the press will wonder...," Mark said uncomfortably.

"She looks Asian and doesn't bear much resemblance to Josh," Joe finished, and Mark nodded as he sipped a cup of decaf.

"Exactly." Mark hurried on, "And then there is Mary."

"What about her?" said Elizabeth defensively.

"Nothing bad. From all accounts, she seems like a nice young lady, but the arrangement in the contract is...unusual. Thinking from the press point of view, once it becomes known...,"

"It raises questions," finished Joe again. He began to understand the picture Mark was painting.

"Now look, I have a good background on the fact we found and introduced Miss Mary to fulfill the Greens' nanny and homeschool teacher role. I will use this information when the time comes if the press insinuates otherwise, but it's still odd to have the daughter and nanny travel with the team," said Mark.

"Do you think the press will try to make something out of it?" asked Joe.

"I don't know. It depends on how Josh comes across these first few weeks and how he plays. Strangely enough, the better he plays, the more scrutiny the press will bring. They'll come in numbers and pressure with more difficult questions. We need to be ready."

"And we need Josh to be ready, most of all," said Joe. Mark nodded and sat back in the chair, looking into his cup of coffee.

Elizabeth looked at them, then turned to Mark. "Mark, one thing we have already learned about Josh is he seems to be a man of deep faith. I don't know if you are a praying man, but Joe and I are. I will pray strongly for the Lord to guide you in defending Josh and his family against these press vultures. It seems you have your work cut out for you."

"Well, Miss Elizabeth, I need all the help I can get. Hey, look—this is a good thing. We are worried about this because Josh's play is incredible. When you pray, pray for him to continue to excel. One thing the press has a hard time defeating is a player the fans love, and the way he played so far is something this town has been waiting for, well..., since the original Pops was placing stars on everyone's hat singing, 'We are Family.'"

"That may be before you were born, Mark, but to Beth and I, it's like yesterday. Let's hope this family can rise to the occasion," said Joe, and they all relaxed with the feeling it was going to be a special season in Pittsburgh.

Forty Two

The evening meal went well at the Arimas' house, but Mark's hope of getting background from Josh failed to produce. He managed to pry little out of him beyond he was from this part of the country, his dad passed when he was in high school, and his mother and younger siblings were still alive. Josh deflected much of the intervening years, other than he lived overseas, where he met Ruth's mom, and they were married when Ruth was young. Try as he might, Mark couldn't get more details, only that Josh worked in government service and left when his wife passed from cancer to move to his old home state and raise Ruth.

It wasn't much to go on, though Mark tried. "Josh, you know the press will try to get your background story, and they will be persistent, especially since you don't fit the profile of a Major League Baseball player," Mark said finally in slight desperation. "They will want to know how you got to play for the Pirates," he continued as he munched on something Beth called rugelach. It was a delectable dessert of chocolate, hazelnut, and fruity jam, wrapped in delicious, flaky, rolled, and spiraled dough. Old Pete was right. Beth's cooking almost made him forget why he was there.

"Divine providence," said Josh and smiled. "Look, Mark. I understand the press will ask these questions. My past is my own. I am not ashamed of it, and there is nothing you need to worry about there, but I want people to see me as I am. I am a Christian who lives to honor and glorify God. I love my family, country, and fellow man and try to serve them as Christ grants me the opportunity. I am a ballplayer, not a politician running for office. If they want to ask me questions, I'll try to answer them honestly, but my private life is just that." Josh finished and sat back, relaxing on the porch chair, sipping a cup of traditional cooked Israeli coffee as the aroma of cardamom brought an old warmth to the evening.

Mark nodded, and he stared out onto Beth's garden. He understood now this was all he would get from Josh, but he knew Josh might find it more difficult facing a reporter like Roman Josephus.

The next day dawned bright and clear for the Pittsburgh Pirates home opener. The game started at 1:30 PM, and the enthusiastic Pittsburgh crowd waited excitedly with anticipation. Inside the locker room, the players went through their pregame ritual, or rather, established it since it was their home opener. The Pirates enjoyed more luxury options than the spring training ballpark or visitor's locker room. Josh's locker now displayed a printed name placard. He was at the end of the row, with the Thunder Brothers, Juan, and J.J., to his left. They dressed quickly and moved out to run some energy down in the outfield. Next to their lockers was Zach, the shortstop. He sat with his eyes closed, leaning back in his chair. Josh noticed Zach occasionally moving, waving his arms to avoid unseen obstacles. Josh finished dressing in what he now referred to as his "old guy" underwear Doc Luke and Pete gave him. He leaned back, watching Zach quietly. In response, Zach stopped his smooth, fluid motions and opened his eyes, seeing Josh.

"All right there, Josh?" asked Zach, smiling.

"Yep. Just got dressed a little quicker than expected. What's that you're doing?"

"Oh, I just try to focus myself, quiet my soul and visualize good things happening in the game, you know, turning a good double play, or making good contact on a swing. What do you normally do before a game?"

"Never thought about it much. I guess when I was getting ready...to take the field, I would check my gear and pray."

"Sounds like a good routine—looks like you already checked your gear out. You could walk into Cy's lounge area. If I know him, he's probably in there reading his dear grandma's Bible."

"Maybe I will," Josh got up, put his cap on, and grabbed his glove as he turned to walk to the lounge. "You want to come, Zach?"

"I am not sure God wants to hear from me anymore, Josh. I kind of find my own way through life."

"Well, the God I know loves us all equally, Zach. I could do the praying if you want while you envision those good plays for the both of us." Josh smiled kindly at Zach, catching Zach off guard. Josh showed no preconceived expectations other than Josh genuinely wanted his company. Zach never received an invitation to a religious service or anything remotely religious since he told the world he was gay. Even in the short time he knew Josh, it was clear he was a Christ-follower. Still, Zach's expectations of some unfriendly feelings never occurred. Josh treated him like a friend, genuinely interested in him and his company. Unexpectedly, Zach found himself wanting to accept the offer.

"OK," said Zach, "I always like Cy's lounge. It's a peaceful place to meditate." He got up and followed Josh.

Cy afforded the players his services in the player's lounge whenever needed. Today, he sat reading his Bible softly but aloud as one of his assistants gave Andrew an upper back massage in one of the massage chairs with a cradle for relaxing with your head face down.

"Mind if we join you, folks?" said Josh as he and Zach walked in.

"Come on in, Josh," said Cy in a deep voice. He was a study in contradictions, sitting there, a giant man gently cradling his grandma's Bible in oversized hands, wearing delicate half-rimmed, almost old-timey, wire glasses.

"Hope you don't mind hearing about Joshua," said Andrew, not looking up as the PT worked on him, "I always like to start the season remembering the battle of Jericho."

"Sure," said Josh as he and Zach took two comfy seats next to Cy.

"Andrew and I usually just hit a few verses before each game while Boaz, here, works on loosening up his upper back," Cy explained.

"Yeah, I find I can stretch out everything but my neck and shoulders now that I have become one of the more 'mature' players on the club," Andrew said through the face-down massage chair.

"Sounds like a wise idea, and I think I still got you beat by a few years, Cap," said Josh with a twinkle in his voice.

"That may be true, Josh, but Boaz's already taken. You will just have to enjoy the reading," Andrew said, half smiling, half gritting his teeth as Boaz worked out a kink in his neck. "Who's with you?" Andrew asked, unable to look up while Boaz worked on him.

"Just me," said Zach.

"Zach, glad to have you," said Andrew recognizing the diminutive man's voice. "You guys should like Cy's readings. He plans out the exact number based on our baseball schedule. We start with Jericho and go on from there. Sorry, you missed the beginning."

"That's fine. Just keep going, Cy," encouraged Josh.

Cy nodded and began, "On the seventh day, they got up at daybreak and marched around the city seven times in the same manner, except that on that day, they circled the city seven times. The seventh time around, when the priests sounded the trumpet blast, Joshua commanded the army, 'Shout! For the Lord has given you the city! The city and all that is in it are to be devoted to the Lord. Only Rahab, the prostitute, and all who are with her in her house shall be spared, because she hid the spies we sent. But keep away from the devoted things, so that you will not bring about your own destruction by taking any of them. Otherwise, you will make the camp of Israel liable to destruction and bring trouble on it. All the silver and gold and the articles of bronze and iron are sacred to the Lord and must go into his treasury.' When the trumpets sounded, the army shouted, and at the sound of the trumpet, when the men gave a loud shout, the wall collapsed;

so everyone charged straight in, and they took the city."[1] Cy finished, closed his Bible, set it aside, and took off his delicate glasses, placing them in a small hard case.

After a few moments without talk, Zach asked curiously, "So what do you take away from this?"

"There's a lot there," said Cy.

"Sure is," said Josh. "Sometimes, I think about the faith it took to trust God. They marched around the city for a week. The defenders derided them. They could have become discouraged, wondering why God commanded them to do it. But Joshua led them, and they obeyed God. In the end, they won the battle without earning the victory. God fought for them. Their job was to keep the faith and obey. The city's inhabitants thought they were safe based on the grand city and wall they built. They trusted in their own handiwork and the gods they made. Nothing man builds will stand against the One True God. Rahab put her faith in the Jews and their God because she believed they served the True God. Her faith led her to act and save the spies. She received the guarantee God and Israel would spare her and her family. God won the battle for the Israelites and redeemed Rahab, the foreigner, and harlot, who became part of the lineage of David. She is an ancestor listed in the lineage of Christ's parents. I think, in general, we see God fights our battles and preserves those who put their faith and trust in Him, even when it seems foolish to the world."

"So, God saved Rahab, who was both a sinner and an outsider?" summarized Zach. That touched a note with him.

"That's right, Zach, we are all sinners needing redemption," said Josh.

"But what's the difference between her and the rest of the people in the city? Why weren't they saved."

"As we understand, she was the only one who turned to God. Many of the rest may have feared God's judgment and even understood it was coming, but they never repented of their sins and turned to God. They remained in rebellion, trusting in themselves. In the end, it's our choice. Turn to God and ask for redemption, or continue making our way and rebelling. It's a choice we all must make."

"She was saved because of what she did?" asked Zach.

"No, you got it backwards, I think—as evidenced elsewhere in the Bible. Rahab first put her faith in God and then was led to protect the spies. Her faith dictated her actions. Paul talks about this in Hebrews, where he says, 'It was by faith that

---

1. Joshua 6:15-20

Rahab the prostitute was not destroyed with the people in her city who refused to obey God. For she gave a friendly welcome to the spies.'"[2]

Andrew spoke up as Boaz completed his massage, and he got up to put on his shirt. "That's an impressive memory, Josh. How'd you manage to remember that verse?"

"I could always memorize when it came to Bible verses. It's just something I studied and practiced as a kid and kept up as I got older. I find, the more I knew and could remember the Bible, the more it spoke to me in everyday life. By the time you reach the end of Genesis, you pretty much see every good and bad thing man will ever do. We find ways to wrap the same old sins in modern clothing."

"Well, we usually end in prayer, and it's nearly time to hit the field. Since you led the discussion, Josh, why don't you finish us with a prayer?" asked Andrew.

"Sure," replied Josh and bowed his head. "Dear Lord, Thanks for this reading of your word. Let us remember You are with us and fight our battles when we put our faith and trust in You. No matter what walls life raises against us, they don't stand a chance against us if we trust in You. Thanks for Rahab's example and reminder no matter who we are, what we've done, and where we come from, You are ready to redeem us when we turn to You. Please, Lord, like Zach's vision of good plays, let us do our best today for your honor and glory. In Jesus' name, I pray, Amen."

"No prayer for a victory, Josh?" said Zach with a little good-natured jibe.

"The Lord's already won our victory, Zach. We're just supposed to go out there and play a good game," smiled Josh back. Zach was a little apprehensive when he followed Josh into the "Christian Club" room as he thought of it. However, these three men and what they read and talked about didn't seem to show a God trying to weed out the bad people, but rather a God inviting everyone to come to Him. That was not something Zach expected. The discussion made him think a bit differently about Christians.

"Amen," agreed Cy, in his deep bass voice. They all got up feeling refreshed and renewed as they headed out to the field.

---

2. Hebrews 11:31

Forty Three

The afternoon was bright and cheery in Pittsburgh, a perfect setting for opening day. A brilliant blue sky, dotted with white puffy clouds and a cool 64 degrees F, provided a beautiful backdrop with the skyline scene beyond the stadium outfield. The Pirates' opponents, the Chicago Cubs, became a powerhouse in recent years. Historically, the Cubs versus Pirates rivalry was one of the better ones in the League. Over the years, one team held the other in check, swapping back and forth on who gained the upper hand. All true rivalries require two things: each capable of defeating the other, and some honest dislike between the two. The Cubs and Pirates history made for exciting baseball. The Cubs opened their season with a three-game winning streak, tied with the Pirates atop the division.

"Well folks, it's a beautiful day in the burgh here for the Buccos' home opener," Bob started the radio broadcast.

"Yeah. We'd tell you to stop listening to the radio and get your butt to PNG Park, but it's a sell-out, so you're stuck with us," said Greg on the Pirates Radio broadcast.

"You always know how to motivate the listeners, Greg," added Bob with a hint of sarcasm.

"Yes, well, Mom says it comes naturally, Bob, from my dad's side of the family."

"You can't argue with genetics folks, but we are glad you are tuning in, and who wouldn't? It's the Pirates' home opener. They've started the season 3-0, tied for the top of the division, and are playing one of our favorite 'love to hate em' rivals, the Chicago Cubs," stated Bob.

"Yep, it's always a good day when the Buccos are playing, Bob, and an even better one if they have a chance to beat the Cubbies, eh?" Greg opined.

"It sure is, Greg. The Cubs have started their own win streak with a season-opening sweep of the Marlins at Wrigley Field. Guess the fish didn't like coming north for some low 40s wind chill up there in the windy city."

"Yeah, the Florida teams seem to be like my dear old Mom."

"Gray-haired and hard of hearing?" quipped Bob.

"Wanting to snowbird in Boca until the forecasts up north stop showing chances for snow flurries," Greg replied.

"Speaking of which, the apparent cold front that's due tomorrow night isn't here yet today," added Bob. "It's a glorious bright 64 degrees, blustery with the winds sweeping out of the west at about 10 knots, according to our KDKA weather experts. They tell us we should have a nice, clear afternoon with the cold front rolling in late tonight, making our weekend game a bit of a pill."

"I guess we can wear our long johns if need be this weekend, but right now, it's a beautiful day in the neighborhood. Shoot, I see a bunch of Pittsburgh crazies in shorts, although a few do have Steeler sweatshirts on out there. They must have been leftovers from Heinz field and last year's playoffs," piped Greg.

"Yeah, well, after the Steelers' unceremonious exit, maybe they spent a few months crying in their Iron City Light 12 pack in the Winnebago out in the parking lot and wandered over here to see what all the ruckus was about, with this Green fella," commented Bob.

"As ole Myron would say, 'Hum-hah. If you'ns haven't been payin' attention, this kid, Green, is on fire! He's the Jack Splat[1] of baseball players. Have you heard the sound his bat makes when he connects? Yoi and Double Yoi!'" mimicked Greg, doing his best impression of Pittsburgh's legendary football commentator, the late, great Myron Cope.

It would be elder statesmen against youth to start the game as the Pirates sent a veteran left-hander, known for his off-speed stuff and ability to paint the corners, to face the Cubs in the home opener. In contrast, the Cub's lead-off man Ittai Gittite was Rookie of the Year two seasons ago as a twenty-year-old from Japan and led the majors in stolen bases each of the last two years. Like the Pirates lead-off man, Zach, he was a switch hitter and led the Leagues in both runs and stolen bases. Many compared him to the former Japanese MLB switch hitter, Ichiro, because of his nationality. However, his numbers were more like Ricky Henderson, stealing bases and hitting for average and power. He averaged 26 homers and a .305 batting average his first two years. After winning Rookie of the Year, his numbers increased slightly, and he also won his first gold glove in right field, finishing third in the League's MVP voting in just his second season last year. He was one of two Cub players to start last year's all-star game.

The Pirate pitcher started Ittai with a changeup low for a ball, followed by a fastball on the outside corner for a strike. At 1-1, Thomas called for the ordinarily

---

1. Jack Splat was Myron Cope's nickname for Pittsburgh Steeler Hall of Fame linebacker Jack Lambert.

reliable curve from his lefty pitcher, but unfortunately, he hung the pitch, and the Cub's lead-off man belted it down the left field line for a stand-up double.

Much like the Cardinals, the big-budget Cubs fielded a strong lineup. Their number two man, their center fielder, was probably a number 3 or 4 hitter on most other teams. The lefty hit for power, with 33 homers and 28 doubles last year. Thomas started him off with a similar diet of changeup, fastball, but both painted the zone's edges this time. Twice, the batter swung and missed. At 0-2, he looked for and got the pitcher's curveball. Unfortunately, like the first batter, it hung over the outside corner, and the batter pulled it, lining it to right field.

"There's a *hard* line drive to the wall in right!" shouted Bob. "Green's back...the ball's deep, and it *careens* off the wall and back towards Green. He barehands it and turns. He guns it—What?—He's throwing toward home plate!" shouted Greg, exasperated, thinking he would throw to second as Ittai's speed should let him score easily.

However, Ittai hesitated momentarily, unsure if Josh could catch the ball. That delay meant he was rounding third as the ball hit the wall. Still, Josh began his throw with the fleet-footed runner heading for home. It shouldn't have been close, but it was.

"Holy Cow, did he get him? Yes! He got him, folks!" shouted Greg. "Green just threw a frozen rope and pulled a Bo Jackson, getting Ittai trying to score from second! The crowd is going crazy. The Cubs manager is on the steps with his hands on his hips. He wants to protest, but we're looking at the replay, and the ball beat Ittai into Thomas's glove just as he started his slide to the plate," announced an incredulous Greg.

"Folks, Bo Jackson is about right, that famous throw he made years ago," Bob followed. "Off the bat, this thing looked like it had RBI all over it. Green was just a few steps from the warning track and threw an absolute bullet straight into Thomas's glove at home. Ittai slid right into it. There was nothing he could do!"

"What a thing of beauty, Bob. I don't think anyone thought Green would attempt a throw home. He threw it well over the head of any would-be cutoff-man. J.J. came out but was shading toward second, thinking Green would go there trying to get the batter, but Green never hesitated. He grabbed it bare-handed on the rebound and fired it home on the fly, no hop, nothing, just straight into Thomas's glove as he caught it while Ittai began his slide. Ittai was dead on arrival. No question about it on the replay. Hey Greg, did you notice Ittai tipped his cap towards Green as he walked back to the dugout? Those Japanese players, very polite, very proper," commented Greg.

"Yes, as you said, Ittai saw the ball come into the glove right in front of him as he slid. I think it surprised him that it got there that fast. Thomas just needed to hold onto it as Ittai kinda' looked up after he slid with a "where'd that come from?"

look. The Cubs decide not to challenge the ruling on the field. Ittai was out, and if there was any doubt, they just showed it on the big screen. Ittai is a class act, much like his countryman Ichiro for all those years. He's a superb young player, but we got him on that one, and Green's throwing arm reputation grew about three sizes, I'd say," added Bob.

"You know, older Pirates fans may remember Dave Parker's throw from right in the all-star game back in the day, but I think the only one I've seen like this one was the Bo Jackson throw against fleet-footed Reynolds," said Greg.

"Yes, when you said that, I immediately drew the same thought, careen off the wall, bare-handed grab, turn and throw to get a fast runner most thought Bo couldn't possibly get. Bo was a freaky strong guy and nailed him. Many people call that 'The Throw.' Maybe we just saw a new, 'The Throw,' right here in Pittsburgh," stated Bob.

"Honestly, folks, I know you might think I've overblown this for radio's sake, but set your DVRs for Sports News highlights because, in nearly 30 years of broadcasting, that may be the greatest throw we've seen here in Pittsburgh," finished Greg.

Josh's stunning play seemed to settle the Pirate pitcher down. He induced the next Cubs batter to hit into an inning-ending double play, and the Pirates escaped the inning without damage after the first two batters hit them hard. Excited fans gave a standing ovation as the Pirates headed in for their at-bats. All eyes were on Josh as he trotted in, and the pitcher waited to give him a glove-to-glove high five before walking into the dugout. Several teammates added a few slaps on his back for good measure.

Pops kept the batting lineup the same as the last game in St. Louis. Zach would lead off, followed by J.J., who drew three walks with no strikeouts in the first three games. Andrew was hitting .333, followed by Josh in the cleanup position. Juan batted fifth with three clutch hits, including a powerful home run and two doubles yielding 5 RBIs. Nathan Fisher was hitting in sixth position, starting the year with one hit in each of the three games in 12 at-bats. Judah posted a better average and on-base percentage than Nate but was hitting seventh as Pops told him he was trying to get some action with the bottom of the lineup, much to Judah's displeasure. He couldn't complain too much as Thomas hit behind him with similar numbers in one of the best starts to his long journeyman career.

The Pirates started quickly. Zach got a first-pitch fastball from the Cubs starting left-hander and swatted it down the left field line into the corner for a hustling double to open the inning. The Cubs tried to go after J.J. with a few high fastballs and a breaking pitch, but J.J.'s good eye, something he worked on since last season, held off swinging at balls, and after a fouled-off fastball on the outside corner, he took ball four, a breaking ball into the dirt, for a walk. It seemed the

Cubs lefty was having some control problem with his breaking ball early, like the Pirates starter in the top of the inning.

The captain, Andrew, was next. He watched two breaking balls outside of the strike zone, and at 2-0, Pops figured the Cubs wouldn't want to load the bases for Josh, so he put the hit and run on. It was an unusual gamble for Pops, but Saul discussed it with his captains and Pete this morning, and they all wanted to be aggressive with their play calling this year. Andrew also sensed this season was their time to strike, relishing the bold call.

"Here's the 2-0 pitch to Andrew," said Bob. "Runners are going! There's a sharp hit down the third baseline. Oh! The third baseman makes a diving stop to knock down the ball. There's a long throw... Nope, Andrew is safe at first!"

"Yeah, the third baseman laid out flat to knock that ball down behind third base skidding into foul territory, but he had no chance to get Zach at third, running on the pitch. He tried to recover and throw out Andrew, but Andrew still has decent speed and beat out the long one-hopper to first," added Greg.

"Wow, an unexpected hit and run the whole way," commented Bob. "The third baseman was playing back and did a good job to stop the ball, or it would have likely been two runs scored and a double for Andrew. Still, Andrew hustled to beat the throw by a half step."

"Pretty aggressive for Pops to start with a hit and run with no outs, but he called it, and Andrew got a fastball he could handle. Now we have the bases loaded for Josh, who's been hotter than a Ghost Pepper!" announced Greg excitedly.

Josh walked from the on-deck circle, taking his now customary kneeling position just outside the batter's box, and bowed his head. The crowd was already enthusiastically clapping in anticipation with the prospect of seeing the rookie for the first time with the bases loaded, but there were a few catcalls for what some saw as theatrics on Josh's part. Still, he stayed motionless, head bowed, right hand in the dirt, and left hand held his bat pointed down. He rose, and the noise increased with more than a few fans swinging terrible towels throughout the stadium. The large flags in left-center were billowing from the winds blowing from right to left field and slightly in as if the wind was blowing straight up the Ohio and Allegheny rivers, foretelling the cold front heading in from the west.

The Cubs found themselves between a rock and a hard place with Josh's recent shows of power in St. Louis. They did not want to give him something to hit, but Juan was behind him hitting .300 and a homer to back him up.

"Green settles into the batter's box after a few catcalls for that kneeling prayer again," called Bob.

"Yep. The crowd seems eager to get on with it, eh, Bob? Perhaps they want to see if this 'Big Mean Josh Green' lives up to the hype they saw in St. Louis?" delivered Greg.

"Well, if he puts anything in play, there's a good chance the Bucs can put something on the board," replied Bob.

"C'mon, Bob. They aren't lookin' for some little RBI single from Green. This crowd wants a Grand Salami, or I'm a monkey's uncle!"

"That would be something, Greg. What I would give to see that to start the Pirates opener! I'd eat my hat to see that one, Greg!" exclaimed Bob.

"That's not sayin' much, folks. He got it for free when he bought a bowl of soup at the clubhouse." quipped Greg.

"OK, Rodney, let's see what the Cubbies do with Green, shall we? Besides, my wife gave me this hat for my birthday."

"Looks good on you, looks good on you...," Greg said, doing his best Dangerfield impression. "Ahhh, I'm not gonna' lie to you, folks. I know you can't see it, but she really mustn't like him much. Trust me on this one."

"Green's ready," reported Bob, trying to reel them back to the present. "And here's the pitch."

The Cub pitcher chose to bust Josh inside with a fastball, but Josh wasn't intimidated and took the pitch for ball one. Next, he threw a fastball high and outside for ball two. The crowd was anxious, and the Cubs knew they didn't want to take the count to 3-0. Cautiously, the catcher called for a changeup low on the outside. He wanted Josh to see a similar ball as the previous pitch but knew a changeup would drop down in the zone, causing most batters to swing early or over it. The pitcher delivered as requested, but Josh saw the pitch and its slower downward arc clearly. He waited on the pitch, making a full, uncoiling swing, smashing into the ball as it crossed the bottom of the strike zone, sounding like lightning striking a tree.

CCCRAACCKKK!

"THERE'S a DRIVE! DEEP! to LEFT CENTER. NOOOOO DOUBT ABOUT IT!" yelled Bob into the microphone. "HO-LY COW! GREEN with a TreMENDOUS Drive WAAAAYYY out of here, and where did it go? I lost it in the big screen."

"He BELTED it right over the TOP, did Ole Green," followed Greg. "YOI, and DOUBLE YOI. WHERE'S the SALT and FORK, Bob? You've got a HAT to EAT!"

"HE BLEW that thing right off my head, Greg. It's in the wind and on its way to Philadelphia!"

"Well, your wife could probably replace it 2 for 1 'dahn' Pechin's in Connellsville, so don't fuss about it. Listen to this crowd screaming over the fireworks in the background; They're going Coo-Coo crazy, here in the Burgh!" finished Greg as the Pirate cannons fired off behind the outfield wall.

Josh rounded the bases as fireworks exploded over the Pittsburgh skyline. His teammates waited for him—no silent treatment or casual acceptance for this prodigious blast to bust open their home opener. First, Zach, J.J., and Andrew met him at home plate. Then Juan high-fived Josh as he passed the on-deck circle. Finally, Pops led a parade at the top of the steps. Josh's smash produced a big smile on the coach's face like a proud papa in little league. The crowd was electric. Many high-fived each other or twirled terrible towels in the full-to-capacity PNC Park. The entire stadium was awash with jubilant fans, and the players in the dugout finally forced Josh back up the steps, pushing him out for a reluctant but well-earned tip of the cap.

The game continued with Juan's at-bat, but the Cubs pitcher was more than a little rattled by the grand slam. He gave up a double to Juan and walked Nate unintentionally on five pitches. The Cubs manager saw enough and pulled his starter in favor of relief. However, the reliever fared little better, giving up two more runs before ending the inning, and the Pirates were up 6-0 after the first inning.

The Pirates continued to play well, with Josh continuing his torrid streak despite the Cubs pitching around him. Josh finished the day 2-2 with three walks, including two intentional, a double, and the Grand Slam. He was still perfect on the year, yet to make an out. The entire Pirate's lineup showed dramatic improvement, winning their first three games handsomely and their home opener in a blowout 11-3.

The team and fans of Pittsburgh were understandably jubilant at the game's conclusion. Excitement filled the locker room as the players reveled in their play. Josh wasn't the only story, as several on the team started the year with the best Pirate offensive output in decades. J.J., Andrew, Juan, and Judah were hitting over .300. While not perfect, the pitching gave up the fewest runs in a four-game stretch to start the season in years. Still, all the success seemed to stem from the phenomenal play of the unknown rookie sensation Josh Green.

"Josh, what's your secret? You seem to be on an unstoppable hitting streak?" asked a reporter from the Pittsburgh Post-Gazette® during the post-game interviews.

"I'm not sure there is a secret," replied Josh. "I am seeing the ball really well right now, trying not to anticipate, just react to what they are giving me."

"Yeah, but Josh, you have now started the season 10 for 10, including four home runs and a whopping 16 RBIs in your first four games in the big-leagues. There's got to be something behind this prodigious production," followed the reporter from the Tribune-Review.®

"There's no magic going on here, guys. I am just happy to get a chance to play and contribute. My teammates played some great ball against some good teams. I am glad to get off to a fast start against these teams. It's fun trying to keep it going. Bottom line, everyone's playing well, and it shows in the wins and loss column, which is what counts."

"Josh, talk to us about the throw home in the first. Some say that's one of the best throws we've seen at PNC Park," asked the KDKA® sports reporter.

"Well, it was a hard-hit ball; a line drive. I realized early on as I went back that it was too high to catch before the wall, but I didn't think it would clear it. I set up to catch it off the wall—something Coach Phil worked with me during home field practice. This particular hit flew so hard it surprised me with how far back it bounced. As I turned, I caught it barehanded. I thought early on it was hit hard enough I might have a chance to make the play at home. While it was in the air, I glanced at the runner at second and saw him hold up initially. When I saw that, I thought if I fielded it cleanly off the wall, I'd throw home. I got the ball even faster off the wall than I hoped, in stride, so I already committed to going home with it when I turned."

"Did you see J.J. as the cutoff man?"

"No, I didn't. I knew J.J. would shade toward second to cover the batter if we went there and let the run score. No, my focus was only on Thomas as soon as I turned. You saw my momentum and movement toward home with the way the ball rebounded, setting me up perfectly to make a direct throw. It was a bang, bang, play."

"People are comparing your throw to Bo Jackson back in the day. What do you think of that, Josh?" mentioned another reporter.

"Wow. Well, that's high praise, certainly. I got a little lucky with the bounce and let it fly. You know, it was the first inning, and again, like I said the other day, Pops encouraged us to take good risks, good chances, and be aggressive. If the ball came off any other way to delay me, I would have gone to second, but... everything went our way today, and I took advantage of it. I put the throw out there, and Thomas made a good tag on the runner."

"Did you notice the tip of the cap from Ittai as he walked back to the dugout?" asked Roman Josephus from SPNN.

"I did not see it when I was out there, I think my back was turned to the infield at the time, but Andrew told me about it back in the dugout after the inning.

"Don't you think that's unusual? Maybe something in Ittai's Japanese culture learned playing in his home league before coming to our Major Leagues?" followed Roman, seeing if he could get an ethnic angle on Josh.

"It's pretty amazing, but from what I hear about Ittai, it's consistent with the type of player he is—a real class act. I hope I have that kind of sportsmanship when I play the game," replied Josh, not taking the ethnic bait and keeping it at the individual level.

"Josh, how long can you keep this hitting streak going? You have yet to make an out, and you have homered in your first four games." continued Roman.

"Well, Roman, like I think I said a few days ago, I take each game and each at-bat, one at a time. I look for good pitches to hit. I am not thinking about streaks or anything like that. Just make good contact when I swing, look for a pitch to drive, and help my teammates and pitchers with solid play in the field when I get the opportunity. We are all playing really well. It's a team sport, and as long as we keep playing well together, I think we have a great opportunity to do good things this season," answered Josh.

Mark Johnson and Pops were in the background listening to Josh's answers, and Mark gave a raised eyebrow look to Pops after that last question. Pops nodded back. So far, so good. Josh kept fending off Roman's attempts to find a wrinkle in the story.

Roman prepared for Josh's rebuffs and decided to try a few tricks he kept up his sleeve.

"Josh, you talk a lot about the team and their play. Since you only joined the team two weeks ago, how are you getting along with so many new teammates?" queried Roman. Saul glanced concernedly at Mark, who nodded back and began to slide around the outside of the press ring to cut in if the interview went "off-topic."

"We've all been getting to know each other in the last couple of weeks. There are just a lot of talented players and coaches. They have impressed me with their professionalism, to say the least," said Josh.

Roman did his homework. He also knew personalities on the team, with many "off the record" discussions garnering individual opinions before this season. "So, for instance, you took over from Judah in right field, his normal position the last couple seasons, and start higher than him in the batting order. Did that cause any friction between you two?" probed Roman.

"Look, you will have to ask Coach Samuelson about position and lineup questions. I play where I am told. I think all the players made adjustments with me coming late to spring training. Hopefully, I am rewarding their understanding and the coaches' confidence in me with good play."

Mark worked his way around the fifteen or so reporters and recording gear set up around Josh. Until now, Josh had done well, but Mark knew some reporters would continue trying to stir something up.

One of the other reporters chimed in, trying to keep Roman from monopolizing the Q and A. "Josh, are you comfortable in the number four position? Have you discussed Pop's thoughts for future lineups?"

"Coach Samuelson makes the lineups, and I am comfortable wherever he thinks is best for me to play. It seems to be working well right now. Everyone is hitting well. I think we have, what, five people hitting over .300? We're generating a lot of offense."

"Pops changed the lineup once already since the start of this short season. He's got young players like J.J. hitting at the top of the lineup while a veteran like Judah bats seventh. Is this to accommodate you?" Roman made another jab to get a rise out of Josh or trip him up in his response.

"Look, I am sure that's also a question for Coach, Roman. Again, I came in late to the start of the season. The coaching staff tries to adjust for the best team fit. The results speak for themselves. We all want to keep the momentum going. Whatever lineup does that, the coaches will keep working to produce results. It's about what makes us the best team with the best chance to put runs on the board. Same with the defense, I think. It's about the wins and losses, and so far, Coach Samuelson's led us into the win column. Everyone's doing their job helping us be the best we can be. In my short time here, I can say that everyone, both coaches and players, works hard to give us the best chance at winning. It's a long season, but I think you must say we're moving in the right direction," finished Josh.

Roman was a little stymied as Josh seemed to dodge the landmines he laid out for him. Mark saw his chance. "Folks, any last questions before we let the players finish their post-game routines and get going?"

"Thoughts on tomorrow, Josh?" queried the AP reporter.

"Sounds like it's going to be cold—dress warm, everybody!" replied Josh.

Most of the press laughed at that, but Roman was not amused. Roman could use Josh's great plays to secure national time with SPNN, but Roman still didn't have that edge he needed over the competition to get everyone's attention. Roman knew he needed to step up his game, and there were many more tricks and snares in his arsenal for this unknown phenom. He needed more background—and an angle.

Mark ushered the press out of the locker room, and Pops talked briefly to the team about tomorrow. "Go ahead and complete your post-game work as soon as you can. The weather front is supposed to be coming through tonight, dropping temperatures into the upper thirties, and game time is supposed to be 40 degrees and breezy. It gets worse into the weekend, with a chance of snow the next day. See Pete if you need help with any cold-weather gear. Great game out there today, folks. Let's start our warm-ups tomorrow at 1030 AM to ensure we are ready for the cold. Any questions for me?" Nobody said anything, as most were happy to call it a day. "I'll see you all tomorrow then," finished Pops. After most returned to their post-game rituals, pops walked over to Josh. "Josh, when you get ready to leave, come see me in my office, would ya?"

"Sure, Coach," replied Josh. Saul walked over toward Pete, who talked with a couple of pitchers on the other side of the locker room. He tapped Pete from behind and said in his ear, "Let's talk in your office as soon as you can." Pete nodded and grabbed one of the trainers, giving him instructions about what cold-weather gear he should distribute to whom, then turned and walked over to his office where Pops already waited. Saul was sitting in the old leather chair in the corner with his back to the windows as Pete closed the door, walked over to his desk, and took his seat amidst the collection of baseball gear, boxes, and other extraneous baseball objects. He grabbed a half-chewed cigar from inside his desk drawer, snipped the end with a cutter, and chewed on it as he reached for an old bat with a taped handle.

"What's up, Pops?" said Pete. He studied the old practice bat he liked to hit fly balls with and started peeling the badly worn tape off the handle to replace it with some new tape.

"What do you think about our team so far?"

Pete glanced up at Saul and half laughed, taking the cigar out of his mouth and pointing at his old friend. "Geez, Pops, we sure look like we got a winner here," he said, waving the cigar at the windows and the locker room filled with players behind Saul's back. "At least as much as you can tell in four games," he said, placing the cigar back in his mouth and looking back at the bat.

Saul looked at Pete as he tried to unwind the old tape for a few seconds. "What about Green?" he asked.

"What about him? He's hitting lights out, and you and I ain't seen nothing like it," responded Pete. He paused for a moment, searched his desk for some reading glasses, and threw them on to see the tape better and find the edges. "Why do you ask? What's your concern?" he said without looking at Saul.

"Look," began Saul, "First, in St. Louis, at the end of the road trip, and now Chicago, and how they treated him today, has me concerned. He hammers that homer in the first. They try to pitch around him in the second, with one out and nobody on, I might add. He promptly lifts a curve, probably off the plate, down the line for a double. After that, he doesn't see a hittable pitch. They walk him three more times."

"Yeah, well–that's gonna' happen when you're hitting like he is. It won't take much more of this before no one wants to pitch to him at all," said Pete.

Saul sat silently. Pete continued to pick at the tape for a few seconds. When Saul made no movement or sound, Pete suddenly realized what Saul was talking about and looked up at him over the half-rim glasses. Saul, still silent, stared at Pete. Now Pete stopped with the bat, sat it across his lap, took his cigar out, and gestured toward Saul. "And *that's* exactly what you're afraid might happen, is it?" he said, half question, half statement.

Saul just stared at Pete and nodded slightly. He let it sink in. Pete chomped down on his cigar again. "Son of a gun," Pete said softly, bat forgotten, leaning back and looking at the ceiling as the full impact of his statement sank in.

Finally, Saul began quietly, even though no one else could hear them through the thick glass.

"Look, Pete, I think we are entering uncharted territory here. Remember when I told you about Josh facing Goliath?" Pete nodded and looked back at Saul, concentrating now on him. "I really meant it, Pete. Josh hit everything, and I mean *eve-ry-thing* I threw at him. And when I turned on the targets, after one near miss, he even hit them. We've used Goliath for what, four seasons? We've gone through every non-pitcher multiple times, right?" Again, Pete nodded. "That includes our all-star, Andrew, who won a batting title and the MVP. You've watched them in that batting cage nearly as often as me. Has anyone hit more than 50% of the balls into play against that machine, ever, even on their best day?" The question from Saul hung in the air in Pete's office.

Pete thought about it for a moment. Goliath was a mechanical monster, and he never saw another like it. He knew the answer. They ordered the machine built as challenging as the best pitchers in baseball. He knew no one, not even Andrew during his MVP season, hit it even half the time, let alone controlled the hits into the field like a menu selection the way Pops described: No one, that is, until Josh. And for the first four games, Josh was perfect. Literally perfect. Baseball was a game of statistics, much more in the modern era. It amazed Pete how they now tracked everything about a player's hitting stats. Yesterday, Pete reviewed the players' numbers with the hitting coach for the first three games. Josh not only went 10 for 10, he did so with exactly 10 swings. Pete suddenly realized how odd the stats were for Josh: even today, two more swings, two more hits. Teams in modern baseball based much of their decisions on these stats, much more than in the olden days, just a few decades ago when Pete first coached. Pete looked back at Saul, who still sat staring at him.

Pete leaned back in his chair. "Odd problem to have," he offered, much more subdued than usual.

"No one believes a guy can hit every pitch in and around the zone, Pete, because no player is ever that good. If he were...," started Saul, pausing at the obvious conclusion.

"He'd never get a pitch to hit again." Pete finished for him. He looked down at the bat in his hands, not seeing it.

Nothing flustered Pete for long, and he was finally ready to speak. He leaned forward in his chair over his desk, took the unlit cigar out of his mouth, and gestured pointedly to his friend, "So what are you prepared to do, Saul?"

Now it was Saul's turn to hesitate. "I think I need to talk to the boy."

The mentor in Pete returned, "He's no boy, Pops, far from it. If I get what you are angling at, and I am not going to say it, how do you get him to understand?"

"I don't know. I have to see if what he's shown is what I am thinking. If he can hit each hittable pitch and place it in play without getting out, he will go from giving us a chance for the long ball or timely hits and driving in runs to a walk king like we've never seen before. Baseball, as we know it, can't exist with a perfect hitter. Other teams will just give him a pass, which doesn't help us nearly as much."

"You got to be careful how you and he change what he's doin'," warned Pete.

"I know. I think it's doable. Do you remember back in '01 when Bonds was at his height? He was hitting every, what?–Eighth or ninth at-bat into the stratosphere?" reminisced Saul.

"Yep, I remember. Of course, he had some *help*, so to speak," commented Pete with thinly veiled ire at the period of baseball tainted by the steroid controversy.

"Yeah, but not the point; the point is, while teams were playing him to pull with the shift on and he saw few good pitches each game, teams still believed if they pitched him conservatively, they could get him out. They would try to pitch him hard and hit their spots where he wasn't quite so strong but not always give him intentional walks. He was still hitting homers at the end of the season."

"Because he got just enough decent pitches to hit," Pete finished Saul's thought and sat back in the chair.

Saul nodded as he thought over the ramifications of what he was saying, silently trying to focus his thoughts. Finally, he said, "We got to help Josh find the sweet spot. And he's got to pick his moments, or he won't get a chance to hit when the game's on the line."

Pete chomped on his cigar, relaxing finally, and started peeling the tape off the bat again. "I'll say it again. Heck of a problem to have, eh, Pops?" he said through clenched teeth and cigar, glancing at Saul over the glasses.

Saul half laughed and nodded, shrugging his shoulders while putting his hands on his chair to push himself up.

Pete added one more thing as Saul rose to go, "Just be sure you explain it to him the way you did with me. He's a lot more seasoned, in some ways, than we give him credit for. Lay it out. He'll understand. And oh, by the way, if someone at some future point asks. You and I never had this conversation."

"What conversation?" Saul smiled at his old confidant as he walked toward the door.

Forty Four

"You wanted to see me, Coach?" Josh asked, knocking on Saul's open office door. Josh arrived after receiving a rub down from one of Cy's assistants. While not quite the "Special" Cy delivered, he still felt both relief and soreness. However, he learned it would help him recover quicker for tomorrow's game.

"Yes, come on in, Josh. Close the door and have a seat," said Saul as he gestured toward a chair. The coach's office was more expansive and more private than Pete's. While the office was about twice the size of Pete's, Saul only used about half the space and could quickly vacate it should his fortune change. Rather than displaying wealth or position, it conveyed the sense of a humble man who eschewed the easy pleasures or luxuries someone in his position might take. Pops sat at a well-traveled, large wooden desk with an equally old but cushioned office chair. His one nod to modern conveniences was a big screen TV behind his desk. Attached were several recording and playback devices connected above what looked to be an old sideboard stereo console. It looked like something out of your grandparents' 1970s living room you weren't supposed to touch. Several mismatched second-hand filing cabinets stood off to the side. An old leather couch lined the opposite wall, with a lumpy pillow covered with a hand-embroidered pillowcase and a crocheted blanket folded at one end. It looked comfy and slept on more than once. Next to it was an end table with a built-in lamp from the same time frame as the sideboard. In front of the desk were two inviting oversized chairs with a 1970s post-modern coffee table in between. It was a big office and still felt empty, with furniture only on one side. The rest of the office was bare except for a couple of old moving boxes, half-packed, near a door to a small bathroom.

Josh did as asked and sat in one of the two oversized chairs. What the office lacked in modern amenities, it made up for in comfort. The big old chairs held even Josh easily, and he felt relaxed.

Saul wanted to put Josh at ease, so he started off-topic. "Well, quite a start for you, Josh. How are you feeling?"

"I feel great, Coach. I'm doing well and pleased with the results so far," replied Josh.

"Ruth and Mary getting along? The trip went well to St. Louis? Everything OK with the family?" Saul asked rapid-fire, and Josh nodded yes to all in reply. "Everything's been great, Coach, better than I expected. The medical folks in St. Louis were wonderful, and Mary is working with the St. Louis Patient Advocate on a good game plan to set us up for the other cities on our away schedule," answered Josh. Saul nodded thoughtfully, looking first at Josh, then down at his crossed hands.

Finally, Saul continued, "Well, I am happy the family part is going well. That's always important to get squared away. And Mark and I have been impressed with how you handle yourself with the press. Keep it up, as they will continue digging for a story. Watch for them trying to get into your head about things other than baseball, and bring them back to the game and your play when you can. Guys like Roman will do anything to get something he can use as front-page news, and he'll do just about anything to get it," finished Saul.

"I understand, Coach, and I'll try to think through what the press is after when they ask those kinds of questions," replied Josh. Saul hesitated. He wanted to broach the delicate subject, but was concerned about how to proceed. Josh sat there watching him with those kind dark eyes, older than his years conveyed.

Finally, Josh broke Saul's reverie. "Coach, is there anything wrong, something you want to ask me?"

"Josh, I think your play, these first four games, has been outstanding; on the field and certainly in the batter's box. In fact, it's been phenomenal in the batter's box. It's a start like I've never seen," stated Saul, then stopped, unsure how to proceed.

"That's a good thing, right Coach?" replied Josh.

"Of course, it's great, but..., well, this is just between you and me, you understand?" Saul looked seriously at Josh. Josh nodded. "Josh, when I first saw you hit at the cages, you hit my mechanical pitcher ten times in a row. Do you remember?" asked Saul. Josh again nodded. "OK," Saul continued, "When we spoke right after, I don't know if you remember, but I said no one has ever hit the machine like that."

"I remember, Coach," said Josh, waiting patiently for Saul to explain.

Saul pressed on, "Josh, I need you to tell me honestly, you've gone up to bat, and you're 12 for 12, plus now what - about seven walks? You've hit everything you've swung at for all those at-bats without missing." Saul hesitated, then hurried on, not wanting to lose courage with the question he must ask. "Josh, look, what I am getting at is–do you think you can go up and get a hit each time you're at bat?" asked Saul.

"Well, that's the plan, Coach," said Josh.

"No, Josh," said Saul seriously. In his head, what he would say next sound-ed crazy, but if he was right.... "That's the plan for *normal* players, Josh. Great even. I want you to think about it. The way you see the ball, the way you swing, does it seem like you can get a hit *every time* you go up?" asked Saul.

Josh's face changed slightly, and Saul thought he began to realize what Saul was asking.

"Coach, I guess I never really thought about it like that. I see the ball...dif-ferently," Josh hesitated, "Than when I played ball all those years ago." Saul watched as Josh looked down at his hands, contemplating what to say next, perhaps truly seeing his incredible play the last week. "When I hit the machine, it was twenty years since I picked up a bat. I felt like I could see the ball much better, differently than when I played when I was young." Josh was quiet now, looking off into the blank screen behind Saul's desk.

"Josh, is it the same way when you see the pitches now live?" asked Saul, already expecting the answer.

"I guess so. I just see the ball. I know where it will cross the plate, almost like it slows down. I see the possibilities of where I can hit it, and I pick a swing to send it back out the best way available."

"You choose a hit, so to speak?" Saul asked back, trying to keep his voice even, but this idea was incredible.

"I guess you could say I choose whichever hit I want, within the options I see in my mind's eye, yes," Josh replied.

"So again, Josh, I am ask if you can get a hit every time you swing?" Saul's mind was incredulous at the thought, but he worked hard to keep it out of his voice and almost succeeded.

Josh contemplated his answer. Finally, he looked back at Saul, "Coach, if the ball is hittable, yes, I can swing and hit it." Josh paused but replied with understated confidence, "Every time, and I know pretty much where it's going to go before I swing," finished Josh.

Saul was thunderstruck. Though he suspected it, he dared not believe it. No sane player or coach would think it was true, but as Josh said it aloud, Saul knew it was. The coach got up from his seat and walked around the half-empty office. He came to rest at one of his few pieces of memorabilia. It was a picture he took with the original Pops, Wilver D "Willie" Stargell, the Pirate great, soon after he, Saul, was traded to the Pirates and shortly before Pops passed all too soon. He kept it to remember; time was short. Even this office showed the mindset he could be gone tomorrow. Pops Stargell gave him one important piece of advice that stuck with him. "The Pirates will always be a team of characters," Pops said, smiling fondly at his memories. "If you let them, they'll be your family like they were mine—enjoy the ride because it's the family you'll always remember and miss when you're gone."

Josh waited patiently, following Pops with his eyes. Finally, Pops turned and sat beside Josh in the other leather chair. Pops took a deep breath, then looked deep into those dark old eyes next to him.

"OK, Josh. You and I need to understand that this conversation should not occur outside this room." Josh nodded passively, still the picture of calm. "Josh, this kind of ability, well, you must realize, it's not normal. I knew some of the best hitters of my generation, and I've read most there is on baseball greats of the past. I've never heard any of them describe what you just did—the way you see the ball. Sometimes, a star hitter will say they temporarily found themselves in a different zone. But you seem to be on a whole different level. You're currently batting 1.000. That's unsustainable. After you, the best average in baseball is currently .350 for anyone with ten at-bats this year. Last year's highest batting average for the League was the kid from LA with a .346 average, the best in five years. No one's approached .400 in decades; again, you're talking about hitting every time up. While that's incredible, it's not normal and will soon be a problem."

"What do you suggest, Coach?" said Josh, understanding the dilemma.

"We play the game hoping to be the next Splendid Splinter, like Ted Williams, hit over .400 and win the triple crown. I think you can do that. But look, and this is important Josh. You can't hit everything. You can't bat 1.000. If you do that, well, that's not human, and if other teams start to think you can, you'll never see another pitch over the plate," Saul sat back and let Josh chew on what he said.

Josh looked down at his hands for a moment. The pause gave Saul time to look over the man; Josh's quiet strength, the scar, the wavy dark hair, and the slightly hooked broad nose. Again, an echo of the distant past reached out to Saul. Something in the back of his mind he couldn't quite remember. Then there were those eyes. The rest of the man seemed to step out of some epic, a dark warrior, ready to battle, but for those dark brown eyes. They spoke not accusation and judgment, but ancient kindness and wisdom, the contrasting visage of a warrior chiseled from Michael Angelo's favorite dark piece of marble, imbued with grace-filled eyes of loving humanity. Indeed, Josh presented like an unknown masterpiece, stepped into time, scarred for sure, but with the gentle eyes diffusing his otherwise formidable countenance, casting a caring, knowing look back at Saul, gently piercing to his soul.

"I got it, Coach," Josh said finally, bringing Saul back to the moment, "So how do we proceed?"

After a brief pause, Saul replied, returning to the moment, "Do what you said you could, *but*," he paused with emphasis, "You pick your moments."

"And how do I know when those moments are?" asked Josh.

Pops nodded at Josh. That was the right question, and he knew how to answer. He rested his hands on the chair's leather arms and proceeded.

"I was coaching in the minors when Barry Bonds made his run in the early 2000s. No matter what you think of the steroids debacle, I still studied his at-bats with my hitting coach." Pops sat back, remembering. "Bonds was nearly perfect. Perfect in the way he could patiently wait and pick his pitch. He might go the entire game and only get one good pitch to hit. But we calculated that one pitch, the only one he might see over several at-bats, was hammered about two out of three times when he was in his prime. That's why he was hitting both home runs and hitting for average."

Pops continued, "We need to be situational with your hits. When no one's on, hit for base hits or doubles, and occasionally, I hate to say it, take an out." Saul cringed at this but hurried on. "Save the big hits for runners in scoring position, etc., when we need it most. The one thing I never thought I would tell a player, and I can't believe I am saying it now. You must pick times when you need to swing and miss. We must pick times to let the other team believe you're a great but still beatable batter. Even Bonds, Williams, heck, Micky, DiMaggio, or Rose; all got out. You haven't got out yet, and today, after your two hits, you saw what will happen. You will become the walks king, and that's not good enough to make this team a champion," said Saul.

"So, you want me to get out sometimes on purpose," asked Josh.

"Josh, you haven't even missed a pitch yet—do you realize that? When I told you no one hits the machine like you did, I meant it. Every player, except pitchers, went through that batting machine at least ten times over the last four years. Everyone, Andrew included. Andrew's a prime example. He's hit over .300 in four of the last five seasons and barely missed the fifth. He hits that machine maybe four or five times out of ten on a good day. Most of the players try to get three good hits out of ten. You hit *all ten balls!*" Pops said the last slowly, letting it sink into himself and Josh.

"There's a difference between being a skilled player on a hot streak and hitting everything," said Pops. "When the League thinks you've crossed that line, they won't think you're a superhero to admire. They'll think you're a freak and stop pitching to you. The other players are playing well right now around you, but trust me, teams will soon take their chances by walking you. It almost happened to Bonds. He's the only one in my lifetime to come close to what you are doing, and after a year of it, he saw over 200 walks. We must make them think you're not perfect, or your opportunities will vanish."

Saul watched closely as Josh sat looking down, thinking about what he said. Finally, he nodded and looked up and smiled. "OK, Coach, how do you want me to do this?"

They spent the next half hour talking it out. Saul wanted as much as possible to let Josh decide, but they came up with a few signs to use between Josh and Saul when Saul felt the need to either hold him back or let him turn it on. Saul also cautioned him about practice. "Miss a few balls and foul some off in batting practice. Our players and others watching need to see you're good but not perfect," said Saul.

As they finished up, Josh stood up, and so did Saul. "Look, Josh, one thing's for sure. Your skill and this ability are unlike anything ever seen in baseball. It's a great problem to have. I don't plan to tell you too often to pull back. I suspect you can make good decisions without much help from me. And hey, you have to really be unstoppable before the league stops trying. Just be a little human in your at-bats. Let them see you work for it even when you get a hit. I know it's odd to say that, but you have to be smart about using this gift. Make the most of it when the team needs it most." Saul finished.

"I got it, Coach."

"Good. If all goes well, I probably won't talk to you about this again, at least until we need to adjust," said Saul as he stood and reached out his hand.

"Don't worry, Coach, it will all work out," replied Josh, and he smiled, returning Pops' handshake as he too, stood.

"Good, now go on and get out of here. I'll see you at pregame practice tomorrow." Saul shook Josh's hand warmly. Josh smiled and nodded. Josh left Saul with a last reassuring look from those kind ancient eyes. Saul's final thought as Josh walked out of his office was a good one. He knew, with confidence, the Green era in Pittsburgh was off and running. Oh, what an era it would be!

Forty Five

J osh took to heart what he discussed with Pops. In the next game against the Cubs, he went 2 for 3. Josh swung and missed and fouled a pitch off before singling in the first inning, with Andrew on and two outs, driving in a run. He was next up in the 4th, fouling off a few balls, then grounding out sharply to shortstop, making his first out of the season. Saul watched to see what the Cubs made of it. In the seventh inning, Josh came up with no one on, one out, and the Cubs pitched around him, walking him on four straight balls. At least it wasn't an intentional walk, thought Saul.

Pete, as usual, reminded Saul of Josh's decent speed, and Saul discussed looking for steal opportunities as part of the plan with Josh. Saul realized Josh's base-stealing threat was nearly as unusual as his throwing. Saul directed Coach Phil, his game-day third base coach, to let Josh run in most situations. Sure enough, Josh came through with his second steal of the season, later scoring on a Judah base hit, and Pete winked at Saul with a knowing look. If Josh threatened on the base pads, teams might think twice about walking him.

The Cubs led 5-3 in the bottom of the ninth, on the verge of giving the Pirates their first loss. Josh was due up fourth. Zach hit sharply for a single, followed by a walk to Andrew. J.J. delivered a lengthy at-bat, working the count to full. He fouled off two would-be strike threes, finally drawing a walk on the tenth pitch. The excited crowd cheered enthusiastically, and the Cubs called a time-out to bring in their righty closer they traded to get from the Angels late last year. While he waited, Josh, Coach Samuelson, and Thomas chatted on the dugout steps.

"What's the line on this guy, Tommy," said Pops.

"Fireballer. High 90s with slightly wild control sometimes. Got a real good high-quality cutter. It's his 'out pitch' against righties—same release, but breaks late off the plate—top 2 or 3 in the League."

"Right," said Josh.

"He likes to throw the fastball down and in, or up and out, then lace a couple sliders for you to chase, depending on the count. Oh yeah, he will occasionally drop a changeup out and down, usually not for a strike, to see if you'll chase. He's a lot like Sammy, actually. If I were you, I would attack his fastballs if they are in the zone. The slider's almost unhittable."

"Got it," said Josh.

The young pitcher nearly completed his warm-ups, and Josh was getting ready to walk to the mound. He looked over at Pops and smiled. Pops smiled back and said, "Do what you do, Josh." Josh nodded as the ump signaled it was time to play.

No doubt Josh's out earlier broke some of the mystique he held in the first four games, and even his one hit today was only a single to right. He was still a rookie, and maybe the first four games were a fluke. It was hard to tell for the Cubs. Walking him meant a run, but they still would have the lead. However, Juan, still hitting over .300 behind him, was also a tough out.

The young fireballer was true to Thomas's prediction. The first pitch was hard and inside for a ball, measuring 98 on the gun. Next came a head-high fastball, outside for ball two. They were still leery of Josh hitting for extra bases. As predicted, the righty brought a hard slider, and Josh could see it would break well off the outside of the plate for a ball. Even though he could have taken it, Josh swung as if fooled by the pitch for a 2-1 count. The catcher and pitcher decided this might truly mean the rookie was finally playing like a rookie, but their coach specifically told them not to let Josh beat them with one pitch. The next pitch was the changeup on the outside. Josh could see it would drop down into the dirt and let it go. The catcher made an excellent play to smother it and keep a run from scoring on a wild pitch.

With the count 3-1, Josh figured they would return to the one pitch that fooled him, the slider. He set up ever so slightly closer to the plate. Josh was 6 foot 4, with a long upper torso and somewhat shorter legs for his height. He was deceptive in his power and reach for such a big man. Josh waited as the catcher gave the sign, slider off the plate. They thought they would either get a second strike or walk Josh and go after Juan. The pitcher executed the pitch well, knee-high, looking like a fastball on the corner but breaking late away from the batter. It should be impossible for right-handed Josh to reach it other than to foul it off; If he was an ordinary player; if he was anyone else.

Josh was not anyone else. He shifted his body down, bending low to the ground, reaching out, right knee low, almost touching the dirt with a compact, Tony Gwynn-like swing. However, Josh's powerful long arms displayed uncanny strength, and despite not pulling the ball, he lifted the 94 MPH offering in an arc toward the corner in right field, one of the shortest right fields in all of baseball. The right field foul pole at PNC Park is just 320 feet from home plate, and only the 21-foot Clemente wall, the same height as Clemente's number, protects against short home runs.

Because Green's swing was not his customary bombastic tape measure shot of previous days, the radio announcer's call started subdued but grew like a crescendo.

"Green connects. He's lifted one to right. BACK goes Ittai... IS it DEEP enough? It's hugging the foul line..., YESSSS, IT'S GONE!" shouted Bob into the mike. "Right over the 320 Ft sign, just inside the foul pole and out the exit stairs!"

"Yessirree Bob! Fans are scrambling 'dahn' the stairs after that ball, I suspect," added Greg. "This one didn't nearly make the river but might have made the North Shore Hot Dog stand after a couple bounces. But you don't get bonus points for long or short home runs. This one counts just the same! It's another Green Grand Salami, and look at the Cubbies. They are either crying or trying to get off the field! It's pandemonium at PNC Park! Fireworks explodin', cannon-balls all over the place. The crowd is going crazy! Green just hit a winner-takes-all, walk-off, grand-slam home run to steal this one from the Cubs. Game over, my friends! Raise the Jolly Roger!" finished Greg with a flourish, hardly able to contain himself.

"Look at the Cubs, Greg. The pitcher and catcher are looking up at the big screen replays as they walk off the field. They still can't believe what just happened."

"Yes, and the Pirate dugout is going wild while the Cubs dugout looks like someone told them their Aunt Bertha just died. You know; the aunt who always kept your favorite candy in her apron pocket? Look, their manager is standing on the stairs with his arms crossed. He still hasn't moved. He can't believe what we just witnessed!" exclaimed Greg excitedly.

The announcers sat back for a moment to take it all in, letting the radio audience listen to the cacophony of PNC ballpark celebrating a walk-off grand slam victory. As the base runners rounded the bases, the entire team gathered around home plate. The team, a makeshift huddle of bodies, piled on Josh as he crossed last, like a human great pyramid. Even the mascot, the Pirate Parrot, was doing cartwheels nearby, and the rest of the umpire crew tried to get out of the way after ensuring everyone crossed the plate, finalizing the win.

Finally, Greg summarized how they all felt. "Good grief, folks. Just when you think Green is mortal, with only a weak single early in the game, grounding out, and some bad swings and misses, he comes back, fights off some tough pitches, and does the kind of magic you only read about in storybooks. It was another good slider, like the one he missed badly earlier in the at-bat, maybe just a little closer to the plate, but he got low and lifted it just over Clemente's wall. UN-BE-LIEVABLE! I know the Cubs thought that pitch was unhittable, but Green continues to defy the laws of physics. What's with this old rookie? I just don't know. One thing's for sure, we have seen amazing things these first five games. The Pirates are 5-0 for the first time in, well..., my 26 years of broadcasting! This story's headline is a 38 years young rookie out of nowhere, playing a game the rest of the world can only dream about. What'll he do next?" finished Greg, genuinely shaking his head in excited disbelief.

Forty Six

T he press conference was chaotic as the Pirates locker room became a fighting match on who could outmaneuver who, to ask Joshua Green a question. Pittsburgh historically lacked a national baseball audience. However, the country started to take notice. Although a Friday day game early in the season, the Pirates received a marked increase in national sports reporters. Mark's hands were full, trying to keep the newly arrived press in check with their unfamiliarity of the Pirates' post-game setup. Unlike the previous games this season, there was no dilution of the media talking to other people after this game. There was Josh Green, and there was everybody else.

"Josh, the Cubs held you in check for most of the game. What changed in that last at-bat?" started a local reporter from the Post-Gazette.

"They were pitching me well throughout the game. I fought off some tough pitches here and there, and I managed the RBI single in the first to get Andrew home, but I would say they were doing a good job minimizing my chances."

"Yes, but Josh, what about the last at-bat? You were up against their best closer from last year. He's historically posted a stingy ERA against righties. Despite all that, you still beat him. How'd you do it?" launched a national reporter.

"Well, he threw a couple of good pitches against me, but I kept looking for something I could handle."

"We're you thinking walk at all, Josh? It would have meant a run," asked Roman from SPNN.

"No, Roman, I generally don't look for walks," replied Josh.

"Even with Juan hitting over three hundred with two homers next up?" followed Roman quickly, ready with a series of leading questions prepared for his quarry.

"It's precisely because of Juan and the others around me, we don't worry too much outside our own at-bat. We trust our teammates to pick the team up when we need it. No out and bases loaded. I was looking for something to get us back in the game."

"Yeah, well, you ended it, didn't you, Josh?" interrupted the reporter from the Gazette again before Roman could follow. Several laughed, and Josh smiled slightly underneath his camo Pirates cap. Josh's baptism with Gatorade at some point in the raucous post-game forced a shirt change after coming off the field. He wore a loose white sweatshirt cut off at the sleeves and slightly short—one of Pete's hand-me-downs. Josh also wore knee-length compression shorts covered with some Pirates loose training shorts and changed out his damp socks to put on some calf compression socks Doc Luke gave him. He was unaware his large scar, traveling down his left leg and continuing to just above his knee, was slightly visible where the compression shorts ended. As Josh changed out his socks, Roman, who commandeered a spot up front, noticed the scar, making a mental note.

"Josh, so not looking for a walk. You made some bad swings in an earlier at-bat and missed badly on a previous swing against the slider in the same at-bat. How'd you manage to not only hit the ball but hit it out?" said Roman, taking the lead back.

"I try to learn the pitchers as best I can, seeing them all for the first time as we go. Yeah, he had my number on the previous slider. I knew I would need to adapt to hit it. I figured I could either expect the slider or the fastball. Coaches always challenged me to adapt to the breaking pitches and let my body react to the fastballs. Tommy talked with me about him, and we thought his out pitch would probably be the slider as it's a good one. He got me once, but I guess I made the right adjustment."

"And you lifted it just fair on the line," said another local reporter.

"Being a righty, I know you can't do much if you get his outside slider. I just wanted to go with it. Try to put it in play. I got just enough of it but almost didn't keep it inside the foul line. I watched it for a while, curving away. But the Good Lord was helping with a little no-wind moment, and she stayed fair."

"Are you citing divine intervention then, Josh?" said Roman.

Josh, who pulled on his right sock, bent over and briefly exposed his left ab under the somewhat short sweat top. Roman observed the light scar on his dark skin, similar to the scar protruding to his knee. Could this scar be one continuous injury from his head and cheek clear to his leg? Roman pondered while waiting for Josh's response.

Josh sat up and smiled at Roman. Those dark eyes always caught people by surprise when he focused on them. Roman saw him up close for the first time, just a few feet away, dark complexion with wavy dark hair peeking out from underneath that Pirate camo hat. Chiseled face with a relatively broad nose. Everything about him made Roman think of a dark, swarthy god, fierce in form, except for those eyes. They were pools of peace, even with the scar, yet with piercing understanding. Roman found them disconcerting somehow, as if they looked right into him and, for a second, saw directly into his heart. For the first time in a very long time, Roman, ever the hunter, stalking his quarry for the story, was unnerved—exposed even. He did not like thinking this ball player might know more about who and what he was than Roman knew about him, and perhaps more than Roman cared to admit to himself. Josh stared at him knowingly. It wasn't unkind, but Roman's questions vanished from his mind, and he dropped his gaze, looking down at his digital recorder, suddenly at a loss for words.

"Or maybe it was Clemente's spirit helping you get that one over his wall, eh Josh?" said the reporter from the Post-Gazette, happy to take the initiative back from Roman while making several other reporters chuckle.

Josh turned and smiled, "Well, let's just say tonight, I am sure glad he wore 21 and not 22," referencing the height of the right field wall, which Josh's ball barely cleared. Most reporters laughed at that, and the mood softened. Roman was still off his game.

"Josh, you finally ended your consecutive hits streak at 13, but you've played five games in a row with a homer. How do you plan to keep this torrid pace going?" one of the national reporters, usually following the Cubs, asked from the back row.

"Not up to me, really. I go up with the same attitude every time. I try to see a pitch I can drive and hit it. So far, it has paid off. This is a team sport, and the team has found a way to win this season with a lot of excellent play across the board. I think we are growing as a team, trusting each other to get the job done when we each have a shot individually. Today, it was just my turn at the end. God willing, we can keep up the good focus and attitude. It's a long season. I am not thinking about streaks. Just trying to get it done and get the W."

There were a few other questions before Mark asked the reporters to wrap up all too quickly as far as they were concerned. Roman, unusually did not continue pressing with questions. He was driving blind here and needed answers of his own before he could think of better ways to come at Josh. Roman studied him contemplatively, thinking up new ideas and angles to approach this taciturn enigma whose past was still a closed book. Roman would not forget that scar—perhaps he could find out where it came from and use it to his advantage.

The evening was cold, turning blustery even as the Pirates were glad to keep their win streak going. They looked forward to tomorrow's evening game, but the weather front threatened not to cooperate.

Forty Seven

Retired Master Sergeant Gabriel "Gabe" Rodelo carefully carved the turned bowl of wood as he worked on a flower relief along one side. What started as an exercise to learn to manipulate his prosthesis where his right hand once was, turned out to be a passion and then a satisfying post-military occupation. Scattered around his shop were everything from bowls to chairs and different size tables he built and sold in a specialty store in town. He got the peace and satisfaction of building and creating his art, and the customers marveled at the handiwork of an unknown artist, once the terror of evil men around the globe, now missing his dominant hand.

Nearly ten years had passed since Gabe lost his hand and forearm in combat as one of the nation's most elite special forces. Nine months of rehab brought him back to health, but losing his right hand forced him to leave behind his beloved Green Berets and forge a different path. Like all things life threw at him, Gabe developed a sense the Creator was leading him. Even when he saw no positive future, he chose to follow, one step at a time. With the loss of his hand, Gabe walked a rocky road to recovery.

After his injury, Gabe endured painful rehabilitation and fought many demons pressing upon him. He began to rise only when he gave it all to the Master and Creator, who held all the world in His hands. He finished each piece with a small verse, discreetly applied, reminding all of God's promises for any who chose Christ. Gabe fought the good fight, every day, to hear the Lord's quiet voice and follow Him into the future. Slowly, Gabe rose out of his near brush with death and the loss of his military calling. With hope born from faith, Gabe trusted in God's promises, and in time, God showed Gabe his life still carried promise and value as a new chapter began.

Though removed from his military life, Gabe never forgot his military brothers. Shortly after his recovery at Walter Reed Hospital, Gabe began volunteering with the wounded in Virginia, where he lived. Over the years, while he talked to vets often about his recovery road, he spoke little of his military history. A quiet man like many on his team, Gabe kept the dark world of black ops a well-guarded secret from the public. It would be decades until the classification lifted when he was too old to care or already dust. His only reprieve to talk freely was those special days when one of his former teammates would visit. He always tried to stay close with his brothers even though they, too, remained private. Still, the memories were never far away, as a vivid memory would suddenly interrupt Gabe's solitary work invading his peaceful sanctuary.

As he smoothed the flower carving, his mind returned to the day he lost his hand and nearly his life in an ambush on the outskirts of Ar Ramadi, Iraq. His team saved his life that day, a story he would only learn long after the fact, as the explosion that took his right hand mercifully left him unconscious with numerous injuries. Despite multiple men wounded, Gabe's teammates performed flawlessly, saving Gabe's life in the process.

Gabe was a five-foot-eight fireplug of a platoon sergeant. In contrast, their platoon leader was a thick-chested, huge Chief Warrant Officer 4, Todd Michael, whom they all called Chief Todd. Chief was a living SOF legend, rising through the enlisted ranks in the SOF world, only deciding to become a warrant officer after making E8, Master Sergeant. Starting over, Chief Todd wound up doing another 15 years, working his way up the warrant ranks in the SOF community. The two were friends ever since the chief, as Sergeant Todd Michael, took a very green Corporal Rodelo, brand-new to SOF, under his wing when Sergeant Michael was a SOF platoon sergeant himself. Years later, Chief Todd asked Gabe back as his "old sergeant" to lead his platoon. Honored, Gabe jumped at the chance to work with a man he knew he could trust implicitly.

The two were quite the team, Chief Todd Michael, the giant leader with an unflappable demeanor, and Sergeant Gabe Rodelo, the trainer, who could chew wood and young noncoms but expertly brought out only the best in his men. As good as they were, the enemy pushed them to the limit that spring day in Iraq. The superb team came together with great skill and courage, holding off the attackers. Chief Todd would later recount to Gabe how they fought desperately until their wounded air force combat controller targeted a bomb from his high-flying comrades, uncomfortably close to their hard-pressed position, ending the attack.

Gabe often missed the camaraderie of his team but kept up as best he could, trying to offer them some view of the life to come once they left the military. Sadly, some didn't make it home, while others, like him, were now retired or moving on, civilians trying to cope, often sharing only rare conversations with a few special teammates about their true struggles. Chief Todd retired after nearly thirty-one years of service, moved back to his home state of Missouri to become a cattle rancher, and was one of the more reclusive team members. Gabe understood the desire for peaceful isolation, as the chief probably saw more bad things in the world than most people would in two lifetimes.

As Gabe stared at the fine sandpaper in his hand, almost forgetting where he was, he heard the house phone ring. Gabe kept all electronic devices out of the backyard shop and his cell phone in the house. He liked to work without distraction. Louisa, his wife, left earlier that morning to meet with some fellow master gardeners. Few knew the old landline phone number, and he walked over to see the caller ID. It carried no name, but the area code and number looked vaguely familiar, albeit one not seen in some time. He picked it up, hopeful it was his old friend.

"Hello?" Gabe said, still with a slight Spanish accent he never entirely lost.

"Gabe, it's Todd Michael. How are you doing?" his mentor's familiar voice spoke warmly.

Even though he suspected it was Chief Todd, Gabe was still pleasantly surprised. Usually, he was the one who called his old friend. Chief Todd was a private person, a man of few words. Gabe could picture him sitting a horse, quietly wandering his 70 acres tending to his small cattle farm, spending days without seeing a living soul except for his wife Hope back at the homestead.

"Great, Chief," replied Gabe, genuinely glad to hear his old mentor and friend's voice. "To what do I owe the pleasure? Everything OK with you and Miss Hope?"

"We're both doing fine, Gabe. It's been a good spring. I got several young calves birthed, and the herd is doing well. Busy but good. I know it's unusual, me calling, but I just saw something I thought you should hear."

"Oh really," Gabe responded, "What's that?"

"This may seem strange, and I know you don't do much more TV watching than I do, but I have to ask you, have you watched any of the first week of regular season baseball?" asked the chief.

"Can't say that I have. You know football was my game as a kid, and I am not talking about that American game!" It was a running joke with Todd and Gabe. Todd was a big fan of American football and baseball. On the other hand, young Gabe was something of a phenom. He played soccer for the junior national Puerto Rican team and came to mainland U.S. on a soccer scholarship. When he mentored young people, Gabe admitted he was a bit of a wild child. He would tell them how the young Gabe foolishly squandered his scholarship. Rather than returning to Puerto Rico and the slim job opportunities for a college dropout, he joined the U.S. Army. It was a perfect fit for Gabe, bringing the discipline he sorely needed and putting his mental and physical skills to use in a worthwhile endeavor. Gabe excelled as a young, enlisted man in the army. He also restarted his education about four years into his active duty time, using military tuition assistance, and eventually graduated with a bachelor's degree just before his injury.

With his medical discharge, Gabe used the GI bill, adding a master's in business to help start his successful cottage industry. He often thought of what a strange road the Lord laid for him, with the failure of his early college life, when he seemed to have lost everything given to him. He suspected the Lord saved him from going down a dark road of easy earnings and the temptations that would have come his way. Gabe viewed the military as God's path for bringing him back to a life worth living. In retrospect, the military, especially the world of special operations, and the thick of the fight, while not for most, saved Gabe, even though it cost him his hand. Gabe let God lead him down a path he would not have chosen, yet it made all the difference.

Chief Todd continued, "Yeah, well, there's no soccer going on over here in Missouri as far as I know, so I'll stick to football, American style. And baseball—you've heard of baseball? It's one of Puerto Rico's favorite pass times, remember?" The Chief always good-naturedly gave Gabe grief, but truth be told, Chief was right. Baseball was well-loved in Puerto Rico—although soccer was still king, as far as he would admit. Gabe let it slide, as he could feel the chief wanted to tell him something.

"You know I always follow the Cards when baseball season gets going." It was an understatement as the chief was notorious for wanting Gabe to get the games broadcast, at least on radio, and piped into the team rooms when they were downrange, on the off-chance they caught a break and could watch an inning or two. Gabe's comm troops always amazed him at their ability to figure out how to get the St. Louis baseball or football feeds to Chief Todd and his platoon of special operators, even in some of the most austere locations.

"Yes, Chief, I remember."

"Well, I've been out and about on the upper forty with all the spring birthing and other various cowpoke stuff, so I really have to work to hear the start of the season for the Cards. I managed to listen to them on an old transistor radio I carry with me. Long story short, they got off to a rough start against, of all teams, the lowly Pittsburgh Pirates."

"Uh huh?" said Gabe, unsure where the chief was going.

"Didn't think much about it because some rookie hit a home run in each game, and the Pirates won them all. While they said his name on the radio, it's a fairly common name and didn't register. Anyways, I got back and was out with Hope for a rare night on the town, so I set the third game to record on the DVR. As I heard they lost, I ended up not watching it, and I figured I'd pick up with their next series against Milwaukee. I did see a couple of innings of those Milwaukee games, and they won two out of three."

"That's good, Chief. At least they are almost back to .500," said Gabe, wondering idly if the chief were a little off on some of his old guy meds.

"No, No, Gabe, that's not it; I mean, 2 and 4 is not a good way to start the season, but that's not the point. I was about to delete game three with the Pirates from the opening series, but last night I heard the announcers during our game talking about the Pirates as if something big was happening over there. That's unusual for St. Louis commentators to be talking about a small-town rival to the Cards, and it seemed a little odd. When they mentioned the Rookie's name again, as I said, while it might be common, it's not *super* common," commented Todd, almost as if he dared not say the name to Gabe. Gabe thought this conversation was truly strange. Chief Todd rarely, if ever, showed any doubt or hesitation about what he needed to say. Still, Gabe waited for the chief to explain.

"You know I don't watch hardly any TV or even the internet about current events or news anymore," explained Chief Todd. It was common for many of his old teammates to have this desire to separate from current events. Gabe, too, tired of the politics of his country and the endless political babble. He often retreated from all the hubbub and political correctness as he worked in his sanctuary of wood and sawdust. He and fellow vets frequently found they no longer held much tolerance for the things constantly headlining TV, yet were of little lasting value to our world.

"I understand, Chief, but what's the problem?" said Gabe, still confused.

"Well," Chief Todd said somewhat hesitantly, finally coming to the point. "I ran the tape of the third game and watched this Pirate rookie hit another clutch home run to beat my Cards. But that's not the reason I called you. The real surprise was the rookie himself. He wasn't a young rookie, after all. He was an old rookie, and I now know why the name was so oddly familiar."

"I still don't understand?" Gabe realized he hadn't watched ten minutes of news in a month, and he certainly wasn't following baseball. What was Chief getting at?

"Gabe, this so-called rookie, is tall, dark, has a broad hooked nose, and carries a scar on his left cheek just by his eye."

Gabe paused for a moment. Something in the back of his memory was surfacing.

"Gabe, I sat and watched this guy play like, well..., like no one I have ever seen play ball. It took me two or three reruns when they showed him up close to believe it. He's older than when we last saw him, but I finally knew my eyes weren't deceiving me. Gabe, it's Flash. It's Josh Green."

Gabe tried to comprehend what Chief was saying. His last remembrance of Joshua Green, his team's only USAF member, was just before the RPG knocked him unconscious. He had been standing talking to Josh, who, looking over Gabe's shoulder, saw the RPG shooter a split second before he fired. Josh tackled Gabe barely in time to save Gabe from a direct hit from the RPG. The impact lifted them both off the ground, knocking Gabe unconscious and severing his hand. Chief Todd himself, told Gabe the rest of the story when he visited Gabe in rehab at Walter Reed some five months later. Chief Todd said the same RPG explosion that nearly ended Gabe's life and cost him his hand, ripped down Flash's own body, tearing a nasty gash down his torso and thigh, cutting like a fillet knife from his cheek almost to his knee. Their medic initially worked to stop the blood flow from Gabe's missing hand with a tourniquet, then moved to help Josh.

Chief Todd shouted orders to the team to grab defensive positions as multiple enemy fighters now fired at them from the nearby building. He thought one or both men might have been killed or were dying, but when he finally looked back, he saw an amazing sight. Gabe remembered how Chief Todd described the scene.

As their medic worked on Josh's leg, Josh held a bandage over one eye and used his push-to-talk radio with his other hand to call in his air cavalry. Josh, or "Flash" as they all called him, was a trusted and experienced teammate. Chief Todd specifically requested Josh, their combat controller from their previous deployment, as they prepared for another stint in the sandbox. As the battle raged, Chief Todd described how the entire team heard Josh's calm voice inside their headsets, vectoring aircraft on target. Those who couldn't see Josh were shocked at his extensive injuries after the battle because Josh's voice conveyed the same calm, measured directions they always heard on the radio. Chief commented how he listened to the aircrew read back the fire mission, identifying the distance between their position and the target was inside of the safe distance for dropping the weapon.

Such a "danger close" drop was used only in extreme conditions and required the ground force commander's clearance. Chief Todd knew they were in a desperate situation, and Chief turned back to Josh when the pilot asked for the commander's initials. He could see Josh's one good eye look over at him for confirmation, and Chief nodded and gave him a thumbs up. Josh passed the initials, finished the clearance, and the aircrew perfectly hammered the enemy, as they always seemed to when Josh called on his air knights to save the day, successfully ending the engagement in their favor.

But for Gabe, that day lived in his memory as a slow-motion freeze frame of Gabe's last view of Josh. Gabe remembered wondering why Josh moved lightning quick towards Gabe to tackle him without explanation, as Gabe's back was toward the enemy. Only after Chief Todd's recounting of Gabe's near-death experience did Gabe realize Josh's split-second decision saved his life. Though no one else saw, Gabe's vision remained crystal clear of the landscape near Josh in those last moments before the explosion. Frozen in Gabe's mind's eye was a short but substantial wall to Josh's side. During rehab, Gabe began to remember those last few moments before the explosion more clearly. Gabe slowly recognized

Josh made a split-second choice. Josh leaped away from the safety of the wall to tackle Gabe, exposing himself to the explosion. Chief Todd's description of what happened was unforgettable, as was the picture in Gabe's mind of the big man who willingly lept toward danger rather than dive to safety so that Gabe might live.

"Are you sure it's him, Chief?" Gabe pleaded, trying to wrap his head around it as the memory flooded back. With quiet awe in his voice, Gabe asked softly, "Are you sure it's Josh?"

"Gabe, I'll never forget the look in that man's eyes when he concentrated on bringing down fire from above, even when he only had one good one. It was the exact same look when he stared at our pitcher before blasting his pitch into orbit. It's him."

Forty Eight

T he weather turned from bad to worse overnight, as is wont to happen in Pittsburgh during the first week of April, and light snow fell during the morning hours before Saturday's game. The League quickly called for cancellation, and the Pirates suddenly received two days off before heading out again for a night road-game on Monday. Mary previously scheduled a treatment for Ruth at Children's Hospital on the University of Pittsburgh campus. Usually, they used a pediatric branch closer to their Greensburg home, but the Pittsburgh Children's Hospital included openings on weekends, and Mary and Ruth planned the treatment intending to head to the game afterward. Instead, the Arimas invited several friends from the Pirates organization, including the Greens and Mary, to celebrate the beginning of Passover with them. The three planned to head to nearby Squirrel Hill after Ruth's treatment.

Ruth's appointment was the first at the sprawling Children's Hospital campus, surrounded by Pitt University in Pittsburgh's suburb of Oakland. They took a while, asking for help from the various staff they ran into, trying to find the right office. As the season just started, few healthcare staff or patients saw much baseball, but as the three searched for their destination, providence placed them with one knowledgeable baseball fan. He was a late-twenties medical administration staff member in a wheelchair.

Adam finished talking to a young couple whose son was undergoing on-site treatment for an injury. He said goodbye and turned his wheelchair around in the hallway to look up at the Greens and Mary. Their backs were to Andrew as they studied a wall placard office listing.

"Can I help you, folks?" Adam said since they seemed lost.

Mary turned first and said, "Yes, sir. We are trying to find the physical therapy reception center. It's supposed to be here on the third floor, east side."

"You're not too far off, miss. Just follow this hallway all the way down, go through the double doors, and the reception area is immediately on your left," the man said kindly. Just as he spoke, Ruth and Josh turned to listen. The man finished his directions to Mary and looked over at the other two. His eyes opened wide when they fell upon Josh.

"You're the rookie! You're Josh Green!" he exclaimed, surprised.

Josh smiled back, "Yes, I am. Thank you for your help, Mr....?"

"Adam, I am Adam Shewtick," Adam said. He seemed slightly in shock and struggled with what to say next.

"Thank you for your help, Adam. We have an appointment we're trying to make, so I am glad you were here to direct us," said Josh kindly. Adam stared at the star player come to life. Adam could scarcely believe it. Although he used a wheelchair after a fall as a child, he was a passionate baseball fan, dreaming of the sweet science of standing in the batter's box and hitting a baseball. Adam loved the Pirates since he was a kid, and their lackluster performance during his lifetime didn't deter his passionate support. Even his family thought he was a little nuts for supporting the perennial loser. As the big man nodded at him and smiled, a brief glimpse of peaceful dark eyes mesmerized Adam.

The Greens and Mary started down the hallway, following Adam's direction, breaking his reverie. "Wait a minute," Adam waved desperately, springing into action. "Here, I'll come with you. I was planning to head there, anyway."

Adam wheeled up next to the Greens and Mary, "I don't think I have seen you folks here before," said Adam as he escorted them down the hallway after mustering his courage again to speak.

"No, you haven't," replied Josh. "We usually go for treatments closer to our home, but we expected to play a game today, and this hospital offered weekend appointments, so we thought we'd try it out."

"Well, we have some of the best PT staff in the tri-state area. I think you will be pleased," said Adam as they continued down the hall.

"What do you do here, Adam?" Josh asked politely.

"I am one of the medical administrators, Mr. Green. I've been with the hospital for nearly two decades actually, in one way or another."

"Oh, you don't look old enough," commented Mary.

"Well, miss, I started as a patient a little younger than the young lady here," said Adam, nodding toward Ruth.

"I'm Ruth," she said, "Are you a patient here too?" Ruth asked.

"Yes, and I can tell you firsthand, this hospital has wonderful people trying to help every patient who enters our doors. I felt so strongly about it I attended Pitt University to learn and work here and give back to other patients the way I received help. I stayed on as a full-time administrator when I graduated," finished Adam.

"Did you receive Physical Therapy, too?" asked Ruth.

"Yes, Ruth. I was paralyzed from the neck down from a fall when I was eight years old. Although I never recovered feeling in my legs, the PT did wonders for me, getting my upper body back into working order and giving me a chance at a better life," said Adam as they approached the double doors. He hit a button on the wall, and the doors swung inward so they could move through. They saw the PT check-in desk on the left, just as he described.

"Thanks for getting us to the appointment, Adam," Josh said and reached out to shake the man's hand goodbye, while Mary walked forward with Ruth to check in as they were just in time for the appointment.

As Adam shook his hand, he gazed up at Josh. As an avid Pirates fan, he saw all the fantastic things Josh did this season. But this was different, getting a good look at the man in person. With his dark complexion, broad, slightly hawkish nose, and wavy brown hair, Josh looked down at him. It was hard to tell where he was from, but Adam looked into those kind dark eyes, a stark contrast to his chiseled, muscular frame, and he stared as the big man shook his hand warmly. Josh's eyes reminded him of his Jewish Grandmother, Svatá Remy, and her kindness when he was a boy. The rest of Josh looked like some dark-skinned warrior out of an epic, but those eyes showed only compassion and said all would be right with Adam's world.

A young man in purple scrubs came out of a door next to them and called out Ruth's name. "We're all ready for you, Ruth," he said.

"OK, let's do this," said Ruthie, and Mary turned to walk with her back into the hallway.

As Josh turned to follow the others, Adam had a sudden inspiration and spoke before his courage failed him.

"Mr. Green, I don't suppose there's any chance you would visit with some of our hospital-bound children, could you?" The Greens and Mary turned toward the man who used a wheelchair and almost let them go. "I know it's probably a lot to ask," he hurried on before he lost his nerve, "But, well, they're the kids I work with the most, back down the hall we came from, and I was going to check on them. I just thought how excited they would be to meet a Pittsburgh Pirate star like you...," Adam said, trailing off.

Josh turned to Mary and Ruth, but before he could ask, Ruth said, "Go ahead, Dad, go see the kids. Mary can stick with me while I do my PT, and we can meet up afterwards.

Josh smiled and hugged his little girl, "You take good care of her now," he said to the scrub-clad attendant who stood expectantly holding the door, and he nodded in response.

Josh went with Adam, and a similar scene to St. Louis played out. Although Josh brought no paraphernalia with him, he wore a Pirates baseball cap, and now that he played a few games at home in Pittsburgh, several of these young people saw him on TV. When they first arrived at the ward, an idea came to Adam. There was a play area for the kids with electronic tablets to draw and print out pictures. Adam asked Josh if he could take a picture of Josh with each kid using the tablet's camera. Then he printed the photo. Josh signed each, giving each kid an autographed photo with Josh to keep. It was a big hit with many of these young patients who fought challenging medical issues. On more than one occasion, Josh talked with the parents of a child, and Adam watched as he would stop to pray a brief prayer with the patient and their family. Josh was the physical specimen of a professional athlete, thought Adam, but he seemed far more down-to-earth and very unassuming for a star athlete. In many ways, Adam thought he was not what he would have expected, and he drew in child and adult alike, seeming to understand their pain, giving words of encouragement, or just sitting and listening to their struggles.

Time flew by, thought Adam, as Mary and Ruth returned after Ruth's physical therapy. Together they exited the children's ward, and Adam escorted them toward the hospital entrance. They all said their goodbyes.

"Thank you, Josh, for all you did today. I am sure the children and families will never forget it. If you ever get a chance to bring Ruth and would like to stop and visit, please do. Our patients would love to see you again." Adam said.

Josh took and shook Adam's hand again and turned those ancient-looking kind eyes upon him. "Thank you, Adam. I am grateful for the opportunity to meet all your patients. And I hope to see you again." What a fantastic day, Adam thought as he watched them leave. Somehow, he felt he would never be entirely the same again.

Forty Nine

Warm and friendly light and the sound of laughter seemed to spill out of the Arima house doorway and roll down the front porch beckoning to the Greens and Mary when they arrived. Joe met them and welcomed them into the living room, where he, Saul, and Mark Johnson talked with J.J., Juan, Zach, Thomas, and Barney. Another guest, Nechemia Demus, the Pirate legal advisor, sat beside Joe with Pops on the other side. The Greens and Mary heard Pete and his wife in lively conversation with Beth in the kitchen. Mary decided to join Beth and was surprised to see Samson sitting at the small table from their previous visit with Andrew sitting beside him. Dwarfed by the big man, Andrew laughed at a story Pete told, with Pete's wife shaking her head, while Beth chuckled as she poured coffee. Although Samson seemed too big for the chair and teacup he held, he appeared at ease, smiling as he sipped his cup. Back in the living room, Mark made room for Ruth on the couch next to him. Ruth joined the conversation as Mark spoke with the young players, asking various baseball questions like a seasoned sports reporter for one of the city's newspapers.

"Can I get you a drink, Josh? Beth made a pot of traditional coffee just before you got here, and there should be some left if Pete and Samson haven't drunk it all," said Joe.

"Sure, I'll take a cup," replied Josh as he sat on a chair Saul pulled in from another room beside his. "Everything go all right at Children's Hospital?" asked Saul as Joe went to retrieve a coffee for Josh. Josh told him they would come straight over after Ruth's appointment.

"Yes, fine, but I wonder if you would mind having Mark load me up with some Pirates' paraphernalia, something I can carry in a bag with me," replied Josh.

"Oh?" said Saul.

"Seems like when I go with Ruthie to her appointments, I end up taking a detour to the children's ward. I'm glad to represent the team, but it would be nice to have some Pirates gear to give to the kids," said Josh.

"Hmmm, sounds like you're going to be an ambassador for us, too. You know you don't have to do anything you don't want to," said Saul looking at Josh earnestly.

"No, Pops, it's fine, a great opportunity actually, and I am glad to do it," finished Josh.

"I am sure the Pirates PR guys would love the good publicity," said Nick, who listened quietly to the two men talk as Ruthie, Mark, and the players kept their own conversations going.

"I'd rather keep it as low-key as possible. Say hello to the kids and their families and give them a brief break from everything they are going through in those wards." Josh said. The two older men nodded, and Nick looked down at his coffee, contemplating Josh and his statements. Joe returned with a coffee cup for Josh, and the smell of fresh coffee and cardamom permeated the room.

"Beth is almost ready with the meal, so I will go and prepare for the Seder," Joe said, leaving the group to themselves. They discussed the team, the upcoming trip, and their families and friends. Soon Beth came into the room and invited everyone into the dining room. The Arimas made one alteration to the house when they first purchased it: the dining room. They combined two rooms into one large room with a long table accommodating over twenty guests. Gracefully aging, Joe and Beth entertained many celebrations over their younger years, including Joe's clients and some of the city's various charitable organizations.

Though they slowed recently, the Arimas could still host quite a dinner. Joe welcomed everyone, dressed in his Kittel, a traditional white linen robe, and Beth donned a modest head covering. Joe asked Josh and Ruth if Ruth would mind reading the child's portion of the Seder and welcomed her to sit beside him. He also gave all the guests a script to join in as the Seder progressed.

Joe began, "My friends, thank you for coming tonight. I know you planned to be playing baseball, but since Yahweh has seen fit to give us the day off with some late winter weather, I thank you for coming to celebrate Passover with us. As Christian Jews celebrating Passover, you should know that we gladly welcome you all as our friends, Jew or Gentile, regardless of your beliefs. Beth has created a wonderful meal, but first, we will celebrate the traditional Passover Seder ceremony. As Messianic Jews, we also celebrate the Lord's supper and His death and resurrection, which occurs next Sunday this year. Passover is a remembrance of when the Lord saved his people and foreshadowed Christ saving us on the cross. The little program we distributed is something Beth and I use and incorporates part of Haggadah, the traditional Jewish text for the Seder of Passover, plus the relevant biblical verses from the Old and New Testaments. We know many of you are new to this, and you can certainly just watch as we conduct the Seder, but if you would like to participate, please do. The script will lead you along."

Joe watched as Beth lit the two candles of observance and remembrance. After lighting the candles, Beth waved her hands over them three times and, covering her eyes, sang the following prayer in Hebrew and repeated it in English, found on the pamphlets so all present would know the words. "Blessed are You, Lord our God, King of the Universe, Who sanctified us with His commandments, and commanded us to be a light to the nations and who gave to us Jesus our Messiah the light of the world."

Joe thanked Beth, then directed everyone to the script. "We drink four glasses of wine or grape juice, if you choose, during the Seder, the first being the cup of blessing or sanctification. This Kiddush means to set apart or make holy when the Lord said He would take Israel out from bondage in Egypt." Joe then sang the blessing also in Hebrew and repeated it in English, "Blessed art thou O God, King of the Universe, Creator of the fruit of the vine." Joe continued to lead the group through the Seder. For many of the guests, this was their first time celebrating Passover. Some found it fascinating and were occasionally surprised by the form or content. However, Joe kept it light with the occasional explanation, often reminding people of the extensive use of symbology in both the meal and the actions, such as washing their hands. "Remember Jesus washed His disciple's feet—I won't make you take off your socks. We will stick to our hands," said Joe with a twinkle in his eye. Ruth particularly liked reading the ten plagues during the cup of the plagues and the loud-sounding of each plague as Joe encouraged everyone to repeat them loudly as he read. "You see, when we Jews are children, our elders teach that all sin comes with great cost, for though God is loving, He is also just. Only Christ's perfect sacrifice could pay the penalty for our sins."

To many, the salty water, parsley, and horseradish tastes seemed odd compared to the sweet taste of the charoset and sweet wine. Joe explained how each represented part of the escape from Egypt and bondage. Even the three pieces of Matzah, or unleavened bread, bore an apparent reference to the sacrifice of Jesus. The middle of the three Matzah pieces, representing the trinity, was broken, just as Christ, the Messiah, must come to be sacrificed on the cross, an atonement for our sins. As Christ was in death, hidden, until resurrected on the third day, Joe left briefly to hide the piece of bread wrapped in a cloth bag called a Matzah Tosh for Ruth to find later. This tradition, Joe said, represented Christ's death, burial, and resurrection when we find Christ, and the bread is then passed to all to eat. Amazingly, this Seder tradition, though not specified in Exodus, the book of Jews escaping Egypt, was already in place by Christ's time, the symbolic prophecy of what Christ would do before Jesus came and fulfilled all the Old Testament prophesies.

As Joe and his guests completed the first half of the ceremonial portion of the Passover, Beth brought out the meal with Mary's assistance. It began with traditional hard-boiled eggs in an egg drop soup, then some matzo ball chicken soup, and finally, Beth brought roasted lamb with vegetables and a sweet chili brisket. Beth also served something she called Miriam's red cabbage and artichoke, a delicious vegetable side that went well with both main dishes. Finally, a dessert of dried fruit compote of peaches, apples, and dates delightfully finished the meal. To those new to Passover, the meal was a somewhat strange but delicious mix of tastes and delights.

Joe finished by helping Ruth, hinting where he hid the missing piece of matzo or "lost Afikomen." As was the tradition, Ruth happily traded it for the gift, Saul's rookie baseball card, which Saul then signed for her. Joe began to complete the Seder with the Tzanfun, breaking the found Afikomen and giving it to anyone who wanted to partake. He explained it represented Christ breaking the bread with His disciples, saying, "This was His body which is for you," and reading the biblical text. Joe followed this with Baruch, the third cup or the cup of redemption. He read how Christ told His disciples, "This cup is the new covenant in My blood which is shed for you." Followed by the Hallel, the fourth cup, known as the cup of restoration, which Christ said He would not drink until He returns and restores all Israel.[1] Joe finished, "This cup represents our great hope someday soon, the Messiah will come back to take His followers to be with Him and to restore the kingdom and promises He made to the nation, Israel." They finished by reading First Thessalonians[2] and the second coming of Christ.

Finally, Joe said, "As is traditional, I end Seder with this shout, 'Next year in Jerusalem!' Thank you all for celebrating Passover with us."

The teammates and friends continued to talk well into the evening about all the things they saw, discussed, and remembered with Joe and Beth that evening, an evening few of them anticipated but cherished the experience and friendship just the same.

Ruth, Josh, and Mary helped the Arimas clean up after most guests departed. Ruth, ever the inquisitive type, asked Josh something she thought about as Mary, Joe, and Beth washed dishes in the kitchen.

"Dad, I enjoyed coming here to celebrate with the Arimas tonight, but do you have to be Jewish to celebrate Passover?"

"That's an interesting question, hon. What do you think?" Josh replied.

"Well, I guess, since we're Christian, we believe Passover represents God's protection and plan for our lives."

"Yes, I think that's right, and it's also His provision for us as well. Like Joe explained when we started tonight, Israel was justified through faith by applying the blood to the doorposts and trusting that God would protect them from the

---

1. Matthew 26: 26-29; Mark 14: 22-25; Luke 22 19-20

2. 1 Thessalonian 4:13-18

angel of death in Egypt. So too, we are justified through faith in Christ for what He did on the cross. In the Seder, we see the Jewish tradition of remembering the sacrifice of the lamb and the blood that was shed. Even in its very form, Joe showed in the Seder—this was Israel looking forward to the sacrifice Christ would make on their behalf—the perfect sacrifice, one time for all."

"So, the blood on the doorposts represented Christ's blood on the Cross?" Ruth confirmed.

"Yes, Ruth. Without Christ's perfect sacrifice, there's no salvation. Christ was the perfect lamb who paid the price for all our mistakes. Now, God sees His Son's perfection when He looks at us if we accept Him as savior. Remember, the angel of death did not look inside the houses with blood on their doorpost to see if the people were worthy of life or even if they were Jews. This symbolized how God the Father sees only His Son's righteousness when He looks at us if we accept Christ as our savior. Christ's blood makes us worthy even more than the blood on the doorposts meant those inside received life. In simplest terms, Christ died and rose , so we might live a new life forever with Him, as his blood redeems us from all our sin," replied Josh.

"I guess we can remember Israel's salvation and freedom from Egypt the same way we remember Christ rising from the dead on Easter," stated Ruth.

"That's right," Josh continued. "The salvation from the angel of death in Egypt pointed to Christ's sacrifice on the cross. His sacrifice wouldn't just save the nation of Israel from the one-time slavery of Egypt but would offer salvation for all time, saving us from the slavery of sin and death and God's just wrath upon us because of our sins. If we believe and put our trust in Jesus, we too can receive salvation and become children of God."

"Does that mean Passover can be a time for all to remember God's promise to send Jesus, and Easter is a time for remembering Jesus fulfilled that promise?" asked Ruth.

"Exactly right," said Josh.

Finally, it was time to leave. Elizabeth escorted the girls to the car with some goody bags as Josh paused on the porch to thank Joe for inviting them to the Seder and Passover observance. "Joe, it is so good to do Passover again. It's a joy and privilege to sit down, break bread with fellow believers, and worship the Lord. This is the first time I have brought Ruth, and it was an enjoyable evening and a chance for her to learn from you and Elizabeth."

Joe replied, "Josh, it is always a pleasure for Elizabeth and I to have company for Passover. Thank you for the wonderful explanation of Christ and Passover. I've often tried to explain this to others, but you did so clearly and concisely. We could use such understanding in our church and our community."

Josh responded, "Ruth and I have been looking for a church since we moved into the area. We haven't found one we fit into well."

"Elizabeth and I attend Shoresh David Messianic Congregation in Monroeville, PA. You would all be welcome to come. It's probably about a thirty-five-minute drive from your home in Greensburg," offered Joe.

"Joe, I think we would like that very much. Send me the address and times, and Ruthie and I, and probably Mary, will come visit," Josh said happily, shaking Joe's hand.

As they rode home, Ruth found new joy in understanding Passover and Easter, with each celebrating God's perfect plan of salvation. In all, it was a wonderful, blessed day.

Fifty

The Pirates set out on a ten-game road trip to the west coast the following Monday. The first stop was LA, as the Pirates faced a Major League powerhouse, the Los Angeles Dodgers. They won the first game as Samson Gibson pitched another stellar outing for his second win of the season, and Josh hit a two-run homer in the sixth to score the only two runs of the game. However, in game two, the Pirates suffered their first loss of the season, as the Dodgers blew out Pittsburgh early with six runs in the first two innings, winning 10-1. Josh's hitting streak ended with his first "O-for" game going 0-3. With the early blowout, Josh never stood a chance to do much damage, and Pops was hoping it might pay off with better pitches for him the next day. The Pirates came back to win the third game 5-4, and Josh collected three of the five RBIs with two timely doubles. Josh sprinkled five hits in 12 at-bats over the first three games, dropping his overall average considerably, but still managed five of the runs batted in for the first and third games, with timely hits. After the second double in game three, the Dodgers walked Josh in his last two at-bats. Still, the West Coast reporters looked for a sign of weakness as Josh managed just two hits in the previous two games. The Pirates would play the fourth and final game before a max-capacity crowd on a glorious LA Friday afternoon.

Before the 4:15 PM start, Ruth, Mary, and Josh visited Children's Hospital of Orange County, or CHOC, as it was known, for Ruth's treatment. Even though these visits were to new facilities, they seemed to become almost routine, as Nurse Richards from St. Louis stayed faithful to her word and worked with Mary to set up the appointments well in advance. As far as Mary was concerned, Nurse Richards was a godsend, but Mary began to notice Nurse Richards also wanted to know if Josh would accompany Ruth to the appointments. Mary suspected Nurse Richards was telling her hospital colleagues they could persuade Josh to visit the inpatient children, who could do with some cheering up. When Mary hinted at this to Josh, he smiled and said he enjoyed meeting the kids. Mark Johnson set them up with a bag of Pirate goodies Josh now knew to bring along in anticipation of the visits. Sure enough, when they got to CHOC, Ruth got ushered into her physical therapy session as Josh got corralled into a visit to a children's ward. Josh provided the same kind, gentle greetings with the children and their families. Mary noticed Josh often came across a family or two with a very sick child. Josh would talk with the family and offer to pray with them over their child, and the families often welcomed Josh's prayers.

Pops pulled Andrew and Josh into his office when they showed up for the game. "Gents, I want to try something a little different today. I want to start Josh third in the lineup and you fourth, Andrew. I want to make them think hard about pitching around Josh, and right now, you're hitting .348, Andrew, second only to Josh in the League. With J.J. and Zach hitting over .300 up front and getting on base, this makes it difficult to walk Josh and then have to pitch to you and Juan."

The Captain, as usual, was all about what was best for the team. "Sounds fine, Pops. Let's mix it up and see what happens."

The game began on a glorious California day, with both teams starting young pitchers for the final of their four-game series. Zach slapped a single back over the pitcher's head to center to start the game. J.J. worked a long at-bat but eventually popped out to foul territory on a 2-2 pitch. The stadium announced Josh, and the crowd gave more than a few catcalls as he walked to the plate. He took his customary kneeling prayer position, bringing more boos and jeers. Josh watched the first pitch, a high outside fastball, for ball one. The pitcher came back with a hard fastball clocking 98 MPH at the knees but still just outside, and Josh again passed for a 2-0 count. It looked like the Dodgers would pitch around Josh. However, their approach changed abruptly on the next pitch. Whether it was the lineup change and Andrew's hitting after Josh or the young pitcher simply made a mistake, he delivered a changeup on the outside corner, perhaps thinking the look of the fastball would fool Josh. Josh, as usual, was not fooled and made an even smooth stroke, connecting with the pitch and lifting it into right field. It didn't clear the right field fence by much, but it was a home run nonetheless, giving the Pirates a 2-0 lead. The Pirates sent seven men to the plate in the first, but the Dodgers ended the inning without another run when Thomas grounded into an inning-ending double play.

Meanwhile, the Dodgers scored a run in both the first and the second inning, and their pitcher settled down in the second to record a 1-2-3 inning, bringing Josh up to start the third inning. The pitcher and catcher adhered to their pre-game plan using what worked against Josh in the first three games. For this at-bat, he started Josh with a fastball on the inside. The young pitcher threw upper 90s power, and the lively two-seam fastball would stifle most players. Josh moved his hips swiftly through the pitch, placing the bat's barrel squarely on the hard fastball, yanking it deep to left. Josh's drive rocketed into the Dodgers' left field bleachers just a few rows from the top for another home run, putting the Bucs back on top 3-2. Again, Andrew and Juan both got hits, and this time, Judah doubled them home, and the Pirates' advantage was 5-2. Judah's hit chased the Dodgers' starting pitcher to the showers.

With some of the best depth in the League for relief pitchers, the Dodgers brought on one of their better middle relievers and stemmed the tide by retiring the next three Pirates to end the inning. The Dodgers countered in the bottom of the third with a three-run homer of their own. It was beginning to look like batting practice for both teams. The Pirate starter was gone after two more dodgers reached base, and the Pirates reliever gave up another run before getting the third out, making the score 6-5 Dodgers to start the fourth inning. Both relievers did well with a quick 4th inning that saw three up and three down for both sides.

J.J. started the fifth with an infield single, bringing Josh back to the plate. Again, the Dodgers were reluctant to put Josh on with a walk as both Andrew and Juan were two for two behind him. The middle reliever stayed away from Josh, working a curve and fastball off the plate. Josh decided to swing at the curve and missed it cleanly, as it was too far outside to reach. Perhaps, confident that he may have found a weakness, the pitcher threw another curve, just catching the outside of the plate, breaking low out of the strike zone. For most, it would have been another miss, but Josh's range was far greater than seemed possible, and bending his knee lower than his usual swing, he picked the ball up below the knees, lifting it down the right field line. It was reminiscent of the foul line hugging home run he hit in Pittsburgh a week earlier, staying just fair but dropping nicely, like a 345-foot golfed nine iron, into the fourth-row seats in right field, just beyond the reach of the right fielder. As the Dodgers and their fans moaned, hanging their heads, Josh circled the bases with his third home run in as many at-bats on the day.

The seesaw game continued as the Dodgers scored a run in both the 5th and 6th inning, taking back the lead 8-7 in the seventh. The Dodgers were on their third pitcher, a reliever who pitched well in the blowout game and got Josh out twice with a weak ground out and Josh's only strikeout of the season. He was a hard-throwing righty with a lot of action on his fastball and an excellent changeup.

Zach caught the Dodger third basemen flatfooted and dropped a perfect bunt for a base hit to start the seventh. The Dodger faithful responded to the tension, cheering loudly against J.J. The Dodger pitcher responded with two very good fastballs for strikes. J.J. did not catch up with either and was looking for another fastball when the pitcher dropped his sinking changeup. J.J. swung far out in front and over the wicked pitch, striking out. Now came Josh's turn. The question was, would the Dodgers pitch to him or walk him and go after Andrew?

The catcher discussed this scenario with his pitcher before the inning started, and they decided to throw outside of the strike zone to see if Josh would chase. If he didn't, they would walk him. If he did, then they would go after him.

The pitcher started with a high fastball, out of the zone. Josh saw and swung at a similar pitch in the second game and missed, and he did so again. The pitcher was confident and threw his changeup pitch down and outside, and Josh chased it into the dirt for strike two. Both pitches looked to have fooled Josh, like his misses in game two, against this same pitcher. The next pitch was another fastball high and outside, but Josh let it go for ball one. Perplexed, the pitcher threw another changeup in the dirt. It was just off the ground, and Josh swung at it, fouling it off weakly to the right side. The pitcher and catcher went after Josh, thinking his slow reaction to the off-speed pitch might mean he would be too slow for another fastball in the zone. They were wrong. Josh was waiting for a pitch he could hit, and this was the first he saw. The fastball clocked 100 MPH on the outside corner shoulder-high, and Josh hammered the delivery with an earsplitting "CRAACCCKK." It flew with minimal elevation, a solid high-speed bullet, into the Pirates bullpen in right field. Josh now tied a select list of Major Leaguers for the record of four home runs in a single game.

In the bottom of the eighth, the Dodgers would again strike back with a two-run homer, and the fans exploded as they wrested the lead back, 10-9. The Pirates were down to their last at-bats in the top of the ninth. Judah, their number seven batter, was first up, flying out to left field. Thomas then grounded out to short. They were down to their last out, and Pops went with a pinch hitter for the pitcher. Nathan Fisher, who Pops gave the night off after going 0-8 in the series, responded with a clutch pinch-hit, doubling neatly to left-center. That brought up the top of the order. Zach hit a ball deep into the hole at short, just beating out the throw for an infield single. Fisher, not known for his speed, held at second. J.J. came to bat, wanting a hit to score the run. He delivered a great at-bat, fighting off several wicked pitches with two strikes and finally drawing a walk, somehow laying off a cutter breaking barely outside the strike zone, much to the Dodger fans' dismay.

The Pirates radio broadcast booth called this incredible, action-packed game, with emotions on both sides running high.

"Good grief, Greg! Could we get any more drama than this? In a game where both sides exploded for 24 total hits, it's been back-and-forth play. Now Josh Green comes to the plate as one of very few players in baseball history with a chance to hit five home runs in a single game," announced Bob.

"I don't know what to think, Bob. If it were any other situation, the Dodgers would certainly walk him here, but a walk now means the tying run scores. Unbelievable. What do you do with Green here, Bobby?"

"I don't know, partner, but the 57,000 fans in the stadium either want a strikeout, or they are screaming bloody murder over that ball four call to J.J.," stated Bob.

"Let's recap, folks," explained Greg. "Josh Green delivered a career performance today, by anyone's book. Our stat man tells us he's just the nineteenth MLB player to hit four homers in a single game to go along with his seven RBIs. He comes to bat with two outs, top of the ninth, bases loaded, and the Pirates down by a run. The Dodgers' fans are looking for an out to end the game. For the Pirates, a hit or a walk here would mean at least a tie game, but let's face it, folks, Josh has the chance to become the first player to hit five homers in a single game. Heavens to Betsy, Bob, I can't take the pressure!"

"Maybe you shouldn't watch, Greg, 'cause if you have a heart attack, I'm not giving you mouth-to-mouth!" exclaimed Bob.

"Well, if Josh hits a home run, I think this entire stadium might need CPR. Listen to 'em yell!"

Josh entered the batter's box with a calm, relaxed stance amid the storm of excitement from the crowd. Like the St. Louis and Chicago catchers before him, the Dodgers catcher looked sideways up at Josh and felt unsettled at what he saw. Josh was a man unlike any they faced before. The catcher wanted to believe their closer, an all-star in two of the last three seasons, could beat this batter, but in his heart, he doubted. He called for a high fastball, typically one of his pitcher's best first-strike pitches. The pitcher nodded and began his delivery, rearing back and throwing a piercing fastball to the top inside corner of the strike zone.

"Here's the pitch!" Bob bellowed excitedly.

Josh did not hesitate or wait for a better pitch. For him, it was like a bolt of lightning coursed through his veins as he swung harder and faster than ever since returning to baseball. The sound of the bat barrel contacting the ball was truly otherworldly. Even with the crowd yelling at fever pitch, it was unforgettable.

"KAAAPPPPPOOOWW!"

"OH—MY—SOUL!" shouted Bob in a slowed-down incredulous monotone. "GREEN, CRUSHES IT! DEEP to LEFT CENTER, It's High! It's Fair! It's OUTTA HERE! Holy Moly! It just went CLEAN out of the STADIUM!"

"Goodness gracious, Bob. Have you ever seen the likes?" Greg said, completely awestruck.

"No," Bob said, shaking his head and pausing in near disbelief to watch the scene for a few moments, "Not ever."

Both announcers were struggling for ways to convey what they witnessed. As Josh rounded the bases, Bob finally added, "You know, Greg. I've read about our own Willie Stargell hitting a ball here that left the stadium on the fly. The farthest ever hit here—until now, that is. The Statcast® is showing..., WHAT?! Oh, my goodness, can that be possible? Look at that, Greg!"

"What? What is it?" asked Greg, still stunned by what he saw and heard.

"562 Feet!" replied Bob.

"WHAT!?" Greg said, genuinely astonished.

Bob continued to read the Statcast's® mind-blowing numbers. "The pitch came in clocked at 101 MPH. It exited at, get this folks, 120.6 MPH! and traveled 562 Feet! That's got to be a record," Bob stated, sitting back in his chair, shaking his head in stunned disbelief.

"I've never seen anything..., No, Bobby, I should say I have never even *heard* anything like it. That sound when Green hit it. OUCH, the poor bat. Say, Bob, I remember reading Don Sutton, the Hall of Fame pitcher for the Dodgers, comment on our great one, Wilver Dornell Stargell's home run in '69 you mentioned. Do you remember what he said?

"No, Greg, but did that ever stop you from telling us?"

Greg ignored him and continued, "He said Willie didn't just hit pitchers. He took away their dignity. That's what Green just did today, folks. The sound of that hit made me think someone shot a gun! It was incredible. Heart-stopping comes to mind. The Dodgers and their fans appear absolutely deflated. They have the look of a team defeated," observed Greg.

Josh completed his home run trot, and his teammates mobbed him as soon as he passed the on-deck circle. The stadium crowd took on the look of zombies, unsure what to do. Some stood still while others fell back into their seats, gobsmacked, holding both hands to their heads, dumbfounded over what happened.

"Well, folks, the Pirates have just taken back the lead, 13-10, over a stunned Dodger team and crowd. Once again, Josh Green turned from being just good enough in the first three games of this series, into something out of this world. Oh yeah, and don't forget. Green just did something no one in baseball history has ever done. He's now the first Major League player to hit five home runs in a single game," exclaimed an incredulous Bob, pausing for effect. "*Ever!*"

The Pirates ended the game in the bottom of the ninth with a 1-2-3 inning. Perhaps it was good relief pitching finally for the Bucs, but it almost felt like the result of the Dodgers getting blasted by a colossal blow none of them believed possible.

Fifty One

The post-game interviews of Josh started on the field as SportsNet LA® announcer, a former Dodgers star, corralled Josh as he trotted in from the outfield after the game's final out.

"Josh, can we get a couple of questions with you, please?" the announcer asked.

Josh looked to Coach Saul, and Pops nodded his OK to speak to the reporter. Josh changed direction, walking over to the broadcaster.

"Josh, you just came off the field after a historic day in the batter's box," Orel led, opening the interview. "Five home runs in a single game, the first time in Major League Baseball history. How does it feel?".

"Well, Orel, it feels slightly surreal, to be honest. It was an incredible day for me and a great day for the team. I am excited to contribute to another hard-fought win," replied Josh.

"Yes, but Josh, no one has ever hit the ball like you did today. How do you do it?" the reporter pushed Josh to answer.

"Well, every at-bat is different. I felt locked in during batting practice today, and it carried over to the game. It was probably the best I have seen the ball all year."

"Josh, your last hit, in particular, was a tape-measure shot. Can you talk about it?"

"Yes. He threw me a high, inside fastball, but it was in the strike zone. One thing I try to do is take advantage of the good pitches to hit."

"But it was a 101 MPH fastball on the inside corner Josh; is that what you call a good pitch to hit?" the reporter interjected.

"You don't see a lot of hittable pitches from this reliever. I thought I could put the barrel of the bat on this one, and, like all fastballs I swing at, it's reactionary. I saw it pretty well, but I needed to swing hard to catch up with it. It's just pure muscle memory at that point," replied Josh.

"To the tune of 563 feet," continued the reporter. "That's the longest home run ever recorded by the Statcast® system—in any Major League stadium, not just here."

"Wow," said Josh, surprised. "That's amazing. You know, the pitch's high-speed, inside position required my best, my fastest swing. You try to match velocity and timing. Plus, I had to shift a little inside to get the barrel where it needed to be, so I twisted my core hard. Honestly, it's kind of, 'he's throwing so hard, I have to rev my swing up a notch.' Either it's a big whiff, and I give everyone a big laugh, or I connect, and...," Josh said, shrugging his shoulders. "It sure was fun to connect!" he finished, smiling back at the reporter. As Josh made his latest remark, J.J. and Juan snuck around behind him with a drink cooler. Before he could ask another question, Orel sidestepped away, escaping the deluge of cold beverage raining down on Josh.

Coming back into frame, the reporter said, "It seems like even your teammates think what you did today was pretty special, Josh."

"I should have followed you on that one," Josh laughed while trying to shake off the cold dripping drink. Someone threw him a towel from off-camera as the interview continued.

"What about the five homers today, Josh? No one's ever hit five in a game before. What do you have to say to opposing pitchers in the Pirates' future?" asked the reporter.

"Tomorrow's a new day. You get another chance to earn it. Each at-bat is another opportunity, but the only guarantees are from the Lord, win or lose. Today, however, was fun. It feels like being a kid in little league again, where you have that one perfect game. I thank my teammates and the good Lord for letting me play such a wonderful game. I mean, you saw it today on both sides–everyone having fun but the pitchers," Josh said with a good-natured grin. "Putting on a good show for the fans. What a great day–what a great game. Anything can happen. You gotta love baseball."

"You're hitting over .500 right now, Josh. You lead the League in homers and RBIs as well; it seems like you're earning it and having fun at the same time."

"Hopefully, we can continue putting Ws on the board as we move forward. I am glad to get 3 out of 4 wins to start this road trip, and I hope we can keep it going." Josh shivered, and he tried to towel off.

"OK, thanks, Josh. I guess we ought to let you go clean up after getting that cold shower. There you have it, folks," Orel said, speaking into the camera. "Josh Green of the first-place Pittsburgh Pirates after his historic day at the plate. Five home runs in a single game. No one has ever done that before. What will Josh Green do next?"

Josh dodged the locker room interviews thanks to the Gatorade deluge, much to the chagrin of the clamoring press. However, Roman Josephus, the SPNN reporter who followed the Pirates, cornered Mark Johnson after the interviews with Pops and a few other players ended. "Mark, my network wants to interview Josh Green one-on-one. We are televising the Sunday game you have in San

Francisco. How about an interview, either tomorrow after practice or before the game? Just give me fifteen minutes?"

"Roman, you know Pops does not like making the players face the press outside the normal team interview periods."

"Mark, c'mon man, this is not a normal situation. Green's playing at a historic pace. We've never even met the guy until this season. Even outside the sporting world, the public wants to know Green better. What are you guys trying to hide?" Roman half pleaded, half coerced.

Mark wanted to say that he was trying to keep Josh from the vultures, like Roman, but he refrained. "We are trying to let a rookie focus on baseball, Roman, that's all," he said.

"The Pirates will have to let him speak eventually," responded Roman. "Look, Mark. I promise, just a basic background story. Nothing too deep. Just give the fans something about him. It'll be good for him and the Pirates. Besides, you know the League deal with SPNN guarantees exclusive access and team interviews for our 'Game of the Week.' You're not coming close to meeting those obligations, and the League contract specifies granting these interviews," pressed Roman.

"I'll talk to Coach Samuelson and see what I can do, Roman," responded Mark, knowing Roman would do whatever it took to get the story, regardless of what Coach said or Mark wanted.

"You'll call me after you get into the hotel in San Francisco?" Roman kept on him.

"I'll call you after we get in, but no guarantees on the interview time," Mark said over his shoulder as he walked out.

"Sooner or later, he will have to talk to the public, and you're at that point where the reporters will start camping out everywhere he goes!" warned Roman.

Mark didn't answer back, but for everything Roman was, in this case, he was correct. They could not head off the press forever. Better to choose the time and place, or risk one not of their choosing. Mark didn't want Josh to get blindsided. He would have to talk to Coach Saul on the short flight from LA to San Francisco.

The Pirate team was happy but tired as they boarded the flight at LA International Airport bound for San Francisco. Mark flagged Pops down and asked to sit with him to discuss some team business on the way. Pops had an inkling of what was coming, as he could tell the media was at a fever pitch after Josh's incredible game. Even for a seasoned baseball veteran and coach, Pops was in unfamiliar territory. The Pirates were now 9-1, with the entire Pirates organization caught up in the Josh Green story. The story was difficult to contain for the first nine games, but Josh's historic five home run game elevated the situation to national news. There was little time to think after finishing at the ballpark, but Pops saw highlights of the game on the airport TV. The reoccurring story was two-fold; Josh's record-breaking performance; Josh's appearance seemingly out of nowhere.

Tomorrow was an off-day, which Pops planned to use for light practice at the opposing field. They scheduled the 1-5 PM timeframe with the Giants organization to run their usual off-day practice drills. Pops feared practice, normally a time for the team to decompress away from reporters, would become a media circus trying to get Josh for comments and interviews. Pops felt trapped, afraid things were building to a head no matter what he did. As he achieved the success he always dreamed of, Pops' unease grew, and though he tried to shrug it off, he couldn't get rid of the feeling it was all going to slip away. As the plane took off, Mark began the discussion. "Coach, we need to figure out a new game plan with Josh and the media...."

Fifty Two

San Francisco, the City by the Bay, sparkled beautifully in the Pacific moonlight as the plane touched down. It was a short flight from LA, and it barely gave enough time for Mark Johnson to convince Coach Saul to let Roman interview Josh before practice. Pops didn't like Roman forcing the Pirates into granting the interview, and he certainly didn't trust Roman's motivations, but SPNN's contractual rights left the Pirates little choice. Saul also knew the press wouldn't let a story this big go. Hopefully, Pops could limit Josh's exposure to this fifteen-minute interview, and they could get back to baseball.

Mark met Josh, Ruth, and Mary at the baggage claim after talking with Pops on the plane and calling his counterpart at the San Francisco Giants. The Giants confirmed their press area could accommodate a more one-on-one interview for the SPNN fifteen-minute talk with Roman. Mark told Josh he would have to arrive at the stadium early for the promised interview. Josh seemed to take it all in stride. Mark called Roman, gave him the details, and told him to call the Giants' PR man to finalize the setup for the interview.

The next day, Josh arrived as requested and changed his clothes into his practice uniform while Mark waited to lead him the short distance to the interview area. Pops wanted Josh dressed to practice and purposely scheduled the interview close to the start, limiting Roman's opportunity to extend the interview time. Mark sat in the posh players' locker area, reviewing some paperwork in a business folder he always carried containing his notepad and appointment scheduler while Josh got ready. As Mark poured over the schedule, he noticed Josh dressed, then bent to tie his shoes and remained kneeling, praying silently for some time. Mark could not hear any words from Josh, but he could see Josh seemed deep in thought and conversation with God. Mark wondered what weighed so heavily on the man to pray such an earnest prayer. Surely, his play these last days would make him an overwhelming fan favorite for the interview and subsequent sports press to follow, yet Josh seemed to pray fervently for help and guidance. Did he know something of troubles to come, Mark himself did not? Mark's unease increased, yet he knew he did all he could and must hand it over to Josh and the Lord. As

Josh finally finished his prayer, Mark said a silent prayer, "Let this interview go well, Lord," and watched as Josh stood up.

"Ready to go?" Mark asked Josh, trying to sound relaxed. He was not successful.

"I am now," said Josh placing his hand comfortingly on Mark's shoulder. Mark would never forget this moment as Josh gazed at him with ancient, kind eyes, dark pools of wisdom, and a gentle smile of a man at peace. "Lead on, Mark."

Roman, for his part, held a well-formed plan of attack. He was a shrewd man and knew to ride this story from the small-time sports market into national news, he needed to turn Josh into a story with staying power. Josh's fantastic game yesterday burned hot in the country's imagination, but knowing their attention would soon move on, Roman must seize his national audience with a more lasting story. He ruthlessly planned to catch the wave of public interest in any way possible and ride it to national syndication. The public was a fickle customer, and his window of opportunity would vanish quickly. Roman needed something more than a player on a hot streak, for it must inevitably end. No one could maintain Josh's numbers for long.

Roman coveted lasting power. He would create a story to titillate the temperamental public and lift him out of small Pittsburgh, vaulting him to the national stage. The easiest path to news glory was controversy. Josh's superb play was just the setup. Roman's prodigious news nose smelled a deeper story here, with this 38-year-old rookie phenom from nowhere, and where there was smoke, he could make fire. He prepared his questions to pull information from Josh and expose any secrets the man held; the more sensational, the greater the chance to pique public interest. Of course, his game plan included simple setup questions to put his quarry at ease, including a syrupy introduction of flattery to pump up Josh's ego. Josh Green didn't know it, but he was a lamb led to the slaughter, thought Roman. "You're my ticket to the big show Mr. Green, and I will make sure you get me there, one way or the other."

Roman smiled warmly as Mark and Josh entered. Mark always thought Roman looked like something of a painted doll. His beard was exquisitely groomed and carved, like a precise work of art. His dark hair slicked back. He was small in stature with a bronze tan complexion any European vacationing in Monaco would proudly display. His hooked nose, deep-set, coal-dark eyes, and trim beard gave Roman a mysterious, shifty look. Coupled with his ornately made, expensive, three-piece suit, Mark always thought Roman looked out of place in a baseball locker room, like a diminutive crime boss missing his henchmen. Mark knew, henchmen or no, Roman was dangerous, just as likely to slide a stiletto between your ribs as smile at you.

"Mark, Josh, thanks so much for coming." Roman smiled as he shook Mark's hand, and Josh followed him into the room.

Mark shook Roman's hand firmly and held him momentarily as Josh turned to shut the door. "Thanks, Roman. Please remember to keep it to fifteen minutes. I need to get Josh back to the team for practice."

"No problem, my man," Roman said with an insincere, perfect, white-toothed smile. "We'll get Josh miked up with our soundman here, get the interview, and get you back to playing ball in no time!"

Roman ushered Mark to a table in the back of the room as the techs set up for the interview. Mark noted they turned down the room's overhead lights, and although he could see Josh and Roman clearly, Josh could only see Roman as the angle of the camera lights would blind Josh from seeing Mark. He suspected it was Roman's way of isolating his interviewee, despite the fact he and several technicians were nearby in the room.

Once the soundman finished placing the mikes on Roman and Josh, they did a quick soundcheck. Roman and Josh sat in business chairs with a low table between them with two mugs of water filled from a cooler off-camera in the room's corner. When the technician determined all was in proper working order, he told the two men they were ready to start. Even though it was not to be a live interview, they recorded it as such, giving the men a countdown for Roman to begin with an introduction so SPNN could air it during their prime-time sports center broadcast later that day. The soundman counted down from five, and Roman began.

"Good evening, folks. This is Roman Josephus reporting from San Francisco, where the Pittsburgh Pirates continue their west coast road trip starting tomorrow with our game of the week on SPNN at 6 PM Pacific. The Pirates are on a hot streak, taking 3 of 4 in LA against the Dodgers, and we have a real treat today. I have the pleasure of interviewing Joshua Green, the Pittsburgh Pirates rookie slugger and right fielder. Josh, welcome!"

"Thanks, Roman. It's good to be here."

"Josh, let's start with your stats in this young baseball season. After just a few weeks, you lead the League in batting average, extra-base hits, home runs, and runs batted in. Let's talk about your hitting, Josh. You're batting over .500, setting the Major League record for most consecutive hits without an out earlier this season. These are some pretty heady numbers. How have you racked up such impressive stats as a rookie?"

"Well, Roman, the good Lord, and Coach Samuelson gave me a wonderful opportunity to play for the Pirates this year, and fortunately, I've managed some good play so far for my team."

"Josh, that's pretty modest, especially given yesterday's performance. The entire country is talking about it. You became the first Major League player to hit five home runs in a single game. That's not just good; that's unprecedented. What set you up to take the big-leagues by storm in such a fashion?" Roman would press Josh harder for a story, even if he must get down and dirty.

"I've just been seeing the ball especially well this season. Don't forget. My teammates have put me in a position to make a big impact with their superb play. Several guys are hitting over .300 around me, making it difficult on the opposition. My teammates' play generated my opportunities, and I'm glad to contribute to our great start this year."

"C'mon, Josh, how do _you_ do it? You are the oldest rookie in baseball this year. Where have you been, and what kind of background set you up to be an immediate superstar for the Pirates?"

"Well, I always loved baseball and possessed a knack for it since I was young, but I haven't played professionally until this season."

"How is it possible, Josh, as a 38-year-old, you haven't played professionally before, yet you're breaking all-time records? Your previous life must really be something else to keep a talent like yours from playing baseball until now. The public is dying to know where you came from, Josh. What's your story before exploding onto the scene this year?" continued Roman, not letting up.

"It's true I haven't played professional baseball until recently. I grew up in Western Pennsylvania and worked in government service. I lived overseas and just moved back to the Pittsburgh area," answered Josh.

"Josh, what kind of work did you do for the government, as you say?" pried Roman.

"I don't have much to say about that, Roman," Josh said politely, leaving little room for Roman to maneuver. Josh made it obvious he would not willingly talk about his prior employment. It appeared Josh wanted to talk baseball and the present, but that wasn't enough of a story for Roman to build into a national reputation, and it wouldn't last longer than this fluke hot streak. Roman needed something more, something that wouldn't go away, to secure his reputation as an investigative reporter. He could not get that with Josh's softball answers to his sports questions. Roman would have to pull another string in the Josh Green story to snare his quarry and pry it out of Josh.

Roman looked at the big man sitting across from him. He was a looming figure, more imposing in person than even his physical build suggested. He was dark-skinned; probably some African American in his background thought Roman. His broad nose and curly dark brown hair sticking out from under his Pirates baseball cap made it possible. Still, maybe something else, perhaps middle eastern? Not European, thought Roman, he was too dark-skinned for that, and then there was that white scar, such a contrast to the dark skin, on Josh's left cheek running jaggedly up to his eye. Yes, his eyes, shattering the rest of Josh's otherwise strong, almost stark countenance with their incredible depth. Dark and penetrating, those eyes looked ancient and perhaps...sad? Yes, they sadly looked at him.

Roman could feel Josh's eyes penetrating his armor, seeing right through to his soul. It was not a good feeling. Roman paused longer than he meant, finally breaking eye contact, trying to focus on his notes. His technician was momentarily concerned. Roman usually never delayed his questions, using his rapid-fire nature to keep the interviewee off-guard. Something about Josh unsettled him, questioning the morality of his plan, but no longer. Josh wasn't giving Roman what he needed, and there was something about the man he didn't like.

Roman collected himself, stilling the conscience of his soul, and made his decision. He resolved to go with the most passionate, vocal viewers, for they promised the path of stardom. Pittsburgh was just a baseball backwater, mired in decades of mediocrity. Few outside her hilly confines rooted for their lowly Pirates. Roman must get out, he must escape, and he would do whatever it took. He would give the mob what they wanted. "Since Josh won't cooperate with me, I'll make him someone the public can root against! There is always dirt somewhere. 'Family and Faith' are where you get under someone's skin. Josh holds both closely. Let's see what I can dredge up," thought Roman, and suddenly he was wickedly confident again.

"OK, Josh, what about your family brought you back to Pittsburgh?" Roman began, smiling once more.

"I always loved the area, and when it came time for me to move on from my last employment, I felt the Lord was leading me home to where I grew up," Josh answered.

"Good," thought Roman, "Keep expressing your faith. Your faith will lead you to your ultimate end. Let's see if we can get some dirt on this guy. Surely that daughter of his can't be biological."

Roman continued, "I understand you have a daughter that moved with you to PA?"

"Yes, that's right, my daughter Ruth. She's twelve years old."

"Did you want to bring her back to be near family?"

"Well, she is my family, Roman. We go everywhere together," replied Josh.

"And her mother...?"

"My wife passed away," said Josh matter-of-factly.

Roman needed to be careful here, or the viewers might sympathize with Josh. He thought, "Best not delve into that story until I have the facts and know where it goes. Let's change gears and hit him blindside with that faith of his."

Roman adjusted tack. "You talk a lot about your faith, Josh. You've been prominently kneeling before your first at-bat of each game. Pulling a 'Tim Tebow,' as people call it, right next to the batter's box. Are you trying to demonstrate your faith plays a role in how you play?"

"My faith in Jesus Christ is central to my life, Roman. I do everything in life based on what I think He is leading me to do."

"So, Jesus led you to play baseball for the Pirates?" asked Roman.

Josh smiled and shook his head slightly, "I don't think of it in exactly those terms, Roman, but I felt led to move back to Pennsylvania, and the Lord opened an opportunity for me to play ball, thanks to an invitation from Coach Samuelson."

"And now, here you are playing on the biggest stage just a few weeks later. So, God wants you to be here on this team, for the Pirates to win?" continued Roman. Mark sat in the background, not liking where Roman was leading. Mark deeply suspected Roman was taking Josh down a path where he laid a trap, but he could not signal Josh his concern in the darkened room.

"God wants us to do our best to glorify His name. I don't think He cares about baseball wins and losses, but I certainly feel blessed to be here and happy to be a member of the Pirates," replied Josh.

Josh still fought to stay on baseball, but Roman wouldn't give up. Roman asked a carefully planned series of questions, laying his trap for a blindside follow-up.

"How about your new Pirate teammates, Josh? How are you all getting along?"

"Fine. We have a lot of great players, and they all contributed to our winning start," said Josh.

"You took over right field, moving Judah to left and supplanting him near the top of the batting order. That must have caused some contention?" picked Roman, setting the groundwork for future division.

"I am sure everyone made adjustments. Hopefully, it continues to pay off," Josh still replied without a show of emotion, frustratingly unflappable to Roman's attempts to get a rise out of him. Never fear, I know where to go, thought Roman.

"There are other players besides Judah who made adjustments. Despite his League MVP and batting championship, Pops gave you Andrew's spot in the batting order. Pops also replaced veteran starters with the two Thunder Brothers, J.J. and Juan, almost as new to the League as you are. There seems to be a lot of upheaval early this season for the Pirates?" Roman said, knowing Samuelson was on thin ice with upper management. He might work an angle for some more controversy in the future.

"Well, Coach Samuelson makes the lineup he thinks is best for our chances, and I would say it's worked."

"What kind of adjustments have you made, Josh, coming to the team?" asked Roman innocently. He almost felt sorry for what Josh undoubtedly did not see was about to happen.

"In what way, Roman?" asked Josh. He acted neither surprised nor alarmed but waited patiently. Josh's lack of emotion disturbed Roman, almost like he knew Roman's intentions.

"For instance, your teammate Zach stepped out as one of Major League Baseball's first prominent gay players. How has that affected your relationship as a Christian?" Here we go, thought Roman, take the bait and run with it, Christian, or be exposed as a fraud.

"My teammate's sexual orientation does not impact how we play baseball. We are teammates, playing well together. We get along just fine," answered Josh, again no visible emotion, nothing uncomfortable about his response, thought a frustrated Roman.

"So, as a Christian, you have no problem with the gay lifestyle," pressed Roman. He stalked like a panther, setting up for a kill.

"Roman, I am a Christian, which means I've accepted Christ as my savior. I was, like all men, lost in my sins. Jesus loved me so much, He took my penalty and sacrificed His perfect life on the cross for me. Jesus commanded us to love one another, as He loved us, and to go, tell the world the good news.[1] I believe everyone is free to make choices in life on how they live. For me, I was a lost sinner before I accepted Christ. When He saved me, He gave me a new life, not because I earned it, but because of His love and grace, and what He did on the cross."[2] Roman could feel the jaws of his trap closing, and Josh didn't even know it.

"As a Christian, are you saying Zach's lifestyle is a choice? And that it's a wrong choice, in your words, 'a sin,' then Josh?"

"I am saying, Roman, everyone I meet, like myself, chooses how to live their life. The Bible clearly states we are to flee all forms of sexual immorality.[3] I trust in Christ's atonement for my sins in His death, burial, and resurrection. He verified

---

1. John 13:34; Mark 16:15; Acts 1:8

2. Ephesians 2:8-9

3. 1 Cor 6:9-20; Matt 5:28; 15:19; Lev 18; 1 Cor 10:12-13; 1 Thes 4:3-5; Gal 5:16-22

the Bible as God's Holy Word[4] with authority proven by His resurrection. All humans choose how to live their life. The Bible instructs us that all have sinned and come short of the glory of God. The cost of sin is Death.[5] We are all justly damned, and God's wrath is justly upon us. But God loved us so much, He sent His Son Jesus to be our sacrifice, living a perfect life we could not live. He died innocent on the cross, as both our perfect sacrifice and our scapegoat, so we might not have to die but have eternal life with Him. I have chosen to accept His grace, His forgiveness of sins, and His gift of new life, and I hope all sinners would repent and find new life in Jesus."

Not precisely what Roman wanted for painting Josh as a homophobe, let's refocus on the controversial stance, thought Roman, "So Zach needs to repent, that's what you're saying, Josh?"

"We all choose, Roman. I chose Christ's forgiveness and salvation to follow Him. Every man must make that choice himself."

"And does following your faith trump who someone loves, Josh?"

"I have faith the life Christ wants for us is our best life, Roman, and we should seek His guidance on how to live our lives. 'Love the Lord your God with all your heart and with all your soul and with all your mind and with all your strength.'[6] Jesus told us this is the greatest commandment. We keep this commandment through prayer and reading God's word, putting our faith in God in obedience to His word. His word is clear on the life choices we must make to remain in His will and not sin. Sin always hurts us and those around us in far greater ways than we imagine," replied Josh.

"I think most fans would say calling Zach a sinner just because he's gay is unkind and bigoted, Josh. But let me follow up with a related question to your faith. Why do you kneel before your first at-bat for each game?" continued Roman. Roman was calm outside but relished exposing Josh's critical weak point, harsh dogmatic Christian ideals, and clinging to God against modern morality. Roman knew Josh's strict faith would draw ire and backlash in public opinion.

"It's my way of giving glory to God and His Son Jesus. Everything I do, everything I am, I want to bring glory and honor to the Father and the Son. I pray that I might do so," said Josh plainly, as all his answers showed not anger but

---

4. Matthew 5:18

5. Roman 3:23, 6:23

6. Mark 12:30; Leviticus 19:18

a graceful kindness. Roman liked the ammunition Josh gave him in his responses, but it irked him that Josh's delivery was so serene and unruffled.

"Doesn't that violate the League's bylaws on player public displays?" Roman intended to get him on the record admitting he was a rule breaker.

"You'll have to ask the League, Roman, but I hope a simple expression of faith is still allowed in this country. As for me, I serve the Lord first and always," answered Josh calmly.

Yes! Roman thought, a perfect segue for him to get the League officially to weigh in on Josh's Christian display and now, his gay stance. Either way, forcing the League to take a stance would generate controversy, and controversy, like adding gasoline to the fire, guaranteed Roman a bump in ratings. This interview opened doors and pointed to other avenues for Roman he knew would keep him at the front of the sporting and possibly all news headlines for days to come.

Mark was increasingly uncomfortable and angry at Roman's straying into Josh's personal beliefs. Just as he was about to say something, Roman moved to end the interview, looking back at the camera. Before he could speak to end it, Josh spoke up on his own. "Roman, I know you want to paint me as a Christian zealot who holds others to impossible ideals, but nothing could be further from the Truth. The Truth is precisely what's at stake, that Christ loves us but that we are lost in our sins. That's why He came to earth; To restore us and our relationship with God by taking upon Himself the Father's righteous wrath against our sins, living a perfect life, and dying in our place on the cross.[7] He offers us new life through His resurrection and victory over sin and death. We all need salvation, and Christ offers it as a free gift to all who repent and call upon Him.[8] I hope everyone considers the free Salvation gift Jesus offers. I have nothing but the love of Christ in my heart for all men. Accepting Christ's sacrifice changed me forever. Once, I was dead with sin. Now, I am alive in Christ.[9] I hope you will choose life and accept Christ's gift.

"Well, unfortunately, that's all the time we have to talk with Josh; certainly, a man who holds strong views. His play has been amazing. Josh, I am sure the fans can't wait to see how you do the rest of the season, and maybe the Pirates can ride your offense back to the playoffs. Good luck tomorrow against the Giants. Back

---

7. Philippians 2:6-11

8. 1 John 1:9; John 1:12; Romans 5:12-18; Romans 3:24-26

9. Ephesians 2:4-5

to the studio," Roman finished, looking directly at the camera with a gleam in his eye.

The interview ended abruptly, and Roman called for the lights as one of the technicians brought up the lights in the room.

"Sorry, Josh. I hope you don't take it too personally; just trying to get your story out there to the people," Roman stood and held out his hand.

"I am sure you got what you wanted," said Josh as he stood and shook Roman's hand, "But I wonder, once you receive what you want, will you find it worth it? You remind me of when Christ warned us, 'What profits a man to gain the whole world and lose his own soul?'"[10]

"Well, just keep that unwavering hold of your Christian ideals, Josh, and I think we will both find out before the season's over," said Roman with a wicked-looking smile.

Josh held the handshake for a moment longer and nodded to Roman, "I will, Roman, and indeed you shall see." Roman looked up into those dark eyes, thoughtfully looking back at Roman, and his smile faded despite his best efforts to keep it in defiance as he pulled his hand away. Again, Roman thought, something about this man was unsettling. Even though Josh willingly went where Roman wanted, like a sacrificial lamb, the man seemed unfazed by the backlash from fans and the LGBTQ community that would inevitably follow. Roman wanted to write Josh off as a fool, inviting the wrath of public opinion he knew Josh's comments would incur, but somehow, Josh's eyes told him the opposite. They seemed to show a wise old soul who understood fully the cost of what he was saying yet was unfazed by it, resolute in his stance. Still, Roman would get him, and Josh would play the villain, Roman's villain. Roman would see to it, painting Josh as the zealot who stood against society's values.

As an added bonus, Roman could now force the League to answer up, and Josh would probably be cast against Baseball as well. This kind of story practically guaranteed staying power for him as a reporter, even if Josh's stats decreased, which Roman knew they must. After all, no ballplayer could continue to hit everything. Roman could ride controversy like a surfer catching a wave, leaving Josh behind when he either struggled to maintain his offensive output or drowned in negative public opinion. Roman also formulated a few ideas on casting Josh as a hypocrite. He must first investigate the many flaws he exposed today in Josh's character.

Roman's thoughts flew by quickly, and he almost forgot the reality of the man standing before him. But then those eyes of Josh upon him snapped back into

10. Mark 8:36

Roman's focus. They warned him of something different, something reflecting back upon himself. It shocked his system, and he tried to turn quickly away from those eyes, looking straight through his guile, right to the truth of who he was and what he was planning. Before he could turn away, Roman saw sad kindness in their knowing gaze and something akin to loving pity.

This was intolerable. Roman could not bear it. "Who was this guy anyways?" thought Roman angrily. It doesn't matter, he rebuked himself. He controlled the narrative. The public would see what he wanted them to see. Yet, something worried Roman; a truth that would not leave him. Despite his best efforts, he could not squash the memory of those knowing, sad eyes.

Roman turned and locked sight with Mark as Mark moved to escort Josh out. Mark glared back at Roman. "Time to go, Josh," Mark did not try to hide his disgust as he turned away from Roman. Ushering Josh out in front of him, Mark turned to pull the door shut behind him but glanced back at Roman. "Be careful, Roman," warned Mark. "Trying to hang a star won't win any prizes for SPNN or yourself."

Roman shot back, "On the contrary, Mark, it will win the viewers' attention, and that, as you know, means ratings. Besides, they're with me on this issue, and your player is the one who's walking to his own crucifixion. I am innocent of his blood, be it on his head. I am just giving the people what they want," smiled Roman malevolently as he replied.

"No one believes that Roman. Not even you," said Mark, and he closed the door. Roman's smile evaporated. Again, he hesitated for a moment as a quiet voice of conscience pressed him to consider why he still felt troubled despite his interview going to plan. He couldn't quite shake the memory of Josh looking back at him, deep into his soul. Forget it! Roman chastised himself as he tried suppressing the voice. He was a pro on his way to the big time, and nothing would stop him—this was no time to lose focus. Much work was needed to prepare this interview for Sports News Network evening news in a few hours. He must stop dwelling on these niggling concerns. He banished the voice of his conscience and instead planned what he would do to fan the public's emotional response.

Fifty Three

Mark walked Josh back towards the players' dressing room. At first, he did not know what to say. However, Josh quietly intervened, saving his loss for words.

"Mark, I would like you to find a room for me to talk to Zach for a few minutes before we take the field. Can you do that?" asked Josh quietly.

"You can use my office. It's just down the hall from the locker room. I will get him and bring him to you. Look, Josh, I am sorry you got railroaded into those questions from Roman. He is a predator looking to make his mark. I didn't think he would go to such lengths to make a controversy," Mark said quickly as they walked.

"It's not your fault, Mark. Roman searched for what my faith means to me, to find something controversial. To be honest, it's not that hard or unexpected. Christianity is always controversial and divisive whenever and wherever it meets the world. Jesus said as much when he said, 'I did not come to bring peace, but a sword.' You remember Christ then quoted the Prophet Micah; For I have come to turn 'a man against his father, a daughter against her mother, a daughter-in-law against her mother-in-law—a man's enemies will be the members of his own household.'" [1]

Josh paused as they approached Mark's small office. "I know Roman will portray Christian faith in the worse possible light. However, I want to let Zach hear where I stand and why, so he knows I care deeply about him. I want him to know I believe in God's word and his design of marriage and sex as biblically defined for our benefit and best destiny.[2] I trust Him and His word knowing what is best for us, even when it doesn't always align with what we feel or what others think."

---

1. Matthew 10:34-36

2. Gen 2:24; Romans 1 18-32; Matthew 15:18-19

"That's a dangerous stance to take in today's society, Josh. The public and the League will make trouble for you," Mark said soberly as he opened the door to his office.

"I agree with you, Mark. It is dangerous. But one of my heroes once said it this way," and Josh quoted,

"'Cowardice asks the question, 'Is it safe?'

Expediency asks the question, 'Is it politic?'

Vanity asks the question, 'Is it popular?'

But conscience asks the question, 'Is it right?'

And there comes a time when one must take a position that is neither safe, nor politic, nor popular because conscience tells him it is right.'"[3]

Mark watched as Josh paused thoughtfully after the quote. Josh continued, "Jesus died and rose from the dead. By His authority, He told us we could trust the Bible as God's word, and though I could avoid unpopular ideas, doing so would only harm those I care about. It's fake compassion to tell people falsehoods, even when they don't want to hear the Truth. Christ taught us about the destructive power of sin, especially sin that disguises itself as good, as equal to righteousness.[4] I must stand for the family as God proclaimed in Genesis; 'A man shall leave his father and his mother and hold fast to his wife, and they shall become one flesh,' or I care neither for them, their children or all the future generations to come. History demonstrates a society that protects and honors the family as God defined grows in strength. Those embracing other relationships as equal to God's creation of marriage ultimately break down, suffer with each successive step away from God, decay, and fall. Every study that honestly looked at traditional marriage and all the alternatives shows that families with a married mom and dad have children who grow up better emotionally, economically, and live more productive lives."

"I love my fellow citizens, including Zach. Suppose I lie and say homosexual and heterosexual relationships are equivalent and equally moral, when every piece of evidence proves God's word as the only Truth. In that case, I doom those I love with a false narrative. God warns us against all forms of sexual immorality,

---

3. Martin Luther King Jr. A PROPER SENSE OF PRIORITIES; February 6, 1968, Washington, D.C.

4. 2 Corinthians 11:12-15

including homosexuality.[5] We will destroy our society's primary building block if we lie about same-sex marriage and validate its equivalence with God's plan of marriage as the sanctified union of a man and a woman, for life, before God. The evidence is clear to anyone willing to look with an open mind and heart, and the Bible explains what I must do. Loving like Christ means modeling His example and proclaiming the Truth, especially regarding family. To do otherwise will only hurt the ones we claim to love."

Josh's stance was unwavering. But the compassion Mark saw in the man made all the difference to Mark. There was no hatred or anger in his eyes, just the opposite. But Mark feared few would ever see Josh as he now saw him. Fewer still would accept Josh's opinion, and those vocal in society, those having the public's ear, would paint him as a bigot. Mark could already imagine the crowd turning on him and calling for his censure, if not for his head. Still, it was clear Josh thought out his views, and it was almost as if he prepared all his life to stand on his faith in Christ and hold fast to Biblical Truth, even if it meant he lost all life offered.

At that moment, Mark didn't know if such a stance was worth the pain in life sure to follow, but he must admit, he admired the courage and faith he saw in the man. What surprised him the most was how Josh seemed not to be argumentative in the interview or this discussion. Instead, his words proceeded with a loving spirit, speaking words of wisdom and truth. It reminded him of a doctor with a cure, and perhaps the world was the patient holding on to fear brought by the disease, afraid to reach out for help.

Mark realized he stood for some time looking at Josh, thinking, while holding the door handle. He shook himself and nodded at Josh, opening the door for him while staying in the hallway. "I'll get Zach and bring him back. How much time will you need?"

"Just a few minutes, ten at the most, I think," Josh replied calmly.

"That's fine, Josh," replied Mark.

"Mark, after you drop off Zach, can you please find Coach Samuelson? Tell him what transpired during the interview, so he can prepare the organization, and tell him I am talking with Zach one-on-one," said Josh.

"I will," said Mark. Josh surprised him with his wisdom and clear thinking at this moment. He turned to shut the door to leave and find Zach while reflecting on all Josh said. Before he closed the door, a curious thought crossed his mind.

"Josh, your hero, you quoted about taking a position your conscience speaks to you. Can I ask who it was?" questioned Mark.

---

5. Matthew 15:19, Mark 7:21-22 and extended discussions refer to 'Correct not Politically Correct,' Frank Turek, CrossExamined 2017

Josh smiled and said, "Dr. Martin Luther King, Jr."

Mark nodded and shut the door behind him. There was still much work to be done.

Fifty Four

After leading Zach to Josh, Mark tracked down Coach Samuelson sitting in the visiting manager's office, and gave Saul a brief about all that happened. Saul listened intently, concerned. He tried to remain calm as Mark recounted Josh's interview with Roman, but it wasn't easy. When Mark finished, Saul looked at his watch for a few moments, collecting his thoughts, calculating the time of the first showing of the interview later that day. Mark was upset because he failed to stop the interview or help Josh, but Pops knew it was his call, and there was little more either could have done. Roman was out for a story, and Josh gave it to him. He must tell the boy—no young man, Pops corrected his thinking, recognizing Mark's growth and maturity over the years, that he was not at fault.

"Mark, don't beat yourself up on this. Allowing the interview was my decision. The only thing that could have stopped what happened was not to give the interview, but Josh must face the press, eventually. Regardless, that decision rested with me, not you. Just be prepared to answer questions about this from the rest of the press corps. We've got a few hours at most before this hits the airways. Go get your head together and work on some responses to the questions we know are coming," directed Pops.

"What about Josh...and Zach...and the rest of the team?" asked Mark.

"Something tells me Josh can handle himself better than we give him credit for, but yes, we will have to check on Zach and talk to the team. I'll talk to everyone together at the start of practice here in a few," replied Saul, and he patted Mark on the shoulder as he ushered him out of the manager's office.

It was about ten minutes since Mark dropped Zach off, and as the two men walked out into the hallway, the door to the office with Josh and Zach opened. The two men walked out, first Zach, then Josh. To Pops, the scene was a picture in his mind that would stick with him forever. Zach turned back toward Josh, and to Pop's surprise, Zach held out his hand tentatively. Josh took Zach's hand, then pulled him in for an embrace, releasing Zach to just a hand on his shoulder. Saul could see Josh looking down at Zach kindly, saying something to Zach that neither Mark nor Pops could hear. Zach smiled up at the big man and nodded, then turned and walked towards Pops and Mark heading back to the locker room. Pops was in front of Mark, and as Zach approached, Pops said,

"Everything all right, Zach?"

"Fine, Coach, we're going to be fine," and he continued past, nodding to Mark as he went.

Pops looked at Josh as he approached. He let Zach get ahead of him, then asked Saul, "What can I do to help you, Coach?"

"Well, let's stick to baseball as much as we can today, Josh. I will talk to the team to start warm-ups, as always, and try to put them at ease. The most important thing is how you and Zach get along after this, which will set the tone for the team. It looks like you have gone a long way to ensure that area is in good shape. But know this. Roman is a guy that thrives on controversy, Josh. Causing division inside the clubhouse is right up his alley."

"Yes, I know, Coach, and I'll do my best to serve as a friend and good teammate in every way I can," said Josh.

Saul nodded and let Josh pass on toward the locker room. Practice would begin in a few minutes. Pops turned to Mark and said, "Go work on some canned responses to the questions that are coming. I will get with you after I get practice started. We can talk later, but we don't have much time as I need to call the owner."

"Do you think that's wise?" said Mark.

"I'd rather Cai hear it from me and know we are preparing a response to questions. But yes, I am sure he'll have something to say about it." Saul paused, not relishing the thought of that conversation. Best not to overthink it, Saul said to himself. He hurried on. "In the end, the League will have something to say, and I don't want Cai to learn about it by watching SPNN."

Mark sensed the wisdom in getting ahead of the story and nodded. "OK, I will get to work and see you in a few minutes," Mark said, turning on his heel and heading to his office and laptop.

Pops walked back into his office and sat down to make the phone call, pausing to say a brief prayer under his breath. "Lord, help me say the right things to the team and the owner in the next few minutes. This will not be easy, and I don't want to let anybody down." Saul swiveled in his chair, reaching for the phone, but it felt as if God stopped him in his tracks. *Wait, Saul, listen!* came the quiet voice, speaking to Saul's heart in more than just words. Saul paused instead and reached into a small personal bag sitting on his desk. He rummaged through until he found the pocket Bible he started carrying again recently. Saul got the idea from watching Cy cradle the old Bible he often read. Saul recently got up the nerve to ask him where he got it, and Cy told Saul it was indeed his grandmother's.

It reminded Saul of his great-uncle's pocket Bible. Saul's great-uncle received it in the army somewhere in France and carried it into Germany during WWII. Saul was young when his uncle passed, but he remembered him well, a quiet yet confident man with a kind, knowing smile. His smile said he knew all about how difficult life could be but still found joy in tough times. Despite its age and history, the Bible was in good shape. Saul opened the cover, stopping to touch the red semi-circle stamp with a white lightning bolt from left to right embossed on the inside cover page. He remembered asking his uncle what it meant. Saul's uncle explained it was the patch of his final unit, the 78th ID.

Saul's great-uncle volunteered for the unit as a reinforcement troop when the rules in the European theater changed in 1945, allowing black infantrymen to fight alongside whites in combat. His uncle's platoon was one of the first black replacement platoons in the "Lightning" division, joining the Remagen bridgehead as the division fought across the Rhine into Germany.[1] Saul could still see the pride in his uncle's eyes, remembering his younger days as an American combat soldier, fighting for his country and proving blacks could fight equally alongside other Americans. Saul gratefully received his uncle's Bible after he passed. His mother told Saul she found the Bible on his uncle's nightstand, with a note asking her to give it to the boy to carry him through life's toughest battles.

As was typical for the military Bibles of the era, the hand-sized Bible contained the New Testament and Psalms. The print was small, but Saul's eyes were one thing undiminished over time, and he let the book fall open as it often did to the Psalms chapter 13. It seemed his uncle must have read them often, and he noted it was one of the shorter psalms read many times, evidenced by its well-worn page. Saul began to read, and the verses spoke to his soul as they once did his uncle, in a foxhole late at night, looking out into the unknown darkness.

"How long wilt thou forget me, O Lord? forever? How long wilt thou hide thy face from me? How long shall I take counsel in my soul, having sorrow in my heart daily? How long shall mine enemy be exalted over me? Consider and hear me, O Lord my God: lighten mine eyes, lest I sleep the sleep of death; Lest mine enemy say, I have prevailed against him; and those that trouble me rejoice when I am moved. But I have trusted in thy mercy; my heart shall rejoice in thy salvation. I will sing unto the Lord, because he hath dealt bountifully with me."

Saul finished reading, and his eyes now spied a dark thumbprint in the margin. It was as if Saul's uncle squeezed tightly, perhaps with a slightly bloody thumbprint, while reading this passage. As he looked closer, he saw a faint pencil

---

1. https://www.historynet.com/african-american-platoons-in-world-war-ii. htm

underline of the fifth verse ending at the fingerprint. "Mercy" was circled, and his uncle faintly wrote "Jesus loves _me_" in the margin. He never noticed it before. Saul sat quietly, eyes closed, thinking about all his uncle lived through and survived, even after returning home. Saul's heart was soft and genuinely humble now. He took a deep breath, bowed, and replied to his heavenly father. "Forgive me for the focus of that last thought, Lord. Please help me and give me the right words and courage to say to them, so I don't let _You_ down." It was as if God spoke over Saul, something said to him many times before, but Saul failed to hear. *If you let me, I've got this, Saul. You are weak, but I am strong. Remember, my love is perfect. I love you, and I will never let you down.* This time, Saul listened. There were things in life more important than baseball he needed to get right, and Saul remembered this for the first time in a long while. He returned the Bible to his bag and picked up the phone to call Cai. As he did so, the thought struck him; maybe God was using the best player he ever coached, indeed ever saw, to show him what God wanted Saul to know was truly important.

Fifty Five

After a brief conversation with an unhappy owner, Pops met the team on the field to start practice. He briefly addressed the team as the players and coaches gathered in their customary circle for warmup stretches in the outfield. While he didn't go into the interview specifics, he told the team that Roman interviewed Josh and tried to use Zach's personal life and Josh's Christian faith to drive a wedge between the two men and therefore fracture the team. He reminded the team they all came from different backgrounds and beliefs. Still, like this country, the team was founded on men accepting their differences as free men while working together to accomplish great things. Such was the mark of champions.

Saul asked everyone to focus on their play and team goals while respecting each other's right to live their lives freely. He expected his coaches and players to be of one accord regarding the team, but life in America meant teammates should respect each other's right to disagree on what they believed and how they lived those beliefs. America's foundation was individual freedom to live life and pursue happiness as their right granted by the Creator. As far as the team was concerned, he implored them to respect each other and have each other's back, even when someone like Roman tried to cast their differences as weakness.

Saul said, "I rely on the grace and love given by God when I didn't deserve it. I ask you to give grace to one another, even when we disagree. And remember, as I have told you before, the press are not your friends. They don't care about your success or failure, just about getting the story, any story, even if that means the team gets hurt." Saul looked around at each man and finished with a nod. "Refer further questions about the interview to Mark Johnson or me." For their part, the team seemed to shrug it off, probably waiting to see the interview for themselves, Saul thought, and he nodded to the captains to get started with warm-ups.

Practice went surprisingly well, despite the somewhat ominous discussion by Pops to start. Most of the team seemed happy to remember their recent superb play on this west coast trip. There was a subtle undertone, however. They seemed tentative around Josh, unsure what happened and not as playful with their usual banter. Judah, in particular, put in a jibe or two when he could.

"Put your foot in your mouth, eh slugger?" Judah smirked. "Perhaps you're not such the perfect golden child after all," Judah said as they jogged in from the outfield after a round of "catch and shoot" with Coach Phil. Thinking he would get a rise out of Josh, Judah's evil grin faded as he looked over at Josh and saw only sadness and pity in Josh's eyes staring back at him. He turned quickly away, feeling the heat of emotion flaring up in his reddened face.

Barney, the utility player, was the only one close enough to overhear Judah's comment as they jogged into the dugout, and he put his hand on Josh's shoulder as they slowed. "Don't listen to him, Josh," Barney said softly, "Don't let his words trouble you. We're all behind you," he said, encouraging Josh.

Josh turned back and replied to Barney, saying, "Thanks, my friend. I'm glad you are, but I still worry about all of you, even Judah. I want you all to have a good life and spare you any pain if I can." Josh carried a distant look in his eyes as he gazed out over Candlestick Park for a moment. He continued, "The world, however, is lost, and fights against us when we stand for the Truth." He paused for a moment, then looked back at Barney, and now he put his hand on Barney's shoulder, focusing those dark, knowing eyes kindly on him. "But I am always grateful for kind words from a true friend." Barney smiled back at Josh. Barney intended to assuage Judah's harsh words meant to wound Josh, yet he found himself comforted instead by Josh's response. Barney, surprised, thought, "What manner of man is this? I try to comfort him, and yet it's I who am comforted?"

Practice finished, and Coach Samuelson cut everyone loose until tomorrow's afternoon showtime at the hotel. The players completed their post-practice regimens and arrived at the team hotel in separate groups, with some taking longer than others to finish their workouts and physical therapy. As the last Pirate got to their rooms, the Roman Josephus interview led off the SPNN sports highlights on the west coast and across the country in prime news time. Mark noticed Roman cleverly edited the interview before it aired. Roman cut out his lengthy pause after Josh failed to give details about his government work before coming to baseball. Even worse, Roman removed other parts, including the question about Josh's wife and the end explanation Josh gave about what it meant to him to be a Christian and why he held his beliefs. Of course, the removed footage showed a different Josh, with love and concern for his teammates and all people. In short, Mark realized Roman shortened the interview, enhancing his portrayal of Josh as Christian zealot and bigot.

It was an old trick of yellow journalism tainting a story by manipulation through omission during editing. Mark knew he should not be surprised. Still, it made Mark angry at just how much Roman wanted Josh to be the villain in the public's eyes. It was more than Mark could stomach as he shut off the television in his hotel room. Mark knew the questions from other news agencies would pour in, and it was his job to field them. He sat down at his computer, prepared for the onslaught. It was going to be a long evening.

Fifty Six

J osh talked to the girls that night about the interview, and they watched it on television together. They both posed questions for Josh, and he spoke with them about what he believed and why, clarifying some of the interview parts SPNN and Roman cut out before airing the interview. The next day began early for the Greens and Mary as they took Ruth to an appointment at the local Children's hospital. They went to the treatment center, and as was their routine, Josh met with a nurse's aide who asked if he would visit the ward while his daughter received treatment. He never questioned these requests, pretending he didn't know that Mary made the arrangements while working with Nurse Richards.

Despite being busy with her job in St. Louis, Nurse Richards helped Mary make all the appointments. Her long career brought Nurse Richards' friends at nearly all the facilities around the country the Greens would use, and she talked to each facility about using Josh to visit their critical care children. While handing out Pirates souvenirs, he would speak with them, and Josh's visits encouraged both the children and their caregivers. As was his custom, Josh often found a family and child who was especially in need of help and hope, with late-stage cancer or other life-threatening illness. Josh would ask to pray with the family as little Ruthie did on the first visit to the hospital in St. Louis. As Nurse Richards saw for herself, Josh's visits did wonders for the kids at her hospital, and after talking to the other hospitals the Greens visited, the reports were similar.

Linda Richards thought about Josh's visit a few weeks ago as she walked down a children's ward hallway. Today was usually an off-day for Linda, but Dr. Thyatira invited her to say goodbye to the Sidon family as they were due to be discharged this morning. Young Tyre Sidon was something of a celebrity in the hospital. Tyre's recovery was truly miraculous. The nurse in Ms. Richards smiled inwardly at herself, thinking she still learned miracles can and do happen after nearly half a century seeing patients. As she approached Tyre's room, she could hear a small gathering of people celebrating, and Ms. Richard's friend Dr. Thyatira was in the middle of it all, talking with Tyre and her parents. Everyone donned birthday hats as Reuben hid a pink bike from Tyre's sight outside the door. The celebration was complete with a birthday cake that said, "Happy Birthday Tyre."

Dr. Thyatira said, "Mr. and Mrs. Sidon and Tyre, it is my privilege to sign your hospital discharge papers," which she did with a flourish, "but there is just one more thing we have to do. You were just starting to recover when your birthday came some two weeks ago, and we couldn't give you a proper birthday party. So now we have a cake," she said, signaling to one helper who brought it in, "And even a surprise gift." Tyre looked on expectantly. "But...," Lydia paused dramatically, then smiled, saying, "First, we must sing happy birthday!"

Nurse Richards joined in the singing as Tyre sat on the edge of the bed, half-listening, half wanting to see her surprise gift. It was amazing how much better the little girl looked. So recently, she appeared gaunt and waning, near death. Yet now she looked flushed and lively, eating full meals again, well on the road to recovery. Dr. Thyatira told Linda she never saw anyone come back from such advanced cancer when the turnaround began. Still, perhaps the chemo and radiation created a more pronounced, if delayed, effect. Two days ago, Dr. Thyatira caught Linda late in the day, and for the first time in the twenty years they knew each other, Linda would have to say Lydia Thyatira was both excited and slightly flustered. "Linda," she said, "I can't believe it, but three consecutive tests prove beyond all doubt Tyre Sidon's cancer is in full remission. We can't find it in any of her blood or biopsy tests. I think we will discharge her in a few days!"

As they finished singing happy birthday, Tyre's mom and dad kissed her and cut the cake for everyone to eat. It was chocolate with white and pink icing, Tyre's favorite colors. Dr. Thyatira was accepting a piece of cake when she saw Reuben signaling her from the hallway. "Oh, I almost forgot! Tyre, all the nurses and doctors, and other aid workers are so delighted to see you get better, they wanted to get you a gift. Your mom and dad told us you just wanted to go home and get a chance to ride your bike, which you haven't been able to do for quite some time. We understand your old bike is a little small now that you have grown since last you rode it, so everyone pitched in to get you a new one as a going-away present. Reuben!"

With that, Reuben brought the pink bike into the room. It came equipped with a pink and white basket and a little old-fashioned ringing bell on the handlebars. Tyre's smile grew as she jumped up to examine her new bike. Where recently slept a frail, dying child, now bounded an exuberant girl whose zest for life was infectious. She gave Reuben, the closest to her, a big hug, and everybody laughed at his surprised expression as he hugged her back. As the minutes rolled on, everyone congratulated and wished Tyre and her folks well, and slowly the crowd thinned as many returned to their duties. Soon just Nurse Richards, Reuben, and Dr. Thyatira were left. "Well, Tyre, how do you like your bike?" asked Dr. Thyatira finally.

"It's the coolest thing I've gotten since Reuben brought me my cap," said Tyre excitedly. Linda noticed Tyre, who wore a beanie cap on her almost bald head, was wearing a Pirates baseball cap that was too big if it weren't for the crocheted beanie under it.

"You gave her a Pirate cap, not a Cardinal?" Linda asked, surprised.

Reuben wrinkled his nose, "Ah, I just delivered it, Ms. Richards. It's Josh Green's hat. Josh tracked me down right before he left after visiting our kids and told me to give it to Tyre when she woke up," he said, with a furrowed brow, remembering.

"And she's been wearing it every waking moment since," said her father. "We are lifelong Cardinal fans, too!" he added sheepishly, smiling at his healing daughter, "But what can we say? Our daughter appears to want to change our allegiance!"

"Oh, Dad, you've got to be a Pirates fan now. I mean, I can hardly even remember Josh's visit, except for someone touching my foot and the voice of a girl praying. This hat is my lucky hat now. Look, Josh Green even signed it."

Tyre held out the hat, and on the inside, Josh wrote, "Phil 4:13, I can do all things through Christ who strengthens me. Until we meet again, Joshua Green."

"I guess we can root for the Pirates now, too, sweetie, especially since you recovered and healed after Mr. Green's visit," said her father. The Sidon family picked up the rest of their belongings and proceeded to the elevator to leave, with Tyre proudly walking her bike and wearing her Josh Green Pirates ball cap. Dr. Thyatira, Nurse Richards, and Reuben saw them to the elevator and waved as the doors shut.

"Once in a great while, we get a good ending to what seems like a hopeless situation," Dr. Thyatira commented after the doors closed, and the elevator started down.

"Yep," said Reuben. "It's a miracle." His furrowed brow smoothed out suddenly as he looked at the two women, and he smiled, beaming at them with some newfound understanding.

"I might have to agree with you there, Reuben. I can't explain it medically, that's for sure," said Dr. Thyatira. "Well, I have to catch up on rounds. I will see you later." The three said their goodbyes and waved to each other. Reuben returned to the ward where he still needed to finish his shift, and Linda Richards said goodbye as she turned back to her office to grab her coat and head home. While she walked, she thought about Tyre's incredible comeback, and her walking out of the hospital healed just two weeks after all hope seemed lost. She contemplated Josh Green's words to Reuben when he gave the hat. "Give it to Tyre when she wakes up." When Josh visited, Nurse Richards remembered little Tyre near the end. Anyone who saw her would have lost all hope—anyone except, it seemed, Josh Green. Now here Tyre was, healed and heading home. As Reuben said, it did seem miraculous. Leaving for home that night, Linda couldn't help but think it all turned around after the visit from Josh Green.

Fifty Seven

J osh's interview inspired some very negative press in the hypersensitive American news cycle. Activists holding signs met the team outside the stadium in San Francisco in the days following the interview and the Pirates' next stop in Seattle. The relatively small but vocal contingent of protesters shouted anti-bigotry and LGBTQ slogans. While the League allowed protests outside the stadium, inside the stadium, staff quickly removed any fans displaying protest signs if they were determined to be disrupting the game. Though limited, the protests received considerable coverage from local media and Roman's reports on SPNN. What did not stop, notable on the televised games, were rainbow colors worn by many fans for the rest of the Pirates' west coast swing.

Roman kept up the pressure. First, he tried to sow dissent within the team and stoke the flames of contention, attempting to get more one-on-one time with the players. However, Mark Johnson and Coach Samuelson refused and would not allow Roman to interview any players privately. Saul filed a grievance with the League for the editing by SPNN of the interview. Saul claimed Roman altered the meaning of what Josh tried to say by cutting out parts of the interview, including Josh's explanatory comments. It was within the League's capacity to penalize SPNN financially. The press contract restricted the network from altering player interviews, but SPNN claimed a time constraint caused them to air a shortened interview. The League decided it would be bad press to censor SPNN, hoping the story would disappear.

Roman continued to dig, pressing individuals during the post-game interviews. His first attempt was to ask Zach specifically about his feelings towards Josh after the next game. Zach answered Roman's baited question with a simple reply. "Josh and I are on good terms. He's been a good teammate and honest friend. I don't have to agree with everything someone else believes to respect them, and I honestly feel Josh has nothing but the best interest at heart for each of us and the team. Josh shows it every time we take the field and how he treats each of us, myself included." When Roman tried to pick more out of Zach, he said, "Asked and answered, Roman. I have nothing more to say." That answer rankled Roman, but he was far from done.

The League's response to Roman ran more to his liking. First, Roman got the League to go on the defensive when he asked them to comment on Josh's interview the next day. As the League's commissioner, Quint Pilate knew there was no upside to offending the LGBTQ community. They held powerful social support, and their organizations could impact the League's financial bottom line. First, Quint delivered a lengthy admonition to Cai Annason on the phone. He demanded Cai get control of his player and team. Quint warned Cai the League would punish both the Pirates organization and Green with financial and disciplinary penalties should the player make similar statements in the future. In truth, Quint wasn't sure if the League tried to enact a penalty under the collective bargaining agreement, the punishment would withstand arbitration. Still, he knew Cai was pliable to his threats. Quint expected Cai to stop problems internally rather than risk taking on the League.

Quint decided he must also make a swift, public rebuttal to the "Green Interview," as his staff called it. After a lengthy office call with his legal and public relations teams, Quint released an official League statement from the commissioner's office.

"Major League Baseball continues to support its players, coaching staff, and fans to ensure their freedoms and right to privacy. As clearly stated in our governing guidelines and the League policy of nondiscrimination, Major League Baseball does not discriminate based on race, country of origin, religion, or sexual orientation. While Major League Baseball does not tolerate discrimination of any kind, we recognize the right of individuals to express their personal beliefs as long as those beliefs do not infringe upon others' freedom, provide a hostile workplace, or show bias in violation of League policy against discrimination. According to the collective bargaining agreement, we hold a higher standard of maintaining the player's code of conduct and representing the League in a positive image that includes statements seen as disparaging or diminishing another human being's personhood through negative comments of discrimination. If a player voices their opinion, insomuch as it infringes or indicates possible infringement of the League's anti-discrimination policy, the players' collective bargaining agreement requires the League's ethical oversight committee review player conduct and whether it violated the governing contracts and League rules. The Roman Josephus interview with Joshua Green is currently under review."

Thankfully for Josh and the team, the next few weeks saw the Pirates' hot streak continue. They finished the west coast swing 12-2. Returning to Pittsburgh for an eight-game home stand, they swept Baltimore in four games, then took 3 of 4 against Boston during interleague play. Next, they traveled to Philadelphia at the end of the month and swept the Phillies, finishing April with a historic team-best record of 29-4 to start the season. Josh continued to play at a pace unprecedented in baseball history, at least for the first five weeks of the season. He hit in 56 of 92 at-bats, posting an incredible .609 batting average. He led the League in multiple categories, including the triple crown stats of runs batted in, batting average, and home runs. With 28 home runs, Josh was such a threat to go deep that teams now intentionally walked him 36 times. His walks may have been higher, but Josh was an unexpectedly speedy base runner and was also in the League's top 5 for steals, going 11 for 15 in stolen base attempts. Likewise, the team continued to play well around Josh's play, with four other Pirates hitting over .300, making the Buccos the best hitting team in baseball after being near the bottom of the Major Leagues for years. In particular, both J.J. and Juan, the Thunder Brothers, were having break-out years, with J.J. hitting .327 and Juan going deep 14 times, second in the National League only to Josh. Uncharacteristically, the Pirates became a run-generating juggernaut and were a genuine threat of blowing teams out.

To the well-trained eye, Josh saved his best hitting when a victory was in doubt, always coming through in the clutch when the game was on the line. One of the most recent examples was the Bucs' final game in Philadelphia at the end of the four-game trip in which the Pirates won the first three games. Josh played such an excellent series the Phillies walked him three times, including in the top of the ninth with no outs and the game tied. He promptly stole second, then advanced to third on a single by Nate Fisher and scored what turned out to be the game-winning run on a sacrifice fly.

Quint Pilate sat in his office with the investigation results of the League's ethical oversight committee on the Josh Green interview. It took a little over two weeks to get the internal report back. Quint secretly advised the board to take due diligence in reviewing Josh's interview, even allowing SPNN to delay sending the full unedited video while they sought legal counsel on its content. Behind the scenes, Quint and his deputy, VP for Operations and Media, Herald Gripp, watched both the public response and Josh Green's actions, on and off the field. Quint was no fool. He discussed with Herald, if the Pirates made it through the west coast swing and got back home without too much negative press, the League could ease their response as all the furor died down. Also, Quint watched Josh's play and knew his powerful offensive output would persuade fans to overlook remarks in favor of cheering his record-breaking play.

Though ostensibly approved by the owners, Quint chose and appointed all members to the League oversight committee, and they all owed him for their appointments. Although they came from varied backgrounds, they shared one thing in common: the League paid them handsomely. Quint discussed responses to the interview with his legal team even before the board ruled. Regardless of what the ethics committee found, he and Herald agreed the League's progressive stance required clear public support and validation of the LGBTQ community's equality or risk tainting MLB's image as bigoted or discriminatory. The League lagged behind previous historical, cultural, and societal shifts in mores and values. Quint and Herald understood that poor, outdated decisions or even the hint of being stuck in the past when society's values evolved, hurt the League's reputation and, more importantly, its revenue.

The League's legal team laid out the commissioner's options at a private meeting for him, Herald Gripp, and his ever-present assistant Cassius sitting in the corner taking notes. His legal team discussed punitive options and Green's available recourse, should he or the Pirates object. With this advice, Quint read the confidential report from the ethics committee. The board focused on two possible infractions: the League's nondiscrimination policy, which applied to all employees, and the "detrimental conduct" clause in the players' collective bargaining agreement. For the first, the board found Josh's controversial remarks did not constitute a direct violation of the League's nondiscrimination policy. While broad and similar to most for-profit organizations in the country, the policy required a high legal threshold and met precedent before finding an employee at fault. Quint's legal team warned Josh's actions and words were unlikely to cross the legal threshold of discrimination.

Furthermore, the legal team advised Quint, Josh Green's defense lawyer would likely claim freedom of speech rights on religious grounds. Quint knew that was a battle he did not want to fight. Even if they won, the League risked losing in the court of public opinion, once again hurting the League financially. However, the player's "detrimental conduct" clause potentially provided a lower threshold, more vaguely written in the player's CBA, with less legal precedent. Green could appeal for arbitration, advised Herald, in a dispute, but that could go either way, and the player often chose not to challenge if the punishment was relatively small. The final report found Josh violated the player's conduct clause by making derogatory remarks toward his fellow teammate, a League employee, reflecting poorly on the League. The ethics committee recommended fining and suspending Green for two games by a 6-3 vote. It was the ethics committee's way of showing community understanding, thought Quint, but also a veiled warning the punishment for this first-time offense should be light to stand up if arbitrated. The public would never see the vote, which was not unanimous, as the League only released the summary findings and recommendations. Quint knew he needed to balance the penalty for Green's actions to appease the crowds without imposing a penalty Green or the Pirates would likely dispute. As long as he meted out a reasonable fine with a public press release as both rebuke and a warning, he perceived a way out of a public relations jam. Quint must be careful and walk a fine line. He knew, in the weeks since Green gave the interview, Green's offensive production continued at a record pace, and Quint feared the people still favored him.

Hoping to placate the public but give Green and the Pirates little reason to appeal, Quint fined Green $12,000, the equivalent of two games' salary, but chose not to suspend him. Quint felt this would set precedence against Green or anyone else not to offend the LGBTQ community. They were vocal and held the ear of many influencers, impacting fan support and the League's financial bottom line. Green's interview was a headache that needed to stop before it gained momentum.

Quint directed Cassius to work with legal on the wording of the press release rebuking Green's conduct while reiterating the League's nondiscrimination policy. He intended to show the League in lockstep with the public's concerns on equality and community, hopefully satisfying the small but vocal outcry after the interview. Already, with the Pirates home, some press coverage dropped off, and Green's extraordinary play continued unabated. Quint worried about that. If Green pushed back or continued to espouse his Christian views, it could become a bigger problem and harder to counter if he continued posting incredible offensive numbers. As it was, it was hard overcoming a fan base captivated by his on-field heroics. Quint must play this carefully, he thought. Hopefully, the hubbub would die down, and they could all get back to playing ball and continue with a financially successful summer.

If push came to shove, Quint might need to harness the press to combat Green's offensive output. It would take a seasoned pro working carefully behind the scenes, a skill Quint expertly cultivated and practiced patiently for nearly three decades. Either way, he would keep a close eye on Green. He still knew next to nothing about the man. "Cassius," Quint called to his assistant after he walked Herald Gripp out of the office, "I have a special job for you. Come see me when you finish drafting the press release, and we'll discuss what I want you to do...."

Fifty Eight

The League released their findings, stating Josh Green's actions expressing his position on gay lifestyle, while not illegal, were nevertheless callous and irresponsible, poorly representing Major League Baseball. They judged the issue a violation of the collective bargaining agreement, and Major League Baseball supported the LGBTQ community's admonition of Josh's comments. The collective bargaining agreement detrimental clause allowed the League to censor players who spoke adversely against their teammates as other League employees. Josh's disparaging remarks impacted his teammates and the LGBTQ community, violating the League's policy of a fair, safe, and discrimination-free workplace. While player opinions were their own, stating moral judgments and derogatory opinions during League interviews reflected poorly on the League. Therefore, the League fined Green $12,000 and cautioned him not to make further derogatory statements against someone's sexual orientation or cast a League employee's personal life in a derogatory light while representing the League.

Pops pulled Josh into his office when he arrived for their game at home against Cincinnati at PNC Park. Mark Johnson was already there as the League released the findings and fine, moments prior. Saul asked if he wished to appeal the League's findings. Josh said he would like to talk to Joe Arima before he answered but asked the two what would happen if he did.

"The player's union or the player's attorney of choice represents the player in front of a court-appointed arbitrator. The arbitrator has the final say. They can uphold, decrease or increase the penalty," Mark replied matter-of-factly.

"Josh, it's up to you. Talk it over with Joe," said Pops. "There is something you need to contemplate. There's the official process you can use to fight the fine, and there is the court of public opinion. I recommend you talk with Joe about what's best for you, considering both. They both impact you, but frankly, the monetary fine is probably less of a long-term impact than what the public, the fans, can do to make your life, well,—easy or hard. Baseball is a very fan-driven business, and the fans can be fickle, making life difficult."

Josh nodded and thanked them both. "How much time do I have to decide?" asked Josh.

"The player's agreement gives you 72 hours to ask for arbitration," replied Mark.

"Thanks, both of you, I'll talk to Joe after the game, and I expect to let you know tomorrow," replied Josh.

Josh got up and shook their hands. Pops added, "Unfortunately, this out-side-the-game stuff can pop up, it's not the end of the world, but best you can, set it aside when you take the field. Mark and I will do our best to help with the press, as you can expect their questions after the game. I suggest we say you aren't giving interviews today, and legally you have every right for that until you discuss it with your agent."

"Got it, Coach, don't worry about the gameplay. I know how to set aside the distractions and get the job done," said Josh as he smiled back at Pops when he said it. There was a look of focus and determination in Josh's eyes Pops rarely saw, even in his most gifted players. Josh exhibited calmness though he was in the eye of a brewing storm. His look was one, not of a rookie unaccustomed to stress, but of someone who experienced far worse situations and held true to his purpose.

Josh turned to walk out, then spoke over his shoulder to both men. "One thing you should know. The things I said during the interview were not rash, heat-of-the-moment ideas. While personal, the words are what I believe to be *the truth*. They are not my opinion. They are the reality of the good and loving God, what He declares right and wrong since creation. Telling the truth is the only way people know God is the standard of love and goodness, displaying man's need for repentance and a savior. I won't retract or change what I said, even though Roman tried to twist it and cut out my explanation of what I understand to be the only truth. To say otherwise is not being kind or compassionate. To deny the truth is not loving or helping my friends or my fellow man. If I were to retract or change course to appease the public, the fans, or even my friends here on the team, only then would I be doing something truly hurtful and wrong. I won't hurt people by telling them lies and showing them an easier path down the broad road to their destruction—not even if it costs me my life. That's something I know quite a lot about, as I have seen the destruction of lives and people who follow such a path. I will continue to love my fellow man and speak the truth, as it is the only way to find life. I will love them by walking the path the Lord sets for me, not just for myself, but so others might hear the truth and choose life."

Mark and Saul said nothing as Josh turned, opened the door, and quietly closed it behind him. "That's a hard path Josh sets for himself, isn't it, Coach?" commented Mark.

"I think he sees it as a path set for him by the Creator—one true path among many false paths he could choose. Life is about choices when there's a fork in the road or obstacle in the path," said Saul. "I think Josh has chosen to follow God's path for his life for a very long time, and those choices sometimes cost Josh dearly. He just affirmed he again chooses to follow Him in faith, despite the costs."

"What's at the end of the path, Coach?" asked Mark.

"Josh says it's the choice between destinations; destruction or life," replied Saul.

"It seems the path to life can be a tough choice, a difficult road," Mark commented thoughtfully.

"Yes, I think you're right, Mark. Judging by Josh's scar—even dangerous," said Saul, voicing something unearthed deep inside his conscience.

"Let's hope we don't need to see the dangerous part again, eh Coach?" said Mark, trying to break the seriousness of the discussion.

Coach Samuelson smiled and nodded thoughtfully. Mark got up to leave. "I will see if I can head off some questions from the press on this release, at least until Josh tells us what his response is tomorrow. Anything else you want me to do?"

"No, Mark, thanks for your good work. Right now, let's just play baseball."

"Right, Coach, that's the good news we can keep coming back to," said Mark as he walked out of the office and pulled the door closed after him.

Saul hoped Mark was right. The Pirates owned the best record in baseball and a decent lead in the standings. That should be reason to celebrate, but something unsettled Saul. He couldn't quite put his finger on it. Best to head out to the field and get into the flow of the pregame practice. He grabbed his cap to head out. It was sitting on his desk, covering his great-uncle's old pocket Bible. "Show us how to walk the path you have set for us, Lord, just like Josh," prayed Saul, and somehow, he heard a quiet answer.

I will, Saul. Keep your eyes on me.

Fifty Nine

J osh continued to play well, and the Pirates won two out of three from Cincinnati. After talking with Joe, Josh told the Pirates he would appeal the League's ruling and ask for arbitration. Since the hearing would be in New York, Joe called in a favor from Ezra, Nick's son and Joe's former protégé, who knew better the ins and outs of the arbitration court. In their first discussion, Ezra told Joe several of his firm's clients went through arbitration, and Ezra thought he could help Josh's chance for success. "Honestly," Ezra said, talking to Joe and Josh on speaker, "I think you have a solid case against the League ruling, and I don't say that lightly. First, you drew a conservative judge I know well, and second, the League's position is very tenuous, unlike some of my other clients. Besides, I don't like it when the League wields the players' collective bargaining agreement and its detrimental clause to club players in their effort to win public favor or PC points at the player's expense. In my estimation, that is what this is. The League wants to protect the bottom line, and they've judged upsetting the LBGTQ community will cost them popular support and revenue. The League still has wounds over its past discrimination. Although it ended segregation 75 years ago with Jackie Robinson, the League is still afraid of not being seen as progressive."

Meanwhile, the Pirates began a lengthy road trip through their central division rivals, splitting a four-game set with Milwaukee. Josh played well in the first two games when the Brewers pitched to him, going 4 for 8 with three RBIs, including the game-winner in the second game. The Brewers then walked Josh in six of eight at-bats for the next two games, limiting Josh to one hit and a stolen base as Milwaukee gave the Bucs their first back-to-back losses of the season. However, the Pirates headed into Chicago for an important four-game series against the division's second-place team. Josh immediately impacted the game against Chicago's ace by again hitting a three-run homer in his first at-bat of the series. After ending Chicago's eight-game winning streak with a win to start the series, the Pirates rolled over Chicago, sweeping the series. The Pirates were firmly cemented as the team to beat in the division, if not the entire National League. After the second game in Chicago, the arbitrator decided on Josh's case with the announcement made to the general public shortly after the team returned to their hotel that evening.

SPNN sportscaster Guy "Tac" Cornelius led off the baseball segment of SPNN's "Sports News" broadcast, reading the arbitrator's decision verbatim.

"In the case of Joshua Green versus Major League Baseball, the court of arbitration issues the following judgment. Under the Player's Collective Bargaining Agreement (PCBA), Major League Baseball may use pecuniary authority to fine and/or suspend a player if a player's actions on or off the field negatively impact the League. Precedent includes illegal and legal activities that negatively affect the League or individual teams and/or disparage or otherwise abuse League employees, including other players. However, the League must ensure it respects the individual's rights because of the broad nature of this so-called "Detrimental Conduct" clause and a limited outline of what legal conduct it precludes. The burden of proof is on Major League Baseball to prove its image was unnecessarily damaged or sufficiently unprofessional conduct against another employee warrants censoring the player's actions. In the case of Joshua Green and his interview with Roman Josephus, we must consider two protected concerns: An individual's privacy and self-determination concerning their sexual orientation and an individual's genuinely held and expressed religious beliefs. After a thorough review of the unedited interview with Roman Josephus, this court of arbitration finds the following: Josh Green's speech is consistent with his legitimately held religious convictions. Freedom of speech and religion are fundamental individual rights protected by the Constitution's first amendment. Furthermore, as a player, Joshua Green has no oversight authority whereby his statement may be construed as prejudicial against another employee's freedom from discrimination in the workplace, as already admitted by the League Ethics and Oversight Committee in their previous finding. When taken in the full context of the questions and responses of the interview, Josh Green's comments do not, in and of themselves, rise to the level of defaming or derogatorily singling out a specific person. Mr. Green treated all people equally when responding to questions, according to his belief in man's nature and his religious convictions. As such, Mr. Green's speech remains protected.

This court of arbitration finds Major League Baseball overstepped its authority under the PCBA, choosing one protected group over another, infringing on Joshua Green's religious beliefs and the protected freedom to express them, both essential tenants of the first amendment to the U.S. Constitution. While such speech may be objectionable to some, the League failed to show quantifiable damage directly or indirectly or prove Mr. Green's actions injured its public image greater than what would occur should Major League Baseball censor speech on religious grounds, against the foundational laws of this country. In short, the League failed to meet the burden of proof required using the detrimental clause of the PCBA to censor Joshua Green, and Joshua Green's fine is hereby overturned."

After finishing the lengthy statement, Tac Cornelius sat the paper down on his desk and sighed dramatically, looking back at the camera. "Wow, that's a whole lot of legal words for me," said Tac as the screen split to reveal both Tac in the studio, and Roman Josephus at Wrigley Field after the Pirates-Cubs game. "You're there with the Pirates, Roman. What does it mean for Josh Green and Baseball?"

Roman, as usual, was impeccably dressed in a dark blue suit and tie with his closed-cropped beard styled to perfection. "Well, Tac, it appears to be a victory for Josh and a loss for the League. The Pirates and Green refuse to comment on the interview or its fallout, continuing their silence since the fine and subsequent request for arbitration. But the commissioner's office already released a statement after the court's ruling. It reads, 'While Major League Baseball was disappointed today with the arbitrator's verdict, MLB stands behind its policy of protecting the rights of the individual to work and live without prejudicial or discriminatory conduct. Furthermore, Major League Baseball continues to support anti-discrimination based on Race, Religion, Country of Origin, or Sexual Orientation. It will continue to support the LGBTQ community by ensuring an environment of tolerance and freedom for our employees, teammates, and fans. No one should feel diminished or defamed for being who they are, and we want everyone, when they come to our ballparks, to be in a place where all people feel equally treated and respected, safe to live life and love without judgment. We support our employees rights and expect them to respect the rights and freedoms guaranteed by this country and adhere to League policy guidelines and governing contracts.'"

"Another slightly shorter policy statement Roman. Break it down," Tac said.

"Tac, basically, MLB failed to punish Green for what many call homophobic remarks. MLB sits in a tough place. According to the judge, Green's speech is protected, and the League has a public relations problem. Meanwhile, Green continues to pound opposing pitchers as he ignores his detractors."

"What can we expect next, Roman?" asked Tac.

"My sources say several LGBTQ groups plan to stage more protests outside of Pirates games, and they get their first chance tomorrow here at Wrigley. Meanwhile, Twitter® and other social media have blown up over the arbitrator ruling. MLB has little recourse, and as far as Green and the Pirates are concerned, the matter is closed, at least for now."

"And the Pirates continue to win?" finished Tac.

"Yes, Tac, the Pirates won again today, blowing out the Cubs, with Green going two for three, with two walks and two RBIs."

"It will be interesting to see how this develops, Roman, and we're sure you'll keep us up to date."

"Count on it, Tac!" said Roman as his side of the screen faded out, and Tac was back by himself on the broadcast. "And...you're out," said the cameraman, who held Roman's camera. Like a switch, Roman's painted-on smile evaporated, and he tossed the mike to the nearby technician and hurried out of the emptied ballpark to a waiting car. Roman did not like the ending of this story or the stonewalling Green and the Pirates did since his interview, but he chased an interesting fresh development and a new prized source. Politics, it was said, made strange bedfellows, and he just gained contact with someone inside the League's front office who may give him the edge he needed. Who cared if the League got what they wanted, thought Roman, as long as he got the story? Roman needed to be careful, as it would never do to have anyone know he was collaborating with the League against a player. As Roman walked to his waiting car, he enjoyed being the SPNN beat reporter of the hour. It came with an upgraded perk of a personal driver here in Chicago, and while not the biggest limo, it was one with a privacy screen between the driver and the backseat passenger. Roman got into the Lincoln and asked the driver to take him back to the hotel. Once he was sure the privacy screen was up, and the driver couldn't hear, he dialed the new number in his contacts saved under "X." "Cassius, glad you contacted me. I have a few ideas to go over with you, but why don't you tell me what you've got...."

Sixty

The final two games in Chicago saw a return of protesters similar in numbers to the San Francisco games right after Josh's interview first aired. About fifty people, many dressed in colorful rainbow garb, were holding signs, and a few with bullhorns tried to stir up the crowd of fans attempting to enter the stadium at the Marquee and Bleacher gates. The busy Chicago streets, the close confines around Wrigley Field, and the relatively small number of protesters made it difficult for demonstrators to impact the arriving fans. However, many national news outlets and some national syndicates, including SPNN, carried their message, interviewing many protesters. Regardless, Josh's prodigious accomplishments made him a story as the press followed the Pirates in greater numbers than even some big market teams. The Pirates arrived thirty minutes earlier than usual. Wrigley Field security ushered them inside through the Wintrust Right Field gate with little notice by the few fans nearby before the protesters could organize and confront them.

Josh's offensive output paced the Pirates throughout May, as the team led the League with a 41-9 record. The Pirates got even better in June. Their outstanding batting led the "Bigs" in multiple offensive categories, losing just three games all month. They entered July with a staggering 63-12 record, the best in Major League history at this point of the season. While his walks increased, Josh continued with phenomenal batting average and timely hits, propelling the Bucs well out in front of the competition. They were 12 games up on the second-place Cubs. Josh's numbers of .523 batting average with 42 home runs, 38 doubles, ten triples, and 116 RBIs were all historic highs. He also led the League with 116 base-on-balls and was third in the National League with 25 stolen bases in 33 attempts.

The press approached a frenzy trying to one-up the competition by adding something to the Josh Green story, but his back story remained largely a mystery. However, Josh's play was fuel to satisfy most reporters as he delivered no less than 23 game-winning hits in the seventh or later innings. He was hitting for power and production, with less than a half-season in the big-leagues, surpassing what many star players hoped for in an entire season. Of course, the press wanted more, and nobody more so than Roman Josephus. He got his first break after the Josh Green interview by bringing up the question of Josh's daughter and live-in nanny at a rare off-day press conference between games. While the rest of the reporting staff were still asking Josh about the game-winning double he hit to finish yesterday's comeback against the Milwaukee Brewers in Pittsburgh, Josh was nonplussed responding to Roman's line of questions in the Pirates locker room.

"Josh, our viewers would like to know a little about you and your incredible life this season. Some note your young daughter accompanies you to all the games and practices. Can you tell us a little about that?"

"My daughter and I are a team. She and I lost her mom just recently to cancer, as we previously discussed, Roman," Josh reminded Roman of one of the things Roman cut out of his sit-down interview back in May. "One thing I've tried to do is let Ruth participate in my life as much as she wants, and she loves watching me play baseball."

"How does she keep up with school, Josh?" said Roman innocently, knowing the answer.

"Well, schools out now, Roman, but we have a qualified teacher as a nanny who homeschools Ruth and helps me take care of her while I play baseball."

"So, this nanny, I believe her name is Mary Dalene, correct Josh?" asked Roman.

"Yes," said Josh expectantly.

"She accompanies you throughout the season, giving Ruth a chaperon and teacher all in one. Is that right?"

"Yes, that's correct, Roman. She helps Ruth, as she homeschools her, and helps us get Ruthie around when we are on the road."

"Does the team make allowance for all of this, Josh? It's an unusual setup, as teams rarely make such accommodations for their players." Roman needed to nail this down and get it out there for what he planned later.

"Yes, Roman, my contract with the team speculated an allowance for Ruth to accompany me, and the team also pays for a nanny with teaching credentials to accompany us. It was part of my contract with the Pirates when I came on board. Ruth and I are pleased to travel together with the team, and we couldn't do it without Ms. Dalene's help."

Mark Johnson cut in as he feared Roman was up to something. "Can we get a few questions from another reporter now, to be fair here, Roman?"

Roman acquiesced since he made Josh go on record, laying the foundations for his future interrogations. Now he would look for an opportunity to corner this Mary Dalene and use the additional information he held against her to get her to talk.

Sixty One

The Pirates' day off came on Thursday, the last day of June. It was their last free day before the All-Star break. Starting Friday, the Pirates first half season schedule finished with 12 games in 12 days. Eight games were at home against the Cardinals and Braves before heading to New York to play the Yankees in an interleague four-game series. Thursday evening, events would transpire to test the Pirates and the nation, as the entire country began a difficult summer. First, a death in an officer-involved shooting in New York City a few days earlier on Monday birthed spontaneous protest in New York when bystander video on the internet showed a white cop fall on one knee, wrestling with a black man. As the man pulled away, the cop drew and fired on the man as he backed a few paces away. Next to the kneeling cop, another cop lay on the ground with his back to both men.

With no lead-up video or body cam, it was hard to tell what happened. The cop claimed he and his partner stopped the suspect due to suspicious activity after a reported nearby mugging. An altercation ensued, and the police officer claimed the black suspect stabbed his partner, and he wrestled trying to control the knife, but the man managed to break free, and the officer shot him, fearing he would stab him. The suspect later died at the hospital. Then tragedy struck much closer to home for the Pirates in Pittsburgh's Oakland suburb. Reports of gunfire between two cars prompted a police response, with the first patrol car on the scene moments later. A witness described the vehicle, detailing its direction of travel. Another patrol car a few blocks away spotted a vehicle matching the description running a red light. The two officers pursued, and the suspect vehicle soon stopped, caught in traffic at a subsequent intersection. Four black youths exited the vehicle ignoring the police commands to surrender. Two each ran in different directions, with each officer chasing a pair. One youth was shot in the back after the pursuing officer said he saw him turn, raising what he thought was a gun in his hand. As it turned out, it was a cell phone. Emergency responders transported the youth to a nearby emergency room, but he succumbed to his injuries late Thursday evening. He was sixteen years old. The news reported the officer involved in the shooting, Jezreel Naboth, was a rookie cop just months out of the police academy.

The story riveted Pittsburgh Thursday evening, and by Friday morning, various groups planned protests throughout the city. Already galvanized by the ongoing NYC protests, the nation took to social media, and the news discussed the national outpouring of concern as emotions ran high. Spurred on by the violence, many groups around the country called for protests in Pittsburgh, New York City, and many other major metropolitan areas such as St. Louis, Chicago, LA, and Seattle, to name a few. These towns held something in common with Pittsburgh. They saw their share of violence and protest against police action, and many were home to Major League Baseball teams. By Friday afternoon, there was a growing consensus brewing within the Major League Players Union that something must be done to show support against racism in America.

The Pirates contributed three player representatives for the union. Thomas was the primary representative, and Andrew and Barney were alternates. The Players Union asked all MLB player representatives to join a Zoom call hosted by the player's union executive committee at 2:00 PM Eastern Time. The meeting began as most of the other Pirates arrived at PNC Park for the 5:10 game start time for Friday night's game against St. Louis.

After the meeting ended at 2:45, the Pirates three player-reps asked Coach Samuelson to call a player discussion in the locker room at 3:00 PM to discuss what transpired during the Zoom meeting. Coach Samuelson assembled the players as requested. Both player captains, Thomas and Andrew, asked Mark Johnson and Coach Samuelson to attend. Besides Pops and Mark in the room, Dr. Luke and old Pete were in Pete's office. Though they weren't in the room, they could see through the glass, and they left the door open to hear the conversation. In the training room just off the players' locker room, door open, Cy sat alone. As was his custom before a game, he read from his grandmother's Bible waiting to see if any player needed his help.

Thomas and Andrew briefly discussed and agreed on how to start the meeting. Andrew, as the team's long-term star and an African American, would speak first. With all eyes on him, Andrew began.

"Look, we've all seen what happened this week in New York City, and now we've seen what happened yesterday here in Pittsburgh. The entire country is energized against these shootings. The Commissioner's Office and the Players Union Office in New York received media requests for their response. The commissioner's office wants to release a joint statement with the Players Union. Tommy, Barney, and I joined a conference call with the Players Union and all 30 teams' reps on the Zoom call. This is the bottom line. The Union wants to make a visible response to the shootings. They look particularly to the Yankees and us as teams of great interest because the most recent shootings occurred in our backyards.

"What is the union suggesting we do?" asked J.J.

"The union wants to take our inputs but would like whatever we decide to do, done in unity across the League," said Thomas.

"Yes, while they didn't give us guidelines, I can tell you what some other representatives discussed," said Andrew.

"Surely they discussed kneeling for the anthem," said Judah, speaking impatiently on impulse.

"Yes, many teams suggested kneeling during the anthem," Andrew affirmed.

"And what has the League said about it?" asked Nate Fisher, the Oklahoman third baseman.

"Who cares," snapped Judah quickly before anyone could respond, through clenched teeth, "We need to do something," he added, seething with frustrated anger.

"Well, here's the kicker on that account," continued Andrew. "This is the Union's direct quote of the commissioner's office discussion with the Union leaders. According to our leadership, the commissioner is 'Receptive to a show of unity if done in a way that can positively reflect on the League's concern with racial inequality in America,' end quote," said Andrew.

"What does that mean?" asked Juan questioningly, voicing what most of the other players also saw as a perplexing statement.

"Well, we asked exactly that to the Union President and VP who led our Zoom meeting. They said it's all unofficial, meaning the League won't admit this, but they have a direct line to someone inside the commissioner's office. This source claims the commissioner assessed the public is against a passive, do-nothing response and worries it will seem callous towards public anger opposed to the shootings and rising sentiment against police brutality and racism. They fear fans will stop watching, possibly in droves. Basically, they want the players to do something they can get behind and say they were supporting players' freedom and rights to highlight injustice in the world, while we players take the blame if the fans don't like it."

"In other words, they're cowards either way," said Samson.

"They are playing both sides, trying to protect revenue for sure," replied Andrew, "And that is what the union said as well. Look, you all know the union president. He's a former player and, as a black man, has supported minority issues throughout his career. He told us this is the first time in his eight-year tenure as union president, the commissioner showed a willingness to support some player protest, as long as it's reasonable. In his opinion, MLB is reading the tea leaves and their own polling. They've judged the old policy of not reacting to current events will lose fans and money."

"So, they are worried about the bottom line," scoffed Judah, shaking his head.

"Let's be honest, for owners and most of the game's executives, Money is *the* powerful motivating force in the League's and team's front offices," said Andrew soberly. "To them, this is about business, and it's always about the bottom line."

"What about signs supporting the movements against racism in America? Why not have those on display?" asked one of the young relief pitchers.

"The union leaders asked about that. Apparently, wearing altered uniforms with supporting writing was not off the table with the League. Our union leaders suggested wearing a different shirt before the start of the game with words of support or the names of the recent police shooting victims."

"What if not everyone wants to take a knee, wear, or do whatever? Why not let each individual decide?" one of the other pitchers asked, and several others nodded.

"Look, the players' union would like us to show solidarity, so they want us to try hard to come up with something everyone can agree upon," said Andrew. Then he paused.

Andrew's thoughts returned to how he, Thomas, and Barney discussed this meeting and their brief plan on presenting the Players' Union and League's view during the Zoom meeting. Andrew and Thomas trusted their friend and sounding board, Barney, to give sensible, levelheaded advice. Though Andrew reluctantly agreed to lead the team discussion about to take place, he was concerned his voice, or even their three voices, would override the freedom of all the players, and this situation affected them all. He didn't want to impose his feelings on others. Andrew was a calm and experienced vet, rising from a poor background, knowing what it was like to carry his family and dreams of a better future from life of a dirt road, barely making ends meet, Louisiana family upbringing. His grandfather was a sharecropper, and his mom and dad worked multiple jobs to give their kids a chance at a better life. He traveled a tough road, becoming a Major Leaguer through hard work added to superb, God-given talent. Once he turned pro, he continued bringing up his extended family by constantly sending money home even before becoming a star in the Major Leagues. He earned the Team Captain title, and the entire team looked up to him, but as they discussed what they should do, Andrew felt his voice should not override others.

Andrew knew Thomas, a white guy with a middle to upper-class upbringing, went to a great college. Though he became a pro ballplayer, he also led a life full of other options outside of baseball. Andrew's upbringing experienced more of the life of poor minorities, and the other two looked to him for his lead on how they should talk to the team. Barney was also a black man, and though he wasn't a Team Captain, Thomas and Andrew liked his workmanlike background and attitude, as he always seemed to understand and voice how the average player on the team felt. After discussing several options for addressing the team, the three settled on Andrew leading the conversation. Andrew still felt like he shouldn't be the only one talking, and before meeting with the team, Andrew turned to Barney and asked, "Barney, you haven't said what you think of what the union is suggesting. What do you think we ought to do?"

Barney was thoughtful, and he looked back and forth to each, then said, "I don't know if I know what to do, but I do have one thought, and I mean no disrespect to either of you. I think, whatever we do, we ought to ask Josh. I understand why the union reps want New York to be one of the leaders. However, I think they are looking at Pittsburgh, not just because of what happened yesterday but because of Josh. Everyone's eye is on us because of our record and his play this year. As the year progresses, we all have come to look up to him, not just because of his play. Something tells me he has a perspective everyone needs to hear."

Andrew thought about Barney's comments as he sat before his teammates, and the discussion continued around him. Barney's profound statement struck a chord with Andrew, giving voice to Andrew's unconscious discomfort. Andrew knew Barney was right. Josh became their unofficial team leader in this most incredible first half-season in baseball history. Andrew surprised himself that this revelation didn't bother him. On the contrary, he felt a little relieved. While it made him proud, leading this team was a difficult burden. Andrew struggled to give the team what it yearned for, what it needed. With Josh's arrival, he not only felt better about the team on the field, he felt better about the team off it. The pressure lifted off his back, giving his career a resurgence, with his best season since becoming the League MVP five years ago.

Andrew snapped back to the present, realizing everyone looked at him as he sat silently, thinking about all these concerns. Their eyes were on him, looking for him to proceed, but he found his eyes locked on Josh. The oldest player in the room, Josh, sat in the middle yet very back of the players in the semi-circle facing Andrew, Thomas, and Barney. Still, Andrew saw clearly those deep, penetrating ancient eyes. Josh waited patiently as Andrew realized he had been staring at Josh for some time, and Josh had yet to say a word. Andrew made a decision. In his heart, he gave the team over to Josh. Andrew knew he could trust Josh to take them where they needed to go. Later in life, Andrew often said it was one of his best moments, which made him glad when he thought about it long after, and he never once regretted it. "Josh, I think it is important for us to hear from you. Would you tell us what you think is the right thing to do?" With Andrew's words, the team's focus shifted as everyone turned their eyes upon Josh.

Sixty Two

A s the crowd of players turned toward Josh, the other onlookers rose to make themselves able to see and hear the man as he finally spoke. Dr. Luke, Pete, and Cy quietly moved into the room, joining Saul, Mark, and the players. Although they could all hear what was being said by the previous speakers, it seemed everyone wanted the best possible vantage to listen, see, and remember.

"Bear with me for a moment before I answer what I think we should do. First, I want to tell you a story," Josh began. "There was a young man, not particularly smart, wise, or talented. He began life simply and though not wealthy, was blessed with the good fortune of a loving family, living in a prosperous and free country. What this family lacked financially, they made up with a firm foundation of love, caring, and teaching the boy what was important in life. He learned much from his mother and father. Most importantly, they taught him God loved him and had a plan for his life. When he did well, they complimented and encouraged him; when he did wrong, they disciplined him in love. He grew up knowing his family's love, though imperfect, reflected God's love. What became evident to this young man was his need for God's love and redemption. As he grew, he chose to follow Christ and put his trust in Jesus as his Savior."

"Now, this man's father died young, and he was left to help his mother raise his younger brothers and sisters. He put away any hopes or dreams centered on his personal advantage and instead served his country, thereby serving his family, who raised him so well but needed his help. He traveled the world, and God taught him how unique and precious his family and his country were, for he saw so many without a family who knew God's love or a country guarding and guaranteeing God's freedom to choose how they lived their lives. Each time he came home, the man remembered he, his family, and his fellow citizens were so fortunate to live in a country that respected individual freedom and accountability, where all were equal under the law. His country was not perfect, and there were no guarantees of a bright future, but there were, as his father taught, always opportunities. If any citizen worked hard, followed God, did justly and mercifully to those around him, and loved others as Jesus loved, then life in his country was full of hope for the future."

"When his nation sent the young man abroad, he saw a world and many places where people knew nothing of love, peace, or justice. His home wasn't perfect, but much of the world languished in hopelessness, brought on by dictators and tyrants, both religious and secular. Only his homeland and its ideals, an oasis of freedom, guaranteed the freedom promised by God through Christ. The founders trusted the Creator's wisdom of endowing man with free choice and the right to pursue happiness as free-willed individuals. This man saw what happened when men forfeited their freedom to a government or a false god. Inevitably, they lost all hope, and the few men at the top took all the power. Soon, they wound up with no freedom, security, or happiness, as their lives and entire society descended into a nightmare of despotism, poverty, and physical and social slavery."

"Eventually, the man returned home, first taught what was true and sound as a boy, now, an experienced witness of the reality of a world turning its back on this truth, without God, and bereft of freedom. He knew God and Jesus held the truth of humanity's freedom. Apart from God, man has no moral compass, and when anything goes, and a culture's morality becomes based on opinion, God's good and wise counsel is forgotten. Truth is traded for expediency and finally ridiculed as men elevate their base desires, becoming their own gods, deciding what is right in their own eyes."

"Our man, throughout his journeys, saw when humanity turned their back on God, they always set up false gods with false beliefs. Soon they abandoned their freedom for promised security, becoming slaves to their leaders of false religions and the despotic governments who wielded their false beliefs. [1] Some followed false gods, some claimed no gods, but all followed the same broad paths of self-righteous destruction. There are no limits to the destruction and evil done by these relative morals, chosen by men, created by their false beliefs, to them and their society. When humanity rejects God, they become selfish and self-centered. They replace the truth with man-made idols of false religions or place their faith in their governments, praying to them for salvation. Their end is always the same. Children are destroyed and sacrificed, and brutal sins become commonplace, hidden within twisted beliefs and corrupt laws. Within a generation, man descends into debauchery and destruction. Their elders scoff at history and examples recorded in the Bible repeatedly, as if it were inaccurate fiction, yet watch as their children and grandchildren do the same."

"This man, however, remembers history replete with examples. Hitler rose from an 'enlightened' nation, yet he and his followers destroyed their society and almost the world in a single generation. Ultimately, our man learned the truth of

---

1. 1 Thessalonians 5:1-3; Romans 1:24-25; Isaiah 1:1-31

the Bible's warnings, not just from his parents' teaching but from his experiences traveling the world. Since Adam sinned and his children followed in his footsteps, when man forsakes God and goes his own way, he destroys himself with his sinful actions wrapped in his warped, self-serving morality. His self-appointed leaders, unconstrained by God's word, are often the most wicked and destructive of all."

Josh paused and looked around. The men were more than a little shocked, but because he spoke with authority, they held their peace and remained fixed on him.

"Now, let me tell you about the present and what I see here in our country," Josh continued. "When we began our journey this season, I was an unknown player and person to you. Today, just a few months into this season, we've grown to know each other better. I try to convey who I am and how I care deeply for each of you with honest words and actions."

"We are all ballplayers, but we come from many different backgrounds. The Creator has blessed us. He blessed us with the talents and abilities to play a sport well. He blessed us with the opportunity to live in a country where we are free to pursue this sport as our occupation and receive great rewards. We must draw an honest and true conclusion; such a country, built on the expression of people yearning to be free and the promise to protect those individual freedoms, is precious and rare in this world. Every man, woman, and child, every citizen of this country, despite their background, where they come from, how much money they have, or how difficult their particular circumstance, all have freedoms few in the world enjoyed a mere 250 years ago. Even 60 years ago, many of our citizens were denied equal opportunity due to race, color, or sex. The United States is a beacon on a hill to the rest of the world. She stands for freedom and personal liberty. She leads by example, trusting in this truth; man only prospers when he respects every individual's freedom, protected by government, but created as a birthright by a loving God."

"I believe America, and its foundation of liberty and equality, starkly contrasts most of history. Man often forfeited his freedom, granted by God, sometimes to war and oppression, but often through his own corruption inherent in his sinful nature. Make no mistake, America is far from perfect. It began not as a perfect nation but with right and true ideals, expressed by our founding documents, af-firming individual freedom granted by the creator, not the government. America held these ideals as its 'crown jewels.' They were not physical treasures, not a force of divine right to be wielded by leaders, but a belief in man's freedom to choose his destiny, given free will by God as an individual right. In the stated truth, All people are endowed by the Creator with inalienable, unremovable rights of life, liberty, and the pursuit of happiness.[2] We became a country by fighting for the right to promote, protect, and establish our nation to uphold the right and freedom of the individual."

"God created the individual in his image to exist free, not a slave or servant, but a free person. We, as a nation, struggled to ensure our country continued toward that lofty goal. We failed many times. In the past, we failed many citizens by not treating them as equals. We wrote hundreds of laws against our core ideal that all are created equal. Even our founders' actions failed to meet the standards their words of truth espoused. Blacks remained enslaved, and women were treated as second-class citizens. Poor struggled; their vote suppressed. Throughout history, we Americans have constantly called ourselves out to rise to the promise of those original good ideals. We fought a civil war to bring freedom to the enslaved. We continued to struggle for another century, working to see liberty guaranteed with equality of opportunity, regardless of race. Indeed, we failed throughout our history. Sometimes our government, laws, or institutions failed the high standard of the simple founding American truth; all are created equal by their Creator to be free."

"We must acknowledge the failures of our history and the strides taken by all Americans, ensuring the blessings of liberty and bringing the promise of freedom to all our countrymen. We should not forget how unique and rare this country is, founded on individual freedom. Man's nature is to rebel against his Creator, denying the freedom of his fellow man in pursuit of his self-interest. Man's natural state leads to domination and enslavement, not the Creator's intention of freedom and equality. We made a country based on ideals and fought for those ideals against man's nature. We fought and stood and raised, with God's blessing, the freest, most equitable, though imperfect nation in the world's history. Each generation refined the laws, government, and institutions, ensuring freedom's blessings are guaranteed to all."

"However, this is what we often fail to understand and admit. We cannot change the character of natural man, and despite our country's institutional progress, individuals continue to fail. We treat one another not as individuals and equals but as 'us against them' and more often as 'me before you.'"

"Here is the crux," Josh said, as they all searched his words, "The seed of our current situation. The actual problem we face is the same one faced by man since Adam's fall. Man's nature is morally corrupt. Our country's brilliant and God-acknowledging constitution set boundaries to protect the individual from the government and unfair, unequal treatment. Still, laws are only guardrails and

---

2. Paraphrase of the Declaration of Independence, July 4, 1776

cannot change man's nature. Man's heart is exceedingly wicked,[3] wanting to dominate and take steps to promote himself at others' expense. Fear and misunderstanding continue. Even though our government is built and established to protect freedom against prejudice, imperfect individuals still fail to live up to the standards of our ideals."

"We, in America, must not give up on our ideals or our attempts to guarantee them to all our citizens by seeking to tear down our institutions trying to uphold them. What is good and hopeful in this country comes from generations molding our institutions to meet those ideals. We must pick ourselves back up and try again to meet them for all. We must hold all our people to the high standard set in our foundation. The enemy of the Creator's free creation is man's immoral response and misuse of his freedom. His sinful nature often begins with his denial of his fellow man's freedom. The enemy fights us and uses our flaws to deceive and trick us into thinking it's the other guy's fault. The enemy I speak of is two-fold. Satan, the prince of this world, seeks to deceive people and use lies to cause them to destroy each other. Also, our sin can destroy a nation built on Godly ideals when our sinful self-serving actions bring hurt and pain to those around us. The devil uses lies and our failures to enslave man and ultimately lead us to destruction."

"I believe these deaths in New York City and Pittsburgh are tragedies. I don't know yet, as the facts are unclear, if they were failures by the police or police trying to protect us in a difficult situation. We must stand for an honest accounting of what happened. So, I say to you, I don't know where the fault lies, but I know where it doesn't. Since the 1960s, our country has taken great strides toward protecting the individual and each person's freedom, regardless of background or race. We represent the different paths traveled to get to where we are today. We are living proof the opportunity exists for all to benefit from this country's freedom. We all owe our own life of liberty to this nation and the promise she keeps. Where else could we live with such opportunity to live free and build a prosperous life in any other place or time in man's history?"

"We won't solve our problems by tearing down our country, but by protecting the freedom of all citizens. Our goal should be to press on toward the ideals enumerated in our foundation, not throw them away."

"Our problem is not our country. These tragedies reflect individual failures. Our laws in place guide us back to the truth and provide justice. Our country and our countrymen must pursue the truth by following the law to meet the promise of our founders to all people and hold each individual accountable for their own actions."

---

3. Jeremiah 17:9

"In the end, our true problem originates in our hearts. Our problem is our individual sins. The solution comes from the Creator's actions and our choice: The free choice God gives us to follow Him. We are imperfect and cannot save ourselves, but He is perfect and came to save us. My Lord, the Creator, is Jesus. He is the only way. He showed us his love in that while we were sinners, Christ died for us. His new commandment was to love one another as he loved us.[4] This is how we save our country and each other. We love and obey God. If we love God, we keep his commandments, and we love our fellow man.[5] We follow God and ask for his redemption to free us of our sins. I hold to this truth above all others. Jesus is the Christ and our only hope and salvation. We all choose to accept or reject His free gift. If we accept, we must and will love our fellow man and pursue the Godly ideals of life, liberty, and their pursuit for our fellow Americans."

All were silent for some time. Finally, Judah asked, "But what do we do to stand against the injustice in the world."

"Kneel," was Josh's immediate response. "Not against this country, for its ideals are good and true, not against the police, for they are a reflection of us and our imperfections. The police aren't just like us; they *are* us."

"Instead, we must kneel and ask God to forgive us and save us, to save our country, to save our police, to save our minorities, to save us all. We must ask God to forgive us and change our hearts to love each other instead of denying each other the same basic privilege the Creator built into us: The right to live free and choose. He offers us His love and salvation. If we choose Him, only then can we truly love our fellow man as He loved us, even though it cost him so much. Even though it cost him death on the cross."

After a few moments, Andrew asked quietly. "How do we show this love, Josh?"

"I would say we come together before the start of the game and show our country what we believe. The problem isn't our country, our police, or anything other than our individual sins. We need forgiveness. We need a savior. He is ready to show His love to all. I will kneel and pray, asking the Lord to heal us, heal those these tragedies have hurt, and save this country."

"You're suggesting we kneel and pray as a team in front of the crowd and the other team?" asked J.J.

"I suggest we invite the other team to come and kneel with us," stated Josh.

"And if they don't?" said Judah in disbelief.

---

4. Romans 5:8; John 13:34

5. John 14:15-24; John 13:35

"All must choose, Judah. I have chosen in my heart already, and I will stay the course of that choice. I choose Christ, so I choose Truth."

"You won't kneel for the anthem, against prejudice, against police brutality?" added a skeptical Judah.

"I am against prejudice and brutality, but it's not our country, its ideals, and its institutions that are to blame. That is a lie. You have the right to kneel during the anthem, but I won't kneel for a lie," Josh said, looking at his fellow Pirates as he let his statement sink in.

"Our country stands against prejudice and bigotry. Since our founding, over a million Americans sacrificed their lives for our freedom. We should not kneel against our country and the sacrifices made to protect our ideals. Instead, we should stand with America to remind everyone what we, as a nation, 'of the people, for the people, and by the people,' believe. We must stand for those freedoms to secure their promise, so no one is denied their freedom by tearing down our country and discarding our ideals."

"What if no one else follows your example or understands why you stand for the anthem and kneel after to pray?" asked Samson.

"All I can do is tell the truth," Josh replied. "Just as Christ told us to tell the good news. Salvation is the Lord's. Conviction comes from the Holy Spirit. Convincing or conviction aren't up to me. It is my responsibility to follow Christ where He leads and to tell the good news in both word and deed. Here I stand. I will trust and follow God and kneel to ask Him to save us according to His riches in Christ Jesus."

"It's a tough road, you hoe, son," said old Pete. Josh looked back at him, and Pete again saw the Gunny Sergeant Marine who guided him as a green troop just out of basic on a hostile jungle hill long ago.

"Perhaps, Pete, but I have seen many hard roads and few easy ones in life. Choose the hard road and the narrow gate that leads to salvation. It's not about how hard the road gets. It's about who you are following. Therein rests your destination. I will travel His road even though the way is difficult because I know only His way leads on to life,"[6] said Josh.

Josh turned back to the rest of the team. "Choose what you will do and who you will follow. Do so based on the Truth. Hold to it. Don't kneel for a lie, no matter who shouts or sings to you. No matter how easy and well paved, no matter how many walk it, for there lies the broad path to death and destruction.[7] Truth

---

6. Mathew 7:13

7. Mathew 7:14

is sharp, like a two-edged sword, and will cut through the fog of the devil's lies. Christ, and His word, speaks to all who hear the truth. I and my family choose Christ."[8]

"Your family? Will you bring your daughter out onto the field to kneel?" said Judah sarcastically, hands crossed over his chest.

"My family is whoever chooses Christ with me. They are my mother, my father, my sisters...," said Josh to Judah, then looking around the room, finished, "...and my brothers. "[9]

Again, there was silence in the room. Finally, Andrew stood up. "The Players Union executive committee asked us to reply...," Andrew paused, looking at his watch, "About now, actually. I will tell them whatever you decide. I think Josh has proposed an idea some are interested in, myself included. Can I get a show of hands of those that would like to do what Josh proposed?" About half the players raised their hands, including Pete, Dr. Luke, and Cy, who stood in the back. Mark also raised his hand. After a moment, before Andrew could speak again, Coach Samuelson waved at Andrew. Saul had stood at the back, leaning against the wall, without speaking the entire meeting.

"Coach, you have something you want to say?" asked Andrew.

"Yes, thank you, Andrew. Look, folks, I want you to know I will support whatever you choose. Think it through carefully. What Josh proposes might not gain public support or approval. We have a great team and a great season going. We also reflect our society. Over fifty percent of this club is black and Latino, a significantly higher percentage than the League average. Not to mention I, as the head coach, and my bench coach, Pete, are both black, which is also rare. Look, all I am saying is that the League is looking at us because of yesterday's incident, but so are the fans. They will judge what you do as your stance on race and minority issues. Make sure you send the message you want to send. The media will be all over this, and baseball can get much more difficult when you have your mind and the media focus on things outside the foul lines."

"Are you telling us what you want us to do?" asked Samson.

"Nope," said Saul. "I only remind you, your life decisions and behavior are a reflection, an extension of what you believe. The public will scrutinize what you do next on this team; so will every media pundit in the country. Make sure of what you believe and why you believe it—that it's worthy. You're about to show

---

8. Joshua 24:14-15

9. Matthew 12:48-50

it for all the world to see. Finally, I want you to know, as for me," said Pops as he looked at Josh, "I'll be standing for the Anthem, and I'll be kneeling with Josh."

The players were silent, but Pete, who chewed on his unlit cigar, said gruffly and emphatically, "Me too!" Dr. Luke and Mark both nodded and smiled. Cy looked on at Josh and raised his grandma's Bible in salute.

Many of the men in the room seemed ready to stand with Josh. Whether that held true outside the room, in front of the world, was anybody's guess.

Sixty Three

Before the game, each team took the field for warm-ups and pregame practice. Andrew and Thomas spoke to the union representatives, as did the reps for the other teams. There was no unanimous decision, but all other teams had players planning on kneeling during the national anthem. Andrew addressed the team as they returned to the dugout before the game started. "Based on the majority of teams and players, the Union recommended to the League everyone kneel in unity against prejudice during the anthem. They warn those who choose *not* to do so will be in the minority. They asked players to wear black shirts before the game and during the anthem out of respect for the deceased victims of police shootings. Like the anthem kneeling, the clothing change received tacit approval from the League. I told them that more than half of our players chose to do something different, and I discussed what we proposed to do. Though they understood our position, the union did not support it. Still, after a brief call with the League contact, they signaled the League will not stop reasonable demonstrations before the game since they already support the anthem kneeling and clothing wear change."

"What's our plan then?" asked J.J.

They all looked at Andrew, and he spoke, looking at Josh. "I think we all need to decide in our hearts what is right to do. Thomas and I discussed this, and we will back each individual's choice. This is America, and that's the rights and freedoms we have. I have thought about it, and I am following Josh's lead. I will not kneel for the anthem. I know we are hurting as a country, but we need to try something to cure what truly is causing all our problems. Taking a knee in prayer before taking the field, with those willing to do so, seems to me to be the best place to start. If you want, I will go talk to St. Louis about what we are doing and invite the Cardinals to join us."

"We will be seen as outcasts, standing against the victims of racial violence and kneeling after the anthem, for what? How will anyone know why we are kneeling? They'll think we're traitors to our people, cowards who won't stand against injustice, and they'll be all over us in the press," said Judah shaking his head, hands-on-hips.

"Judah," said Josh, "You're half Jewish and half black. Your great-grandmother on your mother's side died in a concentration camp, and your great-great-grandfather, was it? Was a runaway slave?"

"That's right!" said Judah hotly. Then asked suspiciously, "How'd you know that?"

"You put it in your bio in the team program," replied Josh, and Judah flushed, having forgotten. "Judah, the world will always find fault with us somehow. We can't let it dictate what we do and stand for. We must know what we believe and examine it, making sure it's right and true. Then we must act on our beliefs regardless of what the world says. Your ancestors knew that, and I think they stood against the world. You aren't a coward or a traitor unless you bow to what others do and say, when you know it's wrong."

Judah, who bowed up against the others at first, seemed to relax a little. "So, you are saying you want me to follow your lead? Not kneel during the anthem and go out and pray for God's help?"

"I am asking you to search out the truth. Seeking God is the first step in finding out what we should do. Without His help, we will fail. We won't solve anything when we go our own way, regardless of our intentions. But if you want a simple answer, I would gladly have you come and pray with me."

"I don't know if I believe in a good God. You just mentioned two of my ancestors who suffered terrible lives just because of who they were born. One died horribly, and the other traveled a hard road to get free. What good God would allow that?"

"All the more reason to love a country based on our freedoms of life and liberty and stand, declaring our nation's ideals to defend those freedoms. Regardless of our failures, always remember, there is One who loves us and never leaves us, no matter what the world throws at us," replied Josh.

"What if I don't have enough faith to believe He can fix this situation?" questioned Judah.

"Faith is a willful act, choosing to trust even when you can't quite see the way forward, and taking a step anyway, Judah. Faith is not blind, and God shows He is worthy of faith and trust, as time and time again, through His word, He faithfully carries His people through every hardship. God may not choose to fix our immediate problems, but He promises to lead us on and carry us through. God showed He is faithful to us by sending His only Son to lead us even through death. I hope you'll come with me, but whatever you do, God offers you His love and His salvation. You must decide—to choose to follow Him."

"Josh," Andrew said after Josh finished, "Thomas and I would like you to join us, walking over to the Cardinals, and we don't have much time."

The two captains and Josh walked over to the other dugout. The game would start with player introductions and the National Anthem in just a few minutes. The Cardinal captains were their All-Star catcher, a Puerto Rican legend who saw Josh's hitting prowess on opening day, and their All-Star pitcher. Both were nearing the end of Hall of Fame careers. The threesome of Andrew, Thomas, and Josh caught up with them in their dugout. Both were silent initially but soon asked a few questions about Josh's plan to lead the team in a prayer after the anthem. Both the Cardinals seemed a bit incredulous with the idea. Though surprised, they agreed to pass on the Pirates' offer to join in the prayer.

As was tradition, the teams took their position on each opposite foul line as they announced their names before the playing of the national anthem. Several of the Cardinal players donned black shirts. The Pirates radio announcers described the scene.

"On a normal day, folks, we'd be making small talk about what the Buccos might do against their National League Central Division rivals, the St. Louis Cardinals. This, however, is no normal day. With the events in the news in New York and Pittsburgh spilling over into our baseball world here at PNC Park, we find the world's problems weigh heavy on our hearts," stated Bob, more somber than his usual jovial self.

"That's for sure, Bob. As we watch the announcement of the starting lineups and the National Anthem, we see signs baseball is looking to make a statement about the shootings. But what the statement is, we're not quite sure," offered Greg.

"Yep, as the announcer introduces the Cardinals, it looks like some players have donned some kind of T-shirt that's not part of the standard uniform. It's all black; definitely not Cardinal colors. Many of the shirts have various slogans and support for some protest groups, while others are plain black," commented Bob.

"Some in this 36,000-plus near-capacity crowd wear similar shirts showing their support, and we see dozens of signs and slogans displayed. Here comes the Pirates starting lineup. No one from the Pirates seems to be deviating from the normal uniforms," stated Greg.

The Pirates all wore their standard uniform, while many St. Louis Cardinals, including their coaches, wore some version of black shirts. After the introductions, each team stood on their respective foul line as they played the National Anthem. More than half the players and some coaches took a knee on the Cardinal side while the Pirates all stood. Some in the crowd booed, but many clapped as well.

After the anthem finished, Bob announced on the radio what he saw. "Folks, if you're listening on the radio, what we just saw is fascinating. Many Cardinals took a knee during the National Anthem. Some wore black shirts over their uniforms, often displaying slogans supporting various organizations aligned against the police shootings. The Pirates, however, did not alter their garb, and no Pirate took a knee during the Anthem."

"Yes, Bob, strange to see the visiting team do that and not ours, especially given the shooting yesterday here in Pittsburgh," Greg replied.

"Quite a mixed reaction of cheers, jeers, and booing to it all, wouldn't you say, Greg?" asked Bob.

"Yes, and the thing is, all for different opinions. It's hard to tell—are they booing or cheering for or against which behavior? Are they for or against St. Louis with their shirts and kneeling or the Pirates for not changing anything?" replied Greg.

"Honestly, folks, we can't tell, but the crowd seems pumped up and vocal. Now, what is this?" said Bob, watching the scene.

The Pirates, who were in the field to start the game, gathered just behind second base. All the Pirates starters, Coach Saul, and Pete as the bench coach, gathered. Now the St. Louis Cardinals catcher, their perennial all-star and one of the few Cardinals who chose not to take a knee during the anthem, along with one of his teammates, jogged out to join the Pirates.

"Well, Josh, I am sorry there are only two of us, but as you saw, most of our teammates wanted to go another way," said the St Louis catcher.

Behind him, his young teammate, a pitcher from Cuba, said something to the catcher in Spanish, and he nodded.

"Javier here, says to tell you, 'Thank you for the opportunity.' As you may know, he only escaped Cuba last year on a small sailboat and still doesn't speak good English, but he said he loves America and Jesus, and he never could say that when he was playing ball in Cuba. Now he won't stop saying it..., literally! He's my roommate on the road, and he won't stop talking about it!" said the Puerto Rican superstar, half laughing, half shaking his head. This seemed to relax the rest of the Pirates. Juan waved the two men over to him, warmly shaking their hands in greeting. The St. Louis catcher was a personal hero of Juan's, as one of the great Latin American stars, and Juan also followed the young Cuban pitcher's story as a kindred spirit. They both knew true poverty and humble beginnings more than the average American, with Juan's difficult journey from the Dominican Republic to America and the big-leagues.

"Shall we all pray?" asked Josh.

Up in the radio booth, Greg described the scene. "Now the Pirates starters and Coach Samuelson, and it looks like Coach Pete, are met by two Cardinals who have walked out. They're all circling up just behind second base. They're taking a knee, holding hands, and bowing their heads. Apparently, they are praying?" questioned Greg, more than a little surprised.

"Well, it sure looks like it. Again, it's all our Pirate starters, including today's starting pitcher, Samson. And look, it looks like much of the bullpen and even the Pirate dugout. I see players, a couple of other coaches, and maybe some other Pirate personnel also circling. They, too, are kneeling and appear to be praying now, Greg!" Bob said, amazed at the scene.

"Yep, it's mass kneeling by the Pirates, folks, but not during the anthem as some might have expected," commented Greg.

"We're also seeing a lot of confusion from the crowd as this goes on. The umps seem slightly baffled as well. Wait! Now the ump by second base is taking a knee outside the circle. Looking at our camera, it appears Josh Green is the one praying in the large circle of men by second base."

"Yes, he's centered with Coach Pete on one side of him and Andrew on the other. The two Cardinals are also in the circle. Everyone is kneeling, holding hands, or hands on backs, with heads bowed. I wish we could hear what's said, but there's no mike out there," said Greg as he watched. Both radio announcers remained silent as the seconds passed. Finally, Josh appeared to finish.

"Green is wrapping it up folks, and the team is standing again," observed Bob.

In the circle, Juan and J.J., on either side of the two Cardinals, shook their adversaries' hands as they prepared to head back into the Cardinal dugout.

"Dios te bendiga, amigo mío," Juan said as he shook the young Cuban pitcher's hand. Translated, it meant God Bless you, my friend.

The young black man replied with a face-splitting smile, "Gracias a Dios por América, por la libertad y por Jesús!" Juan translated for those listening, "Thank God for America, for freedom, and for Jesus!"

Sixty Four

For the next eight days, the Pirates played eight games against some of their biggest National League rivals, the St. Louis Cardinals and the Atlanta Braves. They continued their winning ways, taking three out of four games against each team. Pittsburgh's PNC Park remained near capacity, unusual for the Pirates in recent years when they were much lower in the standings. The Pirates also drew a lot of scrutiny from fans, and non-fans alike, with their response to societal events of the moment. With the League's tacit blessing, nearly every League team now produced, distributed, and wore unique shirts during pregame activities. The clothing displayed minority and racial justice organizations and their slogans, often with the names of black men killed by the police emblazoned on the players' backs. The organizations advertised on the clothing led many demonstrations throughout the country, including in Pittsburgh. Some protests remained peaceful, while others turned into riots, with violence against police, government facilities, and the looting and burning of businesses to the tune of hundreds of millions of dollars in damage across the country.

About half the League teams knelt in unified solidarity during the National Anthem, with the other teams all producing various numbers of players kneeling; All that is, except the Pirates. The Pirates continued to buck the trend as the only team not wearing shirts celebrating race-based causes or anti-police protests and standing for the anthem. Instead, they continued kneeling together in large numbers and praying before the start of the game. In the first few games after the death in Pittsburgh, the fans in attendance jeered and booed them loudly. Some fans booed during the national anthem, but it was hard to tell if they were booing the Pirates for standing or the opposing team for kneeling. Each time the Pirates kneeled for their prayer, they invited the opposing team to join ahead of time. Besides the two players from St. Louis, others also joined. During all four games against the Braves, the Braves long-time skipper, a white man, came out to kneel and pray. He knelt next to Coach Samuelson, his old friend he coached in San Francisco as a young skipper when Saul first played. The men traded games of placing an arm around the other's shoulder as each alternated in leading the prayer circle. It made quite a sight to see. The crowd's reaction was confused and very mixed. After the first Braves game, the press asked Coach Samuelson about the Pirates' response to the country's problems during a post-game interview.

"Coach. You and the Atlanta coach seemed to make a statement today," started a local sports newscaster.

"Coach and I go way back to my San Francisco days," began Saul. "He was a great Coach for me and is a good Christian friend. We are glad to pray together for our nation's healing and God's help in these troubled times. Like most Americans, we are very concerned with race relations and what we see happening across the country. As I said a few days ago, the players and I discussed our response. We believe the right response is to come together and pray," Pops responded.

"Coach, has management or the owners curtailed or told the players they can't wear black shirts supporting the various groups or kneel during the anthem?" a Pittsburgh Post-Gazette reporter asked.

"Not at all. Management told the players they were free to express themselves and exercise their right to free speech. We ask it to be in good keeping with our team's values, appropriately representing the Pittsburgh Pirates."

"Yet we see nationally other teams kneeling and wearing shirts supporting protest groups. Why not here in Pittsburgh?" cut in Roman.

"It's true. The players chose not to follow what other teams are doing. They chose a different path to show their concerns, and the coaching staff supports them."

Before anyone else could pipe up, Roman continued, "Coach, you now have demonstrations outside the stadium from racial justice organizations you don't support, plus continuing demonstrations by the LGBTQ community opposing Josh Green's statements against Gay America and your Gay player, Zach. Why don't Pirate players want to end discrimination?" The demonstrations Roman referred to were limited to about thirty people, but the media, including SPNN, featured the protest prominently in taped broadcasts. Roman, in particular, conducted taped interviews of the small protest groups, and SPNN broadcasted them during their prime-time sportscasts so that the numbers of protesters were often hard to count. Roman highlighted the Pirates' unusual response to social problems, and the major news affiliates began to carry similar reports.

Pops answered, "Roman, first of all, Josh was clear about this in his comments. Josh considers all of us as equals and loved by God, so I reject your characterization of Josh and his comments despite your station's deceptive cut and editing job on his interview." Roman started to protest, but Saul said, "Let me finish, Roman. I don't speak for the players. Each determines how they express their concerns and beliefs. I can tell you this, no one in this organization supports discrimination or prejudice of any kind. We know bad things happen here in our community, and we want to help positively impact the community. That is precisely why we are doing what we are doing. To solve our problems, we must identify the *true* problem. Only when we understand and appreciate the reason for our country's problems can we seek a proper solution. We see the root of the problem differently than many of our contemporaries. Our nation and its institutions are not to blame. Rather, the core problem is individuals choosing to sin against God. That's why we look for a solution to the problem by placing our faith in God, seeking his help and forgiveness to change man's heart."

Many other reporters now asked similar questions to all the Pirates. The media seemed bent on defining the Pirates' unique stance asking the players why they weren't following the pattern of kneeling against racism and bigotry in America. Although Josh continued his torrid offensive production, Josh now received these questions most of all, as Roman treated him as the de facto ringleader and instigator of the team's position. Though Josh neither denied nor confirmed Roman's charge, the other reporters saw Josh's lack of rebuttal as tacit confirmation he was the ringleader and treated him to numerous questions about the displays of faith and standing for the anthem, with few about his historic play.

For Josh's part, he continued to be the center of the prayer circle and still kneeled before his first at-bat of each game, as he did all season. His brilliant play continued unchecked. After a great series against St. Louis, he went three for four against the Braves to open the series, including a seventh-inning home run that broke open the game and chased the Braves number one starter to the showers. Yet the questions post-game focused on Josh's stance and his kneeling.

Roman Josephus led the offensive. "Josh, you played a great game tonight, but before the game, you again led your teammates in prayer, with some significant booing by your hometown fans. The Pirates continue to buck the trend and stand for the National Anthem. You, in particular, seem to hold the anthem in high regard, turning to the flag with hand over heart. Can you tell the fans why you and your teammates are doing this?"

"Roman, I speak only for myself. You will have to ask the others about their reasons. I stand for the anthem because I believe in the founding principles of our nation; freedom and equality for all. I know we have problems, but we Americans recognize the great strides toward those principles we have made based on the struggle of our fellow citizens to meet such lofty goals. Our democracy and free market brought us the greatest prosperity and freedom the world has ever known. I know we're not a perfect nation, but many have died trying to secure and uphold our freedom. We live in an incredibly blessed nation that promises us the blessings of liberty and equality regardless of who we are. We expect our country to ensure those blessings to all citizens. Our country's laws and institutions guarantee all citizens the opportunity and freedom to make a better life for themselves, regardless of their beginnings, more so than any other country on earth."

"Throughout our history and even today, I see many people trying to make this country better. Our ideals and laws allow freedom and justice to flourish. Just because we have bad actors doesn't mean we tear down our democracy and throw away its values. We expect the bad actors prosecuted and justly punished, but it's not our country or our democracy at fault. I won't condemn what I know is a good and honorable foundation of freedom, fought for and built by millions over decades and centuries to produce this great free country, this land of opportunity."

"We have come so far in my lifetime, as we did for more than a century before I was born, as each generation strives to move forward towards those high ideals spoken in our original founding documents. There is still more work to be done, but I will honor all the sacrifices made to get us here. I love our country and all its citizens, the greatest melting pot and guarantee of God-given rights in history. Liberty is rare and fragile on this earth. We must defend it, not tear it down. I will do my part to uphold the expectations of freedom for all our citizens as God grants me the wisdom and ability to do. I remember the soldiers and freedom lovers who stood, marched, and fought in decades past to gift us our freedom and bring us to this point. That's why, when I hear our national anthem and see our flag, I stand, hand over heart, and hold my country dear.

Roman cut in accusingly, "Why aren't you kneeling, like all these groups, because of the police failure to protect these same rights you supposedly honor and protect the rights of the LGBTQ community?" Roman added the last for good measure, hoping to paint Josh as both racist and bigot.

Josh answered calmly, "When individuals fail, it means we need to work harder to meet the promises our flag represents. I see the flag and the anthem, our country's symbols, representing the high standards of individual equality our forefathers expected when they penned our founding documents. Our founders admittingly didn't reach those standards, but that doesn't mean the standards are wrong. We have come a long way in the centuries since. I stand to promise I will do what I can to ensure those lofty goals. I stand to honor those that fought and sometimes died doing the same." As Josh finished, there were a lot of reporters scribbling notes or looking down at their various recording devices, but there was an atmosphere of quiet contemplation considering Josh's words. The silence gave time for Roman to try yet another angle of attack.

"Josh, why then, after the anthem, do you lead what appears to be a group prayer with your teammates before the game begins."

"That's simple, Roman. I believe our country's true problem today, at its root, isn't the laws or practices of its institutions, and it's not one group oppressing another. The core problem lies with the individual. It lies in each person's heart. I believe everyone needs God's help to be the kind of person God created us to be. The Bible teaches us man's heart is exceedingly wicked. Racism pits us against each other in an 'us versus them' world. It stems from a misguided heart, judging someone based on their outward appearance. This is a sin. Our bible warns us that man looks on the outward appearance, but God looks at our heart.[1] Each of us must be convicted of this sin. God teaches us we are supposed to love one another as God's son Jesus loved us, all of us, equally. But sin gets in the way. Our problems in this country aren't our ideals. Our ideals acknowledge God created us with the rights of freedom and liberty *inborn*, not granted by the government. Our right to life, liberty, and the pursuit of happiness come from a Creator God who sees us all equally as his children, who He loves with a supernatural love. He knows we are lost in our sins and wants to redeem us."

Josh continued, "You see, Roman, I kneel in acknowledgment only God has the power to change our hearts. I kneel and pray God turns my heart to him and my fellow man's heart back to him. He alone holds the good and just future for us and our country. It starts with admitting our mistakes and asking His forgiveness for our sins and each other. Our problem, Roman, isn't what our country stands for. Our problem is rooted in each man's sin."

"This is our fundamental problem: Man doesn't reach the standard of freedom and equality set forth by our founders because of our individual bad choices. We all need forgiveness, forgiving others, and loving others equally as children of God, just as Christ loves us. This is what I pray for when I kneel before the game. I pray in the name of the only one who can change man's sinful heart, save us, and redeem our nation. I kneel and pray in the name of our Creator God to our redeemer, Jesus."

Roman said skeptically, "Are you saying that all those kneeling with you must believe this as well, that they also stand for the anthem and kneel to ask Jesus to save us against racism and bigotry?"

"You must ask them what they choose to believe. Every human being must make this choice. I invite all who would join me to come and pray without stipulation or condemnation. Each comes of his own accord, and each must choose where he places his trust and faith. That is both man's right and obligation, given by the Creator. None escape the requirement to choose. First, seek truth, then strive to hold on to that truth. Reject the lies, regardless of whispers or shouts and how appealing those lies might be."

"First, I believe the truth is Jesus. He proved this because only He lived a perfect life, died for our sins, and rose from the grave. Only He holds the answers to our

---

1. 1 Samuel 16:7

problems. Only He can save us. I choose Jesus Christ. I accept his salvation and payment for my sins and follow His holy word and example."

"Second, I pray for His help and blessing to love this country and its Godly values. Like no other country on earth, its foundation declares the freedom God and Christ gave us when they created man. I reject any person or organization espousing a different story. There is only One Truth, and the rest are lies hidden in clever half-truths, trying to deceive men with seductive falsehoods appealing to man's sinful nature. We must discern the truth, even when it exposes our failures. I know this. Our country and its ideals are good. They guarantee us freedom and prosperity, fought for and paid in our citizens' blood since our nation's creation. I don't discount when the nation fails to live up to the promise of those ideals. Instead, I remember those who sacrificed to make the changes to ensure equality and justice for all. We are responsible for securing the blessings of liberty for all our citizens. When someone fails, we must ensure they are held accountable."

"Our problems now lie in individual hearts. Only by acknowledging man's true nature and the Creator's endowment of individual freedom can we understand our freedom demands personal responsibility. If we do not grasp this truth and keep judging people by their outward appearance while ignoring the problems of the heart, we cannot progress towards the benchmark of equality and freedom for all. Each person must decide to live up to our country's promises, one person at a time. We have come such a long way on the road to liberty's promise, but when we fail, we must ask forgiveness, pick ourselves back up, and turn away from the actions that led to our failure. I look to Christ's example of love and righteousness and ask Him to help us follow Him and His example. Only then will our freedom be fully realized."

"Sounds awfully religious, Josh. Not all people believe as you do. Not all or even most are followers of Jesus Christ. What about the rest?" objected Roman.

"I can't speak for them, Roman, but I fight for their right to be free, by holding on to what I know is True. Christ alone can save us and set us free. Our nation is a city on the hill, a beacon of freedom and prosperity to all the world. If we want to bring these principles of freedom and justice for all, we must continue to seek God through Jesus, the source of all good and the Creator of our inalienable rights. If you see good in my actions, it is solely because I follow Jesus and what he does in my heart and life." Josh finished, and no one asked him any more questions because they could find no fault in his words.

Though the reporters tried similar conversations with other players, few would go into as much detail. Roman turned to Zach, hoping to drive a wedge into Josh's hold on the team.

"Zach, despite what Josh said about you in his interview with me, you are joining with him, standing for the anthem, and kneeling in prayer. Many from the LGBTQ community are protesting outside and inside the stadium. Why join Josh in prayer?"

"Josh invited me to pray with him, as he did the others. I told you that even though we don't always see things the same way, I still believe Josh has the best interest in mind for our team and me personally. I believe he's correct when he says we need healing in the hearts of men. The mistakes and terrible losses the black community endures, I think, are because of individuals making terrible decisions. We each must be accountable. I have begun asking God to help me understand this. I ask for him to help me, to help us. So does Josh. That's why we pray."

"Zach, you're black, and you're gay. Aren't you standing against both when you take this approach?" Roman accused bluntly.

"Roman, you are neither, so don't tell me how I should act or feel," snapped Zach. It shocked Roman. Zach softened slightly as he continued. "Look, I am sorry, Roman, but I have seen Josh's heart in action, and I have also seen hatred against me in ways you never have. In Josh, I see his life and what his beliefs in God mean to him based on how he lives and treats all of us. He invited me to come and pray with no expectations, no requirements."

"I decided to seek God because, to tell you the truth, nothing else seems to work for me or my community. No one else offers true solutions to correct the problems in our world. I'm not kneeling against our country because I believe that's not where the problem lies. I am unsure how to fix our problems, but I know tearing down our country or tearing it up..., well, it just isn't the right way. Look, I want our country to stand up for all people as it promises. I stand, just like Jackie Robinson did. He stood despite the systemic racism and awful things going on for many African Americans. I stand to ask our country and my countrymen to see me as an individual, as an equal. Sometimes individuals fail, and I want to hold those who hurt others accountable. But I know man fails at the individual level, even if the laws are in place to protect us from racism and bigotry. You can't fix men's hearts by fighting and tearing us apart. As Josh says, you can't fight evil with evil; instead, we must overcome evil with good."[2]

"We all fail sometimes. Josh is fond of saying so, but he points out Jesus alone never fails. I remember reading how Dr. King warned us, "Returning hate for hate multiplies hate, adding deeper darkness to a night already devoid of stars. Darkness cannot drive out darkness; only light can do that. Hate cannot drive out hate; only love can do that."[3]

---

2. Romans 12:21

3. Dr. Martin Luther King Jr., Strength to Love, 1963

Pausing, Zach smiled while collecting his thoughts momentarily, then hurried on. "Josh teaches us how Jesus is the only one who always loves us all the same, all the time, even when we fail. Josh read to us how Jesus is the way in every sense of the word, the way to freeing our hearts from the chains of bigotry and prejudice and all the other sins that bind us. I've known for a while that men's hearts make them do the bad things they do, but recently I've realized I need help too. If I want to love and live as a good and loving human being, I've got to start with my own heart." Zach hesitated, formulating what was happening in his heart and mind for the past few weeks. He continued, "I guess what I'm saying is I realize I need that from God. I can't tell you all the answers, but I now kneel and pray to ask God..., to show me the way." Zach paused, searching, then said slowly, "Because I've tried everything else and still haven't found the love and hope I see in Josh. I love my community. I love my black and my gay brothers and sisters, but we all need help just like everyone else," Zach shrugged.

He grabbed his shoes and began to put them on. "I see too many seeking to hurt, fight, and tear down, but to what end?" Zach asked the reporters in the room. They all remained silent, looking at Zach. "Look, that can't be the solution. If you know me, you know how I grew up under tough circumstances in a border town in Texas where crime, gangs, and drugs were rampant. I won't demonize the police," he said, shaking his head as he slipped on a shoe and began tying the laces. "More often than not, they were the only ones who fought *for us*—just to survive, the drugs, the gangs, all of it," Zach said, gesticulating with his free hand as he popped on the second shoe. "Look, cops aren't perfect, and occasionally some do bad things, but not most of them. Without the cops, my community would fall apart." Zach shrugged honestly, "My big brother, who grew up taking care of us, became a cop because he saw what they did to help our community and us. He's been a cop now, back in that same neighborhood for more than a decade, and he fights **eve–ry–day**," he said slowly with emphasis. "He fights for those kids, like us, who just want a chance to grow up! We talk often, and sometimes it's like he fights a losing battle. He prays for protection, and honestly, even when I wasn't sure there was a God, I prayed for God to keep him safe from all the bad things in this world. I prayed for God to keep all those back home safe, to give them a *chance!*"

"I know the problem is in the hearts of our fellow man and our hearts. And now I must admit, in my heart, I think." Zach said as he shook his head, raising his hands with a shrug. Shoes tied, Zach sat on his hands, thinking, then said, "I *think* we need a supernatural intervention. I *think* we are lost without God. Just look at the world; look at history. I think Josh is right when he says only Jesus can change a man's heart."

He looked back up at the room of reporters and was now more resolute. He focused firmly on Roman, crossing his arms and leaning back committedly. "Yes!" said Zach, "I *have* begun to kneel and pray to God, to ask this Jesus for a solution to our problems. But most of all, I ask him to fulfill His Promise and change our hearts, help us, heal us, and heal our land. I want and need someone to do that for me, so I pray; so does Josh."

Zach looked around at the reporters and shrugged. In all the years they watched this young man, they never saw him quite like this. Zach finished honestly, "If anyone says I am a traitor to my people, to the cause of freedom and justice, to an end of bigotry, well, they don't know me very well, and they don't know my heart. But God does!"

Zach smiled at the thought, but the reporters, including Roman, remained silently astonished.

Sixty Five

J une departed, the peace of spring long forgotten. In came July, sweltering and restless, a roiling pot threatening to boil over. As the Pirates' four-game series against the Braves concluded, just a week since the men's deaths in Pittsburgh and New York City, the League remained embroiled in the tumult spilling over from cities throughout the country with protests and displays supporting various causes. Though many voices contended for supremacy, there was no clear consensus on how players should display their sentiments. Many chose to kneel during the anthem, wearing logos supporting different movements. However, these movements were contentious and often confrontational, with their public demonstrations sowing violence and discord.

Each held their agendas, moving far beyond racial equality or anti-bigotry. The various movements seemed to only agree on their denial, to varying degrees, that the nation's founding was freedom and equality. Prejudice and privilege were the touchstones many in the movements used to call for change to the basic principles of the government, its institutions, and American society. The interest groups increasingly called for wholesale abandonment of free-market and democratic tenets, rejecting fundamental American ideals. They set up chaotic "police-free" zones and championed government reparations in payment for injustices of even the distant past. Often the movements focused only on the failures of the founding fathers, rejecting and refuting their ideas, calling their motivations inherently racist. They pointed to the struggle of minorities throughout the country's history as evidence the police, the justice system, and even the government as a whole were the cause of the problems for African American and other minority groups in the past and present day. Some within the movements called not just for justice for individual failures but an end to the police entirely. They wanted to radically change the government in form and function as the root cause for all the problems of their communities.

Not all teams or players showed support by wearing the interest group slogans; some stood during the anthem, though they were in the minority. Those few individuals often heard a vocal and growing contingent of movement supporters booing from their lofty positions.

Josh led the Pirates in their pregame kneeling prayer in Pittsburgh, joined by a few visiting players from St. Louis and Atlanta for the eight home games. Elsewhere in the League, some players began to pray similarly in small groups before their games. One such series receiving heavy press coverage was the Texas Rangers versus Seattle Mariners series in Seattle. Support for the anti-police and anti-fascist protests in Seattle was strong. When five Texas Rangers and two opposing Seattle Mariners stood during the anthem, unlike their teammates, many booed. When they then proceeded to kneel together behind second base before the start of the first game and pray, the crowd booed louder, leaving no doubt about their feelings. On the third day of the four-game series, a fan jumped out of the stands, ran up to the kneeling players, and threw two bottles of red liquid at them before being caught and arrested. The liquid turned out to be harmless, but the teams and fans in the stadium were uneasy for the rest of the game.

The news of the fan actions broke as the Pirates arrived at their hotel in New York City after winning the final game at home against the Braves. They were tired from playing eight straight days and looked forward to a good night's rest before their evening matchup with the Yankees for their four-game series before the All-Star break. However, they could not miss the west coast Seattle mayhem reports as national news affiliates reran the video. The Pirates watched the replay of the prayer circle dousing, looking at each other in disbelief.

The following day, not far from the Pirates hotel, the commissioner of Major League Baseball, Quint Pilate, brooded as he hung up his phone. He leaned back in his expensive desk chair, high above the streets of Midtown Manhattan, watching the latest morning newscast. Though muted, Quint again saw the disturbing Seattle video. Quint didn't miss the fact that the news channel he watched was not a sports station. The Seattle video headlined multiple national news broadcasts. At just past 8:00 AM, Quint already fielded six calls from worried owners asking where these demonstrations were leading. The last call came from an owner of one of the League's large market star teams. The owner's not-so-thinly veiled comments still rang in Quint's ears. "When this started, you told us to allow our players to support anti-racist movements. You promised it was the best way to gain the support of the paying customer with the least problems for us. Now we're seen as a politicized organization, no longer neutral, and we're losing more fans than we gained. Plus, you've got these religious folks kneeling and praying, causing even more trouble right in the middle of our ballparks. You opened this can of worms. Fix it!"

Quint sat for a few minutes, tapping his fingers together in front of his face, elbows resting on the padded leather arms of his tailor-made chair. He too, worried these movements were spinning out of his control. On the one hand, he judged the mood of the country. His polling offices clearly showed public discontent over the police shootings. Therefore, he sanctioned kneeling and wearing altered clothing, supporting the slain men and the organizations springing up to champion their cause. This should appeal to a broad public consensus, so the polling suggested, but nothing seemed to follow the logical path.

First, no one predicted the stance of a minority of players led first by the Pirates. Who would have thought the perennial bottom dwellers from a small market with a usually pliable owner group would become such a lightning rod? Quint bristled as he folded his hands under his chin, reading the New York Post front page. It displayed a photo of the players in Pittsburgh kneeling and praying. Superimposed was the snap of the man throwing the red liquid on the Texas/Seattle kneelers with an inset shot of the stands, replete with sign-wielding fans angrily shouting against who knew what. Quint winced as he reread the headline, "America's Pastime, the New Battleground for Zealots, Racism and Bigotry."

If this were a typical year, few would follow the Pirates bucking the trend, but this year, the Pirates sat atop the Major Leagues with an eye-popping winning record. Worst of all, the leader of this counterculture group and counter-protest, Josh Green, continued knocking the baseball socks off the record books. Quint felt caught between a rock and a hard place he never saw coming. The League's star of the moment, Josh Green, prominently discussed his religious ideals, stood for flag and country and kneeled, praying to his unseen god. "I backed the majority's will," thought Quint. "I backed the side with the most influence on popular sentiment. I brought baseball along the growing cultural divide to fight against the old establishment. Baseball will be on the right side of history this time," Quint vowed. Still, Green and his followers continued to cling to contrary ideals long gone and out of fashion. I should be in the driver's seat, successfully placating the public, giving them what the people demanded. Yet here we are.

It all comes back to Green. He stirs dissension, Quint thought, exasperated. By every count, Quint did what seemed wise in his own eyes. He listened to the counsel of those closest to him in the organization, including most owners, yet things now seemed worse. His former supporters tried to distance themselves, and some even threatened to oppose him. Suddenly, Quint felt very alone in his decision, besieged on all sides as the crowds appeared poised to act against the League.

Come on, man! Quint scolded himself as he sat up, opening his laptop, trying to break out of his funk. All that happened actually increased most teams' attendance as more and more people noticed what was happening at the ballpark. More people showed up to either support or deride one side or the other. The entire country seemed caught up in the shootings, with protests and counter-protests nationwide. Quint's concern, however, was he unwittingly allowed the public sentiment to spill over into the ballparks, and now it was tough to control. The real question was, could he ride out this demon and keep a lid on the powder keg? Should he change tact and use the League's power to curtail the demonstrations, and what would that do to the League's bottom line?

Quint's phone buzzed, and he hit the speaker out of reflex. His assistant, Cassius, spoke, "Herald Gripp to see you, sir."

Quint expected his rival and deputy for some time, "Send him in, Cassius," he replied, "And hold my calls."

Herald walked in with his usual confident and relaxed demeanor. He was a middle-aged, slightly rotund man with black wavy hair and a mustache. Impeccably dressed as always, his three-piece suit and double-chained vest held his grandfather's gold watch, which he loved to show and tell. He always carried an air he belonged here, a crown prince awaiting his ascension to the throne his family once owned. Quint knew the nature of Herald's family pedigree made him feel that way compared to his own "up-by-the-boot-straps" rise to prominence in the League. However, today, Quint couldn't shake the feeling, either way, his success or failure probably worked to Herald's advantage. Quint knew Herald always played the game, intent on improving his hand. Still, Quint held the League coffers in a strong position despite the current crisis. Things were still his to control, and he wasn't done yet, not by a long shot.

"Herald, what do you make of all this commotion with Seattle? What are our sources saying?" Quint started.

"Well, Quint, it's not good news, I'm afraid," replied Herald with his usual too-familiar address of the commissioner. He took out the other of his two vest pocket chains, connected to a pair of reading lenses like someone from the 1930s, and read from a well-worn little black book, "From what my agents tell me, Seattle is just the beginning. There are likely to be more attempts at demonstrations against the so-called 'religious right' if players continue to buck the norm and don't stick with the 'on bended knee' approach to the anthem. The good news is most players are doing so, with our tacit support, per your guidance."

Herald Gripp paused while he flipped ahead a few pages, but Quint wondered if he did so to let that last remark sink in. Herald Gripp would let it be known, he was sure, the decision to support kneeling and wearing the various logos of support for the racial equity causes and the men killed by police was strictly Quint's decision. Yes, Herald would gladly serve up his head on a silver platter if the public or the owners turned against the commissioner's office and needed a scapegoat.

Quint's thoughts were interrupted as Herald continued. "Apparently, besides Seattle, you should expect more demonstrations in many of the League's cities, including Baltimore, D.C., Chicago, and worse yet," Herald hesitated with effect, looking over his antique tortoiseshell pince-nez reading glasses, "Right here in New York."

It was a rather ominous pronouncement as Quint took it all in. He leaned back in his chair, listening to Herald's report. He noted Herald said "my agents" instead of "our agents." The League scouted the country for more than a century for young baseball prospects, but the League's agents expanded under Quint. As he attained rank in the organization, he built a stable of what he called "public relations specialists." Their task: monitoring business and understanding public penchants to buy particular products and everything relating to League revenues, including reactions for and against League decisions and actions.

Herald clearly built his own set of informants, like Quint himself cultivated, and quite frankly, Herald wasn't telling him anything he hadn't heard from his network, but it galled him that the man would express it so overtly. Of course, he also understood it was something he may have done if he was in Herald's position. Quint tried to focus on the current dilemma.

"Options?" Quint said finally.

Herald was ready, "Three that I see. One, maintain the status quo and hope it dies of natural causes."

Quint replied, "Wait and see?"

Herald nodded.

Quint asked, "Two?"

Herald replied, "We could eliminate all public displays of politics and religion. Since we have made no official statement supporting either side, we end all demonstrations with something like this. 'Baseball is meant for all fans and players as a respite from the world in a friendly environment where politics and life's problems are left at the gate while we all enjoy a baseball game. We ask our players and fans to keep baseball America's favorite pastime and not display political or other areas of community strife, so all can participate in a family-friendly way....,' Something to that effect. Then we outlaw all displays, including kneeling for any reason."

Quint thought about it for a minute. Could he put the genie back in the bottle? What seemed like a good idea, to get out in front of the public's emotions and show the League's racial equality, now grew to represent the anti-bigotry and anti-racist movements. Yet it was still not enough. He need only watch the nightly news to see the increasing demonstrations and public frustrations. How could he ignore the growing blowback personified by someone running on the field and dousing players with unknown liquids? It was a pressure cooker building up steam. To close the relief valve now was suicide.

"No," Quint said finally. "I think that ship has sailed," he paused, "and three?"

"Well, this one's tricky," said Herald. "If we achieved unity throughout the League's players and all were bowing and wearing some form of support for the various agendas, maybe we could finally gain the support of those organizations calling for and leading the most vocal protest."

"You mean if all the players were *kneeling?*" said Quint, and Herald looked up at him, slightly confused. "You said if all the players were bowing. You meant kneeling."

Herald replied, "Did I? Yes, kneeling."

Quint considered this last option Herald brought. He let himself think out loud. "This all comes back to the different responses we're seeing with *some* players." Quint emphasized, "*some.*" He continued. "When this started, the union assured me the players would all follow our tacit policy of supporting the anti-racist movement. I thought the worst we would see was a few players not showing any support by not kneeling. But we immediately got this counter display, an entire team not kneeling, and not just any team, the Pirates."

"And right after the last black man is shot and killed on their city streets," added Herald with disdain.

"Precisely. Not only do they refuse to kneel during the anthem, they conduct a pregame 'Prayer meeting' in the middle of the field. And they're inviting the other team to join them! And by golly, some have, even if just a few! The Pirates, in turn, inspire a few other teams' players to break ranks. Not many do, but enough to be visibly prominent to fans and the media. So, the Pirates' stance against our consensus emboldens a small but visible dissension in other teams' players and coaches to stand for the anthem and kneel afterward in prayer," Quint finished his thoughts out loud.

"Making the League look tacitly complicit or racist," added Herald.

Either way, Quint thought silently, it makes me look weak, unable to control my organization. This unsettles the owners, who ultimately hold the only power greater than the commissioner; The power to hire and fire me. They need confidence in my judgment, decisions, and ability to run this organization. For the first time, the owners are telling me I am failing despite our prosperity because they fear a loss of control more than even temporary monetary gains. This is the problem. I must act to retain my position, and my actions must send a message. I am still in charge, and the owners can trust me to keep the League solidly in their control through me.

Quint looked back at Herald finally, then stood and stared out at his Manhattan million-dollar view. He loved his view. He had no intention of losing it to Herald or anyone else for that matter, not for a long time, not until he was ready to exit on his terms as an old and respected commissioner, like his predecessors. Quint resolved to do whatever it took to stay on top. With that resolute thought, he turned back to Herald. "This all comes back to the few holdouts not towing our unofficial line. The vast majority of the teams are compliant. Those few players that aren't following suit did so *only after* the Pirate stance that first day. It's the Pirates' initial response and their continuing refusal to go along, making this all go awry. The Pirates! They're such a backwater team normally," Quint stated in a forceful and slightly more exasperated tone than intended, sitting back at his desk and shaking his head.

"Yes, but of course, this season, they are off the charts, leading the League, and, unusually for them, filling their stadium. You can't ignore what they are doing on the field. Even their merchandise sales are at the top of our League growth this year," Herald commented.

"Yes, but that's not the problem, is it?" Quint said out loud. Then he took it back a step, thinking aloud, looking back out the window. "No," Quint said, pausing, arms still crossed as he turned, focusing on Herald. "Maybe that *is* the problem."

"What do you mean?" asked Herald.

Quint went on faster, placing two determined fists on his desk, leaning toward Herald, causing him to sit back deeper into the leather chair.

"This all became a problem, thanks to the Pirates and their unexpected prominence this year. To whom do we owe the bulk of the credit for their play and the disruption to our planned player response?" asked Quint, barely waiting for an answer.

"That's easy," said Herald without hesitation. "Josh Green. Without him, the Pirates are, at best, a .500 team."

"Yes, and my source in their organization says it's Green the team is following in this 'prayer stance,'" said Quint, almost spitting the last word as he stood again, folding his arms.

"Source?" asked Herald, eyebrows raising slightly. Quint winced ever so slightly. He didn't mean to let on, he owned someone in the Pirate locker room.

"Yes, Cai Annason," Quint said, looking away, trying to cover his slip up with a drink from his glass, "That man can't wait to tell me it's Green's fault every time we talk and when it's not Green, he's trying to throw Samuelson under the bus." Quint hoped Herald would forget the source comment as he wanted to keep that to himself. Well, that is, except for Cassius, who knew. He used the young man to run much of his network to bypass Herald and the rest of the League's official channels. Cassius was good at keeping secrets and owed his position and future to the commissioner, thought Quint.

"So how do we stop the Pirates and Green from bucking our order? Especially when their owner can't seem to?"

"How indeed," said Quint, as he rubbed his chin thoughtfully. If he was to come out of this situation on top, he had to be clever and careful. Whatever Quint decided, he needed subtlety and caution. He must leave no trace his office pulled strings to hurt the game's most prolific star of this season. He would start by making life difficult for him and the Pirates.

"Here's what we are going to do...," began Quint to Herald. Herald raised his eyebrows in surprise as Quint explained what he wanted.

Quint's brazenness shocked Herald, but he nodded and said, "I'll get right on it, Quint."

As Herald got up to leave, Quint knew he surprised Herald with his forthright approach to the problem. "That's right," thought Quint, "I still have a few tricks you haven't seen, Herald, and what's more, I'm not even telling you the full plan. I'll use my network for that. Cassius is much more loyal, of course, because I know his price well and pay it handsomely. But I'll use you in all this, Herald, and make sure you're hip-deep in it with me. No one will knock me off my throne before I am ready to step down; Not you, Herald, and certainly not an upstart unknown like Josh Green. Green will either 'play ball,' or he'll have to go."

Quint finished his thoughts unemotionally as Herald walked out of the office. He held nothing against Green personally, but Green wasn't being reasonable, and he wasn't being practical. Quint never let his beliefs cloud his judgment or get in the way of good business. He didn't see his plan as a threat, he told himself. It was just an honest response to the situation. After all, Quint was a practical businessman, and baseball was still a business. Whatever internal voice spoke to him, nagging deep down with moral concern against his logical approach, was quickly suppressed. What he did was for the good of baseball, which was good for him, Quint countered his inner voice. As Herald pulled the door shut behind him, Quint leaned back in his chair, looking out over the magnificent city as he quieted his troubled conscience. It truly was a spectacular view, he thought, and I'll have my fill of it before I'm done. It was shaping up to be a beautiful bright sunny day, and the Big Apple never looked better.

Sixty Six

T he Pirates came into New York riding high with a good team vibe and a
winning attitude. At 69-14, the Pirates led the majors, taking six of their
last eight games against good teams and still not losing a series all year. They
were now set to play the most storied team in baseball, the New York Yankees.
Major League Baseball added interleague play in 1997 to generate new rivalries
and revenue. Because the two Leagues previously only met in the All-Star games
and the World Series, the interleague games were a special time for teams, who
may not have played against each other in years, to compete. The Pirates would
play the Yankees for the first time in nearly a decade. For the Yankees, there was
good reason to play well. They battled their division rivals, the Boston Red Sox,
for first place in their division. Plus, the Yankees carried added incentive playing
Pittsburgh. The Yankees organization held baseball history in high esteem, being
the baseball franchise with far and away the most championships. As baseball's
vaunted and most valued franchise, if one historic loss, in particular, marred the
juggernaut franchise's resume, it was the 1960 World Series loss to the Pirates.

The 1960 World Series stuck in the minds of many a Yankees fan as an unhappy
memory that never went away, passed down to the next generation. They didn't
like to talk about it, but old Yankee fans lamented the 1960 series loss in the dark
corners of their favorite New York haunts. Perhaps the late great Yankee, Mickey
Mantle, who suffered the loss at the peak of his Yankee career, best summed up
the disappointment to the collective Yankee psyche. He called the 1960 series
his greatest regret. Many aficionados of baseball, and all sports for that matter,
called the Pirates' victory over the Yankees one of the greatest upsets ever in
sports history. Yes, when Bill Mazeroski hit his home run in the bottom of the
ninth inning over Yogi Berra's head and the left field fence of fabled Forbes Field
in Pittsburgh, he "walked-off" the Pirates as World Series Champions and into
Pittsburgh immortality. The Pirates' unforgettable victory made this rare Yankees
and Pirates meeting an instant rivalry. This interleague series portended serious
drama as both teams showed real prospects for making the playoffs, and both
clubs realized if they were to meet again, it would be in the World Series come
October.

The Pittsburgh fan base turned on their favorite radio broadcast as the pregame banter began at 4:00 PM sharp. "It's a beautiful day here in the Big Apple, folks, and we welcome all the fans back in Pittsburgh and around the world joining us on the broadcast for the start of a four-game series between your Pittsburgh Pirates and the Bronx Bruisers. I mean the New York Yankees," began Greg. "Well, Bob, what can we say about today as we renew one of baseball's great yet rarest rivalries?"

"That's a good question, Greg. You know, ever since Maz hit the shot heard 'round the world to win the '60 Series, the two teams have had little chance to renew their rivalry," replied Bob.

"True Bob, the two teams remained perennial League contenders through the late '70s yet never met again.

"That's right, Greg. The Yankees would win the championship in 61 and 62, then again in 77 and 78, while the Pirates added championships in 71 and 79, but neither team quite synched up, if you will, to play each other in the series again," stated Bob.

"Yep, and of course, since then, the Yankees have won a couple more while the Pirates, well...," Greg hesitated.

"Let's just say, it's been a while since the Pirates earned a chance to play in the ol' fall classic, Greg, and leave it at that," replied Bob with an easy quip helping his colorful teammate out of a broadcasting jam.

"Well said, Bobby, well said. As for this year, it's a different story, though. Both teams approach mid-season and the all-star break as their respective League leaders," replied Greg.

"True, but while the Pirates sit comfortably atop the National League with a whopping ten-game lead over their closest rival, the Yankees have a mere one and a half game lead over Boston, with the Red Sox breathing down their neck as we approach the All-Star break," explained Bob. "Let's not forget this history between the two clubs is short but memorable. In baseball's first one hundred years, the clubs faced each other in two World Series. The first meeting was the 1927 World Series. In the heyday of Babe Ruth and the rest of the so-called 'Murderers' Row,' the Yankees swept the Pirates in four games. The '27 Yankees are often voted the greatest team in baseball history."

"Ah, but Bob, that sweep was all but forgotten when the underdog Pirates won arguably the greatest upset victory in World Series history with Bill Mazeroski's immortal home run. It's still the only game seven World Series walk-off home run in baseball history and is consistently listed in the top two or three greatest sports moments ever."

"In Pittsburgh, you mean?" Bob asked somewhat sheepishly.

"I mean period, Bob!" responded Greg. When Bob rolled his eyes over the radio, Greg responded, "Well, name one better?" he said with ire.

Without hesitation, Bob replied, "How about Franco's immaculate reception, Or Mario's first Cup?" bringing up still other Pittsburgh-specific sports moments.

"Well, I did say top two or three, didn't I? No need to pick just one," Greg replied.

"There you have it, folks, something to argue about with the neighbors as you fire up the charcoal, throw a couple of bone-in ribeyes on, and add a couple of kielbasas for the kiddos before crackin' open a cold one," Bob commented.

"Make my steak black and blue and get me a *Yingiling*, Bob. I just found out Rolling Rock is now made in Jersey, for crying out loud!" cut in Greg, acting more than a little offended.

"Where've you been for the last decade, Greg? Rolling Rock's been imported for years! But why Yuengling? Why not IC light?"

"I'm in New York, Bob. Got to go a little highfalutin while I'm here since the per diem's up. Besides, we're east of Philly. They don't let 'Cold Arns' past their western border,"

"True, and 'Smokey and the Bandit' passed away some years ago, as I hear it," reminisced Bob.

"Yep. Dang, now I'm hungry and thirsty. Does Primanti's deliver to the Bronx?" asked Greg thoughtfully.

"Don't think so, partner. Maybe we can order pizza from Ray's?" he suggested.

"Well, I guess that's better than that excuse for a sammitch from Philly we got when last we were out east. What do they call it?" asked Greg.

Bob shook his head. "Don't know. Not worth rememberin'."

"True, True," agreed Greg. "Well, folks, we have to take a break and see about ordering some New York zah while you all discuss those great sports moments over that sizzling moo-cow—remember black and blue now! We'll be right back after we pay some bills and find what passes for food here in the house they still say that jolly-old-slugger with the beer gut and a giant bat built. Stay tuned. We'll be right back!"

Sixty Seven

As the Pirates went through their pregame routines, Andrew and Josh made their way over, as they customarily did, toward their opponents' dugout to invite the other team to join them when the time came for their team prayer behind second base. The two teams the Pirates played since they began the team prayer showed small individual support contributing a few players and even one coach during their previous series. However, the Yankees, as it turned out, would be different. As Josh and Andrew approached, the Yankees shortstop and captain, one of the League's biggest stars, met the two Pirates on the field before they reached the Yankees dugout. Walking just behind the Yankees captain was the Yankee designated hitter. He was a large man, equal in height and twenty pounds heavier than Josh, looking more like a bodybuilder than a baseball player. Though he was still relatively young, he signed a multi-year contract after coming over from the Angels in a blockbuster deal last season.

The Yankees captain and undisputed team leader was a well-respected baseball player nearing the end of a lengthy, Hall of Fame career. Earning hundreds of millions in salary and endorsements over the years, rumors abounded of his intent to retire and become one of the first minorities to own a baseball franchise. As Josh and Andrew began walking toward the Yankees dugout, the Yankee captain whispered in the ear of the muscular designated hitter gesturing at the Pirates walking their way. It quickly became apparent the Yankees planned their response as both men walked out to challenge the two Pirates before Josh and Andrew reached their dugout. If anything, the other Yankees players moved farther away, and most refused to look at or acknowledge the approaching Pirates.

The Yankee captain held up a hand before either Pirate got too close or could speak. "Look, guys, we know what you're going to ask, and our answer is unanimous. The Yankees play and stick together as a team. We will again be kneeling during the anthem as a team to protest the treatment of African Americans in this country, and the death of those killed by police whose names you see displayed prominently on our warm-up gear. We won't support your counterprotest by kneeling after the anthem in the outfield. We ask you not to do so. It's an insult to our city and our losses at the hands of racism."

Andrew stood still, hands-on-hips and wrinkled brow, shocked at the harsh words of his fellow team captain, "It's not a counter-protest," Andrew said, sounding surprised and defensive, "It's a prayer for our country and all our fellow citizens." He would have said more, but Josh calmly reached out, gripping his shoulder, and Andrew held off.

"We don't see it that way, Andrew," the Yankees captain said forcibly as he folded his arms over his chest. He continued more quietly, but no less sternly so only the four of them could hear. "Quite frankly, as a fellow African American, I've got to ask you and the others on the Pirates, how you can kneel with this guy?" said the Yankee captain, nodding at Josh without looking at him, "And think you're not betraying your people?" Andrew leaned backwards in surprise as the Yankee captain delivered his last words menacingly.

Before the Yankee baited Andrew into a response, Josh replied, "We understand you see things differently. We kneel in prayer to the Lord, asking for His help and guidance to bring us together in forgiveness and brotherly love as He demonstrated with His Son, Jesus, who loved us all equally, even unto death. We only ask any who want to pray for this country and the hurt they feel from prejudice and discrimination to meet with us when we take the field for the bottom of the first inning. We welcome anyone who may want to join us regardless of who they are or where they come from," finished Josh.

The Yankees captain shook his head, refusing to look at Josh, instead directing his response to Andrew. "*No* Yankees will participate," he replied slowly and with finality, clearly indicating dissension was not allowed. "We ask, as the League asked, for the Pirates to show solidarity with the cause and kneel during the anthem."

Josh replied, "All our teammates make their own decision to stand or kneel for the anthem, just as they freely choose to join us and pray. We choose to honor what our country stands for and those who sacrificed to make us free. Many of us choose to bow to the one who can truly heal us and our country, and we pray to the Lord for help and forgiveness. Our team respects each person's right to choose."

"We see it differently," came the Yankee captain's reply, "As do the people of New York. We kneel in solidarity against those in our country that permit and encourage these racist acts. None of us are free as long as any are denied freedom, and they continue to kill our brothers and sisters. Until we get justice, we will kneel and be heard!" finished the Yankees captain, turning abruptly without waiting for a response. His giant teammate stood silently like a statue with two large bats over his shoulder, glared menacingly at them both, then turned to follow. As they walked away, the Yankees captain took one last parting shot over his shoulder. "Andrew," he said, again ignoring Josh, "Be careful and choose wisely whose side you're on. Even a star needs friends in this League."

"I thought we were all on the same side?" said Andrew.

"Your actions say otherwise," said the Yankee captain, "And remember, we are not responsible for the reactions of New Yorkers to your little display of opposition, regardless of what you claim it to be. It's time you realize you're either for us or against us."

The two Yankees continued walking away without looking back, leaving Josh and Andrew standing there alone, staring. After a moment, Josh turned back to their dugout, and Andrew slowly did the same. Andrew played in this league a long time and interacted with the Yankee captain several times. He never expected this chilly response and didn't understand the Yankees' animus toward his and Josh's invitation. Josh extended his arm around Andrew's shoulders. Quietly Josh said, "Sometimes you do your best to speak the truth in love, but even when you do, some people will choose to reject the honesty of what you say. They choose to go their own way, and there is nothing your words can do to change their hardened hearts or open their muted ears. Only the Holy Spirit can change such hearts. It's not up to us. We must choose to do what the Lord shows us to do. At times like this, all we can do is stand our ground and pray." Andrew nodded, looking up at Josh. Josh's kind smile displayed wisdom and understanding while reflecting Andrew's sadness and disappointment at the Yankees' response. When they returned to their dugout, they told their teammates all that transpired. The other Pirates listened, saying little. The mood was suddenly more somber, and most became quietly introspective.

"I thought we were the good guys, just inviting all people to come together?" Thomas stated in a dismayed, confused voice.

Old Pete, who sat as he often did, chewing on a large wad of sunflower seeds at the end of the bench, replied, "There's a cost for standing up for what you know to be true. Get used to it. Many don't want to stand up to the mob, and truth often cuts deep. People often hate and fight the truth when it means they must change. When you walk the walk, expect to be challenged, and don't let the bullies intimidate ya."

Josh nodded, turning to the others, "What we do, we do because it is good and right and because we have faith in God's plan for us and for healing our nation. We must love in both gentleness and truth. For God has not given us the spirit of fear, but of power and love and of a sound mind."[1] Josh quoted Paul writing to

---

1. 2 Timothy 1:7

Timothy, reminding those who knelt and prayed with him of the promise behind their faith.

Samson, the Pirates starting pitcher today, eyed Josh from the bench before heading to the bullpen to warmup. He came out a little late from the locker room while Andrew and Josh replayed their chilly conversation with the Yankees. Normally a gregarious, easy-go-lucky fellow, something curtailed his outgoing personality after the Pirates returned from their last road outing two weeks ago. Samson listened to the discussion, and as it ended, got up to walk out to the bullpen. Josh walked to pass him and placed his glove with his bat in the cubbyholes at the end of the bench. Samson asked Josh, "Got a moment to walk with me, Josh?"

"Sure," Josh nodded and followed as Samson headed towards the bullpen. "What's on your mind, my friend?"

"I am not sure why I am coming to you with this. I know it may not be the best time...," said the big man, who made even Josh look small.

"Samson, it's OK," said Josh encouragingly, as he smiled that old and kind smile. Samson's view of Josh grew as the season progressed, and he began to see Josh as a big brother. Josh reminded Samson of a picture his grandma kept of her veteran uncles from WWII. Large, strong, black men, proudly dressed in their military uniforms. Samson looked into those dark eyes, remembering how Josh lived his life, and Samson knew Josh was someone he could trust.

As they walked toward the bullpen for warm-ups, Samson began, "Look. I got some news when we got home from our last road trip. I am not sure how to handle it. You see, there's this local girl I've seen in Pittsburgh, on and off..., Anyway, she told me she's five weeks pregnant with my child."

Samson let the statement sink in, but it was almost he who needed more time to think about it. Josh waited patiently for a few moments, then Samson continued. "You may think this was just a chance encounter because of how I act, but, well...it's not. She's a nice girl. When she told me, I didn't know what to say. She's not the kind to be going around with other guys. Honestly, I am not sure what she sees in me. Unlike other girls around me," Samson hesitated, "Who seek the celebrity or, you know, the money and fame. This girl is different. We met about the time I met you in spring training. Honestly, Josh, you made me think about some things..., like my grandma too!" Samson laughed at himself as he looked over at Josh, smiling kindly back at him. "Anyway, I went back to church for the first time in a while, to the First Baptist Church of Pittsburgh in Oakland, where I went a few times. I thought it would be a good way to reconnect and stay grounded, like you said."

"And you met this girl...," said Josh.

"Her name is Kevuda," said Samson, "Yes, she is a member there and active in some of their outreach programs. And she sings in their choir."

"I see. What does Kevuda say about your baby?" asked Josh.

"She said she will have the baby and raise it by herself, if need be, but she hopes I want to be a good father to the baby. I never wanted any of this, but I know what it's like to grow up without a father."

They approached the bullpen. Samson stopped, reluctant to get within hearing distance of the other players and coaches. He turned to Josh, hanging his head, arms crossed, not quite able to look at him. "Josh, I don't know what to do," Samson stated honestly. "I want to stand up and be a man, but I realize I'm not sure I know what that means." Samson looked down as he said the words, shuffled his feet and pounded his empty fist in his glove.

"Samson," Josh said, calling him by name, and Samson finally looked up into his loving, kind eyes. Josh placed a gentle hand on Samson's shoulder. "You have a father. You have always had a perfect, loving father. He promised never to leave you or forsake you. He's ready to help; to help you, to help Kevuda, and to help your baby. He loves you so much, before the foundation of the world, He thought of you. Jesus knew your name and what you needed. He loves you and is ready to help. You just have to ask Him. First, you have to ask Him to forgive you and save you. Have you done that?"

"Yes, Josh," Samson said without hesitation. "I know it seems like I make light of it, but my grandma led me to the Lord when I was a kid. I seem to stray away on many occasions, but I don't want to do that anymore," he said firmly, knowing his heart was ready for a change.

"Well, Samson," Josh said, a twinkle in his eye, "I think you've heard of the prodigal?"

Samson smiled, "Yeah, I guess I have. He was a bit of a hell-raiser too."

"Yep," said Josh, nodding, "But when he finally realized how much trouble he caused himself and others, he turned back, repented in his heart, and came home to his father. His father was waiting for him every day, looking for him, and saw him from a long way off. You know his father ran to meet him! He brought him back into the family and restored him. How much more your perfect heavenly father wants to do for you."

"How do I do it, Josh? Where do I start? What should I do?" asked Samson, looking back into the eyes of the man he saw as his big brother, almost pleading.

"Samson, like the prodigal, you run to the father and ask him to save you and give your life into his hands."

"I have made some big mistakes. How will He ever fix all the things I've done?"

"Samson, you know your Bible as well as I do. But now, you need to remember! It's full of imperfect people making some whoppers of mistakes. God wants you to turn to him. He forgives you. That doesn't mean the consequences in this life aren't real because of your actions. But it means He's got you. Follow Him, and He'll show you the way home."

"He'll show me the way to do right by Kevuda and my baby? To be a good father to our child?"

"If you let him, Samson, He will help you build a life of blessings and meaning beyond anything you can dream. He can take you and make you the dad you always wanted. We can do all things through Christ who strengthens us.[2] There's no problem God can't handle if we let Him lead the way."

Samson looked up and around at Yankees stadium, contemplating what Josh said. The stands were nearly filled, and the Pirates in the bullpen watched, wondering what kept Samson. But he was miles away. He remembered his life and those moments when he needed his dad and didn't have him. Somehow his granny, who raised him, sufficed, but he always knew a child needed a good father. Josh *was* right. God was the Good, Good Father. No matter how Samson strayed, the Father always offered to forgive and bring him back with open arms. But until today, Samson rebelled and resisted. His days of running were over. He was turning to the Lord fully, asking the Lord to make him the man and father he should be for Kevuda and his child.

"OK, Josh," said Samson, surrendering to the Lord. He was ready. "Let's pray." Josh smiled back, facing Samson, and put both hands on Samson's shoulders. The Pirates in the bullpen couldn't hear the words, but they could see both men close, bowing their heads. It was a short prayer but seemed of deep meaning, finished with an embrace. Samson felt light as a feather as he turned, and Josh patted him on the back before returning to the dugout, each man heading in opposite directions. Samson entered the bullpen, and pitching Coach Eli Aaronson said, "You ready to go there, Sammy? Everything OK?"

"Everything's great," said Samson smiling as if a giant weight lifted from his spirit. "Let's get to work!"

---

2. Philippians 4:13

Sixty Eight

The Pirates became the focal point of the crowded stadium even before the game started. While they met some resistance to standing for the anthem and praying in Pittsburgh, it paled in comparison to what they experienced here in New York. Outside, over 250 vocal protesters gathered in organized groups, deriding the team as they arrived at the stadium. Now inside, fans filled the stadium with signs supporting the various racial justice organizations, many displaying the names of those killed in confrontations with police. Here and there, rainbow signs indicated protests against Josh's comments on gays.

When the National Anthem played, the Yankees all wore black shirts, many with racial justice organization names and slogans or names of the New York man recently killed by police. A few even wore the name of the man killed in Pittsburgh. All the Yankees, players, coaches, and anyone else on the field and dugouts took a knee during the anthem. In stark contrast, the Pirates stood and faced the flag, removed their hats, most placing their hand over heart. The two teams took their polar opposite approaches as the anthem began, and more than half the fans sat in their seats. The fans were not silent, and the boos rained down onto the field. Several Pirates, shocked by the loud boos, looked concernedly up at the fans, whose catcalls and angry faces displayed their feelings toward the Pirates' unwillingness to bend a knee to their will.

"If you're just joining in," a subdued Bob whispered into the Pirates radio mike, "We're here in Yankee Stadium, where the anthem is playing, the Yankees are all kneeling, and the Pirates, who are all standing, are getting an ear full of Bronx hospitality. Just listen." The crowd boos were as loud, if not louder, than the music. Finally, the anthem ended, and the Pirates returned to their dugout as the Yankees took the field.

"Well, that was disturbing, Bob," said Greg, "And here I thought we were coming to play a nice friendly game of America's favorite pastime!"

"Yeah, Greg, it feels more like Russia under Stalin, and everyone's out of Borscht. These teams don't have enough of a recent rivalry, you'd think, to cast a lingering animosity, but you wouldn't know it based on the crowd's welcome in the pregame."

"Evidently, the grudges of the current day override the old baseball history, or else Maz's homer sixty-plus years ago really stuck in the Yankees' memory! Let's face it, folks, this is the world we live in, and I, for one, find it perplexing. I hope that's not a sign of things to come," Greg opined.

Bob nodded and added, "We may get a chance to see. From what our Pirates sources say about their somewhat unique take on the country's problems, they plan another little prayer meetin' behind second base when they take the field."

"Think they will get anyone from the Yankees to join them?" asked Greg.

"If the anthem and pre-game response is any indicator, I think we'll be lucky not to have a little brew-haha," answered Bob.

"Seems even baseball isn't immune to the country's unrest, eh Bob?" replied Greg, slightly sad.

"Let's all pray we can keep the conflict to the play inside the lines and settle this one on the field. For now, the Pirates are up to bat. It's the top of the first in the first game of four, here in Yankee Stadium. Now for a brief word from our sponsors," Bob concluded.

Sixty Nine

The commissioner watched the game from the MLB offices on Park Ave. He refrained from attending the series opener in person, opting to wait for the third game this weekend. Quint's absence served two purposes.

First, he took certain steps to place the attention directly on the Pirates and Josh Green, specifically, what he saw as Green's antagonistic opposition to supporting the progressive policies of MLB. Quint led the MLB stance embracing the racial equality movements and anti-bigotry organizations holding the public eye and ear. He vowed to distance MLB from its racist mistakes before League integration in the 1950s, joining the public's fight against white privilege in American society. The commissioner must ensure the fans view MLB's image in lockstep with the growing public sentiment of the country or risk alienating the consumer fan base. It was a simple calculus. The commissioner must do everything in his power to stem the flow of fans from leaving baseball for the other more Twenty-First Century sports. Quint committed to appeasing the masses and did not want MLB seen as being on the wrong side of history.

Second, Quint stayed away from the series opening game because he did not want to be visible when his own secret and unofficial network, extended into practically every team, acted. Quint's network was strong inside the Yankees. Over the years, he cultivated key people through various financial incentives and strong-arm tactics. Frankly, it was relatively easy to coerce even star players once you discovered their weaknesses. One of Quint's most effective tactics was to show players evidence of misdeeds and let them think about all they would lose should the evidence become public.

Quint identified his biggest problem started when the Pirates refused to back his agenda. More specifically, Joshua Green wasn't playing ball. Tonight, Quint released the power of his network. It was in the stands and on the field. Josh Green and the Pirates would get a clear message. Quint felt confident he could weaken or eliminate the resistance to his leadership and rule by the end of this four-game series, possibly by the end of this game. Yes, Quint carefully planned multiple contingencies to solve his problem on the field or behind the scenes. Quint knew the sway and pulse of the masses in New York, and for thirty years, he groomed his network to cover all the essential bases. The network was almost impossible to trace back to him as he used instigators in the stands and secured key Yankees staff. Quint cashed in a long-term marker, owning the Yankees ace pitcher on the mound today. Yes, thought Quint; bought and paid for, he is mine.

Quint would watch games 1 and 2 from the comfort of MLB offices. He hoped he would not have to carry out plan B. Quint shook off the thought. With any luck, things would shift firmly in MLB's favor, and Josh Green and the Pirates would be on a losing streak, discredited and derided, heading into the All-Star break.

Meanwhile, back on the field for the start of the first game, Zach strolled to the plate in his customary lead-off position. The Yankees ace started Zach with a fastball outside just off the plate for ball one. Next came a breaking ball, down and inside. Zach pulled it foul down the first baseline, evening the count at 1-1. The pitcher followed with another outside fastball, but it was on the corner at the top of the zone. The pitcher threw the pitch as game-planned with the Yankee pitching coach based on Zach's problems in previous years hitting high outside fastballs, but Zach, like much of the lineup, was having a breakout year. He slapped the ball hard, not trying to do much with it, and it arched down the third baseline staying just fair. The Yankees played the spray-hitting Zach in neutral fielding positions, and although the left fielder got a good jump on the ball, Zach was off like a shot at the crack of the bat and just beat the left fielder's hard throw into second for a game-opening double.

Pops changed the lineup to try and put pressure on the opponent not to pitch around Josh by moving Andrew to second and J.J. to fifth position in the order. This gave the Pirates 2-3-4 hitters with Andrew's second best League batting average and Juan's second highest home run total sandwiched around Josh. Andrew came up to bat second with first base open with Josh waiting on the on-deck circle. The pitcher, aware he faced a good hitter, knew Josh and Juan followed in the Pirates' suddenly powerful lineup. The pitcher started Andrew with two hard sliders getting him to swing and miss the first but not the second. With the count even at 1-1, the pitcher busted Andrew in and low with a hard fastball clocking 98 MPH. Andrew fought it off, hitting the ball just outside a diving second baseman into right field. Hit sharply, Zach held at third as the strong arm right fielder quickly fired the ball back into the infield. The Pirates now had runners at the corners with no outs.

In Pittsburgh, Pirates Chief Partner, Cai Annason, left the Heinz field offices in his private limo, listening like many Pittsburghers, to the Pirates radio broadcast. He just completed a rather uncomfortable meeting with the owner's group. He rode in the back of his limo, alone with his thoughts and computer tablet, staring at quarterly financials. The numbers were the best the Pirates produced in decades. Team sales were up almost 35%, and hometown fans' attendance was at an all-time high, as the box office take this half-season was about to surpass all of last season. Yet the owners weren't happy with Cai. They interrogated him on why he could not control the team's response to the shootings, especially with one right here in Pittsburgh. They criticized his handling of Josh Green from the beginning. First, with his million-dollar contract, then Cai's inability to curtail his Christian comments, kneeling before his first at-bat, and now his leading the team in a public prayer meeting. Cai thought the interview disaster was bad, but he feared the owners' escalating ire with the latest team displays, counter to public opinion and League demands. Despite his protestations that the players' actions were within the legal contract guidance, as team lawyers advised, the owners were unforgiving and pressured him to take control.

It wasn't his fault, thought Cai. He tried to appease the League, but the players, led by Green and backed by Samuelson, stubbornly resisted Cai's cajoling behind the scenes to fall in line. As usual, Coach Samuelson, Cai's primary direct contact, refused to implement Cai's wishes. Instead, Saul declared the players were within their legal right to choose freely. The coach, and Green, in particular, refused to face facts. Whether they liked it or not, the Pirates were a backwater territory, and the MLB commissioner ruled. Cai didn't like it, and most of the time, he could act like he alone was in control, but he knew better than to go against the League. Here Cai was, with the owners on one side and the League on the other. Green and Samuelson were fools, threatening to pull him down.

With one of the largest minority rosters and minority coaching staffs in the League, the Pirate players and coaches still swam against the current. They refused to kneel or wear the specialized clothing supporting the victims of racial injustice and the organizations at the forefront of the protests. Cai was incredulous at the thought and furrowed his brow as he looked absently out on the city as the limo left the parking lot. His plans to sell racial justice sportswear alongside the regular Pirate gear became a costly mistake, as the reticent Pirate players politely but obstinately refused to wear it. The sales were not even enough to cover the costs. To add insult to injury, the team appeared to be holding a counterculture prayer vigil on the field as a "come together" religious display.

Cai was a devout Jew, but there was a time and place for religion, and displaying prayer and faith as an answer to these issues, was, in Cai's estimation, a foolish act guaranteed to incite public anger. Predictably, the progressive organizations adamantly opposed the Pirates' actions, deluging the front office with calls, emails, and increasingly vocal public outcry. Already they saw a significant uptick in protest outside the stadium for their last home stand. Despite their stellar play, Pittsburgh, where the community reeled from the shooting, began to boo its own team in substantial numbers. The progressive national press vilified the Pirates, criticizing the organization for failing to stand against the shootings when one was in their city, incredulously lambasting their counter-protest.

Adding to Cai's headaches, the MLB commissioner's discussion with Cai was even worse. Despite a public image stating players were free to express themselves, the commissioner exerted severe pressure behind the scenes. Quint Pilate levied thinly veiled threats at Cai, chastising his lack of success in pressuring his team to comply with the League's plan. In their last telephone conversation, the commissioner insinuated Cai exhibited weak and incompetent leadership, reminding him of the commissioner's long friendship with his father-in-law. Quint ended the conversation by telling Cai he would hate to call the old man with his vote of "No Confidence." The commissioner knew Cai's position depended on his father-in-law's support, and the loss of his support would be fatal to Cai remaining the Pirate President. Cai fumed privately, recalling the humiliating conversation as the Pittsburgh skyline passed by silently.

The Pirates' response destroyed what should be an excellent year for Cai. He finally gave the owners a real chance of a championship while holding a tight budget. Adding to his frustrations, Cai planned to get rid of the problematic Coach Samuelson when the Pirates posted another losing season. Yet Cai knew getting rid of the hometown skipper would be impossible if they continued winning at this record-setting pace.

How could this happen? It was maddening. Cai was getting what he wanted, a profitable and winning team, yet it all felt like it was slipping away. He needed to focus, thought Cai. He was a shrewd businessman. Identify the correct problem and eliminate it. What caused all his headaches? That was easy, he thought absently. It all began with Saul signing Josh Green.

Cai dwelled on this thought, trying to unpack it. Josh Green was indeed Cai's real problem now. Green refused to cooperate and conform, starting with his stubborn kneeling before his first at-bat. Cai's inability to stop Green's actions snowballed into a series of rebellious choices and public miscues. Cai checked them off in his mind; the Green interview, refusing to promote or at least give tacit approval of the gay lifestyle, and now the kneeling disaster. Kneeling, not conforming with popular opinion during the anthem, but demonstrating his faith in God. Yes, Green stood in direct conflict with the League, public sentiment, and Cai's admonition.

How in the world was a prayer vigil the correct answer to the country's problems? Could the man not read public opinion was firmly against him? Cai admitted to himself finally, it was becoming a nightmare. He almost slammed the electronic tablet down on his lap, looking out the tinted window of the limousine. His inability to get the team to conform to the League's progressive response toward civil unrest made the owners and the League nervous and hostile to Cai's continued tenure.

Cai needed to figure out a way to force Green to conform or get rid of him. Meanwhile, he must do all this without being *seen* doing this from the public viewpoint. Yet he still must convince the owners he was the man who could run the organization efficiently and with public support. That meant winning enough games to keep the fans coming. Cai shook his head. It felt like an impossible position. These competing issues made Cai even more determined to get Josh and Saul to toe the line or ship them out. But how could he, as they seemed to have created a League Championship contender? Josh's miraculous play on the field made him next to impossible to oppose openly.

How could Green, coming out of nowhere, put up such numbers? No one ever saw the likes of Josh Green, and Cai could not understand how to extricate himself from the man without becoming a villain. He sat silently, brooding in his musings, shutting down the tablet and drawn back to the game on the radio. The announcers continued as Cai listened.

"Well folks, here we go," said Bob on Pirates radio. "The Bucs have runners at the corners to start the game, with no outs, and Josh Green is coming to the plate having an other-worldly first half in his first season of baseball."

"Yep, the Yankee ace is between a rock and a hard place now, with Green hitting .500, going 12 for 24 in his last eight games, including three more added to his League-leading home run total. And he's followed by Juan, who's in second place in the League homers, hitting .296 on the year. Pick your poison," explained Greg.

"Well, I think I wouldn't go anywhere near Josh because with runners in scoring position this year, he's hit a whopping .775. Is that number right? That's unbelievable! Seems like the only time he gets out is when it doesn't matter because no one's on or the game is not in question," said Bob.

Sitting in the back of the limo, Cai's eyes snapped back inside to stare at the speaker as if looking through the radio at the announcer's stat sheet. If anything, Cai was a numbers man, and he understood the statistics of baseball almost as well as the Pirates' bottom line. Why did he not realize this particular Green stat before? Hitting as Josh did much of the time was hard to believe, but if Josh was hitting when it counted most and not when it didn't, made Cai think Green's skill might be something truly never before seen. It was as if Green could hit whenever he wanted and chose to hit only when it counted. What did that mean? If it were true, could Cai use it against Green? He would have to do so in a way it never got out. Cai began to formulate several options on how to use this information. As he thought about what he should do, the game continued.

"Here comes Green, up to bat," continued Bob with the play-by-play, "And here he goes with his customary first at-bat kneel just outside the batter's box."

"And listen to the boo-birds on that one, more than a little anger in those catcalls," said Greg as the two announcers sat silently, letting listeners hear the loud boos coming from a boisterous crowd.

"Well, Green is back up and entering the box. I guess we'll find out what this pitcher thinks."

In his Manhattan office, Quint already knew what was coming, and he watched intently as his pitcher delivered the message. It was a high fastball at Josh's head.

In his peace of the moment, Josh saw the ball streaking at his head. Perhaps it was a split-second decision or a self-preservation defensive reflex. Even he wasn't sure today. Josh moved to protect his head and upper torso from the high-velocity pitch, jerking the bat in an unusual quick chopping motion. His upper body swiveled and bent down almost simultaneously. Just before the ball could reach Josh's head or upper chest, the bat intervened and deflected it foul toward the Pirate dugout. Josh's movement knocked him, twisting down and out of the batter's box.

"Green fouls off a would-be headshot from the pitcher and winds up face down in the dirt!" exclaimed Bob.

"Wow, that was an awkward swing, as Green swatted the ball away like a fly while he tried to bail out. The pitch came right at Green's noggin, and he deflected it sideways using the bat as his fly swatter. I don't know if he did that on purpose, but either way, it's still strike one," said Greg.

Bob added, "Yeah, and now he has to dust himself off and step back in to take another one."

"Let's hope we don't see a repeat. It could do some serious damage if Green failed to intercept it with that awkward swing," said Greg.

Josh got up and dusted himself off as the Pirates looked on, concerned. There were more than a few jeers from the crowd.

Quint, in his office, watched, perplexed. He directed the pitcher to send a clear message to Green at his first opportunity, ensuring the League would take no action against him. After that, the pitcher was to do what it took to make Green irrelevant. Quint wasn't sure if Green got the message with that strange swing. Quint watched to see if his pitcher would repeat the message, but mostly he watched to see what Green did next.

The pitcher, too, was stunned by Josh's deflection of his head-hunting delivery. He never saw a batter do something like that with a beanball pitch. He was in this uncomfortable position of having to throw at a batter because of his own poor decisions, coming back as leverage from somewhere high in the commissioner's office. How they found out, he didn't know, but the evidence, presented by the churlish man whose name he still didn't know, was indisputable. He had little choice but to comply. Perhaps this concern made his focus less than optimal on the first two batters. With his first pitch to Josh, he expected to be warned by the umpire, but surprisingly, he was not. Did the League leverage the umpire as well? Still, he wasn't sure the clear message pitch would placate whoever held his fate, especially since Green knocked it foul. He felt hopeless looking in for the next sign but decided he must repeat the high and tight fastball. He reluctantly began his delivery, but his heart was not in it.

Josh saw another ball coming in high but not quite at his head. He thought the first might be accidental, but this clearly was another deliberate, if weaker, attempt to take Josh out or scare him off. Josh reacted defensively on the first pitch but was now more prepared. He could have pulled back and let it go for a ball. Instead, he gave another version of the choppy swing, this time connecting more inline back over the field, pulling the ball using mostly arm strength hard down the left field line just over the third baseman. Josh effectively placed the ball into fair territory despite such an ugly swing. Zach scored, and Josh and Andrew were on first and second base with no outs.

Quint sat back and shook his head, bemused as he watched. It was inconceivable that a batter could fight off two head-hunting pitches in such a manner. In his 45 years in baseball, Quint never saw the like. He planned for Josh to be intimidated by getting plunked, or at least weakened in everyone's opinion. Quint even prepared to accept Green might get knocked out of the game. Instead, Green fought off the pitches and hit the second for a base hit and an RBI. It was maddening! Even if Green dove into the dirt and the umpire warned both benches about throwing at the batter, all would get the message, and the hostile crowd could berate Josh and the Pirates' impotence. Quint posted many instigators in the crowd, ready to lead the jeering. Yet because Josh swung and knocked away both pitches, there was little the ump could do, and now the crowd sat largely silent, stunned by Josh's hit. Quint never envisioned Josh intercepting the pitches, let alone hitting one for an RBI.

With Quint, his pitcher, and the crowd stunned by what transpired, Juan came to the plate. Perhaps the pitcher lost his concentration, reeling from the impossible hit, but the next pitch was out over the plate. Juan extended his arms through the swing making perfect contact with the sickening sound dreaded by every Yankees fan. He deposited the 96 MPH offering into the second deck, and with the three-run blast, the Bucs took a first-inning 4-0 lead and never looked back. The Bucs batted around in the first, with the number nine batter finally grounding into an inning-ending double play. The damage was done, however, as the Pirates scored six runs. Silenced by the Pirates' offensive explosion, the deflated crowd's few boos seemed directed at their team as the Yankees left the field for their dugout.

As the Pirates took to the field for the first time, they met behind second base for a team prayer as in their previous eight home games. Perhaps things would have been different if the top of the first went 1-2-3 with no runs, but the Pirates 6-0 lead seemed to take the air out of the pregame fired-up crowd. Quint watched, seething, as his instigators tried and failed to lead the mob to curse and rebuke the Pirates' prayer, but the subdued and disheartened fans could barely give some half-hearted boos as the Pirates closed ranks.

Meanwhile, Cai arrived at his family home in Squirrel Hill North and went straight to his private study, oblivious to the greetings of both his butler and wife. Cai turned on the game, immediately mortified to see his team kneeling in prayer in the middle of Yankee stadium, on SPNN in prime news time no less. He thought miserably how this would reflect on him as a failure to control his team.

In Pittsburgh, radio listeners heard the announcers describe the scene. "So, what we have here, folks, is a bunch of kneeling Pirates, having a little prayer vigil like they did the last week after the shooting in Pittsburgh, not during the anthem, but out behind second base as they take the field for the first time. It's a bit more hostile environment here in the big apple, however," Bob said in a massive understatement.

"Yeah, I don't think the League quite knows what to make of the Bucs' response. This one is different because the Pirates were doing this pregame at home, starting in the field. Many of the coaches and even the trainers joined them in Pittsburgh. Because it's the bottom of the first, only the Pirate players are allowed on the field this time. However, I see in the dugout the Pirates coaching staff and some of the other players having a little prayer time get-together as well," Greg continued.

"Clever way of not breaking any League rules there, Greg. However, the Yankee crowd doesn't seem to appreciate it, regardless. They were unusually silent after that humiliating top of the first. Our six runs by the Buccos quieted them down somewhat, but this prayer vigil has them a little riled up now, I'd say," commented Bob.

"Yep, lots of boos when the Pirates didn't kneel for the anthem or wear any of the various 'Cause Celebre' these Yankees and the crowd are wearing and showing in the stands," responded Greg.

"Wow, 'Cause Celebre,' eh Greg? Impressive vocabulary there, partner," Bob opined.

"Well, my wife has been trying to get me to take up some highbrow culture with her as of late. Went to the Pittsburgh Symphony last week, and we watched Masterpiece Theater on PBS just the other night."

"My goodness, how'd that all go?" asked Bob.

"Best sleep I've had in weeks," Greg deadpanned. "But seriously folks, the displays by the Pirates versus the New Yorkers are mixing about as well as me and highfalutin society. Maybe worse!"

Unlike their two previous opponents, the Cardinals, and Braves, where several players joined the Pirates in prayer, the Yankees allowed no support as their captain warned. In fact, the Yankees captain, who batted second in the order, approached the home plate umpire complaining about the delay he felt the Pirates were making in the game.

The radio announcers continued the unusual play-by-play. "Looky here, Bob. Even the Yankees captain looks peeved and now is having a conversation with the home plate umpire gesturing toward the prayer circle in the outfield. Uh oh! The ump is now walking out toward the Pack of Pirate Players in Prayer, or as I like to call it, the quadruple P!" said Greg with a flourish.

Bob responded sarcastically, "Well, that's another one of your sayings that won't catch on, Greg!"

"They can't all be winners, Bob!" explained Greg.

The umpire reached the Pirate prayer circle, but Josh, who led the prayer today, was just finishing.

"...Lord, we close by giving you the honor and glory. Change the hearts of those that would do evil and harm in this world. Let them turn back to you and seek forgiveness. Help us all to turn to you and put our faith and trust in your Son, the only true source of peace and justice in this world. Help us do your will, and love one another, as you, our savior, loved us, even while we were still your enemies. In Jesus' name, we commit all things, Amen."

Josh finished, and the rest of the players responded with an "Amen" as the ump approached. The players stood up, smacking each other on the back or bumping gloves in high fives. Samson caught Josh in a bear hug, his spirit renewed, ready to face the world with a new lease on life and hope for the future.

It may not have been evident to those watching, but all of this spelled doom for the Yankees and their fans today. What the Yankees intended as a statement game, to show the Pirates and the public they were better in both social correctness and play, instead became a Pirate blowout. Quint's well-laid plans to deliver a diminished Josh Green, and a demoralized Pirates team, evaporated in a Pirate rout.

The Pirates fired on all cylinders, leading 9-0 by the fourth inning, chasing the Yankee starter by the second. "Slayer" Samson Gibson returned to early season form with a dominating performance, striking out a season-best 15 batters, pitching a complete-game two-hit shutout. Josh hit just two singles in his first two at-bats, not exactly a heavy-hitting display, but both hits produced early runs. Notably, the Yankees' pitching never really figured Josh out. Josh walked twice and grounded out sharply in his final at-bat, but by then, the game was well in hand.

After the game, the Yankees and their fans left feeling the "message balls" aimed at Josh's head, backfired. Instead, Josh and the Pirates sent a clear message to the Yankees and everyone watching. The Pirates and Josh Green were in a League of their own.

Seventy

The Pirates endured their largest post-game press conference of the season. The New York press was larger than just about anywhere, and the Yankees closed their locker room to interviews without notice. It was hard to say whether the Yankees were second-guessing their approach to the Pirates and Josh Green or just embarrassed by their lackluster play, but they weren't ready to talk to the press. Samson's gem of a shutout, coupled with the Pirates' offensive onslaught, made the press coverage in the Pirate locker room even more raucous than anticipated. Before they could start, Coach Samuelson grabbed Mark Johnson and said, "Look, we have more press in here than players. Each news agency gets one person and one technician, max. Kick the rest out. Just because the Yankees aren't talking to the press doesn't mean all their press gets to pile on our guys."

Mark did his best to remove redundant news people before letting them into the players' area. Nevertheless, the press still felt like a wave hitting the Pirates when they opened their doors. Despite brilliant play from several Pirates, including Samson with his complete-game shutout, and Juan with five RBIs, the press still focused on and surrounded Josh Green with most of the questions.

"Josh, can you explain how the Pirates humiliated the Yankees here in Yankee Stadium?" started a reporter from the NY Post with a strong Brooklyn accent.

Josh answered, "We set out to win the game, for sure, but no one's trying to humiliate anyone. Honestly, it comes down to Samson pitching a great outing and Juan leading us with a homer, a double, and going four for four with five RBIs. You need to talk to them. They're the stars for us tonight."

"Josh, what about that first at-bat? It looked like the pitcher was trying to take your head off?" asked another New York reporter.

Josh shrugged his shoulders. "What matters is I got the job done. I did what I needed to defend myself and keep the inning going."

Roman Josephus, who was more than a little hot over almost being trampled by the aggressive New York press, finally took control of the conversation with his barrage of planned questions. "Josh, Roman Josephus here from SPNN," Roman started, not for Josh's benefit, but for all the New Yorkers who saw him on their local affiliates for the first time. "Do you think the Yankees were trying to send you a message, with not one but two fastballs at your head in your first at-bat?"

"What message would that be, Roman?" Josh replied. By the way he asked it, calmly with arms crossed, almost seemed to invite Roman to give the answer he already knew.

Roman was ready, and Josh obliged, "Well, Josh, it seems the Yankees and their fans don't like your response to the racial strife in this country. The fact that the Pirates follow your lead, not kneeling for the anthem or wearing any race or equality organizational clothing supporting the victims of police brutality or anti-bigotry against the LGBTQ community."

"Roman, my words and actions this season and throughout my life have never shown racism or bigotry. I believe God created all humans as equal in His eyes, equally loved, above all His earthly creation. I believe God and His Son Jesus are the answers to our true problems, the problems in each of our lives and hearts. I choose to show my faith in God and ask for His guidance and help in all our problems by prayer and following Him. Each person chooses how they live their lives, and in this country, we are fortunate to choose with as much freedom as ever in the history of humanity. I understand not everyone thinks or believes as I do, but I will always invite others to the help, healing, and hope Jesus offers to all. He's the answer to our problems as a nation and as individuals."

"Do you reject the stance, or in this case, the kneeling others are taking against the country?" followed up Roman.

"Why are people kneeling against this country?" asked Josh.

"Well, they believe the country is racist and bigoted. We have all these shootings of unarmed black men, Josh. Doesn't that bother you?" pushed Roman.

"It bothers me and should bother everyone anytime someone is shot, Roman, regardless of their skin color or who's doing the shooting. But while our country had a bad history of systemic racism from its early days of slavery through Jim Crow into the 1960s, I believe systemic government racism no longer exists. Our laws, policies, and the way our governmental institutions ensure equal treatment and fairness under the law and in all public institutions guarantee equal rights."

"Then how do you explain the recent deaths?" Roman said adamantly.

"I would have to examine each death based on each individual situation. That's precisely what our justice system does. Every loss of a human being in a police shooting has to be, and is, reviewed. If the policeman did something wrong, we have laws to deal with misconduct, which we must uphold. However, I don't see a pattern of systemic racism. Some 680,000 cops in America from all backgrounds respond to millions of situations. The number of police shootings is extremely small and equally likely to be distributed across the races. Based on the number of violent crimes committed, police shoot blacks and non-blacks in similarly small numbers. One life, every life lost, needs to be evaluated as each is a tragedy, but the police are, by and large, doing their best to protect and serve our society in very tough and dangerous situations. More so than ever before, police are a reflection of us. Perhaps that was not true before my lifetime, but we have changed as a society, and now our police are a representative cross-section of our communities. They are our brothers and sisters trying to protect us."

"Individuals are responsible for their actions, and that includes their misdeeds. Police shootings are tragic events, and my heart goes out to those who lost a loved one. But I don't believe the facts and the numbers support blaming our country or even the police force, as a whole. Police do America's toughest job well, placing their lives on the line to faithfully serve. They keep us safe at home, work, and throughout our communities. But they can't change the hearts of individuals, and once they get involved, it's usually because we have failed, as individuals, to do what we are supposed to do. Man's sinful heart is the ultimate problem and the cause of all our strife and death."

"Our country is not perfect, but it holds high the standard of freedom for all our citizens, an example and beacon of liberty, freedom, and opportunity to the world. We sometimes miss the mark as individuals, but the country maintains its ideals of life, liberty, and the pursuit of happiness, and every one of its citizens has a chance to live their lives in freedom and make their life better."

"There is a lot of suffering in the African American community, Josh. What do you say to them?" Roman continued to press.

"I say the same thing I say to all who ask. It starts with each individual. Like the mistakes of the few policemen who do something wrong, we each need to look at ourselves and how we live our lives and hold ourselves accountable. For me, I would be lost if not for giving my life to Christ as a young man. When I follow his teachings and seek his will, I live a life worth living. When I go against his will and rebel, my life falls apart, I do wrong to myself, and in turn, I hurt those around me. Our problem isn't our country. Its promised foundation is freedom for every man, as all are created equal. Each generation must continue to reach for the high ideals of liberty and justice for all, more than the last. Today, we have more opportunities for freedom and prosperity than any previous generation for all citizens. Our problem is when we use our free will and go against what's good and just; what the Creator has told us is right and true. Our failures come from disobedience to God as individuals, and our decisions to rebel against God causes strife and destruction in our society."

"Look," Josh said, looking around the press corps with eyes of compassion, "I know many people have hard, tough times in their lives. When my life turns difficult, only God can pick me up. Christ is the answer, He's the Truth, and His way is the only way to find peace and justice. Only through Christ can our problems in this world truly be solved, and only Christ promises to see us through our greatest difficulties. I kneel to Christ and pray for His healing and guidance. I work daily to exercise the freedoms given by God and guaranteed by this great country, to treat all people with the love and care Christ shows me."

When Josh finished, even Roman was silent for a few seconds.

Another reporter asked, "Josh, what do you say to others who want our government to take the lead and make things more racially fair, who want to eliminate bigotry and racial inequality? To make people stop racism in their jobs, like the police shooting blacks?"

"What law, what government policy, what police precinct is allowing either through a bad law, a bad procedure, a bad policy or something else, systemic racism or bigotry?"

"Many of these movements would say there are many," answered Roman before he could stop himself.

"What are they, Roman? What do *you* say? Give me one example of the policy or law that allows or condones bigotry or racism?" asked Josh.

Roman remained silent, and the extensive press corps held their peace.

Josh looked around and waited, but they were without an answer. Therefore, he continued, "The government or society cannot change an individual's heart. To the best of my knowledge and understanding, we stamped out the laws allowing racism and bigotry by the 1970s. We have also rooted out institutional policies, like segregation in our government entities. For thirty or forty years, we've pushed for fairness in hiring, education opportunities, government agencies, and even in sports. You cannot ask the government to change the hearts of individuals. The government is not God, and we certainly don't want to treat it as if it should be—that is when totalitarian governments arise, destroying nations and ruining people's lives. Our current problems stem from the heart of man."

Josh continued, "Only God can change the heart. We need to look at our hearts and take responsibility for our actions. Christ alone offers the promise of a new life and a new heart. I would challenge my neighbors, those listening, to start by seeking Him. Let Him change your heart and give you a new life, and then help your neighbors by showing them the love Christ gives to us. That was His commandment 2000 years ago, and it's still the only true solution to all our problems. Our country sets the standards of freedom and justice based on its foundation and practices. Our founders wrote the Constitution to keep government out of our lives to the maximum extent possible and allow us the freedom to live as God created us, with free will and choice. These mirror Christian thought, representative of what we once valued, even when we failed to meet the high standards stated in our founding documents. However, only God can put right the standard of goodness and love in each person's heart. Christ is the standard.

No one can reach it without Christ. And no new government, policy, or law will change the heart of man."

Roman fought back, trying to pick apart Josh's beliefs, "You say this, yet in the same way you stood against the gay lifestyle. Doesn't Christianity support bias against gays and tells slaves to keep their place? Isn't it just an old trope to say Christ can solve our problems when Christians show prejudice against blacks and gays over the centuries?"

Josh replied, "Christ said, 'Come unto me all who are heavy burdened, and I will give you rest,' Roman. He saw all equally. He made it a point to be with those who needed him most, those who were rightly called sinners, because he knew we all are sinners and all need him to overcome sin and its penalty, death. Jesus loves me and you, despite our sins. He offers salvation to each, equally. But as God, He also allows us to reject Him. He gives us that freedom. As for slaves and the gay lifestyle, I say to you, you distort what the Bible says if you proclaim it approves of racial slavery or says one race should be slaves. Christ and his followers were not revolutionary in changing society by force but by changing the individual's heart and life by the power of Christ's forgiveness. He never supported enslaving people based on race and rejected someone based on immoral lifestyles and sin. He knew and told us, we all had sinned and come short of the glory of God, but as God, He came and offered himself as our perfect sacrifice to repair our relationship with God. In simple terms, He said we all are lost and can't meet God's standard, for He is the Perfect Standard Himself. We need a perfect savior, and Christ is that savior. He came to us and still meets us where we are, offering forgiveness and a new life if we accept him."

"It seems you have a lot of Sunday School in you, Josh," said one of the New York reporters, "But what New York wants to know is if you support the anti-racist and anti-bigotry platforms."

"I am against racism and bigotry in all forms the way Christ is, sir. The only way I see successfully fighting against both is through prayer and learning of and following Christ, our Lord. He is the only one who can set people free. Free of racism, free of sexual immorality, free of all sins. As far as society and our government, I want our government to continue to strive to meet the high standards outlined in our founding documents. It's been nearly 250 years, and as a nation, we still have to work every day to meet those lofty ideals. But we have come a long way since ending slavery through a bloody civil war 160 years ago. We stamped out Jim Crow before I was born. Look at what this sport went through nearly 75 years ago with our greatest sportsman, Jackie Robinson, and all he suffered as the first black baseball player in the Major Leagues."

"Today, this nation is still the beacon of freedom and justice shining in a dark world. We are the envy of the rest of the world with opportunity for all to enjoy life, liberty, and the pursuit of happiness, and I stand with this country as it continues to fight for those high standards set in our Declaration of Independence and our Constitution. However, I know the truth and will continue telling it to you. It's man's heart in each person driving our problems today, and only Christ can heal a man's heart. The government isn't the answer because the problem isn't our laws or institutions. Our problems come from sin in our hearts and our choices. Christ is our redeemer and the only solution."

"No kneeling for the anthem, then, Josh?" asked Roman. "Aren't you saying to African Americans, they don't matter, Josh, just as you said to the Gay community when you chose not to support your teammate?"

Josh replied, "I care about my teammates equally, as I care about everyone I meet regardless of their race, Roman. I won't separate people into groups. I see them as individuals. In Christ's eyes, as the Son of God, He died for all. His love for us is so great, despite knowing our sins, He loved us and became man to live the perfect life and be the sacrifice necessary to redeem us. He showed us the truth: One race, the human race, in the same condition; lost and separated from God, needing a savior. Jesus told us to love God with all our heart and our fellow man as He loved us."

"Our country stands for freedom, justice, and all those good things created by God. I can't kneel against the ideals guaranteeing all freedom and equality under the law. Americans for generations have struggled, fought, and died for these ideals. Instead, I must ask for God's power to change each man's heart, starting with my own. Christ is the true hope for our country, freedom, and future. To say anything else is untrue. The cause of our problems is not our country, its founding ideals, or our laws and institutions, including our police. This is a lie from the pit of hell. Our problems come directly from our hearts. Our laws and government only regulate our behavior. They can't change a man's heart; only Christ can. I will not shift blame, and I will never kneel for a lie. Instead, I will stand for the Truth and kneel to the one in whom my hope rests."

The news reporters remained silent, and even Roman couldn't think of a way to get Josh to respond differently. He hoped to pick Josh apart, but Josh would not take up or directly oppose "the cause" in a way that allowed Roman to make it an "Us versus Them" battle. Roman found this incredibly frustrating. He needed Josh as a villain or as a champion. Instead, Josh was just a Christian and repugnantly, stubbornly, would not pick a side Roman could use to generate the momentum for Roman's promotion. Well, it didn't matter, decided Roman finally. He would continue portraying Josh as the villain, regardless. Roman would keep attacking until he showed this Christian stance was just a lame smokescreen covering a life of lies. To do so, he needed dirt on Josh to show him a hypocrite, and he hoped an old source just brought him such information.

The sportswriters scratched their heads, grumbling as they left the Pirate locker room. They wondered how a post-game interview became a political and religious discussion. Roman, however, was already thinking ahead to his next move. As he returned to the hotel room, he checked his incoming messages and began to smile.

Seventy One

Quint Pilate hung up the phone and sat back in his chair, brooding. Things were going decidedly against his plans. What was he to do? He hoped to attend the third game of the series on Saturday evening as the series ended on Sunday before the League headed into All-Star week in Atlanta. Unbelievably, in a few short months, the owners went from solidly behind him to nervously concerned with the League's direction and public discontent. This latest phone call from one of the league's powerhouse owners was one of three he fielded as the Yankees succumbed to the humiliating defeat by the Pirates. Not only were the Pirates winning, their rebellious stance placed them at odds with the League and Union position, public opinion, and, most importantly, the owners' bottom line. Television viewership plummeted, with the fan base split on their support of the League's reaction to the country's unrest. Box office and ratings now fell, a cardinal sin in the eyes of Quint's bosses, the owners. The owner who just hung up on him made it clear, Quint's position depended on righting the reputation of the League and, in turn, the owners' revenue stream. If the owners doubted Quint's ability to lead them back to profitability, Quint's job would be in serious jeopardy. He needed to end the first half showing himself in complete control of the situation, but today's game in New York was a bad omen. It came down to this: something must be done about Josh Green.

The commissioner paced and waited for the dailies. Quint's network of staffers busily worked with the relatively unheralded and unadvertised commissioner's polling department, used much like a major political organization but focused on MLB's image with their fans. He already ordered a series of poll questions conducted nationwide to determine what fans wanted the League to do and ask how well they were doing it. First indications were not good. For most ballparks, after initial upticks, attendance now dropped since the League took its aggressive stance supporting racial justice and anti-police brutality themes. Despite echoing liberal themes, the groups voiced only moderate support, indignant the League did not come down on what one group called disturbingly bigoted dissenting displays. Quint was dismayed at the response and the League's lackluster economic performance. He could not understand how the country, when polled, seemed to be for race equality and against bigotry yet voted with their dollars by staying away from the game when the League tried to show its support.

Quint answered to the team owners. While they publicly spoke out against racism or bigotry against sexual orientation, he could tell they were uneasy with his decisions and the League's falling market share. As it turned out, public support was mixed for teams kneeling against racism and wearing the names of those slain by police and other anti-racial, anti-bigotry gear. It was a polarizing topic. While some fans adamantly supported the movements, many turned away because of the demonstrations, often citing the loss of a family-friendly atmosphere. Worrisome was the significant number of respondents' comments in the optional section of the polls saying players and teams were now anti-American and hypocritical. Usually, they cited the League average salaries and the opportunities minorities found in American baseball. The responses didn't stop there, however. They also showed those who were for the protest weren't happy either. To Quint's surprise, those who strongly supported the organizations MLB backed with visible displays of support were upset the League allowed what they cited as a counter protest by not kneeling and not wearing their gear.

While there were many negative indications, one theme was consistent throughout the polls. Public sentiment indicated the League appeared weak in support, and the prime example cited was the Pirates and Josh Green's rejection of progressive displays. Surprisingly, the Pirates were the one team, at home or on the road, gaining revenue as fast as fan passion, both good and bad. Yes, these same perennial losers and usually irrelevant Pittsburgh Pirates were now a thorn in Quint's side and a major problem for baseball's image. It started first with their superb play and Josh Green's unprecedented historic season. Quint feared what might occur if the Yankees didn't bounce back, especially if Josh Green's Pirates continued to stand against popular opinion while dominating the League. Quint knew something must be done.

While the commissioner stewed, Roman Josephus returned to his upscale hotel, finally alone, able to check out the fruits of his investigative report. Roman returned a call and listened intently to the voice on the other end of the line. It was an old source, a private investigator of sorts, he used to find seedy and salacious background details about players on more than one occasion. Roman paid handsomely for this information, based on its value. Getting information through a third party could be tricky. Still, it gave Roman plausible deniability in the means and methods of garnering the data he needed to stay clear of the scandal. Besides, it allowed Roman only to pay if the information found was worth it. This source came through on more than one occurrence with a valuable report, even when Roman didn't use it directly. While the information may be incomplete, some would even call it hearsay or gossip, Roman found it suitable for his purposes. He was a sports journalist, not a lawyer, and this wasn't a court of law but the court of public opinion. "Anything goes" wasn't something Roman would admit openly, but behind closed doors, getting a story was the only bottom line that mattered.

Even when only minimal circumstantial evidence supported the report, he often used it to pry open an otherwise uncooperative source. If they still refused to open up, an "innocent" release of the information to the public, done in just the right way, could show enough smoke so fans could surmise the fire present without direct evidence. As long as he piqued public interest and increased his ratings, who was he to quibble? Roman need never claim the innuendo as fact. If no one knew who started the rumor, he was in the clear. The investigator continued relaying the story as Roman busily scribbled notes. He stopped the investigator periodically with questions to clarify his story.

"So, you are telling me this guy was essentially a pimp before getting busted eight years ago and just got out? OK, and he swears the girl was one of his workers? That she ran away just before his business got shut down?" Roman continued scribbling in his notebook listening through his blue tooth earpiece. "And now she shows up as the nanny to Green's kid? Are you sure it's the same girl? This is important. Right, OK. So..., You confirmed it from someone with her in...what did you call it, the Light of Life rescue shelter?" Roman wrote the name down and underlined it with a question mark to look up later. "So, two positive identifications of the photo and the girl's name. OK, just first name and photo. Yes, got it."

Again, Roman paused and listened to the oily voice at the other end of the line. "Yes, yes. I got the part she was a recent graduate of Grove College from the PA certificate and licensing website. Yes, my Pirate source confirmed it appeared to be a Pirate hire they made without Green's help or prior knowledge, but they couldn't confirm how they discovered her for employment. Well, not as far as anyone knows." Roman sat forward during the following few details. "And you're sure she's actually *living* with the Greens at their home as well?" he said, listening to the response.

Roman smiled as he wrote that tidbit of information. He didn't say anything but thought to himself greedily, "Well, this helps my position when I talk with them. Perhaps Green isn't the saint he portrays to the public. I can use this to get to the girl or even make Green himself answer my questions. Even if they don't play ball, the right-timed 'leak' of this information will surely stir the public's imagination. Who am I to change their opinion? After all, I only deliver the report. What the public infers is up to them."

The voice on the other end of the line was now starting to give Roman the costs of getting all this information, but Roman quickly cut him off to protect himself from ever knowingly supporting funding witness testimony, just in case he did end up in court. "Look, how you do your business is your business. I pay for your time and associated expenses, understand?" Roman emphasized that last word in case his investigator was recording the conversation, just as he was. Roman went further, "You know I have never paid you for any expenses outside of standard business practice.... Yes, I would be interested if you find any photos or videos supporting the claims, but for what I've got planned, the information is enough to get started.... OK. Give me this Christian teacher's name again. No, I'll only use it in person if I need to pry something out of her." He listened to the voice with one final warning and said, "Well, your source's credibility will not come to light the way I plan to use it anyway, but if you find out more, let me know," and hung up.

Roman sat back, formulating a plan. He knew how to use this information himself and knew his friend in MLB's front office would likely find this information valuable. He would give it to him only in good time and at a price. Yes, Roman smiled to himself. What started as a miserable and frustrating day at the ballpark in front of the camera turned out to be a good day for the future reporting of this soon-to-be nationally syndicated SPNN sports news reporter, Roman Josephus.

Seventy Two

G ame two of the Yankee series promised to be even more intense than game one. It was another late afternoon game with a capacity crowd. The charged atmosphere began outside the stadium as demonstrations heated towards full boil. Coming in from their nearby hotel, the Pirates ran a barrage of angry crowds exhibiting more hostility than typical fan support of the Yankees. The Pirates hurried into the stadium under a buzz of angry fan chants and numerous unruly displays during pregame activities.

Finally, game time arrived. During the anthem, the crowd again booed and jeered the Pirates for standing and showing respect for the flag. The Pirates, batting first, started the game with three quick outs after some good Yankee pitching. They walked Josh intentionally and ended the inning with a sliding catch on a sharply hit ball by Juan to left field. Taking the field for the bottom of the first, the Pirates' prayer circle behind second base received an even greater show of hostility than in game one, with a loud wall of boos like a football crowd trying to disrupt the opposing quarterback's play calls. Josh and the two Pirate captains decided to have their pitcher and Thomas start their pitching warm-ups while the rest of the team prayed. This temporarily appeased the head umpire, as they weren't delaying the game. When the other umps felt the rest of the fielded players should take positions, the Pirates completed the prayer before the umps could confront them. The bottom of the first inning was similar to the top, as the Pirates also got three quick outs without advancing a player past first. Josh came up again in the third, receiving another free pass, but the Pirates couldn't get anything started. The game remained a tight pitching duel between the Yankees' number two starter and two of the Pirates' young pitchers, who combined for just four hits and two runs through eight as Josh's day remained quiet at the plate.

The game stayed close, but the Yankees held a 2-1 lead entering the ninth inning. Josh was due up fourth. The Pirate lead-off hitter was the number nine hitter, the Oklahoman Nate Fisher, batting for the pitcher position as designated hitter under American League rules. Nate drew a walk to start the inning. Zach followed with a sharp single up the middle, placing runners at first and second. The Yankees replaced their pitcher with a lefty closer to face the right-hitting

Andrew. This Yankees closer pitched only one blown save all year, back in May, and was 3-0 with 22 saves and a minuscule 1.28 ERA, leading the League. The only surprise was the Yankees didn't start the inning with him on the mound.

Andrew's at-bat was difficult, but like the all-star he was, he fought off a 2-2 count with several foul balls. Then Andrew showed remarkable restraint holding off on two curveballs breaking down, out of the strike zone, drawing a rare walk against the Yankees closer.

With the bases loaded and the tying run at third, the crowd was almost apoplectic, loudly cheering and booing both as Green came to the plate. The Pirate radio broadcast described the scene.

"My goodness, that walk to Andrew drew the worst moaning and crowd frustration we've seen in a while, Bob," commented Greg.

"Yeah, you would have thought the home plate ump's ball four call was the worst in history. Honestly, though, it wasn't as close as the ball three call, making the ump's job easy. However, the fans wanted a called strike even though it ended up in the dirt."

"We'd let you hear a little more of the fan noise, but frankly, we know the kiddies are listenen', and it's a little R rated!" explained Greg.

"This is it, folks. The Yankees have to pitch to Green or walk the tying run home," said Bob.

"Green's batting has been only human in these last two games, going two for five, two singles, and two RBIs. That's not bad for anyone else, but for Green, that's shutting him down pretty well for the Yanks. Green's O for 1 with two walks and a ground out today. The crowd is really letting him know; they still don't like him. In fact, they are the definition of a hostile crowd right now. Wouldn't you say, eh Bob?" understated Greg.

"Yep. I hear some things that would make a sailor blush. I sure wouldn't want to be walking toward that batter's box, Greg!" Bob replied.

"Well, that's because you batted .196 in Tee Ball League as a seven-year-old and never recovered, Bob," Greg opined.

"I was short for my age, and that tee was too tall!" Bob whined.

Despite the Pirate radio crew's jovial banter, the anger felt palpable as the crowd shouted select epithets against Green as he approached the batter's box. Josh appeared unfazed, taking his normal neutral stance, with quiet hands, staring calmly at the pitcher. The pitcher started him with a hard fastball just off the plate, and Green took it for ball one.

"Do you think they are willing to walk the tying run in by pitching around Green?" asked Bob.

"I guess you've gotta be careful. A walk is a tie, but the Yankees get the last at-bat, anyway. However, if Green takes you deep, that's a tough road back. Then again, Juan's up next, and as he showed yesterday, he's no easy out either," replied Greg.

"Let's see how this goes, folks. The pitcher comes set again.... Here's the pitch...," Bob paused.

Josh knew this pitcher was famous for his fastball velocity, a big looping curve, and a cut fastball, similar to retired Yankee Hall of Famer Mariano Rivera, except from the left side. Often the cutter would jam right-handers, breaking their bat. As Josh watched the pitch, sure enough, it started on the inside part of the plate and continued to slice in towards Josh; hard, fast, and tight. Most hitters would hit the ball on the bat's handle, but Josh was not most hitters. He pulled his hips quickly through as he swung, bringing the barrel inside and swiping the ball down the left field line.

"Hit hard down the line in left field! Fisher and Zach will score. There's a strong throw to home by the left fielder, and Andrew will hold at third! Green's into second with a standup double, and the Pirates take the lead 3-2!" yelled Bob excitedly.

"Yes, folks, he came inside on him, but ole Green swatted it down the line just fair! The crowd is really not happy. What can they do except try to halt the damage and make a comeback in the bottom of the inning?" Greg finished.

A Yankee comeback was not to be, however. Juan flew out to right field with a deep fly, and Andrew tagged at third, beating the throw to the plate. Two batters later, Judah added a single, scoring Josh. The bottom of the ninth inning was a touch-and-go affair, with the Yankees getting back one run and threatening with another runner. It ended meekly with a softly hit grounder and a pop foul ball caught by Thomas behind the plate for a third out. Despite a closely contested game, the Yankees now dropped two in a row to Pittsburgh, and the fans could only manage some weak boos as the Pirates left the field, once again victorious.

Seventy Three

The following morning, Mary, Josh, and Ruth took the subway to the Columbia University Irving Medical Center, just a short distance from the team hotel, for Ruth's 10:00 am visit on Saturday. The treatment was one of the many Nurse Richards helped Mary arrange when the Pirates finalized the team schedule at the start of the season. When they planned the visits in April, Nurse Richards encouraged the Greens to take advantage of the New York stop for Ruth to see one of the world-class doctors at the famous hospital, the only scheduled stop this year for the Pirates. Yet spring seemed almost a world away in light of the last few weeks of upheaval. For the first time during his travels, people recognized Josh in passing, not always in a good way. While the threesome expected a relatively short and uneventful trip to the hospital, Josh was alert for possible unpleasantries. This was the first trip since Josh and his fellow Pirates took their controversial stance. Whether it was a sign of things to come for Josh and the Pirates or specific to New York, more than one passerby recoiled when they recognized Josh. Perhaps Josh's play, defeating their Yankees, fueled the animosity. More likely, Josh and the girls suffered the cost of standing against public sentiment and society's mores. Recognizing Josh as the baseball star who refused to kneel for the anthem or support the gay lifestyle, many scowled, and one young woman even cursed them under her breath as they passed.

Ruth was excited to take the Subway, a new experience for her. The ride started pleasantly enough as they made their way to a subway entrance close to the hotel. They took a quick ride across town on the D train, transferring to the A train, followed by a ride uptown to the 168th Street stop on Broadway. From there, it was a short walk to the hospital entrance. While the trip by subway was relatively short, Josh, Mary, and Ruth left the hotel just before 9:00 AM to ensure they arrived early. Like it or not, Josh's now familiar face continued receiving second glances. Though Ruth mostly missed the responses, Mary looked a couple of times at Josh, and his eyes told her he understood. Mary's concern grew as the city felt unexpectedly brooding and unfriendly despite the sunny day.

Upon arriving at the hospital, it took Josh and Mary some time to figure out where to go, and despite the excitement of riding an actual big city subway, Ruthie was a little tired from the ride and walk. They experienced more stares from the hospital employees and the occasional visitor inside the hospital complex. Finally, they navigated to the correct hospital wing and corridor and sat waiting for the doctor's visit, followed by a physical therapy appointment. Their waiting area was relatively large, and despite being a Saturday morning, nearly two dozen patients waited for appointments with the various orthopedic practitioners. While they waited, those around him eyed Josh. He wore his camouflaged Pittsburgh ball cap Pete gave him, which he often donned at the post-game interviews and was soon recognized.

An older black man with a scruffy beard and hair graying at its tips sat across from Josh, apparently waiting for someone already being seen. He wore a Yankees baseball cap and looked Josh over appraisingly. "Aren't you that Pirate baseball player?" said the man accusingly. "Aren't you Josh Green?"

"Yes, I am," answered Josh politely. "How are you today?"

The man did not respond with the easy banter Josh formerly encountered on public outings. Instead, he came right to the point, stating critically, "I was fine until you showed up. What are you doing here?"

"We're here to see the doctor," Josh replied, trying to defuse the situation but still protect their privacy. "I see you are a baseball fan," Josh said, nodding at the man's cap.

"Of course, I'm a fan. I've lived here all my life. But I am more of a fan of standing up for what's right. Many of us don't like how you've been playing the game, with your stance supporting racism and bigotry!" said the man, almost spitting the accusation.

"Well, I am sorry you feel that way, but I assure you, I don't support either. I stand for equality and justice for all people."

"Yeah, well, apparently you've missed it, but my people are hurting, and the world doesn't seem to care."

"I haven't missed it, my friend. Your people are my people too."

The older man raised his eyebrows at this. After all, he did not expect Josh to call blacks "my people." He was a proud New Yorker but, more than that, a proud African American. He traced his ancestors to the Harlem Hell Fighters of the World Wars and farther back to the civil war when his ancestor escaped slavery and joined the 29th Connecticut (Colored) Volunteer Infantry Regiment. Angry when he first recognized Josh, the man hesitated, looking at him anew. He only recently saw him on TV. Previously, he listened to the New York media outlets talk negatively about his racist stance. The media referenced the SPNN interview and his charged remarks against his gay teammate, though they never showed the interview. He assumed this Josh Green must be another privileged white guy, but now he saw him up close for the first time. He was struck most by those dark brown eyes staring kindly. Despite displaying anger toward Josh, Josh looked at him with a disarming look of peace. The man saw Josh's dark face and broad hooked nose more clearly in person. Josh's dark curly hair peeked from under the camo Pirate ball cap. Suddenly, almost shocked, the man realized this man didn't appear to be a white man but looked mixed race, perhaps African or Middle Eastern, or both. His skin appeared more of a coffee-and-cream hue.

Still, the man remembered what the New York announcers on TV said about Green's position on current events, and he tried to shore up his animosity towards Josh. Was Josh a traitor to his heritage? The media's picture of a racist bigot became hard to maintain as the man looked across at Josh, the coffee-colored warrior, displaying not hatred but a calm serenity, with kindness in his eyes. Was Green really someone who believed their problems stemmed from something other than what society did to his people, was doing still? Now the man was unsure. Despite his best efforts, there was just a hint of a softening in his heart as Josh nodded, finally starting a conversation.

"That's why I kneel and ask the One who always cares for all. I pray for His help and understanding of His love for each of us. I ask His guidance on what He wants us to do. I kneel and pray for our country and our fellow citizens, and I honor the Lord and ask him to bring His hope and peace to all people," said Josh.

"Since when has God worked to help us?" The man's wall of hurt and regret went back up as he thought sadly of his difficult life of more than fifty years, and his only child, his one true blessing in life, was now a twenty-three-year-old confined to a wheelchair because of a wretched disease.

"Have you asked Him?" said Josh quietly, sensing the man's pain.

The man tried to shake off Josh's kindness, holding onto his defiance by turning back to the plight of the black community instead. "I don't believe God has helped our people. Did he help us when we were brought as slaves here against our will? My family fought for the white man and this country. Despite that, we worry about getting killed by a cop just because of our skin color. How has God helped us against racism to this day?"

"The Lord knows all about our struggles," Josh said, and it struck the man that Josh made this personal. Josh continued, "He went through a life of sorrows and felt the scourge of oppression and hatred for who He was. Jesus knows your pain and wants to lift your burdens. He says, 'Cast all your cares upon him, for he cares for you.'[1] He tells us that if we turn to Him, ask forgiveness for our mistakes, and accept His sacrifice for our salvation, we share in His victory over death and this world. If we do, He promises us, no matter our situation or station, no matter

---

1. 1 Peter 5:7

what the world does and says against us, He will never leave us or forsake us.[2] He loves us with an everlasting love."

"I just want my kid to be healthy," said the man, finally admitting for the first time out loud the core source of his hopelessness and despair. "I want him to be able to live free in a just world that gives him an equal chance like everyone else, yet all I see is a world that rejects him, either because of his disability or because of his skin color."

"I don't know what God will do for you and your child's situation, sir, but I know whatever you are going through, God sees you, and He sees your son." Josh paused until the man looked back up at him, deep into his eyes, and saw nothing but kindness and love looking back at him. As he did so, the man began to release his anger, the anger he held against God for allowing his son to travel such a difficult path, a path the man was helpless to make better.

For the first time, the man thought truly and fully, who was this man Joshua Green and this God and Lord he worshipped? Could God really be there for him too? How could God understand what it was like to love his son and have to watch him hurt so badly for so many unfair reasons? Finally, Josh continued as if reading the man's thoughts. "The Father knows what it's like to see His own Son suffer horribly and unjustly. His Son, Jesus, knows what it's like to be rejected, ostracized, and suffer unjust, painful punishment. I don't know what you are going through or why, but I know God has a plan for your family. He can see you through the worst storm. By accepting Him, He heals your soul and gives you a life worth living."

The man hesitated, then asked quietly, skeptical, "How do you know what I've been through? How can you understand?"

"I don't know, but the Father does. He sees you. God knows you and your child by name. In my own life, He carried me through the worst situations when all hope seemed lost. He brought me through the valley of death. I have lost friends and even my most beloved wife. But through it all, He never left me. I know He wants to help you, and He alone brings true peace and justice to this world. He will heal you, but you must choose to let Him."

The man realized Josh did not say God would heal his son. Instead, Josh implied he, not just his son, needed healing. The man now admitted his wounds began as a child growing up in a fallen world. He longed for something, no, *someone*, to come into his life who truly loved him, to heal him where he hurt, deep in his soul. Could there truly be a God of the Bible who cared about him and

---

2. Deuteronomy 31:6; Joshua 1:9; Hebrews 13:5-6; Psalm 55:22; Philippians 4:6-7

his son personally in this evil world? What's more, would God save such a wreck as he? It was hard to believe this late in life, after all his mistakes, God would even want to save him. "I don't have enough faith," said the man quietly, but honestly, the heat of anger cooled from his face and words, replaced by an ember of hope.

"My friend, you only need enough faith to take the first step. Choose Christ. Choose to put your faith not in yourself or this world, not in the government or other people, but in the only name under Heaven, whereby you must be saved.[3] Accept you need salvation and no one else, not you, not good deeds, nothing in this world can save you. Only Christ is worthy. That's where faith begins. Accepting you can't do anything to change your destiny. Only Christ can. He loves you. He wants you to turn to Him and find peace. With His love and sacrifice on the Cross, he bought your redemption, and He is what you need to come through this lost world and find new life in Him. He'll carry you through the journey and lead you home."

As the man sat struggling, listening intently to what Josh proposed, across the room sat a woman traveling a very different road. She, too, was late middle-aged. She wore large, oversized sunglasses with loose black hair flecked with gray surrounding her face. Adding more cover, she wore a wide-brim floppy hat, making it difficult to see facial details to describe her. She sat quietly, a world away across the room from Josh and the man, reading a copy of the Times. While it was becoming rare to see people with newspapers, this woman was old school. She enjoyed getting her information from the crinkled pages smelling of ink and reclaimed paper. Besides, it allowed her a portable cover, if you will, to hide behind as she spied out her quarry. Still, the modern age had its uses.

After one quick, invisible glance at Josh from behind the dark glasses, the woman got up from her seat, turned towards the exit, and walked around the corner, quickly covering the short distance to just inside the hospital entrance. She made sure she was at least temporarily alone before making the call. "Yes, it's Sana Ballat," she started, "I wanted to let you know the buck is out and separated from the herd. We're currently at Columbia Medical Center on 168th Street with just his two does. Yes, they appear to have an appointment. No, I've been following him from the hotel. He took the subway. Yes, the 168th Street station. Whether he goes back to the hotel or directly to the stadium, the 168th Street station works. OK, I will let you know when they are leaving.... Yes, but once they start down into the station, that's where I part ways. It's better for both of us if I am not around. Remember, payment, regardless of the outcome, by the means discussed. Right. I'll see you at the café tomorrow. Wait for my call."

---

3. Acts 4:12

Shabana Ballat, or Sana as she preferred to be called by anyone outside her family, hung up and returned to the waiting area. Sana again sat across the room from the Green threesome and resumed reading her newspaper as a nurse walked into the busy room calling for the Greens.

As Sana watched, the little girl and the woman got up to walk back into the office. At the same time, Sana noticed Josh still talking to the older black man, joined now by a young man of indeterminate age in a wheelchair. Sana could not hear what they said as Josh bent down on one knee between the older man and this young man. Or was it a teenage boy? Either way, what started as a heated conversation, at least for the black man's part, when Sana first watched, became a quiet, almost intimate one. Sana could see all three men bow their heads in quiet prayer.

Meanwhile, the nurse waited impatiently as Ruth and Mary stood by the door waiting for Josh before entering. Josh finished and stood up. He reached into a large bag he carried over his shoulder, pulled out a baseball, wrote something on it, and handed it to the kid sitting in the wheelchair. Like the older man, the young man wore a Yankees cap, and Sana harrumphed at the thought of a Yankees fan taking a baseball signed by the Pirate star. It surprised and confused Sana to see the older man now smile as the kid beamed at Josh. The older man seemed hostile when first meeting Josh, yet now he thanked Josh with soft words Sana could not hear over the hubbub of the patients in the waiting room. Josh shook the man's hand and walked toward the nurse and his waiting daughter. Sana noted Josh, the last to enter the hallway, turned back once more and waved to the two people with whom he prayed. The older man seemed shocked as he watched the boy in the wheelchair wave back.

Sana waited until the door closed behind Josh. As the man pushed the boy in the wheelchair towards the exit, Sana got up, pretending to walk out, and struck up a conversation as they walked away from the noisy waiting area down the relatively quiet hallway.

"Excuse me, sir. Was that man you talked with, that ballplayer for the Pirates?"

The man took his eyes off the boy in the wheelchair, who talked and gesticulated with him somewhat energetically. "You mean Joshua Green? Yes," said the man smiling at Sana, "Yes, he was."

Sana pretended to be put out, "I am surprised to see him here. With all the negative things I've seen about him in the press, you'd think he'd have enough sense to keep a low profile until the Pirates went home."

"I know, me too, but I've gotten to talk with him today," the man commented, "And I've got to tell you, he's not what I expected. I mean, my son, here, and I, are big Yankee fans. But my son hasn't been doing well. His illness has taken a toll on him recently and I, well...," the man hesitated. His voice cracked as he seemed to tear up at the thoughts he tried to express.

"You would think Green would be a little more sensitive to not bothering you and your son," said Sana consolingly. Sana was used to American men opening up to a soft female touch, and she often got information just by allowing men to talk to her, whereas a male in her profession might use less subtle ways.

"No, no, just the opposite," said the old man emphatically. "I wanted to be mad at him and give him what for, but instead, he offered words of encouragement. Then, when my boy came out of the physical therapy," the man hesitated, searching for the right words. He continued, "My son's been going downhill a lot recently, like he'd given up. He's had this condition since he was ten, but he's twenty-three now, and it's become much worse lately. I could barely get him to move or speak for the last several months, but when Mr. Green started talking with him, he came to life! After he prayed with us..., well, look!" The man gestured happily toward his son, who waved the ball around and occasionally switched it from hand to hand. "He's talking and moving like I haven't seen him do in a year or more!" Indeed, the boy or young man, Sana corrected, now said something about meeting the ball player showing off the signed ball to a hospital employee who passed by as they approached the exit. "I have got to tell you," said the old man smiling back at Sana, "This is nothing short of a miracle for us, for my son to move and talk like this."

The man shook his head lovingly at his son, smiling in disbelief. He turned back to Sana, tears in his eyes, "I can't tell you how wonderful it is to see. We have season tickets to the Yankees' home games, but I haven't been but once or twice this year because my son didn't seem up for it. I think I am going to take him tonight." The man seemed to talk as much to himself as Sana, looking lovingly at his son. "Yes! I think we both can go, and we might even cheer Josh on!" he said, smiling at his boy. As they approached the exit, he turned back to Sana. "I guess you never know how God will help you when you need it most, even in the form of a Yankee nemesis! Who would have thought? Have a nice day!" the man said cheerily as he pushed his son out the exit.

Sana watched the man head down the sidewalk with his son, both smiling and talking as they headed off into the bright sunny day. She stood perplexed at what happened but soon realized she needed to get back to the waiting room to catch the Greens and their companion before they came out of the appointment.

Sana was unsure exactly why the Greens came to the hospital, but she guessed it was an appointment for the little girl. After about an hour, the daughter walked out with the nanny. Sana thought she heard one of the Greens call her Mary. A man in green and blue scrubs escorted them. They walked further into the hospital, down a corridor away from the entrance. Sana was unsure what to do but decided she must follow them because Josh was nowhere to be seen. As the bustle of the crowded waiting room gave way to the quiet corridor, Sana became afraid she might lose them or stray too close and get asked where she was going, so she prepared the excuse she was looking for a restroom. A woman desperate for a bathroom worked almost every time. Just as she was about to give up and head back to catch Josh coming out, she overheard the man say, "Just keep going down this corridor until you come to the elevator, head up to the third floor, and you will walk right into the cancer ward entrance. Doctor Weinberg phoned, saying he would have Josh there as soon as they finished visiting the children's cancer treatment center. Thank Josh again for visiting the kids. I'm sure they enjoyed seeing him. And good luck Ruth. I hope to see you again the next time the Pirates play in New York—maybe in the World Series!"

Sana stopped at a water fountain and got a drink to avoid making contact with the man as he let the two ladies go and turned back towards the physical therapy clinic. This may prove problematic, thought Sana, as the hallway remained empty. Still, she needed to follow the Greens as they left the hospital but wasn't sure they would return to the entrance they used initially. However, she couldn't go upstairs without a good reason. Sana decided to head to the elevator area described and see how it looked. It turned out to be a relatively open part of the hospital with a little atrium, some greenery, and a coffee shop with a few tables and chairs; a perfect place to wait. She got a coffee and sat at one of the tables, hoping the Greens would leave the way they came.

Sana sat and contemplated all she saw and heard today. As she walked and let the old man talk, Green must have left the PT area to make this visit, perhaps escorted by this Dr. Weinberg, up to the cancer ward. What was Green doing there all this time, she wondered? Sana furrowed her brow. This was not Sana's first disconcerted feeling about her predicament in the last twenty-four hours. She knew too little background when hired to track Green, far from her usual meticulous study of a mark before taking a job.

Usually, Sana did extensive homework before getting involved in a case, but hired only yesterday, and despite her considerable skills and best efforts, she couldn't find much about Green. Of course, she used the word "hired" loosely. She would never normally accept such a job, especially with the latest stipulations from the client only this morning. Yesterday she was told it would be a "follow, observe, and report" job. However, this morning the client added the stipulation Sana identify when Green moved away from the other Pirates, becoming relatively isolated. Sana bristled just thinking about it, saying she wanted no part of such work, especially with a public figure like Green, but her client had two things going for him. One, he paid unusually well. Two, and far more decisive, he held damning information over Sana. Sana tried to forget their phone conversation, but the client was quite effectively blackmailing her, and as much as Sana hated that thought, it was the truth. From time to time, Sana used dirt dug up about others to get the job done, but this was her first time on the receiving end, and it did not feel good.

Somehow this client, whom she never actually met and still didn't know their true identity, obtained information with evidence that could genuinely ruin her and even land her in jail. How they acquired the information and evidence was a mystery, and it did not bode well for her future to have some malevolent power with such a hold over her. She must figure out who it was. Perhaps she would get a clue when she took the rest of the payment tomorrow? Yet, there was nothing she could do about it now. Besides, thought Sana, her client gave assurances their actions against Green would be superficial and never traceable back to her.

After nearly thirty minutes, Sana became increasingly concerned Green and the girls may not return this way. Just when she feared she must call her client to say she lost Green, inducing an involuntary shudder, Green and the two women magically reappeared out of the elevator. Thank goodness, Sana thought. She breathed a sigh of relief, pretending to read the newspaper, and waited for them to start down the hallway for the exit. When they were a dozen paces down the hall, Sana folded her newspaper, picked up the cold coffee cup, and tossed it in the waste can, following a safe distance behind the threesome.

The hallway was still relatively empty, and Sana could overhear the conversation. "...always nice of you visiting the sick kids, Dad," said Ruth.

"I wish I could have stayed longer, but we have just enough time to get back to the hotel to change and catch the team bus to the game," said Josh.

"Looks like we'll need to get with Mark and refill your goody bag," Mary said, motioning to what appeared to be an empty athletic bag. When Green arrived, it was bulky and slung over his shoulder. Now it was limp and folded in his hand.

"Yes, all that's left are a few of the stickers. I was down to signing them for the kids when I left. I needed more. We might need to ask Mark to give us a rolling bag to carry more when we get to these big hospitals. So many kids to help here...," Josh continued to talk, but Sana could no longer hear as the hallway opened past the noisy waiting area where they sat earlier. The Greens and Mary continued toward the exit. Sana thumbed back to her contact list to the no-name entry denoting her unknown client's burner phone. She knew this because she checked the number, trying to get a bead on who hired her, but someone purchased it with cash only a few days ago, making it untraceable.

Sana keyed the call button as she followed the threesome discreetly. They retraced their steps, turning out of the exit, heading back towards the subway entrance they used this morning. "Yeah, we just left the hospital, taking the expected route back," Sana said to the disembodied voice on the other end of the phone. "Yes, I will. Be there in 5 to 10 minutes at this pace. It's only two or three blocks."

Sana followed while blending in with the standard New York fare of a Saturday midday crowd. The pedestrian traffic was relatively light here in midtown. In these quiet moments, Sana became conscious of her doubt about the path she traveled since the "voice," as she thought of it, ordered her to look for an opportunity where Green was by himself, ideally somewhere out and about in the city. When Sana first told her client that Green took the subway and would likely use it again, the "voice" said he just needed to know where Green would be, and he would take care of the rest. This chilled Sana's heart thinking of it now. Despite her client's assurance Green would only receive "a tuning up," Sana wanted no part in hurting Green. She only agreed when the voice reminded her of the evidence against her. The voice assured her they only wanted to send Green a "warning."

Sana thought about that comment. What exactly did it mean? Sana was not happy. She worked for thirty years in this male-dominated domain and thrived. Her father and family would probably disown her had they not needed her on more than one occasion, working for the family business. That, of course, led to the evidence this client now wielded over her. Her father always wanted a son and often let her know what a disappointment she was, along with two younger sisters. Even more disappointing to her father, Sana, as his oldest, was a plain-looking daughter, unlikely in his eyes to win a man without his intervention. His selected and likely paid-for suitors were all the worst stereotypes of her culture. She was glad to be a third-generation Ballat living in America, able to refuse her father's pressure to marry. Still, she did the only thing left to her, becoming her own person, working the seedier side of New York City as a private investigator.

She became successful at it, tiptoeing on both sides of the law, keeping one step in front of the police and her heavy-handed, arm-twisting father. Yet here she was. Though she survived more than her fair share of tussles, she usually came out on top, much to the surprise of more than one testosterone-filled mark. She often rationalized that the lug-heads she routinely encountered got what they deserved. She even took a life once when some unsavory characters attacked her, thinking she was an easy mark while working near central park. Her disguise was a little too good that night as she was tracking a divorce case, and the would-be thieves thought she was a businesswoman walking a little too late alone. Still, she could easily justify all her somewhat unsavory moves over her career as part of being an investigator of lowlife in a big city. After all, she thought, surely, she was not as bad as those she usually tracked and cataloged for the right price.

This job, however, was anything but typical. Sana could not understand why her unknown client wanted Green warned. She found nothing during her day of research implying this man deserved such a warning. Green's short public history as a rookie baseball player looked clean, despite his rejection of the public's various progressive causes. It seemed absurd to the pragmatic Sana that someone would worry about what a baseball player did or did not kneel for, let alone risk a warning. For what?—to make him change his stance? Why?

When Sana started in this business, things were straightforward. It was all about man's weaknesses revolving around power, money, or sex. Now, it seemed people got upset about all the wrong things and for all the wrong reasons. Perhaps it was still the big three wrapped in a new disguise Sana didn't recognize.

This question of client motivation kept nagging at Sana since the unknown caller first called. Why Green? What did Green do except hit a bunch of home runs? Why was he a threat? Why was Green's perceived position against the public tide of opinion on racism and bigotry a problem worthy of such a response? Sana herself was of mixed heritage, with much of her family coming from Arab and Persian descent. She held her own racial opinions and hang-ups but wrote them off as residual feelings inherited from parents and grandparents who emigrated to America in the 1950s. Her grandparents fled the middle east as they were from Sunni and Shiite families, and the clash between the two was too much for them. Her grandfather came to New York, earned a degree in civil engineering, became a citizen, and started his own business. Still, her grandparents would be downright racist by today's standards. Now, three generations of Ballats lived and witnessed decades of New York City's struggles with race, gender, and sex.

Sana could admit to herself she still held some stereotypes. She justified herself, thinking it protected her against trusting the many unsavory characters she encountered during her professional activities. Still, when she was honest, Sana fought suspicions of people based on her own classifications. She was so much like her father, she surmised, somewhat angrily. He denied her a chance to take over the business, insisting only a man could do the job. Her father would have her marry some slimeball and be the power behind the throne, as her mother told her. No thanks, Sana thought, shaking her head. Look what an idiot her father was trying to groom, married to her younger sister. The family was in the construction business, which was highly competitive in NYC. Sometimes it meant building the wall, but with the Ballats, it could be just as important to keep someone else from building it. It was all about power, and the Ballats continued to thrive only with help from their shrewd investigator daughter.

Sana increasingly acted on behalf of the family, as her father tried to bring her brother-in-law into the business, bailing them out after mistakes by that arrogant moron. Still, her father thought *she* was the wayward daughter who had become too Americanized. Her family exclusively called her by her birth name given by her father, Shabana, meaning "Belonging to the Night." It was not exactly an endearing or optimistic name for a baby girl, though perhaps it suited her adult occupation and demeanor. Still, as she grew, she chose to tell her friends and now her clients her chosen name, "Sana," meaning almost the opposite. "Light or Radiant, like the sun." Though she longed to be that person, she found more and more recently, perhaps as her father predicted, she became the name her father gave her.

Yes, she was still her father's daughter as she thought now of her family's issues towards Jews. With Jews, she bought into the stereotype they were trying to sneak something by her with their shrewd business dealings, despite the similarity to her own transactions. Also, she conceded she often stereotyped blacks, thinking they wanted something for nothing or not wanting to work hard for their money. She chastised herself again, knowing that for every group stereotype, she saw so many different individuals over the years, both the good and the bad. She knew well no group kept a monopoly on behaviors.

Why did she hold to stereotypes handed down from her grandparents' generation? She caught herself thinking consciously of Green, whom she shadowed all day. When she first saw him in person, she found it difficult to guess his background. Was he Jewish? Or Black? Perhaps both? Was this just a defense mechanism, her way of warding off feeling like the bad actor she became in accepting this hire? What little personal history she hastily accrued yesterday on Green and Green's actions today showed only a decent man of moral character. Certainly not someone deserving of anyone's hostility. Sana became acutely aware of a growing dread she could not shake. She faced mounting evidence, *she* now played the bad guy working with a client with obvious ill intentions towards an innocent man.

How did it come to this? Should it matter? When she wondered if Green were Black or Jewish, she now wondered if she tried to justify another of her stereotype prejudices taught by her family and the negative experiences chasing unsavory characters during her career. Admittedly, her profession often placed her with rather poor examples of any culture, and she knew she should not apply stereotypes to an individual without reason or proof. Green did not seem to meet whatever stereotype Sana chose while she followed him. Green's ethnicity was difficult to tell, but everything about this situation felt wrong. Nothing seemed to make sense now as people found new reasons for bigotry. Sana did not understand it. She dismissed it for much of the last decade. Now the world seemed ready to explode with culture clashes she only heard about from stories her parents told from the 50s and 60s when she was too young to remember and never expected to experience in her lifetime.

Still, Green somehow became a focal point of a hostile force, one with deep pockets and substantial reach, but why and more importantly, who? Was it some group he stood against or failed to support? The caller didn't make her feel that way. He lacked the emotion of a cause-driven motivation. There were no words or rhetoric against Green. Instead, there was an over-calm demeanor, like old school mafioso, when someone threatened their business. Sana contemplated, walking the last block behind the threesome towards the subway entrance. Yes, she thought, her client's words betrayed motives more in line with a strong-arm business deal. Coming from her family, she knew what one felt like. This usually stemmed from someone concerned with power or money. The mafioso could draw from all three of her clientele's typical motivators; money, power, and sex. Power came first in precedence, followed closely by money. Sex would be more overtly emotional, but she didn't sense it with this client. So, it must be a power play, someone's business or position threatened, probably with money to lose, thought Sana. Yes, that's how it felt.

As the threesome looked to cross Broadway to the 168th Street subway entrance, Sana followed this line of thought as she thumbed her phone to the unknown contact one last time. Who held the most power or placed the most money on the line and needed to change Josh's ways? He seemed an unlikely target. Who would gain, no, not gain, who would lose, if Green continued to stand against public opinion? The old mafioso only acted like this when they felt seriously threatened, when someone on their turf was not doing what they demanded. Who would go to such extremes where Green was involved? I mean, Green was just a ballplayer from a small market baseball team, no less. Who cared? Green was no one's pain other than Baseball's.

Sana was thunderstruck, like someone just slapped her face; hard. If any were now looking at her, they would see the blood drain from her middle eastern complexion, turning her almost pale white. Suddenly, Sana felt heavy-footed as she walked slowly behind the Greens, crossing with several others to the subway entrance. She tried desperately to think how she could lead the Greens away from the rendezvous awaiting them. Sana did not know who in MLB was pulling her strings, but whoever it was must be connected very high up, and she knew this kind of thing put her in a perilous position. Sana wanted nothing to do with it. Yet she felt genuinely powerless against the evidence held by the unknown voice. What could she do? For the first time in a long time, Sana was desperate, but she was out of time and options. She must comply and hope for the best. Her time was up, and she reluctantly thumbed the call button as the Greens and the lady started down the subway entrance elevator. The phone picked up on the first ring.

Sana said haltingly, "They're at the entrance now."

What she heard from the other end chilled her to her bones.

"We'll take it from here," then the phone hung up.

Sana walked hurriedly now, past the entrance. She wanted to be far, far away from this place. From what she saw of the man, Green was just a guy, perhaps even a good guy, trying to do good things. Green was innocent of whatever hatred or fear others held towards him. Sana prayed silently whatever happened to Green would not be too bad or, at least, untraceable to her. Sana was devoid of the usual solace she took during less than charitable dealings in the somewhat dirty underground of private investigation. This time, she was not going after a bad guy. Instead, she found herself on the wrong side of what was turning out to be a very dangerous, powerful, and ruthless client. Hurrying away, Sana couldn't shake the feeling her conscience named her "Shabana," a woman belonging to the night, not "Sana," the radiant light of day she longed to be, and she feared her guilt would only continue to grow.

Seventy Four

Josh, Ruth, and Mary walked to the subway elevator entrance and took the elevator down to the subway turnstiles. The A, C, and 1 trains stopped at the station, and they needed to catch the A train. It came every 10 minutes according to the schedule Mary downloaded, so there was no need to rush. Passing the turnstiles, they followed signs past a small newsstand store on their right and headed for a slight uphill tunnel collecting several hallways, narrowing as it approached a bend. Half a dozen other people were in the vicinity, and they paid little attention to a man in a gray hooded tracksuit looking at a magazine rack just at the edge of the newsstand. As they started up the hallway, the man turned from the magazine rack as another man, coming up the subway stairs to the left, exited from the subway below. He also followed the threesome into the hallway leading further into the subway complex.

While the ladies didn't notice, Josh remained vigilant in the unfamiliar surroundings. The man caught Josh's attention since Josh didn't quite understand why someone exiting one train would turn back in the opposite direction to get back on another. Perhaps they were transferring between lines, thought Josh, but he remained conscious of the man's footsteps slowly closing the gap behind them. As the Greens and Mary approached the right turn in the hallway where it narrowed, the two men behind almost caught up to them. Josh felt, rather than saw, the men close as the girls rounded the corner facing another two men walking shoulders abreast towards them down the hallway. One was tall with dark glasses and a scraggly beard, the other shorter, stocky with a dark blue baseball cap on backwards and reflective sunglasses. It suddenly struck Josh, the two men in front and one behind wore sunglasses obscuring their faces, and the fourth man wore his hoodie up, despite it being neither bright nor cool in the constricting tunnel. Something was off.

The men in front were just three or so steps from them, and instead of sliding to a single file, so they could pass, they appeared to spread out, line abreast, blocking the narrowed hallway. Adding to Josh's alarm, he saw each man wore a barely visible, single-wired earpiece in their left ear, running down inside their shirt. The ladies slowed, expecting the men to move and allow them to pass. Josh realized their restricted movement allowed the footsteps behind him to finish closing the gap. He looked over his right shoulder just in time to see the man who climbed the stairs from the subway, swinging what appeared to be a blackjack toward his head. Josh's barely dormant combat reactions kicked in as time slowed.

Josh's previous life as a combatant began with USAF special tactics qualification training. While the training was some of the most extensive and challenging in the military, there was little more than rudimentary instruction in hand-to-hand combat. Yet this was only the beginning. Josh spent a career embedded with special forces preparing for and engaging in combat, adding skills and altering his demeanor in dangerous situations. In particular, Josh experienced a repeat role with one specific Green Beret team, unusual for a USAF combat controller. Green Berets operate in small 12-man units known as an operational detachment alpha, or an ODA. Typically, combat controllers are assigned when the ODA deploys to a contingency, usually on a first-come basis. Josh received an unusual "by name" request after one combat stint with a particular ODA to rejoin the same team because of his great work on a previous combat deployment and their very persistent Chief.

The ODA's Chief Warrant Officer ran the entire team like a mama bear watching her cubs. This included their bright but young team captain, a First Lieutenant, smart enough to trust his experienced Chief for training and personnel recommendations for much of their combat preparation. The Chief leveraged his Lieutenant's contacts to get Josh back for a second and third deployment. The Chief also planned the team's training drills, including weekly workouts with their third-degree black belt team member, a former U.S. Army martial arts champion. Early in his first deployment preparation with this ODA, the chief made clear he expected Josh to attend these training events, despite Josh being "the Air Force guy." Josh never wanted to let Chief or the team down. Besides, the martial arts trainer spared no one in his training, not even the chief himself, preparing everyone for hand-to-hand combat if the situation turned desperate.

After multiple deployments together, Josh, with his athletic build and talent, grew into the equal in hand-to-hand combat with even the best Green Berets on the team. By the time of Josh's brush with death, during his third and final deployment with this ODA, the team looked to Josh to demonstrate much of the hand-to-hand training with the black belt teacher, and he was often the chief's pick to help the new and youngest ODA members. Much to their chagrin, the chief would openly laugh at the cocky newbie Green Berets the first time the "USAF pug" flipped them over like an off-balance tumbling sack of potatoes. Only the chief, a monster of a man, and his black belt trainer could regularly hold off Josh, but even they remained evenly matched. The other team members trusted Josh to handle himself if they needed him to do something other than call down aircraft strikes.

In the present, Josh reacted to the man's attacking blow. There was little warning, but in that split second, Josh deftly sidestepped to the left. He felt the man's attack more than he saw it, instinctively rotating just enough to avoid a direct blow to his head, likely rendering him unconscious. Instead, the impact fell heavily on Josh's right shoulder, causing an immediate numbing pain. The man was surprised by Josh's quick deflection. Josh continued to rotate, grabbing his attacker, using the man's falling strike as momentum to pull him with his other arm as the attacker overreached his follow-through. Josh threw him by rotating and pulling him, with a hip toss, hard toward the wall. It was a narrow corridor and the man's momentum, combined with Josh's pivot-spin, caused him to launch headfirst toward an emergency fire exit door. He struck the door head-first, just below the push handle, with an audible metal "THUD!" as the door held firm. The man collapsed in a heap, unmoving.

The second man from behind was more toward the right side of the hallway. He froze as he was about to grab one of the girls, momentarily surprised by Josh's defense against his partner. Instead, he now turned and leaped at Josh with a heavy-handed right hook. Josh's lightning-quick consciousness seemed to slow the man's movement like receiving a pitch in the batter's box. In his mind's eye, he caught the flash of brass knuckles. He stepped lightly to one side, a dancer whose movements blurred to those watching, moving past the wild roundhouse of the man's punch and jabbed with a quick, short, left-handed finger strike straight to the man's right eye. Josh's strike was lightning fast, catching the man lunging forward, adding to the jab's force. The man never landed his punch, collapsing to his knees with a piercing scream as Josh's strike caught the corner of his eye socket, completely dislocating his eyeball. A sound of pure agony escaped the man's lips, the kind of sound released involuntarily from a wounded beast, and he clutched his face with both hands, dropping to his knees.

The two men from the other direction were still advancing towards the women, initially focusing on them. The first grabbed Ruth by the shoulders while the other grabbed Mary's backpack slung over her shoulder. When they heard the other man's unexpected scream of pain from Josh's strike, both men froze and snapped their gaze to the man on his knees. Unknown to the Greens and Mary, the man Josh just took down with the eye strike was the group's leader. As the boss, he planned to knock Josh out with the help of the first attack while the other two men robbed the girls and chased them away. Then they could kick and beat Josh while he was down, giving him a few broken bones and ribs, likely ending his season. However, with the eye strike and their leader down screaming, the remaining two men hesitated.

Initially surprised, Mary now used their hesitation, yanking on her bag. Distracted by the scream, her attacker leaned forward at Mary's pull, still holding onto the bag. Mary spent several unfortunate years on the street, and though she seemed a meek and gentle girl, those years taught her one significant maneuver that served her well. She instinctively brought her knee up as hard as she could into the man's groin, then down just as hard with her heel to his foot. Unprepared for her to fight back, the man took Mary's knee full force, yielding an audible "Harrumph!" from his surprised face as he instinctively bent over, releasing the bag. Mary's heel to his toes dropped him to the floor on all fours, gasping with pain.

This left only the man who grabbed Ruth still standing. As his partner went down, he spun Ruth around, holding her backwards by her backpack, taking a tentative step away from his three downed partners. She tried kicking back at him wildly with her braced legs, and though he held her momentarily, the leveling of his three compatriots made him realize the odds unexpectedly now stood against him. He hesitated, then let the squirming and kicking Ruth go. However, he didn't run, but took a defensive stance as Ruth ran back into Mary's waiting arms. Josh focused on the man who locked eyes with him, then squared up to Josh, preparing to attack. Josh saw the man reach behind his back, an evil look on his face, but Josh was already moving. He closed the three paces with lethal speed, and just as the man pulled a switched-bladed knife out of his back pocket, Josh, now at full velocity, leapt feet first toward the astonished man. Josh's horizontal flying kick lifted the assailant off his feet and flung him backwards like a rag doll. The man lost his grip on the knife, and it skidded back down the hallway along with his flying baseball cap. Now, only the two women were still standing.

Before anyone else moved, Josh jumped back to his feet, moving quickly towards Mary and Ruth. He saw the man who attacked Mary trying to recover and get up from his crouch. Josh stepped up quickly, swinging a hard left fist at the man's head as he tried to stand. This second blow fell squarely on the man's right jaw below his ear with a satisfying crunch. He collapsed flat on the floor and was still.

The man Josh just kicked rolled to his knees, trying desperately to catch his breath. He held an arm across his chest as if a rib or two might be cracked and looked hatefully toward Josh. Josh returned to Mary and Ruth, who stood gripping each other. While able to handle himself, Josh knew that one or two men would likely be back in action in a few moments. He needed to break contact now.

Josh stepped up to the women and spoke commandingly to get their attention.

"Mary!"

Josh's intensity snapped Mary out of her shock and fear, and she looked away from the attackers, still clutching Ruth tightly but now focused on Josh's eyes. They were still those kind eyes saying all would be well, only follow me. "Let me have Ruth," said Josh, more quietly and kindly now that he held her attention. He took Ruth gently, easily picking her up with his good left arm, and firmly told Mary, "Now, let's go!" Josh cradled Ruth with his left arm while his right arm hung to his side. "This way," said Josh as he nodded back the way they came, moving Mary and Ruth back around the corner towards the subway newsstand and entrance.

As they hurried away, the man Josh drop-kicked rose to his feet, holding his chest, watching them walk away. He considered following, but the sounds of other people approaching from other connecting tunnels changed his mind. He knew their brief seclusion would be over soon. Instead, he turned to his comrades, trying to rouse them and retreat.

Meanwhile, Josh walked Mary and carried Ruth some fifty yards back toward the hallway entrance. There, the newsstand owner stepped out from his store to peer around the corner in their direction. Though the attack occurred out of sight, he heard sounds echoing down the corridor. He moved from behind his counter, stepping into the hallway to see what was happening. The man was a Sikh with a traditional Dastaar head cover, and he looked at Josh and the two girls with concern. He remained by his store, holding his cell phone. Josh spoke first as he carried Ruth almost one-handed with his left arm as his right throbbed in pain from the blackjack blow. "Namaste!" Josh used the traditional Sikh Punjabi greeting he learned while training with an Indian force during a deployment in the Asian-Pacific theater.

The Sikh, frozen with indecision while Josh and the girls approached, was not used to non-Sikhs using their standard greeting. It brought him to life, and he responded in kind to Josh, "Namaste," continuing, "Are you all OK?"

Josh immediately responded, "No. Four men attacked us around that corner. Can you call the police?" Josh nodded to the phone in the man's hand. The man forgot he held it, while the other hand thumbed his traditional Sikh Kirpan knife, invisible to others, inside the waistband of his pants beneath his loose-fitting shirt.

The man nodded quickly and said, "Of course. Please, come in here while I call." He waved them into the small store and stood outside defensively, watching back up the hallway for signs of their attackers. "Yes, officer, my name is Bakht Singh. I am the owner of the 168th Street subway newsstand. I need police here right away. There was an attack on a man and two women, and I don't know if the attackers are still nearby...."

Josh could hear Bakht talk to the 911 operator as he sat Ruth down on a stool behind the counter and looked her over.

"Are you OK, hon?" he said. Ruth hadn't said a word, and she just nodded. Josh looked over at Mary, who stood farther into the newsstand, looking back toward Josh. She still clutched her backpack with a look of shock.

Josh said, "Mary?" questioningly.

Mary nodded finally, managing a quiet, "I'm OK, Josh," then she looked at him, noticing as he sat Ruthie down, he held his right arm close to his body, gripping his right forearm with his left hand. "Is your arm hurt?" she asked, concerned.

"I'm not sure. I took a blow to my right shoulder when one of those men hit me with something. It initially went numb, but now I'm feeling it. I can still move my hand and fingers," he said, wiggling them but still not releasing his arm, "I hope nothing is broken, but I'll need to get it looked at." Both the girls were now concerned, but Josh continued. "I'm OK, really. I want to make sure you guys are all right."

Finally, Mr. Singh turned back in their direction, letting the phone down but not done with the call. "The police should be here any minute. They are asking do you need an ambulance?"

Before they could say anything, Josh shook his head, "No, I think we are OK," he said to Mr. Singh. As the girls began to protest, he said, "I can walk back to the hospital and get checked out once this is over."

The police arrived five minutes later, coming down through the same entrance Josh and the girls used. They hastened up the hallway once they got a description of the four men from Josh and Mary. Despite only a few minutes since the attack, the men all fled, and the police found only a baseball cap and a pair of broken aviator sunglasses on the floor, plus what appeared to be some drops of blood where they fought. Even the knife and blackjack disappeared, and it was hard to tell the attack occurred.

The police officer said Josh should get his arm checked out as they finished their report. Josh nodded his thanks, and the officer commented, "Probably a gang looking to rob you. They do this from time to time, although usually not during broad daylight."

Josh replied, "Do they usually talk to each other over two-way radios wired to earpieces?"

Both cops looked up at that. "What do you mean?"

"All four men were wearing earpieces in their left ears. I saw it on the two men who came from behind, and when I punched the one Mary kneed, his fell loose out of his ear when he hit the ground. The one I kicked also lost his as he flew backwards, and he instinctively put it back in when he rolled to his knees. They must have been coordinating their attack."

The two cops looked at each other. The older one looked back and shook his head. "No. That's a little more sophisticated than what we're used to seeing, and we'll note that. Are you sure you didn't see any of these men before coming downstairs to the subway? None were behind you outside or earlier as you walked along the street?"

Josh said no, and Mary and Ruth shook their heads.

"OK, look, we'll get a team in here and process the scene, but it still was probably a random, though coordinated, mugging. While we usually don't advise fighting back the way you did, Mr. Green, it sounds like you and Mary had little choice. We will look to review the surveillance tapes, but with the construction going on down here," he said, motioning to ongoing work in the area, "The one camera in the hallway seems to be out of commission. It's got a bag over it and won't be much good. We have your contact information, and you have ours and the case number. Here's my card," the older police officer said, handing the card to Mary since Josh was still holding his arm. "We'll start an investigation with this information and see what we can find. In the meantime, I can tell you we have two foot-patrols and two cars canvasing the few blocks in and around the station. Unfortunately, they've found no one matching your description, so the attackers appear to have fled the general area."

"OK," said Josh. "What do you want us to do?"

"Why don't we escort you three back upstairs and across to the emergency room? It's a few blocks away, and we have our car upstairs and can drive you there," replied the senior officer.

Josh nodded, and the three followed the police, taking the elevator to Broadway. The three squeezed into the back of the patrol car, and the police drove them the short distance to the emergency room entrance. They piled out, and the older officer in the passenger seat rolled down his window. "You stay safe now, Mr. Green. I have your number and will call you in a day or two to see how you are doing and update you on our investigation. If these guys try this on someone else again, we'll get 'em. Consider yourself unfortunate for being in the wrong place at the wrong time."

Josh thanked the officer. He was grateful the girls were not hurt, yet Josh remained unsettled. As the car pulled away, he couldn't help but think this was not a random occurrence. And if that were true, what did it portend for their future?

Seventy Five

D r. Luke held the hospital report in his hand Sunday morning as he and Josh talked with Dr. Levine at Columbia Hospital. Dr. Asa Levine came highly recommended by Dr. Luke. Dr. Levine spoke at a sports medicine conference Dr. Luke attended nearly a decade ago, hosted by Major League Baseball in New York. Back then, Dr. Luke cared for an aging pitcher with a shoulder issue and worked closely with Dr. Levine on his treatment, giving the man an additional two seasons of productive baseball before he finally retired. Josh even talked to Nurse Richards, and she knew the doctor by reputation, saying he was one of the country's best shoulder specialists. The doctor sat with Josh and Luke as Mary, Mark, and Ruth waited outside. Doctor Levine concluded, "Well, Josh, I am sorry this happened to you, but the good news is, if there is such a thing as a minor collarbone fracture, you've got it. No surgery, and you can follow my prescribed rehabilitation plan under Dr. Luke's care back in Pittsburgh. Your season's not over. I think it's realistic to say if you follow this regime, you'll be back in no more than six weeks, and I wouldn't be surprised with some luck to see you get back a week sooner. We must check the bone periodically. My biggest concern is for you not to overdo it. As slow as it may seem, this plan is what your body needs to allow the bone to heal fastest."

"I understand, Doctor Levine. I have done my fair share of rehabilitation before, just not of my collarbone," said Josh, "I am sorry to have to give the team the bad news."

Dr. Levine nodded. "OK, I'll let you get ready to go, and Dr. Luke and I will be in regular consultation, but the facilities you have at home should do fine. You can both call and check in with me as we discussed and call me if you have a problem crop up."

"Thanks again for your help and good advice, Asa," Luke said.

"No problem, Luke, but I'll probably regret it!" The other two men looked concerned. "When Josh gets healthy and beats up on my Yankees again, I'll never live it down!"

All three men laughed as Josh relaxed. A long twenty-four hours passed since the attack. As the two men walked out of Dr. Levine's office, Ruth, Mary, and Mark looked up with concern.

"Are you going to be OK, Dad?" Ruthie said as she jumped up and held onto Josh's good arm with both hands. The other two stood and looked kindly at her, holding back their questions.

"I will be fine, but I will be out of playing for a few weeks. Don't worry; the doctors say that with some rest and rehab, I should be as good as new in no time." Josh replied as he bent over and hugged her tightly with his good arm. "We will stay at home while I rehab."

"But you'll be back in time to finish the season?" Ruthie asked hopefully.

"The doctor seems to think I should be back before the end of the season, as long as my recovery goes as planned, yes," Josh answered. "Now, what do you say we head back to the hotel and get ready for tonight's game?" Dr. Luke and Mark looked questioningly at Josh, and he responded. "I want to go see the team, let them know I am going to be alright, and tell everyone to play well tonight." Mark nodded, and Josh led the group out of the waiting room with little Ruthie tightly clutching his left hand.

Mary followed quietly behind Josh and Ruth as Dr. Luke and Mark brought up the rear, conversing quietly. Josh cleared Dr. Luke to talk to Mark and Coach Samuelson about a public statement of Josh's condition and timeline. Josh was quick to warn them about making anything out of the attack. He talked to both men and Coach Saul and Pete after leaving the hospital yesterday. The team was noticeably distracted as word of the attack reached them shortly after they arrived at the stadium without Josh. They subsequently took the field under a cloud of suspicion from the Yankee fans, and Josh's condition was the subject of lots of wild speculation. The series' third game featured seven pitchers total between teams, 21 hits, and a walk-off victory for the Yankees 11 to 10 over the Pirates in 10 innings. Josh spoke to Coach Saul and Pete back at the hotel in the wee hours and asked them to keep details of the attack to themselves. They would stick with the police story of a random mugging. He warned them, however, that it felt like something more. Pete and Saul showed concern but agreed to keep the information private.

Tonight, the Pirates would play their last game of the first half of the season before the all-star break. Josh and the others returned to the hotel and got ready to go to the stadium. The team left for the game by the time Josh was ready. He wasn't used to doing things for himself with an arm in a sling. Mark drove Josh, Mary, and Ruth to the stadium in his rental minivan, and soon he and Josh were in the locker room as the ladies took their place in the stands reserved for Pirate team member families behind their dugout.

Josh was now a national figure, for his historic play, and stance on societal issues. Speculation festered wildly overnight throughout American news and social media, leaving his team confused about his status. Mark moved quickly into an office just off the locker room where he could work on a computer, putting the finishing touches to a press release. Meanwhile, the team gathered around Josh, and many began asking questions until he raised his good hand. Coach Saul and Old Pete walked out of the manager's office and joined the group.

"Coach, is it all right if I address the team?" Josh asked.

"Go ahead, Josh. I think everyone is here," Pops said. Then Pops followed, "Phil," to his outfield coach, "How bout grabbing those doors, please? We don't need any prying eyes." Everyone knew Pops meant the press, as this was a team-only moment.

"Please grab a seat," said Josh. "I know there are a lot of questions about what happened and how badly I got injured."

Everyone circled in a makeshift semicircle on the room's available chairs and benches. After Coach Phil gave the thumbs up, he stood blocking the door.

Josh began. "I know you were all left in a lurch last night. I am sorry I wasn't able to get here until today. Here's the brief story. At about lunchtime yesterday, my daughter, our nanny, and I returned from a pre-planned appointment for my daughter at Columbia University Hospital here in New York City. As we entered the subway to catch the train back to the hotel, four men attacked us. The police believe it was an attempted mugging. Long story short, the girls are OK, but I injured my collarbone in the scuffle. I saw several doctors, and they took a bunch of X-rays and did an MRI. The bad news is I have a fractured collarbone. I saw a specialist today. The good news is, he says it's a simple fracture, and the rest of the shoulder looks bruised but uninjured and should heal nicely without an operation. I should fully recover, and the doctor thinks I can be back to playing in less than six weeks, depending on how my body heals. I'll be able to complete the therapy back in Pittsburgh under Doc Luke's care."

Josh let that sink in for a moment. He continued speaking to the somewhat somber group. "I know this is a shock and surprise to everyone, but I wanted you to know I will be OK. I plan to be with you all as much as I can. For now, please focus on the job at hand. We have one more game before the all-star break. It's time to come together as a team and take care of each other as we go through the break and continue toward our goal. Remember, we all have a part to play in reaching that high mark we set for ourselves in April. We will have our fair share of trouble along the way. But you are not alone because this team is a family. We can count on each other to pick one another up when we have a setback. I plan to be here to help you along the way and help you finish strong."

Josh leaned back and looked at them all, saying, "We've all been through a lot this year. I have urged you to persevere and stand for what's right and good. Most of all, I ask you to follow the Lord. These last several weeks, we chose, as a team, to stand for those things that are good and true beyond baseball and our personal issues. We kneel to the One who brings peace, justice, and forgiveness to all who ask. We know that even when men fail, and the path becomes hard to follow, Jesus never fails, He never wavers, and His way is always the best for each of us, no matter the difficulties we face. As I have told you before, I press on for the mark of the high calling of God in Christ Jesus. He tells us, He will never leave us or forsake us. We can do all things through Christ, who strengthens us. He will take our burdens and give us rest. He reminds us, in this world, we will have trouble but to take heart, for He has overcome the world."[1]

---

1. Philippians 3:14, 4:13; Matthew 11:28; John 16:33

Seventy Six

The Pirates entered the all-star break with two straight losses to the Yankees. Josh's loss hit the Pirate clubhouse hard, but they had a lot going for them as they entered the second half of the season. They set the Major League record for the best first half of a season, going an amazing 71-16. The Pirates' closest competitor, the Chicago Cubs, also with a great first half at 60-26, found themselves just over ten games back. "Slayer" Samson Gibson was having a great season with a 13-2 start and a 1.89 ERA to lead the Major Leagues. Samson led a contingent of Pirates to the all-star game, including Andrew, Juan, and Zach. Josh would have added to the record number of Pirates selected but did not play because of his injury. Still, during baseball's first half, Josh's play was unprecedented, including an astounding batting average of .470.

Initially gaining national attention because of his play, the public saw Josh as the leader of the Pirates' resistance to growing demonstrations against racial inequality and bigotry against the gay lifestyle, among other perceived injustices. Josh and the Pirates became constant headlines in the national news media. Despite MLB's attempt to downplay the Pirates' refusal to kneel during the anthem or wear racial or LGBTQ supporting paraphernalia, the story would not go away. The start of the All-Star game drew stark contrast as only 10 players out of the 68 selected for the All-Star roster stood for the National Anthem. The stadium was full of fans supporting the various movements nationwide with flags and signs sporting protest organizations. Players kneeled for the anthem, and the League stuck by its vow to allow the players to express their supported causes, wearing warm-up gear advocating racial justice, LGBTQ, and names of victims of police shootings.

The national news attention for the game was part of a continuing national trend during the restless summer. Many cities exploded with demonstrations after the police shootings in New York and Pittsburgh. Somehow, MLB's decision to allow and even support these movements polarized and galvanized public opinion and public awareness of baseball in unusual ways. While Josh remained in Pittsburgh recovering from the subway attack, the Pirate players at the all-star game became favorite targets for press questions unrelated to their play. Zach again fielded pointed questions about his sexual orientation, given Josh's interview, and all four Pirates received questions about their decision to stand for the anthem despite being black.

"Andrew, as Captain of the Pirates and your team's perennial all-star, have you foregone your position of leadership for the team and acquiesced to Joshua Green's stance on race and the LGBTQ community?" a reporter from the associated press asked bluntly at a news conference the day before the game.

"First, every player believes, speaks, and acts according to their conscience on our team. We work together for the team's success, but this club gives grace to each other to stand for what they believe. My co-captain Thomas and I stress to all players their right to stand, kneel, pray, or wear clothing supporting a cause, per the League guidelines and the players' collective bargaining agreement. Second, if you ask about our play, I don't have to cede any team leadership to Josh as captain. Josh's leadership on the field comes entirely from his play, which, in case you missed it, is the best offensive first half in baseball history! If you are referring to moral leadership, Josh always makes it clear to anyone who listens. What he does is based on his faith in Christ and trust in the gospel as the inspired word of God. He pressures no one to follow him or do what he does. He invites us to join him in prayer."

"You may have forgotten, but I previously told you, *I* am a Christian," Andrew said with emphasis. "I enjoy Josh's friendship on and off the field, but my beliefs are mine. I stand for the anthem, and I kneel in prayer, like Josh, not because of him but because I, too, have accepted Christ as my savior. I believe in this country and its ideals. In the past, our country sometimes failed to meet these ideals. Many fought, at home and abroad, to ensure our country holds true to those good words promised by our founding documents. Our problems today aren't because our country failed us. Our problems are because individuals fail to meet our country's ideals. That's why I stand for the anthem. I stand to honor my countrymen's sacrifice for our freedom and equality and pledge myself, united with my American brothers and sisters, past and present, to uphold our country's highest ideals."

"Andrew, don't you feel your stance during the anthem is a stance against blacks and our struggles against racism," asked an African American reporter from an Atlanta hometown newspaper.

Andrew replied quickly, perhaps reflexively with some frustration, "Respectfully, I don't need you to tell me what I should feel or think as a black man," the other reporters all seemed to want to jump on the ire they heard in the response. Andrew quickly followed in a more even tone before they could ask more questions, "Look, we have players from all walks of life, and quite a few minorities, including our coaches. One of you reporters recently told me we have some of the highest number of minority players and coaches in the League. I don't know if that's true, primarily because I, and the rest of the Pirates, try not to judge people based on their race. So, I don't talk on behalf of 'our people,'" Andrew said pointedly, looking directly at the reporter who asked the question, "But I do speak for myself. I grew up in the deep south, in what some would say is one of the more racist areas of the country. I've seen racism firsthand since I was a kid. I know what it's like to have a cop pull over and ask what I was doing while walking home from playing basketball at a friend's house or getting pulled over when I started driving. To me, it's always personal, but it's not the focus of my life or our problems. I stand because this country has given me incredible opportunities. My father and mother worked multiple tough jobs to raise eight kids and give them a better life. My mom never let us kids use any excuse to stop us from building a life worth living. I became our family's first college graduate, but it didn't end with me, and now five of my siblings have gone to college. My sister is an ADA in Baton Rouge, and our baby brother is a New Orleans Police officer. Yet, we all saw prejudice as kids. For those of you who want to pit us as victims of oppression, I know what my momma would say to us kids about using that as an excuse."

"What would she say, Andrew?" followed another reporter.

"First, she would ask, 'What happened?' Sometimes we had legitimate stories of racist behavior against us, and momma would usually put an arm around us and say, 'Child, life's not fair, but in this country, you can prove those people wrong. You must show them, not tell them. Become somebody. Make something of yourself. Prove them wrong by persevering. God doesn't make racist people. People are taught it then they become it. Don't let them stop you from becoming what the Creator meant for you to be.' My mom was quick to give a hug of encouragement, but she never let us mope for long or use one person's racism as an excuse for us to fail or quit. My dad rose to become a successful business owner after starting as a stock boy as a kid. Neither Mom nor Dad experienced the advantages we kids enjoyed. My grandpa died after a tough life as a sharecropper a generation before, with only an eighth-grade education, having dropped out of school to help his dad put food on the table. I have seen poverty and prejudice, but my momma would say we've come a long way as a country in her lifetime, and her kids are proof. Our country isn't perfect, but it's still the greatest opportunity any young person in the world would envy."

"Our job is to change people's minds and hearts. We don't do that by violence against each other or the police. The police, like my kid brother, are there to keep us safe. They do a tough job, and the vast majority are good people. We don't help by tearing down the country. Instead, we should help by building up the country. Each of us has a job to do. I know this as a black man and as a Christian."

"Some would say that's easy for you to say. You're a star baseball player," responded the reporter who first asked the question.

"I am, but I didn't grow up that way," Andrew responded, "And I thank God for letting me live in a country that enables a poor black kid a chance to go as far as his talent and drive allow. This country may have its problems, but it's still the land of opportunity, and I want to keep doing my part to make it better and give the next generation a chance for a better future, like my parents did for us. That's what I pray asking Christ to help me do every day."

As hard as the questions were for Andrew, they seemed equally difficult for Zach playing in his first All-Star game.

"Zach, this is your first All-Star game. What's it going to be like?" asked one reporter during press day.

"It's a great honor, and I'm looking forward to being around so many talented players. I hope to represent the Pirates well when I get the chance."

Another reporter followed, "Zach, the Pirates have four players in the All-Stars for the first time. Can you talk about how the team turned it around this year?"

"We've had a great first half, and we feel like we're finally playing the type of ball Pittsburgh fans deserve. It's been fun to be a part of a great team playing great baseball, and I know we all want to keep it going."

Roman Josephus saw an opening. "Zach, the Pirates would have sent a fifth player, Josh Green, if it weren't for his injury. Can you talk about missing him in this game and what it will mean while he's out of the lineup?"

"It's a big loss for us, no doubt, and I feel terrible he missed the All-Star game after his incredible year. As far as what it means to the team, he's been a leader on the field, and we certainly will miss his bat. The good news is it looks like we should get him back before the end of the season."

"Any thoughts on Josh's loss and the Pirate stance concerning standing for the anthem and kneeling for team prayer?" Roman continued.

"On this team, each has the right to do as we see fit. Josh has been an inspiration, but I think the team and players are already doing what they think is right. I plan to continue to stand and pray."

"Zach, as a black man, you have stood during the Anthem, and as a Gay man, you have kneeled following Josh's leadership in the team prayer. Many ask why you, of all people, would do either with the things Josh said, particularly about being gay. What's your response?" Roman hammered his point home.

"Roman, nothing Josh said was meant to hurt gays or me," Roman tried to object, but Zach raised his hand, "Let me finish. Josh is a Christian. Every time I talk to him or listen to him, he is consistent in what he says and does. I don't know if I believe the way Josh does, but I know what Josh says, he says with grace and love. He doesn't judge me the way you make out. He offers what Christ did and the hope He gives to all. I know this world is messed up. But this country is not to blame. My father taught me that, and anyone who knows my story knows my father came to this country looking for a new life, a better life. I stand for this country of hope that shines out to the rest of the world. And as for Josh and praying to Christ, Josh talks with us often about the hope and healing power Christ can do in a person's life. I see our problems, and it seems they all stem from people's hearts. I've come to understand the solution isn't in some external fix the world or the government will do. Ultimately, I think it's something in our souls that needs fixing. I don't know or understand it all, but Josh talks with me about the One person who offers to change our hearts. I pray to a God I want to know, in the hope Christ can change this country and help us."

"So, are you saying you are a Christian now?" Roman followed skeptically.

Zach chuckled slightly, answering, "Roman, let me put it this way. I find no matter how much success I have in life, something is still missing. I think Josh helps me see life differently." Zach shrugged as he looked up in the air, trying to put something into words. "I still seek to find the road in life with real meaning. I want to know the truth. I think there is much truth in Josh's words, what he reads from the Bible, which I never really considered before, and what it means for us today. To find true answers and solutions, you must examine yourself and be open to the possibilities." Then he said more soberly, looking down and collecting his thoughts. "Josh showed me and talked with me about things I haven't thought of in a long time. Mostly though, I see in Josh a life I don't have. I am unsure what it is, but I find my mind and heart open to search out this Christ who changes so many lives. That's why I pray and why I listen. I want to have that kind of life."

Before the game, the four Pirates, with a small minority of players and coaches from other teams, stood for the national anthem. A few other players and coaches joined the same four Pirates on the field for a pregame prayer before the game began, including some players who joined the Pirates' prayers the last few weeks. Both moves brought their fair share of boos and displays of disruption from the stands, not to mention some icy stares from a few other players on the field. However, it was hard to dampen the enthusiasm of the Pirate players as the All-Star game became a highlight reel of Pirates contributing to a National League victory. Samson was the starting pitcher with the League lead in wins and pitched the first two innings, retiring all six batters he faced, including the first four with strikeouts. He won the game's MVP award. But Samson wasn't the only Pirate to do well. Andrew got two hits, the only player to do so during the game. Juan's double in the seventh plated the game-tying run, and Zach's pinch-hit single to start the bottom of the ninth, followed by a stolen base, led to him scoring the game-winning run to end the game spectacularly.

Quint Pilate sat in a box seat for the event with the Atlanta Braves owner, the game's host. He watched stoically, barely able to hide his contempt and exasperation at the prayer circle with a sense of unease. This small but resolute group of men included some League stars. The Braves' aged manager and Pops' old friend was the National League All-Star manager and joined the circle with the players, leading them in prayer. Quint watched with what he knew would be millions on broadcast TV. Those players who stood and prayed, though small in number, were from all different backgrounds. The Pirates were three black men and a Latino. Several others that stood for the anthem and prayed were minorities. Yes, there were whites, including the old white Atlanta coach, but even the great right fielder from Japan, Ittai Gittite, stood for the anthem and, surprisingly, joined the others in prayer. Quint could hardly believe it. Gittite, the starting right fielder after Josh Green's injury, decided to wear Josh's number, telling the press, through his interpreter, he wanted to honor Josh since Josh could not play. In Ittai's translated words, "Josh's brought play to the game we have not seen in my country and perhaps not here in the Major Leagues since legends like DiMaggio, Williams, and even Ruth played. I wear his number three to honor his play and pray for peace and Josh's speedy return to baseball."

Quint brooded. Now some openly prayed for Green's return. How did Green escape the attack of four seasoned men with such a relatively minor injury? If anything, this got the public back on Josh's side. It was not the way he planned things to go. Instead, it seemed as if the All-Star game and perhaps the season refused to submit to Quint's will. Still, he watched the crowd boo the players as they prayed and felt he knew where the public leaned and where their hearts were leading. He just needed to stay in front of the mob to curry their favor and weed out those few who tried to bring him down.

The game turned out to be an exciting, close-fought affair for a change. Even though the All-Star game no longer determined home-field advantage for the World Series as in the past, Quint could not shake the feeling things were spinning out of his control. The four Pirates' brilliant play and heightened attention, even during Green's absence, captivated the country. It threatened to place Josh Green and the Pirates front and center in the public's eye, as they led the League and the country into an unknown future for the rest of a hot and restless summer.

Seventy Seven

With the All-Star break over, baseball began the second half of the season. The Pirates started with a four-game road series against division rivals, the Chicago Cubs. The Cubs took 3 of 4 against the Pirates to close the gap on the Pirates' division lead to 7.5 games. It marked the first series loss of the year for the Pirates. The Pirates would play the next three and a half weeks at just under .500 while both the Cubs and the Cardinals made up ground.

The League and the Pirates experienced more problems surrounding the games. League attendance at the games dropped for most teams as cities nation-wide faced protests and continued unrest. Much to the commissioner's dismay, baseball's stance, allowing and even promoting racial justice and anti-bigotry demonstrations on the field by players and in the stands, made baseball a focal point for the country's problems. While protests around the ballparks and cities in the northeast and western venues grew, fans stayed away in increasing numbers. Cities experienced protest marches and demonstrations, many turning violent and destructive. In Chicago and Seattle, the violence included protests centered around the stadium demonstrations. The Pirates were the unfortunate recipient of one of the first violent outbreaks as protesters during the Cubs series against the Bucs yelled curses at players and began throwing objects at the team as they exited the bus arriving at Chicago's Wrigley Field. The stadium security initially could not contain the protesters, and the Chicago police responded, making over a dozen arrests. One of the Pirate players, third baseman Nate Fisher, received seven stitches after getting hit with a bottle in the back of the head as the players hustled into the stadium during the chaos. The violent outburst delayed the game for over an hour before police restored calm.

Quint Pilate was left dismayed and confused. Attendance declined as protests and violence increased since the commissioner pushed policies supporting overt displays of racial justice and anti-bigotry. He hoped the sidelining of Josh Green, albeit temporarily, would remove the spotlight and take the pressure off baseball. Yet the chaos seemed to spread and increase. America was embroiled in a heated debate that Quint hoped to assuage by standing with the popular sentiment. The country voted with their conscience at the ballot box just last fall, decisively electing national officials who supported the progressive agendas consistent with the anti-racist, LGBTQ, and anti-bigotry platforms. Baseball, politically aware and in step with the times, fully supported players, teams, and fans with the same ideals and expression. Yet despite pragmatic choices, giving the people what they wanted, Quint watched the protests increase, and fan polling showed mostly negative trends. The polls displayed a two-edged sword cutting both the revenue and reputation of Major League Baseball. First, Quint's pollsters warned of substantial resistance by a surprisingly large fan base against baseball's progressive movements as more traditional, conservative fans turned away from the game. Second, many liberal fans eschewed baseball's refusal to tamp down on Josh Green's prayer protest and his leading a rebellion against bending knee to their progressive agenda.

In effect, Quint Pilate now saw the League in a lose-lose position. Worse and most damaging to his tenure, financially, sales of all types, from clothing to ticket sales and TV ratings, all fell. Quint's internal polling showed that at least ten owners would likely vote against him if a no-confidence vote occurred. While this was not enough to unseat him, Quint was worried. Such a vote would undermine his powers and potentially lead to an uncertain future where someone like Herald Gripp might convince the additional owners necessary to bring Quint down. For the time being, Quint used his extensive network to keep any motion to vote on his tenure from coming to the table. However, he quickly used his precious markers to stem the tide. Things would have to change, or his once stable tenure as League boss could be in jeopardy.

The Pittsburgh owner group was even more nervous than MLB. Cai Annason, as Chief of the group, was in an ever-increasingly tenuous position. First, the team's play dramatically fell off the month since the All-Star break. Undoubtedly, losing Green to injury was a blow to the Pirates' offensive production. However, it did not fully explain the Pirates' downturn. Fan attendance also took a hit, with the Pirate hold on first dwindling after their recent lackluster play.

What's more, Cai faced reoccurring and increasing demonstrations before games against the Pirate players and coaches' failure to show support for racial equality. Cai approached Saul Samuelson at the All-Star break to pressure him to reconsider his stance while allowing players to oppose the League's wishes and instead join the rest of the teams.

"Mr. Annason, are you asking me to tell the players to change their actions?" Saul asked incredulously after Cai indicated the League wanted the Pirates to comply.

"No, but I expect you to lead by example," said Cai to the coach in Cai's office, where he felt the coach might show more respect.

"Mr. Annason, begging your pardon, but I have chosen not to wear the gear or kneel. How can I ask the players to do so?"

"Then you're part of the problem!" Cai let out his frustration in an unusual burst of emotion. He reined himself back in quickly. "Look, Coach Samuelson, I will not force you to go against your conscience, but could you consider ending the public prayer vigil? With Josh Green gone, now would be a good time to refrain from showing support for or against a specific political agenda and just return to playing baseball. Don't ask the fans to pick a side. Appear more neutral, and the players would follow. Then we could get past this. Let the city heal," Cai pleaded, trying to sound reasonable.

Saul responded, "First, Josh Green is hurt, but he'll be back. I hope you realize his accomplishments this year are nothing short of extraordinary. He's been the key to our resurgence as a team. Second, the city is hurting. But healing can only begin if we identify our true problems. We need prayer now more than ever. Our problems won't end by ignoring them. Like every Pittsburgher, the players and I must decide what we need to do to bring us together and heal. The way forward is not by standing against our country or blaming the police. That road is a dead-end road to our destruction. Our problems can't be solved by blaming those trying to make our citizens safe. I want to focus on the true problems and true solutions. These race organizations are woven together with antigovernment, antidemocracy, and antifreedom ideals. They pit us against each other. They would have us in anarchy, followed by tyranny, destroying everything good in our world. I don't want to burn society to the ground, and I don't want to lose the precious freedoms we've fought so hard over previous generations to secure. That's not me, and many of our players feel the same. What we do kneel for is prayer to God to forgive, heal, and bring us together as one community, one nation," finished Saul.

"Your stance puts you at odds with popular support in Pittsburgh and around the nation, not to mention Major League Baseball. You're swimming against the tide, Saul. You and your players will find your position becoming increasingly untenable."

Saul finished, "Mr. Annason, I am morally bound in my stance and legally bound in allowing my players the freedom to choose. They must decide for themselves, but I chose to stand for what is true and right, and like Josh Green often says, I kneel to the only One who can save us and make us whole again."

"That is a risky stance, Coach Samuelson. You now have a team without its star player. What happens if it loses its winning ways?"

"I expect the team to continue to play well and win, but either way, we must live and act according to our conscience."

"Remember Saul, your job is to give the fans what they want, not just a winner, but someone they can cheer. Your dropping popularity with the fan base and the city means decreasing revenues, especially if the Pirates lose. Your position as Head Coach would be in jeopardy."

"I understand, Mr. Annason. My tenure is always at your discretion," Saul said as he stood up, realizing his job was genuinely unimportant to his soul. "I neither can nor will retract anything I believe, for it cannot be either safe or honest for a Christian to speak against his conscience. Here I stand; I cannot do otherwise; God help me!"[1]

Cai stared silently at the man, eyes stern, but Saul was unwavering. "Is there anything else?" Saul finished.

"No, Coach Samuelson," Cai said, failing to get up, let alone offer a handshake to his coach. "I hope the next time we talk, it is under better circumstances. However, that depends entirely upon you and the team's actions." Cai finished.

Saul left Cai's office without looking back.

---

1. Martin Luther's defense at the Imperial Diet in Worms 18 April 1521.

Seventy Eight

R oman Josephus was not one to look a gift horse in the mouth, but even he felt uneasy about the means used by his unknown benefactor to get the information he now held. He could never use it openly because he was pretty sure it was illegal to keep someone's medical history, especially a juvenile, and probably illegally obtained. How the unknown voice on the other end of the phone acquired it, Roman didn't want to know. Acquiring such information represented significant expenditures, probably as bribes or nefarious favors. Roman knew this meant a network with reach, willing to push the boundaries of what was legal, let alone ethical.

Here was the bottom line, however. Roman now held evidence on Green's live-in nanny, Mary Dalene, confirming a checkered juvenile past. On the surface, she appeared to be a well-educated and credentialed nanny and teacher. But Dalene's lack of prior history in her background made Roman curious. Roman's investigator uncovered a criminal source claiming Dalene was once one of his "girls." Roman brought this to his mysterious source inside MLB. Sure enough, after a few weeks, the source now brought him irrefutable evidence, though highly charged and possibly illegally obtained, verifying the girl's illicit past.

Roman held the evidence telling Mary's story before coming to Light of Life ministries. It included a sealed juvenile record, since expunged, of two minor drug charges and a solicitation charge, later dropped, all before the girl turned eighteen. Mary was a runaway at a young age. Her sordid past finally ended as a seventeen-year-old when she became pregnant. The information was salacious, and the extent Roman's source went to get it was disconcerting. Possessing the juvenile police report was bad enough, but somehow his contact dug up evidence from a Planned Parenthood clinic the girl visited. He reviewed a copy of the scheduled abortion record, confirmed authentic but highly sensitive. Roman could never admit to them publicly, but he and his source knew that was not his intended use.

Roman set aside his misgivings, remembering his advancement required getting the scoop on Green. He needed something to break Green's aura of invincibility as the good and noble knight. Roman worked for weeks trying to dig up something to show Green was no Christian Saint. He searched for something to titillate the public's interest, stoke their passions and possibly expose Green as a hypocrite. If releasing this information also met some objective of his MLB benefactor, it was almost irrelevant.

Roman hurried his thinking, not dwelling on the ethics to tax his conscience too much about the consequences. He must build back waning interest with Green sidelined and get the story soon. Yes, he must stoke the flames to keep the fire burning hot so he could move up to the national desk. He would use this evidence and follow his road to fame and fortune.

Roman's next step was clear. This Mary Dalene lived two lives, one before, filled with shame and ruin, and a new one since coming to Light of Life ministries. Roman, like his source, believed she would want to keep her past a secret lest she lose the new life she built for herself. Roman would use this evidence as leverage to enter the inner circle of Josh Green through his nanny. Surely, Roman could justify using this information to get the story. "All you did was receive it," Roman told himself. "You didn't do anything wrong. You don't have to report on it. Just use it to get the girl to talk and get the story. That's what good reporters do, right? They get the story!" the voice demanded, overriding Roman's conscience questioning the use of this inflammatory information.

Roman quelled his unease by listening to his greater fear of slipping back into anonymity as the Pirates' play dropped off while Green remained sidelined. News moved fast, and he fought to keep relevant on sports center or sink back into small-town irrelevancy. The Pirates never held a large city fan base, and only the extraordinary play of the team led by Green propelled Roman's in-depth reporting into the limelight. Now more than ever, Roman needed a hook into Josh's mysterious past to spark interest. Roman hesitated, knowing his source was someone with high access in MLB's dark tower and would call in this marker on him someday. However, Roman's fear of falling back into obscurity exceeded all others as he chose to risk paying the price for any sins later after attaining all he desired. Roman needed to strike now as rumors surfaced the network considered promoting him to a regular beat as a nightly MLB lead reporter for SPNN. But, as his producers told him, he needed to close the deal on another scoop of national-level news on Green.

Roman thought of all these things as he waited outside Children's Hospital and pushed away any doubt as he spied Green's vehicle entering the parking garage. It was difficult to find Green's rehab schedule until Roman thought up a "Good Samaritan" approach. Instead of trying another backdoor bribe, which failed on more than one hospital employee, he posed as a reporter for the local newspaper, looking for photo opportunities on one of Green's many visits to the children's ward. Green seemed to do this almost every week when his daughter received treatments. While the person on the other end of the phone ultimately refused to let Roman come himself, he promised to take pictures of the event, if Mr. Green allowed, and send them to the newspaper. This did Roman no good, but the reply came with an anticipated date and time, allowing Roman to estimate Josh's scheduled visit.

Josh arrived with Ruth and Mary at Children's Hospital at the University of Pittsburgh campus. They scheduled the downtown therapy because both Josh and Ruth could get what they needed at the same time. It was a month since the attack, and Josh's broken clavicle mended nicely. Dr. Luke approved Josh to move forward with rehab, arranging treatment at sports medicine in the same hospital complex Ruth visited at the beginning of the season in Pittsburgh's Oakland district. Roman watched as Mary, now driving the Greens in Josh's old green Cherokee, pulled into the parking garage by the hospital.

Roman wasn't beneath some subterfuge and scheduled an appointment under a fake name to get a look at a fictitious injury. Now that the Greens were here, Roman quickly entered the hospital before they exited their car. Roman wore a disguise of an oversized floppy fishing cap and dark sunglasses, with his left arm in a sling. The hospital was relaxed with their security, and fortunately, no one challenged Roman as he followed the signs to a large waiting area for physical therapy. When he saw no one was paying him much attention, he slipped off the sling and placed it in a small bag slung over his other shoulder that kept his recording gear carefully packaged and ready to go with just a push of a button hidden on the strap. The bag's strap also hid a small camera with a recording device. It captured sound and video, and Roman rehearsed its use to perfect his technique. He could aim the mini-camera that looked like a small lapel pin forward or move it to right angles. This allowed Roman to video to his front or side with a simple innocent-looking adjustment of the strap and pin. Roman kept his hat and glasses on, appearing to be one of twenty or so patients waiting for an appointment in the busy facility. He read an old sports magazine as he awaited the Greens and his chance with Mary Dalene.

The Greens and Mary soon arrived, and Josh Green checked in at the counter. Roman noticed Josh's shoulder was no longer in a sling. Green's shoulder rehab must be proceeding well, as he was only a month removed from his strange accident. Roman put that thought in his mental notebook. He must press Mark Johnson on the timeline for Green and his return to baseball activities. Still, he wasn't here for Green today.

As expected, first Josh, then Ruth were called back for their appointments. Mary sat waiting outside. The gods must be favoring him, thought Roman, as Mary sat with her back to him and was relatively alone with empty seats around her. Now was his chance. The plan was simple: strike up a conversation, see what the girl revealed about Green and his background, and if she resists, start dropping the information that shows he knows her past. Roman adjusted his camera to the angle he would use when he sat next to Mary and keyed the power button to record. He looked inside his bag to see the record light shining before zipping it shut. He figured he had at least thirty minutes before Green or his daughter came out. That should be more than enough for this first installment. Oh, this wouldn't necessarily be anything he could use, but it was bound to sow the seeds for using Mary as his pliable inside source if she wanted to keep her past hidden and not jeopardize her new life as a successful nanny. As Roman stood to move, he almost felt sorry for the girl. She wouldn't know what hit her.

Seventy Nine

Josh's physical therapy went well, and although he was still sore, his week since removing the sling showed reasonably rapid progress. He gladly did the work, happy to do something other than ride the stationary bike, and the soreness remained mild compared to his range of motion tests evaluating his progress. After Dr. Luke checked the scans from yesterday, he gave Josh approval to start some power drills and light throwing next week and told Josh he could be back to the field soon if all went well.

As Josh exited the PT area, back to the waiting room, he found Mary by herself toward the back with no sign of Ruth. Generally, their therapy took the same time, and Josh returned first. As he walked over towards Mary to wait, he noticed Mary seemed withdrawn. She usually greeted Josh with a smile and hello, yet she didn't say anything when he sat down, avoiding eye contact.

"Everything OK?" Josh said, looking at the girl, or he should say, young lady, who became a part of their family in the last few months.

Mary hesitated, still not looking over at Josh. Finally, she nodded, keeping her head down. Something was off, but Ruth came out before he could ask more. She was smiling and gave her dad a warm hug. The three left the way they came, but Josh noticed Mary hanging back, more introverted and withdrawn than usual. The ride home took about forty-five minutes, and Mary continued to say very little for the rest of the day. She left before dinner, saying she needed to run an errand, and returned to the house just as Josh put Ruth to bed. Mary usually kept the evenings to herself, and her attic apartment, with a separate entrance, meant Josh didn't know when she returned. Mary came down the stairs and told Ruthie goodnight, but before she went upstairs, she turned to Josh and asked if she could speak to him when he finished putting Ruth to bed.

Mary went to the kitchen, waiting for Josh with great trepidation and sadness. Her past caught up to her, and now, all these years later, she feared it would ruin her present. Whenever she thought these dark thoughts through, she remembered Ms. Phoebe. It was Ms. Phoebe she went to see this afternoon. Phoebe was one of the few people from her "new life," as she called it, who knew of her past, and all its dirty details. Perhaps more than anyone, Ms. Phoebe understood how far she'd come. Phoebe reminded her that her life was new, made new by the One worthy sacrifice that made all things new. Though Mary could not forget her past and the hurt and pain she endured and caused, Christ forgave her and took her shame and punishment.

Today, as she drove to visit Phoebe, Mary reflected on her life. Mary met Ms. Phoebe so many years ago in despair, ready to end it all. Mary, forced to live on the streets after running away from an abusive stepfather at just fourteen, fled to nearby Pittsburgh. She became trapped in drugs and forced by threats from her dealer into prostitution. Three years later, her life seemed over. She was pregnant, and her dope-dealing pimp took her to get an abortion.

Scared and all alone, the clinic offered little in the way of comfort or alternatives. Pressed by her drug dealer and seeing no alternative, she succumbed to despair and had the abortion. She regretted it immediately and ran away, trying to hide from the mess she made of life. But she could not shake the shame and the utter hopelessness of ending her baby's life. A few sleepless nights later, hungry and alone, she was lost, in every sense of the word. She thought of her child. Yes, she knew the baby was her baby, a human life entrusted to her by the Creator. Precious and unique, no matter what the clinic said, the child was a life, and she ended that life. She hoped there was a heaven, and her child was there, but she feared her child would never forgive her for what she did. Broken and despairing, she prayed to a God she never knew and wasn't even sure existed, to forgive her, doubting she could ever forgive herself. The pain was too great, the burden too heavy. She knew she could not save herself. Devoid of hope for salvation, still she prayed.

She wandered somewhere on Pittsburgh's north side, deciding she must end it all. Evil forces she could not see whispered damnation and shame upon her. They condemned her for her many bad choices, none greater than ending her baby's life. They told lies she was unloved and unlovable, reminding her of her abused life, whispering she was better off dead. She saw no hope and no path out of the ruin of her life. It was just better to end it all, and she walked aimlessly, planning to find one of Pittsburgh's many bridges and fling herself off it.

Stumbling blindly and turned around, Mary found herself passing one of the cities many churches. She was cold and weary, and she could see lights inside and a few women were exiting the door talking about God's amazing love as they walked away. Though Mary passed the church many times, she suddenly felt the need to enter. She hoped for one last bit of warmth and perhaps one final desperate prayer, one last cry for help, before heading to her destiny. Collapsing into a pew, she wept silent tears and beseeched the God she did not know and could not see for help she did not deserve.

Late as it was, Mary had stumbled into the church just as Ms. Phoebe finished leading a weekly women's bible study. After Ms. Phoebe tidied the side classroom where the women just departed and moved to turn off the lights, she noticed the young girl by herself in the pews. Mary met the gentle Ms. Phoebe that night and poured out her life story. Today, Phoebe reminded Mary, she actually met Jesus in that pew. On that first night, Ms. Phoebe told Mary, neither Mary nor Phoebe held the power to change her life. Only Christ offered her new life. Tonight, Phoebe reminded Mary it was Christ who saved her that night. And the same Christ placed her on the new road she traveled and would never leave her.

Instead of ending her life on that dark night years ago, Mary accepted Christ as her personal savior. She began this incredible new life leaving the lost streets behind for the Light of Life mission house, thanks to Ms. Phoebe's kindness and help. Even though her life completely changed, one big hole in Mary's heart still haunted her, a void left by the child she would never know. Though the Bible promised Christ forgave her, Mary sometimes fell into the trap brought on by evil forces, reminding her of her seventeen-year-old self. Mary longed to tell her younger self there were other options that Planned Parenthood never led her to consider. If only she'd met Jesus and Ms. Phoebe before that fateful decision.

Today brought such thoughts after the ugly encounter with the reporter, threatening to reopen a wound she sometimes feared would never heal. But Mary grew in her faith. The Holy Spirit taught her, and gradually she understood the forgiveness taught by Phoebe and the ministers visiting Light of Life. Someday, she would meet her baby in heaven, but until then, she knew Christ, who knew all things, also knew she needed to forgive herself as He did, taking both the penalty and the shame for even this, two thousand years ago, on the cross.

Mary waited for Josh to come downstairs. Though she dreaded this discussion, not knowing what Josh's reaction would be, she was now steadfast in her determination to tell him her complete story, the one almost no one else knew. That reporter didn't understand. Mary no longer feared what someone like he could do to her. She did the worst to herself and would never return to being that person, not because of anything she did in contrition or good works, but because of what Christ did in her life. She would not allow any man to abuse and threaten her again like her drug dealer often did and many men before him.

Somehow, she felt Josh was different. From the beginning, she saw Christ in this small family, and Christ's love seemed to shine between father and daughter. It was the same love she felt the first night with Phoebe when she accepted Christ, and like the Greens, Christ's love took hold of her heart and life. No reporter would bully Mary into betraying the love and trust of this family, even if it cost her job and position, for she grew to love the Greens as well. Mary resolved to tell her story to Josh. No matter what happened, she learned she was a new creation in Christ, as His word described, and He gave her a new life, a redeemed life. Whatever came, she would hold on to Him, as He would hold her for all eternity.

Josh came downstairs. Before she could say anything, Josh asked if it was OK for him to make them some hot cocoa. There was some apple cake Miss Elizabeth sent home with them last Sunday when the three ate a late lunch with the Arimas. Mary watched Josh silently fiddling with her cup of cocoa as he heated the apple cake in the microwave for a few seconds. The smell of apples and cinnamon filled the air as Josh took out the plate, set it on the table, and sat down. He bowed his head and blessed the cake saying, "Dear Lord, bless this food and drink. Let it nourish our bodies. Be with us, Lord. Let us feel your presence. Help Mary, be with her, let her know your love, and let the love and grace of Jesus be with us tonight and always."

When he finished praying, Josh cut the warmed cake, giving Mary a generous piece and taking one himself. He took a bite and sipped his cocoa, and Mary did likewise. When they ate a little, Josh sat back and looked at Mary. His eyes were especially kind tonight, and old, Mary noticed, not in age but in wisdom. He smiled and said, "I want you to know, whatever you need to talk to me about, Mary, it's OK. The Lord prepared my heart to receive whatever it is."

Mary began. "Josh, something happened today, but to explain it, I must first tell you about my past life."

Josh nodded. He would barely talk over the next hour, just an occasional word of encouragement to Mary when she reached a difficult pause. This was the first Mary told anyone her story since Ms. Phoebe at the Light of Life ministry. She feared looks of pity, derision, or righteous indignation if others knew, yet Josh's eyes remained kind and understanding. When she feared condemnation, Josh offered encouragement. When she deserved judgment, Josh extended mercy. He often listened without comment yet conveyed acceptance and support as he nodded. Mary explained all that happened leading up to her meeting with Phoebe at church that fateful night and how, in turn, she gave her life to Jesus.

"After Light of Life and following Christ, my life changed. It truly was a new life. But not a day goes by that I don't wish I met Ms. Phoebe before going to the abortion clinic. I don't know why Christ would accept someone like me. I know He did, and I know He forgives our sins. It's so hard for me to hold on to His promise of forgiveness. I know my child is there with him, and I am afraid they know what I did and won't forgive me. Today, I was reminded of this. It is my greatest fear and regret."

Josh nodded, and after a thoughtful pause, he finally spoke.

"Mary," Josh began, "Christ didn't just take our place on the cross to offer himself a perfect sacrifice for our sins. He also took our place on the cross to take away our shame. The Bible says God the Father, because of what Christ did, removed our sins as far as the east is from the west and buried them in the deepest sea.[1] Christ stood before God on the cross in our place, taking everything upon him that was justifiably due to us. His atonement was equal to our sin and our shame.[2] It was fully and completely sufficient to wash us clean. All God sees is Christ and his perfect sacrifice when He looks at us.[3] Remember Jesus when they brought the women who committed adultery? He took on her accusers, and they were humbled one by one. Each, remembering their unrighteousness, fled. He alone remained, and He forgave her sins.[4] He has taken your sins, but he has also taken your shame, and he knows your regret. Your child is with him in a glorified body. They know what Jesus has done for you, the price paid, the stain and shame of sin removed. Your child will see you through Christ and the new life He has bought for you. They will know your love of them and forgive you as Christ has forgiven you. You cannot bring them back. Remember what King David said when his child perished after David's sin? He knew they were in heaven and waiting for the day their repentant father would be reunited with them in love,[5] by the love and grace of the Lord Jesus Christ, who gave His life a ransom for ours."[6]

"I know what you say is true. Thank you, Josh. I just slip back into listening to the devil's lies sometimes," replied Mary.

"That's exactly what they are, Mary; lies from the prince of lies. But he used someone to get at you today. What happened?"

Mary described her encounter with Roman Josephus. She finished, "He ended with the threat of exposing my past to the press and the entire world if I didn't start passing him information about you and those around you. I told him I would never betray your trust, but he told me I would be the one who would pay the price when the media found out where I came from and what I did." Mary trailed off. She didn't know what more to say.

---

1. Psalms 103:12; Micah 7:19; Psalms 31:1-2

2. 2 Corinthians 5:21; Hebrews 10:12-14

3. 2 Corinthians 5:17

4. John 7:53–8:11

5. 2 Samuel 12:21-23

6. Matthew 20:28

Josh responded, "Mary, I can't stop Roman from giving away information on you, but I can tell you that everyone who cares about you, including Ruth and I, will never stop caring and believing in you. I know you now, Mary, and I can see the work of Christ in your life. We all have a sinner's past. Sometimes it tries to raise up and pull us down, but Christ redeemed us, once, for all time.[7] Even when we fail again, Christ won't let us go, and He won't leave us when we go through tough times. Even when someone tries to remind us of where we once were, Christ says the Father only remembers His Son when he looks at us."[8]

Josh continued, "Never forget, God said He is with us and goes before us to fight our battles. Who then shall we fear?[9] As for me, I can handle Roman if you let me. I will make it clear to him, I know you, and I know you are the best person to watch over, teach, and love my Ruth when I am not around. I don't know anyone better for helping us through this season and beyond than you, Mary. The Lord has a plan for you. Ruth and I are both beneficiaries of the fact the Lord brought you to Him and then to us when we needed you most."

Mary smiled at Josh and nodded as she cupped the mug of cocoa Josh made. It cooled considerably since he made it, but that was OK. She was warm with the thoughts of Christ's love Josh displayed and demonstrated through his words and actions. Once again, she remembered Jesus's promise in John of a new life, and she would hold on to that life for all eternity.

---

7. Hebrews 9:12

8. Deuteronomy 31: 6, 8; Romans 8:1; Ephesians 2:13; Hebrews 8:12; Romans 8:30; John 1:12-13

9. Isaiah 41:10-11; Romans 8:31-35

Eighty

As Josh's rehab progressed, Dr. Asa Levine and Doc Luke conducted bi-weekly consultations with Josh. Today, Doc Luke asked Josh if it was OK if Coach Samuelson sat in as Josh wanted the green light to begin baseball activities. Doc Luke prepped the video consult in Pop's office with Dr. Levine. Luke ran Josh through range of motion tests and reported the strength tests done with the physical therapists. Dr. Levine examined several data files Doc Luke passed, including an MRI, and was satisfied with what he saw.

"Well, Josh, I'll say this, you are definitely on the front side of the curve when it comes to healing. The bone looks good, and I understand the soreness decreased considerably. I suggest you start slowly, as the muscle loss will still be a good 5-10%, even with the PT you've been doing. Doc Luke and the coaches can ease you into practice. Restart with caution and restraint. I am more concerned with your throwing than your hitting. Batting practice is fine. Keep your reps down at three-quarters speed, especially when throwing the first few days. I've emailed Dr. Luke my detailed recommendations on your exercises and reps. Three on, one off, for eight days should get you back to a starting point for easing you into game situations. That will place you at the 35-day point after your injury, and believe me, that's probably a record for the dozens of professionals I've seen with this injury, so don't cut any corners. Based on what I see, you shouldn't have any problems, but if you feel anything but the expected soreness we discussed, call me."

Josh thanked both doctors for their help as Dr. Levine ended the video conference. Doc Luke asked out of the office to go back to his computer and get a printout of the workout Dr. Levine sent. Pops turned back to Josh and said, "OK, partner. Looks like we can start working you out based on the doctor's program. How do you want to proceed?"

"I think the doc's warning about the arm strength and throwing matches how my arm feels, at least as far as the PT is concerned. I would like to keep my practices out of the limelight until I am ready to play," Josh said tentatively.

"What's on your mind, Josh?" Pops could tell something wasn't right.

Josh, who talked with Mary about what he would tell the coach, gave Saul a shortened version of Roman's attempt at strong-arming Mary for dirt on Josh. To say Pops was not happy was an understatement, but he could tell Josh seemed to have a plan.

"This is the part of the business I truly hate," Pops said, more angry than surprised. "The press can surely make people's lives miserable. Some press more than others. I always knew Roman would do just about anything to make a name for himself, but this is extortion, plain and simple." Josh nodded. Pops followed, "I take it you have some idea of how you want to proceed?"

"Pops, I would like not to talk to the press until we're ready for me to play or even until my first game back. Is there some way we could keep the practice out of prying eyes?" asked Josh.

"OK, let me think." Pops paused for a few moments. An idea came to mind, and he leaned back in the chair. Crossing his arms, he said, "Why don't we see about heading over to my alma mater, Trinity Christian High School, for catch and throws in the mornings? I am good friends with their coach and sponsor his clinic each year. Coach Eli works a couple of our relievers every day, so we could bring in one a day to work BP for you after you get your throws in with Coach Phil, Pete, or me there. We'll keep it on the down-low, so the press can't find us easily, and the school is pretty small and tight-knit."

Josh agreed with the plan, and Pops made all the arrangements. After his first three days of workouts, Josh felt ready to move from three-quarters to closer to full speed. Josh worked hard on the treadmill and cross-trainer the previous week and finally started getting his wind back, feeling like he did before the injury. The Trinity baseball coach asked Pops if some of his upperclassmen could work out with Josh. Saul said they could participate in some of Josh's drills but asked them to keep it off social media, hoping to stay below the press radar. Pops sent a pitcher due to go through an off-day routine, who pitched 30 or so hard pitches to work Josh's batting back up to speed. Saul instructed his players not to let on where they were going, and only the pitcher and one other player would show up to play catcher. The high school coach, Saul's old friend, agreed to caution his kids to keep it to themselves.

The practices started well with about a dozen players who showed up to run some sprints, and Josh joined them. He got back to beating all but one by day three, and the young man, who was also the school's best sprinter, kept him working hard through the week. Josh gave them encouragement and pointers as they worked through drills Coach Phil directed. Josh often thought back to how his dad taught him during many days playing catch and hitting his dad's pitches. Like always, he missed his father, but now he thought he missed a bit not having his own son to pass on what he knew. Ruthie was a wonderful daughter, and Josh enjoyed all they did together, but Josh was thankful for these days with the young men who became more comfortable around the gentle giant as the practices progressed. Josh encouraged the ballplayers to work on their fielding skills as he worked with them while Coach Phil and Pops or Pete and their coach worked around Josh's rehab drills.

Samson was due to pitch on the third day, and he brought Zach, his roommate, since the Pirates had a rare off day. The student players were all about getting autographs from Samson, and many loved taking a picture of him, hand to hand with them, as his giant hands dwarfed mere mortals. He was a natural at getting the kids to open up with his easy, affable way. Samson's presence and gentle kindness put the kids at ease. During a water break, the young man, who challenged Josh's speed in the wind sprints, got up the nerve to ask Josh about life and what made him successful. The rest of the players listened intently, as all previously were a little afraid to ask too many questions outside of baseball.

Josh stated, "My parents taught me as a young man to seek to serve the Lord and His will in life. When we follow Jesus and study His words and life, we see He came to serve others. I think for me, the Lord spoke quietly through the circumstances of my life growing up and even today as an adult. He gently shows me how I should serve and do his will. I want you to know it's not always a clear voice, and sometimes, it's been hard to understand what He wants me to do. But I would say first, seek God's will for your life and follow it.[1] He will lead you in developing and using your gifts to serve others."

"You sound like Coach and my Sunday School teacher," the young man replied, nodding to the high school coach who sat listening in the bleacher nearby next to Pops, Coach Phil, and Zach. His coach smiled back at the young man. "But my question always is, how do I know God's will for my life? How do you answer that?" he asked, genuinely concerned.

Josh smiled and nodded, "It's a great question; perhaps the most important question after you have answered the question of will you put your faith and trust in Jesus. I asked the same question when I was your age. The answer always starts with two things: prayer and reading God's word. It sounds simple, and it's easy to say, but it requires a lifetime of perseverance and truly seeking God's wisdom and will. God's power is available to us through his word and prayer with him. This is the same God who created everything, knows all things, and loves you so much, He sent His Son to die in your place. You find God's will on occasions, during life-changing moments, but most of the time, it's in the quiet of prayer

---

1. Matthew 6:33

and reading His word. In such times I have learned to hear or sense God's gentle leading and encouragement in how I should go and what I should do."

"In fact, it's been the story of my life. Ask and seek—that's prayer, reading the Bible, and listening with our minds and hearts while doing both. In my experience, God rarely overpowers us with blinding flashes of guidance. He wants us to seek Him in the quietness of our hearts. God doesn't want to overwhelm us, but He wants to fill us with His spirit and guide us to our decision points. Then He wants us to choose to take the step on the road He lays out for us. I'll be honest. It's hard sometimes to know. That's where faith comes in, with lots of prayer along the way. I can tell you I have walked the path and chosen to follow God's will and rely on his promises, even though I haven't always been sure of the path. In life, we face tough choices, big and small. You already see some choices right here in High School. Each day, we have many small choices about how we approach life. Do we turn to God and follow Him and His guidance, or do we rely on ourselves or listen to man's way? I must choose to follow the Lord every day. I must ask the Lord to help me be more like Christ. Every morning I get up and then, by the Holy Spirit, walk the walk. Sometimes, it can seem foolish by man's standards."

"Like the fact, you choose not to kneel for the anthem, and yet you kneel and pray to God?" another boy asked.

"Yes. Often the way God leads me isn't popular. Many may say I am doing the wrong thing for the wrong reasons. I constantly go back to praying to the Lord, reading His Word, and studying its lessons and history. I must understand when the authors, inspired by God, wrote it and what it meant in their culture while asking God what it means to me today. Following the Lord can be difficult to know and difficult to do; having the fortitude and faith to follow His way, keeping His commandments, and walking the path He sets for us. Following God's plan even brought me to a hair's breadth of death," and with that comment, Josh pointed to and traced the scar that ran down his cheek with emphasis. Even the coaches, Samson and Zach, now listened intently. Josh continued, "But I tell you, when I have stepped out in faith and obedience following the Lord, He has always led me down paths that made life worth living, giving me the best opportunities to serve Him through serving others. The times I chose what seemed an easier way, not what I knew God wanted for me, I always ended up regretting it. The Lord's path may not be easy, but it is always our best path with our best destiny."

"Even when it leads to injury or danger, even if it costs us something dear?" pressed the young man who asked the first question.

"Following the Lord is a choice. All choices come with costs, but I would rather follow Christ and God's will and reap rewards in heaven than follow man's will or my own and have my life not count for anything, even if it brings me short-term gain. Jesus asked, 'What does it profit a man if he gains the whole world but lose his soul?'"

"Even if it cost you your life?" the boy asked finally, quietly, head down. The other boys looked at their young friend, knowing something the Pirate players and coaches could only guess: some trauma deep inside him.

Josh looked over at the young man. He was aware this question turned inward, not just for Josh. Josh put his arm on the young man's shoulder. "I *have* walked through the valley of death, but it was the path the Lord laid out for me. I tell you, though it cost me my life, I will walk it as the Lord leads. I do this because I know it is the only path worth walking. You all are young, but you realize as you grow older, we all face challenges in life, and we all come to the end someday. The question is, will you live the life worth living while God gave you the chance to follow him? I want my life to be lived for the Lord, no matter where He leads. Following Him has always been the best choice and my best life."

"You sound like my dad did," the young man said. Many of his teammates looked down at their feet. "He lived the life you suggest, following the Lord and taking us to church all the time. He owned his own business, a small corner store. He told us how he followed the Lord as a young boy. How it kept him out of the trouble many of his friends and family got into, and how the Lord gave him a life worth living. He worked hard, raised our family, and was an example in our community. Many people looked up to him as a black kid from Pittsburgh who grew up, made good, and gave back to the community. Then one day, some kids tried to rob our store, and Dad tried to stop them. He told them to get out, and they shot him dead. Why should I put my faith in God when He let my dad, who followed him all the days of his life, die like that? Now we are a family without a father, and my mom struggles to keep us all together and make ends meet."

Many were silent after the young man's story and waited for Josh's answer. With the dark eyes of a man who saw so much, Josh somehow knew the words of compassion and understanding this young man needed.

"What's your name?" Josh asked kindly.

"Jadyn," he replied.

"Jadyn, what you are asking is perhaps one of the toughest questions in life to answer. Namely, why does God allow bad things to happen to good people, even Godly people He calls his own? First, and this is very important, we don't always receive a clear answer to why God allows evil to win even a temporary victory in life against good. We know God's word promises His plan will come to pass and bring all of us who accept Christ home to be with Him in glorious final victory. Yet it seems unfair to have the people we love taken from us too soon. He warned us, 'In this life, you will have trouble.' God loved us so much that he created men with free will to love Him and follow Him or reject Him and go our own way.

The Bible tells us and demonstrates all men sin. When men sin, that sin has deadly consequences. Just as Adam, the first man, would eventually die, so do all men. And good men, men who have put their faith and trust in Christ and followed him all their days, sometimes have their lives shortened because the world is full of men who sin against God. I can't tell you why your dad died, but I can tell you I understand your pain and hurt. You see, when I was 16, my father, also a Christian who followed the Lord his entire life, suffered a heart attack and died far too soon. I, too, questioned why God would let this happen. Why did my dad have to die so young? Why would my mom have to raise me and my younger brothers and sisters by herself?"

"What was the answer?" Jadyn asked expectantly, finally looking up at Josh. Could this man truly have the answers he sought? He was such a fantastic athlete, thought Jadyn, but what was at the heart of it? Was this tall, dark, professional athlete who sat before him, not just the unreal talent they saw this year? Was there more to him, something personal and close to home? Jadyn saw the scar on Josh's face, the dark hair flowing from under his hat, but most of all, those dark eyes of kindness and concern seemed to deflect Jadyn's sorrow and replace it ever so slightly with a glimmer of hope.

"I never got a full answer," Josh said kindly. He continued, "I don't expect I will until I join my dad in heaven and see God face to face, Jadyn. But this one thing, I am assured. What Satan used against my family and meant for evil, God took and turned into a way for my family to see how God never is surprised and always makes a way, His way, my best way, to live life.[2] I've grown in the faith because I have a Father in God who is perfect, ever-present, and never left me, not once, since my dad died young and went home to be with Him. My family's needs were great. It seemed we needed a miracle just to get by, yet God did that and more. My heavenly father will be with you and your family as He is with me. He never leaves or forsakes us; He never fails, and He always provides a way for us. When we reach the end of our time on earth, when He fulfills all His promises to us, He takes us home to be with him and our loved ones who trusted in him. We live with Christ, life eternal."

Jadyn chewed on this as he looked at the big man. Somehow Josh was not the untouchable "Hercules" he saw on TV. Somehow, he was human again, someone who knew his pain and lived it, coming through the storm. He began to understand, "So even though my dad died, you're saying God's plan is still in place?"

---

2. Genesis 50:20

"God didn't want anything bad to happen to us, least of all death, and He told Adam this. But He always knew, even before He created time, space, and matter, that man, who He created perfect but gave free will, would choose to sin, and sin would bring his death. Even before He began creation, God's plan wasn't for the Garden of Eden. It was for the Garden of Gethsemane. God knew your father would follow him. God knew your dad needed a savior, just as we all do. He knows your pain, Jadyn, and though I know you'll never get over losing your dad, I can also tell you, God, the Father, can lead you through the pain each day when you let Him. He has a plan for your life, a great plan. Like Christ said on his way to Calvary, after He told us we would have trouble, he reminded and commanded us, '*Fear not!* for I have overcome the world!' God is our perfect Father. He will never leave us. If you let Him, I believe He will give you the great life your dad always talked to you about and, I am sure, prayed for you to have."

All remained quiet. Jadyn looked back out over the ball field and pondered Josh's words. He realized he was angry with God. He knew what Josh said was true, but his heart was hurting. It was time to let the anger go.

"I need that kind of relationship with God like you have, Josh. I need the Father."

"Have you accepted Christ as your savior?" Josh asked.

"Yes, but I think I've been pushing him away since I lost Dad."

"You know, when Jesus told the parable of the prodigal, the father saw the son when he was a long way off. It was Jesus's way of saying, He's always right there beside us, waiting for us to turn. Jesus never leaves us, Jadyn. He's waiting for you to turn back to Him. He knows and understands your pain and is ready to heal your broken heart."

After a few moments, Jadyn nodded, "I think I am beginning to understand because I can feel Him talking to my heart right now."

The entire team seemed to ease and lighten, like the load lifting off of Jadyn was also lifting a cloud over them they didn't know existed. Suddenly Jadyn smiled and said, "You know, my dad always loved to watch me play baseball. He loved it. He used to take me out and have me hit or shag fly balls until the sun went down. We would catch a Pirate game, and he said it was a lot like life, full of ups and downs with a few hits surrounded by a bunch of outs. When I played, if we lost a game, he used to ask if I did my best. Then he would say, that's all you can do, but remember, it's just a game. Enjoy and learn from it but leave it all on the field."

Josh nodded and smiled back, "Sounds like your dad was a lot like mine."

Jadyn looked back at Josh. "He loved the Pirates."

"So did mine," Josh replied and smiled at Jadyn. He paused and looked around at the other young men and coaches sitting around him. Finally, he looked back at Jadyn and said, "What do you think he'd be telling you now?"

Jadyn replied easily as he stood, a thousand times lighter than when he first sat down. "He'd tell me to get off my butt and get back in the game!"

"Sounds good to me!" Josh replied and stood along with Jadyn as the others followed suit.

The players were not quite the same as before. Each seemed filled with new life and purpose as they took the field. The specter of sadness and death lifted off their shoulders, wiped out by God's promise of new life. They played with a loose and joyful exuberance like the game was meant to be played.

Josh hit some easy hits they fielded during his batting practice against Samson. Pops warned him to take it easy, and both Samson and Josh worked at 90%. Josh hit the ball all around the field. The student players got a good workout with Josh, as even his slightly muted swings put balls consistently into play. At some point, they realized he was purposely hitting balls to each of them equally, despite the fact he worked against live pitching, and he finished the third day by hitting balls from one side of the field to each player in sequence finishing with three home runs to left, center and right fields. After the third home run, Samson laughed and turned to Pops, saying, "I think he's good to go, Coach."

It was the end of the eight days of Josh slowly increasing his physical activity back towards his pre-injury level. Josh felt confident he was ready, and with one last medical examination, Josh returned to the active roster.

Eighty One

J osh completed his final rehab, but there was still one thing to do before returning to play. After a month of negative public displays and mediocre play, the Pirates finally found something to celebrate. Samson was getting married.

Josh, Ruth, and Mary arrived at the First Baptist Church in Oakland. Coach Saul put Mark Johnson and Martha in charge of preparations, decorating the beautiful cathedral church in tasteful black and gold flowers. Working with the bride-to-be, they found a brilliant florist, ordering arrangements of Black Eyed Susans, Kevuda's favorite local flower, combined with Black Hollyhocks, a beautiful velvety blackish purple flower with gold centers. They were simple, elegant bouquets. Ruth gave a little squeal of delight, and Mary commented, "Oh my, those are wonderful!" as Josh escorted the ladies to their seats before heading off to find Samson. He was, after all, the best man.

Josh joined Samson in a Sunday school room off the main sanctuary, finding Saul, Zach, and Andrew already there, all getting changed or helping the groom-to-be, try to stay calm and collected.

Before Samson could say anything, Josh raised his hands in a mea culpa expression. "Sorry I am a few minutes late, but Dr. Levine was late coming out of surgery to get to the video consult, and we needed his blessing to end my rehab officially."

"Well, Bro, I thought the groom was the one to get cold feet, not the best man!" laughed Samson easily.

"I wouldn't miss this for the world, my friend," said Josh, "And somehow, I don't think we have to worry about you, eh?" said Josh looking at the big man leaning back on a cushioned chair, probably brought specifically into the room to fit his oversized frame.

"Nope. Best decision I ever made. I only hope my bride hasn't changed her mind," said Samson, and he wrinkled his eyebrows a little.

Zach laughed, "Don't worry. Old Pete's misses told Pete your Kevuda passed your grandma's test last night with flying colors. Pete said if his misses and your granny gave their approval, you've got yourself quite a girl there, my friend!"

"Good, that's good," said Samson relieved. "I am glad Mr. Pete agreed to walk Kevuda down the aisle. With her daddy passing and all, she was unsure what to do.

Pops chimed in, "Ol' Pete was overwhelmed when you introduced Kevuda and asked if he would walk her down the aisle. He may have even shed a tear or two when you two left. He plays the tough guy, but he's quite a softy at heart."

"Well, besides Granny, you are all the family I have. I am glad you and the team could come and support, with it being, you know, short notice.

Andrew piped in, "You are our family too, Brother."

Thomas, already dressed, walked in carrying a large box. Josh finished changing and put on his jacket. "Hey, everybody!" Tommy began and turned to Samson. "Mark Johnson knocked the setup out of the park. Sammy," said Thomas setting the box down, "Wait till you see it!" Thomas looked around to see Josh buttoning his jacket. "Bout time, best man! Hey, so good to go?"

"All good, Tommy. Back with you all on the road," replied Josh,

"Great! Then I guess you're cleared to help me put these on. What are they called?" Thomas asked as he opened the box of groomsmen lapel flowers Mark Johnson gave him.

"Boutonnières," answered Andrew. Everyone looked at him. "What? I've been best man at three of my brother's weddings!"

"Cool!" Tommy replied. "Well, my fellow captain, you can help me with these. Josh, here's the special one for the groom."

The groomsmen's boutonnières were all made from the same Black Eyed Susan's, beautifully offsetting their black suits, but the groom's was unique, one gold and one black rose on Samson's full-tail black tuxedo.

"How do I look?" Samson asked Josh as Josh placed the flowers on his lapel.

"You look like a man ready to lead your family and follow the path the Lord has laid for you," Josh replied.

Samson smiled sheepishly, "Thank you for helping me think it through," he said quietly.

"Oh Samson," said Josh, "The quiet voice you listened to wasn't mine. It was the Father's. Remember to pray and listen to Him for every decision, and you won't go wrong."

They each helped the other put on their flowers, Thomas and Andrew, Zach and Saul, Josh and Samson.

Finally, a tall, gray-haired black man with a beautiful short gray beard entered. "Everybody ready?" he asked.

"Just one thing left to do," said Samson himself. "Pastor Manoah, can you take a picture of me with my brothers? I want to remember how they all came to join me on our big day before we get all formal and everything out there," he gestured toward the main sanctuary.

"Sure thing Samson. Who has the best phone? Mine's a few generations too old, I think," he said as he displayed an archaic flip phone. They all laughed, and Thomas handed his over after setting it up for the Pastor to snap some pictures.

When he walked back, Samson wouldn't leave him go to the edge of the picture. Instead, he pulled the aging white catcher on his side opposite Josh. "Tommy, I wouldn't be the pitcher I am today if it weren't for the way you brought me along. More than just about anyone, you've shown me patience and how to win, and I am more than grateful," Samson looked at the five men, "I mean it," said Samson to them all. "If it weren't for all you five did for me, showing me your kindness, teaching me your grace and wisdom, having so much patience with me," they all smiled at that, "I wouldn't be the man I am today. I am blessed to have you here with me as Kevuda and I tie the knot," Samson said and bowed his head. "And I want you all to stay with me and help me be the man Kevuda and our baby need me to be."

"It's all right, Sammy. The Lord gives us brothers to watch over us and stick by us, and that is what we promise to do for you," said Coach Saul.

"I am beginning to remember, Coach!" said Samson happily. He turned back to Josh, "Brother would you pray for me, that I might be the man the Lord wants me to be, for my family and my friends."

Samson kneeled down on one knee, and Josh gathered the men in a circle around him. They placed their hands on Samson, dedicating him and his life to the Lord as a husband, father, and Christian friend. As Josh prayed, Pastor Manoah took silent pictures. After they prayed, the men all stood, still surrounding Samson, who now stood the tallest in their midst. Surrounded by his brothers, Samson's smile beamed with hope and new life.

Eighty Two

J osh's return was none too soon for the Pirates. After 31 days since the all-star break, the Pirates went from an incredible ten games up on the second-place Cubs to just three games in front of Chicago and five games ahead of surging St. Louis. While their record of 85-33 was still the best ever in the big-leagues at this point in the season, they managed only a 14-17 record since the break, and both the Cubs and the Cardinals were setting their own franchise records in the National League.

The Pirates began another western road trip with a stop first in Colorado. The Rockies were a .500 team this year. Pops hoped not to have to use Josh for a few more games, deciding to keep him on the bench, holding him as a possible late-inning substitute pinch hitter to ease him back into game situations. He didn't bother to speak to Josh or any of his coaches about it. Pops still worried Josh might get hurt. He brought his roster to his bench coach, Pete, to give to the head umpire.

Pete looked it over and looked back at Pops. "You sure this is what you want to do?" Pete said, questioning in a low voice so no one else could hear.

Saul was a little taken aback, but Pete was the one guy who occasionally questioned what he did straight to his face. Pete didn't pull punches much, which was one reason Saul trusted him as his bench coach, but the question this time bothered him because he wasn't so sure.

"Yes," he replied hastily before Pete's squinty-eye-stare, chomping on his unlit cigar, could make Saul reveal his fears and uncertainty. Saul knew he didn't fully trust Josh when Josh told him he was ready to play again.

Meanwhile, the Pirate radio announcers discussed the situation in the radio broadcast booth. "Well, Bob, here we are in ole 'Mile High Stadium' where the Pirates will take on the Colorado Rockies."

"Actually, Greg, this is Coors Field. Mile High stadium's a few blocks that way, where the Denver Broncos play."

"Well, it's still way too high here, Bob! I've been huffin' and puffin' ever since I stepped off the plane."

"Maybe that's all the Primanti® sandwiches you've been eating."

"Naaah, it's not the Primanti.® I switched to BRGR® the last couple of games. I even tried their 'Fire in the Hole' last game. It was good goin' down, but kept me up all night," said Greg, as he punched his chest slightly with the back of his fist and cleared his throat.

"Maybe you ought to try something a little healthier there, Greg. I think you've packed on a few the past few weeks."

"Can you blame me?" Greg said incredulously, "I mean, the Bucs were up by ten and cruisin' before the break, but then Green goes and gets into some fist-e-cuffs with a bunch of New Yorkers, and what happens?" asked Greg.

"He fractures his collarbone, and the Bucs play poorly for a month as the Cubs and Cards climb back into contention?" commented Bob.

"Not just that, the Pirate offense goes to sleep, and they keep finding ways to lose games in late innings! I am telling ya, my poor heart can't take it, and I need my comfort food!" Greg said with a harrumph.

"Maybe there is a light at the end of the tunnel, folks, because ole Green is back on the active roster and joined the team here on the road trip," commented Bob.

"That's great news, Bob. Then again, if he is so healthy, why has Pops decided not to start him?" said a slightly annoyed Greg.

"Hard to say, Greg. Maybe Coach Samuelson wants to use Green sparingly since it's barely been a month since his kerfuffle and fracture," answered Bob.

"Well, I hope the Pirates play better than they have recently, losing five of their last seven games and looking like the Pirates of old, and not the good old either!" finished Greg.

Despite good pitching, the Pirates' offense still slept, and they failed to score during the first seven innings. Their best chance came in the top of the seventh when they placed their first runner in scoring position with runners on first and second after a double and a walk with no outs, but the Rockies starter settled down, getting a key strikeout followed by an inning-ending double play. Meanwhile, the Rockies scored twice, one solo home run in the thin air of Denver that barely got out of the stadium in the fourth, and now an unearned run scored after a lackluster play in Josh's right field position by his replacement.

"Good golly, that right fielder flubbed that line drive, and now we're down by two," Greg commented after the right fielder took one step forward and then could not get back to a ball over his head, bouncing onto the warning track. The runner on third, who walked, stole a base, and advanced to third on a ground out to second, scored on the error to make it 2-0.

"Yep, these winds might have fooled him for a second as that ball was more of a line drive than it looked and made it all the way to the wall," commented Bob.

"All I know is, this is not looking good. The Pirates are playing mediocre, like the last couple of series. Is it just me, or does it look like they are sleepwalking?"

"I'd have to agree with you there, Greg," Bob replied, shaking his head.

"It's as if they are waiting for a spark to ignite them, and that spark is sitting quenched in the dugout!" said Greg, more than a little anxious.

"Yes, folks, Green hasn't moved since he took part in the team's trademark prayer meeting before the game."

"What in the heck is Pops waiting for!"

"Don't know, Greg. Maybe he's not sure if Green's ready?"

"I don't know, Bob, but there's no time like the present! Pops better hurry up and figure it out because the way the Pirates are playing looks alarmingly like it has for the past month. And they're running out of innings!" Greg finished with frustrated emphasis.

Pops brought in a middle reliever, a recent trade just before the break, Jude Keriothson, one of the Florida Marlins' former starters. He began with a much-needed double play, but a long hit to right-center threatened to go for extra bases. However, Andrew got a good jump on it and, with a full-body dive, made a great catch to end the inning without further damage. Still, it was the top of the 8th with the Pirates down 2-0 and their relief pitcher due up third.

Again, Pops doubted himself. The team struggled to get base runners, and Pops was unsure what to do. First up was third baseman, Nathan Fisher. Unlike the rest of the starting lineup, Nate quietly increased his batting average after the break by almost .20 points and was the only Pirate to get to second tonight, hitting a double last time up. Colorado did not have a good bullpen, and the starter still looked good, so the Rockies manager kept him in the game. He started the Oklahoman off with two fastballs, low and outside. He went with a changeup a little too high over the plate, and the blond-haired, Mickey-Mantle-looking young man drilled it into right field for a hard single.

Thomas, the catcher, was next, and the Pirate reliever would follow if Pops didn't pull him. Jude nervously looked at Pops and reluctantly headed to the on-deck circle. Jude shook his head, thinking, "I'm a pitcher, not a hitter. What am I to do with us down by two runs? What is Pops thinking? This isn't my job, and I shouldn't be asked to do it."

With the team to his left past Old Pete, Pops leaned forward to spit some sunflower seeds he uncharacteristically borrowed from the Thunder Brothers to calm some of his nerves. As he bent, he glanced sideways, not wanting anyone else to see, towards Josh sitting alone near the opposite end of the bench. No one seemed to notice as they watched Thomas approach the plate. Josh sat quietly, arms crossed, and it appeared, eyes closed.

Pops leaned back and crossed his arms as well. What was Josh doing? Not sleeping for sure, thought Saul. Nope, Saul sensed Josh was fully aware of all that was happening, maybe more so than anyone in the stadium. Saul became introspective. "What should I do?" he wondered.

Saul almost jumped when Pete, in a low voice, asked quietly through the side of his mouth, "What are you waiting for, God to tell you to put him in?"

Saul looked at his old friend and mentor, once again surprised. Past Pete, the team sat. No one else acted as if they could hear Pete and Saul, and all but Josh seemed intent on Thomas's at-bat.

"Maybe I am," Saul said quietly back to Pete, with more defiance than he felt.

Pete, who spoke under his breath while still looking at the field, now looked directly at Saul and, with emphasis in his low gravelly voice, said, "Have you asked Him?"

Saul looked back at him, momentarily confused, and raised his furrowed eyebrows questioningly. What did Pete mean?

"Saul," Pete continued so only he could hear, "Are you still trying to figure this out all by yourself? If there is one thing I've learned, or maybe relearned this year, it's to not rely solely on my own judgment, not when I have a clear line to the Maker. Josh reminded us with both words and deeds on more than one occasion this year that the Master of the Universe is ready to hear our pleas for help and understanding. He knows what we need, He's never surprised, but He wants us to ask Him. Jesus is ready to make intercession on our behalf. Come to Him and let Him show you, His will."

Prayer, thought Saul. Josh was praying. Saul's heart softened, and he nodded to Pete and sat back. Pete, again, was right on the money. Ever since Josh cleared the Doc's examination and returned to the roster, Saul was worried about playing him too soon. He hadn't prayed to the Lord to ask him for wisdom and guidance. Saul worried about the team, about the funk they were in. He worried if Josh got hurt again, the team might not recover. Suddenly Saul realized he carried this for days, weeks maybe. He knew he must stop worrying, rebuke the fear and give it all to the Lord.

Saul leaned back, closed his eyes, and began to pray. As Thomas took the first pitch for a ball, Saul prayed, "Lord, I carry way more burden than I should. I want to give this burden to you. This team is yours, and so am I. I want to do what you want me to do for your honor and glory. Watch over us today. Please help me make the right decisions in your plan to let these players play their best game. Help me know how to use Josh and when to let him play, so he can do his part in all of this as You have prepared for him. In Jesus' name, I pray."

"Amen," said Pete. Saul was a little startled as he didn't quite realize he was saying it loud enough for anyone to hear. "My hearing's not that far gone!" said Pete without looking back at Saul, who smiled anyway.

Saul was at peace for the first time in weeks. He would go talk to Josh. As he leaned forward and looked down the row, Josh now looked directly at him. Saul got up, and as he passed Pete, he said, "Thanks."

"No problem," Pete replied, never taking his eyes off Thomas. "That's why you still keep me around."

Saul walked down the bench as Josh waited calmly. After passing the other players, he approached Josh and sat down on his far side, away from his teammates. Saul said quietly, "I am sending someone in to pinch hit for our pitcher. How are you doing? Do you feel ready to go?"

"I'm here, Coach. Send me," Josh said resolutely and without doubt in a voice echoing to Saul from antiquity.[1]

"OK, Josh, grab your bat and get out there."

Josh stood and walked towards the end of the dugout. Pete was already up, holding his helmet and bat retrieved from the cubbyholes. The three men came together. "About time you get back to work, Son," Pete said, handing him his batting helmet, which Josh donned, and then his bat. Still chomping on his unlit cigar, Pete clasped him on Josh's formerly fractured shoulder, "Lord knows, playing this game and hitting that confounded ball is what you were built for, what you were put on this earth to do. Now go do it!" Pete said, giving him a little squeeze. Josh knew it was Pete's way of saying, "You're all right!" and indeed, he was. Josh smiled at the older man he, like many of the team, came to love and respect. Then Josh turned, walked up the steps, and onto the field.

---

1. Isaiah 6:8

Eighty Three

"Ball four!" yelled Bob into the mike as Thomas walked on four straight pitches. As Thomas trotted to first base, Josh Green came out of the dugout, and Jude Keriothson, the pitcher still in the on-deck circle, looked very relieved. He smiled and gave Josh a handshake as he returned to the dugout.

"Bring 'em home, Josh!" Jude said.

"Woo-Hoo-Hoo! Looky here, Greg!" Bob continued excitedly. "Out of the dark recesses of the Pirate dugout comes one old rooky, Josh Green."

"About time!" replied Greg, sitting forward in excitement. "And now the entire park is noticing. The Rockies have called a time-out, and it looks like the manager is coming out to the mound. His pitcher pitched a gem of a two-hitter, but he seemed to lose some control this inning and put two aboard. It appears his night's over, and they'll go to a reliever as soon as they announce Green."

After the loudspeaker announced Josh Green as the pinch hitter, the Rockies called for their closer. He threw a solid upper 90s fastball with good movement but had a history of control issues. He was a bit of a wild card but was hard to hit when he threw strikes.

After the warm-ups, the umpire signaled to play ball, and as he did all season, Josh approached the batter's box and took a knee before this, his first at-bat. It was a quick prayer. Still, the crowd filled the stadium with boos.

"Josh picked up where he left off, folks, as he completes a kneeling prayer to a chorus of boos here in Denver," stated Bob.

"Yep, I just hope the good Lord likes what He heard: from Josh, that is. We could use the old Josh Green bat tonight," hoped Greg.

The pitcher let the first ball fly. It was fast and high at 100 MPH on the gun, and the catcher barely reached it to hall it down for ball one.

"The Rockies' pitcher is getting the 'OK, take it a little easy and try to locate it in the strike zone, not up in Telluride' sign after that one, Bob!" Greg commented.

"Yeah, the catcher asked for it high but didn't expect to have to climb Pike's Peak to catch it. Ball one to Green, and who knows where the next pitch will end up!"

Josh was at peace. Though he hadn't been in an actual game for over a month, the last few practices told him his feel for the pitches was still there. He was seeing the ball and seeing it well.

The second delivery from the fireballer clocked 99 MPH, still a little high and slightly outside, but it didn't matter. It was close enough for Josh. Josh rose slightly as he swung, extending to his full height to ensure the ball contacted the bat's sweet spot. Josh drilled the ball, hammering a frozen rope into the thin Colorado air.

"THWAACCKK!"

"There's a DRIVE! to DEEP Right-Center field. That ball is..., Out-a-Here!" Bob announced excitedly.

"Hal---Le---Lujah!" sang Greg in relief.

"Green is circling the bases while the stunned Rockies can only shake their heads. That ball either went into the upper deck, in right-center, which I don't think any ball has at that angle, or it just missed it and went high into the second deck under the third deck overhang," commented Bob.

"I'll say. Looky there, Bob! The ole Statcast® is showing 528 Feet! I think that thing wasn't quite high enough to get into the upper deck, but it was hammered on the button and disappeared in a hurry into the restaurant section between right and center. Say, isn't that where they make those Smash Burgers,® Bob?" asked Greg.

"I think you're right, Greg," Bob replied.

"Well, Josh delivered a Pirates smash of his own, with some extra hot sauce on it, I suspect, did ole Green!"

"I guess we got our answer, eh Greg?"

"What's that, Bob?"

"Whether or not Josh Green is back!" replied Bob.

"Oh! He's back, all right, folks!" Greg said emphatically, "And maybe, just maybe, this is the spark we need to light a fire under the Pirates and get this team back in gear and on track for the playoffs!"

The two Pirates in front of Josh high-fived him as he crossed home plate. His teammates were jubilant upon his return to the dugout. There was still the rest of the eighth and ninth innings to complete. The Pirates' top-of-the-order bats finally awoke and added two more runs before chasing the relief pitcher for the Rockies. Saul brought in another new reliever, Justus Barabbas, called up from the Minor Leagues after being sent down in Spring Training. He shut down the stunned Rockies for their final two at-bats, earning his third consecutive save, and the Pirates won the game 5-2. However, the most important outcome was the Pirates were once again in their comfort zone. Josh Green was back.

Eighty Four

The following day Josh returned to the starting lineup, and by the end of the four-game series, it was clear Josh was indeed back. The Pirate slugger went seven for fourteen with a single home run in each game, good for either a go-ahead or game-winning RBI. Every time the Rockies thought they might have Josh's number and got him to hit into an out, he seemed to come back and hurt them with a timely hit. The last game was typical as they started walking him after his first-inning home run to start the game. After an intentional walk in the fifth, Josh stole second, and for the fourth time this season, Judah doubled to plate Josh after his intentional walk and steal, putting the Bucs back on top 3-2. Josh eyed Judah after crossing home plate, giving his teammate a thumbs up, and Judah responded in kind.

The next at-bat, in the seventh, they pitched to Josh, and he struck out on a good slider from the pitcher. The Rockies then scored two off the Pirates and threatened to win the final series game, but in the top of the ninth, the Pirates put two aboard, with a pinch hitter on second and Zach on first base. With the strikeout fresh in their minds, the Rockies decided to pitch to Josh rather than face Juan, who swung a suddenly hot bat again, hitting a torrid 7 for 12 in the series. With the count 1-0 to Josh, Coach Samuelson put the hit and run on, and the gamble paid off as Josh reached out and slapped a similar slider to the one that struck him out to the opposite field wall. Fast-running Zach scored easily from first to put the Bucs back up by a run.

In the bottom of the ninth, Pops brought in their new reliever, Justus Barabbas, who was becoming the Pirates closer, saving 4 of 5 opportunities since his call-up. He quickly got the first two batters to ground out. The one question mark for opponents, and perhaps the Pirates, might still be the health of Josh's throwing arm since his injury. They soon received their answer.

"The Pirates look to close out a sweep of the Rockies here in Denver with two outs in the ninth and a one-run lead," Bob observed on the Pirates radio network.

"The Rockies are down to their last out. Let's see if our Buccos can close it out and move on to LA!" said Greg cheerily.

"Barabbas gets the sign from Thomas, and here's the delivery," stated Bob.

"Crack!"

"There's a drive to deep right field!" shouted Bob, concerned, as Josh hustled toward the wall in right-center. The ball carried high into the thin Colorado air. "Green's back to the wall and!..., it careens off the screen just above Green's glove! Green's after it! The runner's rounding second! Josh picks the ball up just inside the warning track and throws towards third..., He GOT HIM!" shouted Bob into the mike. "WHAT - A - THROW!" Bob gushed with enthusiastic slow emphasis. "That ball seemed to hang up forever, allowing the runner to almost be at second when it hit the wall. It hit a few feet above Green's jumping attempt to catch it and careened at an angle off the screen above the 375-foot sign. The runner could've held with an easy standup double, but it seemed he could make third easily as the ball rolled to Green's right. Green got after it, picked it up bare-handed, and threw all in one motion. It was a perfect strike in the air straight into the waiting glove of Fisher at third, and the runner was diving right into that glove as he caught it. The only question was would he hang on? He did! WOW!"

"Wow's an understatement, Bob! Good Golly, Miss Molly! Green's throw had to be seen to be believed, folks. I thought there was no way he catches the fleet-footed Rockies lead-off man as it would take a perfect pick-up and throw even to be close, but that's exactly what we got!" gushed an enthusiastic Greg. "That was almost as amazing as Green's throw against Ittai Gittite early in the season!"

"The Pirates are scampering off the field after completing a series sweep for the first time in over a month. They're high-fiving all the way to the dugout while the Rockies are still trying to figure out what happened these last four nights!" stated Bob.

"I'll tell you what happened, Bob. The 'Old Rookie' is back with a vengeance, and you can put away questions about the health of his arm after that throw! He threw a dime, and the Rockies may find their pockets emptied of all their loose change!"

"Greg, aren't you mixing sports metaphors there? Dropping a dime, picking pockets?" asked Bob.

"Don't get technical on me, Bob. I'm on a roll—and so, fans, are your Pittsburgh Pirates! Four wins and their lead in the NL Central is back to five games. Now on to the West Coast, where they take on those Cali crazies who happen to be one and two in the NL West. We will see you tomorrow night in the City by the Bay."

Eighty Five

The Pirate locker room was jubilant and lighthearted again for the first time in a month, and it felt as if the Pirates were back, moving in the right direction. Pops directed Mark Johnson to constrain Josh's press time, and the reporters started with mostly "How are you feeling?" questions. However, Roman Josephus intended to go deep.

Roman listened, testing his limited patience as the rest of the press corps gushed their usual trope when things were going well for a player and team. He almost sneered as he thought of how common and predictable they were. This wasn't reporting, Roman silently scoffed. This was a coronation, kid's gloves on a player supposedly coming off hard times from an injury to a decent four-game stint. "Where were their journalistic guts?" thought Roman derisively. Where was their resolve in asking the tough questions, in digging deep? Were these journalists or court jesters playing to their prince on a pedestal? He waited for his opportunity to show the world what real investigative reporting was all about. And he was sure the world would not forget him.

"Josh, you had a long layoff while recuperating from your injury," started a reporter from the local sports channel, "How did you manage to come back at the same level you left before the break?"

"I had a lot of help while I was recovering. The team and doctors came up with a good plan to work me back in as my body healed, and of course, my family helped a lot, too," Josh replied.

Finally, Roman saw his chance. "Josh, by family, you mean your daughter and your nanny, Mary?"

Josh looked at Roman somberly as if he knew what lay ahead. That look and the pause Josh gave Roman made Roman hesitate, but he was committed to his path, regardless of what Josh said.

"Roman, I am fortunate to call many good people part of my extended family, both in Pittsburgh and beyond. My brothers and sisters helped me throughout my life in many difficult situations. But yes, my most immediate family, with me through my healing, are my daughter Ruth and our nanny, Mary. Ruth and I have been through a lot over the years, and Mary has been a great help to us both since we joined the Pirates this spring."

"Ruth and Mary have been with you every step of the way, through your recovery?" led Roman on, "How were they able to help?" he questioned.

"Well, believe it or not, things get more complicated one-handed when your arm's in a sling. Ruth and Mary made up for that and helped me adjust while my body healed."

"With Ruth's medical issues and your injury, was Mary able to help at the Green home to get you both through this?" again Roman pressed, and the rest of the press corps wondered where he was going.

"Mary's been a great help for us since she moved in with us and became our nanny at the beginning of the season, yes, Roman," Josh said and again waited for Roman to make his move.

"Does Mary have any specialized medical training, Josh, for taking care of Ruth or you?"

"Mary's trained as an educator and working with children with special needs, Roman, but not specialized medical training. The Pirates provided us with Mary as a wonderful nanny to Ruth and access to medical professionals both in Pittsburgh and on the road. Many specialists oversaw my rehab."

"But Mary lives with you and cares for you and Ruth."

"She's our nanny, yes. Mary's become part of our family. We are fortunate to have her as Ruth's nanny."

Mark Johnson listened to the various interviews around the locker room but paid closer attention to Josh's cluster as it was often the largest group. Coach Samuelson talked with him about Josh and Mary's concern after Roman's strong-arm attempt with Mary a few weeks ago. Mark started to work his way around in front of the press, but the packed locker room slowed him, and Roman continued unabated.

"Josh, we know you've put your Christian values front and center since you began playing in the pros. You've made it a point, saying it's your 'foundation.' But I think our listeners and your fans deserve to know more of your life's details as you have made this Christian stance a priority on display for all to see."

"What do you want to know, Roman?" Josh replied as if he knew what was coming but showed no fear. Roman wondered if Josh was the fool he took him for but was concerned it might be something else. Still, he pressed on.

"Well, Josh, Mary has quite an interesting past, doesn't she? I mean, I've been told she has some pretty shocking police records indicating she was quite a troubled youth, including arrests for petty drug possession and even charges of prostitution. Yet you brought her into your house to be a nanny for your child, Josh?" As Roman dropped his bombshell, the press corps leaned forward, and the side conversations ceased. Whatever they were, Roman knew, these reporters were like sharks in the ocean, docile until there was blood in the water, and then they couldn't help but strike and feed. It was in their base nature, and Roman smiled on the inside as he delivered the cutting blow.

Meanwhile, Mark Johnson's heart sank as he felt he left Roman attack Josh. Mark wanted to move to intercept the damage, but he looked at Josh, who seemed calm in the storm. All waited as he stated his reply.

"You're right, Roman. I am a Christian, first and foremost. Christ is my core foundation. That is because I am imperfect, and only through Christ am I redeemed to start and live a new life on the path He set for me. In that way, we are all equal, for all have sinned. Mary is dear to our family because we have met her, a young lady whose tough childhood was filled with hardship most of us can't imagine. There came a time in Mary's life when she realized she was lost and needed a Savior. Though Mary's life started with tragedy and heartbreak, like many before her, Mary finally met the One who loves unconditionally, despite her mistakes. You see, Roman, Mary met Christ. The person you describe was the person Mary was before meeting Christ. Mary gave her life to Jesus, and He, in return, gave her a new life."

"So, you're saying, even knowing her very unchristian-like life growing up, you forgave and forgot her past? What about your daughter Ruth, Josh? What does she say about this woman raising and caring for her? Does she know of her past and what she did?"

"Roman, I believe God through Christ can and does change people. Mary shows us daily that she is a new person, able to take care of us. She does a wonderful job helping me care for and raise Ruth," Josh said without hesitation.

"So, you tell your fans, as a Christian, you hold nothing against Mary? You let her care for your daughter and be an example to her?" Roman continued, waiting with his last malicious fact to drive home.

"Ruth and I both see Mary as the life changed by Christ, and we see her devotion to us and the Lord daily. If anything, Mary is an example to everyone of what Christ can do for each of us."

"Josh, how can Mary be an example to and care for your daughter when she, as a young woman, chose to have an abortion instead of giving birth to her child? Isn't that the ultimate sin for a Christian woman? How can God forgive that? How do you justify your position as a Christian letting this woman live with you and raise your daughter?" Roman twisted the knife as fully as it would go and waited for the sharks to feast.

Instead of anger, Josh returned Roman's triumphal stare with one of sadness, not for himself, but for Roman's hard heart and the damage Roman did to Mary to get his scoop. Josh responded with grace and compassion for Mary and all women and families who suffer from past choices and the loss of a child, never replaced.

"Roman," Josh said with clear discernment, "You try to disparage my family and friends, but what you fail to understand is we choose Christ as Savior and become Christians because we know we are not perfect, not even close. We are redeemed. Mary is our nanny. We have complete faith and confidence in her because she proves herself every day. Long before she met us, after terrible loss from what the world did to her and because of her choices, she held no hope. Death awaited her, but someone far greater, the only One to champion over death, Christ, awaited her as well. Mary chose Christ. Jesus saved her, and He has done so much more for Mary. He's given her new life with a new purpose, and He's forgiven her for all her sins. No matter what you have done, Christ will forgive you if you turn to Him and confess, as He forgives us. Though heaven awaits us, the ramifications of our sins on earth often seem too deep for us to scale and overcome. God doesn't always change our circumstances, but Jesus always delivers us through the problems created by our sinful failings. He always makes a way. Then He walks that way with us. He goes before us and never leaves us. When we are too weak, too brokenhearted to carry on, He carries us onward. He loves us when no one else does. Even when we can't love ourselves, He does. He calls us worthy. He claims us and loves us as His own."

"Together, Ruth, Mary, and I are a family of redeemed Christians, as are all my Christian brothers and sisters. They are my true and everlasting family. With God's help, they continue to help me move forward in my walk with Christ. You must understand, Roman, Christ came not to make bad people good, but dead men, alive." Many reporters who looked on seemed to stop taking notes and listened now with intently puzzled looks.

"I'm alive in Christ, with new life granted by a God who knows all things, forgives even our worst sins through Jesus's sacrifice, and makes all our lives new and worth living," Josh continued. "I can think of no better example of what Christ does for any who accept Him, than Mary. Such is the offer of new life Christ makes to all. No matter what you have done or how far gone you think you are, Christ is ready to meet you in the depths of despair and sin. You, too, can choose Christ—just like Mary. There is nothing you can do that would separate you from the love and forgiveness of Christ.[1] I hope all who hear about our lives and what Christ did for us would turn, believe in Christ, and be saved."

Roman looked confused and wrinkled his brow as Josh spoke. He expected Josh to be wounded and defensive. He expected Josh to be surprised at least,

---

1. Romans 8:35-39

maybe even to deny or deflect. Yet Josh answered as if he knew all Roman said and still held to his so-called Christian values, defending his nanny and beliefs. How was this possible?

The press corps around Roman was silent, without further questions. More surprising for Roman, he could not think of a follow-up to strike down Josh's words. He tried but failed to think of any avenue of attack to catch Josh in a contradiction of his Christian beliefs. It was infuriating. Roman dropped his costly and deviously acquired bombshell, but like the others, Roman could find no way to exploit Josh's life or use his words against him. Unable to trap Josh in what he said in public and astonished by his answer, they all became silent, for they could find no fault with either his actions or his beliefs stated and lived so clearly.[2]

Mark moved to intercept the press questions on Josh's behalf but slowed as Josh proved again, he was more than their match, undamaged and undeterred despite the attack waged against him. When Mark reached the front, Josh already laid bare their threats, and their silence showed Roman's attack shallow and empty, ending with his defeat.

"Is that all? Is there nothing else you want to fire at Josh?" Mark asked with a wry note of condemnation evident in his tone. He paused for effect as he looked across the twenty or so reporters. Those closest in motivation to Roman looked to scurry away lest they, too, be shown feeble in their queries.

Finally, Mark spoke to the suddenly quiet group. "No? Well then, that will be all tonight, folks. We'll see you in California."

---

2. Luke 20:26

Eighty Six

Though the trip to California from Denver was short, it was long as far as the news cycle was concerned. The taped press conference, carefully edited and cut before reaching the airways, limited Josh's explanation and remarks. Roman demanded the last word, as he always did, preparing an overview of his evidence against Mary ahead of time. SPNN played his investigative background clip covering Mary's juvenile record and her Planned Parenthood abortion without giving away his sources. Roman skillfully avoided the nature of the documents to avoid legal questions he didn't want to answer.

Roman downplayed or ignored Mary's life since turning to Christ. His clip insinuated Josh's complicity in employing Mary, despite her juvenile record, exposing Mary's living arrangement with the Greens and questioning Josh's Christian values. It seemed to those who watched Roman's video or read his accompanying print article, complete with Mary's mug shot, that Josh essentially employed and lived with a young woman of ill repute. Though parts of Josh's response made the news, few broadcasts showed his complete statements. Most downplayed or ignored entirely, Mary's credentials for teaching and other evidence pertinent to her qualities as both a licensed teacher and caregiver in Pennsylvania.

The Pirates, as an organization and with Mary's consent, responded with a statement trying to counter Roman's account. Though it proved her qualifications and stellar recommendations from multiple sources, many drew their conclusions based on Roman's carefully crafted version, picked up by most news agencies. Several op-eds followed, most painting Josh in a harmful light. They reignited and reinvigorated calls against the Pirates, with Josh as the focus, judging based on a cursory review of the facts.

As a result, when the Pirates arrived at Oracle Park for their evening start against the San Francisco Giants, they faced an energized crowd inside and outside the stadium. Largely negative views permeated the crowd's attitude after Roman's investigative report hit the country overnight and during the day leading up to the game. The Pirates faced many of the same protesters that plagued their appearances but with new enthusiasm fueled by Josh's implied duplicity. Adding to the protests with racial and bigotry causes, people now held anti-Christian signs, many showing pictures of Josh and Mary with the word "Hypocrite." Even the pro-abortion lobby took Josh's words, or at least those cut onto Roman's report, as a condemnation against Mary's abortion and opposed Josh with pro-abortion and women's choice slogans. Many of these new protesters gained airtime with interviews discussing how Josh tried to convict Mary of sin, condemning Josh as a typical pro-lifer trying to shame women and deny their personal choice.

The Pirates, to their credit, pressed on. As the boos and chants of the crowd turned more accusatory, the Pirates took their customary stance of respect to the national anthem and kneeled as a team to pray. In the first game, Josh saw only one pitch to hit. It came during his first at-bat in the first inning, which he promptly drove into the deep corner of Oracle Park's uneven right-center-field wall. His line drive hit the wall wildly, careening back towards the right field line, allowing Josh to make it to third with an easy standup triple. Juan then singled to drive Josh in for a 1-0 lead. It was the last hittable pitch Josh would see for the game as the Giants walked him the next three at-bats. The game became a pitching duel as Samson and the Giant's ace traded great pitching until the eighth inning when the Giants put two aboard with no outs and the score still 1-0. The Pirates sent Jude Keriothson, the lefty, to the mound, who walked one in a shaky start but then got an infield pop-up followed by an inning-ending double play. In the ninth, Pops went with Justice Barabbas, who pitched a 1-2-3 inning, including a final decisive strike out against the Giants cleanup hitter, sealing the 1-0 victory.

The first game turned out to be the only close game in the first three as the Pirates beat the Giants handily in the next two games, 9-4 and 12-2. The crowd seemed to gain antipathy and ire against the Pirates as they won, but the Pirates followed Josh's lead, staying quiet off the field but loud on it. Josh's teammates seemed to play with a renewed sense of purpose, hitting as a team like the Pirate lumberyard of old. The Giants tried to pitch around Josh for the most part as he was walked ten times in the four games, eight intentionally, but he still went 5 for 9. The fourth and final game was close, and just when it looked like the Giants might win the finale, Josh hammered a low outside fastball with two on in the seventh to put the Pirates back on top with his only home run of the series. All of San Francisco seemed to moan in response, booing yet not deterring the Pirates as they swept the Giants for four straight and moved on to the National League West leading Los Angeles Dodgers.

The Dodgers series was another four more games against a west coast powerhouse who fared no better, cementing the Pirates' status as the class of the National League. They narrowly lost the first game to a late-inning loss charged to the starting pitcher but given up during relief work by Jude Keriothson, who came in with the bases loaded, giving up a sacrifice fly for what turned out to be the game-winner. Josh never got a chance to bat again, and the Dodgers held on for a victory. However, it was a false hope for Dodger fans as Samson started the second game, and the Pirates won the final three games in stellar fashion. The Dodgers pitched sparingly to Josh, trying to curb his impact, but he again wreaked havoc on the base pads going three for three in stolen bases. Josh led the League in walks by a country mile and crested an incredible .496 Batting Average for the season. Despite his 30 days off during rehab, Josh led the League in home runs, hitting one each in the final three games in LA, including a monster grand slam in the third inning of the finale, breaking the Dodgers' backs and leading to a laughable 15-2 victory. The crowd turned decidedly ugly in the game, chanting all kinds of insults as the Pirates seemed unable to do wrong as even their starting pitcher wound up with a hit tallying his first two RBIs of the season.

While the rest of the country pondered the meaning of Josh's unprecedented prowess, Pittsburgh celebrated their first genuine contender for a baseball championship in half a century. Most Pirate fans waited expectantly for Josh and the Pirates to return to make the final run for the pennant. For now, they were willing to overlook their hometown son's controversial stance and positions, clamoring for Josh to lead them out of the wilderness of mediocrity, back to the promised land of the playoffs and the World Series.

Eighty Seven

Nurse Linda Richards smiled as she looked up at Dr. Thyatira entering with the two delivered meals. The two old friends tried to eat together once a week. It was a ritual that served them for nearly twenty years, as each enjoyed the other's company and found there were things both women could tell each other, professionally and personally, they would say to no one else. Their private meals were often lighthearted releases, with shared experiences in the high-stress, fast-paced life of a major metropolitan trauma center. Often, they benefited from deeper discussions of two women navigating a complex world with a similar foundation. They came from very different backgrounds, yet each became Christians as young adults and used each other as sounding boards for problems discussed only between themselves and God. The ladies often began the meals with a prayer to help them overcome all challenges with God's grace and wisdom. These weekly meals became an oasis of calm and strength for an otherwise hectic and challenging occupation.

It was Lydia's turn to pick a cuisine, and although she didn't always go to her Greek roots for the menu, Linda didn't mind when she did. Even in St. Louis, the small Greek community kept several hidden gems of culinary delight.

"This Moussaka is incredible, Lydia!" remarked Linda as she relished the brilliant flavor and spices.

"I know, isn't it," Lydia said, wrinkling her nose. Linda looked surprised. "I hate to say it, Linda, but I always thought my version of Giagia Aneka's besamel sauce was the best, but this chef puts something in it that makes it..." she trailed off, not wanting to admit what was coming.

"Better?" whispered Linda leaning forward.

Lydia nodded, eyes closed as she took another bite and savored the taste. "And what's worse, it's made by a second-generation upstart child of an old Greek friend of mine who took over the family restaurant I've gone to ever since moving to St. Louis," Lydia replied emphatically.

"So, what's the problem?" questioned Linda.

"Unlike his father, who would tell me everything, 'Paidi mou' will not give me the recipe!" said an exasperated Lydia as she threw her fork down onto her plate in false anger, looking longingly at the delicious food. She finally looked up at Linda, who paused with a piece of Moussaka frozen midway to her mouth. Both women stared at it for a moment and simultaneously burst out laughing.

"It sure is good, though!" said Linda, finally bringing the bite to her mouth.

"So good!" said Lydia with a half-crying smile as she quickly recovered her fork and continued eating her piece, closing her eyes, sighing over its deliciousness.

The ladies could show such emotion easily to each other they often hid from their colleagues, due to their professional demands, and because this job often required potential life and death decisions. Refraining from showing emotions in public was a natural reflex of self-protection. They portrayed a peaceful calm to support and protect the emotions of both their patients and junior colleagues. Here, however, they were in a circle of sisterhood and trust that served them well through the highs and lows of critical care.

"So how goes it this week in the children's ward," Linda asked her dear friend.

"Oh, Linda, we've had a rough week. I have two recent patients admitted with late-term cancers. Different stories to how they got here, but they both seem headed to a rough end." She laid her fork down lightly and quietly this time, as her concern suspended her appetite despite the marvelous flavors.

"I guess it's been a while since we lost someone. Tough to get two difficult cases. But that means we kept quite a good streak going until now," commented Linda trying to encourage her friend.

"I know, I know. It's been quite a summer. With so many youngsters in the spring, even I was feeling a little overwhelmed," thought Lydia out loud, and Linda nodded, nibbling at a grape roll.

"Yes, it was a tough spring, wasn't it?" she remembered, "But look, it turned around in a hurry this summer. No deaths at all, and most of your patients have walked out of here cured!" she said happily trying to will her friend back to good spirits.

"You're right, of course," said the Greek doctor with some pep back in her comment. She picked up one of the dolmades and dipped it in tzatziki sauce. "Our Reuben said the other day, it's because of baseball season. Everyone does better when the Cardinals play baseball."

At that, Linda raised an eyebrow. "Reuben always was a die-hard Cardinal fan," she commented, smiling as she picked at the salad that came with the meal.

"I know. He was exasperated when I replied, 'Well, it must be that Josh Green who visited because I hear his Pirates are still out in front of your Red Birds. How many games is it now?'"

"Oh, that must have hurt!" smiled Linda.

Lydia nodded, "Only a little, I think. Today he was helping me with one of these two kids I mentioned, a precious little girl that reminded us of Tyre. After we left the room, Reuben said to me, 'I tell you, Doc, I would take a Josh Green return right now if it meant another miracle for her like Tyre.' I nodded in agreement. After all these years and medical advances, it still hurts when you see someone you know you probably can't save."

"God sees it too, my friend. He knows," said Linda.

Lydia smiled and sat back, sipping her coffee. "How is our Mr. Green anyway? What's the latest?"

Linda perked up. "Actually, Dr. Melnick out in San Francisco left a message for me to call him back. The Greens were there last week at the start of their stay in California. I was going to call Dr. Melnick back after lunch," Linda said, looking at her phone messages.

"Why wait? Let's call Zachary. I haven't seen him since last year's symposium. Maybe it's good news. I could use some right now," said Lydia.

"OK, I'll put him on speaker. We can both catch up." Linda hit a button on her desk phone, and looking at her contacts on her cell, she dialed the number. He picked up almost immediately.

"Dr. Melnick," answered the voice.

"Dr. Melnick. It's Linda Richards. I am here with Dr. Thyatira in St. Louis. I am returning your call."

"Well, hello ladies. So good to hear from you, Linda. And glad to have Lydia join us. It's been too long."

"I am glad you remembered me from the symposium last year."

"I can't forget your brief on operations there in St. Louis. You gave us plenty to chew on with your holistic approach to your patient's needs."

"You're too kind, Zach, and your research certainly helps many of our patients," replied Lydia.

"Thank you. Coming from you means a lot, Lydia. I am glad you are both on the line. I wanted to thank Linda for setting up the meeting with Mr. Green when he arrived with his daughter for her treatment."

"To be honest, Dr. Melnick, that's all Josh Green. He's been supporting visits wherever the team goes," replied Linda.

"That's wonderful because I tell you, with our busy schedule, I almost missed the opportunity, and I am glad I did not," he replied, a note of excitement in his voice. Both women sensed there was something more.

"Oh?" said Linda questioningly.

"Yes, Josh was nothing short of a miracle worker. I met him and his daughter. Ruth was great, and she happily went off to her treatment while I took Josh around our children's ward, as you suggested, Linda. The kids absolutely adored him. What an impact he made. He was patient and graceful with the children and the parents he met. It was quite amazing. I think I kept him going for nearly two hours. So much so, his daughter and their nanny finished her treatments long before, and he finally stopped so they could get to the ballpark," Dr. Melnick tailed off at the end as if there was something more. Again, both ladies seemed to sense it.

There was an awkward moment of silence, and Lydia chimed in, hoping to reassure her colleague over the phone. "Zach, we are so glad the visit went well. To tell the truth, your story is not unique. We saw the same great response when Josh was with us earlier in the year. The kids light up around him, and the parents seemed to find so much solace in his kind words of understanding."

"Yes, yes. Josh is quite special in that way...," said Zach, still hesitant.

"There is something else, Doctor?" Linda asked encouragingly.

"Well, I hesitate to say this, but the reason I called, what I wanted to say...." Finally, he hurried on. "Look, Dr. Thyatira, I remember you showed how your hospital incorporated a holistic view of treating your patients in your presentation. I was very intrigued, but as a thirty-year-plus veteran and researcher, I am also a healthy skeptic. I must be. With my studies, we want to recommend and promote only treatments that show true promise. In a way, I almost missed out on the goodness of Mr. Green's visiting our patients, or should I say, *they* almost missed out." The two women could tell the Doctor was not finished.

"Yes?" asked Lydia.

"I may as well say this before you think I am just a California crazy, which I am *not,* by the way!" the doctor said emphatically. "In thirty years of practice, I've seen some patients and treatments that seem to defy the odds, but I also wrote them off as the 1 in a 100 that got better and were healed when many others weren't. But as of today, Josh Green is the first to leave me truly dumbfounded."

"What makes you say that, Zach," Lydia said, leaning forward as both women were now very attentive.

"At the end of the visit, I almost skipped our last two patient rooms. We have a section for our terminally ill. Frankly, I am a realist, and their diagnosis was clear. I knew one would be gone in a few days and the other..., I did not expect them to live through the night."

"What happened?" asked Linda, hands now on her desk, leaning towards the phone as both ladies forgot their food, with the memory of Tyre foremost in their minds.

"That's the thing. Both patients, kids I believed, did not even have the 1 in a 100 chance, defied all odds, and did a total 180 after Josh Green prayed over them."

"What kind of 180 do you mean, Zach?" Lydia could barely ask.

"Lydia, the one I thought at most had a few days, walked out of here this morning, and the other who was at the end of life, comatose and on a DNR with a priest already giving last rites, is now sitting up, smiling and eating ice cream this morning. I just got the third repeat test back from the lab. I don't know how to say this other than her cancer screen is completely negative. All her organs, which previously shut down, are all back to normal range and function," the doctor said haltingly. Composing himself, Zachary continued, "She appears completely healed. I can't explain it. Each case is impossible by itself, but together...," he trailed off again.

"It's a miracle," said Linda in a quiet voice, looking across her desk at Lydia, who nodded. They both became silent, staring at each other equally dumbfounded.

Over the phone, the ladies could almost hear the doctor nodding in agreement. Finally, Dr. Melnick continued, "Believe me, I am more than reluctant to say it, but yes, I can only describe it as a miracle." After a moment of contemplative silence, he followed. "You know, I got into this business partly because I lost a dear friend after a terrible bout with cancer when I was young. I think I stopped believing in God because I convinced myself no good God, no supreme being, who claims to be the standard of good, would let something like that happen, especially to an innocent child. I wanted to be a doctor to find the cure and save everyone," Dr. Melnick said almost sheepishly. "I know, after thirty-plus years, it sounds even more cliché, but it was true for me. I specialized in pediatric cancer to save children going through cancer and the pain it causes to their family and friends. Despite all my efforts, I still don't win all the fights. Sometimes, we struggle, and in some cases, we fail. This week, I was convinced I knew the answer for these two young people, and the answer was without hope. I could do nothing but watch with the families, watch my failure in many ways—and I tell you, deep down inside, it hurts like it did when I lost my friend. But here, after all hope was lost, after nothing but a supernatural occurrence could change the outcome, along comes Josh Green. Ladies, Josh has this hope in his eyes, this faith...." Zachary paused as if remembering, then continued. "Josh comes in and prays to the God I didn't believe existed." Dr. Melnick's voice wavered as he fought for composure. Softly he said, "I don't know exactly what happened, but I know I can't explain it. It was nothing we humans did, that's for sure."

Dr. Melnick hurried on, "Look, it may seem silly, and I don't know what you think of me now, but this is a new day for me. My wife asked me for 25 years to go with her to church, and I always refused. When pressed, I told her I couldn't accept a God who lets kids die like this, even if I believe. Somehow, now that seems wrongheaded. I think it wasn't that I didn't believe in God. I've been angry with him all these years for letting my friend die. But now I must wonder. Maybe God offers us something even when death is all around. I'm not sure," he said honestly. "Still, I have decided to go to church with my wife this weekend for the first time since we got married. This I know; I don't have all the answers. Last week,

Josh Green showed me maybe the answers are there. Maybe there is something more, something I missed. I watched Josh, even before we came to those last two patients, how he helped everyone he met and knew just what they needed. But two kids living and breathing today when all my training and experience said they wouldn't survive? That erased any doubt, and now I want to find out who God is and what He's been waiting to show me all these years."

The line was quiet for what seemed a long time. Finally, Linda spoke.

"Dr. Melnick. I think I speak for Dr. Thyatira when I say we don't think you're crazy at all. Now that we hear your story, it sounds remarkably like one of our patients who met the Greens here in St. Louis. I think we both wrote it off as a one-of-a-kind miracle when it happened...," Linda trailed off as Lydia stepped in.

"But we were just discussing today," Lydia continued, "How the entire ward Josh visited seemed to respond in a similar, if not as immediately obvious, way. It's been two months since Josh Green's visit, and our patients who were there," Dr. Thyatira shrugged her shoulders, and Linda nodded, "Well, they all seem healed, one way or another, as my ward now only has new patients who came to us after Mr. Green's visit."

The other side of the line was silent as both women looked at each other, more than a little shocked at what they began to consider, as unbelievable as it sounded. Dr. Melnick broke the silence. "I don't know what another reasonable explanation is. I will keep track of all the patients Josh visited while he was here. I don't know if he visits all the towns the team plays, but I'll tell you this. I hope he comes back to San Francisco before the season closes out. I, for one, would love to have him visit us all again!" The three agreed to keep in touch, then said their goodbyes, and Dr. Melnick hung up.

"What do you think?" Linda asked Lydia.

"I have known Zachary Melnick by reputation for nearly his entire career, which is almost as long as mine," she said smiling. "He's always been a good doctor, driven but caring. Slightly arrogant, but as you know, that's not a bad thing. It's something you want in your corner if you're a patient—his confidence he can and will do everything on earth to help you. He is one of the few I've met who doesn't allow his arrogance to get out of control. He always remained open-minded to new ways of fighting cancer, which allowed him to try new things, yet critical minded to back away from other treatments if they proved inadequate. I guess I am saying he is a brilliant thinker of medicine. But he strikes me as a person who has come to find; if there is a God, he is not it. Perhaps that's one thing we, who see life and death daily, must comprehend from our failures and lost battles. He's certainly not one to exaggerate. I think he saw something he knows he can't explain, and in fact, it is contrary to all his not insubstantial experience. I must be honest. I think I saw the same thing with Tyre."

Linda nodded at her friend and lamented, "Why didn't we realize it when it happened?"

Lydia sat back and smiled now, thinking out loud. "You remember the story in the Bible in Acts when the people gathered together praying for Peter, who was in jail."

Linda nodded and said, "The Angel of the Lord came and escorted Peter out of the prison. When he came to the home where the church was praying, they didn't believe he was really at the door, set free."

Lydia responded, "Yep. Here they were, praying for a miracle, and when it came, they almost missed it!"

Linda dwelled on that for a moment, hands folded, then said, "You think we witnessed a miracle?"

"My friend, with what Dr. Melnick told us, it may be more than one." She said, picking up her coffee and taking a sip; then she stopped suddenly and set her coffee down. "How much feedback did you receive from the other cities where you booked visits for Josh and Ruth?"

"They all were very positive, saying Josh's visit went well and was a big hit with all their patients, but I didn't get much into details. Several did ask specifically if Josh can stop back when the Pirates come around again...." Linda paused, considering. "Wait! You don't think they might be more than just hospital staff hoping to have a star athlete encourage their patients, do you?" Linda scrunched her eyes at her old colleague, trying to grasp what Lydia suggested.

"My friend, you might want to dig a little deeper into *all* Josh's hospital visits. You and I might have Peter, or maybe even someone else, someone greater, whose knocking at our door, an answer to many prayers, waiting to come in."

Linda raised her eyebrows at that thought as she sat up. "I think I need to make some calls!"

"That sounds like a wise thing to do." The two women stood, and the small Greek woman gave her American friend a firm hug. "I am so blessed to be here with my good friend doing what I do. If Josh did anything, he's reminded us, we are not alone, and God's never surprised. His plan is moving forward, and He always has the whole world in His hands, no matter what a mess we see each day or make of it ourselves."

"I completely agree. Sometimes I start to forget it, but I know you will always help me remember," Linda replied.

"Oh, my friend," Lydia said as she walked towards the door, "It's always and ever the Lord who gently yet urgently reminds us all, Jesus is the same yesterday, today, and forever. We now see again, with God, all things are possible!" She smiled as she closed the door behind her, and Linda paused before starting her inquiries. She prayed, thanking God for her dearest friend and His blessed son Jesus, who conquers even death.

Eighty Eight

After winning 11 of 12 on their road trip, the Pirates returned to Pittsburgh 96-34, holding a nine game lead in the National League Central. With just over a month left, the Pirates looked to top 100 wins in a season for the first time in over a century. Even the 1906 Cubs and 2001 Mariners shared MLB record of 116 wins seemed within reach as the Pirates now needed to win 21 games out of their remaining 32 to break the record.

Still, Pops worried. He didn't know why, as the team's road trip cemented the fact, with Josh back in the lineup, the team once again fired on all cylinders. The Pirates were blowing away the competition as they made the two west coast National League powerhouse teams look like AAA farm clubs. Pops sat in the front of the team plane as Old Pete snored softly beside him. After their final game in LA, the rest of the team relaxed on the late flight home, following Pete's lead. To his left, a few seats in front, Josh was in an aisle seat with his daughter sleeping across his lap. Mary was in the front row, one of the few women on the plane. Next to her, Martha, their PR intern, was on a headset, listening to something Pops was sure he wouldn't understand, busily typing away on her laptop. Mark Johnson sat across from her, also working feverishly on his computer. Those two seemed to be the only ones besides him still awake. Saul once again thanked the Lord for Mark and his unit. They were a good, albeit small, team of media people constantly working behind the scenes, trying to stay out in front of the Pirates' story and protect their image as best they could in today's fast-moving, high-stakes world of sports media.

Perhaps that was what concerned Pops the most on this late flight: The public's perception of the team. Saul wanted to believe you could, as the famous Raiders coach, Al Davis, used to say, "Just Win, Baby!" but Pops knew, probably just as Coach Davis did, public perception and winning didn't necessarily mean the same thing. The Pirates were winning on the field, but Saul worried the public's perception of the team, and all the whirlwind of emotions and publicity this year, threatened to undo the Pirates' stellar season. In the end, Coach Davis was as great a salesman for his team as a coach. In this business, for indeed it was a business, the public's impression was paramount. Saul Samuelson played to win, but the Pirates organization needed the team to produce a product the public would support with their dollars even more than their cheers.

Pops read one of the news rags that came out of Los Angeles. The west coast press always gave a different vibe than hometown news back east in small-market Pittsburgh. Even so, LA was probably second only to New York in influencing popular opinion and, in some ways, led the nation with its vast population and Hollywood status. The progressive newspapers and media were down on the Pirates all year, but with this trip, they reached a new and, if Pop was honest, truly ugly and angry low. He stopped reading the article on the bottom front page of the LA newspaper, disparaging the Pirates with a veracity Pops could scarcely believe. It cited everything from the Pirates' standing for the National Anthem to their use of criminal employees with a barely veiled reference to Josh's nanny, Mary. This both angered Pops and broke his heart for the girl, one of the sweetest young people Pops met. Even Ms. Phoebe called Saul after the team arrived in LA, questioning what the Pirates were doing to protect Mary. Phoebe asked why her young friend, whom she cared for and worried over for the past decade, received such poor treatment. Saul assured Phoebe he and his team would protect Mary and fight back against the misleading and false press releases.

Still, Saul must admit, it was a David versus Goliath situation as the modern mass media, with hundreds if not thousands of people, bulldozed Saul's dedicated but small PR staff. Saul knew it mattered little to Roman and many of the news outlets who twisted the facts heard by the public, including Josh's convincing but virtually ignored and silenced rebuttal. The so-called "free press" were mainly of one accord and seized the chance to hammer Josh for his politically incorrect position, askance with public opinion. A dwindling number of people wanted to accept biblical truth and Christian morals, thought Saul, placing Josh and the Pirates squarely at odds with public sentiment and the humanist press agenda.

Besides the public and the press, Saul spent significant time defending the team to the owners' group and Cai Annason. Saul knew Cai was upset at his inability to mandate the team's actions. Cai feared what the League leadership might do if he could not bend the club to their desires. He knew they could threaten his position as the Pirates President. Saul almost felt sorry for Cai. Even so, Saul staunchly guarded the team and Josh's freedoms. The Pirates played their best baseball in decades, yet somehow Saul felt besieged on all sides. "What shall I do?" Saul almost wondered aloud as he turned off the light. Try as he might, sleep eluded Saul for the rest of the flight home as he could not kick the feeling. The Pirates were on top, but the position seemed precarious, with everyone gunning for them on and off the field.

Eighty Nine

The Pirates enjoyed a free day on the schedule, and Pops elected to give them a well-earned and much-needed day off. He addressed the team before they left the plane after landing at nearly 5:00 AM from their late flight. "Everyone did great this trip. Get some rest, spend time with your families and get away from the game for a day. I'll see you all at the park Saturday at 3:00 PM. Let's all get some rest and finish strong."

Pops owned a three-bedroom condo a few blocks from the river on Pittsburgh's south shore. It was unassuming and understated, like the man. He liked it because he could get up and walk a few blocks to the river. Saul took morning walks east along the three rivers heritage trail, giving a beautiful view of Pittsburgh Point and PNC Park, across the river to the north. Tired from the trip, he showered and went to bed but slept fitfully, finally giving up at 10:30 AM. He made his customary cup of coffee and was going to set out for a walk. It was a gray day outside, unusual for August in Pennsylvania. Cooler than normal, it looked and felt more like fall. He kept a few flowerpots on his front stoop that spilled plants onto his walkway, glowing with vibrant colors of life in the gray late morning overcast. Saul wondered how he managed not to kill them. They were a gift from Elizabeth, and he suspected she and Joe snuck over to water and care for them while he was away. He was tired and didn't feel like walking today anyway and, without much thought, felt the impulse to make a call.

Elizabeth answered the phone on the second ring. "Hello Saul, welcome home."

"How goes it, Miss Elizabeth? Just called to see how you all were doing and tell you my daisies are blooming beautifully."

"Those are New England Asters and Black-Eyed Susans, dear, and yes, they are beautiful. The Virginia Bluebells I planted out back near your lone tree are a little late, but they should bloom in a week or so. I am glad you are home now to enjoy them," Saul could hear her kind smile confirming she was his secret gardener. "How are you?"

"The team's great. They're playing better than ever. Can't complain," Saul said evasively.

"That's nice, but that's not what I asked." Miss Elizabeth had a way of seeing right through you. Saul could give no suitable answer, as he himself couldn't quite put the finger on his problem. Understanding Saul's silence better than he, she said, "Joe asked for some Kuhaona strudel with his coffee today, and I am about to take it out of the oven. I made it with some fresh granny smiths a neighbor brought back from a trip to New England. They are absolutely delicious. The figs are authentic too, carried home by our young missionary friend who flew back from the old country last weekend. Why don't you come over and make sure I didn't mess it up?"

"I'll be over in ten minutes," Saul said, relieved. He truly felt the need to be around some good friends today.

"Joe and I will be out back on the veranda, dear. Door's unlocked," She replied, and Saul could feel her kindness flowing through the phone.

Saul arrived minutes later and found the Arimas on the back porch. Elizabeth sipped a cup of tea, and Joe drank his customary coffee with cardamom and turmeric. However, the smell that dominated was fresh out of the oven strudel. Saul could smell the apples and cinnamon when he walked in, and the wonderfully complex aroma only increased as he neared his friends on the back porch. Elizabeth hugged him and offered a piece of the delectable treat, and he sat down in the chair prepared for him at a small patio table. "Just poured your coffee when I poured mine a minute ago," said Joe, handing him his mug in greeting.

Saul smiled but took a bite of the strudel first to savor the flavors unabated by the coffee.

"Oh my!" Saul said out loud, without thinking. Besides what he smelled, the figs gave a rich, creamy flavor, enhanced by the butter and offset by crushed walnuts, but something else was definitely going on. He raised his eyebrows at Elizabeth, and she laughed lightly, smiling over her teacup.

"It's the rum, eight tablespoons," she said. Saul looked alarmed. "Don't worry. The alcohol is all cooked off. Only the flavor remains."

"This isn't your Jewish Grandmother's strudel!" Saul replied, savoring another bite.

"Oh no, like I said on the phone, it's Kuhaona Strudel. It's our friend from Croatia, Karmela's recipe. She first sold me some in her shop in Shadyside years ago. She agreed to let me have the recipe in exchange for the hamantaschen cookie recipe. I gladly obliged—Safta was always willing to trade recipes with her friends. I may have even made out in the deal. This might actually rival my babka."

"No!" said Joe emphatically, almost as a reflex. Elizabeth looked surprised, "Nothing beats your babka." Then he thought about it as he took another bite and spoke between chews, looking longingly at his nearly empty plate, "But this is very good." He sat his plate down, picking up his Pirate mug, "It goes nice with coffee," he said, taking a sip. "Maybe Kuhaona strudel and Jewish Coffee at breakfast, and then your babka after evening meal. Now there's a menu to die for." Joe said as if tasting it all in his mind while watching the steam rise from his coffee.

"Yes, and that's exactly what the doctor said will happen if we keep eating all this rich food. We can only eat this way once or twice a month." Elizabeth reminded her husband more sternly than she meant.

Joe nodded and sighed, "I know, I know. When I get to Heaven, Isha Ahova, will you make it for me every day?" asked Joe, almost like he was still dating his wife of more than fifty years.

"If you wish, dear," Elizabeth said lovingly, "But not for some time yet, please?"

Saul sat and ate the rich pastry before starting his coffee. It took a few sips to overcome the sweetness of the treat, but he didn't mind. The three sat quietly, looking out onto the garden. It was just a plowed and barren yard when he came here in the spring and introduced Josh to Joe. Now it was peak season. The vegetables were almost out of control, with tomatoes, cucumbers, and colorful peppers of different varieties. On the side growing on trestles were three different types of beans, squash, and even a small pumpkin patch. Somehow, Joe, who picked what he did in the garden sparingly, once again got his strawberry patch to come in full. The strawberries were many, about a week from being ripe for picking. In addition to the vegetables, spectacular flowers of many types bloomed around the yard's edges and pathways. It was hard to believe they were in the city. Even with the large trees that lined the back alleyway and shaded about half the yard, it was an oasis of life, a glorious sight to behold.

"How do you do it, Miss Elizabeth?" Saul asked admiringly.

"Patience," she said, smiling, "And a lot of help from my kids." Elizabeth referred to the children's groups she and Joe sponsored for city kids during the week, treating her yard like a commune. The Arimas not only nurtured the children, they gave almost all the food away, canning what remained for use over the winter by them or one of the city's soup kitchens. Joe and Elizabeth made a jam from Joe's Strawberries and a long row of Blackberries growing along the brick wall separating their yard from the neighbors. It was legendary, and you were fortunate if you were one of the lucky few to find a jar in your Christmas stocking.

"Speaking of which," Joe added since he and Beth considered everyone their kids, "How goes it with Josh Green, Ruth, and Mary? He certainly looked good out west." Joe, like Beth, had a way of knowing when Saul needed to talk but didn't quite know where to start.

"His shoulder seems to have fully healed. He's playing great again. The entire team, really," Saul trailed off, the nagging unseen problem, like a buzzing insect just out of sight in his periphery, still bothering him.

"But?" Joe said, and Saul shrugged his shoulders. "Saul," Joe said, helping to ease Saul's concern, "You're here, hours after a red-eye flight, back from a successful but tough two weeks on the road. I know you, Saul. If things were going well, you'd be sleeping in and walking along the river, enjoying your day off with some peace and solitude," Joe deduced correctly.

"I guess you know me too well," Saul said, setting down his coffee.

"We love seeing you, dear, and you're welcome anytime, but when you called this morning, I could tell right away something was bothering you," encouraged Elizabeth.

Saul nodded. "I am not sure where to begin."

"Sometimes it helps to talk it out loud," counseled Joe.

"OK, here's the best I can explain it." Saul recounted the problems as he saw them. He described how the team came together, led by Josh's stellar play all season and his quiet leadership during and around the game. At the same time, the news seemed to swirl around them. The reporters kept getting more and more antagonistic. Simply standing for the truth, standing for the country, warts and all, somehow made the Pirates more and more outcasts. With Josh and the Pirates' stunning play and historic winning pace, they somehow became a magnet, drawing society's problems into their game. The more they tried to live what they believed, the more it seemed the world railed against them.

"The crazy thing is, we want to stand for what is good and right and turn to God as the answer to our problems, yet the world is fighting us as if we are the problem. I don't understand how baseball has become such a focal point for our society's ills. Why can't they just let our ballplayers play ball?"

Joe and Elizabeth sat and quietly listened as Saul enumerated all the ills and problems the Pirates faced, and his attempts to combat them. Saul had nothing but good things to say about his coaching staff and his small public relations team. "But to be totally honest, everyone else seems to be against us: the owner, the League leadership, the majority of the other teams. It's overwhelming. It's like we're fighting the world right now, not just trying to win baseball games. I know how to build a team and make them the best they can be, playing baseball. But this," Saul gestured, both hands in the air as if it was something he couldn't grasp. "This is something I don't know how to fight," Saul concluded, sitting back silent.

"Saul," said Joe, "It sounds like you have done everything humanly possible to protect your team and to fight back against the enemy," Joe said, sipping his coffee.

"And therein lies the problem," Elizabeth finished for Joe, who nodded.

"Exactly," Joe said, setting his cup down. He leaned back and reached for a leather-bound New International Version of the Bible sitting on the coffee table. It was a large print edition, well worn.

"What do you mean?" Saul asked, a little confused.

"You are such a wonderful coach, and so is your coaching staff," said Elizabeth. "You come up with a good plan, good programs to bring along your talent and make them the best they can be."

Joe nodded and continued, "You understand the game better than just about anyone I have ever known. Let's face it, Cai and his father-in-law before him didn't give you much leeway to get established talent. Yet you, in all these years, put together a team the Pirates and their fans could be proud of because you worked tirelessly to figure out every angle against your opponents and make all the moves available to field a competitive team. You may not have won a championship, but I can tell you other teams don't enjoy playing the Pirates. I know many of their coaches and quite a few owners by their first names. They know Saul Samuelson will give them everything they can handle and then some, whenever the Pirates come to town. As I told you over the years, more than one owner called me and asked if you were interested in moving to one of the big city teams."

"So why, now that the Pirates are winning, do I feel like we're under attack? Why, when we have the best team in the League, and no one can stand against us, do I feel like we're hemmed in on all sides?" Saul asked, bemused.

"Saul dear," said Elizabeth, "You are trying to solve this yourself like you're playing against another team. I can see the coach in you trying to figure out a way to beat them–Like you're facing the Cubs, the Dodgers, or even the Yankees. It's like you are trying to get ready to win the World Series, and you can't figure out why it's not working."

Joe continued in perfect harmony with his wife as if they knew each other's thoughts, "As I said, you have done everything humanly possible,'" Joe paused for effect. "But Saul, the fight you're fighting, the one you feel you're losing? It isn't against another team, at least not a human one. Not even the Yankees could fight you like this." Joe opened his Bible and handed it to Saul. "I know you know this, but I think you need to reread it. It's God's words coming from your namesake Saul. Remember? Remember what Saul, who became Paul, warned us against and what he told us to do? Would you read aloud Ephesians 6 versus 10-18?"

Saul took the book gently and read somewhat tentatively, "Finally, be strong in the Lord and in his mighty power. Put on the full armor of God, so that you can take your stand against the devil's schemes. For our struggle is not against flesh and blood, but against the rulers, against the authorities, against the powers of this dark world and against the spiritual forces of evil in the heavenly realms.

Therefore, put on the full armor of God, so that when the day of evil comes, you may be able to stand your ground, and after you have done everything, to stand."

Saul paused and looked up to Joe, who smiled and nodded encouragement for him to continue. Saul's words grew stronger as he began to see this fight for what it truly was. "Stand firm then, with the belt of truth buckled around your waist, with the breastplate of righteousness in place, and with your feet fitted with the readiness that comes from the gospel of peace. In addition to all this, take up the shield of faith, with which you can extinguish all the flaming arrows of the evil one. Take the helmet of salvation and the sword of the Spirit, which is the word of God. And pray in the Spirit on all occasions with all kinds of prayers and requests. With this in mind, be alert and always keep on praying for all the Lord's people."

Saul sat back, holding his finger on the verses.

"I have been fighting the wrong battle," he said.

"Not the wrong battle, dear. You just forgot what the battle is," said Elizabeth.

"And whose it is," continued Joe.

Saul looked out over the beautiful backyard and thought deeply about what the Arimas showed him and what God was showing him now that he was ready to listen. Finally, Saul nodded.

"I have been so close to it, yet I still couldn't see it. Shoot, we've been kneeling in prayer, but I forgot to give the battle to the Lord. I forgot to look to Him, first. Here, I have been struggling to do it myself. Instead, I should have read this book and asked the Lord to fight the battle for me."

"He fights for us, and when we let Him, He will fight the battle through us. If we turn to Him and ask for the full armor of His making, He will gladly give it to us. You hold the sword right there, Saul," Joe said, gesturing to the Bible. "And you already know how to begin."

"I need to read God's word and pray," said Saul.

Elizabeth nodded. "Give it all to the One who made everything and holds the whole world in His hands. The devil has you feeling surrounded and hemmed in on all sides. It's time to stop seeing only what he wants you to see. The devil's the one who's hemmed in. He's the loser, Saul. Don't be angry or afraid when it seems the entire world is against you. It's not. That's part of Satan's lie."

"Many people are praying for your success and working for it as well. Do you remember Elijah having a pity party under the bush, lamenting he was alone, the only one standing for God?" Joe asked.

"God showed him there were seven thousand still standing for God who would not bow to the false god Ba'al,"[1] Saul said, remembering his Sunday School lesson.

---

1. 1 Kings 19:13-19; Romans 11:2-4

"Exactly," said Joe, pointing his finger. "Almost every game, I see one or two opposing players or even their coach come out and kneel with your Pirates in prayer. Can you imagine the courage it takes for them? How much grief must they endure when they return? You're on a team of players who have turned to the Lord. Don't be upset when the world rails against you—that's what the lost do, Saul. Remember, that's what they are–Lost. The people are sad and confused. They've been lied to for so long, and they can't recognize the lies from the truth. They're defeated in life in every way that counts, and they can't understand why. They fight and hate you because they rebel, not against you, but against God. All they do is rail against the Creator who loves them. Who offers forgiveness and healing, but they refuse. They won't accept because they want their own will to be done. They want to live their lives outside of God's goodness, and they cling to their sinful ways. They're dead in their sins and empty inside. The only thing that will fill that emptiness is what you already have. It's Jesus. It's His battle. The devil is damned to hell, and he's trying to drag all creation down with him. The world doesn't want to admit it, but they know they're lost because of their sins. They don't need you to fight them, Saul. They need a Savior," Joe finished and sat back.

Saul thought about the words of Paul and the life of Jesus. He thought about what Joe and Elizabeth said. Finally, he pronounced, "And I need to be like Paul, when he said, 'I press on for the mark of the high calling of God in Christ Jesus.'"

As if completing his thought, Elizabeth continued, "As Paul strove to let Christ shine through him."

Saul sat still. Ironically, on this overcast August day, it felt like the first time in weeks the fog was lifting, and Christ's Light shone through into Saul's soul.

"I've been going through the motions of being a Christian, too busy worrying about the team and how to fix everything, I forgot to look to Christ for leadership and direction. That ends today," Saul said as much with his heart as with his mouth. "Would you two pray with me to help me lead this team the way Christ wants us to go?"

The Arimas were glad to accept, and they all bowed their heads and prayed. Saul was last to pray, and after praying for his team, he felt he could hear the Spirit speaking to him again, and moved by the Spirit, he finished. "Lord, I don't know what You have in store for us, but I want to ask You to place a hedge of protection around Josh Green. I know You have a special purpose for him in all this, and I feel like he's in the middle of the whirlwind. Let me be the coach and friend he needs to help him see it through to the end."

For the first time in weeks, Saul felt calm, in harmony with the Lord's plan. The day was still and quiet as they all sat looking at the beautiful garden. It was a good, few peaceful moments, but it was a peace in the eye of a storm, still moving.

Ninety

J oe and Elizabeth sent Saul home. With a weight lifted off him, Saul realized he needed the break he gave his team and went to get some proper sleep. He silenced his phone and laid his head down on a pillow. About the same time, back in Squirrel Hill, the Arimas, working in their garden in the cool early evening, heard a police siren in the distance. At first, it was one siren, but soon a second and third siren followed, all moving to the same location not far away. In less than ten minutes, a myriad of alarm whistles started going off around their home, and the Arimas both looked at each other. Elizabeth told Joe, "Let's head inside and see what's happening in the news."

They turned on the TV. News reports on the local channels were sketchy at first, but the first reports claimed shots fired at an Orthodox Jewish Tabernacle in Squirrel Hill. Joe and Elizabeth gripped each other as they saw a brief video, shot apparently by someone with a cell phone about half a block away, hiding in a shop doorway. They instantly recognized the Tabernacle. As one of Pittsburgh's oldest Orthodox Jewish synagogues, it was the worship place for generations of prominent Pittsburgh Jews. More than that, it was Joe and Elizabeth's childhood temple. They grew up there as their families did for more than a century. Joe's Father's words still rang in his ears as they did 50 years ago. "If you follow Jesus, you turn your back on your people and all we stand for," he said. Though Joe tried to explain Jesus was not against the Jews, His people, but the Messiah they waited for, his protest fell on deaf ears. He and Elizabeth were never invited back, though many of their family continued to attend. Though they no longer belonged, Joe and Elizabeth deeply loved their Jewish family and friends who worshipped there.

Throughout the evening, the reports poured in. Two men entered the main hall at the start of the Mincha prayer service, shooting, killing, and wounding dozens in the sanctuary and an adjoining hall where children and women worshipped. It took less than five minutes. At least two dozen people were hurt. Twelve were pronounced dead at the scene. The police arrived quickly, and the men tried to shoot their way out of the building. One died outright, but the second made it to a van. A second police vehicle arrived and rammed the would-be getaway vehicle as he tried to escape. Arrested with multiple gunshot wounds, he was now in critical condition at a hospital. The names of the deceased and injured were not yet released.

Despite being excluded from Tabernacle decades ago, Joe remained friends with some who attended and spoke with him occasionally. Joe and Elizabeth's parents passed away, yet other family members regularly attended synagogue. Worried, Joe reached out to one friend, a cousin he grew up and went to school with, who became a bank inspector for the state of Pennsylvania. Fortunately, his friend was delayed at a bank in Irwin, PA, and did not return in time to make the service. This cousin was getting sporadic reports of the injured and passed on to Joe all he knew. Joe recognized several of the names. As it turned out, one was another younger cousin, Yusef, a baker who lived nearby the Arimas in Squirrel Hill. Yusef always held Joe in high regard, looking up to him and his accomplishments. Yusef bucked the Jewish leadership and remained fast friends with Joe and Elizabeth. Elizabeth went to his shop at least once a month and bought bread and treats to bring home.

Joe's cousin passed Yusef's story. Yusef was near the back of the synagogue when the shooting started, entering moments before the shooters. Joe's cousin said witnesses attested Yusef confronted the two attackers, even reaching one trying to seize his gun, but the other shot him at point-blank range, killing him instantly. Joe and Elizabeth listened, dumbfounded and heartbroken. "You know Yusef," said Joe's cousin with tears in his voice, "He was never one to back down from a just fight."

"Indeed, he was not," Joe replied. "He was fearless. It was, I think, part of the reason he remained friends with us when most everyone else...," Joe's voice trailed off.

"There's more, Joe. Cai Annason's brother-in-law, Zechariah, is among the dead. Apparently, Zechariah was sitting next to Nick Demus," said Joe's cousin. "Nick is wounded and in critical condition at UPMC." Somehow, Joe's heart sank even deeper with this blow. The Annason family attended the synagogue even longer than Joe's, and of course, Cai, being a good Jew, married a girl whose family also attended. Though they were often at odds, Joe was sorrowful the Annasons lost at least one family member.

Nick Demus's injury, however, was too close to home. He was a well-respected Jew, yet a person many of the orthodox Jews held at arm's length. Nick often questioned the orthodox stance and traditions, genuinely searching out what was true and profitable for living a righteous life. Joe always found him among the most reasonable of men. He, like Yusef, was one of the few Jews Joe stayed friends with over the years. They sat down to break bread at least every six months for nearly thirty years, and Joe considered Nick, and his son Ezra, family. Nick often asked Joe difficult but reasonable questions about why he believed and accepted

Jesus as the Messiah. Of all the people he knew throughout life, Joe prayed for no one so long and so much as he did for his friend Nick, who came so close to accepting Christ.

They met a few weeks ago at their usual place, talking much of Josh and what Josh was doing on and off the field. Nick commented on events, saying he never saw such a wave of unjust criticism, and Josh's humble yet firm stance amid the fierce opposition convinced Nick, Josh must be a righteous man. Nick shocked Joe, saying Josh's example, in the storm of the news media, almost convinced him to become a Christian. Joe reflected on how his friend reminded him so much of King Agrippa, telling Paul nearly the same thing in Acts. Joe said to Nick, "Never be 'almost' my friend.—It is the saddest word in the English language. King Agrippa fell soon after he, too, came so close to believing. Please, my friend, don't come so close and miss Messiah." Joe now prayed a most fervent prayer asking God to spare his friend, soften his heart and give him a chance, yet again, to accept Christ and be saved.

"This is all so heartbreaking," Joe said to his cousin on the phone, feeling more than a little helpless. "What can we do?"

"I don't know what we can do. I feel the need to head to the tabernacle. I feel I need to pray for their souls," replied his cousin.

"My friend," said Joe, "I, too, would like to pray. I will call on our community church as I am sure many will wish to do the same."

After Joe said his goodbyes and hung up the phone, he and Elizabeth discussed what they heard from his cousin. Joe called his community church rabbi to pass on what he knew. Joe felt compelled to go to the synagogue in Pittsburgh, where the shooting took place, to pray for and show compassion for his fellow Jews, even though they were no longer members of the Orthodox Jewish synagogue. The rabbi understood and said he would hold a prayer vigil at the same time at their church in Monroeville.

Joe hung up and asked Elizabeth what she thought. "I think we ought to pray right now." Joe agreed and began praying for all the wounded and slain, their families, and the trauma and first responders. As they closed, Joe asked the Lord to help them know how to help. Just then, his phone rang. It was Josh Green.

"Joe, I have been watching the news with Ruth and Mary. Do you have any more insight on what's going on?" Josh asked as he recognized the synagogue as the one Joe mentioned when talking about his childhood. Joe discussed all he learned from his cousin ending with the news about Nick Demus.

Josh was quiet for a few seconds, then he said to Joe. "I don't have to be at the ball field until 3:00 PM tomorrow. Perhaps we could go to UPMC and visit Nick, then swing over and say prayers at the synagogue."

"Elizabeth and I were praying about this, and I think we feel the same. We should try and do what we can."

"Mary, Ruth, and I would like to join you."

"OK, let me make a phone call about Nick, and I'll get back to you," said Joe.

Although the stalwart orthodox Jews rejected Joe for his messianic beliefs, he was still a pillar of the Pittsburgh community. Another of Joe's friends was the head administrator at UPMC. That evening, Joe learned from him, off the record, that Nick was out of surgery, recovering in critical but stable condition. Nick's wife passed away nearly a decade ago, and his only son, Joe's former protégé, Ezra, lived in NYC. There was no other family save for an older sister with dementia who lived in a nursing home. Joe left a message on Nick's son Ezra's voicemail. It turned out Ezra was already flying back using his law firm's contract charter flight with their blessing. He called Joe after he arrived in Pittsburgh about an hour later. Ezra was glad to get Joe's news update from the surgeon, as he was out of the loop while flying and rented a car to head to the hospital. Relieved somewhat, Ezra expected to be at the hospital when Joe and the Greens came the next day at 10:00 AM and planned to meet them. Joe passed this on to Josh, and they agreed to rendezvous at the Arimas' house at 9:30 AM before heading to the nearby hospital.

The following morning, Ezra met the Arimas, Greens, and Mary as they exited the car park into the main UPMC hospital in Oakland.

"Dad's out of intensive care, but he's still unconscious. He was shot once in the lower abdomen and once in the shoulder. The doctor said he was unconscious when he arrived yesterday. They operated for almost four hours as the abdomen shot shattered, and repairing the damage took some time. They are monitoring him closely. We can see him, but only for a few moments."

They went upstairs to the ward where Nick was recuperating. A doctor making rounds was finishing with Nick. She talked to the nurse in charge outside Nick's room as they arrived.

"This is the nurse who talked with me about Dad. I don't know the doctor," whispered Ezra to the rest of the group as they approached.

"The nurse, a middle-aged black man, listened quietly to the Doctor as she wrote notes on the placard and handed it back to him. "I'll check back in about two hours, but if you need me, call me. Don't hesitate. Today will tell the tale of Mr. Demus and how we did last night," she said tiredly.

The nurse saw the group approaching and recognized Ezra. "Understood. Ah, Dr. Shewtick, this is Mr. Demus's son Ezra."

The diminutive doctor, a young thirty-something lady, about five foot two with dark eyes and darker hair, turned and assessed the group, reaching out to take Ezra's hand in her own. Her eyes bore dark rings as if she badly needed sleep.

The nurse continued, "Ezra, this is Dr. Shewtick. She is Chief of Trauma Surgeon Residents. She and a team of doctors operated on your dad and many of the other wounded yesterday."

"It is good to meet you, Mr. Demus," Doctor Shewtick stated. "Your father is stable, but we must watch him closely today to ensure he is recovering properly. He gave us quite a handful yesterday, but we are hopeful he will continue to improve."

"Thank you, Doctor," Ezra said, "I asked Nurse Chris here if Dad could receive a few close friends. They would like to pray over him for recovery."

Doctor Shewtick released Ezra's hand and crossed her arms. Her body language indicated she was concerned about Nick receiving visitors, but she looked up for the first time at the others, and her tired gaze locked on Josh. She put her hands on her hips, tilted her head, and said, "Are you Josh Green?"

Josh smiled slightly, nodded, and said, "Yes, Dr. Shewtick. Might I ask, are you related to Adam Shewtick?"

"Indeed, I am, Mr. Green. Adam is my baby brother. Ever since he met you at Children's," she said smiling, referring to the Greens and Mary's visit earlier in the spring, "He won't stop talking about your visit."

"Adam was a great help to us and a great Pirates fan. We enjoyed a wonderful visit with him and his patients," Josh replied kindly.

"Yes, that boy has been a die-hard Pirates fan since he was little," she said, shaking her head. "Got it from our Zayda Mordecai, who always listened to the Pirates on the radio when Adam was a boy. Much to Savta Remy's chagrin, but of course, she never complained," she smiled at a happy memory. "And Adam certainly was happy to have you visit his kids. But he has continued to talk about your visit since you came, with more than his usual baseball enthusiasm."

Dr. Shewtick trailed off, wrinkling her eyebrows and staring at Josh more curiously, lost in thought. She snapped back after a moment, as if deciding. She turned to Ezra, saying, "We doctors and nurses have done all that is humanly possible to help save your dad. Now it's up to the All-Mighty, and Mr. Demus definitely needs our prayers. I warn you all; he looks rough," she said kindly to the group. "Please don't expect too much from him, either. His body is trying to heal, and he's not awake. I would ask you to keep your visit, as a group, down to fifteen minutes. Ezra, you're welcome to continue to sit with your dad. You can help Nurse Chris and his team watch over him. I just completed my rounds, and I have been up for," she paused, looking at her watch, "26 hours. Technically, my shift ended two hours ago, but I will grab a power nap in our lounge and return. I want to check on your dad and two of our other patients in two hours, before I go home tonight," then she caught her mistake with the sunlight streaming in the window. "I mean today," she said, overly tired.

The group shuffled into the room led by nurse Chris and Ezra, with Elizabeth and Mary bringing up the rear. Dr. Shewtick slid around the group and grabbed Josh by the arm, pulling him aside. The two women could tell Dr. Shewtick was talking to Josh quietly but intently. However, they could not quite hear what she was saying.

As Elizabeth looked back out the door, standing next to Mary, she whispered, "Do you know what that is about?"

Mary looked at Dr. Shewtick talking to Josh, who was listening. Josh smiled and nodded, then she took his face in her hands, in a kind but almost grandmotherly way, even though she was probably a few years younger than Josh. She patted him gently on the chest, and the ladies could tell her brief reply was filled with relief. "Thank you," they read her lips as her stance and shoulders relaxed. She turned and walked away down the hall, weary but reassured.

Mary whispered to Elizabeth, "I suspect she asked Josh if he was here to visit like he did when visiting her brother's ward." Elizabeth looked quizzically at Mary, who smiled quietly and looked back at the rest of the group surrounding Nick.

Even though his father didn't respond to Ezra, Ezra still talked to his father as if he could hear, telling him who came to visit. They all said hello in their own way, and Joe spoke to his dear friend, encouraging him and telling him they came to pray over him and ask for God's healing. Ezra stood on one side with Joe next to him. Josh fell in behind Ruth, taking the opposite side of the bed. Next to Ruth, Elizabeth and Mary stood near Nick's feet. Nick's many bandages, monitoring devices, and an intravenous drip made for harrowing sight as the little group of friends gathered around him to pray.

Finally, Joe spoke again.

"Nick, if you don't mind, we will pray for you now as the doctor wants us to make our visit short so you can rest. Ezra will stay with you here, after we are gone. I will start the prayer, and anyone who wants to pray can do so," Joe said, looking around at the group. "Josh, can you finish for us?" Joe asked. Josh nodded.

Joe placed his hand on Nick's arm, and the group instinctively did likewise, feeling the need to lay hands gently on the man as they prayed. Little Ruth held Nick's hand, and Josh, standing over her, placed his hand on theirs. Joe began praying, followed by Elizabeth, Mary, and Ruth. They were different prayers, simple, but each asking for healing and peace for Nick, asking for wisdom and skill and comfort to his medical staff, and giving God the glory to make good out of what was an act meant for evil.

Finally, Josh prayed humbly. "Father God, Lord Jesus, please bring your healing to our friend, Nick. Help him feel your presence. Give his doctors and nurses wisdom in his care. Give them peace in this difficult circumstance, and let your name be glorified as you place your healing and protective hand upon all. Lift up Nick and the other injured and hold them close to you, Father, so that men might know you, Lord, the God of all creation, have the power to overcome even evil such as this and use it to your glory. We claim this healing in the precious name of your Son, Jesus, our savior. Amen."

As he said Amen, Nick, who, until now, showed no signs of consciousness, squeezed Ezra and Ruth's hand gently but firmly. Ezra, who remained quiet throughout, with eyes on his father, looked up, surprised. Ruth smiled and said, "You see, Ezra, God is always at work, even when we can't see it." Ruth spoke, not as a twelve-year-old girl but as someone who knew the pain and heartache of losing a parent she loved with all her heart.

The Greens, Mary, and the Arimas said their goodbyes to Ezra and Nick, leaving Ezra with his father. Yet both Ezra and Nick seemed buoyed by the brief visit. Ezra did say one thing to Josh and Joe, who were the last to walk out. "Gentlemen, I greatly appreciate you all coming and praying for Dad. I have already felt as if he is improving since you have come. I know you are going to try to pray at synagogue. Joe, you haven't been there since before I was born," Ezra said and hesitated. "I don't know how else to say this, but if anything, their orthodoxy is even stronger than you remember." Ezra hurried on, "I am not sure how they will receive you, but the Rabbis and some of the longstanding families...." Again, Ezra hesitated, but finally shrugged his shoulders and continued. "They don't abide Jews who accept Christ as Messiah. They eschew them more than heathens, seeing them as...," Ezra couldn't finish.

Joe said, "They see them as traitors, traitors not just to their beliefs but to the ancestors who, they say, died rather than accept Yeshua[1] as Messiah and Lord."

Ezra bowed his head and nodded, saying sadly, "Yes."

Joe responded, "One thing you said is not correct, my young friend. Their orthodoxy has not changed. As a matter of fact, it hasn't changed in two thousand years."

Ezra looked back at Joe with tears in his eyes, and he nodded at this as well.

---

1. Symbolically, the name Yehoshua/Yeshua/Jesus conveys the idea that God (YHVH) delivers or saves (his people). When used in this book, Yeshua is meant to be Jesus as said by many modern messianic jews (and many Christians) and a good historical discussion can be found at Yeshua.org, with their best comment ",'But everyone who calls on the name of the Lord will be saved.' -God knows who calls upon His name, whether they do so in English, Portuguese, Spanish, Hebrew or any other language. He is still the same Lord and Savior."

"Well, we will still go and try our best to comfort them and pray in the name of the one man who can bring true healing to their hurting bodies and souls," Joe said, and he hugged Ezra. "Let us know how your father is doing and call me if you need anything."

Except for Ezra, the group walked out of the room with Nurse Chris. Josh paused to talk to the ladies.

"Mary, can you and Beth walk Ruthie down to the car? Joe and I need to stop and talk with Nurse Chris for a few minutes. We will meet you at the cars shortly, OK?"

The ladies agreed and headed for the elevators. They waited in the cars for about twenty minutes before the two men arrived.

As Joe got into the driver's seat, Elizabeth asked, "Is everything OK?"

Joe smiled and nodded, "Everything is fine, and I believe everyone will be OK."

Ninety One

J osh followed Joe to the synagogue, parking on the street a few blocks away. The men donned Kippah's, the traditional Jewish head covering, as Josh did since he, Ruth, and Mary began attending Shoresh David Messianic Congregation in Monroeville, PA, after Joe's invite. Joe's Kippah was black with white stitching, and Josh's was white with blue stitching. Both bore the Messianic Seal, or the "Grafted in Seal" centered on top. The seal was centuries old, dating back to the third century, depicting the Menorah, Star of David, and Fish symbol, connected in miniature, running from front to back. Although not required by the messianic Jewish customs, Mary and Elizabeth placed light head coverings, as they did at their congregation. They knew this orthodox Jewish temple expected it, and they felt wearing modest head coverings was especially important to avoid offending the Jewish members.

As the Greens and Arimas walked towards the temple, they came upon quite a scene. Police tape still sectioned off portions of the synagogue. The media descended in numbers, setting up outside the temple perimeter but close enough to video the scene and filmed several "live reports." At first, their small group went unnoticed as they approached. Outside the buildings, but still in the parking area, were two or three groups of what turned out to be synagogue members wanting to pray, worship, and gather to show solidarity with their fellow Jews. Also, they demonstrated the evil perpetrated here would not intimidate them.

As they approached the synagogue parking lot, one of the news reporters from the TV vans recognized Josh.

"Hey, here comes Josh Green!" the local CBS affiliate newsman said to his cameraman, "Come On!" as Josh and the group passed. "Start filming," he said over his shoulder, "And follow my lead."

Josh and Joe noticed they were now drawing attention but tried to lead the girls on before the news people caught them. However, the commotion attracted the attention of a large group of synagogue members who were outside the building. Several prominent members talked to a Rabbi, but there were also what looked to be several strong men dressed in black suits, doubling as a show of force and security, presenting a physical barrier. In the middle of the group, currently listening to the Rabbi, were Cai Annason and his father-in-law. After glancing at Joe and Josh, Cai said something to the Rabbi and one of the security men. The Rabbi, flanked by several tough-looking men in orthodox dress, walked over and intercepted Joe and Elizabeth, who led the Greens.

"Joseph," said the Rabbi, who looked about Joe's age. "What can I help you with?" said the man, obviously recognizing Joe from the past. The younger men formed an effective wall, cutting off their approach from the sidewalk to the synagogue.

"Rabbi Korah, I am sorry to meet again at such a time as this. We have come to offer our help, to grieve with your families and pray for those who were hurt by this tragic event," Joe said, with Elizabeth on one side and Josh, Ruth, and Mary on the other. By this time, the news reporter and camera operator caught up and recorded the scene. Cai Annason and his father-in-law were safely behind the line of men, including the Rabbi, formed to block the way. Still, they were within earshot along with several well-dressed Jewish members, no doubt some of the synagogue's most respected families.

Rabbi Korah replied. "Joseph, I think it would be best if we respect those who lost loved ones here yesterday from our temple families and let them mourn their dead in peace. You understand our community is still hurting, and we are a tight-knit community that takes care of our own."

"I agree, Korah, and you remember, Elizabeth and I, too, were once a part of that community. You know my cousin Yusef is among the dead," Joe said.

"Yes, many unfortunate deaths have occurred, Joseph, and we will certainly remember Yusef when we pray, but as you said, you and Elizabeth *were* once part of this community. You chose to leave our community fifty years ago," Korah said, emphasizing past tense.

"Korah, surely you want the greater Pittsburgh community with you in this hour of need," Joe said as one of the younger men who talked with Cai walked up next to Rabbi Korah. The man was mid-thirties, dressed in black with a black Kippah and black beard. Wrapped high on his arm was a black ribbon. His expression indicated he wanted to say something and had little time to say it. Joe addressed him first, "Benjamin, we are so sorry to hear about your brother Zechariah," Joe said, mentioning the name of Cai's brother-in-law. This must be another of Cai's in-laws. "Please accept all our condolences for your family."

"Mr. Arima. I know you only by your dealings with our family and the team. Please understand we are asking everyone not part of our community, here at our synagogue, to allow our families to mourn their dead in peace. We don't want any outsiders to interfere. I am sure you understand, as I am told that you were once a member of our community. We take our Jewish responsibilities seriously and ask you to respect our traditions, even if you and your wife no longer share them."

The man said with finality, dictating there was to be no argument and nothing more to discuss. He spoke almost as if he, not Joe, was the elder and Joe was a child needing instruction.

"Benjamin, we only came to pray for the injured and their families and mourn the dead. I too, have a cousin who died and friends who were hurt. I may be a Christian, but I am still a Jew."

"I am afraid, as far as our community is concerned, you cannot be both, Mr. Arima, as I think your own family made clear to you when you forsook them all those years ago. Also, you come with Mr. Green, an outspoken believer in praying to Christ. Such were the men who came here yesterday and slaughtered my brother, as they have done to our people over the centuries."

At this, Josh spoke gentleness and compassion to the angry and hurting man. "Sir, I grieve for your brother and your family, but let me say, no Christian did this act. Christ himself is a Jew and came to save his people, not condemn them. Those men yesterday are not Christians, for their actions are the opposite of what a Christ-follower would do. All Christians mourn for you and this community hurt by those evil men. We simply want to pray with you and ask for God's protection and healing on your family and all the others hurt yesterday," Josh said.

"Mr. Green, our community appreciates those outside it who truly wish us goodwill and want to help. They needed to be here yesterday to keep men like this from thinking they could solve their problems by killing Jews. That is what the rest of the world needs to do. Still, if history is any indicator, only Jews who hold strong to our traditions," he said with emphasis, "and hold to the laws laid out by Jehovah through his Prophet Moses, can truly understand the needs of our community. We don't need prayers to a false messiah for forgiveness. We require your action, not your prayers: restrain evil men from doing us harm and justice against those who commit such heinous crimes. What we don't need is more people inspired to think of us as enemies to their Christ or killers of Jesus like these men."

Benjamin paused, smoothing some of the anger from his face. "Regardless, nothing brings my brother back. Now, if you don't mind, I want to return to my father and uncle and keep our community's customs and laws. Rabbi Korah was about to start a Shiva for my brother, whose casket is in one of the few rooms not still closed by the police, and the rest of my family is already there. Please do not delay us or interrupt our service again."

Joe replied, understanding they would not be allowed further, "Again, we only wished to give our condolences and share in your mourning. We will pray for you and your family."

"Thank you for the sentiment. We will endure, like we always have, as a family of Jews." With that, Benjamin turned on his heels and returned to the older men who moved away from the line of men, leaving only the Rabbi.

Rabbi Korah told Joe, "Joseph, when we were young, you knew scripture even better than I. Surely you must know our observances are traditional and only fit for proper Jews to follow. While I appreciate others, like Mr. Green here, might not understand the affront wearing a Christ symbol and planning to pray a prayer no doubt to Jesus would be offensive at a True Jew's Shiva and funeral, I would have thought you would remember, even after all these years."

"I did know the scripture better than you, Korah, which is why Rabbi Bernie wanted me to follow the path to becoming a Rabbi. I still know and believe the scripture Korah, and I am not here to offend or to convert, only to pray and mourn. I can see we cannot do that now, so I take leave and say we will continue to pray for you all to the Lord and His anointed, the only one who has conquered death."

The Rabbi remained stoic, saying nothing. He turned away, rejecting Joe and Josh's attempt to help. The other men closed ranks, making it clear only those invited could enter.

The Greens and Arimas turned back, and the newscaster and his cameraman, still rolling, finally stepped in and shouted a question. "Josh Green, you've come to the scene of the devastating shooting of this orthodox Jewish Synagogue. Why have you come, Josh, and why are you now turning back?"

Along with these two, who recorded the entire time, several other broadcast journalists and news people also encircled the group. The police, still present, took notice and tried to move the growing crowd back.

Josh tried to lead the way, but the questions now intensified from other reporters. "Josh, why are you here? Are you a Jew? Are you a member of this congregation?" yelled one reporter, blocked now by a police officer.

"Josh, did you know some of the Jews killed? Why haven't you made a statement about the tragedy?" another yelled.

By the time the Greens and Arimas turned back to return to their cars, various other onlookers descended with signs and slogans of all types. Most spoke against the slaying, while others displayed different causes, hoping to gain national TV coverage. The questions flew from many directions in the mixed crowd, asking why Josh Green tried to enter the synagogue, why he was wearing a Jewish cap, and his role in these tragic events.

They traveled back several blocks to their cars. The crowd finally left behind, they took stock of what happened.

"I am sorry it turned out the way it did," Joe said sadly. "Perhaps I should have expected being shut out. Our families forced us to leave the community fifty years ago, but I forgot how hardened the hearts are for Jews who reject Messiah. It is..., very discouraging. I am sorry I got you into this, Josh," Joe said, and Elizabeth put her arm around her husband.

"Joe, I know this has been a hard day, but the Lord does not ask for our success, just our faithfulness," Josh replied. "We tried to convey God's love and His healing powers, as we carry His Good News, as He commanded us to do. Let's pray here for our brothers and sisters. They need God's healing and love now more than ever."

On the quiet side street, the Greens, Arimas, and Mary prayed for those hurt by the tragedy, for their healing, and for their hearts to turn to the great physician who was the only One who could heal their souls.

Ninety Two

T he media coverage of Josh's small group turned away from the synagogue sparked much negative publicity. On the one hand, the video showed Josh and the others approaching the Rabbi and other synagogue members. The distance was too great to hear the conversation. Since Josh did not answer any questions when they walked away, the press felt free to speculate about his intentions and why he turned away.

Roman Josephus saw his chance to splash his explanation and capture the public's attention, which waned somewhat with Josh's refusal to give him more interviews.

In a prime-time exposé on SPNN, Roman began with his update.

"Josh Green likes to make headlines, it seems, as much for his public stance as he does for hitting a baseball. Today, Green and his agent attempted to insert themselves front and center into the tragic scene of the Jewish Synagogue in Pittsburgh. With the shooting less than 24 hours ago, we have footage of Josh and other non-members of the synagogue trying to come onto the premises. Watch them as it takes the synagogue Rabbi to turn them away from a funeral for one of the men killed."

Roman then showed a cut clip of Josh and the others approaching the synagogue. The video cut to the Rabbi waving them away, dismissing them.

"What was Josh Green thinking? We don't know because he refused to answer questions before leaving. However, many commentators point out his Kippah, the little top cap seen here," Roman said as the video froze and blurrily zoomed in on the symbol, "Has the symbols of Messianic Jews. These people claim to be Jews but believe Christ was the prophesied Messiah. We are all well aware of Josh's stance on Christ with his very public prayers in the name of Jesus. His controversial 'Tebow' before each first at-bat is met with ever-increasing jeers and derision. I now confirm Josh attends a messianic congregation with several of the people in this video. Is he claiming to be Jewish? We can only assume Josh attempted to put the Christian stamp on this event by coming to pray openly, as he has done at so many public places throughout Major League Baseball this year. Of course, knowing of Josh's Christian tradition of prayer, he was turned away.

What did he expect at a Jewish Synagogue where ultra-right, self-proclaimed 'Nationalists,' claiming to be Christians, killed twelve Jews and injured eight others just yesterday? Are Josh's actions a pious display of Christian concern, or are they an insensitive stab at grabbing headlines for his so-called Christian virtues at the expense of a Jewish community reeling from another bigoted attack costing a dozen lives and further fracturing our society? You decide."

The Pirates played a short four-game home stand against Cincinnati. Game one was the first game Josh played at home since the injury. Again, the stadium sold out. The Pirates received a mixed welcome. Many fans cheered wildly for their team to continue its recent winning ways, yet inside and outside demonstrations increased. New signs against antisemitism joined the other causes, and a few anti-fascist displays sprang up. Unusual for the hometown crowd, quite a few fans now openly booed the Pirates for standing during the anthem, although many were, in turn, shouted down by fans nearby. In one section, about a dozen anti-fascists changed to all-black clothing upon entering the stadium, with partially covered faces and held up anti-fascist slogans. They screamed obscenities at the team when they gathered for their pregame prayer. The police were called to remove them, delaying the game about ten minutes when it looked like the protesters might fight back. Around thirty security personnel finally showed up, and outnumbered, the protesters went relatively quietly. An anti-fascist's cell phone video made national news showing their disruptions and chants as the team kneeled on the field in prayer in the background.

While tempers were short and the protest became more vocal, the Pirates made the Reds look like a Minor League team. In the first two games, the Reds thought to stifle Josh by shifting the infield to the left side, where he previously made a majority of hits. Josh collected three hits in each game. Only two went to left; home runs late in each game.The other four hits were all to right field, including three singles through the position where the second baseman customarily played. Cincinnati gave up the shift for the final two games and started walking Josh, but he upped his stolen base totals with one steal in game three and two in game four. Pittsburgh won all four games and went back on the road again.

The Pirates played NL East leading Atlanta Braves, winning the first three games by a combined 33-5 score before narrowly losing the final, 5-4. The Pirates then traveled to Philadelphia and saw a lot of protesters of all types. With the crowd at fever pitch and their Ace, Samson, on the mound, they played a tight game for the first three innings with both starters going once through the order, perfect. Zach got the first Pirate hit to start the fourth with a single, and J.J., giving Captain Andrew a day off with a sore rib cage, drew a walk. The Phillies pitcher threw a good changeup and two-finger fastball, staying low on batters with good late movement. They tried to keep the ball down and away on Josh, but Josh saw the pitches well in his first at-bat and now, with runners on, finally got a hittable pitch. He drilled another opposite-field hit for a standup double, plating both Pirates for a 2-0 lead. The pitcher duel would continue, but Samson was the class of the League. After narrowly giving up a single in the fifth inning, he kept the crowd quiet, again getting nine consecutive outs in the last three innings for a one-hit complete game. The win sealed the Pirates at least a wild card position in the postseason, as both the Cubs and the Cardinals struggled to keep pace with the second and third best records in the National League. The other three games in Philly were not as close, with the Pirates winning all three. In the last game, the final nail in the coffin was a three-run homer by Josh in the fourth inning, breaking up a 1-1 tie on the way to a 9-1 rout. It was a memorable game for one reason. The Pirates clinched the division and the best record in the National League. For the Pirates players and staff, it meant reaching their first step toward the lofty goal they set for themselves at the beginning of the season, but it came amid a tumultuous summer of unrest for the League and Nation.

Ninety Three

The Pirates blazed through the League for Josh's first twenty games back from injury with an 18-2 record, and the Pirates were now 114-36, three games shy of setting the MLB record number of wins in a season. With twelve games remaining in the regular season, they had nothing left to prove. They moved from Philadelphia to New York City for one last series on the road before coming home to Pittsburgh for the final eight games. The trip to New York was the first time back for Josh and the Pirates since the series against the Yankees when Josh was attacked and injured. This time, the Pirates played the "other" New York team, the New York Mets, at Citi Field.

The team chartered two buses for the short one-and-a-half-hour trip from Philadelphia to Flushing Meadows and the team hotel. It was late in the evening when they started, and Josh tucked Ruth into a seat in the front of the bus with Mary as it was the closest thing to quiet you could get with a team full of players who just locked up the division and National League's best record. Samson grabbed Josh, asking him to join he and Zach at the back of the bus. Juan was lying down on the rear seats stretched across the back of the bus. A few seats forward, Justus Barabbas slept soundly against a window, and his roommate Jude Keriothson, who pitched to end the game today, wore his headphones and read a book, the only one who seemed to be awake. He nodded to the two men as they passed and returned to reading. Sitting in the next-to-last row, Zach waited, almost anxiously, with a big smile that seemed even larger than winning the game would cause.

"Something good has happened?" Josh said, half question, half statement, trying not to wake anyone as he took the seat in front and opposite Zach.

"You could say that," laughed Sammy quietly over his shoulder. "Well, go on, Bro!" he said as he sat in front of Zach, sprawling across both seats. "You've been bursting to tell since this morning!"

"I did it, Josh," Zach said, "I've accepted Jesus as my Savior!"

"Incredible, Zach," Josh answered, reaching across and grabbing him on the shoulder and smiling, "That's great news!"

Zach hurried on excitedly, "I've been watching everything going on this year, and well, I don't know how else to say it, but God has been talking to me through it all. I've been fighting back, I think, afraid." You could almost see the gears turning as Zach explained to Josh, simultaneously voicing the explanation to himself. "Yes, I was afraid of what it means and what it might cost. I know that sounds crazy, but ever since I watched how people react to us, to you, and all of us praying, I sat back and took stock of what I believe is true. I asked myself what my life is about. Where am I going? Why do I feel like I was flat-out missing something? No matter what I tried, no matter my success." At this, Zach looked up, "And I got everything I wanted this season, Josh!" Josh nodded encouragingly. He could tell there was more. "I watched you and the others, and you know, all the negative, angry, and hateful responses."

Zach continued, "Sammy began reading the Bible with me this spring when you got him thinking about his faith again. There is a change in him. I can see the way people react to you and your faith. I began to see Jesus. He's become real and relevant, not some ancient mythical figure. The same things He talks about in the world so long ago are the same problems today. I am starting to understand. He's here. His love changes those that give their lives to Him. The world hates those who are changed, and now, I know why—why they hated Him, why they hate what you are doing."

Zach continued, "Sammy and I have read through John, Acts, and Romans this season. I became convinced Jesus talked to all of us. Just like Nicodemus, I was lost, struggling. Paul spelled it out again. He knew because he had gone through the same struggle, in some ways, lost but not understanding. He rejected the truth and tried to suppress it as Saul, but then was confronted and became Paul. I felt the spirit confronting my heart. I reread John after that day we came to work out with you at the high school, and a few days later, it all suddenly clicked for me. They hated Jesus because the Truth He told meant they were lost. Like Saul, I knew I was a sinner, too. I knew I was trying to justify myself my way. Like Jesus told those who would listen, and like Paul then repeated as a repentant sinner saved by grace, I finally admitted I could not save myself. It forced me to admit I've been running. I've been fighting, trying to make myself right with God—No, not right with Him. I was trying to make my own righteousness in the world's eyes. I was rejecting Him. The last few weeks showed it to me. It was like all the world's lies were laid bare, and I saw the rebellion against Truth and Goodness come to life. And I see you and the other Christians standing calm in the storm."

"It's not me, you know," Josh said, "I am standing on the Rock. It's the Lord."

"Yes, exactly!" Zach said, leaning forward. "That's exactly what I realized!" He said in a hissed whisper. "I realized you stood not as a self-righteous man but as a man who held the righteousness of Christ. It happened when I watched the reaction to you trying to pray for those wounded and killed at the Synagogue and then those angry, hateful people at PNC Park that afternoon. It clicked for me. I knew the truth like a bolt of lightning. Like," Zach faltered, grasping for words, "Like a shock of electricity went through me! Everything I've seen, all the way back to when I was a kid, is the fight of sin against God in my life. I knew the truth because I used to live the opposite of truth. That wasn't just a lie. It was sin." Zach shook his head and lowered it towards the floor, "But knowing the Truth wasn't enough. I was miserable. These last few days have been hell. Like I was standing right there on the edge. I knew I was in a state of rebellion knowing the Truth, but still, I was so afraid."

"And what changed?" Josh said with kind encouragement. Zach now looked up with tears of joy in his eyes.

"God would **NOT** let me go!" Zach choked up, saying it, as Josh nodded in apparent understanding.

Slowly Zach continued, his eyes distant now, "He wouldn't let me go, Josh. I could hear Him. I heard your words, reminding me of what He said. *Fear Not!* I knew I didn't want to rebel anymore. Before, I feared what I might lose, but now I wanted Christ more. I wanted, no, I *needed* what you have, what Sammy and the others have. Before, everyone in my life kept telling me who I should be, what I could do, and how to do it. I did all those things, and yet, I was still lost. In fact, I wasn't free at all. I was bound in chains, knowing my sins would drag me to hell. How could I come back? How could I break away? Jesus kept whispering through all I have seen this summer. He kept saying, 'I love you; I have always loved you. Come to me, and I will give you rest. I will never leave you or forsake you. Come, drink from the water I give you, and never thirst again.' Through all my fear, it was his voice I heard. More than anything else, I knew I needed Jesus!"

"And now?" Josh asked, already knowing the answer.

Zach looked at him, and his smile was a mile wide, "This morning, I had Samson lead me through the sinner's prayer, and I gave my life to Jesus!"

"Yeah, the turkey woke me up an hour early. You know how I don't like to lose my beauty sleep, Josh!"

"Good thing you aren't staying out late on the town anymore, my friend!" Josh said, smiling, and the three men laughed easily. Then Josh replied to Zach, "Ah, my friend, I rejoice with the angels in heaven over your salvation. You look like you could light up New York City with the smile on your face and joy in your heart."

"I've been on cloud nine all day! It's like, well, it's hard to describe," Zach scrunched up his eyebrows. "Like a giant weight is gone! I feel light as a feather. I feel like going to the top of the empire state building and shouting out to the world. Screaming out, 'I'm Free!' It's like suddenly. I'm, I'm...." Zach hesitated, trying to find the right words.

"Come alive," stated Josh.

"YES!" Zach said loudly, emphatically, and affirmatively. The noise roused Juan, who drowsily sat up in the back row. "That's IT!...isn't it?" continued Zach more quietly. "I was dead, wasn't I? Yes!" he whispered loudly again, answering his own question. "I was a dead man walking, but now I'm reborn. It's just like what Christ told Nicodemus. I'm alive again!"

"Now and forevermore, my brother." Sitting next to Zach, Sammy said these words and reached over, grabbing him and hugging his shoulders with his giant arms.

"Yes," exclaimed Zach, "And now that I am alive and Jesus is my Savior, I want to follow him! Like you all do! What's next? What can I do?" Zach said enthusiastically.

"Well," Josh thought out loud, "As Jesus and the disciples taught us, after you accept the Lord, you are to be baptized in His name. Baptism is an outward sign, to the world, of what's taken place inside your heart. It doesn't save you. It only announces to anyone who will listen, you have given your life to Jesus," Josh answered.

"Yes! Yes!" Zach said emphatically, "That's what I want to do!"

"You can come to First Baptist when we return to the Burgh," Samson suggested. "Pastor Manoah would be happy to dunk you, I'm sure!" he smiled.

"Do I have to wait?" Zach said pleadingly, looking at them both as if he couldn't bear to delay even a few days.

"Yew could ask Pastor Humberto to baptize yew tomorrow," Juan said, yawning sleepily from the back row. The three men looked back at him, a little surprised. "Well, I couldn't help but hear your loud whispers, now could I!" he said, rubbing the sleep out of his eyes. "Crazy Zach and Sammy still keeping me up even as Christians now, Mi Amigos!" Juan said, slapping Zach heartily on his back, and the other men laughed. "Pastor Humberto is de one who baptized me at Faith Baptist in Queens when I came to de States with my family as a thirteen-year-old. He's also da one who got me noticed by the Brooklyn Cyclones when I was in high school in Queens. He's expecting me to meet him at the church tomorrow at 12:00 PM to talk to some of his high-risk kids before we head to da stadium tomorrow afternoon. I could call him in da morning and ask him to baptize Yew?"

"Do you think he would do it?" Zach asked hopefully.

Juan laughed. "Pastor Humberto wanted me to talk to some of de kids to show them how Latino men can serve da Lord as adults and make Christ their leader in all walks of life. What better way to show than have a fellow Latino and Black man give your profession of faith with an impromptu Baptism in front of a room full of minority underprivileged kids? If I know Pastor Humberto, I will say you probably couldn't stop him, even if he has to take us to de Hudson to do it!"

Ninety Four

Jude Keriothson made a phone call as soon as he got to his hotel room, away from the rest of the team. He got upstairs ahead of roommate Justus Barabbas, but knew he didn't have much time. His contact directed him to report anything the Pirates were doing detrimental to the League or its image. He rationalized it was in the best interest of everyone. Of course, there was also the guarantee he would continue to play in the big-leagues and the additional cash bonus. Every time he provided information, since he agreed to work for the commissioner's unofficial agent, he received a cash deposit into an offshore account. Hey, he wasn't rich like some ballplayers, and five or ten grand here or there went quite a ways.

Much more enticing was a guarantee to stay in the big-leagues for at least five years, which tempted Jude the most. There were few, if any, guarantees in baseball. Thanks to being on a winner as middle relief, he pitched decently. Even though his ERA was a little high at 4.21, he did just enough to continue in the Majors. He didn't know how the commissioner's office planned to make good on its promise, but a guaranteed three million dollar contract for the remainder of five years once the season was up, was music to his ears. It bothered him to think of himself as a paid spy, but he could deal with his conscience as long as no team member knew he spied on the team for the League. Besides, he was careful making the calls and passing information, keeping up appearances around his teammates. He could pray as well as any of them, but he knew, in the long term, he needed to be on the winning side.

The phone picked up, and Jude's contact, a person high in the commissioner's office, answered. "Yes, Mr. Keriothson," the voice on the other end of the line said with no hint he was irritated with the 1:00 AM call, "You have something for me?"

Jude began, "I don't have much time, but here's the gist. Zacchaeus Purqana has become an actual Christian. He is going to a church in Queen's tomorrow to be baptized...."

Ninety Five

Three days later, Saul sat in the visiting team manager's office at Citi Field. The last few days were a whirlwind. First, he and the team endured the misfortune of dealing with New York press coverage. It started with the unfortunate ambush outside a Baptist church in Queens, of all places. Had he known the guys would attend church to see Zach baptized, he wouldn't have stopped them. Shoot, he would have joined them. Of course, the press failed to show any good Zach, Josh, and the other players did with the teens and pastor at the church. Josh even took his PR bag Mark always kept filled up for him and gave away a bunch of Pirate paraphernalia, yet none of it made the news. Someone surreptitiously filmed the baptism, a complete immersion by Pastor Humberto in the Baptist tradition, and Zach's proclamation of accepting Christ before it.

Even more disconcerting was how someone found out about Zach's baptism ahead of time. It could only mean one thing. Saul knew most players were not privy to Zach's conversation on the bus and his decision. Whoever alerted the press must be inside the organization. Saul wrinkled his brow at the thought.

Still, what truly dismayed Saul was how the press so negatively portrayed Zach's baptism and Josh's influence. Much of the public was unfamiliar with adult baptism and characterized it as odd, unusual, or cultish by many news outlets. If they filmed the hour afterwards where the teen boys met and talked with the five players, including Josh, the footage never made it in any press coverage. The news videos cut to outside the church when the press first made themselves known, as the men exited on their way across town to the stadium. The reports showed the onslaught of three full-size camera crews descending with microphones in the players' faces, asking why they baptized Zach. The players pushed their way through the shouting press corps and made it to the subway, but not before the disturbing questions were asked and remained unanswered for the evening news.

Since he proclaimed himself a Christian, the persistent question to Zach was if he renounced being Gay. Was he, like Josh, now opposed to LGBTQ equality? What caused Zach to turn against his sexual orientation and his own kind? Was he pressured into becoming a Christian? Many reporters and questions targeted Josh. Was Josh leading a cult of Christian extremism inside the Pirates clubhouse?

Is Josh trying to personally convert Gays the way he tried to convert Jews after the shooting at the Synagogue?

Yes, it was a difficult afternoon the first day, as the players barely got time to tell Saul and Mark Johnson what was coming before the game started. Being New York, it wasn't only local news but national, making at least two major networks evening newscasts before Saul's press team could get in front of it with a press release of their own. Saul thought Zach and Josh did surprisingly well at the post-game interviews. Few questions came about winning their 115th game, one shy of tying the all-time record for victories. The questions were all about Zach's conversion.

"Look, I accepted Christ as my savior," Zach tried to explain.

"What does that mean, Zach?" a reporter asked. "What did you do to become a Christian?"

"Nothing," said Zach, "Nothing at all."

"What do you mean, Zach? Are you saying nothing has changed? I thought you must give up things in your life, like being Gay, to become a Christian. How have you made yourself right with God? How can God accept you if what Josh says is true? If you are a sinner as a Gay man?"

"Look, I don't know everything, but I know this. I finally understood that I don't have to make myself acceptable to God–Because I can't. Christ met me this week. He's been knocking at my heart's door, and I finally let Him in. That's what He does. Like the Apostle Paul, Christ met me, in my messed up life, and asked me to let Him change my life. I realized this summer I can't make myself acceptable to God. God knew I needed a Savior before He created the universe, and His Son volunteered to sacrifice Himself for me. That's the entire point. We are all lost. Christ came for us. He lived life as a perfect man and sacrificed Himself in our place. Christ loves us. When we repent and accept Him, His sacrifice is acceptable to God in our place. Then He takes our heart and makes us new. He gives us a new heart and a new life. Christ met me right here, where I am, and He saved me. I can't change myself, but God, through His Son Jesus, can make me new and alive again.

"So now you're no longer Zacchaeus Purqana?" another reporter asked skeptically.

"Look. All my life, I have been searching; searching for the Truth, searching for where I belong, searching for who I was—who I was supposed to be. I needed answers to the big questions; Why am I here? Where am I going? What is life all about? I came to realize I was missing something. I was lost. A lot of that is my own doing, my own choices. I've made mistakes, but now I understand why. The Truth is, I am a sinner, and I can't save myself. But I am not alone. We all are in the same boat, in the same position. Man is equal. Equally lost."

"I've watched, like you have, the reactions to Josh and Christians this summer. I read the words Christ gave to us through the Holy Scriptures and learned one absolute Truth. God created us, and He created us for a relationship with Him. He loves us, and He wanted us to love him, so He created us all equal with the freedom to choose or reject Him. We all have chosen sin at some point. We have rebelled. The story of the Old Testament is about the children of God, from Adam on down, failing to meet God's holy standard, like all men. All have sinned and come short of God's glory. The Good news is Christ, God's only Son, did what we can't. He lived a perfect life and sacrificed Himself in our place. It's that simple. I have been going down this road, and nothing has ever satisfied me. Nothing I achieved or wanted has taken away the hole in my life, in my heart. I needed salvation. It's not a journey in life or a truth, it's *The Truth*. Truth is a person. Salvation is a person. It's Jesus. But the choice, well, the choice is ours, and it's mine. We each must make the choice. God won't force himself upon us. I finally looked at all I have, and all the world offers and realized that no matter what happens, my old life is the way of the lost, and I was dead. I was a dead man walking. I want life. I want a new life. Only God gives life. He gives it through His Son Jesus, who died to take away my sins. This week, I stopped running. I stopped rebelling. I am still Zacchaeus Purqana. But the man I was last week is gone. He's dead. The man I am today," at this, Zach looked at all the press around him, "I chose Christ, and I am alive in Christ, my Savior!" He finished with a smile and a peace on his face the press could not comprehend.

Saul sat back and thought about that look from Zach. Oh, the press tried to tie him up in his words and ask him twisted questions. "Was he still a Gay man? Did he still support LGBTQ equality? Wasn't he turning against all he stood for?"

Zach smiled and answered the naysayers, saying, "Jesus came and saved me right where I am. Now I am only one day old in this new life, guys. But I will follow where Jesus leads me by his sufficient grace."

Follow where he leads, thought Saul. He dwelled on that for some time. With all the turmoil swirling around them, you would think the Pirates would play poorly, yet they seemed to get stronger as a team. They won three in a row against the Mets. Last night was 117 victories. 117! They were a .500 team before the start of the season, thought Saul. Now they held the record for wins with nine games still to go. Nearly a century and a half of teams playing baseball, juggernaut franchises, legendary teams, many from here in New York, and these Pittsburgh Pirates just played the greatest regular season ever. It was mind-boggling.

The crowd was screaming bloody murder at the start of the game last night. You couldn't hear a thing. Every New Yorker, it seemed, had something to say. Everywhere you looked, signs with the rainbow symbol and words like "bigots" and "homophobe" targeted the team but focused on Josh. What did Josh do to deserve this? It didn't even make sense.

Josh hit a single in the first. The crowd screamed at him. When Josh took the field in right, someone threw a battery at him, nearly hitting him in the head, and he now wore a batting helmet playing the field. Though security arrested the perpetrator, the crowd jeered Josh all evening. Josh needed only a double to hit for the cycle after a triple in the third and a home run in the seventh. The Pirates were up 8 to three in the top of the ninth, but the crowd still screamed angrily when Josh came to bat. Though playoff hopes ended for the Mets with the Pirates winning the first game of the series, the Mets held onto their spite and walked Josh intentionally in his last at-bat, much to the crowd's delight.

After the third game, Saul received another phone call from Cai. Cai told Saul to block the press from talking to the team after the game and get his team directly to the airport. Apparently, the commissioner's office was furious over the debacle of having one of their most prominent Gay players become a Christian on the same team where Josh already stated the Bible equates same-sex relationships as sin. Saul asked Cai if he believed his Jewish Torah's pronouncements, like the Bible, about sexual immorality.

Cai replied, "I don't advertise my faith the way you Christians have, Saul. I don't stand and shove it in people's faces." Cai continued, "And I didn't come to a Jewish Synagogue and try to insert a Christian prayer after two Christian extremists shot it up!" The anger in Cai's voice was as close to rage as Saul ever heard from the usually taciturn man.

"Mr. Annason," Saul said, trying to offer peaceful condolences in his soft words, "I can assure you what Joe and Josh meant was to show their respect and mourn with you. I know you lost a brother-in-law. Joe lost his younger cousin. As you know, one of his closest friends, your employee, was lying near death in a hospital. As for Josh, he meant no disrespect; quite the opposite. He was there to help, to show his concern and love for all hurt by those evil men."

"We don't need your concern, Saul. We need your action and your obedience."

"I am sorry, Mr. Annason. As I said, I won't tell my players to go against their consciences and beliefs. I would be a hypocrite and worse if I did."

"And what about Zacchaeus Purqana? A week ago, he was the lone player whose lifestyle the fans supported. Now he's what—turned straight?"

"No, Mr. Annason, he became a Christian," Saul replied.

"And what does *that mean*?" Cai said incredulously.

"It means, Mr. Annason, he's never going to be the same person again."

"That's what your religion means, Saul? You give up who you are? You lose what makes you, *you*? How in the world is that something you want to be a part of?"

"Oh, Mr. Annason, it's not about religion. It's about the Creator making us who we are supposed to be. Yes, He changes us when we accept Jesus as Savior, but it's not about what we have lost. It's about all we gain!"

"Regardless, just tell your people to keep their mouths shut for once. At least until they get out of New York!" Cai finished with a huff and hung up the phone. "When will these people learn!" thought Cai.

Saul was a little overwhelmed. It was not the phone call he expected. No "great job" breaking the all-time win record or winning the division. Nope. Keep your mouth shut and get out. Saul remembered something a pastor said once. Don't be surprised by lost people acting lost, for that's what they are. Rejoice instead, that the Lord has given you a clear vision in Christ and a new life.

Saul was concerned, but there was still one game left. Saul decided to rest his starters. Pirate fans barely recognized the Pirates playing their last road game of the regular season in New York. With the expanded roster allowed at the end of the season, Pops started five of nine players who had never played in the big-leagues before, called up from the minors. One, John Mark, was cousin to both Mark Johnson and Barney and got to play the outfield next to Barney, the Pirates utility man who announced this would be his last season earlier in the year. It was a special moment for Barney, 36, second only to Josh in age on the team. He played twelve years in the League. Though he got little time on the field this year, he hit .280 and provided a unique ability to play seven of the nine positions during the season. His cousin, 22-year-old John Mark, was a great player for the Pirates AA affiliate this year. Still probably a year or two from making the "Bigs," he held big dreams as he sat between Josh and Barney on the bench.

"Any words of advice?" John Mark asked both men as he stood up to get his batting gear before going to the on-deck circle.

"Have fun and enjoy it." Josh said, "Look for a good pitch to hit and swing away."

"Don't let a few bad swings bother you," Barney said encouragingly. "We all have made some bad swings before, but it only takes one good swing to make you forget all the bad ones!"

John Mark struck out in his first at-bat, lined out to second in his next, and came to the plate with two out and two on in the top of the ninth. The hostile crowd at Citi Field seemed to shout and wail against him. His nerves and butterflies showed during his first two at-bats. This time, he chose not to listen to the crowd and instead looked at his dugout, finding his cousin, Barney, standing next to Josh, both men smiling at him. Barney clasped both hands together and raised them over his head, and Josh gave him a thumbs up. Their smiles and good words were all he thought about as he turned back and stepped into the batter's box. The second pitch was a hanging curve, and John Mark promptly swatted it into the left field bleachers, giving the Pirates a lead they would not relinquish. When he finished his home run trot, Josh stood at the top of the stairs with Barney at his side, happily waiting with open arms to welcome him home.

Ninety Six

The Pirates came home to mixed blessings. On the one hand, they were the National League's top seed heading into the postseason with the best record in baseball history. They also seemed to be the national focal point for the country's turmoil. They heard both shouts of joy and screaming derision as they opened their final eight-game home stand at PNC Park. More and more, the nation watched and judged.

After clinching first place and the top seed, Saul began platooning his starters with the last game in New York. He planned to rest his team, as the final eight games meant nothing for the postseason. As luck would have it, the two teams they played were both out of the playoffs. Saul did have somewhat of a dilemma with Josh. Josh was in an odd position due to his phenomenal year. He was hitting .468, and even if he got no hits for the last eight games, he would finish the season over .400, the first to do so since Ted Williams in 1941. However, Josh also sat at 64 home runs. It was within the realm of possibility, despite missing 30 games, Josh could break the single-season home run record from the steroid era of 73. Even sitting at 170 RBIs, the most hit since the 1930s, it was conceivable he could also break the all-time record of 191. Pops asked Josh what he wanted to do.

"Pops, I'll do what you ask, but if you are asking, do I need to play to break any record? The answer is no. I am here to help the team win and be victorious," Josh proclaimed before the beginning of the final home stand.

"OK, Josh," Saul replied, "That makes it easier on us with what we want to do. I think I'll sit you down and play you sparingly, if at all. I will rest the starters as much as possible and give the other guys a chance to get some good reps. We'll start again with the playoffs."

Although MLB's expanded roster rules were not as generous as past years, the Pirates brought up several prospects and rested their starting pitching rotation. The fans were not happy with Pops' decision, of course, wanting to both cheer and boo their star players on the field in the crazy mix of emotions swirling around the team. The Pirate stars cheered on their replacement players, standing for the anthem and kneeling together in a team prayer vigil, and the crowd didn't know quite what to make of it. Their team played in the rarefied air of clinching a trip to the playoffs and the League's dominant team while playing primarily Minor League players to end the season.

Finally came the last game of the regular season. Pops returned his starters to the lineup to knock off some rust and prepare for the postseason. Josh and his teammates did not disappoint. After a slap-out to center field and a line-drive ground out, Josh's final at-bat ended the season where he began, with a deep drive over the left field bleachers. Despite using primarily substitutes, the Pirates finished the season 4-4 for a final record of 122-40, officially the greatest regular-season record in baseball history. Now they would wait for the wild card game to see who their opponent would be in the first round of the playoffs.

Ninety Seven

Cai Annason didn't like waiting, but the MLB commissioner gave him no choice. Knowing Quint, it was more to make a point than his busy schedule. Yes, Cai knew he answered to the powers ruling the League, but he resented Quint's reminder of who was in charge. In Cai's realm, his little world of the Pittsburgh Pirates, Cai carried all the trappings of lordship. Though he would never admit it, even to himself, Cai loved the feeling of power he held over his world, his team. He was the man in charge. All Pirates bowed to his will, even though some tried relentlessly to buck his rule and rebel.

Cai's manager, Saul Samuelson, was a constant thorn in his side, pressing for a proper budget to field a contender. Just when it seemed Cai finally figured out how to dispose of this popular and troublesome coach and get someone more malleable, Saul finds Josh Green and turns Cai's world upside down. Yes, Cai feared his realm no longer followed his will, threatening to spin out of control. Just as he finally felt established, able to run the Pirates without interference, wresting control from his overbearing father-in-law, Cai felt everything slipping from his grasp. Cai coveted the respect of his position, and now he even owned a winning team. Yet his father-in-law saddled him with Saul. Cai feared the public viewed Saul as the architect producing this winner, not him. Saul added his centerpiece, the intractable Joshua Green, against Cai's wishes, and Josh Green, the outspoken Christian with all his crazy and dangerous ideals, turned Cai's world upside-down.

Green threatened Cai's position as Pirates President and true leader. The Pirates were number one, all right. Number one in the public's crosshairs as the most disliked team, hated by mainstream media and those who followed popular culture. The Pirates were an anathema to the world, displaying conspicuous Christian values and bold patriotic support. Their rise as a baseball powerhouse mirrored a surge in public ire.

Pittsburgh became a focal point, attracting protesters from every social justice cause known to mankind, thought Cai as he waited impatiently to be called on the carpet. Yes, Cai got everything he wanted, yet nothing was going as he anticipated, planned, and carefully manipulated. Now here he sat, the last blow to his ego, shattering his happy illusion of kingship, in the outer office of the commissioner of Major League Baseball. His father-in-law sent him, like a child called to the principal's office, with orders to "make it right, whatever it takes." Must Cai grovel to this heathen?

"The commissioner will see you now," said the executive assistant, a beady-eyed, bespectacled young man, the gatekeeper to the commissioner's office, as he hung up the phone. Despite his youth, the man made Cai feel like he was watching him, observing Cai's flaws, tallying them in notes he studiously wrote on his mobile tablet. Cai tried to shake it off, thinking no one so young could know the intrigues and complicated threads it took to climb to the heights of leadership in this world. Yet Cai remembered seeing the man at virtually all the commissioner's dealings over the last few years. Cai made a mental note to find out who he was and his position of influence.

Much to Cai's chagrin, the little man watched as Cai made his way to the commissioner's office door instead of getting up and opening it as Cai demanded from his Pirate staff. Of course, Quint wasn't coming to open it either, so Cai would have to do so himself. Another indignity suffered to his status, Cai thought, as he opened the door and entered.

"Cai, a pleasure to see you finally. Won't you have a seat," Quint said, without a hint he kept Cai waiting fifteen minutes past the appointed time. "Can I have Cassius get you anything?" Quint said, gesturing to a chair. Cai noticed he did not proffer a hand for a handshake. Was Quint forgoing the handshake because he heard Cai's habit of not shaking hands, or was it a snub? This time Cai suspected it was the former. One thing Cai found with the commissioner was his meticulous study of every situation before entering a discussion. Cai knew the commissioner justly earned his reputation for running a sophisticated network of informants throughout the industry. Even Cai's efforts to keep all his Pirates "his," he suspected, were not entirely successful.

Cai shook his head, "No, thank you. Young Cassius welcomed me with a Perrier while I waited. It was quite sufficient."

"Of course, of course. I am sorry I am running a little late, but I just got off the phone with our good friend, Herald Gripp. He is in Chicago to attend the National League wild card game. I will attend the AL wild card here in New York."

Herald, of course, was part of baseball's so-called royalty, a multi-generational family of one of Baseball's oldest owners, thought Cai. The Gripp family owned parts of two franchises and previously placed a family member in the commissioner's seat. Yes, Cai was aware of this commissioner's ability to garner support in baseball's hierarchy despite Quint's lack of pedigree. Perhaps pulling Herald Gripp as his deputy was putting the fox in his own hen house for Quint, but

Cai expected Quint saw it as "keep your friends close and your enemies closer." Either way, Cai recognized they made a formidable "Team." Only time would tell if Quint managed to manipulate the tiger by the tail.

"I wanted to stay a little closer to home," Quint continued while looking out the window. "What with all the turmoil we've seen this year," Quint said blithely, showing no signs pointing to Cai's Pirates and Josh Green. Cai knew Quint didn't demand this in-person visit for small talk. Still, the man prattled on.

"Yes, the Yankees and Red Sox, quite a classic rivalry for the wild card game," Quint said. "Should garner significant interest. Surprised the Yankees didn't win the division, but they came back after their terrible July and played a great September. They're looking like contenders again. Either way, we will get a big market team to offset Toronto winning the division. The Blue Jays still couldn't manage much of an uptick in attendance, even fielding a contender." Quint turned back from staring out the window and looked unsmilingly at Cai, "Not like the Pirates this year, though?"

"Yes, we've had quite a year," said Cai, carefully trying to swim clear of the shark circling in the water. He suspected he was already bleeding.

"*Quite-a-year,*" Quint said slowly. "Setting the Major League record for wins that may never be broken. And your year-to-year attendance, what..., doubled?"

Cai didn't answer. The truth was, the Pirates' attendance more than doubled, but then Cai knew the commissioner was well aware of his numbers. For all the turmoil, the Pirates posted their most profitable year in history before the playoffs even started. While Cai failed trying to cash in on the League's plan to market the pro-social cause gear, the regular Pirate paraphernalia saw almost a tripling in purchases over recent years. All the Pirates saw their jersey sales skyrocket, especially Juan and Zach, as the African American and Latino communities rushed to buy the clothing of these two rising stars.

However, Green led the way, out-pacing all others. His jersey and even his rookie baseball card were prime examples. Green's jersey sales topped MLB both domestically and internationally. Demand for Green's rookie baseball card was so great, Tops,® a prime baseball card manufacturer, printed and sold a special-edition card at a whopping $20 a pop. They sold out of it after only ten days. Yes, Josh cost him an additional $500K bonus money by winning baseball's triple crown, something Cai wrote off as impossible when he signed the contract before the season. Cai dared not consider the additional bonuses Josh would pocket if he led the Pirates deep into the playoffs. Still, even if Josh won the World Series MVP and the Pirates won everything, Cai knew the Pirates sales would easily make his team the most financially successful club, for one season at least, in franchise history.

Knowing all this didn't seem to help. Instead, Cai felt he was drowning in the shark-infested waters. "Yes, indeed," he responded finally, looking down unable to meet Quint's unfriendly stare.

"Of course, the League has taken a 15% hit in revenues, the largest one-year drop-off in history," Quint commented, sitting forward slightly, his voice itching from neutral to quiet, yet more menacing. "And what do you think is causing that trend?"

Cai wanted to say, "Due to your ill-advised embracing of unpopular themes and encouraging the players union to step out on social agendas," but he feared what such a comment would do, even if it was true. Cai also suspected Quint recorded this conversation. He knew his opinion might cost him his position if it leaked to the media. Cai would keep his peace, hold his tongue from speaking true but unpopular thoughts, and go along with the commissioner's point of view—as long as Quint held the crown steadily. Cai was a survivor if he was anything, and he knew he would eat crow if it helped keep him lord over his dominion.

"No thoughts?" asked Quint, smiling wickedly now at Cai's silence. "Well, let me throw a couple out there. The fans are fickle. They follow the trends, and the trends are clear. Social justice, racial equality, stamping out bigotry, and tearing down our country's old, outdated way of thinking; that's where our fans want to go. Especially the 16-34 year groups. Our polling indicated if we universally supported the popular opinion that our country needs to change its racist, bigoted past and prove baseball is a leader in cultural change, we would increase market share. Instead, here we are, decreasing it. Why is that? What's the most obvious obstacle to our success, the one venue our polls show as _the_ reason people are staying away, not supporting our causes? You want to take a guess what organization that is?" Quint said, lips drawn tight in a sneer.

"I suppose you brought me here for a reason," said Cai looking at Quint, wanting to get on with it. He tired of being the whipped dog. Even his patience had limits.

"It's _your_ Pirates and Josh Green!" Quint spat with intense malice.

"Begging your pardon, Commissioner, but if my Pirates are decreasing MLB revenue, then why are all my numbers at all-time highs? Why are Josh Green's sales the highest in the League? If we are the problem?"

"_You_ are the problem because your team won't play ball," Quint replied, using the ill-thought-out metaphor. "Your players rebel. They make us look bigoted and racist, bucking the trend and standing for the anthem. They make us look like religious extremists by kneeling in prayer. Josh Green gives interviews like a Sunday School teacher out of our bigoted past. He puts everything in the context of right or wrong, truth or lies. What is Truth? Are we to stomach Josh Green's sanctimony, the righteous saint preaching repentance and grace?"

"I don't believe in what Josh Green says, but as you know, we can't stop the players from talking about their faith. I am sure your lawyers warned you, as have mine, about curtailing or fining a player for his religious beliefs," Cai defended his actions rather than Josh's right to hold to his faith and freely speak it.

"What my lawyers have said to me isn't the point. The point is the bottom line is falling. The point is: Major League Baseball cannot be on the wrong side of history. We cannot go back to the days of Jackie Robinson and prejudice."

"Are you arguing for the social agenda or against Joshua Green?" asked Cai.

Quint was angry, but said nothing for a moment. He was no fool, but his statement made the question difficult to reconcile. Who was the Jackie Robinson of this age? Where did the root of the League's problems, or the world's problems, for that matter, lie?

"You can't be for one without being against the other," Quint said, following quietly almost to himself, "And there's the rub." It was Quint's turn to look down at his hands. Swayed by the people's desires, Quint again chose to follow their demands. He looked back at Cai with a less menacing, more conciliatory but confident voice, communicating he alone held the key to Cai's success. "Where do you stand, Cai? Do you want to continue to be the Pirates' President? Whose side do you choose?"

What was the heart of the matter, thought Cai? Where did his heart lie?[1] Cai loved the prestige of being a team president. He loved the power and the status symbols of owning and presiding over a Major League team, even if it was small-market Pittsburgh. The whole town was his as Pirates President. Every door opened, and the chief seats were his at any venue Cai wanted.[2] He was a well-respected man, from a well-respected family, probably with more influence now than the mayor. And the mayor contended with the city council daily. Cai pretty much got his way, and his only real problem was Saul. No, Cai corrected. The problem was Josh Green.

Cai knew all he valued came from the League's and his father-in-law's support. Cai would not give up what he idolized the most, what he coveted for years and finally possessed; holding the title, President of the Pittsburgh Pirates. Cai must take the only lifeline offered.

"I am on your side, of course, Commissioner," Cai Annason said without further hesitation. "What would you have me do?"

---

1. Matthew 6:21;

2. Matthew 19:20-21, 23:5-7

Ninety Eight

Linda Richards carefully set out the covered dishes of chicken pad Thai and beef bulgogi, with the various kimchi and potstickers, aka steamed dumplings, all in covered bowls made hot and cold as appropriate. The food was from a unique Asian restaurant in town, owned by two sisters-in-law married to brothers who held business dealings in the far east and married two women gifted in their native cooking. They subsequently started a restaurant with Thai and Korean cuisine. It was a strange but delicious combination. Linda ate there in person on more than one occasion. The sisters-in-law were an interesting combination of cooking and conversation, with an evident friendship that spilled over in making fun of each other in their unique blends of accented English. They often came out to talk with the guest and sample their opposite's menu, debating which cuisine was better. They never disappointed in their cooking or entertaining playfulness, engaging with each other and their clientele. Today, however, was a takeout day for Linda as she waited excitedly for almost a week after gathering all pertinent data before her scheduled luncheon with Doctor Thyatira. It took her a few weeks and many phone calls and questions to compile the medical evidence from the hospitals Josh Green visited over the season. Last but not least was the unexpected recent information from Pittsburgh.

Lydia was a few minutes late. When she walked in, she looked a little disheveled. "What a day, Linda! I am so sorry I am late."

"Do you have time to sit and eat something?"

"Yes, Yes. I am good for now. It's been non-stop all morning. I need a break," said Lydia, "And some good news, Yes?"

"Yes indeed! First, have a seat, and I'll pour you a chai tea," Linda said, opening an insulated thermos. The smells of ginger, cardamom, cinnamon, fennel, black pepper, and clove all intermixed and flowed in the room, contrasting against the background of peppery curry and the sweet and sour smell of the meats and vegetables already hanging in the air.

"Oh my! I've got to watch out for afternoon heartburn, but I love the taste," said Lydia.

"It's OK, the buffalo milk in the tea will help pre-coat your innards in preparation, and I got the pad Thai mild like you asked. They kept the momoya sauce on the side so you can season to taste. If worse comes to worst, I have a bottle of Tums in my cabinet!"

"Let me get the chai tea in me. I like spicy cuisine, just not heartburn! So, what is the news? What have you found out?"

"Here it is. Take a look," Linda said as she brought up her laptop and cast it onto a flat screen mounted on a wall in her office. Linda often gave briefings or taught interns and other students and was well-skilled in the art of PowerPoint and spreadsheets after years of writing on chalk and whiteboards.

"I polled the fourteen different hospitals Josh took Ruth to throughout the season. There were a total of 218 patients Josh visited. Most were children in critical care, many with advanced-stage cancer. Fourteen were children on an organ transplant list. Forty-two had stage four cancer. Reading the doctors' notes suggested eight were near death." Linda let Lydia digest the note columns as she handed her the mouse to scroll through. Linda could barely contain herself, so she grabbed a bite of the bulgogi. It was warm and slightly sweet, a delicious blend of flavors, and not too spicy. She popped a dumpling in her mouth for good measure. It was steaming hot and a nice offset to the strips of mildly spiced beef; nothing vegan today. It's OK, she felt, well, she didn't know what to feel. She drank some tea as Lydia finished scrolling over the notes and numbers.

"OK, so I see what they were when Josh visited them, including ours," Lydia commented. "And I know what happened with them. What about all these others?"

"Go to the second tab," Linda nodded, trying to play her best poker face.

Lydia selected a tab at the bottom of the spreadsheet entitled "Current as of" with yesterday's date. The columns looked to reproduce the original tab, but many contained no information or dashed lines. Lots of the summaries showed "0." There was one exception. Linda added one new column to the right side of this spreadsheet.

"I don't understand. Where's all the information?" Dr. Thyatira asked quizzically.

"It's there. Scroll over." Linda said.

The added column's title was "Discharged." It was the first column with a number in every hospital entry. Lydia looked back at Linda, confused.

"Now scroll down to the bottom," Linda directed her friend.

Lydia did. The summary number of the "Discharged" column was 218. Again, Lydia looked back at Linda, who sat down her tea and looked at her intently. With a confused, scrunched brow, Lydia said, "Linda are you saying...,"

"Everyone Josh saw is discharged, yes," stated Linda, with a voice that could no longer contain her excitement.

"What about the organ transplants?" questioned Lydia, her voice uncharacteristically shaky as she set down her drink.

"All fourteen were taken off the transplant list and discharged," replied Linda.

Lydia's scrunched forehead smoothed as she digested what Linda was saying and showing her. "What about the stage four cancer patients?" Lydia asked, and Linda shook her head. "And the terminal cancer patients? What about them?" Lydia said emphatically, honestly questioning Linda to tell her she wasn't mishearing her.

"All discharged!" said Linda, smiling and slightly teary-eyed.

"All? No deaths, no transplants?" Lydia questioned, not daring to believe.

"None. All treatments completed or ended, cancer-free," said Linda.

"All...healed, Linda?" Lydia half stated, still with a question in her quavering voice.

Linda nodded, "Once I began to suspect the data, I talked personally to each lead supervisor or administrator from all fourteen hospitals. For some of these hospitals, Josh saw only a subsection of large wards. For others, it was everyone in the children's ward, like yours. It was a little harder to tell for those who Josh met only a portion of their patients. It took me some time, but I finally tracked down the people from the hospital who went with him. For the ones where he saw everyone in a particular ward, many guessed why I was asking. They suspected something unusual happened because all their patients walked out within a week or so after Josh left, all healed. Now that I have been in touch, many are asking what others are seeing. I think they were all afraid to ask or say anything initially...," Linda paused as she finished.

"Because it's impossible. Because if we say it out loud, someone might think we were crazy," said Lydia sitting back, looking at her plate of food, untouched.

Linda nodded and was silent, letting it sink in again. Then she remembered her last piece of evidence. "Lydia, there's more. Something I learned that's not on the list. When I talked with the Pittsburgh hospital, the one Josh went to early on, the administrator there was one who noticed something happened but was unaware of my role in helping the Greens schedule visits around the country. He knew no one to talk to, but he needed to tell someone, and that someone was his sister, the Chief of Trauma and Surgical Residents at a neighboring facility."

"Her hospital received some of the wounded from the terrible shooting we heard about at the Pittsburgh synagogue. They operated on six injured that day, and three were in critical shape. She feared some of them wouldn't make it. Josh Green held some connection to one of the men, apparently an employee of the Pirates organization, and showed up the morning just after she completed rounds. She remembered what her brother said and pulled Josh aside, hoping he would pray over her other two critical patients after his friend, saying she feared for their survival. He agreed, and she confirmed after he visited his friend, he stopped by the other two people, an elderly man, and his thirty-something son, who received multiple gunshots. The son, in particular, was still in intensive care, with one bullet having passed in and out of the left side of his skull, causing brain damage. They believed him to be close to brain-dead. The intensive care nurse said she made Josh stay outside the room, but he and another older man prayed over them both." Linda paused for a moment, and Lydia looked at her expectantly, guessing what came next. Linda smiled, saying, "All three victims fully recovered. They all walked out of the hospital a week later.

"Oh, good and gracious Father. This is nothing short of a miracle, Linda," Lydia replied.

"218 miracles," Linda said.

Lydia nodded, then, thinking about it, corrected, "221 perhaps?".

Linda smiled at that. "Yes, 221—That we know about. How many others are there, and will there be more?"

Ninety Nine

T he Pirates' best record in baseball earned them home-field advantage in the playoffs, meaning Pittsburgh hosted the initial two games of the divisional playoffs best of five series. The Pirates' opponents were the St. Louis Cardinals, who defeated the Cubs 6-1 in the NL wild card game. Before the first game in Pittsburgh, the teams met and shook hands. Surprisingly, St. Louis was the team closest in attitude to the Pirates' stance on social agenda and baseball. From the beginning, nearly half the players and several coaching staff stood for the national anthem, although several wore the paraphernalia supporting racial justice. Six players, including two St. Louis all-stars and three coaches, joined the Pirate's entire team for the post-anthem prayer. Many fans with strong feelings supporting the racial and anti-bigotry causes tried to stir the crowd against supporting the anthem stance and subsequent prayer. Still, mixed emotions flowed from the rest of the Pittsburgh crowd, unsure whether to support the show of faith.

As expected, Pops started Samson in game one. Pops rested Samson, skipping his last rotation at the end of the regular season. The media questioned Pops sitting his starters and stars at season's end, but Pops said it was a calculated risk he and the coaches would manage with proper practice and preparation. After the long season, Pops felt his starters needed the rest and were now well-prepared to make a playoff run. For game one, Samson at least did not disappoint. He went eight innings, giving up only two hits and no runs. The Pirates did not hit the St. Louis Ace particularly well the first two times through the order, but Josh started the seventh off with a double down the left field line. Juan followed with a single, and Judah worked a base on balls to load the bases, chasing the St. Louis ace to the showers. Nate Fisher lifted a deep fly to right to score Josh and advanced a hard running Juan to third. Thomas hit a ball into the hole left of short. The shortstop made a good play, but hard-charging Judah gave a good disruptive slide on the second basemen. His throw went wide of first, pulling the first baseman off the bag, allowing Juan to score. Judah made it back to the dugout to many back slaps and high fives, including Josh, who stood waiting, holding Judah's glove and regular cap.

"Nice hustle Judah. You bought us an insurance run," said Josh handing Judah his gear.

"Well, I may not run as fast as you, Josh, but what I lack in speed, I make up for in ugly, tumbling slides!" he said with a wry smile.

"Hey partner, whatever works is good enough for me," Josh said, extending his hand. Judah was a little surprised both by Josh's offer and his response. He took it greedily and said, "Let's finish this thing, Josh!"

"My thoughts exactly," Josh said, smiling kindly at his former nemesis. The Pirates never looked back. Justus Barabbas did what he had for most of the second half of the season, pitching a no-hit ninth inning, and the Pirates won game one, 2-0.

Game two was a different affair. Both starters were shaky, giving up runs in the first. Josh batted a quiet one-for-three in game one but hammered a 1-1 pitch line drive into the right field bleachers with Andrew on first to give the Pirates a 3-2 lead in the fourth. In the eighth, with the score tied 5-5, Josh was due up third. Both Zach and Andrew got on with singles. Josh was two for two, looking like the Josh of old, having burned St. Louis many times this season. After a mound consultation, the Cardinals decided to walk Josh with no outs. Now, they faced Juan, who finished the season in third place for home runs with 41 and second only to Josh in RBIs.

The Pirates' radio broadcast was in good form as they surveyed the scene.

"Greg, quite a statement by the Cards, not wanting to pitch to Josh with no outs here in a tied game in the eighth. Do they think Juan is an easy out?" asked Bob.

"Only compared to Green, Bob. Third in the League in Home Runs and a season average of .304. Besides all that, one of Juan's many attributes this year is he's a fly ball hitter in these situations, third in the League for sacrifice flies. I hope to see one of those lovelies float right over the fence and bust this thing open," quipped Greg.

"The Cards have brought in their sinker ball submariner, though, looking for a double play. He has been a mixed bag against Juan, who has gone just one for six against him, lifetime," said Bob.

"How is hitting 1 for 6 a mixed bag, you might ask folks?" asked Greg, playing along with his partner, "Well, the one was a mammoth home run. Even a deep fly ball gives us the lead here. Anything but a double-play ball would be nice, and right about now, I'd like to see Juan roll another snake eye, one-fer," said Greg.

"Yeah, but then he'd be a two-fer, wouldn't he, Greg?"

"Yer confusin' me, Bob. Besides, my math ended in Mr. Reily's algebra class, and not in a good way—hey, here we go, folks."

"The St. Louis submariner is ready, and the house that Green built is a-rockin'. I think they also want a two-fer," called Bob, "Here's the windup..., and the pitch."

"CRACK."

Juan's powerful swing connected with a sinkerball that didn't. Outside, but waist-high, Juan belted the hanging pitch deep towards the center field fence.

"THERE's a Deep Drive!" shouted Bob.

"THERE SHE GOES, folks. The Grand SALAMI with Extra CHEESE, to deep dead center, no doubt about it!" chimed in Greg.

"Yes, folks, the cardinal sin of a sinker-baller is to get a pitch up, and this Cardinal sinned," declared Bob.

"But our beloved Juan's a saint tonight, on the straight and narrow with a heavenly swing even the angels are applauding!" said Greg.

The rest of the inning was rocky for the Cardinals, but they managed to get the third out without allowing another run after another pitcher change. The Pirates gave their fans some late frights, almost squandering the four-run lead, as Jude Keriothson got two outs after allowing a home run, then allowed two more base runners. Pops, who tried to save Barabbas, brought him in to finish. Justin got his second save in two nights with a timely strikeout. It wasn't always pretty, but the Pirates were up 2-0 on their way to St. Louis to try and close out the series.

One Hundred

With the series back to St. Louis, Nurse Richards saw her chance. She watched the second game of the series, and even though it was late evening, she made the call.

"Mary, it's Linda Richards. I am sorry for the lateness of the call, but I wanted to talk to you and ask you for a favor...."

The Pirates traveled to St. Louis the following day. Needing one more win in the best of five series, the team looked to finish the series quickly and get a break before the National League Championship Series. Scheduled for an early day game tomorrow, the Pirates settled into their team hotel early that evening. Mary approached Josh while they got ready to eat.

"Josh, I got a call last night from Nurse Richards," Mary started tentatively.

"Yes?" Josh calmly responded as they sat eating Chinese takeout from a restaurant Ruth found their last time in town.

"Oh, I like Nurse Richards," Ruth chimed in, "She was so nice the first time we came to St. Louis; And look at all the nice people she has set us up with on our travels."

"Yep, you're right, hon. Nurse Richards was a Godsend," replied Josh smilingly. He then looked back at Mary. "What did she want," he asked, though Mary felt Josh somehow already knew.

"She was very apologetic, knowing we would be busy and didn't necessarily have much time...."

"No, we don't," said Josh, "What with the day start, we need to be up and out of here by 9:30 AM. We will be traveling home if we win," he added evenly, looking at Mary.

"Yes," Mary agreed tentatively. "She was hoping you could give her and Dr. Thyatira..., You remember the sweet Greek Doctor who showed us around the Children's ward? They both wondered if we end up being here long enough...," Mary trailed off.

"She would like us to visit again," Josh said helpfully.

"Dad, we should, if we can. The kids and all the patients and doctors always do better when you come and spend time with them. They could really use you," interjected Ruth.

"I would love to go. If we have to play another game here, I will. We will have to wait and see. Please tell Nurse Richards I plan to come see them the morning after game three if we're still here," Josh answered. Mary nodded, concerned, knowing if they were still here, it would mean the Pirates lost game three. As she watched without speaking, Ruth grabbed her dad's hand, squeezed it, and smiled after his statement.

"It's OK, isn't it, Dad, if the Lord wants us to stay an extra day in St. Louis. It means we can go get a Smash Burger® from Mac's!"® Ruth said happily. Usually, Ruth was all about the Pirates winning, and she fought frustration every time they lost, especially when Josh was hurt. However, it felt to Mary that Ruth and Josh already knew what the Lord intended to do, and they were fine with whatever lay ahead, as long as it was His will.

Nurse Richards was never much of a baseball fan, and Lydia Thyatira tried to pretend she didn't even understand the game, but Lydia called her out the morning of game three. Linda found her about to make rounds with their friend Reuben, one of their genuinely gifted nurses in the Children's ward.

"Ah, Linda, glad you could come," Dr. Thyatira said. Then she waved to Reuben and three other staff. "Now, before we begin today, we need to pray for a miracle for Reuben," Lydia said seriously, and he looked back at her, surprised. She smiled. Looking at Linda, she continued, "And for us all, I think. There is one of those 'Ball Games' going on today, Right Reuben?" she continued and looked back at Reuben, and he relaxed as a smile replaced his surprise.

"Yes, ma'am," he said slowly, as if he tried to teach the doctor about baseball, yet she refused to learn. She pretended not to notice.

"Well, as I understand, Our Red Birds are not doing well," she said sadly, "And we need them to do well today!" she added emphatically. "Because poor Reuben needs to have them win at least one game, eh?"

"Three, actually," said Reuben.

"Let's not ask God for quite so much today, eh Reuben? One day at a time. But please, we do need this miracle," and she was looking at Linda when next she spoke sincerely, "And I can honestly say, I have never wanted more for our Red Birds to win," she said, and Linda nodded with a little tear in her eye.

"So, now we pray, for all our kids and staff, like we do to begin every day. But we also today make a special prayer for our Red Birds!" As was her custom to start the day, Dr. Lydia led the group, including Nurse Richards, in prayer with a special request for God's blessing on their baseball team.

Game three was a one-sided affair; all St. Louis. The Cards jumped out to an early 3-0 lead, and the Pirates bats fell silent. Josh faltered with his first no-hit game in two weeks. The Pirates uncharacteristically made two fielding errors allowing three unearned runs in the third inning to blow the game open. The Cards went on to a 10-2 victory. Saul was worried, and he brought the team together post-game before letting Mark bring in the media.

"Hey! We were sleepwalking out there today. I think we all looked past these Cardinals to the next round, myself included. We forgot these guys won 103 games this year. They have a lot of pride as a franchise and are used to the playoffs going up and down. They aren't gonna quit, and if you go to sleep on them, we will flat-out get our butts kicked like we did tonight." Pops looked at his team, and more than one was hanging his head.

"This is our wake-up call. We got to do what they did after coming off a tough loss in game 2. There's no one going to give us the championship. We are going to have to go out and earn it," Pops said looking around the subdued locker room. Pops continued with a confident, resolute, voice. "Men. We have gone through a lot this year. We are no longer the up and comers we were in May. I've never been through a tougher season than what we've been through, with everything going on. We've always risen. We've always come together. You think on this one while you get cleaned up, and we finish the day at the ballpark, but that's it. Once you leave, you leave it here. This day is done. Tomorrow's a new day. Let's come back, come together, and give the kind of effort I saw out of you all during the season. Let's remember who we are and who we want to be," Saul finished, reminding the players of something he instilled from the beginning.

The team all nodded at the coach. Juan and J.J. bumped fists. Samson patted Zach on the back, who uncharacteristically made one of the errors in the third, and Zach nodded back at the big man. Judah punched his fist into his glove in determination. Barney slapped Nathan Fisher on the shoulder, smiling encouragingly. "You'll get them tomorrow, Nate. Have a little faith!" Nate was down on himself after striking out with two in scoring position, with the game still close in the second inning. Andrew and Thomas nodded to each other from opposite sides of the players. Andrew started a chant they began early in the season.

"Who - are - we?" Andrew said slowly, almost quietly, looking across at Thomas.

"Pirates," Thomas answered evenly.

"And what are we about?" Andrew continued.

"Team," Thomas said slightly louder.

"And what's that mean?" Andrew finished.

"Family!" Thomas affirmed, leaning forward.

The Thunder Brothers stood up, picking it up.

"Who are WE?" J.J. said, looking around the room.

"Pirates!" the players picked up the chant, sound building with some standing up now.

"And what are we about?" Juan said more emphatically.

"TEAM!" came the louder reply.

"And what's that MEAN?" Samson now finished in his booming baritone voice.

"FAMILY!" was the raucous reply thundering the locker room.

Unnoticed by them all, one sat off to the side, unlacing his spikes, and put little effort into the rallying cry. Jude Keriothson, who pitched in the middle innings, giving up two of the runs in a lackluster performance, barely paid the chant lip service. He wasn't into high school rah-rah motivations. Jude was far more realistic about what this world offered and demanded if you were to succeed. He didn't want to get called out, so he pretended to join in but held little team belief. At best, he saw it as foolish sentimentality from the other players, though they did not know or notice he felt this way. Better they didn't. "If they only knew," Jude thought ironically, laughing to himself. But as the chant finished, he locked eyes with Josh Green. Josh quietly observed the scene, leaning back in his chair in front of his locker. No, not watching the scene, Jude corrected himself. Josh stared directly at him. Jude didn't know how long Josh watched him, but he quickly surmised it was long enough. Josh's dark features, the wavy black hair, the broad nose, all signs of Afro-Arab descent, thought Jude. All those ancient features focused Josh's dark penetrating eyes on Jude, seeing right into his soul. Despite all the noise and movement around him, in the brief moment their eyes locked, Jude felt Josh Green knew what he was about and what he would do before Jude knew himself. Jude quickly glanced away, pretending he did not see Josh notice his fake team support. But Jude was worried Josh somehow knew so much more. Jude's heart beat rapidly; a heart, Jude feared, Josh somehow knew clearly, and he did not want to think what that meant.

The next day dawned anew, and Josh, Ruth, and Mary visited Linda Richards and Lydia Thyatira at the hospital. The two ladies greeted the three Pittsburghers with open arms. Dr. Thyatira and Nurse Richards planned the visit as much as they could. They ran Josh throughout the children's ward, ensuring he saw all the patients. Josh, for his part, pretended he did not notice the more systematic schedule Dr. Thyatira held than when they visited the first time. Josh embraced and prayed with each patient and family. The three visitors handed out Pirates goodies from the large bundle they wheeled that Mark Johnson now provided everywhere Josh went. Dr. Thyatira didn't stop there. Josh saved enough time to visit some adult patients in the hospital's adult critical care wing. The two ladies coordinated the last few days with several doctors to make the visits happen within the hospital protocols. When questioned, the two ladies insisted Josh, as a sports icon, brought a superb bedside manner and dramatically impacted their patient's health the last time he came through. One skeptical doctor questioned why Dr. Thyatira was making a big deal about Josh seeing one of his patients in a coma since having a stroke last week. The small woman put her hands on her hips using her not inconsequential reputation built at the hospital over the past quarter-century. "Where our medicine and actions can do no more, Josh's presence and prayers bring hope and healing." The doctor raised his eyebrows but acquiesced when she said, "Trust me, Thomas. You'll thank me you did."

After more than two hours, it was time for Josh and the ladies to head to the ballpark for their evening game. The four ladies hugged each other, and Josh told the girls to go on ahead. He would catch up with them in the parking lot. Mary took Ruth, and Josh stopped to say his goodbyes.

"Thank you for having us here, Linda and Lydia. It has been a real blessing to meet and pray for all your patients," Josh said as a goodbye.

"Josh, we are so honored to have you. We know our patients are better off because of your being here," Linda Richards said with earnest honesty and hope.

"Linda, if they are better off, it is entirely the Lord's doing, you know? I can do nothing myself."

"Josh, why aren't you showing the gift you have to the world?" asked Dr. Thyatira.

"If I have anything, Lydia, it's the good news. I am here to proclaim the Truth in Love and Spirit. To spread the good news of new life. The news that Christ loves us, that He paid the price for our sins. Though we are dead and enslaved by those sins, Christ wants to make us alive again. He is our hope, and He is the Truth. He is the only way. This is all I have—Christ's offer of Salvation. I give my words and live the life He gives me. He is the Truth we all need, and He is faithful and just to forgive us our sins and cleanse us. But we must choose. Our problem is us. We must either hold onto our sins, rebellion, and death or turn back to God, choose Christ, and live. That is what I have, and I give it all willingly."

"Josh, but the patients, all you have prayed over, live! Isn't that enough to make people choose life?" Lydia asked.

"Oh, my dear friend, even though Jesus did as He said He would, even though He rose from the dead as He prophesied, and conquered death, many still choose not to believe. The children's lives and those who return from death's door are a gift of our Father, through His Son, to all mankind. They testify to the Truth, that the words I repeat are True. Some will believe, repent, and be saved. Those who don't, will be unable, once again, to say they did not know the Truth, for their choice is made clear."

Josh hugged them both. "You are always welcome here, Josh," Linda said.

Josh looked sad for a brief moment but then smiled and answered, "I look forward to that day when I see you again. Until then, love each other and spread God's love and the Good News of His Son, Jesus, our risen Savior."

One Hundred One

T he National League Divisional Series for the Pirates finished in four games as the Pirates bounced back from their poor performance in game three. They looked focused and an altogether different team for game four. The Pirates scored in four of the first six innings, and the game was as lopsided as the last, but this time in their favor, with the Bucs winning 12-2. Josh went 2-2 with a single in the first and a three-run homer in the third. The Cards walked him in the sixth, but he did what he did all year. He got a better-than-average jump and beat the All-Star catcher's throw for a steal of second, then scored on a close call from a double by J.J.

After completing the NLDS, the National League Championship Series placed the Pirates against the Los Angeles Dodgers, a perennial powerhouse. The Dodgers fielded a team with great pitching and hitting yet failed to match up well this year against the Pirate bats. It was a lopsided series. Josh went on a terror. The Dodgers did their utmost to pitch around him, walking him a stunning ten times in four games. However, he came to bat with multiple base runners in each game. Juan hit behind Josh at a torrid .438 pace in the playoffs, giving the Dodgers a tough decision. The Dodgers pitched to Josh five at-bats over the four games, and four of the five ended in a home run, with the fifth, a bases-clearing double. After the last game, the LA Times ran the front-page headline, "Green's Greatest Hits," and the pictures of the four homers led off their sports section.

The Pirates punched their ticket to the World Series, defeating the Dodgers in four straight. Josh's numbers were astounding. Despite accruing 18 intentional walks, in the eight games of the postseason, he was 10-14, with five home runs and 18 RBI. He also scored ten runs going 4 for 4 in stolen bases. There was no stopping him and, as a result, no stopping the Pirates. As the Pirates went home to Pittsburgh to await their opponents for the World Series, it was as if the entire news cycle of the country focused on Josh's Herculean homers and offensive prowess while reminding the public of his off-field controversies. It was clear Josh and the Pirates' dominance in baseball seemed to spill over, becoming a lightning rod for the country's struggling cultural conflicts in the fight for its soul.

One Hundred Two

D ecades after the original "Pops" led the '79 Pirates to their last World Championship, Pittsburgh would again host the World Series. Finally, the day arrived with great anticipation, and Josh led his teammates in a triumphal entry onto their home field to adoring crowds. The city was electric, and the entire country watched with piqued interest as the Pirates took the field for warm-ups before game one of the World Series.

"Welcome to Pittsburgh folks, and PNC Park, where your National League Pennant winning Pittsburgh Pirates are hosting the first game of the World Series!" Bob proclaimed to the radio and TV viewers as part of the combined broadcasting team.

"Yes indeed, friends. Some said it would never happen again, but I've always been a believer, haven't you, Bob?"

"It's been hard some of these years, Greg, but ever since Saul Samuelson seemed to right the ship five years ago, we held hope, however dwindling these last few seasons. But not this year, Greg."

"That's right, Bob. This year would have made the Pops of old proud, as this Pops unleashed his secret weapon, the find of the century, the new Sultan of Swat, the great 'Greenbino,' and, for at least one night, the Prince of Pittsburgh. Let's listen and watch this capacity crowd chanting his name as the team comes out onto the field!"

First, the PNC announcer called out the lineup for the American League Champions. It was a winding road, but the Pirates' opponents for the World Series would be none other than the vaunted New York Yankees. It would be the first time the two teams met since splitting the four-game series in New York before the All-Star break. Of course, the Pirates won the first two games of that series convincingly, only to lose Josh after his injury during the attack in the subway station.

The Pittsburgh crowd greeted the Yankees with a mixture of emotions. Boos led the chorus, but there were also a surprising number of cheers. The Yankees, true to their actions since before the All-Star break, donned various cause célèbre wear. All wore shirts with causes proudly displayed, but it didn't stop there as almost every article of clothing received alterations promoting racial justice, anti-fascist, and anti-bigotry causes for these pregame introductions. Some even wore pictures of the victims of police shootings, including the one in Pittsburgh. Many included rainbow colors. These groups mirrored corollary groups outside the stadium trying to build a fan response, and some inside PNC Park also supported the Yankees' stance, shouting and cheering wildly. Today, Pirate fans largely shunned and ignored them.

Next, the announcer began the Pirates lineup. Leading off and first introduced, Zacchaeus Purqana's name received thunderous applause. Next came Andrew, the Pirates captain, and perennial all-star, and the crowd was even louder though they seemed on the edge of their seats, filled with anticipation.

Finally, the announcer said, "And now, batting third, the Major League's newest Triple Crown winner, the first player to hit over .400 in eight decades, our hometown hero, number 3, Joshua Green!"

The crowd practically drowned out the loud PA as he called out Josh's name. They screamed in anticipatory rapture, greedily awaiting his crowning as king of baseball.

"Listen to that crowd roar, folks. Boy, they really love a winner here, don't they, Greg," called out Bob, trying to talk over the roar in the surrounding stadium.

"That they do, Bob. Ole Josh Green, the aged rookie, has done amazing, some might call miraculous, things this year!"

"We have seen Josh Green do everything from hit five homers in one game to hits in consecutive plate appearances, setting records in his first season and even his first week of play," Bob reminded.

"Yeah, and let's not forget he took largely the same team that went 78-84 for their second consecutive losing season into a powerhouse 122 game-winner, the most, by six wins, in Major League history."

"Well, he did have a little help, now and again, Greg," Bob interjected.

"Even if that's true, Bob, you couldn't tell that to this crowd. They are still screaming so loud we can barely hear the rest of the announcer's lineup calls," Greg finished.

Finally, when the National Anthem played, the crowd seemed split, like a "*Tale of Two Cities*."[1] Some fans actively tried to support the New York Yankees, who all kneeled. Most continued to wear their slogans of support, as the League allowed, and some even raised black or rainbow-colored gloved hands of defiance. But tonight, the crowd seemed with their team as many stood and sang. The Pirates,

---

1. A Tale of Two Cities is a historical novel published in 1859 by Charles Dickens

dressed in their team uniforms without displays, stood with hands over hearts. The Yankees watched as the Pirates took to the field. As was their custom, the entire team met, closed in a circle, kneeled, and prayed. The crowd remained primarily supportive, though some booed.

"What an interesting night here in Pittsburgh, folks. There seems to be quite a difference of opinion. Each team making their own statement, showing what they believe and what is important to them," Bob observed.

"I guess it's all about what you are willing to stand up for," replied Greg.

"And I am not sure what the crowd thinks about it all. It's hard to say which way they choose," said Bob thoughtfully.

"I guess it would be fine if people allowed others to believe what they wanted to believe," said Greg.

"Would that mean they are trying to figure out who's telling the truth?" Bob asked.

"I don't think that's it, Bob," Greg huffed his response. "I think we can know the truth, but I'm not sure the truth has anything to do with it. I just think the crowd is waiting," answered Greg.

"Waiting for what, partner?" Bob truly asked.

"Waiting to see when it's all over, who is lost and who is victorious."

The game was a tight affair. Samson matched blows against the Yankees ace. They each took two-hit shutouts into the ninth inning. Josh was 1-1 with a single to start the fifth inning and three walks. Twice he made it to third base, the only Pirate to do so, but was stranded by some clutch pitching. Samson allowed only one runner to get to second, a solid double from the Yankees captain, leading off the fourth, but he bore down and pitched three straight strikeouts to end that inning. As the game wore on, Samson seemed to get stronger. In the seventh, he was so dialed-in, he pitched what is called a perfect inning. Nine pitches, nine strikes, for three straight strikeouts. He threw two more strikeouts and a weak ground-out to first in the eighth. Samson fired on all cylinders. Fastball upper 90s, changeup dying mid-plate down to the dirt, and a slider on the corner breaking four inches outside.

Pops watched Samson as he came off in the eighth and was going to ask him how he felt, but Samson headed that off, looking at him directly, waiving his open hand, and thumping his glove at his chest, nodding, "I got this." Saul saw enough from his ace to know he would fight to finish, and his last fastball hit 100 on the gun as it sliced the corner. Pops kept the bullpen idle. They would ride their ace into the ninth.

Samson did not disappoint. He got the pinch hitter to bite on a changeup for a weak ground ball to the right side for out number one. He then delivered a three-pitch strikeout to the lead-off man and finished with the Yankee captain's inning-ending strikeout on a 1-2 wicked slider that was simply unhittable.

The Pirates would start the bottom of the ninth, score tied 0-0 with the top of the order. The Yankees starter threw 98 pitches through the first eight innings and was almost as dominant as Samson. Almost. The Yankee skipper decided to let him stay in to start the ninth against the Pirates as Pops had done with Sampson. Zach didn't make it easy on him. After a long at-bat, fouling off three consecutive 2-2 pitches, Zach held off on two balls and finally drew a walk.

Andrew was next. He talked with Josh and Thomas in the on-deck circle as they both stood on the edge of the dugout when he returned for a rosin bag.

"He's at 110 pitches. Conventional wisdom would be to take a pitch and get this guy to wear himself down," said Thomas, "but that last at-bat..." he trailed off.

"Yeah, it was a long one," Andrew replied.

"And what does this guy tend to do when he needs a quick out?" said Thomas.

"He tries to throw a first-pitch fastball high on a corner to get a quick strike, then come back with either change or a slider, same location," said Andrew.

"No time like the present," said Josh, "Don't wait. I'll back you up."

Andrew smiled so that only Thomas and Josh could see, and Josh winked back.

The first pitch was a high fastball outside corner, and Andrew drove it sharply into right field, one-hopping it to the right fielder fast enough to keep Zach from reaching third.

The Yankee skipper knew it was past time and pulled his starter, going with the bullpen to face Josh. They must decide what to do; pitch to Josh or walk the bases loaded to get to Juan. With the score tied and no outs, the Yankees decided to try to get Josh. It was their last mistake of the game. Josh took two pitches that weren't close and, on a 2-0 count, hammered a fastball that was low and inside but in the strike zone out of the park over the PNC scoreboard above left field for one of the longest home runs in baseball history. Just like that, the Pirates won game one of the World Series, 3-0.

The stadium exploded in celebration. Any chance for on-field interviews was drowned out with ecstatic chants of "Josh" and "Green." Josh, pushed by his teammates, made one curtain call out of the dugout and tipped his cap to the still capacity crowd, who refused to leave. They responded with rapturous cheers of delight as their Pirate star, the man who brought their team from mediocrity to the championship series, walked off the first game with a thunderous home run. Indeed, it seemed that the Pirates' long-awaited savior had arrived.

Finally, the team gathered in the locker room. Pops pulled them all together before letting in the clamoring press. He said few words except to give out two game-stars. Saul restarted the old tradition in the playoffs from his namesake,

Wilver "Pops" Stargell. Like the Pirates of '79, Pops handed out stars representing someone who contributed exceptionally to a Pirates victory. Samson got one with his incredible outing, a gem of a two-hit shutout, with some of his most dominant pitching coming late in the game. The second went to Josh. Then Pops gave them a warning.

"All right!" Pops yelled to get the attention of the somewhat unruly players cheering on each other after the victory, almost as loud as the crowd. "Listen up. There is one more thing!"

"This is game one. Don't go drinking the Kool-Aid this crowd, and the press, will feed you. We've won one game, that's it! Tomorrow, it starts again at 0-0. You can't mail it in, and we haven't done anything until that fourth W is in the books and done! We're fighting a proud and experienced team. They took us down to the wire tonight. We can't let up! Go about your business and prepare for tomorrow as you did today. Don't let down your guard, even with the accolades this press corps will throw your way when we release the hounds in a minute. We don't want to give the Yankees any more motivation than a loss like this one is bound to do. Remember what I have always preached; One game at a time. Yesterday means nothing. Play today like it's your last. No regrets, OK?"

The team nodded, and unlike their younger selves at the beginning of the season, they pulled together with sincere resolve, soberly taking Pops' words to heart. They were ready to meet the press with the same quiet composure Josh showed every day.

Samson garnered many reporters today with his great outing and questions about his perfect inning. Still, Josh drew the most attention, ending the game with a walk-off home run.

"Josh," one reporter from sporting news began, "Can you walk us through the final at-bat."

"I went up knowing with no outs and a runner on second, we needed solid contact to advance the runners. Anything through the infield was good. I didn't want to swing at a bad pitch with no outs. I knew they would have to fight through the middle of our lineup if they walked me, and chances were good we'd get the run if they did."

"Yes, but Josh, you yanked that ball out like you were sitting and waiting on it," another reporter said.

"He started me with a fastball outside and a curveball in the dirt. I saw both well. His two-finger fastball has good movement, but I think he threw the four-seamer on the last pitch. I knew he probably didn't want to go 3-0 on me, so I expected something close. It was on the inside at the knees, and I worked to get my swing through it,"

"Josh," Roman Josephus cut in, "The ball went 558 feet on Statcast® and cleared the scoreboard. Some say it bounced onto sixth street, the first ever to do so. Were you trying to make a statement to the Yankees about what happens to them when they cross Josh Green?" Roman asked with an unfriendly smile.

"I tried to hit the ball solid and drive it. It doesn't matter how far it goes as long as it clears the fence," Josh answered.

"Josh, you have to admit this was quite a statement game," said another reporter, this one a Yankee beat reporter from New York. "Samson shuts down the Yankee bats, and Josh Green takes the only good pitch he saw all night and drives it out of the park for the win."

"Only thing we are trying to do is get the victory," Josh countered, attempting to diffuse the rhetoric. "Both pitchers tonight did a great job. We got the upper hand late. I got into a position where I could make an impact. I got a pitch to hit, and I didn't miss. It's one hit and one game."

"The Pirates look unbeatable, though, Josh. You put up the best record in baseball, then rolled through the playoffs and drew a wild card team in the World Series," said the same reporter, looking for more.

"The Yankees are an excellent, very accomplished franchise. I expect them to give us everything we can handle and come back strong in game two," Josh replied, trying not to take the bait.

"And you think they could beat this team of yours, Josh?" Roman injected.

"They beat us twice in the regular season," Josh replied.

"Without you, though, Josh," the New York reporter replied quickly, reminding everyone as if they would forget. "The Pirates were without you when they lost."

"Look, no one's unbeatable, and even we have had our ups and downs," Josh said and was going to say more, but Roman cut him off.

"Yes, Josh, but as he said, the Pirates' ups and downs are up when you play?" Roman said, working another angle to take Josh where he wanted him.

"I am glad to make a solid impact for the team throughout the year, Roman," Josh replied noncommittally.

"Your play has pushed the Pirates to the brink of a championship. It would have been a banner year if it weren't for the off-field troubles," Roman said, veering the conversation.

"I do my best to play the game and help the Pirates win. What happens off the field or around the game," Josh said, shrugging his shoulders, "I, like every human being, try to live my life the best I can and make the world the best place I can."

"Yes, Josh, but today we saw very contrasting styles at the start of the game. The Pirates stuck to their official uniforms, without themes, while standing for the anthem despite the victims of racial injustice." Roman began his well-thought-out series of comments and questions, baiting Josh to express his controversial positions and generate Roman's coveted ratings.

"Each person has to determine where they stand and what they believe to be true, what they put their faith in," Josh said, looking at Roman calmly. Josh did not seem surprised by Roman's line of questions. He acted as if he expected them, resolving to see it through. Roman wasn't sure what that meant. Still, he chose to press on.

"Yet the Yankees were the polar opposite of the Pirates, Josh. Supporting their causes and kneeling to the anthem. The public sees two very different points of view."

"Yes, that's true, Roman, but I think it's more an individual choice, and I see things differently than many of the opposing players," Josh said, teeing it up for Roman.

"The Yankees show their beliefs when they kneel by the slogans and gear they wear. They feel they need to kneel during the anthem, yet you don't. Do you not believe in their causes?"

"I don't kneel because I believe our country, government, and laws are not the problem. I stand because I believe in our country and what it stands for, as I have told you before."

"So, you don't believe this country is racist or bigoted?" Roman pressed.

"No, the country stands against racism and bigotry, in its ideals expressed in its founding documents and current laws and policies."

"What about the police shootings?" Roman said.

"As I have said before, police shootings, though tragic, are relatively small in number. Each is reviewed and investigated. Few are found to be unjustified, and even fewer are judged criminal. We are talking about a few dozen people killed through individual criminal acts against all races each year. That's not a country of 330 million people being racist. That's individuals doing something wrong."

"Lots of Yankees don't see it that way," Roman said, trying to drive his wedge.

"I understand that, Roman, but I try to have an open mind and go where the facts lead me. I try to look for the truth."

"Don't you think they might have a different point of view growing up as black men than you? Don't you think their truth might not be the same as yours?" Roman said.

"What race do you say that I am Roman?" Roman remained silent, wanting him to announce. Instead, Josh continued, "There is only one race in God's eyes, the Human Race, and there is only The Truth—you and I and everyone can't have our own truth. Truth is universal. All else is lies. In fact, the opposite of Truth isn't just a lie. It's sin. Each of us must search and find the Truth, regardless of how painful it might be to our situation and lives. Jesus offers us Truth, and

Truth brings life. If two people or groups see the same thing differently, we must look deeper and discover what is True and what is not. There cannot be two equal and opposite Truths. That is logically impossible. If two groups have opposing beliefs, no matter how much they believe them, only one can be true. I told you I would not kneel against my country because my country is not racist or bigoted; not in foundational documents, government practices, policies, or laws. To kneel for me would be to kneel for a lie, and that is a sin.

Roman was ready to get Josh, and he knew where to go. "Josh, then why do blacks have so many problems in America?"

"Roman, all humans have problems. Certainly, when our country started, it continued a terrible sin; slavery. While it professed all men were equal, it denied that equality to black people. It treated them as less than human. As a 'Not Truth,' this was both a lie and a sin, and a truly egregious and terrible sin. We need to understand when we believe or practice a 'Not Truth' as a society, it has terrible consequences. The consequences for allowing slavery were nearly country-ending and catastrophic. Slave traders did terrible things to blacks pressed into slavery, as did the slave owners. Slavery led to the civil war, nearly tearing our nation apart. After we won the war and abolished slavery, we still held onto untrue beliefs of one race being superior. Again, this is proven untrue by God's word and any scientific examination. Yet we wrote laws as a country and held policies, civil conventions, and norms that kept African Americans from taking their rightful place as equals in every opportunity to non-blacks for another century. This was another terrible sin for our nation. Sin always costs us far more than we can pay. Sin unchecked and a people unrepentant of their societal sin, such as racism, reap a whirlwind of negative consequences, and our black ancestors paid in ways few today can understand."

"Isn't that sin still going on?" Roman questioned.

"Roman, this country underwent major upheaval and social change over our racial bigotry after World War II. We know Jackie Robinson, our most important sportsman in American history, fought the fight for understanding to prove the truth that all men, all humans, are created equal. Jackie and many others understood these words were in our founding documents as the founders attested to God's Truth. All are created equal in God's image, and our skin color makes no difference. We are all sons and daughters of Adam. Jackie showed us we, as a country, sinned against God by holding African Americans down, and because of the color of our skin, we were separating and sinning against one another. Our collective conscience changed with the civil rights movement that Jackie and others spurred, and that great Americans like Dr. Martin Luther King Jr. taught us through their grace and action. America changed our culture as we changed our laws, policies, and practices in the 1960s and 70s. By the time you and I were born, our nation banished racism at the systemic level by law and practice."

"Many say racism continues and even grows today, Josh," Roman reiterated.

"I know racism still exists in many forms but is the nation at fault and responsible? Is the government the solution, Roman?"

"The Yankees think so," the New York reporter piped in.

"Where does the racism come from today? Our laws, government policies, and practices haven't allowed it for over forty years. Show me a law where race is allowed to be a determiner in any policy, practice, or segregation."

"Some might say affirmative action is racist by that claim, Josh," a different reporter said.

"Folks, affirmative action at universities and hiring practices hoped to bridge a gap for blacks who lacked opportunities for better education and make inroads to certain jobs denied during the decades of Jim Crow. The idea was to give blacks a hand up to equal opportunities in the future through education."

"So, you think our country wronged blacks in the past, but no longer, Josh? Is that what you say is true?" asked Roman.

"I say the country is not racist in its police or the laws they enforce. The country is not holding back people because of the color of their skin. Not now and not in my lifetime. In this nation, you can be any race and become whatever the Creator gave you the abilities and the desire to be. We live in a land with the greatest opportunities for all people for all time. It doesn't matter where you start or what skin color you have. You can become a CEO, the President, or even a ballplayer."

"Josh, certainly you aren't naive enough to think the average black man has the same opportunity as the average white man?" Roman almost spat with sarcasm.

"Roman, all men travel their own journey. Some have more opportunities than others, independent of their skin color. You are right to say our minority communities often have fewer opportunities and have a harder path to success. Still, in America, it is far more likely for minorities and even brand-new immigrants to work their way to success and prosperity than most of the world. That's why millions of Africans immigrate to our country to enjoy the opportunities found here. Our Declaration of Independence didn't guarantee equal outcome, only the chance for all to make a better life."

"Why do so many blacks feel like they are suffering? Do you want facts? What do you say about the high numbers of blacks in poverty or lack a good education? The low number of blacks as Fortune 500 CEOs or owners of baseball franchises or even coaches, rather than just the athlete in professional sports?"

"Roman, there are many problems in our poor communities where blacks often live. Minority entrepreneurs are a mixed bag when it comes to the success of one minority group. Still, no minority or majority has a guarantee or a monopoly on getting ahead in America. It's an individual that makes the difference, and you don't have to look far to find every walk of life has every skin color represented."

"Yes, but blacks are often at the bottom rung. Isn't that a sign of America's problem, the problem with our country?"

"No, Roman, it's not," Josh said.

Shocked, Roman and some other journalists stared momentarily, and the Pirates and staff froze with unease. Roman realized this was it, finally. He forced Josh where he wanted him, and now he would turn his words out and show what Josh really believed.

"Whose fault is it, Josh?" said Roman, a wolf ravenous for the kill.

"As I have said from the beginning, Roman, you must start with the individual. We have to take responsibility for our actions and choices. America allows you to improve your lot in life. Our nation guarantees 'life, liberty, and the pursuit of happiness.' It doesn't guarantee the outcome. Some have 100 ways to get to success and travel an easier road. But that isn't because of race. It's far more likely to be those born into wealth. But whether you have three pathways or one hundred pathways to success, you have opportunities. Your choices and your actions dictate how far you go."

"Are you trying to tell black people that their choices hold them back, Josh? Is that what you're preaching."

"I believe everyone is responsible for their own choices and actions. This country guarantees us the freedom and opportunity to choose in a far greater way than most of the world and history can barely comprehend. That's why millions are trying to come here. You have to take responsibility for both your free choices and your actions. It's up to you. Live righteously, live good lives by God's grace, or make poor choices, rebel, and face the consequences of your actions. Our government can't save you. Only God can, and I have told you I myself need salvation. I can't do good in and of myself. Only Christ can do that in me when I turn to him."

"It's always back to Christ with you, Josh," Roman scoffed.

"You keep turning to the Government to fix the problem. The Government can't fix our problems," Josh replied.

"So, you are saying all the Blacks living in poverty, shot by police, lacking educational opportunities; all this is because of something they have done?" Roman spat the words with ire.

"I am saying until we look at the problems we have and truthfully accept the mistakes we are making and turn away from those mistakes, we will continue to have ever-worsening results. We will never find a solution if we hold on to the false truth, the lie, that our government is to blame. It's like any other lie. It's a sin.

Each sin generates more negative consequences. Unadmitted and unrepentant sin never gets better. It's cancer. It must be confessed and removed."

"What are our sins then, Josh?" a black reporter asked angrily.

"Americans of all races are making many mistakes according to God's word. Where do you want to begin?

"Gives us a big one, Josh," Roman said, baiting with glee.

"Easy. The number one problem in America is the destruction of the family and the breakdown of marriage."

"Are you going to preach at us about sex, going to say having sex and therefore having kids out of wedlock is causing the black community problems?" Roman strung Josh along, and he obliged.

"It's what's causing our national problem, Roman. The fact that the black community leads the other communities by a decade or so in this area just means our black communities are more destroyed. 75% and more of our black children grow up with a single parent. 75% and greater of our black pregnancies end in abortion. In the '70s, both those numbers were around 25%. That means that since Roe versus Wade in the early '70s, we've lost nearly half the black population that would otherwise be living. Those two facts alone should absolutely break everyone's heart in two. This is, far and away, a much greater cause of the problems in our black communities today than anything we call systemic racism or even individual racism. If we don't turn those statistics around, we invite the total destruction of our people. And I mean all America. Because while the black community leads, the other communities move in the same direction. It's a gigantic sin on our individual parts, destroying this country. A reckoning is coming, and we see it more and more each day."

"Why should we listen to you, Josh?" one reporter asked, and many nodded.

"I am only telling you what I know to be True. Christ warned us against sexual immorality. When we sin and ignore and now celebrate our immoral sexual behavior and call it entertainment, we destroy the foundation of the nuclear family. Until we rectify that, we will have problems in our society and households. We pass these problems with immoral lifestyles onto our children, and the cycle worsens."

"God shows us sins consequences in the True history of his Word. Blaming the government for the actions of a few police officers, however egregious their actions, belies the problems of millions growing up without their nuclear family. It's so not even close, it's outrageous to think we complain about the speck of wood in our brother's eye and not recognize the tree trunk in our own.[2] We

---

2. Matthew 7:3-5

complain about the two dozen unarmed people shot by cops each year, half black, half from other races, yet we remain mute about thousands shot during violent crimes and almost a million Americans we abort in the womb yearly. We lose thousands, indeed millions, because of how we live our lives and sin against God. We scream for justice while the blood of thousands each year cry out to God but are ignored by man."

"So, besides unmarried blacks having sex and children, you would throw the LGBTQ community in there as the so-called 'Non-Nuclear' family, Josh?" Roman added, knowing Josh would stand firm.

"Again, Roman, you keep saying blacks. God doesn't judge you based on your skin color. He made you. He made Adam with every race color in his genes. No color has a lock on righteousness or sin. It is the sin of man to judge on the outward appearance. God looks on the heart.[3] Immoral lifestyles come in all shapes and sizes. If you ask me about the gay lifestyle, what kind of family questions do you have?"

"Does a gay couple qualify as a family if they get married?" Roman asked, knowing the answer.

"You already know what the Bible says about the gay lifestyle, Roman. Jesus calls all sexual immorality, immoral sexual behavior, a sin. Quoted by Mathew and Mark and repeated by the Apostles in Acts. Paul further details homosexuality as sinful behavior in Romans 1, 1 Corinthians 6, and 1 Timothy 1. The nuclear family starts with God as the standard when he tells Adam and Eve what a family is in Genesis 2. Man leaves his parents when he finds a wife, and the two become one flesh. They, in turn, have children. That is the only family unit, and within such a union, sex is blessed. Society is built on this stabilizing nuclear family to grow in strength and multiply. Many studies show a mom and dad family unit produces children on average with the best likelihood of growing up as productive members of society versus all other families. The Old and New Testaments of the Bible repeatedly warn us against all sexual immoralities, including homosexuality, fornication or sex before marriage, and adultery. Sex outside God's ordinance of marriage always has negative consequences, just as all sin does. Since you ask about the allowance many states have made for Gays to be married, do you know their marriage rate? In other words, heterosexual marriage rates are about 60-65% in the U.S. What about Gays being and staying married?"

"Tell us, Josh?" Roman said. He almost pitied the man digging his own grave.

"In the U.S. and worldwide, where quite a few countries have a longer period to collect data, Gay marriages are generally less than 10%. Something like 6% is a

3. 1 Samuel 16:7

typical average, roughly an order of magnitude less than heterosexual marriages.[4] Again, for all marriages, society loses when marriages break down because children suffer. Ultimately, regardless of race or even sexual orientation, when a single parent raises a child, the child is more likely to live in poverty, do poorly in school, and become a criminal. All the problems we see with our children increase when they live outside of biblically defined family - Man and Wife, for life. It was true in Genesis. It's true today. When man rebels against God's creation of the family, society self-destructs."

"Our government's role in all this is pretty simple. Its responsibility is to promote things that sustain and perpetuate the nation. Instead, our government laws and policies, such as no-fault divorce and social welfare programs, often promote the dissolution of the family and incentivize single parenthood through welfare and tax breaks. Consequently, our society suffers. Most of all, our children suffer when the traditional family is eroded or destroyed. Our own choices and our actions cause the wound. However, using the government as a scapegoat is a poor excuse. Let's face facts. We are the ones who asked for the laws we have. In the end, our laws reflect our desires as a society. It's our fault."

"Look, it's like this. Our problems are a lack of righteousness, denying the truth, and doing the right thing. The Bible tells of how Paul said, the things I don't want to do, I do, and the things I want to do, I don't.[5] He said we know what's right, but our sin enslaves our will. Only God, through the grace of Our Lord Jesus Christ, can break our will from sin and turn us to His will of righteousness.[6] Otherwise, sin makes us lose self-control, and we perpetuate more evil. The more we try to fix ourselves, the more we spiral out of control. Chasing after the lies that government or police cause racial injustices takes us away from the truth and the heart of our problems. God said our hearts *are* the problem, for our actions flow out of our hearts.[7] When we ignore God's direction for our families, our sinful lifestyle choices plague those we love. We've only seen the tip of the iceberg regarding final judgment. God gives us grace right now to turn away and turn back to him, only by trusting in Jesus. Please know, I am only a sinner, saved by God's grace, and I tell you all these things that I have read and heard and lived, that

---

4. For reference studies, see extended discussions in 'Correct not Politically Correct,' Frank Turek, CrossExamined 2017

5. Romans 7:19

6. Romans 6:6-11

7. Matthew 12:34; Mark 7:21-23; Luke 6:45

I know to be true so that you might also know the truth, repent, accept Christ, and be saved."

Roman got everything and more, he wanted out of Josh. He didn't even have to cajole it out of him. Josh volunteered his opinion on what righteousness required. He claimed we all lack self-control, and there was judgment upon us. There was a time, early on, when Roman first saw Josh play, he wondered if he would make a good hero or a good villain. It was so easy now to see. Josh was indeed his villain. A villain of epic proportions the world would hate, and Roman would ride the public's seething wave all the way to the fame and fortune he so desperately coveted. He sat back and could not help but let a thin sneer of satisfaction slip through his mask of a professional, balanced reporter and show on his well-groomed, bearded face.

The response to Josh's answers was felt almost immediately. Of course, since the news conference was not carried live, but edited by each network, it came out in various forms. None was worse or more negatively edited than the Roman Josephus' version on SPNN. Roman led off with an innocent-sounding statement of how for months, the public saw Josh Green and the Pirates buck the cultural response against racism and bigotry but never fully explained why. Now he, Roman Josephus, would let Josh explain in his own words the reasons and how he blamed the sins of Blacks and Gays for the problems of our society. Thus began the show, with carefully edited responses of Josh providing condemnation without explaining redemption. The edits also made it look as if Josh directed his comments mostly against Blacks and Gays, not our entire society, all citizens, indeed all human beings, including himself, as he did.

MLB Commissioner Quint Pilate brooded as he watched from his home on Long Island. He already knew where the polls would go with this final insult. He must confront Josh himself. If Josh would not willingly see the light and turn away, publicly, from this untenable position, Quint would be forced to act. He called Cassius and told him to have Herald Gripp meet with him in the morning. They prepared to meet Josh together and confront him. Quint hung up and thought carefully about what he must do if that failed. He did not like to think of such things, but suspected the man would not change his intractable position. He worked hard to find something against Josh, something he could use as he so often did when he needed to persuade someone to do the right thing. That's all he wanted, after all. Doing the right thing was in everyone's best interest: Baseball's, Josh's, and indeed, Quint Pilate's, for he was the captain shepherding the future of baseball, America's pastime. In a way, Quint thought, he led America's conscience. Unfortunately, Quint could find no dirt on Green. He had tried to use the innuendo of impropriety of his relationship with the nanny, but that failed.

Quint hoped Josh would see reason or understand his threat of what must happen if Josh would not change his course. But he feared Josh would not be swayed. Quint held one piece of information, large that it was, he did not use. Through Quint's specialized services, he found Green was a recently retired military man. Quint's investigator found mostly redacted information, unusual at best. The man evidently saw extensive combat yet never brought it up. His scar was the only tell-tell sign, as Quint received a partial list of Green's decorations. Besides the purple heart, he received several combat awards for valor and bravery. Why Green did not advertise his record and garner admiration from a sympathetic public was a mystery to Quint. Since Green continued to fight against the people's will and the commissioner's office, Quint was happy to bury his military heroics so the public would have no reason to follow his lead. Yet it indicated one thing to Quint. He felt relatively sure Green would not respond to threats or coercion. Still, he must try the easy way, perhaps with a carrot, if not a stick. But Quint knew he must prepare, however reluctantly, if he failed to change Josh's mind.

Quint set down his personal cell phone and used his key for the desk drawer containing his "other" phone, one Cassius purchased for him in cash and replaced every few months. He dialed his contact's number and set up a separate appointment for a discussion tomorrow afternoon. After Quint hung up, he knew even this "Plan B" might not be enough. He sadly hoped they would not have to move to the final plan. That would be genuinely distasteful. Best not to trouble himself about it now, thought Quint. He would wait until the meeting with the people who handled such things, but he knew he must be prepared to discuss it. It took time and preparation to conduct properly and leave no trace. Heavy is the head that wears the crown. Still, it was his decision and baseball's future. What was good for Quint was good for baseball and the country, and Quint was determined to do whatever it took to fix his problem.

One Hundred Three

G ame two of the World Series would be a day game at PNC Park. Though it was less than twelve hours since game one, game two seemed a world apart. The teams were the same, but the audience was decidedly different. The crowd's mood turned against the Pirates and against the stand Josh took the night before. People failed to unite behind one particular cause, but Josh's words drew condemnation on many fronts. There were protests outside and inside the stadium. The unorganized crowd showed rebellious anger and hatred in various forms.

For the Pirates part, they repeated their customary stance for the anthem and kneeled for prayer, but many in the crowd now disapproved and let them hear it. The Yankees, if anything, were even more defiant. Before Josh's first at-bat, he kneeled as was his custom all year long. At least half of the hometown crowd booed him decidedly. Though not all turned against Josh, and many didn't see the interviews, it became clear Josh's off-field and on-field activities outside his play eclipsed his historic baseball achievements.

The Yankees represented those in the crowd who rejected Josh, greeting him with a pitch inside, nearly hitting his head. Shockingly Josh barely reacted. Instead, he leaned back just enough to allow the pitch to narrowly miss him. Even the umpire took a second to stare at Josh, who still was in the batter's box. The ump gave both sides the customary warning another headhunter pitch would result in ejections. It was unclear whether the Yankees threw at Josh because of what he said or the game-ending home run in game one. What was clear was Josh's response. He would not be moved to change what he did or said. The next pitch sliced the outside corner hard and fast. Josh struck it soundly into right field for a single. He then stole both second and third on the first two pitches to Juan and scored on Juan's double to left. The game remained close, and the Yankees intentionally walked Josh the next three at-bats, including in the seventh inning with two aboard, similar to when Josh homered in game one. Juan hit a sacrifice fly for his second RBI of the game. J.J. then doubled to clear the bases, and the Pirates were up 4-1 over the Yankees. Jude Keriothson pitched a scoreless eighth and continued into the ninth. However, he gave up two consecutive hits after getting a quick out, and Pops went to Barabbas to finish the game. Although one run scored, Justus got the Yankees to hit into a game-ending double play on the next batter, and the Pirates won 4-2.

For a team leading the best of seven series two games to none, the Pirate players looked like they were waiting for the other shoe to fall. Deciding to give them a break, Pops did not let the press in after the game, telling the press corps he wanted to let the players prepare for the trip as the series shifted to New York City. They were disgruntled, and Mark Johnson warned Saul there would likely be a backlash of more negative press.

Saul answered Mark, "Son. Do you really think it will be any worse than what we received last night?"

Mark shook his head and shrugged, "I guess not, Skipper. I am sorry I haven't figured out a way for us to look better to the fans," he finished with regret.

"Mark, you can't serve two masters.[1] If Josh has shown us anything, it's often an unpopular position when you stand for the Truth, and there is a price to pay. I think it's up to us to decide what we believe and where we place our faith and trust. We must decide what we are willing to sacrifice and risk to live the Truth. It's not your fault at all. Besides, I don't think the fight we fight will be won or lost in the press. Josh shows us all we can do is hold on to the Truth by exercising our faith in Christ, following where He leads, regardless of the cost."

The Pirates had one thing to look forward to, a special dinner Joe and Elizabeth arranged when the team first earned their trip to the World Series. After all the scrutiny they faced for game two, the players and staff gladly embraced a chance escape the world and spend time with their baseball family. The Arimas hosted the delicious supper prepared by Elizabeth with help from Mary, Ruth, and Joe. Joe told those attending they would make the food hot and ready about an hour after the game ended. Joe passed they should come as they were, as game dress was acceptable at the informal gathering. The Arima hospitality and Elizabeth's famed cooking drew about a dozen Pirate players. Saul was one of the last to arrive, and he nodded to Pete, Mark Johnson, and his assistant Martha, who were already there. Several other staff attended, including Simon Cyrene, the physical therapist, masseur, and gentle giant of a man. Cy struck a sharp contrast to his conversation partner, the energetic, feisty, seventy-something Ms. Phoebe. They were in a deep conversation, probably about a meaty biblical topic, thought Saul. He walked through the living area into the hallway and saw that the study door was open. Josh was conversing with two men, and Saul was pleasantly surprised when he realized it was Nick and Ezra Demus.

---

1. Mathew 6:24

"I'd be happy to draw it up for you, Josh. I could have it ready for your signature in a few days. Certainly, I'll have it ready when you return from New York, even if you win in four straight!" said Nick happily.

"I would like it sooner than that. Any chance you could get it to me in New York?" Josh asked.

Nick paused, taken aback. "Well, I could get it done tomorrow, of course, and I suppose I could fax it, but we need to get signatures...," he trailed off.

"Pop, you could send it to me. Thanks to Josh, I am going to the game. I could bring it to you before the game or even stop by the hotel, where you both could sign," Ezra said.

"I don't want to impose, but I would like to know it's settled. I should not have waited, and I need to complete it," Josh said.

Ezra replied, "Josh, I think I speak for my dad when I say we literally can't thank you enough. It will be our pleasure to help in any way we can."

"Yes, I am here today, in many ways, because of what you did," Nick said.

"You are very gracious, but I am not the one who brought you through to today," replied Josh.

"At the very least, you pointed me to the true path. I am glad Yeshua gave me one more opportunity. This time I did not miss it. Indeed, I have finally made it home," Nick said, reaching out his hand and shaking Josh's vigorously.

Saul felt he eavesdropped long enough from the darkened hallway and continued to the kitchen to say hello to the hosts.

The Arimas' house offered a charming, almost old-world dining room. Nowadays, Joe did not have nearly as many gatherings since he retired, but Elizabeth still held a few with her gardening club and even the children's charity get-togethers once or twice a year. Tonight, though, was a special night, and guests filled the large table to overflowing. The Arimas' became an oasis and shelter from the stress of the world's angry spotlight blazing down on the team. Those gathered left the world's torment and displeasure temporarily behind, if but for one evening.

Soon they all gathered in the Arimas' beautiful dining room. Joe sat mid-table with Elizabeth by his side and Nick and his son on the other. Josh sat across from the Arimas with Saul on one side and Ruth on the other. Mary sat next to Elizabeth, and the other guests, Pirate players, coaches, and staff, sat scattered around the table.

Joe stood and began.

"Today is in Jewish tradition Simchat Torah or the Joy of the Torah. It is the day we celebrate God's great gift of His Word. As Christians, we rejoice in that great gift, none other than the Messiah Yeshua. As our brother John told us, 'In the beginning was the Word, and the Word was with God, and the Word was God.' John 1:1. In Proverbs 13:14, we are reminded, 'The teaching of the wise is a fountain of life, turning a person from the snares of death,' and the Psalmist expressed, 'Your righteousness is everlasting, and your law is true' Psalm 119:142. Finally, our savior Yeshua declares, 'I am the Way and the Truth and the Life. No one comes to the Father except through Me.' John 14:6."

Joe continued, "Today, Elizabeth and I are so glad to welcome you all to a celebration of the Truth that Yeshua, our savior, is The Word, and He offers to save all who call upon his name. I know it's been a tough week, and it will continue again tomorrow, but I pray tonight you will find sanctuary, joy, peace, and fellowship here among friends. Elizabeth, with help from our friends," Joe smiled as he bowed slightly, gesturing to Mary and Ruth, "Prepared this feast."

Joe stopped and smiled across at Josh. Without hesitation, he asked, "Josh, would you bless our food in remembrance of Yeshua, our Lord and Savior?"

Josh rose and paused, looking around the table lovingly at those present. Each person would remember it differently, but Saul couldn't shake the feeling this may be the last time they would all be gathered with Josh. Josh smiled finally and said, "Please pray with me." He bowed his head, "Thank you, Heavenly Father, for giving us Your Word, Jesus, who gives us Truth and Grace in equal measure. Lord Jesus, now grant us:"

"Wisdom, to know what is right to do, today;"

"Courage, to carry it out;"

"Fortitude, to see it through to the finish;"

"Faith, in the only One Worthy and True, and"

"Love, for our fellow man, the way You have loved us, for while we were yet sinners, you loved us so much, you gave your life as our ransom."

"Bless this food and drink as we enjoy each other's company, and remember You, always. In your precious name, Lord Jesus, we pray," Josh finished.

"Amen," said nearly everyone at the table, and Josh sat down.

Most, it seemed, thoroughly enjoyed both the dinner and the company. Genuine laughter and love abounded as each recognized such opportunities for joy and companionship come few and far between. They all cherished this precious gift as a community of brothers and sisters.

As the meal finished, Elizabeth, Joe, Ezra, Martha, and Mary brought various desserts, coffee, and spiced warm drinks as the late October weather turned cold. The guests moved from the table to the living room area, where Joe lit a fire in the fireplace. Josh headed to one of the side rooms where everyone placed their jackets as he felt a slight chill.

Jude Keriothson felt the buzz of his phone in his pocket. He took it out and saw a message he could not ignore. Jude took part in the evening events long enough to give the necessary impression to the team he was "with them," whatever that meant, thought Jude. He did not understand this glorification of religion when practically the entire world, it seemed, was against them. "They will hold onto their outdated beliefs until it drags them all down," he thought. Jude did not have the luxury of talent or faith to stand against the world. He must take care of himself, and the League would overcome Josh and the Pirates one way or another. Jude needed to ensure his future, and Cai Annason and Quint Pilate offered him precisely that, with guaranteed financial security as well. Of course, it came with a price, and it appeared he now needed to pay, as the text directed him to meet his contact shortly to discuss what he must do. He got up to depart. After all, he was barely keeping up the false front to this crowd, and his stomach was bothering him.

Jude eased out of the dining room and headed to get his cloak. He was not alone, as Josh surprised him by coming out of the cloakroom. "Oh, sorry Josh, just getting my jacket."

"Leaving Jude?" Josh said in a neutral tone with those penetrating dark eyes of his.

"Ah, yeah, my roommate texted me. Apparently, he needs a ride back home. He had a few drinks downtown and asked if I would pick him up." Jude roomed with young Justus Barabbas, who was known to be a bit of a partier now and then. He thought it would be an easy cover for why he really must leave.

Josh helped him with his coat and spoke to Jude as he prepared to leave. "You know, we all have a choice to make, Jude. You're not locked into your path. You can choose anew. Christ gives us all the grace to make a new choice."

Jude froze for a second. Could Josh know of his lie? If so, could he know who Jude followed and what they would ask of him? He shook himself. Even he wasn't sure, he lied to himself. Certainly, he wasn't sure what he would do, or was willing to do. Yet here, the man they watched all season, this prominent, dark-skinned leader, stood now in front of him with an offer of kindness and love in his eyes, Jude did not understand or perhaps already rejected. Jude chose again to do what it took and make his fortune his way.

"Thanks, Josh," Jude said quizzically, unsure of how Josh could possibly know anything. There were muffled noises as if others were approaching, and Jude needed to leave before the others, as Jude's direction was opposite his lie to Josh.

As if sensing Jude's choice, Josh nodded with sadness in his eyes. Josh said, "What you are going to do, do quickly."[2] He turned from Jude back toward the congregation of friends and family. Jude watched Josh walk away, back toward the living room's light. Jude instead turned back, following his dark path out of the house.

---

2. John 13:27

The rest of the evening was one of fellowship with the body of believers. Come what may, they were together and in one accord, enjoying each other as brothers and sisters, gifts of joy and love from the Creator.

One Hundred Four

When it comes to World Series Championship history, there are the New York Yankees, and there is everyone else. Game three of the series took place at Yankee Stadium with all the expected fanfare of arguably the most storied franchise in all professional sports. The Yankees owned more championships than the next two baseball franchises combined and refused to see themselves as the underdog, despite losing two to the Pirates in Pittsburgh. The Yankees and the crowd held a feeling of, "This is our house, the House that Ruth, Gehrig, DiMaggio, and Mantle built." Along with the venue change, the crowd was Yankees through and through, supporting every cause their team now embraced. Racial justice and the end of bigotry mixed in with many other smaller yet very vocal protests, all wearing clothing and displaying banners of their various causes along with the Yankee blue.

It may be the house Ruth built, but the Bronx Bombers could not stand against Josh Green and the Pittsburgh Pirates. Despite a game plan to marginalize Josh, there was no doubting his great impact after the game. Josh's first three at-bats came with runners on base and less than two outs. Each at-bat, the Yankees tried pitching Josh differently. Josh swung only once in each at-bat, yet the results were the same: Three home runs. The first homer went to right as Josh lifted an outside curve over the short right field fence three or four rows deep. The second, he pulled through an inside low fastball slightly below the knees, like a golf shot into the left field second deck. In his third at-bat, Josh received not one but two brush-back pitches, with the second bringing a warning from the umpire to both benches. They didn't matter. Josh took the next pitch, hard but high over the plate, and belted it to deep center. It flew deep enough to hit the bottom of the scoreboard on the fly. The capacity crowd became more dismayed and angered with each successive blow, booing Josh loudly. The Yankee players looked away from the Pirates as if trying to deny what was happening. Josh came to bat one more time, but the Yankees intentionally walked him. The Pirates won the game 8-3, and Josh amazingly collected all eight RBIs.

Commissioner Quint Pilate and his second in command, VP for Operations and Media, Herald Gripp, watched the game from the confines of one of the

Yankees individual game boxes high above the field. The commissioner hoped it would not come to this, but Josh's polarizing words off the field, and play on the field, were impossible to ignore. Josh must be stopped, but the commissioner would meet him face to face and give Josh Green one last chance to recant and change his course. Quint already discussed with Herald Gripp how he planned to talk to Josh if the Yankees could not defeat him. After watching Josh's third home run blast into the scoreboard, Herald turned and looked at his boss raising his eyebrows. After a moment, Quint nodded reluctantly, and Herald got up, walked back inside the private luxury suite where Cassius, Quint's assistant, worked on a laptop.

"Cassius, the commissioner will proceed as planned," Herald directed.

Cassius nodded. He closed his laptop and exited the suite to execute all the final arrangements away from prying eyes, as even the few trusted people in the suite were a few too many witnesses.

The post-game interviews were even more unrelenting, filled with the vitriol of the day, and it was telling when few asked Josh about his remarkable three home run, eight RBI day. Josh took the questions but mainly responded he gave them all the answers they sought on his beliefs and stance previously. Still, they railed against Josh as if he would suddenly change his mind. He finally said, "Each must seek the Truth. But that is not enough. Once Truth is known, each must decide to accept or reject the Truth. I accept Jesus, as His life and resurrection from the grave proved He is The Truth and The Way. Choose you this day whom you will serve, as all men must choose. For me, for my house, we will serve the Lord."

He refused to answer further questions, and Saul nodded at Mark, who waved off the angered press corps. Mark, who usually preferred only to give the press prepared statements on the record, instead, raised his hands when they complained.

"Look," he said uncharacteristically sternly, and they quieted, momentarily surprised. "You ignored the game and the incredible historic performance of Josh Green. Instead, you want to berate him for his beliefs and then distort them by cleverly cutting the video you broadcast," Mark said, looking directly at Roman Josephus, whose ratings and name recognition skyrocketed as the playoffs progressed. "Why should we continue allowing questions that have little to do with the game? You want to accuse and condemn Josh with your twisted half-truths and false witness. Go! You can return when you decide to do your job and report on the game, but you're done tonight. By the way, The Pirates are now up 3-0 in the World Series, in case those watching your news reports didn't know, since not one of you brought it up in the questions!"

When the reporters still moaned and grumbled, Old Pete, who rarely talked to reporters, half-shouted through clenched teeth over his unlit cigar. "Everyone not part of the Pirates, get lost!" Whether it was because of Pete's gruff command or because Simon Cyrene, the giant physical therapist, stood towering behind Pete, the press hurried to collect their gear, exiting the Pirates locker room like rats scurrying off a sinking ship.

Mark ushered the last of the press out and closed the door. Saul got up, and there wasn't much to say. "We need one more to finish this thing. Now more than ever, we need to come together." He looked around the locker room, and everyone seemed to sense no matter how hard they fought until now, the last victory would be the toughest. It was as if they were fighting the world. Even Saul doubted as he looked around, until his eyes fell upon Josh. Josh looked back at Saul with his lovely, dark, scarred face. Saul knew in his spirit that Josh saw so much beyond what Saul could ever understand, and Josh showed no doubt in those loving dark eyes. It was as if they told Saul, "Yes, the road ahead is tough, but I am resolved to see it through to the end." Those ancient knowing eyes invited Saul in, silently communicating, "Have faith, Saul," replacing Saul's doubt with hope. Hope and peace. "Give it all to the One worth all our faith, my brother. He is worthy of our trust," Saul heard from the Spirit Josh trusted in, and so too, did Saul.

"Let's finish strong and go home!" Saul announced with conviction, and they all breathed again, slapping each other's backs and knocking fists, only the final victory yet to come.

One Hundred Five

M ost of the younger players finished their post-game routines quickly. Game four would be a short 18 hours later, so most wanted to get back to the hotel, get a bite to eat, and get to bed. However, the season and post-season took a toll on Josh's thirty-eight-year-old body, and he needed a good looking-after by Doc Luke, Pete, and Simon Cyrene. Tonight seemed especially difficult as Josh fielded several balls, diving twice to make a catch, much to the Yankees' chagrin, taxing his body. By the time Cy finished Josh's massage, most of the team had already departed on the bus, and the few players who needed a little extra time got a hotel limo to pick them up. Pete, who worked on some gear for the next day, relieved Cy and told him to take Doc and go. Pete would finish up and head out with Josh. It was an empty locker room as Josh finished with a twenty-minute cool bath in one of the whirlpools.

Pete walked up after finally beating yet another glove into submission for one of the bullpen pitchers who managed to tear a finger in his old glove. "If you're almost ready, I'll go order us a car," Pete told Josh.

Josh's eyes were closed. He looked up, "Thanks, Pete. Just a few minutes left, and I'll change and be ready."

As Pete approached the door, it opened with a large man in a suit who wore a corded earpiece and looked menacing. Pete stopped short of the man a few steps, but before he could say anything, the man said over his head, "Mr. Green, Major League Baseball Commissioner Quint Pilate needs a word with you," and in walked the commissioner with Herald Gripp in tow. They walked past Pete, hardly noticing, and Pete took one step sideways as they passed, almost dropping his half-chewed cigar.

Without looking back, the commissioner said back over his shoulder, "You can wait outside."

Josh got out of the whirlpool, pulled on a robe, and said to the commissioner, "Daily, I've been available, answering all questions in front of dozens. You could have come and talked to me anytime, yet you waited until late at night when no one is around, Commissioner? Like a thief?" Josh moved slowly to his chair and sat down, hands in the robe's pockets, waiting.

Pete looked around as the large man by the door walked towards him. Finally, in desperation about what to do, Pete said, "I'll call a car," and allowed himself to be ushered out unceremoniously by the man who doubled as security and enforcer. Once outside, Pete realized a second security guard of similar build and dress waited and closed the door. The two guards took up posts blocking the door, a significant deterrent to Pete's thoughts of trying to go back. Pete hurried down the hall toward the exit, thumbing through his contacts to locate the number of the hotel shuttle service, trying not to think of what the commissioner and his VP, Herald Gripp, wanted with Josh Green.

In the locker room, Josh sat resigned to wait for the commissioner to explain why he was there. The commissioner sat in a chair opposite him, with Herald standing behind him to one side.

"Josh, I know we haven't met previously, and I am sorry to meet under such circumstances, but I, and my VP Herald Gripp, saw no choice. We need to talk to you now."

"We always get a choice, however difficult it may seem," Josh said unblinkingly as he stared at the commissioner. Quint noted Josh sat back, hands resting in his lap, without emotion or a look of stress at the commissioner's surprise entrance. Most people and players were usually a bit in awe of meeting the commissioner for the first time, and Quint counted on a certain intimidation factor working in his favor. He judged such an entrance would only increase Josh's unease, helping in the negotiated settlement he expected. Instead, Josh, in his bathrobe after his cool bath, appeared entirely unruffled and unafraid. For the first time, Quint saw Josh's large head-to-knee scar as he exited the tub. Knowing Josh's redacted extensive military combat record, combined with Josh's calm demeanor, Quint doubted his plan. Still, he must try to get Josh to see reason. Quint realized, by Herald's slightly nervous shuffle next to him, he paused too long. Gathering himself, Quint continued.

"Josh, let me get to the point. Despite your outstanding play, Major League Baseball pays a heavy price for your actions in and around the game. You have continuously balked at following the League's expectations to provide a uniform front supporting the freedom and equality of the people of this country. You are alienating the fan base by failing to support anti-racist and anti-bigotry stances made by most players. Your over-the-top displays of religious zeal take the League's policy supporting freedom of speech and religion too far, and you seek to impose your morality onto other players and the fans who watch and look up to you."

"I am sorry you feel this way, Commissioner. However, I fail to see how you can, on one hand, say I infringe on peoples' freedoms, and in the next breath, say I take those same freedoms too far. If one such as I can't use my freedom of speech and religion to do as I am morally compelled to do, then how does any fan or player, for that matter, expect to keep their freedoms, even if my views are in the minority?"

"Josh, I don't care what you believe, but I care about the message Major League Baseball sends to the public. Every time someone asks you a question about racism or the gay lifestyle, you turn it into a Sunday church service about righteousness and the ramification of sins."

"I don't mind that comparison if that's what you think," Josh replied before the commissioner could continue.

Quint said exasperated, "Whatever happened to don't judge lest ye be judged?"

"You must read our Lord's entire sermon when he spoke those words. He clearly conveys we are to use discernment in our judgments and follow the determination with God's eyes, not man's."

"But Josh, you attempt to impose your morality on others," Quint replied.

"No, commissioner, I only state what is True and Moral. In God's word, He tells us of His absolute morality and explains what it means to all of us. I only describe how I see those immutable truths playing out in our society. They are not 'my' morality, for if we were arguing a human moral standard, then any person's morality is based on their opinion. That is not what I do. I relate what is God's standard. God is the standard of good, and His morality is absolute. I do not try to impose morality forcefully on any man. When God himself gives humans the chance to accept or reject the Truth, to accept or reject His Holiness and His Son's redemption, then a sorry soul I would be to take away your right to choose. Yet that does not change the fact God's moral law, like His Word, is immutable and everlasting. Anything less than His standard is sin. Someone's morals will define society's laws and cultural stance. The question is, whose? I choose and pray they are God's morals, for He is the only True standard who can provide a good and firm foundation for our nation."

The man is intractable in his position, thought Quint. Perhaps I can convince him to temper his expression. Quint changed tack. "Be that as it may, Josh, it still is inappropriate and detrimental to Baseball to have you express such controversial positions. The public doesn't want to hear they are at fault for the problems in this world because of the sins they commit. Even if you believe it, telling everyone what you believe to be true kills our revenue as fans stay away in large numbers, and our MLB sales are down nearly 20% this year."

"I am sorry to hear that, Commissioner, but I think you are putting two and two together and getting five," Josh replied.

"What do you mean?" Quint said haughtily. Why did he suddenly feel the need to be defensive?

"The Pirates attendance is higher than any time in history. Pirate gear sales are at record numbers, not just in Pittsburgh but around the country and the world. Did you know my jersey made more sales overseas in the last six months than any other athlete in the world?" Josh remarked, somehow not with pride but as poignant evidence. The commissioner knew very well what Josh said was true. "Perhaps it is you and Major League Baseball that need to change," Josh finished calmly.

Was this man calling him out, Quint wondered incredulously? Was Josh telling him he was wrong, and it was his decisions, not Josh's actions, hurting baseball? Like many of the people Josh addressed through interviews over the year, Quint suddenly felt Josh's stare and the irrefutable logic behind it. Josh spoke with authority in his steadfast message of God's love and justice and the judgment awaiting all men. Josh made clear Jesus was the Truth, and his offer of redemption was man's only hope.

Did this man honestly believe anybody cared about the Truth of his words, wondered Quint? People believed whatever they wanted to believe, whatever made them feel good about themselves. They didn't seek the truth. They sought happiness and pleasure. They sought what this world offered, not what was Right, and if Right meant facing the hard reality something you did or wanted was wrong, they didn't want to hear it! Didn't Green get that? Major League Baseball and every other business in the world, indeed, every government, every entity who hoped to succeed, gave its people, its customers, what they wanted. The commissioner wanted to wake Josh up to reality. When it came to peoples' hearts and desires, God was dead. Quint was a businessman and, as such, a pragmatist. Power, money, and sex were far more powerful tools for winning public favor. Yet Quint knew inherently, should he even try to use these on Josh, he would fail.

Instead, the commissioner would try one last compromise.

"Josh, we will not see eye-to-eye on this, so I would ask you to consider apologizing to anyone you offended during your interviews and make a statement that you will hold future displays and comments about your religious faith to your personal time away from baseball. If you were to do that, I can promise you, you would have a very lucrative future in baseball." Josh sat quietly, without response. "C'mon, Josh, give me something to work with here!" Quint finished, desperately replacing his cajoling with an almost pitiful plea for help.

"Respectfully, Commissioner Pilate, I cannot, in good conscience, change my stance on what is True and Right. God commands us to spread the Good News in Truth and love, and I have but one life to live for my God and my countrymen. I would, that all who hear my words hear the Truth of their need of Jesus, so they too might claim His salvation."

Quint sat back in the chair. As he feared, there was no changing Josh's mind. Or his path. Both were captured by his Lord and God, Jesus, and Josh would not be swayed. Quint already felt regret for what he must do. He thought back to earlier this evening as he was leaving his house for the game. His wife stopped him in the hallway. He rarely discussed the business side of his job with her, but she said something almost impulsively, it seemed, somehow knowing his dealings with Joshua Green were coming to a head. "I know that Josh Green player is wreaking havoc for you, and I am sure you are catching grief for it. Even so, I urge you to avoid having anything to do with him." Quint was shocked. His wife never said anything similar about his business for almost thirty years, and he looked at her, surprised. She added hastily, with actual concern in her eyes–fear, Quint might even call it. "I am sorry, dear, but I have had terrible dreams about him as I've never had before. Please, stay away from him. Let someone else deal with this problem."[1] Josh was indeed a problem, but Quint was the Commissioner of Baseball. He must deal with it or lose his position, and his position was all.

Finally, the commissioner returned to the present and relented, sitting forward, temporarily defeated. "Well, I guess there is no changing your mind. I warn you, your stance is bound to cost you everything."

"I understand, Commissioner. But in Truth, my stance comes because I have already gained everything of everlasting value. As I stay this course, I press on for the high calling of God in Christ Jesus where my soul rests, and my reward awaits."

There were a few moments of silence, and Quint got up to leave. Herald locked eyes with Quint as he rose out of his chair. It was both a question and a request. Quint nodded ever so slightly.

"Mr. Green. You don't know the commissioner or me, but I want you to know he has everyone's best interest at heart. As the commissioner's head of operations and public relations, I try to make it my business to follow the players closely, especially star players, such as yourself. It would be beneficial if we could put your actions in a charitable light. Although you are a rookie with no baseball background, I found you served in the military. The public generally considers such information a positive, at least if the service was honorable. Any reason why you have not let the information be made public?"

Josh sat still in his chair and made no sign of a response. Josh's silence was unexpected for Herald, so he tried again with slight frustration growing in his voice.

---

1. Matthew 27:19

"Also, Josh, we hear you visit hospitals in each town where you play. Often these visits are long and involve extensive time spent in children's wards, and you even visit terminally ill patients. I recently spoke to the St. Louis hospital you visited on more than one occasion. I've got to say, Mr. Green, you missed a gold mine of potential positive press in your visits. The hospitals I talked to gave glowing reviews. They all believe their patients loved meeting you, and the visits significantly improved their health." Herald paused, searching for a response. Still, Josh looked at the man and said nothing. "I mean, the one PR event you did have, the attempt to pray at the Synagogue after the shooting, was a disaster, but I checked on the hospital you visited the same day. I know it did not make the press. But a doctor there, like several hospitals I called," Herald didn't want to admit it was all of them, "Claimed your visit caused miraculous effects on the three critically wounded patients you visited. News of such an event would do wonders for the public's view of you," Herald said firmly, then slipped in almost unnoticed, "And, of course, Baseball." Herald waited. Josh did not respond. With a touch of angry frustration, Herald finished. "Look, Josh, we could have a video crew follow you through Children's at Columbia University Irving Medical Center, here in New York, where you took Ruth, and you could revisit the children's ward. If we could get the kids on tape and show them healed, well, that would be a game-changer!" Josh now folded his arms and remained silent. Herald was exasperated. No one ever defied to talk to him in such a way—the gall of the man!

Quint watched the one-way exchange and Josh's refusal even to answer. Quint shook his head finally when Herald looked back at him helplessly. "He's just a ballplayer, Herald, nothing more," Quint said to his VP, then turned to Josh, "That's it, isn't it?"

Josh responded, "I was born to grow up, know, and speak the Truth. I am not the Truth, but my purpose is to testify of the Truth and tell the world. Anyone who has ears, let them hear," said Josh.

Quint said sadly, "What is truth, Josh? Is it not, the world hates what you say, and it will be your undoing?"

"Whoever tries to save his life will lose it, but whoever loses his life for the Lord will preserve it,"[2] Josh replied.

"What kind of horse hockey is that!" Herald said, now letting the anger break through his veneer. Quint knew, but he did not bother to tell his colleague. He shook his head. It was time to leave.

"We're done here, Herald. Let's go," Quint said, motioning Herald towards the door. Quint let him pass, then turned to follow. "I am sorry we could not

---

2. Matthew 16:25

convince you to join us, Josh. Baseball could have used you, but I now fear your career will be a short one," he said as he began to follow Herald to the door. "And I think it will not have a happy ending."

"I am sorry too, Commissioner, that you choose not to join us. As for me, my eternity in Christ is secure. Please remember our Lord warned, 'What profits a man should he gain the whole world and lose his soul,'" Josh quoted, then added, "But to remain the Commissioner of Baseball?"

Quint was no longer looking at Josh as Herald already passed out the door, and his security guard was holding it, waiting patiently. However, Josh's last words cut to his heart, and he ever so slightly flinched as Josh pronounced his question more as a statement. Quint squashed down the memory of his wife's ominous premonition. He must move forward with plan B.

Quint and Herald left through the side entrance, the least visible in the stadium. Few cars waited beside his and Herald's separate limos. "Well, you can't say we didn't try," Herald said, shaking his head, baffled at Josh's intransigence and angry Josh didn't jump at the chance to show Herald something truly miraculous.

Quint replied, "We will do what we need to do."

Herald nodded, "I am heading home to dinner, and my route will show me well away from here. See you tomorrow?" Quint nodded and walked to his separate limo. He got in and sat down across from Cassius. Cassius looked for a sign from his boss, who stared out the window as the car pulled away. How, Quint thought, had it come to this?

Quint sighed, then looked at his assistant. "Make the call," he said, and Cassius took out a cheap flip phone and thumbed its only contact.

"You're a go," Cassius said. The voice on the other end of the line said something and hung up.

The car stopped to let Cassius out by his car several blocks away.

"Do you want me to call you if something goes wrong again?" Cassius asked.

"You better not need to!" Quint said more forcefully than he meant to. Cassius pulled back. "I am sorry," Quint apologized, shaking his head, frustrated at himself. "No, don't call me. I'll see you at 8:00 AM tomorrow. By then, we'll know."

Cassius departed, and the limo continued toward Quint's home on Long Island. He had a feeling it was going to be a sleepless night. As the city passed, Quint tried not to dwell on it, but one nagging thought repeatedly echoed in his head. He hoped there was no need for plan C.

One Hundred Six

P ete was more than anxious. He was conflicted when he let the commission-er's men force him out of the meeting with Josh. Why did he not take a stance and stay with Josh? Pete tried to tell himself it was only a meeting with the commissioner, but something inside him said he should have stayed, stood his ground, and been there for his friend.

He sat in the back seat of the hotel car, anxiously waiting for Josh to come out. Where was he? The commissioner and VP left several minutes ago, and still no sign of Josh. He texted Josh's phone again with no answer. The city was restless, adding to Pete's angst with himself, and there were regular processions of people walking past in groups despite the late hour. Pete knew, somehow, he failed his friend. He should have gone back to get him, but he was ashamed of his fear and failure. "Dear Lord, forgive me and restore my courage," he prayed silently.

Pete exited the car and started walking the 100 yards or so toward the stadium side entrance. It was windy and cold, and he pulled his jacket shut, trying to hold onto the fleeting warmth and safety. Finally, he saw Josh exit the stadium and turn, looking for him. They locked eyes, and Pete waved with relief as Josh took a few steps toward him. A group of people milling about a bus stop directly outside the stadium entrance noticed Josh. One shouted, pointing, "Hey, look, it's Green. It's Josh Green."

Suddenly, as if the words were a signal, people started running toward Josh from the bus stop and several other directions. People who'd been walking or milling about suddenly jumped up and moved. In shock, Pete began running toward Josh as he pulled out his phone. The people were closer and were quickly on Josh in a few seconds. Josh fended the first few off, but the group was too large, at least ten or more, and Pete could see several armed with various types of blunt objects, cudgels, and blackjacks. One even swung what looked like a pipe of some kind. Pete dialed 911 as he ran. As soon as the operator answered, he yelled into the phone, "Send Police to Yankee Stadium Gate 6! Please hurry! There's an attack on a player in progress. Oh, Lord! Please help us!"

Pete closed the ground as quickly as his old body would allow. The mob formed and swarmed over Josh so fast it was beyond belief. Pete's last thought was,

"This can't be happening by accident! It's not random." People beat, kicked, and punched his unseen body in the middle of the pile. Pete reached the mob with a built-up head of steam, and not knowing what else to do, flung himself at the group swarming over top of Josh.

Pete leapt and hit the pile of people on the side, knocking two men into several others. They seemed surprised as Pete's momentum from their backside gave him a momentary upper hand. He saw Josh for a few seconds, uncovered. His arms were around his head, but his face was beaten and bloody, and his eyes were closed. Pete yelled his name in desperation, but he did not move. Pete's leap caught one of the men hard in the back, and the man dropped what seemed to be an expandable police-style baton. Pete grabbed it quickly and jumped up next to Josh's unmoving body. He didn't know how long he could stand, but he must try. "Lean into it, Marine!" came the words of his Gunny Sergeant from Vietnam, "Keep moving. Keep your head on a swivel. Never give up!" The last echoed as the surprise from his initial thrust into the mob wore off, and they gathered themselves.

The first brave soul was the man whose baton Pete grabbed. His face of surprise turned to anger, and he reached to grab Pete's arm. The old marine in Pete exploded, and he let loose a hard left jab, landing successfully on the man's jaw as he overextended, trying to grab the baton in Pete's right hand. The man crumpled to the ground. Pete gained just a moment and realized someone was coming up from behind. He spun, swinging blindly at head height with all his strength, and was rewarded with the sound of a satisfying crunch as the end of the baton caught the man on the side of his head and jaw, relieving him of several teeth. Pete circled back with the strike, slicing the baton down sideways, as hard as possible, into the man's knee. His leg bent awkwardly, and he collapsed with a wail.

Suddenly, Pete could hear police sirens not far away, and so did the crowd. Instead of running away individually, the group began what Pete could only describe as a coordinated withdrawal. Two men each grabbed the two men Pete put down and dragged them toward River Avenue a few yards away. Pete stood guard over Josh, trying to understand what was happening. He heard one of the men yell, "Extract, Extract!" As Pete watched, he saw the man's raised left hand as he talked into his wrist, communicating into his sleeve. Pete noticed he wore a wired earpiece descending down into his shirt. Two panel vans pulled up by the time the ten-plus men got to the curb with their two wounded compatriots. They loaded up and sped north on River Avenue. Suddenly Pete was alone, standing over Josh, and the police sirens were getting loud, coming from the east on 161st Street. Pete turned, dropped the baton, and knelt down. Josh was breathing raggedly, and his left eye was swollen shut. Blood came from both his mouth and nose. When Pete tried to roll him over, Josh moaned but did not regain consciousness. The police arrived, and Pete stood up, waving vigorously at them to get their attention.

One Hundred Seven

I t was five hours since Josh's attack, and Saul was sitting in the waiting room at the New York-Presbyterian / Columbia emergency room. Pete told him the story after the police left. Mary and Ruth sat in a corner seat, and Pete stood staring out a window at the pink horizon as sunrise peaked over the New York Skyline. Several of Josh's teammates came, but the hospital rules limited the number of people who could visit, and Saul sent them all back to the hotel. Although Saul understood their desire to stay, he was glad for the rule as it gave no allowance for the press who caught wind of Josh's attack. The hospital turned away several reporters trying to sneak in and get the story. He knew it would be national news, but how it played out was anyone's guess. He was in contact with Mark Johnson, but had little in the way of additional information. Pete's story was haunting enough. The police wanted to keep it as a random act of violence, an offshoot of the angry demonstrations proceeding the game. However, Pete was adamant his opinion changed when he saw how the attackers made their withdrawal. The police searched for the unmarked vans to no avail and were concerned enough to place a uniformed officer outside Josh's room. Finally, a doctor came out to meet the family, Saul, and Pete.

"The good news is, Josh is stable for now. He's got a bruised spleen and kidney and contusions on his head, torso, back, arms, and thighs, and he has a concussion. We completed a CT scan, and it appears there is no permanent brain damage. Though he's very bruised and in pain, the blows to the rest of his body look like they should all heal on their own. He'll stay with us in the definitive observation unit to ensure we haven't missed anything, but for now, it looks like he should heal after some rest and eventually recuperate at home."

"Thank you so much, Doctor," Ruth said, relieved. "Can we see him?"

"Yes, they are getting him set up in a room, but I warn you, he's awake but groggy from the concussion. We have him on some pain meds and anti-inflammatories. Please understand, Ruth, he was badly beaten, and...," the doctor hesitated, "He looks pretty rough."

The four followed the Doctor up the elevator to a room where a police officer stood guard.

"Not too long. He needs rest most of all. I'll be back in a few minutes to check on you," said the doctor as he opened the door and let them pass. They entered and found Josh lying with an IV drip hooked up. Ruth rushed to her father's side and hugged him as gently as she dared with the multiple monitors attached to Josh.

Beaten and swollen, Josh's face was barely recognizable. He said through swollen lips, "It's all right, hon. It's not as bad as it looks." He held his daughter gently but firmly. She shook and did not speak, but slowly, she relaxed. Saul looked on, finding it difficult to keep his emotions in check and off his face. Josh looked like he fought in a 15-round prize fight and lost. Besides his battered face, Saul saw bruising beginning to show on both arms where he was kicked or beaten with the Lord knew what.

"What in the world is going on?" Saul growled to himself.

You know what it is, Saul

Saul heard the quiet voice reply in his head. Surprised, he looked around at Pete and Mary, who watched Josh and his daughter hug at Josh's bedside. Saul knew no one spoke out loud, yet he still thought he imagined the voice, so he tried again.

"Then what am I to do?" he prayed.

Hold tight to your faith. Watch, listen, and remember.

Josh released Ruth and looked at his three friends. He spied Saul and tried a smile that looked sadly warped because of his contusions. "I think I might have to miss tonight's game, Skipper," Josh cracked, but Saul barely smiled. He wanted to say it was OK and the team would be alright without him, but Saul doubted that was true, especially after what happened to Josh.

"Josh, don't you worry about us. Just rest and get well," Saul responded. He did not want to think about the team without Josh. He continued worriedly, "Is there anything we can do?"

Josh nodded one arm around Ruth, "Please make sure Nick and Ezra Demus are on the visitor's list. There are some things I need to discuss with them."

Saul nodded. He was silent, and Pete moved forward. Josh looked at him. Pete carried a Pirate black flat cap trimmed in gold. Pete called it his cold-weather Pirate cap and now gripped it in both hands, concerned. Saul moved to allow him to come closer to Josh.

"Are you all right, son?" Pete said haltingly. "Please tell me, you're gonna be all right?" Pete's question seemed like a plea, for what, Saul knew not, but he could feel Pete's deep regret.

"I'll be fine, Pete," Josh replied. "I'm so glad you're here."

"I'm so sorry, Josh, so sorry I couldn't stop it, so sorry I wasn't there for you. I..., Please, forgive me," Pete hurried, appealing to Josh like a drowning man, grasping for a lifesaver just out of reach.

"It's OK, Pete. It wasn't your fault; None of it. Besides, you came right in the nick of time. I don't remember much after they hit me over the head, but the police said if it weren't for you calling them and then throwing yourself into the fray, this could have been much worse."

"I should have been right there with you from the beginning," said Pete. "Even before, I should have never let the commissioner intimidate me and push me out of the room. I should have been there, by your side. But I was...," Pete shook his head. "I am sorry I failed you," Pete confessed, eyes downcast.

"Pete, the Lord brought me through, bruised and battered for sure, but then he kept you in the right place to save the day. If you were next to me, we might both be lying there on the ground, even worse off than I am without you to call the police and fend off the attack."

Pete looked up at Josh's eyes of care and forgiveness. He seemed made new and restored right before Saul's eyes. Pete said something earlier and now stirred a thought in Saul's mind: The commissioner's visit. He almost forgot when Pete first told him. But now he remembered listening to Pete trying to impress on the cops how the attack may look random, but the way they all withdrew smacked of organized premeditation. If that's true, how did they know when and where Josh would come out? Was it only a coincidence the commissioner and VP left minutes before? No one attacked them. If it wasn't a coincidence, what did that mean? Who were they really fighting? Suddenly, it struck Saul. He asked a similar question at the Arimas' house not so long ago. He realized the answer was the same, regardless of the physical entity directing the attack.

The doctor returned. "How are we all doing?" he asked. He walked up and hit a button on one monitor, causing a strip to print out a few seconds later. He looked at it briefly, then tore it off, checked several other vitals, and compared them to this current chart.

"Josh, how are you feeling?" he said to Josh while still looking at the chart.

Josh replied honestly with an obviously struggling voice, "I am feeling it a bit, Doc," Josh said.

"OK, any particular place?" the doctor asked, looking at Josh's bandage on his head.

"No," Josh replied, "Just hurting quite a bit all over."

The doctor nodded, "OK, that's probably your pain meds wearing off. You have," the doctor paused, looking at his watch, "About ten minutes before the nurse can give you some more. I am going to add something to help you sleep as well, you need to rest," this last he said looking at the other adults in the room. "OK, Josh?"

"OK, Doc. That sounds fine."

"Josh, I will check on you later this morning. Please, when the nurse comes, try to get some sleep. Gentlemen, can I speak with you for a moment?" The doctor didn't wait for an answer and walked to the door, waiting for Pete and Saul to follow as he held it open.

Once outside, the doctor stressed, "Josh is in for a few rough days. I will do what I can for him, but after taking that kind of beating, we must watch and wait while he rests and lets his body heal. Rest is key. I don't want anyone to come in here and stir things up," the doctor said pointedly. "Can I trust you two to ensure he has limited visitation from anyone, especially someone who might raise his stress levels?"

"Understood," Saul said.

"Doctor, I want to stay here. I promise to watch over him and protect him like a hawk even more than this fine officer is," Pete nodded to the young officer sitting in a chair to the side of the door watching the three men.

"I want to impress on you. Watch, but try not to engage. Let him rest, sir. That's the only way he'll heal. Everything looks OK, but there is much bruising. Even on the Cat Scan, there are some areas where I need the swelling to go down, so I can take another look. His vitals and everything we have say we don't need to do anything drastic. We'll push a lot of fluids, give Josh a quiet place to sleep, and let his body do the rest. He's in phenomenal shape for his age and what he's been through, but the next day or two will tell the tale."

The men nodded. The doctor reached into his pocket, pulled out a card, and handed it to Pete. "Since you are going to stay, call me anytime if you see anything wrong the nurse can't help with or have any concerns." He then turned to Saul, "You and Mary are on his notification list he made when we first talked with him, Coach. Please go to the desk and fill out a visitor form for Josh. If they are not on your list, I will direct security not to let them in. The police require this, but I would do it anyways based on the patient's needs right now, and for goodness' sake, make sure anyone on the list understands they need to limit their visits, especially at first."

Saul thanked the doctor. He turned to Pete. "You sure about this?"

"I am not leaving the boy again, Saul. I made that mistake once; I won't ever make it again!"

Saul nodded in understanding. "Give me your room key, and I'll put a bag together for you. I'll have Doc Luke bring it by. I want him to take a look at Josh and what they are doing here. Make sure everything is for the best. Luke knows Josh's medicals better than anyone, and I want to make sure we aren't missing something." Saul paused, and Pete knew there was something else.

"What's on your mind?"

Saul shook his head. "It's just the way this all went down."

"What do you mean," said Pete.

"I mean the late-night visit from the commissioner and the VP. Followed immediately by the attack."

"Good," Pete whispered, surprising Saul. Pete responded to his questioning look, "I'm glad I ain't the only one thinkin' it. And let's not forget what happened here before the All-Star break."

"Lots of coincidences," Saul said.

"Too many," agreed Pete.

Saul's relief at their mutual feeling immediately became concern. If they were both thinking it, what did it mean? "Pete, we need to know why the commissioner was there and what they discussed at that meeting. And we need to understand it before the press finds out," Saul finished.

Pete nodded. "I'll let the boy sleep, but I will talk to him after he wakes up about it."

Saul nodded wearily and yawned back at him. Pete finished, "You best get going. Try to get some rest. You have a game to play tonight." He reminded Saul as he backed into and pushed open the door. "Oh, and throw some sugarless peppermint gum of some sort in my bag for Doc Luke to bring. These turkeys won't even let an unlit cigar in here, and I need something to chew on." With that, Pete walked back into the room to join Mary and Ruth as they watched over Josh.

One Hundred Eight

G ame four did not go well. The Pirates looked rattled. They got off to a rough start and gave up four runs in the first two innings, two unearned. Their fielding wasn't the only poor play. Their bats went quiet as they collected more strikeouts in game four than the first three games combined. The game was not close as the Yankees, with their backs against the wall, made the Pirates look mediocre, handing them a shutout loss, 6-0.

The following day, Josh felt a little better. Mary and Ruth arrived early, and Josh asked Pete if he could see the two alone. As Pete excused himself, Josh said, "Pete, I expect either Ezra or Ezra and his dad. Could you send them on in?" Pete nodded though he wondered a bit about it and what the Doc might say if he happened upon Josh with so many visitors, but he figured he could handle the Doc.

Sure enough, Nick and Ezra showed up about thirty minutes later, and Pete sent them in. The police officer checked everyone was on the list. Even though Pete gave the officer a thumbs up, the officer raised an eyebrow when Doc Luke arrived. Pete headed off the cop's question and said, "We'll wait out here until they leave." The cop reluctantly nodded his approval. Doc Luke, as usual, wanted to know all the details of what happened yesterday. However, he first went to visit Josh's doctor. Luke previously called their mutual friend, Dr. Asa Levine, Josh's rehab doctor, from July, who recommended Josh's current attending doctor. Doc Luke soon returned, up to speed on Josh's condition.

Doc Luke started asking Pete questions about the little meeting in Josh's room. Of course, Pete couldn't answer any of them and was about to tell Luke what to do with his questions when Nick stuck his head out the door, smiling. He said, "Ah, Pete and Luke, you'll do fine. Won't you come in? Josh needs you," said Nick, holding the door open.

Pete looked at Luke and said gruffly, "Now, I guess you'll get your answers." The cop gave Pete a disapproving scowl as they walked into the room. Pete shrugged his shoulders, sheepishly saying, "I don't think there will be anyone else," and the cop shook his head.

As they all settled around Josh, Nick said, "Gents, thank you for coming in. Josh would like you to witness this document. Josh?"

"Guys, sorry for the bit of secrecy, it wasn't meant that way, but I wanted Mary and Ruth to talk with me about something I've been praying about before Nick and Ezra here could come, but I still want you to be here with us. You see, Ruth and I, well, we are really the only close family each other's got, and ever since Ruthie's mom passed, I've been concerned about Ruth and what would happen if, well...," Josh squeezed Ruth's hand as she held happy tears in her eyes. "You know we're not guaranteed tomorrow," Josh hurried on, trying not to bring up what happened to him. "Ruth and I have been blessed to have Mary here this year. She has been such a help to us, and Ruth and Mary have developed a strong bond. Mary is now part of our lives. We're a team. I need someone I can rely on to care for Ruth," Josh hesitated, "In my absence. So, I asked Mary and Ruth if it was OK if Mary becomes Ruthie's guardian if something should happen," Josh hurried, "And they have both agreed."

Mary squeezed Ruthie's shoulders, and Ruth looked up at her with the same happy-sad eyes. Josh's speech caught even Pete a little off guard. Again, the thought struck him of his years in the Marine Corps and how the few grunts with families worried about who would take care of them should something happen. Pete knew with Ruthie's mom passing and now her dad's close call, what Josh was doing was necessary. While Pete couldn't bear to think of Ruth losing her dad, he was joyful Ruth and Josh found in Mary someone they could count on.

Nick stepped in to relieve the little sadness of such an event. "The paperwork makes it official with the signatures, but, as I am a new Christian," he said, slightly surprising Pete and Luke, but not, it seemed, Ezra and Josh, who were both smiling. "And an old Jew," he continued with a smile. "Then I think it would be good to get your witness signatures," Nick said to Luke and Pete, "While I read you from a particular part of my brand-new, New Testament. Even as a non-believing Jew, I have always adored this chapter, and now I am delighted to claim it as my own, in Christ. Although it's often read at weddings, I think it's for all of us, as a family of believers."

Nick took out his New King James Bible and began reading from First Corinthians chapter 13 as Ezra brought the papers to Doctor Luke and Pete to sign. Nick's voice was warm and clear, like the well-read old Jew he was. "Love suffers long and is kind; love does not envy; love does not parade itself, is not puffed up; does not behave rudely, does not seek its own, is not provoked, thinks no evil; does not rejoice in iniquity, but rejoices in truth; bears all things, believes all things, hopes all things, endures all things. Love never fails...And now abide faith, hope, love these three; but the greatest of these is love." The simple proceedings had a special feeling, and all could not help but feel blessed to enjoy these moments together.

The day was a good one but soon ended as Josh let them go. Doc Luke left for the game. Ruth wanted to stay, but they were there all day, and Mary could tell Josh needed to rest. Doc Luke escorted the ladies out, saying to the remaining men, "You three, let the man get some rest now, Doctor's orders!" Then Luke added, "And Pete, you might want to head back to your room and, you know, freshen up a bit!" in a fake whisper.

"It's all right, Pete," Josh said before Pete could object. "Why don't you head back and get yourself cleaned up? I am feeling a bit tired and ready to get a few winks. I'll be all right. As a matter of fact, why don't you get some sleep? Come back tomorrow, and we can talk about the game."

Pete was concerned about leaving Josh alone, but with the police officer outside, he guessed it would be OK. He begrudgingly left as Nick and Ezra were saying their goodbyes. Pete walked out, and Nick followed when Josh said to Ezra, "Ezra, would you stay a moment? I require your assistance once more...."

Game five placed Samson on the mound against the Yankees ace again. Both pitchers pitched well again, although Samson was not quite as dominating. The game was touch and go, as this was another do-or-die game for the Yankees. The Pirates gave up one run through the sixth and were down 1-0 when Juan took a 1-0 pitch and sent it into orbit over the left field wall in the top of the seventh. After he walked J.J., the Yankee starter's day was done. However, the Yankee relievers were better than the Pirates on this day, ending the inning without any more runs. Tied 1-1, a single and a walk followed by an uncharacteristic passed-ball by Thomas placed runners on second and third. Samson, at 120 pitches, was done. Pops brought in Jude Keriothson to try to hold the tie. The Yankees substituted the lead runner with a pinch-runner; sure enough, the batter hit a fly ball to center. Andrew made a good throw, but the runner on third slid in just in front of the throw. The Yankees made the one-run lead hold up for a 2-1 win, sending the series back to Pittsburgh with the Pirates leading the series 3-2, still needing the elusive final victory.

The next morning, Pete tried to drink an instant coffee in his hotel room before seeing Josh. It wasn't very good, and he would have dumped it out if he weren't so tired. His cell phone rang, and he saw it was Doc Luke. "Good, you're up," Luke said. "I am calling for Josh. Long story short, pack your things. We're heading back to the burgh this morning."

"No, I'm not! I am staying with Josh!"

"Well, if you want to stay with Josh, you'll have to pack your things. He's going back to Pittsburgh."

"WHAT!" Pete was ready to object.

"Look, I don't like it much either, but he's a grown man. He is signing himself out of the hospital. Now before you go ballistic, listen. He added me to a conference call with the trauma doctor there at the hospital. Although he's still beat up, the doctor begrudgingly agrees all his tests show he is on the mend. When the doctor objected, saying he couldn't recommend Josh fly back to Pittsburgh on the team plane, Josh was ready. He got Ezra to charter their corporate jet for him, the girls, you, and I back to Pittsburgh and direct to UPMC hospital in Oakland. The doctor reluctantly agreed, warning Josh the movement risks damaging his internal healing. It should be OK if Josh minimizes his movements and has no further complications."

Pete didn't like it, not one bit, but it did have one benefit. They might manage to keep it from getting to the press as Josh would leave the hospital through an alternate exit and fly out of the Farmingdale-Republic airport in New York, where Ezra's firm chartered their corporate jet.

They were all back in Pittsburgh early that afternoon, with Josh settling in his room at UPMC in Oakland. Doctor Shewtick herself reviewed the chart and tests from New York-Presbyterian / Columbia. She wrinkled her nose as she put down the chart and shook her head. "I can't say I like the fact you chose to fly home, Josh, but I guess I would agree it was a relatively safe risk. Now, I must insist that be all the excitement for you for a few days. I prescribe rest, quiet, and more rest. I will order a few scans to ensure your little adventure back here didn't incur any setbacks." She turned to Doc Luke and Pete, the only ones with Josh besides Mary and Ruth. "Seriously, and I mean this. You can't expect him to heal if he keeps moving, and you two should know better." Doc Luke, who was at least fifteen years her senior, looked like a little kid caught with his hand in the cookie jar. Pete started to protest his innocence, but Josh cut in.

"Evelyn, don't blame them. I gave them no choice. It was my decision. I needed to come home early."

Dr. Shewtick turned back from Pete and Luke, hands on her hips, but like many before her, she looked into Josh's eyes and saw the ancient strength, kindness, and, dare she say it, wisdom and purpose beyond her understanding. She lowered her hands from her hips and dropped her objections. She shrugged her shoulders, resigned to accept what she knew she might not understand, but added, "Very well. But I must insist you rest while here and let me run the tests. In the meantime, only Ruth and Mary can visit but sparingly! Besides, from what I hear, you all need to get home and get your own rest," she said, looking at all four. "Doctor's orders!" She finished, and everyone agreed to do as she said, with the adults acting like contrite good little children.

Pete was last to go, as Josh seemed to follow a step-by-step plan known only to him since the attack. "Pete, a moment," said Josh while Doc Luke escorted the ladies out. Mary and Ruth looked at Josh with worry. "I'll be good, I promise," he said gently to the girls, alleviating some, but not all their concern.

Josh waited until Pete and he were alone. He then told him his intentions. Though the plan greatly concerned Pete as he listened, Pete could sense it reflected a deep understanding and discernment on Josh's part. Something told Pete that Josh knew more about what was truly happening than he would ever know, even after it was all over. Also, as a man who once helped plan dangerous operations, Pete knew such undertakings to defeat the enemy required an accurate assessment of the risks and an understanding of the stakes. You must understand both what it means to act and not act.

When Josh finished, he looked at Pete. Until now, Pete remained silent. He asked, "Josh, are you sure the risk is worth the outcome?"

"Pete, I am on a journey. I now realize it didn't begin this spring. It began a long time ago. I think, perhaps, it began before I was even born. The journey is not of my making. It is the Lord's. I believe He has shown me I am to see it through. My part in this is to choose. To choose to obey in faith or to give up. If I give up, so much will be lost. We are to carry the Good News to the utmost parts of the earth and love our neighbors as brothers, as Christ first loved us. I choose to obey. If I follow God's leading and His will, no matter how difficult and impossible the path may seem, it's the right path for me. It's the only path I want to follow."

Pete listened carefully and nodded. "And you don't want me to tell Saul? Just Doc, when the time is right?" he asked.

Josh nodded. "Pops has a part in this, but we don't need to burden him with this plan. He must get the team to where it needs to be."

"You know, they could win tomorrow, and it could all be over," Pete said hopefully. Josh's expression did not change. Pete knew what that look meant. Pete looked at Josh again like he did the first day in his office. Josh, the dark-skinned warrior, but he wasn't that anymore, not to Pete. Josh was something more. He was his brother. He was a son. He was his Gunny, his first coach, all the way back. Josh was all these things and more. He was the ancient and caring friend. "The friend that sticks closer than a brother,"[1] thought Pete, who now knew something about that famous verse in Proverbs and what Jesus later said about his friends. Jesus didn't just tell them he would be that kind of friend to them. Jesus was also asking them something. Something the Creator asked man ever since the Garden. He asked each person to come back and join Him again. To take his offer of friendship and love and do so freely, yet with their whole heart.

---

1. Proverbs 18:24

God is the God of second chances. Pete wavered at Yankee Stadium. Josh never did. Now, Josh asked Pete once more to be that friend. This time Pete was all in.

Pete nodded and said, "All right, my friend. We will see it through. Together."

One Hundred Nine

Quint sat in his office at MLB headquarters on the thirty-first floor, reading the dailies. So far, his plan was working. The Yankees were doing their part in righting MLB's ship, and the crowds responded accordingly. They now backed both the Yankees' and the Leagues' progressive stance more forcibly. The Pirates, absent the instigator Green, were now a losing pariah, and fans abandoned their cause, and support on the diamond, in equal measure. It was amazing how fickle the public could be and how quickly they bailed when they lost someone to follow.

Cassius buzzed Quint's desk phone. Quint knew Cassius would not bother him during his daily review unless it was necessary.

"Yes?" Quint answered.

"I am sorry, sir, but I just received some news. May I come in?"

Quint also knew Cassius wouldn't ask to walk in from the outer office unless it was the kind of news no one else should know, either because of what it was or the source who reported it.

"Come," Quint answered and hung up.

Cassius entered and closed the door. Quint hit the lock button under his desktop so no one would accidentally walk in. It also activated a scrambler Quint had installed when he first took over in case someone was using electronic equipment trying to listen in from a distance. You could never be too sure.

"Sit and tell me the bad news." Quint could already tell from Cassius's slightly altered demeanor it was not a good surprise.

Cassius sat across from the commissioner and said, "Our source inside the hospital notified me that Green left earlier today," he stated.

Quint sat back. "Are you sure?" he asked skeptically.

"Our contacts in Pittsburgh are a little light, but I played a hunch he might return to the Pittsburgh hospital he's visited previously. Sure enough, he, his family, and a few others showed up a few hours ago. He checked in and is under a trauma doctor's care."

"Anyone with eyes on know his status?" asked Quint.

"No, we don't have anyone inside the hospital. Yet." Cassius replied.

"No, I don't suppose we can build a contact like that quickly," Quint said, thinking out loud, and Cassius nodded in agreement.

Cassius added, "But, If Green got out and flew back to Pittsburgh...," he let the statement hang.

"Then he may be better off than we were led to believe," Quint finished the man's thoughts. Cassius again nodded.

Quint turned and looked out on his million-dollar view of Manhattan. He did love this view and everything that went with it. He would do anything to maintain it. He spoke without looking back at Cassius, "Options?"

"We made the necessary initial contacts for the final solution," Cassius started, but Quint cut him off.

"DON'T—use that term," he said sternly, looking back at Cassius, and Cassius raised his hands in contrition. Once Quint looked back out the window, Cassius continued.

"We've made the initial contacts for plan C. Our contact identified a man for the job. He only needs access."

"What kind of man?"

"Our contact says he is personally motivated, a true believer in the cause, with a personal grudge, and the necessary skill sets. Also, our contact set a payment option to an untraceable third party in our acceptable range."

"Do I want to know what cause?" Quint asked.

"Do you really care, sir? Our contact ensures us the man will carry out the task and disappear. If he gets caught, his cause will suffice for his motive. He also has the kind of background that will ensure he cannot be traced back to us."

"And this access?"

"Our contact has reviewed the possibilities, but the only obvious contact point is...,"

"The ballpark," Quint finished again.

Cassius said, "Yes. Even though this is not desirable, it has one benefit. If Green does not show, it allows us to cancel the plan. We can prep the site beforehand, but we'll need a high-level key card to gain access on the day. We can get that from Annason, but it will require using our inside man. We need your go-ahead to get everything in place."

Quint looked out the window as he listened. He didn't like this nasty business. Why did it come to this? But really, did he have any choice at all? There was only one guaranteed way to keep his position and status. Green stood between him and his continued power and success.

Quint reluctantly turned back to Cassius and nodded. "OK, get everything in place. It's time to use that burner phone we gave Annason. If he tries to wriggle out, let him understand his position depends entirely on seeing it through."

Several hours later, Cai Annason was in his office working late. The Pirates were back in town. He needed to finish some last-minute arrangements trying to survive the possible outcomes of the series as his team's tumultuous season threatened to end either with his greatest victory or his absolute defeat. Suddenly, the phone the commissioner forced him to carry since their meeting, rang in his pocket. It was an old-school flip phone, and Cai felt a sense of dread as he pulled it out.

"Hello?"

A voice Cai did not recognize said, "Mr. Annason, I have directions you need to memorize and follow."

Cai responded, "Now's really not a good time, I am about to sit down to dinner, and we have guests," Cai lied.

"Mr. Annason, you are sitting in your office alone. We have eyes everywhere. You will follow these instructions to the letter, or you will no longer be the President of the Pittsburgh Pirates. Do you understand?"

Cai, frozen by the voice's coolly delivered ultimatum and the fact he was being watched, haltingly replied, "Yes." Cai's eyes opened ever wider as the voice told him what he must do.

Finally, the voice finished, "Do as you're told, Mr. Annason. You will have your team back, and no one will be the wiser. Fail, and we will be coming for you next. Do you understand the instructions?

Cai felt he had no choice.

"Yes," Cai replied, fearfully accepting his fate. "It will be as you have commanded."

One Hundred Ten

Game six at Pittsburgh was a dark, cold, drizzly Friday night. PNC Park was packed. Inside and outside were throngs of people from every walk of life, all with something to say or shout. A few fans noticed Josh Green's status upgraded from "out" to "doubtful" without further details or explanation. Rumors flew, placing him back in Pittsburgh, and it seemed the crowd wanted to see the man, but not necessarily with good intentions. When Josh was a no-show for the game, the crowd grumbled and, in anger, cast many a disparaging comment during the lineup announcements as the team, absent Green, took the field. The crowd seemed unsure where to aim their anger, carrying a disgruntled feeling of malaise to start the game. The Pirates' melancholy mood seemed opposed to the fact they were trying to win the world championship. They played disconnected and demoralized, and the Yankees pounced. The game was a blowout. It took only 2 hours and 53 minutes, and the Pirates lost their third straight, this one a laugher 12-0. The stadium was half empty by the end of the game, and the Pirates could not look each other in the eyes.

Saul pulled the team together in the locker room. There would be no press tonight.

"Look," he began, "I don't know what to say to motivate you or to tell you how we dig ourselves out of the pit it feels like we're in right now, but I feel I must say the feeling you have, is a feeling we all have. And I think it's a lie."

Everyone looked at Saul as he said it. He slowly looked around the room at each of them. Finally, he said, "When Josh was attacked and hurt, we all took a blow. It's a tough blow, I know. No one feels it more than I do. But we weren't meant just to lay down and die. Josh always reminds us how the battle isn't any one person's. It's all of ours, because we are a family. That's what our chant is. I know you don't feel like saying it right now. You want to go home. But I want you to remember something. Family isn't who you pick. It's who the Lord puts into your life. We all come from different backgrounds, and many of you come from pretty tough circumstances. We all have failures, and we have all been knocked down before. That's what's happened to us. We've been knocked down. But here we are, and nothing is decided. Right?"

Saul paused and looked at each person again. "You are my family, and when one of us gets knocked down, we don't give up. We come together, and we fight. Not amongst ourselves, we fight together against the common enemy, and right now, as far as I am concerned, we have 'em right where we want 'em!"

Everyone on the team looked at Pops like he lost his mind. Just then, Jude Keriothson's cell rang. He looked at it, then at the coach. "If you need to take that, Jude, then go. We got things to talk about here," Saul said.

Jude looked around, and a few looked back at him. Justus Barabbas, his roommate, gave him a quizzical look, and Jude looked back defiantly, got up, and walked out.

"OK. Now we can speak about where we stand. The Yankees think we're done. Heck, maybe the entire world does. They think we're dead, and our heart has stopped beating. But I know something the Yankees don't, and maybe the world doesn't either. I think they've forgotten something." The team was focused, looking intently at Coach Saul.

"The only thing the Yankees have won is a reprieve. And it's temporary. They've staved off their own sorry ending three times. But that means nothing to us. We still need one game, just one good game. That's what you've got before you. Forget what's behind and press on to the fight in front of you!"[1]

Saul continued, "Tomorrow night, you are playing for something every ballplayer dreams about their whole life, but few ever get the chance. Tomorrow, you all have a shot at the Championship! One game, winner takes all! And this family is going to give it everything we have. Those Yankees haven't won squat. Tomorrow is a new day. We play tomorrow for each other, for this family the good Lord blessed us with. I tell you, I have never been so proud of a team as I am of you. Everything you've been through. Don't give up, and don't give in. Play until the very last out. Play for all your worth. Love this. Love this opportunity, for it may never come again. Show your family, your brothers, show the world this Pirate family can't be easily defeated. We've got something the world needs. We've been standing all season, despite what the world tries to do to us. We stand for what is right and true. I say to you: Stand fast. Stand for each other. Show the world, when we finish, no matter what, the Lord has done a mighty work, right here, right now, with this team, with this family."

It was quiet for a few seconds. Finally, Andrew stood and walked to the middle of the room. "If Josh were here, I think he would say, 'Let's bring it in and pray to the Lord. Let His will be done!'" The team huddled and, to a man, knelt, and with one accord, asked the Lord to cover them with His grace and peace.

---

1. Philippians 3: 13-14

Outside, Jude Keriothson walked away from his team. He walked towards a black limousine on the edge of the nearly empty parking lot. He obeyed the phone summons and got in the back of the car as instructed, sitting down next to another occupant in the back seat. As they drove away, the man, who wore a strange fake beard with a false mustache and glasses, told Jude to look straight ahead and handed him a manila package.

"Here's a detailed schematic of the ballpark. If you look closely, on page 4, there is a maintenance entrance labeled B52, like the old singing group, that's rarely used along the outer wall on the first sub-level. You can access it through a narrow tunnel running from the handicap bathroom nearby. Tomorrow, Cai Annason will visit the bullpen at 5:30 PM before the game and give you all a pep talk. When he leaves, follow him out. He's going to drop his wallet. Pick it up. The main pocket will have a black and yellow master key card. Make sure no one but him sees you take it, and then give the wallet back to him. Go to the handicapped bathroom. The card will open both the service door in the bathroom leading to the tunnel and the outer stadium door. Use the key card to open both and place a piece of the gorilla tape there in the package over the latches so the doors won't latch when closed. I recommend wearing gloves. Make sure each opens without the key card when you push on them. Understand?"

Jude, who listened while staring forward, forgot the man's warning and looked back at him.

"Yes."

"DON'T—Look at me," the man said in a quiet, intimidating, slow voice, and Jude snapped his head back to look out the window. "When you're done, there will be a battery-powered shredder in the handicap bathroom, inside a blue waste bin—one big slot for the paper map, one small for the key card. Shred the map and key card. This is important. That keycard has a tracker in it. As soon as Annason reports it missing, they will use the tracker to find it. You'll have thirty minutes before he reports it missing. Got it?"

Jude stared straight ahead this time, "I got it."

"Do all these things, and you'll get the other half of the three million in silver bonds to your Cayman account. Mess anything up or get caught, and you can kiss your butt goodbye."

Jude was startled at that. He tried to recover. "Look, what about my contract with the Yankees?"

"The Boss said you'll get it in the off-season when Cai releases you on waivers. Three years at a one million base with milestones from there."

"The commissioner promised me three million a year guaranteed," Jude objected.

"Well, the deal's changed, and you best not say that name again if you want your pitching arm to stay in one piece. There are no guarantees, Mr. Keriothson, and the way you've been pitching in the playoffs, any contract at all, is generous. You want something more, you're going to have to prove yourself worthy. Just concentrate on doing as you are commanded. You screw any of it up, you won't be around to collect on a contract or those Cayman silver coins in the off-season, I'll guarantee that!" said the man as he tapped on the glass and the limo pulled to the curb. "Get Out!"

Jude looked out. "This is Oakland. I live on the other side of town!" Jude whined as he stepped out of the car.

"I know where you live, Jude, get an Uber!" said the man, and he pulled the door closed as the limo sped off.

Jude knew he had made his bed, he realized, and though he now doubted his choice, Jude thought staying on the losing side was even worse. Now that Josh was gone, he held no faith in God or miracles. He put his faith and trust in the commissioner's power. Like Cai Annason, Jude knew with power on his side, he could get what he wanted. However, this was not what Jude envisioned when the offer was generous. The requests began almost innocently for inside info on the team. Soon, however, came more troubling requirements for a few "poor pitches" at critical game junctures. Now Jude was in deep. He felt boxed into a corner. He knew his teammates and coaches were foolish, going against the League and the people's will, but Jude was still sick about it. Why did he feel so bad and conflicted when he made the smart move? Jude's conscience churned inside him as he rode home in the Uber. The real question in his mind, he tried to ignore, was who was he letting through a back door of the stadium, and more importantly, why? No, he didn't want to know, yet the thought plagued him all night through dark dreams and fitful sleep.

One Hundred Eleven

S aul noticed Pete was distracted as the team warmed up for game seven. Finally, as the pregame finished, Saul couldn't take it any longer. "Pete, you've been checking your watch and cell phone more this evening than I have seen you do in the last decade. You don't even normally have your phone out of the office. You hate that thing. What's going on? Game seven of the World Series too boring for you?"

Then, in answer to Saul's question, Pete's phone rang, "Hold that thought," Pete said. He got up from the dugout bench and walked down the tunnel back towards the locker room a few steps. Saul could only hear part of the conversation. "Ya. Yep, I'll grab him. Yep, he's waiting just like you wanted. You're cutting it a little fine, aren't you? Yeah, OK, I understand. We'll be there in a few." Pete hung up and hurried back to Saul, pulling another phone out of his other back pocket.

"What's this?" asked Saul.

"It's your phone. Take it off silent and only accept calls from me," said Pete.

"I hate these things almost as much as you do. That's why I leave mine in my office, too!"

"Tonight, you can't. I got some things to do, and I need to get updates from you!"

"What kind of updates, and what do you mean you've got things to do? Are you leaving?" Saul asked incredulously.

Pete paused. There wasn't time to explain, and he knew Saul needed to focus on the game. For once, Pete got a look in his eyes, a look Saul hadn't seen since he was a young player, and Pete used Saul's nickname, which he rarely did. "Pops, trust me on this. Coach the game of your life. Help is not far away." Then Pete's eyes softened a little as he seemed to remember something. "You remember when Saul had his encounter on the road to Damascus?" Pete said, and Saul nodded. "The Lord told that guy, what's his name? Saul was coming to see him?"

"You mean Ananias?"

"Yeah, that's him. Remember how Ananias said, 'But Lord, are you sure? He hates us?'" said Pete, paraphrasing.

"I don't think that's exactly what he said," Saul replied.

"Yeah, well, it's the gist. I need you to remember what God said back. Again, just the gist. 'Trust me on this,'" Pete said and turned on his heel, starting back down the hallway, "And keep your phone on!"

"What? Now you're comparing yourself to God talking to Ananias?" shouted Saul after him.

"Just coach, Pops," Pete said, looking back one more time, "Oh, and I am takin' Doc with me! We'll be back before it's over!"

Saul stared disbelievingly as his bench coach, friend, and mentor walked out of sight. However, he didn't have time to object as the team came off the field and the stadium prepared for the game's start. Saul needed to reassure his players and get them ready to play.

Pete hadn't told Luke the whole story, just that Josh needed them sometime today. Still, Luke packed his kit up more than two hours ago and almost gave up when Pete stuck his head in Luke's office. "Time to go!"

"Now?!" said Luke incredulously.

"C'mon, Doc, don't you know we're just along for this boat ride, and the Lord didn't say let's go to the middle of the lake and stop? He said, let's go to the other side." Pete turned his back on Luke as Luke scrambled to catch up. Luke couldn't see Pete's satisfied little smile. All that Sunday school growing up was paying off with some excellent metaphors tonight, thought Pete.

It didn't take long to get to the hospital. When they brought Josh home from New York, he was still on an IV and so weak he needed help to get dressed, and they used a wheelchair to move Josh. Mary and Ruth helped on that trip, but today, Josh sent the girls ahead to the ballpark. As Pete and Doc entered the hospital, Pete wondered how they would get Josh where he needed to go. Nearing the hospital room, Pete noticed a strange assortment of burly men in a communal area down the hall. Nearby, Pete saw a very "not amused" Doctor Shewtick standing, looking down the hallway at Josh's room. She turned and looked at them, and her eyes shot silent daggers.

Pete was a bit confused. "What's going on, Doc?" he asked.

"You tell me, Pete! These guys showed up thirty minutes ago and kicked me out of Josh's room. I tried calling security. It seems these gentlemen," she gestured towards the half dozen guys sitting in the waiting room, "And their friends down there," the doc gestured again, and Luke and Pete saw there were two more standing in front of Josh's door, "Apparently, know someone in security. The guards said they can't help me with this and disappeared! Josh said, you supposedly know what this is all about?" Pete noticed for the first time that one of the men was sitting with a leg crossed, but it wasn't a leg. It was a titanium prosthesis. The man next to him wore an eye patch.

Pete forgot that Josh's detailed plan mentioned some old friends going to help them, but wasn't specific about what that meant. When he asked Josh about it, Pete now remembered Josh replied, "They're my brothers, like the ones you knew before you came home, back to the world, from that different life." Now Pete understood. Pete looked around. Though they were a younger generation, these men bore the same look as those in the fading photograph in his office of guys in fatigues surrounded by a jungle from a different lifetime.

"OK, Doc," he said, giving Dr. Shewtick the hands down, let's all calm down gesture. "Look, I'm sorry, but this will all work out. However, we do need Josh's discharge papers," Pete said.

Dr. Shewtick did not look satisfied, but her firm stance softened after a few moments as she realized she couldn't change the course of events. "Against my professional recommendation, Josh has taken it upon himself to sign himself out. Now I need you to understand something I told him. His body is healing, but it's not yet healed. From what I saw in his tests yesterday, he should be in bed for another week, let alone not playing any baseball." After a few moments staring at the two men, she took her hands off her hips, sighed, and clasped them in front of her. "Look," she said slowly, "I know Josh has...," again, she hesitated. "Well, he has a special purpose in life. His actions with the men who were shot," she said, thinking back, then hurried on, "And the children he saw in the cancer ward where my brother worked...," she paused. "Well, they defied our understanding of human health and healing. But I can't say what leaving early will do to him, especially if he plays tonight."

Pete and Doc Luke stood with Dr. Shewtick. Luke broke the silence, gently placing his hand on her shoulder. "Doctor, where our training and understanding ends, there faith begins. You have done all you can. Josh has decided he has something the Lord wants him to do. I don't think hell itself will stop him from trying."

"Is it worth it?" Evelyn asked, eyes filled with emotion.

"I think Josh believes, if it's God's will, it is both the only thing and everything worth doing," Luke finished.

Finally, Dr. Shewtick nodded. She walked a few steps to the nurses' station, signed a form, returned the clipboard back to the nurse. She looked at the men, then turned and said as she walked away, "I am off in an hour. I plan to go home. My brother's already there. We will be watching. And praying." She was at the stairwell when she turned back a moment and said to them, "God bless you," kindly then looking at the rough men who were now circling Pete and Luke like lions, she added, "And take Josh's friends with you when you go, please. They're making my staff nervous!"

Pete and Doc turned back and walked to Josh's private room door. The two men standing guard stopped them. One held up his hand, stopping their movement, while the other turned and knocked lightly twice.

"I'm ready. Send them in," Josh's voice said.

The man opened the door and let Pete and Luke in. Josh was dressed in his uniform. Though he was still the tall figure of a man, there was a gaunt look to him, as if he lost ten or more pounds overnight. His face was bruised, and he rose with some effort and the help of two men. On one side was a short, tough-looking man with a prosthetic right arm ending in a clawed hook. On the other was a man the same height as Josh, but thicker by at least fifty pounds. He wasn't fat. He was, well, formidably big, thought Pete. The kind of guy who likes to go through the door, or the wall, first.

"Hello, fellas. Thanks for coming," greeted Josh. "These are old friends of mine. Pete, Doc Luke, meet Master Sergeant Gabe Rodelo," Josh said, nodding to the short, fireplug Latino, with one arm. "And Chief Warrant Officer 4, Todd Michael. They've come with some of our friends to see we get where we need to go tonight safely."

Chief Todd was wearing dark glasses and nodded to the two of them as he walked past without saying anything. He exited the door, closing it behind him. Pete would have stared after him if he hadn't caught the same look on Doc Luke's face, following the imposing man with his eyes as he passed like he just saw the boogie man. They were both saved by Gabe's melodious Spanish-accented and amused greeting. "Don't worry about Chief Todd, mi' amigos. His bark is mostly worse than his bite. Mostly. As long as you fall in line." Gabe's disarming smile broke the mood as he continued. "He'll have the fellas all moving to their positions. Ready Flash?" he asked, turning to Josh.

"Don't feel quite like Flash tonight, my friend. I am afraid this time you'll have to lead the way."

"Not to worry, partner, we got your back, and we'll get you there. Follow Chief and I." Gabe turned and said to Pete and Doc Luke, "Gents, I need you to stay with Josh. No matter what," he said, smile fading to a serious look. "Stay with him." Both men nodded, and Gabe's smile returned. "Good. Now Chief and I will lead you out, and our two compadres you saw outside the door will follow behind and keep it clear to the rear, OK? Nothing to worry about."

"What about those guys in the waiting area?" Doc Luke said.

"Don't worry," Gabe smiled. "They are already in position," and he tapped his ear where Pete now saw an earpiece.

Luke and Pete wondered what that meant, but Josh was walking slowly. "Best use that for now, Flash. Save your strength," Gabe said, nodding to the wheelchair in the corner of the room. Josh nodded and moved to it, sitting down. Pete didn't question, and he grabbed the handles to push Josh. Doc clutched his bag. "Ready?" Gabe said, and the three men nodded. "Here we go."

Gabe knocked twice firmly on the door, and one of the men opened it from the outside. Josh, pushed by Pete, accompanied by a slightly unnerved Doc Luke, followed Gabe as he exited. The two men outside followed, trailing behind them, carefully checking their rear. Chief Todd was at the nurse's station, and as soon as he saw them come out, he nodded, turned, and moved off down the hallway, past the elevator they initially used. Instead, he led them down the hallway to a corner. He reached his left hand up and said something into a sleeve mike. As they walked by the area where the other men milled about, it was now empty. Pete noticed the nurses were now alone, staring at them as they passed. Chief Todd stayed about 50 feet in front of Josh and the others, clearing the way. It took about five minutes, but they wound up in the back of the hospital at a service elevator that required a key, which apparently the chief possessed. He used it, and the door opened as Gabe, Pete, Josh, and Luke arrived, with the two trailing men behind them by about 25 feet. Pete noticed all the men walked lightly, like stalking lions, with one hand inside their jackets. He did not want to know what was there. The two men bringing up the rear stayed outside the doors looking back down the hallway to each side while Chief Todd spoke into his sleeve again. After a few seconds, he said quietly, but loud enough they could all hear, "They're ready. All clear, we're good to go."

The two other men stepped back into the elevator, and Chief Todd turned the key, already inserted into another keyhole inside the elevator, closing the doors. When the doors opened again, they were on the ground floor near the backside of the hospital. The men walked outside with Chief on one side and Gabe on the other. Chief pulled the key out and flipped it to a wide-eyed janitor who apparently was directed to wait next to the back alleyway elevator. Chief Todd slapped him on the shoulder. "Thanks," he said gruffly. The guy grimaced slightly but nodded, smiling weakly.

A Dodge Caravan with doors opened waited for them, with a police cruiser in front and behind the van. The men directed Luke into the back seat, and Pete helped Josh up as Chief Todd grabbed the wheelchair and shoved it back past the startled custodian into the still-open service elevator. The last thing Pete noticed was the police cruisers were not occupied by police, but by the men he saw in the waiting area—four in the front car and four in the rear. Pete realized one was in the van's front passenger seat, and one was in a rear-facing seat in back next to Doc Luke, who faced forward with a worried look at Pete. Gabe got into the driver's seat while Chief Todd Michael got in last, next to Pete, and slid the door closed.

Pete squeezed in between Josh and Chief and said to Gabe, "Wouldn't Chief Todd be better at driving?" nodding at Gabe's claw.

Both men in the passenger and backseat said emphatically in unison, "NO!"

In a still cheery Latino voice, Gabe said over his shoulder, "We learned long ago Chief's talents lie elsewhere." Chief Todd flashed Pete a wicked smile as Josh stifled a small laugh at what was obviously an inside joke.

"Besides," said Gabe, raising his right hand that was a metal claw, "My trigger finger ain't what it used to be. But don't worry, my driving hand works smoother than ever," he said as the police car in front turned on their flashing lights. Gabe grabbed the gear shifter with his claw and slammed it into drive. "Buckle up, gents. First stop, Bruno's Sports Emporium."

One Hundred Twelve

"Jude, where the heck have you been," said Justus Barabbas. Jude was walking back into the bullpen as two security guards searched the ground around the entrance as he walked by.

"Got the call of mother nature, my friend. What's up?" said Jude.

"Geez, buddy, and I thought I was bad. Did you eat something last night? You were late getting back to the apartment after leaving before me," said Justus.

"Na, but I got some free hot wings from one of the vendors on the way out of the stadium. I think they must have been a bit off, you know."

"Man, I told you not to touch the freebies. No matter how nice you think they are, they're only giving you the stuff they can't sell 'cause it's old."

"I know you warned me, and they were still hot, maybe too much, if you know what I'm saying," Jude said, touching his stomach. "Hey, what's with those guys?" he asked, pointing to the security guys, who seemed to give up and walked out.

"I don't know. They asked about something Mr. Annason dropped, some kind of keycard or something. Whatever, they can't find it. Weird, him coming down here and that pep talk earlier. Just pathetic. The guy doesn't show up all season, then stops by to talk to us before game seven? Got to be a bad omen, I'd say. I hope he doesn't jinx us."

"Don't worry about it, Justus. Besides, I don't believe in good or bad luck. You make your own luck. In the end, we're all on our own," said Jude.

"Sheesh there, Poly Anna. Could you be a little more pessimistic?" said Barabbas.

"I'm a realist, Justus. You should try it sometime."

"You know, roommate, that's one area where you and I disagree. Sooner or later, you got to put your faith in something. Everyone does. It's only a matter of who and where you choose to put your faith. That's what counts. Make sure it's in something that won't fail, in someone that'll cover your butt when things turn grim," said Barabbas, and he slapped Jude on the shoulder as he sat down to watch the lineup introduced.

Jude stared out onto the field. He did what he was told to do, barely finishing it in time. Jude hadn't much time to think about it, but now fearfully questioned to whom he'd sold his allegiance and placed his faith.

One Hundred Thirteen

It was a strange procession that pulled up to Bruno's gates, as Bruno himself opened them wide, letting the three vehicles drive up from the parking lot directly into the park. They drove to the back, around the corner, and parked by the batting cages. Bruno closed the gates and jumped into his golf cart. He sped around to catch up with the strange group of men. Twelve brawny men, including two amputees, plus Coach Pete, Doc Luke, and Josh Green, exited the vehicles. Bruno closed the park at 5:00 PM to kick out the patrons so everyone, including himself, could get home and watch the game. That is, until Pete called him, saying Pops needed him to open up for some remedial work with Green before he went to the game.

Bruno knew better than to ask why Pops requested to bring a player at such odd times, as Pops paid him back handsomely for a few such inconveniences over the years. Still, this took the cake when it came to strange requests, but two tickets along the third base line for game seven sealed the deal. However, Bruno couldn't help but wonder what they were doing here with Green's injuries supposedly knocking him out for the rest of the season. Last he heard on SPNN, Green was still in a hospital in New York City. Yet here he was, in his uniform except for tennis shoes instead of cleats, looking to hit some balls from Goliath, even though the game started almost two hours ago. Bruno couldn't help but wonder why Josh was here and not the ballpark.

Bruno parked the cart next to the shack where he kept all the batting gear, jumped out, and walked through the side door, finally opening the roll-up front awning so his customers could select their equipment, or in this case, Josh's gear. He'd already set aside a helmet and one of Josh's bats based on his previous trips to hit Goliath. He liked watching Josh the few times he came. Josh hit the machine like no other batter, ever. Bruno thought of him as the "Super Man" of ballplayers because he hit Goliath with an otherworldly gift mere mortals did not possess.

Bruno hit the lights for the batting cage, and he could see the group more clearly as the light reflected off the surroundings. Josh approached his booth slowly, head down. He was almost to Bruno when he raised his head, the light finally spilling onto his face. Bruno gasped. "Mr. Green, are you OK?" Bruno asked, worried. Josh looked gaunt and beat up. He looked like someone who should be in the hospital instead of trying to hit baseballs.

Josh smiled, "That's a bit what I am trying to find out," he replied through grit teeth and somewhat labored breathing. Josh leaned on Bruno's booth with one arm as he looked at what Bruno retrieved from the back room. Josh took off his soft cap and donned the batting hat. As he did, he looked into the same backroom he saw last spring and the old picture with the Star of David frame. Josh gestured as he pulled on a batting glove Bruno also laid out. "Tell me about your picture," said Josh.

Bruno looked over his shoulder at the old, faded photograph. It was there so long he almost forgot about it. "Ahh. Uncle Bruno. Or, more precisely, my great-uncle."

"Yes?" Josh asked, waiting.

"Yes, my namesake, you see. We've kept that picture in the family since my grandfather gave it to my father, who gave it to me when I was old enough to understand. Wanted to let me know my namesake, to understand who he was and what I must live up to." As Bruno talked, his eyes seemed to lose focus, and his voice quieted as if he remembered something distant yet deeply felt.

Josh listened and looked back at Bruno with those kind ancient eyes encouraging him to tell his story. Josh's eyes said what Bruno now told was precious because Bruno, too, was valued.

"Bruno Shulz, famous hero, Polish Jew, writer, and artist. Victim of World War II. He was my grandfather's brother. Great-Grandfather Jakub was a merchant, you see. Grandfather continued with his knack for business, while Uncle Bruno was a true artist and dreamer. He wrote, and he painted. Uncle Bruno was talented, and everyone who read or saw his works knew it. He began to be published in the early '30s and became mildly famous for his writings. He received the Polish Academy of Literature's prestigious Golden Laurel Award in 1938. My grandfather could see the writing on the wall and left for safer pastures, but his brother, Uncle Bruno, loved home and stayed in and around our hometown of Drohobych, feeling the need to try and continue his work there with our people.

When the Russians invaded in '39, he stayed and tried to help those he could. In '41, as the Nazis broke the Russian non-aggression agreement and launched Barbarossa against the Russians, they occupied Drohobych. Uncle Bruno was forced, with all the others, into the Jewish ghetto. Most Jews there perished at the Belzec extermination camp, but Uncle Bruno received protection in exchange for painting a mural for a Nazi Gestapo Officer. His reprieve was short-lived as a rival Gestapo Officer shot and killed Uncle Bruno in retaliation for a similar act committed by Bruno's own Nazi protector. Much of what Uncle Bruno wrote and painted was lost. The Nazis took his life from us, and they took much of who he was from the world. Like so many others, Bruno's existence, his exceptional gifts and creations, were nearly erased. What few remain are a constant reminder of all who were lost. May we never forget." Bruno finished his story, and his eyes were distant yet burned with the light of resolve.

"Quite a story," said Josh.

"Yes, quite. Especially when you are an eight-year-old boy, and your father is telling you this, so you stand tall against the bullies you face in your world, small that it is," Bruno thought back to his childhood at school in the '60s and how the children called him those derogatory names, not always behind his back.

Josh patiently watched Bruno. Bruno suddenly realized he had gone silent, still holding Josh's bat. He handed it to Josh. "It has been a while since I thought about my uncle," Bruno admitted.

"He speaks to you," Josh stated rather than asked, as he took the bat. Bruno nodded. "What does he say?" asked Josh.

"I have been trying to answer that all my life, Mr. Green. My father thought it was important for me to know, but what it meant, what his naming me for our uncle and not for Grandpa or himself, I was never sure," he hesitated.

"And now, what do you think your father meant when he named you, Bruno?" Josh said with his ancient eyes and dark face. There was something very familiar and kind about that face, as if Josh might be a distant relative looking down at him through time.

"I think," Bruno said slowly, "I think Papa was trying to tell me, we all stand for something. The money and business success we Schulz's garnered—They are not what was really important. It was what and who we were that counted. What we stood for and what we were willing to risk everything for," Bruno said, not quite finished but unsure he should go on.

"And?" Josh asked, encouraging Bruno with his kind eyes.

"And Papa told me that day, 'Remember Bruno, even if all the world tells you to do something you know isn't right, you should not do it. Even if they laugh and ridicule you and tell you they will wipe you off the face of the earth and erase what you do, you still must do the right thing...,'" Bruno repeated perfectly from his memory.

"Why?" Josh asked, urging him to finish as he gripped the bat and turned towards the cages.

"...Because even if they kill you and try to cover up what you did and what you stood for, all will be revealed. In the end, no one can hide from the Truth."

Josh nodded finally and asked no more questions. He looked back at Bruno over his shoulder one last time. "Thank you, Bruno. Thank you for reminding me. Your father," Josh paused, then added, "And your uncle, would be proud."

Bruno watched Josh as he headed towards the batting cages, then Bruno turned back and walked to the picture on the shelf. He held it for the first time in so very long and lovingly brushed off the dust with the towel he always carried as tears poured down his face. He remembered once again what was truly important.

As all watched, Josh took position inside the batter's cage. His mind and heart remained in a difficult place since the night of his attack. He prayed for long stretches while he recuperated, desperate prayers, asking God to remove this cup if it was His will. It felt more than a little like God remained silent. The road in front of him was fraught with peril; Though it was clear where his team would be and where the Yankees and the world would be, Josh wasn't sure of his role, or perhaps, more correctly, if he could fulfill it. Now Josh felt like a veil was lifting, revealing the full cost of what he must do. Slowly, the Lord brought him around to understand his faith and choice to follow God is what God asked of him. Josh, bolstered by Bruno's own story, knew he was ready to stand for the Truth.

Josh kneeled at the batter's box like he did before each game and bowed his head as the other men watched from the bleachers. "Thank you, Lord, for reminding me of Your Purpose and my Choice within Your will. Help me now," Josh said in silent prayer.

He stood as Pete, holding Goliath's controls, asked, "What do you want?"

"Just let 'em fly, Pete."

Josh was hurting, but he wanted to know if the attack in New York did more to him than the physical bruising and battering. He took up his normal batting stance with some effort. Every muscle screamed in varying amounts. As the red eye of Goliath glowed brightly, Josh let his mind clear, looking to God once more for His peace as he focused on the arm of the one-eyed mechanical monster.

The first ball hurled towards the plate, and Josh stepped lightly, letting the bat fall easily into position, almost like a swinging bunt. Everything hurt, but his vision of the ball was clear. He saw it spinning hard and fast, all four seams turning uniformly down as it left the machine and aimed at the outside low corner of the strike zone, a fastball.

The men watching from the bleachers saw a clean but light hit of Josh's weak swing, and the ball, mainly from the energy of the pitch itself, rebounded back out into right field.

After the swing, Josh turned to Pete, "Keep them coming for a bit. I want to make sure I have the True vision," he said. He then turned ninety degrees and took up a simple bunting position.

Pete took Goliath through its complete gambit. Fastballs, big curves, sliders, and changeups. Josh hit them all; half bunts, half gentle swings. He caught them cleanly and directed them around the field. After a dozen or so pitches, he stepped out of the batter's box, wobbly and winded. He bent over, leaning on the bat like a cane with both hands. Doc Luke jumped up and entered the cage, hurrying to steady Josh. Pete silenced Goliath, and the red light winked out while the whizzing behind Goliath's backstop wound down and became still.

As Pete caught up with Luke, Josh's twelve friends gathered outside the fence. Doc checked Josh with a stethoscope as Josh fought to stay upright, his bat-cane holding him as he took deep breaths. His face was pasty and covered with sweat, and his heart raced despite his mild exertion.

"Come out of the cage, sit on the bleachers, take a breath, and let me check you out," Luke said.

Suddenly, Pete's back pocket rang, and he pulled out his phone.

"Saul," Pete said into the phone, "How's it going?" There was a long pause as Pops gave Pete an update. Pete finally nodded. "OK, Saul, keep it close. We'll be there."

He hung up, and the two men looked at him. "Top of the ninth, and the Yankees just tied it up. They're still at-bat with runners on."

Josh replied, "We've got to go."

Luke tried to protest, but Josh said, "It's OK, my friend. I can see my way clearly now."

Their twelve protectors collapsed around them, leading them toward the vehicles as Josh dropped his bat and helmet back at Bruno's shack.

Bruno still held the picture of his uncle and grandfather to his chest.

Josh said, "Thank you, Bruno," who nodded. "You know," Josh continued, "God surely does remember all your uncle Bruno did and all the beauty he brought to the world. But it wasn't all lost. Your grandfather, your father, and now you, still remember and honor him. Perhaps, it's God's way of allowing the goodness He created in Uncle Bruno to bring good to the world all these years later. His legacy survives despite all that evil did to try and stamp it out. God uses what was meant for evil, for good, in ways we sometimes can't see. You're living proof."

Josh and the three cars sped back out the way they came, leaving Bruno alone in his sports emporium. He said a prayer to God, thanking Him for all the goodness and mercy He gave despite the evil of men. Bruno felt so very blessed. He would not forget his Uncle Bruno's sacrifice nor the words of the man he barely knew who reminded him of the Truth.

One Hundred Fourteen

Josh, Pete, Luke, and their twelve defenders arrived at PNC Park, driving up to the player entrance. Josh said his thank you and goodbyes while Pete handed each of the twelve reserved tickets for seats beside the others already left for Ruth, Mary, and Josh's friends. Pete and Luke watched as Sergeant Gabriel and Chief Todd were last to leave. Sergeant Gabriel paused in front of Josh for a moment. Gabe stared up at Josh for a few moments, searching for words that wouldn't come. Sensing Gabe's need, Josh gently reached out and pulled him close. Gabe seemed to relax and gratefully hugged Josh in a strange, one-hand, one-claw grasp that seemed, to the witnesses, full of meaning.

"Thank you!" Gabe said finally, holding onto Josh for a moment. As he released Josh, his claw and hand on Josh's shoulders, with glistening eyes, Gabe finished, "*For Everything.*" Josh nodded and smiled deeply at Gabe. As Gabriel turned away, Pete and Luke saw Gabe's face filled with peace, as if Josh had given him something beyond their understanding. They could only wonder what Josh had done to warrant such devotion.

Gabriel peeled off to catch up with his other ten teammates, leaving only Chief Todd Michael standing, arms crossed, unmoving, opposite Josh. Pete and Luke watched as the two men spoke silently, not with words, but in communion only those who moved together through death's valley understood. Finally, Chief said, "Do what you do, Josh. What you have always done." With the dark shades of his glasses still concealing his eyes and the bearded, taciturn face hiding any expression, it was hard for the other men to fully understand the giant man's meaning, but they sensed he reluctantly agreed to Josh's will. Chief Todd Michael nodded, lowered his arms, and as he turned to walk away, he said over his shoulder, "See you again, Joshua Green."

Pete opened the gate he left earlier that evening and hustled Josh and Luke along as best he could. They came into the empty locker room. Mark Johnson was there, sitting by himself, watching a TV screen with a look of dejection. When he saw the three men, the surprise on his face as he jumped up carried a tinge of hope mixed with his confusion.

"What in the world? Where have you been, Pete?" Mark said, then seeing Josh, he exclaimed, "JOSH!?" Hope and concern flooded Mark's face as he saw Josh's bruised body under the lights for the first time.

The doctor and Pete helped Josh to his locker, and Pete scrambled for Josh's cleats as Doc removed his sneakers. Pete chomped hard on an unlit cigar that magically appeared.

"What's the situation, young Mark!"

"What?" Mark said, still standing there like a deer in headlights.

"The game, man, the game! What's the situation?" Pete growled.

"Pete! We were winning, but the Yankees scored two runs in the top of the ninth. They're up by one run. The press was all in here, ready to interview the team until the Yankees went up. Then they all tore out of here and headed to the Yankees locker room."

"I don't care about your press bozos. What's going on in the game NOW!" Pete yelled.

"That's just it. It's the bottom of the ninth, and we've loaded the bases! One out, and Thomas is coming up to bat! The crowd, the crowd...," Mark tried to put it all together, but words failed him, and he shook his head. "You'll have to see for yourself."

Pete yelled over his shoulder. "Go tell Saul we're coming and not to send a batter up after Thomas until we get there." Mark was still frozen, standing there, staring. "Go NOW, son!" Pete barked. If Mark had run any faster, he would have run right out of his clothes.

One Hundred Fifteen

As the Pirate players all stood watching Thomas's at-bat, Saul was perhaps the one who felt most helpless. He coached the team as best he could, but now he felt there were no decisions left to make, no moves left in his arsenal. It was now up to the good Lord and his players. One out, down by a run, the Pirates were so close, but they were running out of chances. They needed a miracle.

Something stirred in the dugout hallway coming from the Pirate locker room behind Saul. He turned around to see what was going on. Suddenly, Mark Johnson shot out of the darkness and almost ran into Saul. Saul grabbed him and steadied the young man.

"What is it, Mark?" Saul asked anxiously.

"Doc Luke and Pete just arrived with Josh. Josh Green!" Mark said, looking expectantly at Saul.

"Yes?" Saul replied.

Finally, Mark found his words. "Pete said to tell you not to send anyone up after Thomas. They're getting Josh ready."

As if in answer to the questions in Saul's mind, Pete and Luke appeared, walking up the tunnel. Doc Luke nodded but hurried to the bench without saying anything. He was not used to being seen in the dugout. Saul's eyes fell on Pete, chomping hard on his unlit cigar.

Before he could ask about Josh, someone else made a shuffling sound over Pete's shoulder.

Pete moved aside, and as Saul looked, Josh walked up the tunnel out of the darkness. Saul's surprise and elation quickly turned to concern as he got his first good look at Josh coming up the stairs out of the shadows. Josh looked like someone who'd gone to the gates of hell. His cap was pulled low, and when he raised his head finally, Saul looked into his face. The same face Saul found filled with serenity, kindness, and hope all year was now bruised and gaunt; life nearly drained out of him.

"Josh!" exclaimed Saul, with a shocked, whistling intake of air. "Are you all right, son?" Saul said, alarmed.

"I'm here, Skipper," Josh replied, quickly smoothing his pained expression, forcing a half-smile to ease Saul's concern. Josh stopped and straightened with effort, quickly covering the momentary glimpse Saul caught of his pain. After a moment, Josh said, "I am ready to finish."

"Are you sure, Josh?" Saul questioned.

Saul still carried the fight within, the desire to win regardless of the cost. Was it at odds with his justified concern for Josh stepping onto the field? What will it cost Josh? Finally, Saul committed his will to the Lord in one more prayer from his heart. "Dear God, please show me what I am to do. Not my will, but Thy will be done." Saul finished his silent prayer. He was ready to do whatever the Lord wanted, letting go of his control. Even if it meant losing a World Series Championship, Saul's heart filled with peace in the storm, the kind that only comes supernaturally. He knew it was now up to Josh's decision.

Josh smiled, and as always, he seemed to understand the worries of the older man, who learned to trust Josh's judgment and the Creator's plan. Saul was concerned, but the soft voice inside him prepared him for what came next.

"Don't worry, Pops," Josh placed his hand on Saul's shoulder as he stepped forward, "I still have one last good swing to make." Saul looked into Josh's eyes, dark brown pools swimming with love and just a hint of something else. Sadness perhaps? Saul hesitated. His concern now was not for the game's outcome, but for Josh. The fans, yes, even his beloved hometown fans, sounded hate-filled, as if something or someone whipped them into a frenzied uproar. What would happen if Josh stepped out of the dugout? Why did so many preach hatred for a man who offered only compassion, forgiveness, and friendship?

Throughout the latter half of the season, Saul watched as the world turned increasingly into a raging angry mob, yet Josh responded to all the hatred with patience, compassion, and love. He kneeled and prayed when the world rebelled and hollered. Josh stood and lived truth and goodness while the world screamed to burn it all down. How did the world turn so upside down in less than a single baseball season, Saul thought? Perhaps it was heading this way for a while, and he was too self-centered on his problems to notice. If anything, Josh taught Saul to look at the world differently, to look at himself differently.

Josh stared at Saul with a kind smile on his bruised and scarred face, bat resting on his shoulder. One last choice to make, thought Saul.

"OK, Josh. If you're sure, pinch-hit for the pitcher."

Josh nodded. As he reached the dugout steps, Josh turned back, speaking so only Saul could hear, calling him by his first name for the first and last time. "It's OK, Saul. Don't let your heart be troubled." He knew Saul not as one of his players, but as a comforter, a healer, and a friend. "This is what I was put on the earth to do. Remember?" Josh smiled at him, and Saul couldn't help but smile back. He would hold Josh's smile and words in his heart forever.

Josh began to climb the dugout steps. He would pinch-hit for young Justus Barabbas, who just gave up the tying and go-ahead runs in the top of the ninth inning. Until tonight, many saw Barabbas as a Pirate impact player on the rise. Receiving the call-up after the All-Star break, Barabbas quickly became the Pirates primary closer. He finished the season strong and carried a successful save streak for six consecutive playoff appearances before blowing the save tonight in the top of the ninth. If the Pirates lost, much of the blame would fall squarely on his shoulders.

As Josh walked up the steps to the on-deck circle, Barabbas watched him closely. Being new to the team and coming out of the bullpen, Barabbas rarely observed Josh up close or even thought much about him. Barabbas focused on the world and all it offered him as a new, big-league player. He desperately fought to secure a permanent position in the League and fans' hearts. Now his chance to be the hero who saved game seven would end instead with him, the game's loser who blew the save.

Without warning, Barabbas's fortune dramatically turned. He feared his catastrophic failure would precipitate his fall back to the minors, costing Pittsburgh its first championship in half a century. Barabbas felt numb, trapped, lost, and alone. Bereft of all hope, Barabbas was out of the game, and only a miracle comeback could save him and wipe out his shame. After losing the lead in the top of the inning, he sat alone on the bench, ostracized, as if the others didn't want his failure to rub off on them.

For the first time in a long time, Barabbas stopped thinking about his dreams of being a star. They fell to his feet, crushed and smashed. He looked out at the crazy world he barely considered since his call-up. As he gazed out onto the misty field and the cruel fate he would soon meet, into his view, out of the shadows, stepped this giant legend of a man he barely knew. Suddenly, Barabbas realized the main reason for the Pirates' climb from worst to first, now prepared to walk onto the field. The thought struck him that it wasn't about him. Josh Green made this season a victorious change for the Pirates. For so long, the city lost. The Pirates made the unlikely rise to contender this year because of Josh's extraordinary play.

Woken out of his hapless situation, Barabbas stared intently, finally seeing Joshua Green clearly. Josh's dark brown, almost black, wavy hair greased down his face as if he just fought in some physical battle before getting so late to the game. Indeed, Barabbas now saw Josh's face was battered and bruised, and he held himself gingerly as he climbed the steps. Where did he come from, thought Barabbas? More importantly, could Josh truly be the Pirates savior, erasing the memory of Barabbas's losing effort through some miracle finish? As Josh put his hand on the rail at the top of the dugout steps, he paused.

"Here's the payoff pitch to Thomas," Bob, the Pirates radio broadcaster, yelled. "Swing and a miss, Strike Three. Two Down!"

The crowd roared.

Barabbas, however, never took his eyes off Josh as someone spoke loudly to his heart.

Watch!

Justus would never forget, until his dying day, as Josh turned to him. He looked deeply into Barabbas's eyes with a grace-filled look and saw all of Barabbas's hopes and dreams, fears and failures. Josh spoke no words, but he smiled at him and nodded knowingly. Josh's eyes, ancient and kind, full of mercy, communicated wordlessly, "Don't worry, my brother. I will bail you out."

In the dugout, the Pirates watched as Josh walked to the on-deck circle. The crowd noise rose in a crescendo. Instead of shouting support or excitement, the crowd's voice overflowed with anger and malice. In stark contrast to the adoring crowd one week earlier, it was now an angry mob full of condemnation, screaming a torrent of curses. Incredibly, the crowd's vocal leaders and well-placed instigators whipped the fans into a frenzy, overpowering the hometown's desire to win. They fanned the fires of the virulent protests and burgeoning anger, giving direction and encouragement to voices of division and hatred whispered to the masses by the prince of this world and his lies. Spurning Josh's biblical stance urging faith in Jesus, the mob demanded heaven accept their every choice. Each turned their backs on God's absolute morals, demanding validation of their own ways and blaming everyone but themselves for all the negative consequences sin brought.

They hated Josh. They hated him for supporting the country, despite its failures. They wanted immediate corrections for all the wrongs they felt, all the hurt they received. They wanted to force men's hearts to change, yet they refused to change their own. In the end, they blamed Josh because they hated his love and faith in God. They rejected him for refusing to kneel and yield to public opinion, siding with men against God and Christ. They could not stand to hear Josh's true testimony of a loving but Holy God who came to earth to preach repentance and salvation for the lost. As of old, humanity rebelled against God, against all authority, against any reminder of their sinful nature. It was far easier to blame and denounce others for their failures than admit to their own. The voices of rebellion were many tonight, but they represented the history of man's existence. Filled with half-truths, they chanted twisted narratives, shaking their signs and fists not at this man, but at heaven. Deaf and blind, refusing to own their shortcomings, they denied the truth, railing against Josh with the fury and passion of false witnesses. Screaming at the injustice they saw, their many causes and excuses were as old as humanity. Filled with pain, loathing, hatred, and the pride of unrepentant children, they drowned out the few who dared support Josh and accept God's truth, shouting them into silence.

Thomas walked, head down, back toward the dugout in utter disappointment. He did not want to look Josh in the eye, embarrassed by his failure. Josh, who always seemed to know what his own needed, stepped in front of him and, with a hand on his shoulder, said, "It will be all right, my friend. Hold on. It's not over. Keep the faith, pray, and believe." Thomas nodded and returned to the dugout, but his hope seemed extinguished. Thomas saw loss and failure one too many times in his career. How could he hope and risk being crushed with another disappointment after coming so close? Thomas was ashamed to admit to himself, but only by seeing victory would he ever again believe.

One Hundred Sixteen

"WOW! Bases loaded! Bottom of the ninth! World Series Game Seven, and look who has suddenly stepped out of the dugout to pinch-hit! It's JOSH GREEN!" Greg yelled as the crowd roar raised to a crescendo, threatening to overwhelm his mike.

"Where did *he* come from?" Bob said, taken aback. "And where's he been, for that matter?"

"I don't know, but this crowd is...," Greg struggled for words. The crowd screamed so many things it was hard to tell what they shouted. The ugly sounds were difficult to break into distinct words at first, but none of it seemed good.

The Pirates looked on from the dugout with mixed emotions. They watched Josh warm up with a few swings of his bat, adding a weighted donut. Josh seemed to falter at first as he began to swing, grimacing slightly in pain. The umpire and the Yankee players waited anxiously to get on with play, but Josh took his time, with several successively longer, sweeping, then windmilling swings. Finally, he seemed ready but kneeled gingerly before leaving the on-deck circle. As Josh knocked the donut off his bat, those closest to him in the dugout could see his body wince again, causing him to pause. He did not get up from kneeling but seemed to bow his head instead.

"Green's in the dirt at the on-deck circle, praying, it seems," said Bob, describing the scene. "I guess this is to make up for the fact that he hasn't yet batted tonight. And the crowd...," this time with trepidation, he finished almost apologetically, "Well, they are giving him an earful and then some."

"I'll say, Bob. I'm not a praying man, but perhaps we all need prayer right now. This crowd seems to be screamin' for blood," replied Greg, shocked by his own words.

Bob felt the stinging truth of his friend's honest assessment, replying softly, "Amen, my friend."

The cold October wind flowing up the Ohio River Valley stilled, as the night sky grew dark. So dark, in fact, it seemed a veil was pulled over the stadium as a low mist suddenly enveloped PNC Park, threatening to blot out the lights. The crowd's roar reflected off the foggy darkness, rebounding with an eerie echo, increasing the brutal cacophony of shouts and curses from the irate crowd. They were at fever pitch, yet Josh held his prayerful kneel without moving. The men closest to Josh could see large drops of sweat, like blood, appear on his forehead, with his dark curly hair matted, sticking out from under the hard plastic hat. Face gaunt, dark skin battered and bruised, the old white scar on his cheek contrasting, descending like a salty tear from his left eye.

"Lord, I am hurt, and I am *so tired*."

I know Joshua.

"I don't know if I can do this?"

Yes, we can.

"You will stay with me?"

*I love you, my child. I have been with you, watching over you, since I knit you together in your mother's womb. I love you, *Always*. I am with you, *Always*. To the end and beyond. Your pain will soon end, and you will find rest in Me, forever.*

"And the others?"

*I *cannot* fail those who follow Me and are called by my Name.*

"I'm scared, Lord."

I know Joshua. Fear Not! I have overcome the world.

"I can finish this?"

You will, because I have.

"Thank you, Lord. I love you."

I love you, Joshua, my beloved child. Finish the race, and come home.

The Pirates watched as Josh finally stood and walked towards the batter's box. The crowd roared against him. This same people, who so recently cheered and lauded the man who broke nearly every single-season offensive record and brought the Pirates from last to first, now cursed and swore profusely, drowning out the few who tried to encourage. Josh's daughter Ruth, Mary, and the other Pirates could only watch as Josh walked, head bowed slightly, toward the plate like a lamb to slaughter. Fully aware, Josh stopped purposely and turned around one last time, aiming to give them peace. He looked back at the dugout, at his teammates and coaches. As they all watched intently, they each saw him differently; to some, a brother, to others, a mentor. Still, others saw him as a friend and confidant. To some, he was a healer and comforter, yet some considered him a zealot with extreme ideals, counting him a fool. While they each would remember it their own way, they could not forget the look of kindness in his eyes, looking directly, purposely, slowly down the line at each of them.

Josh then raised his gaze to the stands behind the dugout. As the crowd seemed to yell even more hatred for him to get on with it, he found his brothers in arms, come to see him off. They were the sheepdogs, Josh's guardian angels, ready to defend him when called. The crowd did not seem to notice or care, but the dozen men watched, some with beards and tattoos, one with a missing leg below the knee, and Master Sergeant Gabriel Rodelo with his missing right hand replaced by a claw. All sat together, looking like a hodgepodge old biker gang. Chief Warrant Officer Todd Michael suddenly rose, and the other eleven men did as well, though several did so with painful effort. They all stood tall and erect. Their strength and power, usually hidden these days by age and years of wear and tear, was suddenly, fiercely evident to any who looked their way. Master Sergeant Rodelo, the shortest of the men, to the chief's left, took a step forward in the row. Standing just in front of the rest, he raised his claw to the corner of his forehead in perfect salute, and the rest of the men, in unison, snapped a salute as well, all holding it until Josh reached to his hat and ever so slightly tipped it, so they would know. He smiled at them, and they saw his deep brown eyes speaking volumes once more. "It's OK, my brothers," his eyes conveyed, "I do this willingly. You are my brothers who know my true heart, for you know my heart is true. Tonight is not a night to fight, but a night to finish." Master Sergeant Gabriel Rodelo, Chief Todd Michael, and the others slowly lowered their salutes. They understood and obeyed Josh's wishes, but they would not sit down. They would stand their silent vigil and bear witness until the end.

Next to his brothers were Nick and Ezra Demus, Josh's newest friends, sitting with Joe and Elizabeth Arima, his steadfast supporters. Though he only met them this summer, he knew the love of a family that would last into eternity.

Finally, next to the Arimas, Josh fixed his gaze on his daughter, Ruth, and Mary. They held each other against the force of hatred all around, yet for that moment, the two girls locked gaze with Josh, and he smiled, giving them all his peace and love. It was a supernatural love and an eternal peace shining through Josh. Most could not see the offered love because they rejected the Truth, even hated it. Ruth and Mary each knew it would last them a lifetime. Mary wept silent tears, and Ruth smiled a serious smile at first, then one that simply burst wide, reflecting back the love, despite the hate all around. Such hatred is no match for the daughter's love for her dad and the father's love for his child. It was an everlasting love given to them both, sealed on high.

As the crowd continued to roar with impatience, Josh turned back and walked towards the batter's box, stopping just before the plate. He now looked out onto the field for the first time. But instead of a sweeping gaze, Josh stopped and looked directly at a single point high in left field. His eyes came immediately to rest, and he stared, not moving for a brief moment.

The adversary long laid in ambush in his hiding spot high at the top of the stadium. He watched the game through the high-power scope of his rifle, deep in his dark crevice hidden from all, or so he thought, waiting patiently for his chance.

Finally, his moment arrived. When Josh appeared walking up out of the dugout, his heart rate soared. Over the next few moments, he willed it back to a more reasonable beat to take the steady shot. Now, as Josh approached the batter's box, the adversary knew he would make an easier, anchored target. He would take the shot and end this before Josh could even swing the bat. Josh's time was almost up, thought the adversary greedily. However, instead of his customary kneeling in prayer before his first at-bat next to the batter's box, Josh paused and raised his head towards the outfield.

Though the entire stadium rocked with emotion and seemed impossible with his well-concealed position nearly 500 feet away, the adversary was sure Josh looked directly at him. Josh's eyes unhesitatingly locked on his position, catching the adversary's eye in his gaze right through the scope, going straight to his soul. The adversary's heart froze, and before he could pull away, he saw Josh's eyes clearly, locked on him. In that brief moment, Josh's eyes conveyed not hatred or fear, only pity. Pity towards him. Pity and sadness. In that split-second, the adversary saw the sadness in Josh's eyes, not for Josh, but for the adversary, who chose his own damnation rather than forgiveness. The adversary jerked his head away from the scope with this lightning bolt revelation, his calm shattered. Shocked, his heart raced as never before when stalking a target, and his eyes, tightly shut, could not forget the clear vision of what Josh's eyes showed him. The adversary saw his eternity laid bare. He glimpsed his chosen path leading straight to destruction. Though his eyes remained closed, his mind and heart could not shake the vision. He released his rifle and rolled over, cowering in a fetal position, overwhelmed by reasoned fear. He knew, without doubt, the damnable end he approached, and he lay quivering, trying to rid himself of the truth of his chosen path, deep in the hidden spot, high in the stands.

With the capacity crowd screaming and blind with every imagined hatred, Josh stepped into the batter's box.

One Hundred Seventeen

Nothing prepared the announcers for what they heard tonight.

Bob, used to his partner's jibes and colorful commentary breaking up a tense moment, was unnerved by the lack of any comments in his headset. He finally looked over at Greg. Greg grasped the mike, frozen in unusual silence. Brow furrowed, he remained mute, unable to adequately describe the scene here in Pittsburgh. It was something neither man ever saw in a quarter-century of broadcasting. Their hometown team and their hometown hero were behind by only one run, with the bases loaded in the ninth inning of the final game of the World Series. Yet, here they were, and it seemed as if the crowd shouted louder than ever–against Josh. Neither could understand it, but Bob decided he must try to declare what he witnessed as best he could.

Bob began tentatively.

"Josh Green steps into the batter's box. Bases loaded; Two outs. Down by one run, bottom of the ninth, game seven of the World Series. Can Josh do it one last time and snatch victory from the jaws of defeat? Let's listen to this crowd and watch."

The crowd stood shouting and jumping up and down, incensed. It seemed as if each person carried their own wounds, seeing Josh through troubled hearts and anguished souls.

"Greg, have you ever witnessed such a scene?" Bob whispered nervously into the mike as he gave a sideways glance at his usually verbose and elocutionary partner. Greg retained an incredulous look of perplexity, not quite believing the heavy shadow, now descending to engulf the stadium. Bob was shocked to see in Greg a reflection of his own sense of dread. It jarred him into returning to his play-by-play to cover his partner's stunned silence and his own fears.

"Green settles into the batter's box. The catcher gives the sign, and the pitcher comes to the stretch. He looks the runner back on third. None of the base runners have taken much of a lead...."

Indeed, the Pirates were all close to their bases. Like their teammates in the dugout, they seemed frozen with fear, not wanting to watch the scene unfold.

Having no place to hide, they stood nervously, laid bare and vulnerable, holding close to their respective base for its insufficient safety.

Bob finished the only way possible.

"Here's the pitch."

The crowd watched as the ball hurled towards home plate, fast and hard, threatening to pierce the strike zone like an unstoppable spear. It aimed for the heart of the plate, slicing late violently, its wicked velocity punctuated with a final, hard-cutting movement.

Josh started his swing.

Body uncoiling with life and limb in unity and flawless perfection, the ball could not avoid its destiny. Like a brilliant flash in the darkness, witnesses saw flesh of humanity and smoothed wood of creation meet the invincible lancing orb of starched leather and crimson stitching. Perfectly impacting the hardwood's sweet spot, man's best delivery was overcome and crushed with complete finality. Struck by supreme authority, the lightning crack burst through the curtain of darkness and the roar from the exigent crowd, catapulting the baseball to tear through the black veil of night, exposing Pittsburgh to its skyline.

Though few could fathom the depth of Josh's swing, the sound was unique and devastatingly unmistakable. The "CRACK!', so loud and otherworldly, stunned the crowd into silence. They froze, speechless witnesses to the unforgettable event.

"There's a DRIVE!"

Bob's voice, formerly restrained by some evil shroud, now set free, broke through the abruptly silent crowd, rising in crescendo.

"It's DEEP!... To DEAD Center!..." he yelled, fragile hope daring to overcome his fear.

"The ball...?" Bob hesitated in amazed disbelief at the ball's unending rise. Lost for words, he finished.

"IT'S...GONE!"

Having risen with the ball's flight, Bob slumped back into his seat in the stilled, silenced ballpark, staring after the disappearing ball.

Josh finished his swing.

He dropped his bat.

He did not have to look where the ball went. Like his first home run in practice on this very field so long ago last March, Josh knew when he hit it, it was gone. As in the spring, he was the only one who moved. The crowd, those in the dugouts, and the players for both teams gazed, transfixed by the ball's impossible flight. Higher and higher it rose, quickly passing into the dark night, far past the stadium center field wall, disappearing while seemingly still ascending, way out towards the eternal river, far beyond the stadium. The ball was so hard hit Josh's slow, pained jog towards first barely began as everything suddenly started into motion.

The Pirate base runners, previously frozen near their respective bases, began to move. Released from their fear, they realized the home run brought not only freedom but victory. They looked back at Josh in wonder and began their joyful run towards home.

The Pirate dugout, too, jolted into jubilation. First, young Juan leaped up the stairs, and Old Pete jumped quickly to race him. Yet it was fleet-footed Zach, who was in the on-deck circle, leading. Zach's eyes locked on Josh, the kind friend who loved him like a brother and always offered him Truth. They all jumped for joy, moving toward home plate. However, the Pirates' brief moment of victorious celebration vanished quickly. The crowd, released from watching the thundering strike of the ball disappear into the midnight sky, suddenly exploded in a terrifying cacophony of screams and wailing. It was not the sound of victory but of petty hatred and incensed rage mixed with roaring accusation. The Pirates all cowered in response to the evil in the world loosed upon Josh through the crowd's curses. The team's joy was overcome with a sudden need to brace for some invisible malevolent strike. The base runners hurried for home to join the Pirates leaving the dugout. Fear struck them all as they took their eyes off Josh. Forgetting their movement to welcome him home, instead they backed towards each other as they looked into the fury of the surrounding mob.

Josh ran on, unchanged and undeterred in his slow march around the bases. As he jogged gingerly in pain, the crowd noise, though clamorous, became more and more decipherable as each called him out as they saw him.

As Josh ran towards first base, some in the crowd saw him as "That black man!" shouting their particular hatreds. For some, he was the betrayer of his people, his blood, his race. Blacks and non-blacks within the racial justice movement shouted, "Traitor!" as others accused, "Uncle Tom!" Many jeered, as leaders of the racial movements in vogue led chants with hatred for his lack of conforming to his racial background and their ambitions for power. In direct contrast, others leading anti-black movements saw him with their own bigotry, believing him a black apologist, shouting their opposite accusations. These bigots often finished with hateful epithets of "Ni##er!" or "Ni##er Lover!"

As Josh rounded first, heading to second, others marked him as a Jew. They too, spewed their own epithets. "Filthy Jew!" rang out, and "Jew boy" resounded. Even the derogatory Jewish slur "K##e" came from the Jew-haters. Conversely, many devout Jews, righteous in their minds, saw Josh falsely claiming to be Jewish. They were indignant a Jew would declare Christ as the Messiah. They nodded their heads in appreciation of the condemnation this blasphemer now received. It was the only inevitable end for such a heretic, they surmised. They released their barrage of accusatory shouts in ironic contrast to the Jew-haters by shouting, "Anti-Semite!" Other Jews followed their lead with "Apostate!" and even "Deceiver of Children!" A few conservative Rabbis smiled as their students chanted their well taught and forgone ancient verdicts, "Mumar!", "Poshea," and even "Meshumad!"

To others, Josh was the embodiment of the obscene self-righteous religious zealot. "Bigot!" they called; others "Fascist!" Many screamed, "HOMOPHOBE!" yet their counterparts took the opposite tact and jeered, "Fairy!" or even accusingly, "Gay!"

As Josh rounded second and headed to third, many nay-sayers denied his witness. "Liar!" they accused. "Cheater!", "Delusional!" Many screamed variations of, "Ignorant Bible Thumper!", "Zealot!" and some scoffed, yelling, "You Hy-Po-Crite!"

As he rounded third, the crowd seemed to yell, each in their own tongues, "Who are you to judge us! Surely, your way and your truth are no better than ours!"

Josh rounded the bases with every accusation and curse cast upon him. Yet their testimony constantly contradicted each other, reflecting their biases, not the truth. Though they shouted all the louder, they could not agree on his sins.

Amongst the crowd, carefully sequestered in the best seats and surrounded by plainclothes protective agents, was the commissioner, Quint Pilate, with his second, Herald Gripp. Each sat stone-faced, like hanging judges of times past. Quint leaned over to Herald, offering his pronouncement, "I wash my hands of this," he waved offhandedly, gesturing to the crowd who shouted around their secure perimeter. "They are the ones who accuse him and want him gone. May it be on their heads."

Herald nodded and replied, "We warned him," he shrugged. "He could have reaped fame and fortune, but he refused to listen to reason and give up his outdated beliefs." Herald shook his head with indignant contempt, remembering how Josh refused even to answer him.

Elsewhere, high above the fray in the owners' box, Cai Annason watched in brooding condemnation. With his father-in-law and the other owners nearby, he kept his thoughts private and his countenance hidden. The Pirates were victorious. They were World Champions. Cai plotted to stop Green from being the one to lead the team to victory, yet somehow Josh still managed to strike the winning blow, despite Cai's scheming and best efforts. However, Cai was still master of playing the sides against one another, all to his benefit. Even as he stood there, he formulated a plan to take credit for the victory while distancing himself and his team from Green. Cai resolved not to let this upstart usurp his leadership as club president. This wasn't over, not by a long shot, and while the owners may mistake his forced smile as evidence of his pleasure in the team's championship, Cai held fast to the conviction this was not the end of his influence and position. After all, this did nothing to change Josh's ultimate destination. "Josh will reap his just reward," Cai said silently to himself. "If not today or tomorrow, then soon, surely soon, he will meet his fate! The crowd, indeed this public rabble, will see to it. I will still be here, and I will reap all I have justly earned." Instantly, in his mind, Cai heard a loud and clear voice state:

SO BE IT!

Startled, Cai looked around to see if any of the others heard the loud voice, but they looked on the scene below without change. Surely, he must have mistaken hearing a voice? Yet as Cai watched, a sinking feeling grew within his soul that he prophesied truth for once, and that truth would come devastatingly to pass. Cai brushed the startling thought away nervously and resolved he would make his own truth and make everyone forget Green and what he stood for when this was all over.

On the field, the Pirates stood frozen, gathered halfway between the dugout and home. They watched, stunned, recoiling from the palpable wash of evil embraced by the crowd and released toward the lonesome runner slowly circling the bases. The other base runners already hustled home and continued toward the Pirates coming out of the dugout. Together, they hid in plain sight, watching Josh from afar. They could see him grimacing with pain from his beating, almost stumbling like an unseen burden wore him down, slowing his trot to little more than a walk.

Simon Cyrene, the gentle giant of a trainer, followed the team onto the field. He grew close to Josh over the season and knew the hurt and pain he endured better than most. Now in their midst, Only Cy seemed able to shoulder some of the load aimed at Josh and speak. All the players and coaches recognized Cy's deep bass voice above the din of the shouts and curses as he stood and quoted Isaiah from memory.

"If the world hates you, you know that it hated Me before it hated you. But all these things they will do because they do not know Him who sent Me..., for as the prophet has said, 'They hated Me without a cause.' Surely, He took on our infirmities and carried our sorrows; yet we considered Him stricken by God, struck down and afflicted..., We all like sheep have gone astray, each one has turned to his own way, and the Lord has laid upon Him the iniquity of us all."

High in the recesses of the outfield, the adversary finally recovered. The "Crack!" of the bat brought him out of his own self-loathing as he cringed, eyes pressed shut against Josh's eyes, reflecting his lost soul. He must fight back. He must rail against all the world that caused him so much torment and led him to this moment. He rolled back over to see Josh, the living embodiment of his anger and pain, running around the bases.

Though Josh ran perpendicular from first to third, soon his back would be toward the adversary as Josh rounded third and turned for home, making the shot much easier. Plus, he hoped he would not have to see those eyes, for he only wanted to forget the vision, burned into his memory, of his doomed future. He held his scoped rifle on a spot down the third baseline. He could still stop this. He must! He was full of hurt and jealousy, and it fueled his hate. He must strike back. It didn't matter that the Pirates already triumphed. Josh must not complete his run. He must be stopped, the adversary thought, his twisted heart wanting to flee the judgment awaiting him. Perhaps if Josh were stopped, the adversary could evade Truth and escape his own terrible reckoning. He willfully shoved away the voice screaming "NO!" in his mind. Yet the voice was persistent as he held his scope on the third baseline. The quiet voice of conviction warned this shot would only seal his fate. He denied the voice once more, gave himself to the prince of this world, and took aim.

Finally, the Pirates took their eyes off the crowd and placed them back on Josh. As he rounded third and turned toward home, Josh looked up into heaven, and through his pain and grief, said, "Jesus, forgive them as you have forgiven me, for they know not what they do!"

Josh ran on. He held onto peace, for the Prince of Peace held fast his faithful heart. Josh labored down the third baseline, now just steps from home. Could he actually make it, the Pirates wondered? Was Josh to be spared the ultimate cost of overcoming the evil raining down against him? As a team, they all started to move again towards home plate, joy blooming on their faces, victory at hand. As if hearing their thoughts, Josh looked their way, found them, and smiled at them all, and for a final brief moment, they were once again a family, in peaceful love and harmony.

The rifle shot exploded from the darkness somewhere deep in left field. As loud as the stadium was before that moment, the shot rang out, silencing the angry mob for a final time. The crowd blanched in confusion, like an ice-cold bucket of water doused their face, awakening them from their evil stupor. They watched Josh jerk, hands flung out, parallel to the ground, his 6 foot 4 inch frame snapped fully upright. For an instant, his cross-shaped silhouette burned into the collective memory of the thousands at PNC Park and millions of spectators watching from home. Time froze for a brief moment, then Josh's momentum carried him forward. Stumbling as he fell with hands reaching forward, he slapped home plate, face down, unmoving. A crimson-red bloodstain grew from the left middle of his back, seeping outward on his white jersey just left of his number.

Some would later say it looked like the number one, while others thought it shaped strangely like an arrow pointing at his number three.

Like the crowd, no one on the field moved, frozen in shock. Their hearts pounded, spirits stirred, and souls shook. They were statues of every color, creed, background, and history; every walk of life, stripped of any pretense. For this moment, they saw all around them as they truly were. Equal and equally guilty. They felt like blind dead men, unsure how to breathe, see, and live again.

Some looked into the crowd, some crouched low, trying to hide without cover, hoping to escape, perhaps? Many looked around in confusion. The home plate umpire stumbled backwards, falling as if something struck him. He was without physical harm when he looked himself over, for Josh alone took the full blow. All on the field, like the crowd, stood frozen in confusion.

Seconds ago, the mob of a crowd was caught up in their hearts' hatred, casting all their fears and sorrows, all their troubles and shame, onto Josh. They woke from their self-made nightmare as if slapped by the ringing shot, jolted awake. Yet the nightmare didn't end, only the realization they each cast the unjust curse on an innocent man. Whether frozen by fear or shame, they stood silent or sat down cringing as if afraid the next shot would be righteously cast their way.

The Pirates also stood still and remained stuck in position, either due to the conviction of their waking conscience or the fear of what would happen to them if they tried to come to Josh's aid. However, two people moved quickly toward the bottom of the stands, where a gate stood open to the field. The leader struggled, legs braced, down the stadium steps onto the field, letting out a high-pitched child's cry.

"DADDY!"

For the next few moments, the two women were the only ones moving toward Josh. Despite Ruth's braces, Ruth and Mary were the first to reach Josh's side. Ruth fell to one side of her dad, and Mary kneeled next to her. Both women gently rolled Josh over. At first glance, he showed no sign of life. Sitting at Josh's feet, Mary bowed her head and began to weep, her long dark hair escaping from the bun she customarily wore, extending down to touch Josh's dusty cleats. Seeing the women's actions with Josh, the Pirates finally summoned the courage to move. Juan was the first to reach them, peering over Ruth's shoulder. Pete moved around the women and kneeled on Josh's opposite side, holding his cap in both hands. Zach wanted to be close to Josh and, having no other way to see him, came around to his head, sat down cross-legged, and cradled Josh's head, weeping silently, hope lost. His roommate, Samson, made it in from the bullpen and kneeled behind Zach, tears blinding his eyes with grief. Saul kneeled next to Pete and bent down, holding Josh's hand, feeling for a pulse. The other players joined in, some standing, some kneeling all around. Thomas shook his head, soul crushed. He could not believe Josh was gone. Andrew, Nathan Fisher, and Coach Phil led a group of players off to the side in silent prayer. Each kneeled, holding the players' hands next to them. J.J. joined Juan, arms across shoulders, heads bowed. To Judah's surprise, he too was brokenhearted, and though he rarely prayed, he knelt next to young Nathan and asked if he could pray with them as well. Without hesitation, Nathan made room, welcoming his brother into the circle.

The Yankees players all gathered around their dugout watching. The Yankees captain stood next to his muscular teammate, the same two who met Josh and Andrew when the teams first met before the All-Star Break. "Guess he got what he deserved," said the Yankees captain softly under his breath so only his few teammates nearby heard.

The imposing teammate, the Yankees designated hitter, the silent enforcer at the first meeting with Josh, looked at the Yankees captain, eyes wide and filled with tears. His teammates often commented how few words the big man spoke, his mere presence enough to silence most. He surely never went against the Yankees captain. Now, however, he shook his head as he spoke. "All summer, I followed the crowd's wishes and your demands. Yet I do not know why. Where has it brought us? Everything is worse. And now this man, who we all know is innocent of any wrongdoing," he said, cutting quick all his fellow Yankees who listened, "Is cut down like a dog. Do you not fear God?"

"He claimed God could save him. Why doesn't God save him now and fix all our problems while he's at it?" the captain shot back, sneering.

"I don't know why God allows these things to happen, but I know this. That man has done nothing wrong. It is we who deserve such a fate." The big man paused and looked back at Josh. After a moment, without taking his eyes off Josh, he said, "I am not following this path anymore." He removed his Yankee cap, letting it fall where he stood, and walked onto the field towards Josh and the prayer circle.

"You'll lose everything!" the Yankees captain yelled after him incredulously, hands-on-hips, surprised.

The big man did not look back. Andrew and Nathan saw him as he approached. They watched tentatively, but his demeanor was gentle and, if anything, contrite and ashamed. As he approached, they saw his eyes streaming tears down his face. Hands palm up, in a humbled low voice, cracking with emotion, he asked, "I have nothing to offer, and I know I don't deserve it, but can I join you? I want to pray too, for Josh..., and myself...." His voice dropped low when he said the last, and he lowered his head, hope nearly gone. "I am sorry for all I have done," he said repentantly. Seeing Andrew, he looked up and said desperately, "Can you please forgive me?"

Andrew stood slowly. He too, shed tears, but he smiled in peaceful joy. Andrew reached, clasping the man's hands in his own. "The angels are rejoicing, my friend, as am I, and you are no less welcome or worthy than any of us." The two men embraced, and the relief of forgiveness and new life washed over the man and out of his beaming face. Gladly accepted with the others, he kneeled to pray.

People on the field stood in various states of shock around Josh. Mark Johnson broke away, running lithely through the gathering crowd, shouting for the medical crew. However, any medical help would find it hard to pass through the mass of people as the entire crowd, frozen seconds before, now seemed to all descend onto the field. It was chaos. Police tried to hold back the crowd in vain, but there seemed no stopping them as they rolled onto the field all at once. The umpires closed ranks, and the home plate ump, who rose like Lazarus after his momentary stunned fall, now pushed back, trying to make way for the medical team Mark was attempting unsuccessfully to usher from deep in the outfield.

Without taking her eyes off Josh, Ruth cried out softly again, unwilling to give up.

"DADDY!"

Suddenly Josh, who had been still, opened his eyes and looked up.

"I am here, sweetheart," Josh struggled, sounding like a drowning man.

"Oh Dad, what have they done?" She gripped Josh's strong right hand between her two small ones as she kneeled by his side. Josh blinked against the growing darkness at her. Struggling to inhale roughly, he tried summing his remaining strength for a few more words. "Please, Daddy, don't leave me!" Ruth pleaded.

Josh looked back at Zach, cradling him, and forced out, "Sit me up, Zach."

Zach was afraid to move him because it might end his life, but the look Josh gave him was a gentle command, silently communicating nothing would stop that now. Reluctantly, Zach pulled him higher into his lap and helped him sit up enough to clear his airway. Though the blood drained slightly from Josh's face, he could breathe enough now and spoke clearly. He turned back to his Ruthie and reached up, caressing her face as only a father could.

"The last thing I want to do is leave you, Ruth." Josh said lovingly, "But God has a different plan and a new road for you. Know this. I will be waiting for you. Jesus, who is here now, will always be with you."

Josh looked up at Mary and back at Ruth. "As he gave you to me as your father, now Mary will be your mother on earth." Josh looked up at Mary, "Take care of your daughter," and back to Ruth, "Take care of your mom."

Mary nodded, gripping Ruth's shoulders, and Ruth reached her left hand to hold Mary's right on her shoulder. Still, she held Josh's right hand tightly. "How will I do it? I'm not strong enough!" she cried softly.

"Oh, my dear, I am not strong enough either, but it has never been just us. It is always the Lord. He has overcome all." Then Josh reached and touched Ruth's braces, "A parting gift He gives for me to you. You don't need these anymore." Ruth felt her legs miraculously heal, her lifelong ailment gone, and with the end of her disability, the braces gave way as the straps holding them together dissolved to ash like parchment in an unseen fire. Ruth smiled through her tears and bent to kiss her daddy goodbye, then she and Mary embraced each other looking at Josh, with the rest of his friends gathering close and listening.

The crowd hushed, and Josh looked and spoke his final words to all who would hear.

"Remember the commands our Lord and Savior, Jesus, gave us. Love God with all your heart and love one another as He loves us. And Go, tell the Good News to all people. All have sinned and come short of God's glory. The wages of sin is death. Salvation comes only through faith in our Lord Jesus, Who, with the Father, made all things, and Who, in obedience to the Father, came to earth, lived a perfect life, and died on the cross as the necessary and perfect sacrifice in payment for our sins. Having fulfilled the law and paid our debt, He rose again on the third day and claimed victory over death. Jesus is The Way, The Truth, The Life. No one comes to the Father but by Him! Let every man choose, for all must make the choice. As the Bible states and all creation declares, 'Salvation is found in no one else, for there is no other name under heaven given to mankind whereby we must be saved.'"

Josh's strength was failing him, and he said at last, "I go home to our Lord, but I wait earnestly for your homecoming. I love you all." With these final words, Josh stopped speaking to the crowd and leaned back.

Zach lowered Josh gently back to the earth. Nearby the head umpire who watched Josh for some time said to those around him, "Surely, this was a righteous man."

Josh looked up into heaven. His face filled with the serenity of someone seeing Jesus in eternity, and he smiled pure joy as he went.

"My Lord,
My Savior,
My King!"

Well done, my beloved child. You are a man after my own heart! Welcome Home!

Epilogue

The family of Pittsburgh Pirates mourned the loss of Josh Green, but as Christians, they rejoiced over the life and love Josh lived and the promised hope of eternity with the Lord. The Pirates were victorious in every way, confounding their enemies. They used their position as World Champions with charity and forgiveness, always standing for the Truth. Wherever they went, they were of one accord, spreading the good news of Jesus's love and offer of salvation, as Josh taught them.

Ruth and Mary kept in contact with the team and all the friends they made in their season as part of the Pirate family. They visited the Arimas regularly and often spoke with Saul as he continued leading the Pirates. Saul directed Mark Johnson to see that the girls could travel to any of their games as the years passed. They often showed up behind the Pirate dugout, cheering on the team, much to the players' delight. Mark also kept filling the wheeled bag Josh used with Pirate paraphernalia for the girls. Sometimes, where the Pirates played, a nearby hospital received a visit from two young women. A rumor followed that the sick and hurting received Pittsburgh Pirates gear while hearing the story of the greatest Ballplayer ever to swing a bat, and his savior, Jesus, who offered all salvation and new life. Mark received many "Thank Yous" through Nurse Richards, who arranged the visits as the girls found only new patients wherever they visited. It seemed those patients they previously prayed with all went home healed.

~

Finally, the angel asked the thief, "Then on what basis are you here?"
The thief replied, "I asked the man on the middle cross, and he said I could come."
– Paraphrase, Alistair Begg